VIOLENT MEN

Abbye –

You are

awesome ! ☺

Eric Blore

Aplr. 6. 10

VIOLENT MEN

ERIC FLORE

Library of Congress Control Number: 2006904935
ISBN 10:   Hardcover   1-4257-1778-0
                  Softcover   1-4257-1779-9

ISBN 13:   Hardcover   978-1-4257-1778-0
                  Softcover   978-1-4257-1779-7

To order additional copies of this book, contact:
Xlibris Corporation
1-888-795-4274
www.Xlibris.com
Orders@Xlibris.com
34379

For the intercessor—who privately and without any fanfare, credit, or earthly rewards, changes this world in which we live.

" . . . *the kingdom of heaven suffers violence, and violent men take it by force.*"
—*Jesus Christ*

Matthew 11: 12 (NAS)

ONE

May, 1999

"Big business deal tonight, Honey," Todd Falco politely told his trembling wife. Todd, thirty, was tall with a pot belly in the making. He put on his brown windbreaker as he left their master bedroom. He held an overnight bag which he had just packed full with clothes, toiletries, and a silver 9 mm automatic.

Kay Falco felt his breeze as he indifferently whizzed past her. Kay didn't want to contain her rage, but she didn't want to break down in front of him for the millionth time, either. That humiliation she could do without. Kay, 26, was short and petite, but solid from eight months of post delivery exercise. Her skin was milky white, her hair sandy, and her brown eyes currently bloodshot from anger and pain. She followed Todd out of their bedroom, trying to stifle tears. She took a deep breath and said:

"If this is a 'business deal,'" mocking his low, monotone voice, "why do you have an overnight bag? Most of your business is local, so you swear."

Good! she thought. Firm, stern, and her voice didn't crackle once.

Todd continued down the hallway toward his "office", which was the third bedroom of their two story home. The "office" was locked at all times and commanded forbidden to Kay and all other life forms. As he unlocked the "office" door, very sweetly Todd answered, "This business might take me to a late night meeting in Pittsburgh, if all goes well, Hon."

Still clutching the overnight bag, Todd opened the door and began to enter the darkened room. At two o'clock in that afternoon the blinds were down and the curtains shut. As always.

Kay went to follow him into the forbidden room. "I . . ." she began, but Todd instantly turned with a polite smile. "Honey," he reminded, "no one's allowed in here." He closed the door gently in her face.

Kay broke. The tears welled, her fair-skinned face flushed, and she could no longer contain the hurt.

"I don't understand," she whimpered through the door, "why you have to stay overnight when Pittsburgh is only an hour away." Hot tears rolled down her reddened cheeks.

There was no answer from inside the "office". Kay listened to him rummage through the room. She turned and went into the second bedroom. She looked into the crib at their sleeping eight month old son. Dylon was to be the cure to their severe marital problems, Todd had promised. Things were now ten times worse. Todd was completely consumed with this filthy business and the sinful trappings that went with it. If Kay were to expose his illegal work, she and Todd would likely wind up in jail. Dylon would be parent-less.

She heard Todd emerge. Although Dylon was sleeping fitfully and was only halfway through his nap, Kay snatched him up and carried him into the hall. The baby screamed, protesting his interrupted sleep.

Todd locked the office door. He had his bulky old wooden suitcase with the wicker trim. Kay recognized this ancient luggage from past business deals. She knew it would soon be filled with large amounts of laundered money. She would have been shocked to know that it would soon hold over one million dollars.

Todd gripped the overnight bag in one hand and the wicker-trim suitcase in the other. As he headed for the stairs, Kay stood directly in his path. She held the screaming baby high up on her shoulder so that Todd would be sure to notice.

"He's not a weapon, you know," Todd said as he politely squeezed himself and the luggage around Kay. He never even looked her in the eye.

Kay was convicted. She was ashamed for using Dylon in such a selfish fashion. She was also furious with herself for giving Todd the opportunity to rightly correct her.

"I do know!" she shouted, startling Dylon even more. "He's your son and I'm your wife! But that's all just a bother to you anymore."

Baby in arms she chased Todd down the stairs. Todd ignored her.

"We're just a ball and chain that keeps you from your almighty cocaine business and your filthy women!" Kay cried openly now, no longer concerned about the humiliation.

Unfazed, Todd made his way through the kitchen toward the back door.

Irritated at his coolness, Kay tried to draw blood: "Who is it tonight, Todd? Is it Sharon again? Yeah, I know who Sharon is! Or are you gonna pay for one of those disease-ridden prostitutes again? Yes, Todd! I know all about your social life!"

Todd stopped at the back door and lightly set down the luggage. Kay froze. For an instant she thought she really had drawn blood. But Todd casually turned around, put a hand on Kay's free shoulder, leaned forward and kissed crying Dylon. No emotion. Totally indifferent. Todd had completely contained. He always, always did. At that moment Kay wondered how she could even love this man.

"Look," he said, finally looking her in the eyes. "This is a big deal tonight. Maybe we'll go off and celebrate this weekend. I'll see if I can get something planned."

Todd turned, picked up the bag and suitcase, and silently walked out the door.

Kay felt an iron knot in her stomach. She wanted to tell Todd through the screen door how much he was hurting her. Her mouth seemed seared shut by the pain, however. Dylon cried, Kay could say nothing.

In the driveway, Todd set down the luggage and opened the trunk of his white Camaro. He picked up the overnight bag and unzipped it. He pulled out the 9 mm and stuck it down the front of his pants. He then loaded the luggage and slammed the trunk shut. Kay cried bitterly, watching Todd through the door. She and Dylon traded sobs.

Todd hopped in the Camaro and cranked it. Though Kay was less than ten feet away he ignored her. He never even looked to his wife and son as he put the Camaro in reverse and backed down the driveway.

Kay trembled. The sharp rejection buckled her knees and sent her to the floor. There she sat, crying and rocking Dylon. Todd sped away, leaving a cloud of dust and exhaust fumes. Kay watched through her tears until the car disappeared down the road, leaving her and Dylon completely alone again.

But this time was going to be different . . .

TWO

Detective Ray Kirkland was on his face in his Father's Presence. The faint dawn light shone through the sliding glass doors of his study. The morning rays glimmered on his coal colored skin, emphasizing well developed back and arm muscles. The sheriff's detective was on his knees, bowing forward. He pressed his nose to the carpet in worship to the Creator. Prayer was a daily discipline for him. Ray Kirkland daily wanted God to speak to his heart, order his footsteps, and guide him in his destiny.

Detective Kirkland gave his life to Jesus Christ at age seven. Trained by his parents, Ray always had a hearing ear for the Lord. God recreated him from the inside out and set Ray apart to Himself. God required every area of Ray's life. He gave him a burden for the corrupted and perverse of society. He also gave him an influential and dangerous position in law enforcement. Therefore Ray Kirkland never skipped a fresh opportunity each morning to fellowship with his Father, giving Him the first fruits of his day, his best time. He couldn't afford to miss these divine meetings. He needed Him.

Ray's stance for Jesus had more than once put him on the hot seat at the Beaver County Sheriff's Department. He was unabashed about Christ. He made references to his Savior often. He had prayed with victims and suspects on more than one occasion. Other officers and deputies made fun of him and criticized him for praying with criminals. They did not understand Ray's compassion. Five complaint letters had been placed in Ray's file over his twenty year career. All five letters were from people who were offended at Ray's "open religious discussions about Jesus Christ." He was passed over for promotion several times. He should have surpassed his current rank years earlier. To top it off, Sheriff DeBona pulled Ray out of the homicide division and put him in charge of missing persons cases. These were the most frustrating and fruitless cases a detective could work. Ray knew Sheriff DeBona had done it to discipline him. Yet Ray worked diligently on the missing person's cases, no matter how frustrating they were, and God blessed him for it. The department had to congratulate him several times for putting some tough cases to rest. God blessed what was meant to curse Ray and drive him out of the department. Ray knew the harassment was all for the cause of Christ.

In the meantime, Ray was able to work with a level of society lost and without hope. He had doors opened up for him that he never even dreamt about. He still prayed with some of the people he met through work, and many of them were deeply grateful to him for it. He was honored to have such a privilege, and blessed God for it.

On this morning the detective prayed for the Kingdom of God to be advanced in Beaver County, Pennsylvania, where he lived and worked. He prayed for Christ to guide him on the job, to give him wisdom, discernment, and protection. He prayed for the peace of his wife, Shelly, and their two daughters, Shaniqua, age ten, and Latonya, age six. He prayed for angelic protection around himself and his family. He prayed against the spirit of violence that might come against him on the job. He interceded for all of these things, as he did daily. Yet he still felt a stirring in his spirit that something else needed prayer. He felt a burden for something yet unidentified. It began to trouble him.

"Lord, what is it?" Ray said out loud, his voice muffled against the carpet. Holy Spirit did not lift the burden, neither did He identify it for Ray.

Ray got up off the floor. He adjusted his shorts and walked over to the sliding glass door. The sun was just behind the trees on the edge of his back yard. It looked like a beautiful spring day in the making. Yet Ray Kirkland felt heavy in his spirit.

"What is it, Lord?" he repeated. It was a deep burden.

He felt Holy Spirit directing him to just pray in the Spirit. The six foot five, powerfully built Beaver County Sheriff's Detective got back down on his face before the Lord. He began to pray in his heavenly language. An incomprehensible yet controllable language burst forth rapidly in staccato syllables. Almost immediately he felt the anointing of God pouring through him. He didn't understand what he was saying. But now that his carnal mind was taken out of the way his spiritual discernment greatly increased. He prayed and listened intently for Holy Spirit's unmistakable voice to speak to his heart.

God gave Ray a vision: in his mind's eye Ray Kirkland suddenly saw the outline of a woman and a baby in a baby carrier. The woman and her baby in the carrier were like a lighted silhouette. Only their outlines were discernible. Neither could he make out the baby in the carrier. The burden Ray'd felt suddenly seemed to lift. He stopped praying. But the silhouette of the woman with her baby was imprinted in his head.

"Who's that in the vision?" Ray asked God out loud.

Silence.

"Hello?" Ray called out again. "Please tell me what I'm seeing."

No answer.

"What am I supposed to do with this vision, Lord?"

No answer. Ray knew from his lifelong walk with Jesus that he probably wasn't going to get an answer right now. God would reveal the vision to him when He was ready. That was the hard part. God always required patience that the human mentality didn't naturally produce.

"This isn't funny, now!" Ray said. "You know this'll drive me nuts until I know who it is and why it is you're showing them to me!"

He already knew that wouldn't change anything.

Ray leaned his tall frame against the glass door and sighed. Spiritual visions usually bring great responsibility. It would need to be bathed in intercession. Ray would have to be faithful over it. As senseless as the vision seemed, it was obviously important to God.

"All right, Jesus, I'll wait 'til you show me," he proclaimed aloud, trying to be patient.

Across town, Holy Spirit awoke fifty-two year old Audra Dutton from her sleep again to pray for *her* burden. Audra did not have to work. Her late husband left her a comfortable sum of money. Therefore, the widowed woman groaned and rolled over under her covers.

"Please, Lord," she whispered half asleep, "let me sleep and I'll pray when I get up."

Yet Holy Spirit stirred up the burden all the more within her.

Unlike Detective Ray Kirkland across town, Audra Dutton knew what this burden was. She didn't know the faces or names of those for whom she was praying, but she knew that God had specifically laid His burden on her heart five years ago. He'd given her this burden during a time of great heartache and grief in her life. He asked her to be faithful over it. She had been. He promised it would bring healing and life. It had. Frequently Holy Spirit would stir up this burden within her heart, at various hours of the day, and she would faithfully pray.

But today Audra only wanted to sleep. She groaned, knowing she was under conviction.

"Please let me sleep!" she pleaded, sticking a pillow over her face.

No dice. Holy Spirit pressed her.

"Give me one more hour, Lord!"

No, Holy Spirit was gently telling her. Now.

"Oooooohhhhhwaaa!" Audra shouted in frustration. But like a little girl who had been asked to do a chore by her daddy, Audra finally gave in and began to pray in her prayer language. Quickly she felt God's holy anointing moving through her spirit like a river. The burden wasn't lifted, but she knew God was doing something about it now.

Feeling a little more energized by His presence, Audra Dutton sat up on her bed and continued to pray. As she addressed her burden, she felt the cleansing, joyous power of God wash over her soul.

She wound up praying for over an hour.

THREE

"Rome burning."

That's what Joseph Vero said aloud as he navigated his silver Porche up Route 51 outside Beaver Falls, Pennsylvania.

Disaster looming. Destruction inevitable, he thought. The fifty-six year old man couldn't shake the feeling. Anxious thoughts pervaded him. Joseph Vero watched the sky as he drove. The sun was nestling behind the trees on the horizon. The golden-orange hues were breathtaking. However, the beauty of this springtime dusk couldn't shatter the dreadful malaise creeping through his soul.

"It's all coming down around us," he thought, "and there's not one thing we can do to stop it."

Joseph Vero was a strong man. Despite his age, he was strong physically and mentally. He was stoic, logical. Negativism was not a part of his psyche. Work hard and conquer was his philosophy. If a problem arose he tackled it head on until it was defeated.

But this dread he could not shake.

Joseph felt he had merely survived this past winter. It was one of Western Pennsylvania's worst in recent years. The harsh ice, cold and snow of the past six months had only compounded Joseph's incubating anxieties. Just as the ice and snow had swept through this region, the first rumblings of chaos had begun to shake the illegal business for which Joseph worked. As he looked to the western sky, Joseph Vero meditated on how things had begun to sour for the first time in the twenty year history of the secret criminal empire to which he belonged. It hadn't happened in any grand fashion or explosion. It began with subtle tremors. He saw some "business deals" in their illegal empire go somewhat awry. Not severely askew, but just enough to make a discerning eye take notice. Rifts had begun among those who worked in the Family, the nickname those involved called their criminal empire. Unity that had once been the strength to keep such a powerful criminal organization secret had begun to dissolve. Along came distrust and backbiting. Joseph was even beginning to distrust Carmichael Vero, the leader of the Family and Joseph's own flesh and blood relative. Carmichael Vero might be trying to rearrange the Family power structure. Give himself more power. Maybe eliminate some of the positions close to the top. Including Joseph's. Again, Joseph had no concrete proof, but he sensed that Carmichael was secretly planning. He was a marvelous schemer. As he drove up Route 51 Joseph noted those peculiar changes in Carmichael that began to manifest over the past winter. Joseph's sixth sense about people was as uncanny as Carmichael's business talents. Joseph knew something was up. He just knew it. And he had to be wary of it.

Then there was Joseph's nephew, Tony Vero. Twenty-four years old. "The Kid," his relatives called him. Joseph Vero still looked after Tony Vero and his older sister, Gina. Their father, his brother, Pete Vero, died several years earlier. Their mother had died several years before Pete. Joseph watched after his brother's kids, even though they were of age. Tony was a local football hero. A quarterback. But a college injury ended his career. So when Tony wanted into the Family, he went to his Uncle Joseph. All the other Family members first said no. Tony persisted. Joseph convinced Carmichael to give in. Everyone worked so hard to get Tony into the Family business. Great risks to security were taken. They paid for Tony to go to a special private investigator-body guard school out in California. The intelligent, athletic Kid excelled there, graduated, and came on board the Family payroll as a private investigator. The Family even paid to set up his business. Tony was first given a series of minor assignments. He blew them away. He impressed *everyone* in the Family. He was the Kid! The Family took notice. Carmichael gave him a couple of other assignments. After much hard work and sacrifice the Kid was given his first official "business assignment." The Family sent him to Ft. Lauderdale. He carried out his assignment like a champion. But when he got back, Tony changed. He holed himself up in his house and wouldn't come out. He refused all phone calls and visitors. He refused even Carmichael. No explanations or apologies. He was like a hermit or something. Joseph was the one who had really stuck his neck out to get Tony into the Family business. Now Tony wouldn't even speak to him. Gratitude. Figured. Joseph had to answer to the Family about the Kid's current mental state and had won no favor about the whole thing.

That was all quite enough trouble, thank you very much.

But now this.

Joseph steered the Porche right onto a long, winding black-topped drive leading to a two-story hilltop business complex. The entrance had a huge stone-laced sign that read:

VECO

Vero Company Industries

"Business Builders and Leaders"

Joseph Vero looked at his watch. 7:58. VECO usually shut down and locked up by six o'clock nightly. However, this night there were five vehicles in the half-acre VECO parking lot: a Cadillac, a Mercedes, another Porche, a B.M.W and a Harley Davidson motorcycle. These were the vehicles of the VECO executives that made up the Family. VECO was the business Carmichael created to cover his criminal empire, The Family. The Family ruled the narcotics and pornography industries in Western Pennsylvania. VECO was the business front for these illegal industries. This night the Family was present for a hastily arranged emergency meeting. Rarely did they actually meet at their office complex together after hours. Secrecy could never be compromised. The average VECO employees didn't even dream that meetings like these occurred. This, however, was a crisis situation.

Todd Falco had disappeared. Completely. Hours after Joseph Vero had loaded Todd's old wooden suitcase with a million and one hundred thousand dollars for a cocaine buy. All Family money. All gone, now. Todd Falco, the million and some dollars, the suitcase, Todd's white Camaro, everything—vanished without a trace. Todd Falco was the Family's top narcotics dealer. He was also the primary buffer between the illegal drug rings and the true Family members, a VECO employee who worked for the Family. Todd Falco protected their identities and made them incredible amounts of drug money. Now he was gone without a trace.

Joseph Vero parked the Porche. He sat for a moment. Inside the Family waited for him. He would be in the spotlight tonight. Joseph Vero headed up the narcotics business for the Family and answered for it. He had no answers tonight, though. The Family was not going to be happy. But Joseph was a strong man and VECO's attorney. He had the awesome load of keeping VECO legally afloat in order to camouflage the Family empire. Joseph usually ate strife and chaos for lunch—and loved it. Manhandling that pressure was intoxicating to him. It made him feel virile. And he always faced the music. Fear could never be a factor. Never. Not even tonight. He would boldly face the Family.

Even though his intuition told him that this was the beginning of the end.

He got out of the Porche and walked up to the modern two-story office building. Using his master key Joseph Vero unlocked the mirrored-glass entrance doors and disappeared inside the building.

"Rome is burning," was all he could think.

FOUR

Tony Vero was becoming a living corpse.

The twenty-four year old lived by himself in one of the nicest homes on McKinley Drive, a posh rural neighborhood outside of Beaver Falls. At three in the morning he sat in a recliner in his living room with his feet up. His head rested on his left fist, he held a mug of beer in his right. The TV was on. His eyes were aimed at the screen, but he did not see it. Tony had black hair and a lean, athletic build. He wore old jeans and a flannel shirt with the sleeves cut off. His ethnic good looks were obscured by a two month growth of unkempt hair and beard. His skin, tanned in the Ft. Lauderdale, Florida sun two months earlier, was beginning to pale. He hadn't been outside his home in weeks. His green eyes, eyes which usually shimmered with warmth and determination, were now dull and glazed. Dark circles were forming under them due to constant drinking and little sleep. His once confident demeanor was being replaced by a careless slouch. His lifetime dreams had been shattered. Tony, a local football hero with uncanny talent, a person whom many locals envied for years, was quickly becoming the antithesis of all he'd ever dreamt of becoming. Once he had been surrounded by friends and loved ones at all times. Now he was alone. And he didn't even know that loneliness was such a bad thing at this point. Maybe someone as bad as him truly needed to be alone.

A few weeks earlier Tony started the habit of staying up all night and sleeping during the day. He could no longer stand the nightmares. Soon after returning from Ft. Lauderdale the recurring visions began tormenting him nightly. Those awful dreams, spawned by unbearable guilt, would wake him up, leaving him gasping for breath in the darkness. He soon found that if he stayed up at night drinking and went to bed drunk in the early morning sunlight, he wouldn't have the nightmares. Instead of sleeping at night, he'd catch four or five hours of sleep in the morning after the sun was up, and maybe take a two or three hour nap in the afternoon. It was as though the alcohol and sunlight were a barrier against horrible dreams and a guilty conscience.

Along with the binge drinking and change to his sleep patterns, Tony Vero made one more severe alteration to his life: he stopped leaving his house. Completely. He had developed a serious fear of leaving the safety of his home. He didn't want to be in open

16

areas and he surely didn't want to face any people. He'd stay home, lock the doors, and bar the world and its harsh realities. He refused all visitors and paid no attention to the telephone. Things seemed better that way. He wouldn't even go out to get the mail. He had a once a week housekeeper, Lula Johnson, who would do that for him. Lula would also go to the supermarket for Tony and buy his groceries and home supplies. The beer distributor would deliver him a new barrel of beer every four or five days when he called. He had everything he needed in his one big spacious house. He no longer needed to leave. He no longer needed to fear the night time. He just stayed locked in his house and slept during the day. Problems solved. He knew it was a screwy way to be, but these were the changes he made to adapt to his newfound turmoil. His home became both his fortress and prison.

Tony inherited his house from his late parents, Peter and Dorothy Vero. Dot Vero died of a sleeping pill and wine overdose when Tony was a ninth grader. His father Pete died of a heart attack when Tony was a sophomore in college. Pete and Dot Vero raised Tony and his older sister Gina in that house. Both Tony and Gina Vero graduated from Beaver Falls Senior High School. Gina was always the black sheep, rebellious and rejected. Tony had been the ideal son: a fun-loving overachiever and his father's pride as Beaver Falls' quarterback hero. So when Pete Vero died he willed Tony the house and property and a one million dollar insurance policy. Pete left Gina a hundred thousand dollar policy and some minor family heirlooms, but she was not welcome to any of the property. So Tony got the big five bedroom, three bath house with a three car garage and swimming pool. He also got his father's prized '88 convertible Mercedes. He had it and a blue, mid-sized Ford pickup truck he'd bought with his inheritance money, both sitting in his garage. He had always been the golden boy in his family. Now he was the golden boy holed up in his family's huge house.

He'd made one change to the interior of his house, too. In the well-lit foyer of the house lay the shattered remains of a what had once been an impressive glass trophy case. The case originally stood nearly four feet high and was covered with countless trophies and award plaques of all shapes and sizes. There were trophies with inscriptions such as "Tony Vero, Pennsylvania Press Corps' Quarterback of the Year," "Beaver Falls Senior High School Athlete of the Year: Tony Vero," and "Beaver Falls Tigers, W.P.I.A.L. Football Champions; Quarterback: Tony Vero." Sports articles read: "Vero the Hero!" The trophies, awards and athletic photographs from a stellar high school career had been stacked three shelves high, abundant icons in this former shrine to Tony Vero. However, the shrine was now demolished. Only shards and splinters of glass, toppled aluminum and plastic trophies, chipped wooden plaques, and torn pictures remained. On top of the remains lay the aluminum baseball bat that was used to reduce the case to dangerously sharp rubble.

His father's death had been strike one for Tony. Soon after, a college injury that ended his NFL dreams had been strike two. The events during his recent trip to Ft. Lauderdale were strike three. Ft. Lauderdale triggered an unwelcome revelation within Tony. His eyes were opened and turned inward. He suddenly saw awful darkness within himself. He was not golden. He was not the all-American boy. That was a deception. *Local football hero* meant nothing to Tony, now. He may have been a tremendously gifted athlete in high school and college, surrounded by friends, admirers and girls. That was no consolation, anymore. That's when Tony destroyed the trophy case. After several weeks of being holed up in that house, all of those trophies and awards meant to praise him had become a mockery to him. So Tony ended the mockery. He brought down that baseball bat on the Tony Vero Shrine over and over again, devastating it.

"What should I do about this mess?" a shocked Lula Johnson asked the next morning when she found the demolished trophy case.

"Sweep the glass up underneath it and leave it alone."

People used to slap him on the back, congratulate him, praise him, buy him a beer and tell him how great he was. All that meant nothing now, for Tony Vero knew who he truly was. His experience in Ft. Lauderdale revealed who he and his family really were. And no athletic career, no slap on the back, no praise of any sort could change this one fact that had completely overtaken him: Tony Vero was not a good person. At all. He was *bad*. He was worthy of hell. And nothing could change that fact.

FIVE

Joseph Vero walked up the inside steps of the Vero Company Industries two story office building. The VECO office complex housed two powerful Western Pennsylvania business entities: VECO, a widely acclaimed enterprise, and the Family, a covert and sinister criminal operation. Carmicheal Vero led them both.

The other five members of the Family were waiting for Joseph Vero in Carmichael Vero's plush second story VECO office. Their ages varied from the late thirties through the early sixties. All were dressed in expensive business suits. All looked stressed. No one spoke a word.

Carmichael Vero leaned back in his swivel chair, his hands pressed together in front of his face as though in meditation. The sixty-two year old man had stylish salt and pepper hair that accented his dazzling green eyes. Crow's feet and wrinkles on his face were scarcely as defined as they should have been for a man his age. His skin was attractively olive from his French/Italian background. He was lean. His hands were manicured. He wore a Rolex on his left wrist and a gold bracelet on his right. He looked impeccable, as usual, in a dazzling silver-gray suit.

Half-seated on top of Carmichael Vero's desk and chomping gum like a teenager was a bulky, beer-bellied linebacker of a man named Ed Larsky. Ed Larsky, 39 years old, was the office manager at the VECO office building. In the Family, Ed Larsky was Carmichael Vero's right-hand man: bodyguard, enforcer, advisor, confidant. In the biker gangs Larsky had been known as "the Russian," because of his parents' ancestry. He had steel blue eyes and blond hair that was crewed on the top and shoulder length in the back. He was six foot-two and 270 pounds, mostly muscle. He looked like something out of the World Wrestling Federation. But games were not Ed Larsky's interest. He was one of the most dangerous men in the tri-state area. Violent, and a master of weaponry, he was one of the main reasons the Family had flourished unscathed and camouflaged for so many years. He had earned his place under Carmichael's wing. Carmichael was the brains, Larsky the brawn that protected him at any cost.

Anthony Zann, 48, and his brother Warren, 46, were both accountants. Their VECO firm was Zann and Zann. They both acounted for VECO's finances. But Anthony laundered the Family's money, and Warren ran their pornography businesses. Some were legal. Some were illegal, and quite vile. Marv Lenstein, 56, worked with Joseph Vero in their law firm. The attorneys both handled VECO's legal matters. But Lenstein covered for Joseph while he ran the drug business for the Family.

None of the five men said a word when Joseph Vero walked into Carmichael's office. He acknowledged no one. The atmosphere was grim. He closed the two oak doors to Carmichael's office and went to sit down. The other four Family members silently eyed Joseph as he settled into one of four chairs that faced Carmichael's desk.

When Joseph was seated Carmichael lowered his hands from in front of his face and gently nodded at Larsky. The gum-chomping man slid his hulking frame off the desk and sauntered over to one of the shelves. He turned on a CD player and popped in a disk. He set the volume on ten and pressed "play." Rock music suddenly blasted from an outdoor sound system. Carmichael had the massive outdoor speakers installed in the exterior walls of the VECO offices. The rock and roll echoed throughout the fifteen wooded acres that surrounded the VECO complex. Carmichael's sound-proofed office windows shook from the bass vibration. Larsky sauntered back over to Carmichael's desk. The music was for the benefit of outsiders trying to use spy devices to listen to the Family's conversation. All spying from without was now thwarted. Larsky had already swept Carmichael's office for bugs. The inside was clean. The silent men could now safely speak.

"Gentlemen," Carmichael spoke, "Joseph is leading this meeting."

All eyes were on Joseph Vero. He leaned back in his chair, drew a deep breath and paused.

Todd Falco was his underling and responsibility. He shouldered this pressure.

"I called this emergency meeting at Carmichael's request," Joseph calmly began. "The Family has a crisis. You were all present at our meeting two weeks ago. I brought before you Todd Falco's request that he be allowed to start buying his cocaine from a new source. A guy by the name of Bernie Lokawski. Todd had checked him out thoroughly and he looked clean. This man gave Todd a cocaine sample that was out of this world. This stuff was pure. We could stomp this stuff twice over and our drug rings would still have to buy it at top dollar. We could have really increased our earnings with this deal."

"We remember," Carmichael prodded him along.

"Well, we all voted and agreed that Todd be allowed to start dealing with this Bernie Lokawski. Yesterday was to be their first deal. Lokawski wanted one million and one hundred thousand dollars for ten and a half kilos, which was a righteous price." Joseph waved a hand at Anthony Zann. "Anthony gave me the cash from our Family account. I met Todd yesterday afternoon and loaded him up for the buy. I have no idea where he was meeting this guy. I never do. Todd went to the buy. Then he completely disappeared. He never came home, never called his wife, never came back here, he never called me. No one's seen or heard from him since. I've checked all his local hangouts for his car, but I never saw it. He's gone."

"This is serious," Warren Zann said shaking his head.

Carmichael calmly leaned forward and folded his hands on his desk. His green eyes met Joseph's brown eyes. Despite the fact that he was only four years Joseph's senior, Carmichael Vero was Joseph Vero's uncle. Carmichael was the youngest of eight children. His oldest brother Danny was seventeen years older than Carmichael. Danny's wife gave birth to Joseph when Carmichael was four and a half. Three years later they had Joseph's brother Pete. Their families treated the three as though they were brothers, rather than uncle and nephews. They had always been that close. In their childhood Carmichael was always Joseph's protector. When things got serious in the tough Pittsburgh neighborhood where they grew up, Carmichael would call Joseph "nephew" to show his authority and protection over him.

"Nephew of mine," Carmichael now said to Joseph in all seriousness, "what could possibly have happened to this Todd Falco and all of our money?"

"I see three possible scenarios for Todd Falco's disappearance. Two are plausible, one is not."

The hardened men stared silently at him.

"One," Joseph said, "Bernie Lokawski is a lawman and Todd was set up and arrested . . ."

Warren Zann snapped out from Joseph's right, "If Falco had been arrested we'd've known it. It would've been plastered all over the news . . ."

Carmichael pointed his finger at Warren Zann and fired off, "Warren! You let him finish!" Carmichael's face turned crimson. The younger Zann had been visibly nervous since the emergency meeting had been called. "You're showing your lack of mettle and I'm not impressed." Carmichael relaxed a bit. "We're all upset by this, but we're not going to take it out on Joseph. Now shut up and don't interrupt."

Warren looked down in disgust, but did not dare aim his anger at Carmichael.

"The first possibility," Joseph repeated, and this time he turned his head slightly toward Warren, "is that Bernie Lokawski is a government agent and he's arrested Todd Falco. FBI, DEA, either one of them. If Todd had been careless recently he may not have realized they had him under surveillance. They could have staked him out, planted Lokawski, set up the deal yesterday, arrested him and now have him under interrogation."

Silence.

"Who's his lawyer?" Carmichael asked. In order to further insure a buffer between Todd Falco and the Family there was no way that Joseph Vero or Marv Lenstein could be his personal attorney.

"Guy by the name of Banks. From New Brighton." Joseph shook his head. "I checked on him. It's been business as usual for Banks during the last twenty-four hours. Todd knows better. He knows the procedure I told him to follow. If he gets busted, he immediately calls Banks for counsel. He tells Banks to call his wife Kay and office manager Larsky here at VECO, since he's employed here. That way everyone knows he's been busted. He's to do this especially if the feds bust him. I told him if the feds busted him they're probably already onto us."

"We have no reason to believe the Feds are on to us at this point," Marv Lenstein added. Carmichael nodded knowingly.

"So," Joseph said, "the only reason I doubt this scenario is that Todd hasn't contacted anyone. His wife Kay hasn't heard from anyone. Todd, Banks, cops, the Feds, nobody. She's livid. Really ticked that Todd's not called. If Todd had been arrested the Feds would have had to let him contact someone, unless they are seriously working him over in the interrogation and are about to smoke us. Then they would delay letting him talk to anyone for fear that someone might try to tip us off."

"But even after twenty-three hours?" Ed Larsky asked.

Joseph shook his head grimly. "No. That's why I doubt this scenario. The Feds can't kidnap a suspect and hold them hostage. They could blow their whole case. If they arrest you, they have to allow you to contact someone, especially a lawyer. Not unless Todd's turned on us and is giving us over to them. But he knows the penalty for that."

Todd had a wife and baby. He did indeed understand the penalty for ratting on the Family.

"Marv and I have checked on Banks and Todd's wife since he failed to report back to me last night. No activity with either of them." Joseph paused and took another deep breath. "And that's why I believe we can eliminate this scenario as an option."

Carmichael nodded. "Next scenario."

"The second one is that Todd took the money and ran."

"Plausible?" Carmichael asked.

"He has a bad marriage, loves the honeys, and cheats on his wife all the time. He's dissatisfied working here at VECO forty hours a week to cover his cocaine business. Then I loaded him up with a million and one smackaroos yesterday. Strong temptation for anyone, wouldn't you say?"

"He's *your* dealer. You know his character," Carmichael replied defensively.

Joseph put both hands in the air. "He was totally loyal to us," he explained with frustration. "He did fantastic business. He knew the ropes. He knew the punks to avoid selling to. He knew the ins and outs of the cocaine business and had finesse about it all. He knew how to avoid the law like a gazelle avoids a lion. Second nature. He was tops and was well paid for it. He knew how to buffer the Family and was quite sure of the penalty for crossing us. If I had two Todd Falcos I'd quit the Family and go into business myself. I can't see Todd doing this to us."

"Why not?" Ed Larsky asked. "He's human and you just listed a whole bunch of his problems. You handed him a million and one, plus who knows how much more he's had stashed from past deals. You told me yourself earlier today that he had packed a bag full of clothes. Maybe he ran off with one of his chicks? You talk about him like he was your son or something. Like he couldn't possibly be capable of such a thing. What is he, a saint? Are you protecting him?" Larsky stared coldly at Joseph.

Joseph glared back at Larsky. Joseph and Carmichael were like brothers, but sometimes Carmichael allowed Larsky to have his way around Joseph, let the watchdog chew on his leg every once in a while. It reminded Joseph who truly was the chief of the Family and pulled the strings. Joseph was well aware of how invaluable Ed Larsky was to the Family's security and power. However, Joseph never put up with young Larsky's arrogant mouth and disrespect.

"I don't protect Falco, Ed," Joseph whispered coolly. "I know he's human and susceptible to temptation. I was giving my professional opinion about the man's loyalty like Carmichael asked. Todd Falco was as loyal as any of us. I said I believe Falco wouldn't run out with our money and it's true." Joseph leaned forward toward Larsky now. "Not every man who's given a powerful responsibility becomes a total jackass because of it."

Larsky's face reddened with fury, his eyes locked on Joseph's.

Anthony Zann whistled a sharp note. Marv Lenstein chuckled to himself. The watchdog had just been beat with a stick and put in his proper place.

"Gentlemen," Carmichael said slowly shaking his head. "Let's all relax a bit, here. It's important that we solve this together." Secretly he was impressed with Joseph's quick takedown of Larsky. It was gutsy. Larsky's ego was as massive as his frame. And he never, never let an insult go unpunished.

"Joe," Carmichael sighed, finally prying Joseph's eyes from the brooding Larsky, "you know I trust your opinion." Carmichael looked at Larsky now, "And we *all* know that Todd was loyal." He waved his hand and sat back. "Please go on."

Joseph turned grim. "The third and final scenario is that Todd Falco is kidnapped or dead. By this Bernie Lokawski. Could be a rip-off, could be a ransom. Both ways this Lokawski stands to make a fortune. This is the most likely scenario, in my opinion."

The office was like a graveyard again.

"This would explain Todd's complete disappearance, car and all." Joseph said.

"Well," Carmichael said, "you all know the reason that Ed and I were so leery about dealing with this Bernie Lokawski was because we knew so little about him. Todd may have checked him out but Ed could find no trace of him anywhere. That's not how the Family usually does business."

Joseph defended himself. "But Carm, we all agreed months ago that Todd needed to start finding some new drug sources, since we don't want to produce our own anywhere. We all said that it's just too dangerous buying narcotics from the same suppliers and smugglers who get their loads at that Philly port and smuggle them the whole way across Pennsylvania. They put us at risk every month. So Todd found this Bernie Lokawski man. He brought Todd that sample. This was some of the best coke we've ever seen! I haven't seen cocaine like this in years . . ."

"Joe," Anthony Zann put a calming hand on Joseph's right knee. He thought that Joseph needed a break. "You don't have to sell us on this coke sample again. You had us the last meeting."

Anthony adjusted his thick black glasses and crossed his legs. The cool, smooth talking accountant put his palm out toward Carmicheal and said, "Here's how I see it. This is all just too simple for us to be mulling over all these scenarios. I agree with Joe's last idea. This Bernie what's-his-face wows Todd Falco with this wonder coke to get our attention. We're astounded by the quality and take the bait. Joe here gives old Todd-boy the cash and sends him to this Bernie Old-cow-ski . . ."

"Lokawski," brother Warren Zann corrected.

Anthony waved his hand. "Whatever. Todd-boy goes to meet Bernie whatever-his-last-name-is, cash in hand for the buy, and Bernie has other plans. This time's been coming for years."

"What're you gettin' at, Zann?" Larsky asked impatiently.

"Mr. Larsky," Anthony said, "Our luck's run out! Drugs and pornography and all this Mafia type business we're involved in, it tends to be pretty dangerous, wouldn't you say? How many people a day do you see on the news who've been killed doing business like Todd? How many different reasons are there why this guy could have ripped us off? How many things could this guy have done with one million, one hundred thousand dollars? Bernie Lokawski may work for another drug ring. Maybe it's another big operation like ours. Bernie meets Todd Falco. Todd is just some kid who works for a living. But suddenly, he can produce millions of dollars. That's not the norm for the average Beaver County white collar worker. Old Bernie may have wanted to get his hooks into Todd Falco to see how deep his cash well ran."

Both Carmichael and Larsky looked uncertainly at one another.

Anthony embellished. "I discussed this with Joe earlier today. We have had it good. No, I take that back. We've had it great! This run of ours had been incredible! The Family has ruled for almost two decades without anyone catching onto us. It's been like we're untouchable. So now, the inevitable has happened. We've been touched! Or I guess I should say Todd Falco's been touched."

Carmichael digested this. Joseph Vero and Marv Lenstein both nodded in unison.

"You've got to admit it, Carmichael," Marv Lenstein said, "it's been twenty years of smooth sailing for us. We're not exactly a run of the mill organization. We've got top security. You had the vision for us to do business like the Mafia, but not live like wiseguys. Low key, you made us swear to it. You never let us go flashing around town like the dons and lieutenants always did. You had to chastise our late associate Pete Vero, no offense, Joseph, when Pete and that Gus Savage he hung around with used to go gallivanting off to Atlantic City on the weekends. We don't go bragging about who we are, showing our muscles. We're in this for the money and power, not fame and glory. We're a secret to everybody. I've met some of the gang-bangers who make drug money for me, whom I ultimately control, and they didn't even know it! They didn't even know who I was! We run this region, but nobody knows it, cops included. And what luck we have! Like when Warren's old puppet president he hired to run his porno businesses got busted and threatened to turn Warren over to the cops, he dropped dead in the jailhouse!

And that one supplier Joe used to buy from before Falco came on board, he got busted and he dropped dead before he could rat us out, too! Man! Someone's watching after us somewhere. Sure, we've had to erase a few people who found out about us. But no one knows it! And we look like great citizens, to top it off. It's almost unreal. This has all been unreal, Carmichael."

Marv looked around for agreement. Most nodded.

"If Bernie Lokawski's involved with some real wiseguys or even some two-bit operation," Joseph said, "they might want to try to bring us down to pick up our business. Or they might just want to rob us blind."

Ed Larsky got a disgusted look on his face and started shaking his head.

"Do we got any proof on any of these scenarios?" Larsky asked Joseph impatiently.

"No," Joseph said.

"Do we got any trace of Falco anywhere? Anything?" Larsky followed, sliding himself off of Carmichael's desk.

"We have not a trace of anything, Ed. Todd Falco has completely vanished," Joseph said.

Larsky threw up his hands in a rarely animated moment and fired off to Carmichael, "Then what in the world are we doing sitting here making up possible scenarios! Our money and this Falco are gone and could be traced right back to us if we don't find out what kind of garbage is going on here."

The others stared up helplessly at Larsky. The atmosphere was thick with anxiety and frustration.

"Carmichael," Larsky said to the senior Vero, "enough of us sittin' around here. We need to find Falco or Bernie Lokawski. We need action. Tell us what we're gonna do."

Carmichael nodded at his enforcer. "Yes, Ed, we need action." He paused for several seconds, gathering his thoughts. Then he spoke with executive authority: "There's three things I want done. First, we need to keep the cops and everyone completely ignorant of the fact that there is a missing person named Todd Falco." He turned to Larsky. "Ed, the first thing you do is put Falco on personal leave here at VECO, in case anyone in the office starts asking about him. Fill out the form, give a bogus personal statement and reason from Falco and I'll sign it. Tell all the employee's here who might ask about him that he's called off for the next few weeks. Shut them up now. They're all so nosy. Then if the cops do come snooping around here looking for him, you can show them the phony leave form. That'll throw the police off our trail."

"Done," Larsky nodded.

Carmichael continued with Larsky. "The next thing you do Ed, is go visit Falco's wife and convince her not to go to the cops and sign a missing person's report on Todd. I don't know that she would be stupid enough to do such a foolish thing, but the minute she did, the cops would come straight here snooping around. I want nothing to do with that!"

Larsky grunted in agreement.

"What's her name, Joe?" Carmichael asked.

"Her name's Kay. And once Ed meets her tomorrow, he'll not forget her. I called her today to ask about Todd," Joseph said. "She melted my phone. She knows Todd deals drugs. And she knows about all his women. She may suspect my involvement in the drugs. The real problem is she somehow thinks I go around setting up Todd's extramarital sex life. She's a real pistol."

"Ed," Carmichael redirected, "Don't go out there making violent threats. Try the sweet approach with her first . . ."

Anthony Zann snickered out loud. Larsky glared the head accountant.

Carmichael, disgusted, waved off Anthony. "Anyhow," he continued, "there's no use riling her up any further. Try the easy approach first. Tell her that we're going to send our own man out investigating Todd's disappearance and that there's no reason to get the law enforcement agencies involved. Then if you need to, frighten her with what could happen to her if she goes to the cops. Tell her she's like Todd's accomplice. Tell her if the cops investigate Todd's life and find out what Todd really does for a living she'll go to jail too."

"Tomorrow morning," Larsky promised.

"What if she still goes to the cops?" Joseph asked.

"Well, then she goes to the cops. We have nothing to hide here at VECO. As long as that's all they investigate in Todd's life. The third thing that needs to be done . . ." Carmichael went on. "As Marv here pointed out a few moments ago the Family has had tremendous success at staying camouflaged. But that poses our next problem. A problem for which I already have the solution." Vero rose from his seat and stepped away from his desk while he spoke. "To keep the Family a secret and keep the cops from catching onto us, we in this room need to do what we always do: nothing! We can't poke our head out from our shell or we'll get it cut off. We as Family members can't investigate Todd's disappearance. The six of us personally cannot do a thing."

"Then the Family will have no one looking for Todd," Warren Zann said.

"Wrong, my friend," Carmichael pointed at Warren. He walked around to where the four others were sitting. "The Family *will* have someone looking for him. One of our *own*."

"Who?" Larsky asked.

"Tony Vero," Carmichael said.

Tony Vero, the Kid, was Joseph's twenty-four year old nephew, and Carmichael's great nephew.

"Tony?" Joseph asked, shaking his head with uncertainty.

"The Kid, Joseph," Carmichael commanded. "I want the Kid working on this. He's perfect for finding Falco and this Lokawski guy. He's stealth, you know? He has a knack for getting information and tracking people down without making a ripple in the law enforcement world. That's just what I'm talking about. He knows how to get around without stirring up trouble for us. Tony's just what we need right now to find Falco and our money. Or just the money! Look at that job he did in Ft. Lauderdale. He was unreal! Like a pro. He's the one. Get him in here, Joseph."

Joseph paused, then explained, "Carmichael, Tony's not *right* at this point in time."

"'Not right'?" Larsky snarled at Joseph.

"Hush, Ed!" Carmichael ordered. "Just what's going on with the Kid, Joe?"

Joseph shrugged, embarrassed. "I don't know. He's holed up in Pete's house and won't see anybody. He's been that way for a month now. He won't answer his phone, he won't come to the door to talk to me. As far as I know, he's not talked to anyone. He's been funny since he came back from Ft. Lauderdale in March. I don't know what his problem is."

"Well I'll tell you something," Carmichael said, angrily. "I don't know what Tony's problem is, either," rage crept into his voice, "but you went through so much trouble to get him into Family business. He does that job for us in Ft. Lauderdale, and a fantastic job he does, I'll give him that, but he comes back home and then acts like this to *me*? He won't come see me, he won't return my calls, he's refused to work. After the risks we . . . *I* took to get him into the Family, he shows me no respect! Tony's disappointing me almost as bad as his sister Gina!"

"And with that," Anthony Zann stood up smiling uneasily, "I'll leave! I think this is now 'family'-Family business." Everyone knew that Tony's older sister Gina was a sore subject for Carmichael. "Some of us should bug out of here. Just in case someone spies us all here together this late after VECO's closed shop."

Carmichael waved off the Zann brothers and Marv Lenstein. "You three get outta here. Go about your business as usual. You'll be contacted if the situation changes."

The three men gladly left. A minute later Joseph Vero faced Carmichael and Larsky alone. "Nephew," Carmichael said, "You vouched that Tony would commit to the Family to the death, like his father. I gave you the money to send him to that private investigator's school and then to get his license and set up his own personal business. We put him on that Ft. Lauderdale job. But now that he's back, he refuses to have anything to do with us. This isn't some McDonald's we're running here, Joe. Tony's not showing gratitude and devotion. This is a slap in my face! This is our *lives*, and it could be our death. The Family risked vulnerability by letting him in. If it wasn't for his father Pete, with all due respect to your brother, the Kid wouldn't even know about the Family."

"I know Tony's a risk, Carmichael," Joseph explained. "But you know as well as I he has the potential to be a great asset to us. He is sharp. He's just been a mess since he returned from Florida."

Ed Larsky chuckled. "The Kid couldn't handle what happened in Ft. Lauderdale. The Kid's soft. He's like a girl. I warned both of you that he couldn't handle real Family life. He may have been some football legend in Beaver Falls, but he's a little girl at heart. A total loser."

"Well Ed," Joseph boldly stepped forward, "Why don't you teach Tony how to kill and murder? Then he'll be a real man like you."

Larsky reddened with rage and stepped toward Joseph. That was twice in one evening that Joseph jarred his ego.

Carmichael stepped between them, on fire.

"Enough! Both of you!" he shouted at his feuding underlings. "You two are like kids," he said, gathering his composure. "Ed, go outside and have a smoke. I'll lock up the building."

Larsky eyeballed Joseph and then turned and trudged out of the office. He slammed Carmichael's oak doors behind him, leaving them rumbling. He was the only person who could get away with something like that.

Carmichael looked at Joseph. "Ed plays hardball twenty-four hours a day, Nephew. Watch your step with him. Sometimes he acts without my authority."

Joseph sighed and sat back down in one of the four chairs. Charmichael joined him.

"Joseph, we trained Tony to work for us at great expense. I don't care what his current problem is. He is a Family member now, and he works for us. I want you to go get him and bring him in here tomorrow morning. He's going to work on this Todd Falco mess. Tony's a Beaver Falls boy. He's knowledgeable of Todd Falco's crowd and will fit in with the type of places Falco hung out. He'll blend in fine. I want him in this office by ten o'clock and I want him working by noon. I'll pay his usual salary. But he *will* do this job and he *will* respect my wishes. Tony does what *I* tell him to do. He will obey. I will not be insulted by Tony like I was by his sister Gina."

Joseph nodded silently.

Carmichael got up and shut off the CD player. The windows suddenly stopped vibrating. He walked over and stared at the dark sky out the giant window.

"Nephew of mine," Carmichael began. He never turned around to look at Joseph.

"Yes?" Joseph replied.

"Tony belongs to me. Don't ever forget that. Don't ever let your loyalty to Tony override the fact that he is *mine*."

Joseph didn't reply this time.

Carmichael still didn't turn around to look at his nephew. He simply repeated: "Tony's mine."

SIX

The spring sun had completely disappeared below the western horizon. A private investigator named Edgar Waters stood hidden in the dark woods about a hundred yards behind the VECO office building. Edgar was in his early forties, of medium height and build. He was dressed in black and wore a black ski cap on his head. He had an arsenal of electronic spy equipment. He packed an automatic pistol at his waist. He watched through binoculars as Carmichael Vero and Joseph Vero exited the VECO offices, bathed only in the dim VECO parking lot lights. They met Ed Larsky, who was smoking a cigarette on his Harley Davidson.

Edgar Waters spoke softly into a tape recorder as he watched through his binoculars.

"May fourth. It's 9:13 p.m., Captain. There's Charmichael and Joseph Vero. They're heading toward their cars."

He held up a parabolic dish. It looked like a gun with a radar dish on the end, one long antenna protruding from the center of the dish. He pointed it toward the three Family members in the parking lot, a hundred yards away. He had an ear piece in his right ear. He listened.

"They're not saying a word," Edgar reported into his recorder.

He watched through his binoculars. Joseph Vero went straight to his Porche without even acknowledging Larsky. Carmichael just nodded at his large henchman as he slipped into his Cadillac. Larsky spit out his cigarette onto the asphalt and casually climbed onto his Harley Davidson.

Edgar lowered the parabolic dish and switched it off. "No one said anything," he recorded.

Larsky's Harley rumbled to life in the distance. Edgar watched the lights of the Porche, the Cadillac, and the Harley as the three remaining Family members sped away from VECO. He spoke into the recorder again. "They've all driven off now, Captain. My investigation this evening was fruitless, once again. They blasted Led Zeppelin from those outdoor speakers. Do you know what Carmichael Vero tells his VECO employees those outdoor speakers are for? He tells them they're for company picnics on those office grounds back there. Do you want to hear the funny part? They don't have company picnics on VECO property. They have them in Brady's Run Park. VECO insiders say he tells them they're for corporate spies. But actually, those loud speakers are only for the benefit of people like me. And it works. This was the fourth time in six months that all six Family members met together after hours. All four times they blasted that music. Even state of the art spy equipment couldn't compete with music blasting at jet airplane decibels. I need a bug planted in Carmichael Vero's office. But good luck with that."

Edgar stopped the tape recorder and pocketed it. He put on a set of night vision goggles and began to pack up his spying equipment into a military knapsack. When he had it all loaded he flicked the tape recorder back on.

"All I got after they shut off the speakers was a minute or two of Carmichael and Joseph talking about Tony Vero. But something's up. They were definitely on the scramble today. Our insider at VECO said Carmichael was not himself today, and that he and Ed Larsky had many closed-door meetings and several private phone calls, each. Then tonight they had the Zann's, Marv Lenstein, and Joseph Vero meet them for this late meeting that lasted over an hour. Someone called off the outside security guard so they could meet privately here, too. He usually shows up near about seven o'clock. It's after nine and he's still not here. Things were really different here today. Something's gone wrong. For five years of investigation I've never heard of them running around like they were. Now's when they're weak. We'll have to be patient and let them slip up. They will slip up. Nobody's perfect. Pete Vero slipped up before he died and I got it on tape. We'll stick to the remaining six Family members and get them."

Edgar glanced back at the VECO parking lot. He saw headlights turning into the complex. A black Ford Expedition pulled into the lot. He pulled out his binoculars again. Through them he could see "Dalling Security" written on the side of the truck. This black Expedition was new. This was not the usual private night security guard who kept an eye on the VECO grounds from 7:00 p.m. to 7:00 am.

"Hey, Captain," Edgar spoke again into the recorder, "VECO's hired Dalling Security. They're a shady bunch of characters. Bunch of mercenaries and cop wanna-be's. But they're tough. And they're expensive, too."

The Expedition stopped in the middle of the parking lot. The headlights went out. A Dalling Security agent got out and surveyed the area. He pulled out a cellular phone and spoke to someone.

Edgar clicked off the recorder and put it away again. He was about to undo his backpack and pull out the parabolic dish to hear what the man was saying. But the Dalling Security agent suddenly popped open the back of the Expedition: out shot two German Shepherd dogs, barking frantically and running wildly across the parking lot toward the woods.

Right in Edgar Waters' direction.

Even though he was one hundred yards into the woods, he knew he had no advantage over the dogs. He took off running through the forest, zigzagging trees and stumbling over forest debris. He could hear the barking canines come thrashing into the woods. The canines quickly picked up his scent. Edgar broke through branches and bushes on a dead run. Tree branches stung his face and scraped up the lenses of his night vision goggles. He knew the dogs were gaining. They would catch him and tear him up. He heard them about twenty-five yards behind him. They weren't close enough to hit with pepperspray. Edgar stopped, whipped around his knapsack and sunk his hand deep inside. He pulled out a plastic peanut butter jar. He took off running again, unscrewing the lid as he ran. Being a snoop, Edgar Waters was always ready for guard dogs. Bullets were too noisy and could be traced. Mace or pepper spray required almost point blank contact with an attacking dog. That was too dangerous. He could fix it so they never got that close. He stopped, pulled off the lid of the peanut butter jar, and dumped its contents on the forest floor: twelve ounces of cayenne, red, and black pepper spilled on the ground. Edgar took off on a dead run again. The dogs sniffed his trail just yards away. The canines rushed to the spot where he had been standing. They both shoved their noses deep into the pile of hot pepper spices. The high acid content of the pepper scorched the sensitive inner linings of their nostrils. The dogs went insane with pain, yelping helplessly. They split up and ran to and fro, bumping into tree trunks, getting caught in thickets. As he ran Edgar could hear the Dalling Security agent shouting for the dogs to come back to him in the VECO parking lot. The dogs were thrashing and yelping helter skelter in different directions. Edgar heard the Dalling agent continuing to yell for them to come back. It didn't sound like they were obeying. After several minutes Edgar Waters was almost a mile into the woods. He could no longer hear the dogs or the agent. He had escaped unidentified.

He stood still, panting wildly, soaked with sweat. He turned back and saw nothing through the goggles. He bent over and put his hands on his knees while he caught his breath. After a moment he stood up and quickly made his way back to his car parked near the highway on the far side of VECO's property. He cranked the engine and drove off before Dalling sent a car to patrol the vicinity. He drove in the safety of his vehicle for a few minutes, letting his heart calm down, trying to get his breathing back to normal. He pondered the whole situation, then pulled out his recorder and turned it on.

"That Dalling truck had two German Shepherd guard dogs. I just barely got away." He shut it off, panted for another minute; turned it back on.

"Captain, you've had me on these folks for five years. In five years we have had two potential witnesses drop dead on us. We have a twenty second recording of Pete Vero talking about the Family. Pete Vero actually makes three dead witnesses, I guess. And they weren't killed, they all died of natural causes! But you have next to nothing on the Veros. You have spent a lot of your own money all this time and you still can't convince the SBI to investigate VECO. You and I know they're rotten. But it's like there's some sort of protection over them that we can't see. It's like that one Klingon ship on *Star Trek* that had that cloaking device. It went around doing evil, but you could never detect it. The Family is like that. They go around doing evil, but no one even knows they exist. No one can get close enough to them to hurt them. How can Carmichael Vero and the Family have been operating illegally like this all these years and leave no evidence or clues of their guilt? I can barely trace a residue of illegal activity, and I'm a pro. The public sees VECO as totally legit. No one wants to be suspicious. It's that force field that protects them, I tell you. It's spooky. Not even Gotti had such protection, and he was tops. It's what makes the Veros and the Family invincible."

He got goose bumps on his neck as he spoke into the recorder one last:

"I'm serious, Captain. I've been investigating criminals for years. I've never seen anything like the Family. I'm starting to get spooked about this whole investigation. These Vero's have something on their side that ain't human."

SEVEN

Father God stirred up the burden in Audra Dutton as she was talking on the phone. Audra called Sharon Harrison almost every night before bed. Audra and Sharon had been sisters in the Lord for over twenty years. Sharon was there for Audra when her husband Arnie Dutton died in 1976. Sharon, who had been divorced, spent much of her time with Audra, praying, consoling, helping around the house. She was faithfully there for Audra through a time of great grief. Audra had never been ministered to in such a way. She and Sharon bonded and the two were inseparable ever since.

That night Audra and Sharon were chattering about their church. Audra felt God's power suddenly flood her spirit as she spoke.

". . . 'cause Darrin Jennings always flirts with Pastor's daughter and . . . Ooohhh! Sister!"

"Audra! You okay?" Sharon said, alarmed.

"Holy Ghost just came all over me, Girl. Jesus wants me to start prayin'."

"Is it your burden again?"

"Yes! I'll tell you what, Sharon, He does not play when it comes to this. He comes on so forceful and strong. Everyone says, 'Holy Ghost, He's a gentleman.' But I tell you what, He ain't no gentleman when it comes to this burden. He's serious! Like a man wantin' lovin'!"

Sharon guffawed and heaved, and then burst out in long, deep laughter.

"I'm serious, Sharon. You gotta pray with me now."

After violent laughter, Sharon heaved and caught her breath and said, "I've never heard Holy Ghost described like *that*!" She burst out laughing again. She laughed on and on.

"Oh, you know what I mean! I didn't mean Him any disrespect. I just meant He's serious."

Now Audra giggled, too.

"Stop it, you silly girl! You gonna get me laughin', too!"

This did not calm Sharon Harrison's laughter.

"Seriously, Sharon! He's on me *hard* now. I'm gonna start prayin'. You better join me, now."

Audra Dutton began praying in the Spirit. His anointing came on strong, instantly.

"Whoa!" Sharon said. Holy Spirit came upon her now, and her laughter waned a bit. "You do have the anointing on you, Audra. I felt it as soon as you started praying in the Holy Ghost."

Audra quickly paused and blurted: "Then cut the laughin' and start prayin', girl!"

Sharon started praying in her prayer language. There was unity between them as Holy Spirit spoke through them in the languages they could not understand. His power was released from their mouths. They started praising the Father and worshipping His Son. They praised and prayed in tongues intermittently. After several minutes of this agreement in the Spirit, Audra Dutton broke loose:

"My Father in Heaven! Let the power of your Son, the risen Christ, break the chains of bondage off of those people who killed my son! Let your power free them from bondage. From sin and death! Oh Father! from the very powers of hell itself!"

The whole time Sharon Harrison was vehemently saying, "Amen!" and "I agree, Lord!"

"Have mercy on those people, Father, and save them!" Audra said. "I don't even know who they are, but save those people, Lord. Save their children! They took my son, but My Father, I bless them now and ask You to save *their* children! In Jesus' mighty name!"

Their prayers transcended time and space that night, directly touching a life in Ohio.

EIGHT

It was raining in Columbus, Ohio. A woman in her late twenties sat silently on her bed reading her Bible as the rain pelted the roof of her small apartment. She was stout, with long, curly black hair and olive skin. She had big, dark eyes with thick lashes and full, pouty lips. There were some lines on her face that she considered premature. Not many people noticed, but she, having spent years of vanity and insecurity, did indeed notice. She knew that she had put those lines there. Premature age lines. Lines of death, she referred to them. She had incurred every one of those lines. Her former lifestyle had all but killed her. She was just glad to be alive right now. She was so grateful to Jesus Christ.

She thought of those lines on her face as she read the words of Paul out loud from the book of Romans:

"'For the wages of sin is death,'" she spoke as she read, "'but the gift of God is eternal life in Christ Jesus our Lord.'"

She glanced up at the large mirror on her dresser. She looked at the crow's feet around her eyes.

"Those are the wages of sin," she said aloud, this time she was talking to Jesus. "Lord, those are the lines of death because I was killing myself. Because I wanted to die," she explained to Him. "Drugs, men, booze, men, partying, men. Men, men, men. Lord," she looked puzzled now, "why would you create such creatures as men? They are most hateful!" She giggled aloud, then sighed deeply.

Then there was the shame from being a part of her horrible family. She had always wished she could be someone else, not have her identity.

She read back a couple of verses. "'What fruit did you have then in the things of which you are now ashamed? For the end of those things is death.'"

Ashamed. *Ashamed.* "There was no fruit in those things," she said, "except what Paul says there, 'The end of those things is death.' I brought death to myself through my actions."

Ashamed. Man, she thought. *This Paul guy sure can hit the mark.* She had been wrought with shame and guilt. She knew their sting and destruction. Once you do the things you hate doing, the very things that bring shame and guilt, you wind up doing them *again*, for some stupid reason! The promiscuity, the drugs, the alcohol, you just keep doing them. Then those shameful, guilt-ridden activities wrap you up like unbreakable chains of bondage. You become imprisoned in the lifestyle that you hate. The lifestyle consumes you. It becomes part of your identity. People know you for your trashy lifestyle. People stare at you. People point to you and whisper, *there's that person, you know, the one who . . .*

Bondage. Guilt. Condemnation.

"But no more, Jesus!" she said out loud to her Savior.

She flipped over a page in her Bible to the eighth chapter of Paul's letter to the Romans.

She read the verse aloud, excitedly: "'There is therefore now no condemnation for those who are in Christ Jesus, who do not walk according to the flesh, but according to the Spirit of God. For the law of the Spirit of life in Christ Jesus has made me free from the law of sin and death.'"

She had read this a few times before when her pastor had taught on this verse, but recently Holy Spirit had opened up her understanding to it. Since then He was patiently teaching her the true meaning of the verse. He was calling her to accept the truth of these words. But she was very slow to receive them. Eleven years of guilt and shame made her skittish of even God's genuine unconditional love.

"There's no condemnation for those who are in You, Jesus," she said aloud, inching closer to the truth. "If then, Lord, I'm in You, because You have saved me and made me Your dwelling place, made me your temple, then Your Spirit had set me free from sin and death. That's what Pastor said that Sunday."

She opened her heart a little more. He began to fill her heart with this truth. She began to receive it.

She remembered a recent counseling session with an associate pastor and his wife at their church. She honestly had confessed to them about all of her promiscuity and the troubles that came with it. She explained her pain and confusion. She told them about how dirty and sleazy she felt as a woman who was trying to give her life over to a holy Jesus Christ. This associate pastor and his wife had the answers she was looking for. They explained to her how Bathsheba, the woman who committed adultery with King David, was listed in the Bible as being one in the lineage of Jesus Christ Himself. "God cleansed her," they told her. "When God forgives He wipes the slate clean." They also told her about the woman who was caught in the act of adultery and brought to Jesus. "He didn't condemn her," they explained. "And He doesn't condemn you. If Bathsheeba and the adulterous woman could be cleansed of their guilt, you most certainly can be, too!"

"Then," she now said out loud on her bed, "there's no more room for condemnation and guilt. You've taken it away from me Jesus. If You're in me, and Your Word says You've removed the condemnation and guilt and shame, then I don't have to put up with it! It has to go!"

Light flooded her heart. Release came to her soul. Guilt and shame suddenly fled from her as the presence of God increased in her heart. Like manacles and shackles falling to the ground, the bondage of guilt and shame fell. There truly was no room for them there if He was present. Tears poured down her cheeks. She leaned forward on the bed, tears dripping all over her Bible as raindrops dripped outside her apartment.

Gina Vero was suddenly free.

God had used His Word and all of those people in order to loose her from the condemnation that was killing her. It had been a slow process since Gina had given her heart to Him a year earlier, but tonight was a night of breakthrough. Holy Spirit had ordained this time for her deliverance.

"Thank You, Lord," Gina sobbed, in the midst of her revelation. "You've removed all my guilt."

She pushed her Bible aside, laid face down on her bed and began to thank Jesus, over and over. Gratefulness bubbled up in her heart like a spring. She couldn't believe what a loving God He truly was. In all the years of her life no one had ever even told her about Him.

"I'm free," she said. "From my sins, from my lifestyle, from the guilt and the shame, and from the guilt of my family. I'm free."

On that evening, God moved Gina Vero one step deeper into His kingdom. He knew that guilt and shame would try to return and get back inside her, but He would raise others who would pray for her and speak truth to her that would keep her free. Gina Vero was His daughter now, and no one, absolutely *no one*, would snatch her from His hands.

Gina remained on the bed for the next twenty minutes, sobbing, laughing, thanking, praying. She felt so fresh and clean. She felt pure for the first time in her life. She was so blessed to be saved and to be so intimate with God. Jesus was so good . . .

Tony! Thoughts of her brother suddenly swept into her heart.

"I've got to tell Tony about Jesus," she said to herself as she shut her Bible.

Poor Tony, she thought. She had never known him to be in the state of depression he was in now. He had always been so bright and outgoing. The consummate athlete, the consummate winner. But Tony Vero was no winner now. He was a recluse. Something very traumatic had happened to Tony that winter. She had no idea what, and Tony surely wasn't sharing any personal information with her. She had only seen him once since March. He was a mess. She knew he was drinking heavily. Recently her Uncle Joseph Vero told her that Tony wasn't even leaving his house. For awhile he had been answering his phone. She would talk to him. She would try to tell him about Jesus, but Tony was so out of it he wouldn't respond. Now Tony wasn't even answering his phone. Her watressing job wasn't permitting her much time to take the two and a half hour drive from Columbus, Ohio to Beaver Falls, Pennsylvania. She would drive over and check up on him this weekend, though, even if she had to take the time off. She would just have to risk seeing Uncle Carmichael Vero, too. Carmichael had cut her completely off months ago when she told him that she got saved. She had gone to see him again that winter. Carmichael became enraged and openly cursed her. He wanted to hear nothing about Jesus Christ. Carmichael had become to her what her own father had been years earlier when he was alive. Her father would have nothing to do with her when she became so lascivious. Carmichael was the same to her now that she was saved.

"Boy," she thought, "you just can't win in my family."

Which was more the truth than Gina Vero even realized.

She hopped off her bed and grabbed her phone. She had to talk to Tony. She had to snap her younger brother out of whatever had happened to him. She had to introduce Tony to Jesus and let God light him up the way He'd lit her up.

She speed dialed Tony's number. His phone rang. And it rang. And it rang.

What if he just plain has the phone disconnected, now? she thought.

"I'll find out!" Gina Vero said out loud. She let the phone keep ringing.

Gina waited.

NINE

Joseph Vero parked his Porche in his nephew Tony Vero's driveway. It was 10:15 p.m. The two story house sat about twenty yards from the road, hidden behind a huge barrier of tall pines and shrubs. Tonight that barrier would serve Joseph well, for he knew he would have to go to war with Tony to even get the young man to speak to him.

For the past two months Joseph had pounded on both the front and back doors, yelled and screamed, and had even considered calling the police on Tony. His key to his late brother's house was worthless. Tony put new locks and dead bolts on all doors. He tried to sneak in with Lula Johnson the house cleaner one morning, but Tony spotted him and refused to let her in until Joseph got in his car and left. Nothing worked. So Joseph was done playing games. Carmichael had demanded Tony's presence at VECO in the morning and had personally put Joseph's butt on the line if Tony didn't appear. Tony was not only being disrespectful and rude to Carmichael but he was spitting in Joseph's face, as it were, by putting him on the line this way. Joseph would have no more of Tony's insolence.

Tony's long driveway was illuminated by a single spotlight on the corner of the house. In the shadows Joseph walked up to the front picture window and looked inside. The picture window was cloaked with white curtains. But Joseph could still see shapes in the living room. There was Tony, sitting in the recliner. All Joseph could see was his silhouette, but it was his first glimpse of his nephew in a month. As angry as he was, Joseph was relieved to see the young man alive. A lamp was on and the television was flickering. He could hear Tony's telephone ringing incessantly. Of course, Tony was making no effort to answer it.

Joseph did not go to ring the doorbell. He did not try to beg, plead, or yell for Tony this time. He had lived out that scene far too many times. Enough. Joseph calmly walked over to a pair of garbage cans beside the garage. He lifted a brick off of one of the lids and stepped back over to the front of the house. He aimed his sights on the massive picture window. In one fluid motion Joseph hurled the brick. It did not shatter the glass. Joseph had hurled it so fast that it simply made a loud *pop* and left a jagged hole in the window as it broke through. Joseph heard it bounce twice through the living room and then thump to a halt. He stepped back and waited.

Tony's silhouette floated slowly over to the broken window, stood motionless there for a moment, and then floated out of the living room toward the foyer. He appeared in the window next to the front door, then disappeared again. Suddenly the front porch light flicked on. Joseph could hear the sound of the locks being undone. The door flung open. Joseph could see no one inside.

"What?" Tony rasped at Joseph from inside the darkness.

"Let me in. There's an emergency."

There was a moment of hesitation, but Tony finally pushed the door all the way open. Joseph saw him walk out of the foyer and back into the living room. That must have been the okay. So what if it wasn't? Joseph was going in. He entered Tony's luxurious house.

The first thing Joseph saw was the trophy case smashed to bits along the foyer wall. The aluminum baseball bat still lay atop the rubble. Beneath the debris Joseph could make out a photo of his brother Pete and Tony both standing next to Joe Namath. Tony and Joe Namath were shaking hands. Pete had his hand on Tony's shoulder, grinning like the Cheshire cat. It was one of the happiest moments in Pete's life. Now the photo was all but destroyed. That trophy case had been Pete Vero's pride and joy when he was alive. Pete had been so proud of his athletically gifted son. He bought the expensive case and built it up year after year of Tony's athletic career at Beaver Falls middle school and high school. Pete proudly displayed the trophy case in his foyer so it would be the first thing visitors would see. Tony had once said it was more of a reminder of his father than a salute to his high school career. To see it smashed so, obviously by Tony's own hands, only made Joseph that much more concerned about his nephew's mental state.

Joseph followed Tony into the living room. Tony had gone straight back to his reclining chair. He'd walked right past the ringing telephone on the table near the living room entrance. Though his uncle stood in his home for the first time in months Tony didn't even acknowledge Joseph. Joseph was shocked at his shabby appearance. The Kid obviously hadn't had a haircut in months. Thick black locks cascaded down to his neck. Tony just sat there facing the television like a zombie. A quarter pitcher of beer sat next to a beer mug on the floor beside him.

The ringing phone got on Joseph's last nerve. He knew Tony wouldn't answer it. Why didn't the Kid just disconnect it? He reached over and picked it up.

"Hello," Joseph said impatiently.

There was a pause on the other end. Suddenly Gina Vero spoke.

"Uncle Joe?" she asked.

"Hello, Gina," Joseph said lovingly. He had not rejected Gina when she gave her heart to Jesus Christ. He didn't know how to handle her, but he still loved his niece.

"Uncle Joe, where's Tony?" Gina sounded very concerned.

"He's right here. Listen Gina, I just got in here. Your brother looks rough."

"I need to talk to him, Uncle Joe."

Joseph sighed. "So do I." He held out the phone toward Tony. "Tony. Your sister's on the phone. Come talk to her."

Tony didn't budge. The twenty-four year old picked up his beer mug, chugged the remainder of it and dropped it on the floor.

Joseph was disgusted. "This is your sister, Tony! Come talk to her!"

Tony just stared at the television.

"Gina," Joseph explained calmly to his niece, "Tony is a real wreck. I'm about to let him have it. Your Great Uncle Carmichael wants to see him so I need to get Tony cleaned up and out of the house. He looks like he's been drunk for weeks."

Gina's voice quivered as she spoke: "Uncle Joe, take care of him. Tell him I'm going to come see him sometime this week."

"Gina, one way or another Tony's going to be very busy," Joseph told her. He knew Carmichael was going to have the Kid out playing private detective looking for Todd Falco and the money. "You might want to give it a week or two before you come driving over here from Ohio to see him."

"I'm coming over there, Uncle Joe. Don't try to discourage me," Gina replied through tears.

Joseph knew she was determined. "I'm not. Just leave Tony to us for a few days."

"Don't let Uncle Carmichael get a hold of Tony, now!" Gina pleaded. "I think Uncle Carmichael has something to do with Tony being so messed up!"

"Gina," Joseph said forcefully, "You leave Tony to us. I'm hanging up now."

"Tell Tony that I'm praying for him everyday!" Gina cried through the phone.

Joseph Vero just shook his head and gently hung up the phone. "Tony!" he called out.

The Kid wouldn't turn to face his Uncle. Joseph couldn't hold back any more. This was his brother's son. He'd vowed to look after Tony and his sister Gina after Pete's death. Joseph felt a hot lead ball in his throat as he stood there looking at the spectacle of Tony. He finally just blurted out:

"Kid, what's wrong with you?"

Tony didn't turn around, but he finally spoke: "You throw a brick through my window, and you ask what's wrong with *me*?"

Joseph stepped toward his nephew. "Don't give me that, Kid! You've purposely avoided me for months. I've got an emergency here and wasn't about to come pound on your door for twenty minutes while you just ignored me inside." Joseph waved his hand at the beer mug on the floor. "You're the one with the problem."

Tony angrily turned in the chair and faced his uncle for the first time. "I've got a *big* problem, Uncle Joe, and it's my business. I'll take care of it. Leave me alone!"

Joseph waved his hand with disgust at Tony. "It's *my* business too! You're not only my nephew, but you came to work for Carmichael and me, remember, Kid? Or has all this beer killed off all your memory cells?" Joseph noticed that Tony had a scruffy beard. His hair was so long it covered his forehead and ears. Carmichael, Joseph and the late Pete hated scraggly, long-haired men.

"Look at you, Tony! Your Father would kill you right now! You're a mess!" He pointed toward the foyer to the demolished trophy case. "What happened to *that*?"

Tony just stared back at the TV.

"What happened to your father's trophy case, Tony?"

"It had an accident," Tony muttered.

"An *accident*?" Joseph said. "You are a Vero, Tony! You need to straighten up and act like a man. You're hiding away like some little boy."

Tony leapt from his chair. "You know, I didn't ask you to look after me after Dad died. And if I'm such a problem to VECO, then I just quit."

"This is all about Ft. Lauderdale, isn't it Tony?"

Tony's face flushed. His hands trembled. Joseph knew he'd gotten to him.

"Answer me! It's what happened in Ft. Lauderdale that's made you like this. Isn't it, Tony?"

"I had Ft. Lauderdale under control!" Tony shouted at his uncle, his hair bouncing up and down off his flannel shirt. Tears formed in his reddened eyes. "I had it under control down there!" He turned around and staggered over to the broken picture window. "I had it under control!" Tony punched out more of the broken glass with one lightning swing of his fist through the curtains. Glass tinkled to the grass below.

"That's great, Tony. Let's wake up the whole neighborhood and get the cops out here."

"Oh boy! The cops! Wouldn't you like to have them snooping around you and Uncle Carmichael and Ed Larsky over there in your little Family world at VECO?" Tony slurred.

Joseph got up in his face. "What kind of operation did you think the Family was, Tony, when you joined us? Who did you think we were? The United Way collecting donations for Mother Teresa?" Joseph stepped even further into him. "What kind of business did you think your father was into?"

"I obviously didn't know exactly *what* my father was into." Tony walked back toward the recliner. "I didn't know Dad was into *this*. I knew you all weren't priests or anything. But I never imagined anything like Ft. Lauderdale." Tony paused and looked at his Uncle Joseph. "How do you live with yourself?"

Joseph flushed with anger, now.

"Tony, this is what made the Family and VECO and Uncle Carmichael in the first place! You knew about Ed Larsky and what he did in your Uncle Carmichael's trial back in '81. Why does any of this shock you? Can you be a Vero and yet be so thick in the head? Do you think VECO would exist if it weren't for Carmichael and his money he made from the Mafia? Do you think I'd be where I am today if it weren't for my business in the Family? Or your father? Why do you think you grew up in this house in this neighborhood? Where do you think all your cars and clothes and money Pete gave you and Gina came from? Are you going to climb up on some high horse and make judgment over your whole family all of the sudden, just because you got a wake up slap in the face down in Ft. Lauderdale? I'm sorry, Kid, but if it took you that long to figure out what the Family is, what we Veros have been all about, that's your own naiveté. And you're too far in now to get out or change anything about us. It's who we are. It's who the Veros are."

"Then I hate being a Vero!" Tony yelled.

"I ought to slap your fat mouth!" Joseph yelled. "Your Father would have for insulting your own blood like that!"

"Well I do hate it! I hate who the Veros really are!"

"So you're going to lock yourself in your house and drink until you die?"

"I might!"

They both took a step back from each other and stood silent for a moment.

"Why did you come here tonight, Uncle Joe?"

Joseph sighed again. He went over to the couch and slowly set his weary body down.

"There's an emergency. A big one. I loaded up Todd Falco for a big buy last night and he's completely vanished."

Tony looked troubled but said nothing.

"He's vanished without a trace, Tony. I loaded him up with one million and one hundred thousand dollars of Family money and now he's gone."

Tony leaned back against a wall. "Who was he buying from?"

Joseph leaned forward and rubbed his forehead. "A new guy. New contact. His name's Bernie Lokawski. Selling cocaine like I haven't seen in years. Beautiful stuff."

"Did Todd even make it to the buy?"

"I have no idea, Kid. All I know is I loaded him up and that's the last I saw of him."

Silence, again.

"What's this have to do with me?"

"What do you think, Tony? What did the Family pay to have you trained for? What did Carmichael hire you to do?"

"I quit, Uncle Joe. I don't work for you or Carmichael anymore."

"Tony, this isn't McDonald's!" Joseph was yelling again. Tony had never seen his usually stoic Uncle shouting like this. "You don't quit the Family! I put my entire reputation on the line for you to get you into the Family in the first place! We sent you to private eye school when you flunked out of college and made you a part of something so big people would die to get in to. And then you do *this*! Carmichael and Ed Larsky want to wring my neck every time I tell them about you hiding out here, ignoring us."

"I want out, Uncle Joseph!"

Joseph stood up and squared off with Tony.

"No."

"I want *out*," Tony said through gritted teeth.

"You don't get out, Tony," he whispered grimly. "I tried to tell you that before you got in! Once you get in the Family you're a part of it, like flesh and blood. You don't get out. You never get out. Your dad's dead and he's still a part of it! I still have to cover Pete's tracks. Now I'm covering yours, too. No, Kid. There is no way out. I warned you before you ever got in!"

Tony turned and went back toward the recliner. He picked up a pitcher of beer beside it and took a long, slow drink. He looked up at Joseph.

"What's Uncle Carmichael want me to do about this?"

"Tony, Carmichael told me to come here, get you, and tell you that you are going to find Todd Falco and our money. You're coming back to work for us. You're going to do your job."

Tony looked disgusted and shook his head.

"And he said you have no choice, Tony. You are VECO's private investigator. I cannot go find Todd Falco. None of us can without attracting attention to ourselves. We're VECO executives. What would we be doing personally looking for a VECO employee?"

"And a cocaine dealer."

"That, too, if it comes out some time. Todd was good. No one knew what he did on the side. So we're going to have VECO hire you to find their missing employee."

"Have the cops been notified?"

"They have not. Todd's wife knows better and we sure aren't anxious for the involvement of law enforcement on this case."

Tony picked up the pitcher of beer. He guzzled the remainder of beer straight from it and tossed it beside his empty mug. He stared down at the carpet. Joseph knew his intelligent nephew was already manipulating the whole scenario in his mind. The young man finally looked up at Joseph and winked.

Joseph cracked a small smile. "You're going to do it, aren't you, Kid?"

"Yup," Tony said, unsmiling. "I'll find him for you all."

"I know you will, Kid. You're the best I've ever seen. They could make a TV show about you. Carmichael wants you in his office first thing in the morning. He's hiring you under the normal conditions. Usual pay."

"Nope. Not this time, he's not," Tony said as he breezed past his uncle and started out of the living room.

Joseph's temper rose yet again. "What do you mean?" He followed Tony. "Don't you mess with Carmichael and Larsky right now, Tony!"

"I'm gonna find Todd Falco and your money. Fast. And I'm going to save every one of you from this mess. But it's gonna cost Uncle Carmichael and the Family. Big." Tony stopped in his kitchen and opened his refrigerator. He pulled out a cola instead of a beer.

"You're not going to use this situation to make more money, Tony! You will accept normal pay!" Joseph blushed with anger.

Tony walked up into his uncle's face, this time. Joseph Vero could smell his nephew's stale, alcohol breath.

"Uncle Joe, I'm going to charge you, Carmichael, that fathead Ed Larsky, and the entire Family something you've never had to pay before. I'm gonna cost you all, *big*."

Joseph crossed his arms indignantly. "What's it going to cost us, Kid?"

Tony smiled big:

"Me."

TEN

E d Larsky pulled up to Todd and Kay Falco's house at 7:30 a.m. He was there to "talk to" Kay Falco, per Carmichael Vero's orders. The Falcos lived near New Galilee, Pennsylvania, a small country town outside of Beaver Falls. Larsky drove his Dodge Ram pickup truck instead of his Harley. He figured the Harley might be a bit intimidating under these circumstances. He sat in his truck rehearsing his little speech he was going to make to Kay Falco. Carmichael wanted Larsky to speak to Kay as Todd Falco's VECO office boss. His assignment was to convince her to stay away from the police and not to file a missing person's report on Todd, since he had been missing for over 24 hours. Larsky was to assure her that VECO was already conducting a very thorough and discreet investigation of its own. Larsky hated that he would have to make friendly with Mrs. Falco. Here was a case where he would need to paint a smile on his face and act all concerned about the disappearance of her husband Todd. *Oh my! What a pity,* he mocked to himself. He would feed her some garbage about some top investigative team VECO had hired to locate Todd. Ed Larsky knew, though, that Carmichael would have only Tony Vero investigating Todd's whereabouts. Or better yet, the whereabouts of the one million and one hundred thousand dollars. And Ed Larsky was angered by the fact that Tony Vero was being brought into this. Larsky always hated Tony Vero. He hated his guts. Tony was friendly, confident. He always had a smile on his face like he was sitting on the top of the world and inviting everyone else to join him. Larsky loathed his congenial demeanor. To Larsky, Tony Vero was a spoiled brat who got his way about everything in the Vero family. Now he even got his way into the Family, a move which Larsky vehemently fought from the beginning. Tony wouldn't even have known that the Family existed if it weren't for his big-mouthed father Pete Vero. Larsky knew the Kid was a softy at heart and did not have the edge necessary to produce for the Family. Larsky warned the Family. He knew Tony didn't grasp what the Family really was. He thought it was all glitz and glamour. But no one heeded Larsky and Tony was brought on board. After a couple of small jobs came the Ft. Lauderdale assignment. The Kid cracked. When he returned home from Ft. Lauderdale Tony got all squirrelly and hid in his house. This pleased Ed Larsky grandly. It only proved his point that Tony was weak and he had been right about him all along. Tony may have been tough on the football field, but he couldn't hack life in the Family.

Larsky convinced himself that he hated Tony Vero because of some weakness he thought he spotted in the young man. But Ed Larsky was jealous of Tony Vero, though that fact would never occur to him. He was jealous of the way that all the elder Veros gushed over the young man. He was jealous that all the girls swooned over Tony's good looks. He was jealous of the fact that Tony was well-liked everywhere he went. And despite the fact that he was ex-Mafioso Pete Vero's son, Tony was thought of as being some clean-cut, all American boy. And when Tony became a local football hero at quarterback, the likes of which Beaver Falls hadn't seen since Joe Namath, this was all Ed Larsky could stand. Attention poured in on Tony Vero at Beaver Falls Senior High. People adored him. Sports networks, national magazines, and newspapers featured stories about him regularly. Finally, West Virginia University gave Tony a full scholarship to train him to be their junior year starting quarterback. Larsky had been a vicious high school player, but because he came from a poor background with average grades, he never even made it into college. Tony's full ride to WVU was a tremendous blow to Larsky's pride. But oh, how time changes everything! When Tony injured his rotator cuff in his freshman year at WVU he was told he'd never play at full capacity again. Larsky gloated while all the other Veros wept for the Kid. Tony attempted to counter the doctors' claims that his career was finished. He trained extra hard, tried to prove himself in the off season. But then Pete Vero had the heart attack and croaked. Within five years Tony lost both his mother and his father. That took all the wind out of Tony's sails. He got Pete's life insurance payment for over a million dollars. He consoled himself with non-stop partying and lost his competitive edge. Soon Tony Vero drank himself to expulsion from college in his sophomore year. He lost his scholarship, education, and his plans to one day make it in the NFL. And Ed Larsky inwardly laughed at him and bade Mr. Football Hero Tony "The Kid" Vero farewell. *Tough luck, Kid. You're a loser now.* Tony had everything handed to him on a platter, Larsky was convinced. So he deserved this tragic end to his great career. He had it coming to him. All was square and even, then. Until Carmichael let Tony into the Family. Larsky's jealousy against Tony engorged more than ever. This made Tony an easier target for Ed Larsky's undying hatred. Carmichael and Joseph commanded Larsky to get along with Tony. But he refused. Tony was an amiable person. He would try and make nice with Ed, before and especially after he got into the Family. But Ed would never play along. Tony knew he didn't have a friend in Larsky. And Ed Larsky liked it that way.

Now Ed Larsky had this new vexation. Todd Falco had dealt the Family wrong and disappeared. To Ed Larsky, even if Todd Falco was dead from this drug deal, it was *still* Falco's stupid fault because his death now put the entire Family in jeopardy. The Family presently risked being exposed, apprehended and shut down. And who was Carmichael gonna put in control of the investigation? Tony Vero. Larsky shook his head and growled to himself. When would this Vero infatuation with Tony end? Why didn't they see him like he did? How long would Tony Vero continue to live and be a thorn in the paw of Ed Larsky?

Ed Larsky did vow one thing to himself that morning sitting in his pickup truck in front of Todd Falco's house: before this mess was over, he would get Tony Vero. Once and for all.

Larsky got out of the Ram. He was dressed for work. He wore a gray sports jacket, white shirt and black tie, with black trousers and cowboy boots. He rehearsed once again what he would say to Kay Falco as he walked up the driveway to the two-story house. He stopped for a moment and painted a consoling smile on his face. He might need to be the comforter to Kay Falco in order to butter her up. He meditated on his speech one last time. He reached the front door and rang the doorbell. Half a minute passed. No answer. He checked his fake smile in the storm door glass. He rang the doorbell again. This would be his best acting job in years. Still, no one answered. He rang the bell again and then pounded on the storm door. Someone started unlocking the door inside.

I can pull this off, he thought smugly.

Ed Larsky didn't know Kay Falco.

Kay Falco whipped open the inside door hard with a furious face, reddened eyes pouring tears, and screaming baby Dylon in her left arm. Her short blond hair was scattered everywhere with bed-head, and Kay was wearing only a T-shirt and shorts.

"What?" she sneered without even caring to first see who was at her door.

Ed Larsky gasped in shock before he could catch himself. It took a whole lot to knock Ed Larsky off his guard. Kay Falco had. This tornado who answered the door was not the mousy, frightened woman Larsky expected would need consoling. He was speechless. Steam came from his mouth in the early morning cool, but he found no words to say to this underdressed, volcano of a woman. He just stuttered for a second or two . . .

"What is it?" Kay Falco yelled through the storm door, boring a hole through Larsky's thick head with her laser eyes. She had no concern for her appearance.

"I'm Ed Larsky from VECO," was all he could blurt out.

"Good for you!" Kay replied as she switched bawling Dylon to her right arm.

Larsky said nothing for about five seconds, trying to regain his thoughts.

"*WHAT* IS IT?" Kay yelled at him again in frustration, left hand flung out in front of her. "Can't you see I'm trying to take care of my son? Tell me what you want and then get out of here!"

Larsky sobered himself: *Remember your act!*

"I . . . uh . . . I'm afraid it's not that easy, Mrs. Falco. I need to talk to you . . . uh . . . and it's going to take a minute. I can't do it through this glass door."

Kay glared at him for a second, cried out in frustration and then slammed the front door shut.

Larsky was flabbergasted. He made a mental note to write down this date somewhere to mark this occasion when a 90 pound woman left him speechless and intimidated.

He stood there alone on the front stoop for two minutes. He stared at the front door. Was this nut gonna come back and let him in? What was he going to tell Carmichael Vero about this? He was there on a diplomatic mission from Carmichael and his subject hated him after only one minute. No, he wasn't going to be humiliated here. Larsky wasn't about to let this happen. He started getting angry. He went to bang on the storm door again.

Suddenly the inside door opened once more. Kay Falco stood there alone this time. And a bit more presentable. She had thrown on a red flannel shirt and gray sweat pants. Her eyes were still watered and red, and her hair was still a mess. She unlocked the glass storm door and with a disgusted look pushed it open for Larsky.

"You got two minutes, mister!" she pointed her finger at Larsky.

He knew she meant business. He stepped into the foyer.

The house was a mess. Mostly with baby Dylon's things scattered everywhere. Kay had put Dylon in his carseat on the floor and given him a bottle to keep him quiet.

Ed started to step past the foyer into the living room.

"No, no! What you have to say to me you'll say from right there," Kay commanded harshly. She was not going to give him one inch. She crossed her arms and looked at him with contempt.

Larsky realized that all of his sweet talking he had rehearsed in his head for the last ten hours was going to be worthless. His whole act was a crock, anyway. He was a Family business man and was used to threatening, abusing, and killing people. Enough of this attempting to smooth Kay Falco over. She obviously didn't want it and considered Larsky to be trouble anyway. He made a quick decision: forget the act and just let her have it!

"Lookit, Mrs. Falco. Todd's gone. We all want to know where he is. You especially, but so does VECO. We got people investigating his whereabouts already. A special investigation team we use all the time at VECO that's produced a hundred percent for us."

Kay felt herself getting even more infuriated at this man. She knew where Larsky was trying to take her and she didn't like it.

"So what, Mr. Larsky?" she sneered. "What does that have to do with me?"

Larsky glared back at her. "What I'm here to tell you is that you don't need to go to the police. That's what."

Kay grunted in disgust. "How dare you! What business is it of VECO whether or not I go to the police? Todd's my husband and he's missing. If I go to the police that's my business. If VECO's so concerned about him I'd think you'd want me to go to the cops for them to help track him down. Not unless," Kay mockingly acted naive, "you might be one of his drug buddies?" She pointed her finger at the powerfully built man. "Would you happen to be one of Todd's cocaine buddies, Mr. Larsky?" she asked in a Gosh!-I'm-so-shocked-I-can't-believe-it! tone.

Larsky was no longer intimidated. He leaned foreword with a deadly somber stare and repeated: "You don't need to go to the police, Mrs. Falco."

"Does VECO know two of their employees are coke dealers?" Kay continued to lay on the mock innocence. "What would VECO think about that? No wonder you don't want the police involved!"

Larsky turned his head and calmly stared out the window.

Kay refused to be intimidated by this large, muscular man. *I mean, duh,* she thought. *He casually drives up and parks right in front of my house in broad daylight. He obviously couldn't have come here to hurt me.*

"You have nerve, Mr. Larsky, coming here acting all concerned to tell me what to do about my husband when all you're really concerned about is your own criminal butt. You know what? I *am* going to go to the police! In fact, I'll head right over there the minute after your ugly face is out of my house!"

"That would be a terrible mistake on your part, Mrs. Falco," Larsky said calmly and slowly to her.

Kay stepped forward. "What?" she growled.

"If you want things to go well for you," Larsky began, pointing to the floor at Dylon sucking his bottle, "and you really care about your baby . . ."

Kay exploded. "How dare you, you ugly, stupid goon!" Her face was bright red. Plump veins bulged in her neck.

Larsky stood calmly, stone faced.

"How dare you threaten the life of my son!"

Larsky drove his point home: "Mrs. Falco, if you truly do care for that baby and want it to have a happy life with you as its mother, you had better not go to the police."

Kay Falco sobbed first, then broke into tears. "Get out," she said, so choked up that it was barely audible.

"You heard what I said, Mrs. Falco. No police." Larsky coldly whispered.

Like a child who just got hurt, Kay sucked in a long breath, hands over her tear-soaked face, and then screamed, "GET OUT OF MY HOUSE, NOW!"

Baby Dylon jolted with fear in his carseat and began crying.

Ed Larsky pointed his finger at her and softly said, "Remember what I said." He turned around in the foyer and went to open the door.

Sobbing uncontrollably, Kay swiftly bent down, picked up a thick magazine and flung it at Larsky's back as he stepped out the storm door. "Out!" she repeated as the magazines flapped off his back to the floor.

He turned with an evil countenance, halfway out the door, and glared at Kay. Ed Larsky did not let things like this go . . .

But before he could say a word, Kay had already yanked a huge lamp off a living room table near the wall and was charging him. Larsky's eyes widened at the sight of this beautiful, enraged, petite little woman screaming a primordial war-cry as she hurled the lamp at him. He quickly shot out the glass storm door. The bulky lamp, shade and all, shattered the entire glass pane and struck Larsky on the back of his right boot as he high stepped to get out of the way. His first impulse was to go back and break her skinny little body in half. He thought of Carmichael Vero, though, and restrained himself. Carmichael would not accept any public trouble that might tarnish the impeccable reputation of VECO. Instead, Larsky turned and coolly sauntered back to his red Ram pickup.

Kay Falco bounded barefooted out the front door, totally unconcerned about the broken glass on the front porch stoop. She aimed her sights on Larsky and shouted at the top of her lungs:

"I'm going to the police, NOW, you rotten . . ." and the obscenities echoed throughout the wooded areas surrounding the Falco residence.

Larsky, red in the face, could see a neighbor's house visible down the road. He knew they had to have heard Kay's screaming. But he was going to maintain his cool standard. Hey, if anyone questioned him about his visit to Kay Falco, all he would have to tell them is that he was the concerned VECO office manager checking on the well-being of one of his employees and their family. Kay Falco was the one who flipped out. He confidently climbed into his truck, cranked the engine, and slowly turned around and cruised down the road at a gentle clip. Good exit, he thought. He hardly looked like a guilty man. And he was sure that all the neighbors must have known by now that Kay Falco was some kind of nut. He was sorry this assignment didn't turn out better, but Carmichael was just gonna have to get over it. Larsky didn't make Kay Falco the nut that she was. As he was driving off, however, Ed Larsky mentally added Kay Falco to his always expanding list of people he was going to get.

Back at the Falco house, for the second time in so many days, a weeping Kay Falco watched a man who had just rattled her emotions drive off down the road. But this time, with her house in shambles and Dylon crying inside, she vowed she was not just going to sit there. No, Kay was going to do something about all this. She was going to get Ed Larsky and Todd Falco and anyone else who threatened her or her son. This time, Kay Falco was going to stir up all the trouble.

Tony Vero was terrified and fatigued. Not only was he unaccustomed to being up at 8:00 in the morning, but he had barely slept at all last night after his Uncle Joseph left. He was afraid he'd have another nightmare. He didn't want to face one knowing what he had to face today. His head throbbed. He was close to being sober for the first time in over a month. Anxiety was trying to overtake him. But he could do nothing to douse his pain and fear this time. He had to be sober in order to face Carmichael and Larsky. He had to be alert to take on this Todd Falco case for VECO and the Family. But how he longed to have a stiff drink just so he could get himself out of the house! That was his main problem this morning. How was he going to handle leaving the security of his house and step out into the open world? He'd been in his comfortable home so long he'd forgotten how much the idea of leaving it had come to frighten him. He didn't understand this fear that gripped him so tightly. He knew in his intelligent, logical mind that this fear of being outdoors was irrational. But it was still so real to him. He wanted, no, he desperately needed the security of his home fortress to make him feel safe. Depression would set in again if he left. He walked over to an upstairs hall window and pressed his face and hands against it. Outside the sun was breaking through a band of clouds. The spring day looked inviting to the average person. But to Tony, just looking through the window at his spacious front yard made him break out in a cold sweat. He felt nauseated. He couldn't do it! He couldn't leave. Why had he agreed to meet with Carmichael? Why didn't he just tell his Uncle Joseph to forget it? Anxiety swirled in his chest like a twister. Shaking, he staggered down the hall and into a bathroom. He flicked on a light and looked in the mirror. What he saw snapped him up alert. Tony's face was sheet white. His forehead was beaded with sweat. He was trembling all over.

"Look at yourself!" he gasped in realization. "You're terrified like some baby. That's not you!"

Staring in disgust at what he had become, his mind raced to take control of the situation. He needed something within to help calm himself. What was that saying from the Bible Gina had mentioned to him on the phone one night? "God doesn't make us afraid . . ."? "God hasn't given us fear?" Why did she tell him that? This wasn't working. He needed something else. Thoughts twisted and rolled through his mind's eye until he found some sort of strength to focus on within. His mind searched for past pressures that seemed insurmountable, yet he was able to conquer. He remembered Friday nights at Reeves Stadium on College Hill. Nights where he single-handedly took control of football games when the Tigers were down. Games played in front of crowds of thousands. Games played in front of college scouts who had the power of life and death over an athlete's college career. He knew the pain and determination it would take to win on nights like that. He understood the sacrifice. It was he who rallied his team as quarterback. It was he who forced one hundred and ten percent out of everyone on the field when they didn't feel like they had it. It was he who forced the game their way until somehow they got the points on the board to win. *He* had accomplished that. Tony Vero.

"I did that," he said out loud. His voice quivered, though. It wasn't very convincing. Another voice within seemed to remind him what a loser he really was now. The distant voice told him that he'd never make it today if he left the house. Discouragement. He'd heard it before, echoing in the distant balconies of his thought life, in peanut heavens of his consciousness. But now it seemed to be jeering him from front row seats.

He looked in the mirror again.

"If you don't get out there today and do what needs to be done, you'll be blowing the only chance you'll ever have to change your life back."

That was it. The truth. Get out there today or forget about it for good. He'd either walk in that truth, or die a slow death in that house.

"God's not given us fear!" he said again with conviction. Now it meant something. Now it seemed to have a kick to it. Somehow, there was a purpose for Gina sharing that with him. Fear could be his death if he didn't get out and do something that day.

With trembling knees, Tony forced himself down the hall to his bathroom to get ready.

The three men stood over the freshly covered grave. The tallest man was in his early fifties. His face was twisted and homely. He dressed in worn work clothes. He was built like a marble statue, powerfully formed all over. The man beside him was in his late twenties. He walked with a limp. The third man was a stocky twenty-six year old with a crew cut. The big man looked over the grave plot, studying it intensely. The younger two, brothers, watched the big man anxiously. They were worried about his possible reaction. He was quite volatile. If he didn't like this setup, he might explode on them.

There was a temporary golden marker staked in the light brown earth covering the grave. It read, "Mary Louise Gray," and listed her date of birth and the day she died. The big man wouldn't say anything.

The youngest brother chirped up, trying to put a good spin on the work they'd done: "Her name's Mary Gray. She just died Sunday night. She lived in that old folks home on 7th Avenue downtown. She was eighty-nine years . . ."

"I can read how old she was. Shut up!" the big man barked.

The older brother nervously elbowed his sibling, warning him to keep his mouth shut.

The big man looked around Grandview Cemetery. This plot was far off the beaten path and surrounded by many other tomb stones. There was a marble base between Mary Gray's plot and the one adjacent to hers, but the headstone was missing. He pointed down at that other plot.

"That her husband beside her?" he asked.

"Yeah," the older brother's voice quivered. "He died five years ago."

"They have one of those double tombstones? The kind that has both their names on it together?"

"Yeah, Frankie."

"When's it gonna be replaced?"

"It'll take the engraver about two weeks to get her name and death date on it beside her husband's. He'll ship it back over to us and we'll replace it right away."

"So this'll all be looking normal again soon?"

The older brother answered again, pointing down at the earthy plot: "We already got grass seed planted in this dirt. The headstone'll be replaced soon. Everything will be just like you want it, Frankie."

Frankie rubbed his chin and nodded, making a satisfied "Hmmmm" sound. He looked around Grandview one more time and nodded again. He finally announced:

"It's perfect."

The two brothers sighed and laughed, relieved. Their shoulders slumped to relaxation.

"W-w-we knew you'd like this one, Frankie!" the youngest one smiled, his hands trembling.

Frankie stepped back and glared at them both. "Now I suppose you'll be wanting your pay for this," he said with disgust.

They both laughed, embarrassed, like wanting him to pay them for their work was something to be ashamed of. Frankie sighed impatiently. He pulled out a wrinkled envelope filled with a lump of old hundred dollar bills. He took out the wad and meticulously counted it two times in a row, making sure he wasn't accidentally paying them any more than was due. The two watched nervously again. Finally, when he was satisfied with his accounting, Frankie closed up the envelope and threw it at the older brother.

"Four grand," he mumbled unhappily. "You two split it up yourselves."

The oldest brother, Greggy, didn't dare offend Frankie by trying to count it in front of him to make sure it was all there. He'd made that mistake in the past. This time, he simply pocketed the envelope. He and his younger brother, Jimmy, would split it later when Frankie was gone. They simply nodded, smiled, and thanked Frankie. They started to walk off, but Frankie suddenly put out a tree trunk of an arm and clothes-lined Jimmy by his neck. Jimmy "oofed" and they both froze in their tracks. What did he want now?

"You two," Frankie rasped ominously.

They looked up at him, confused but attentive.

He put a long, crooked thick finger in their faces. "Tell me again," he commanded, "What happens to rats?"

They both looked at each other, but neither hesitated to answer: "Rats get stomped," they sadly recited in unison question and answer he'd made them memorize long ago.

He poked them both in their chests, his cold wicked eyes staring down at them like two black coals. "That's right! Rats get stomped! Don't ever forget it!" He went to turn away, but stopped and said, "And don't go spending all that money in one place, makin' people suspicious!" With that, he left them at Mary Gray's grave site. He got into his black Ford Galaxie 500 and slowly drove down the dirt road and out of Grandview.

When the last of his dust settled in the distance, Jimmy spat in his direction and sarcastically yelled, "Been great doin' business with you, Frankie!"

Greggy lightly smacked him on the backside of his head. "Oh, you're a real tough guy! Like you'd be saying that if he was here."

"But at least we ain't gotta deal with him for a long time, now." Jimmy spat again in Frankie's direction. "That psycho."

Greggy grunted in agreement. Now that Frankie was gone, they could enjoy their day.

ELEVEN

The VECO office complex on Route 51 in the Chippewa Township region of Beaver Falls was an electrified hive of activity that week. The coming Tuesday was VECO's annual spring stockholder's banquet. The company's largest share holders would converge upon Beaver Falls and the two story VECO complex to see firsthand how their hefty investments were being handled. The day would be capped with a gala banquet at the posh Wooden Angel restaurant in nearby Beaver. The event was going to be emceed by a famous Pittsburgh comic who'd made it big out in Hollywood. This Thursday morning many preparations were being made. VECO employees were busy creating high tech reports on all their companies' earnings and stocks. Glossy posters and multimedia graphs and pie charts showing the previous year's earnings were visible in cubicles and offices. Time consuming meetings were being held hourly by different VECO departments, fine tuning the preparations for the celebration. Everyone was well distracted by their pressing work for Tuesday's event. That was good for the Family, who were quite distracted themselves, but not concerning a black tie event.

Carmichael Vero waited in his office for Tony. Joseph had left a message on Carmichael's voice mail saying that Tony would be at VECO by 10:00 am. However, Tony phoned later and said that he had to take care of some things and he would be in around 10:30 instead. Carmichael thought of meeting Tony somewhere other than VECO for safety, but he had too much going on at the office that day.

Ed Larksy reported to VECO about 8:15 after his fiasco with Kay Falco. Carmichael was not pleased with the results, but he already had a backup plan in action in the event that Kay Falco would go to the police to report Todd's disappearance. Larsky had gone to Todd Falco's work cubicle the day before wearing gloves. He tidied it up, put things away, and made it look like Todd had gotten his office affairs straight before he left. Carmichael had Larsky draw up a bogus leave of absence form for Todd Falco. This was a standard VECO form issued to employees who needed long stretches of personal time away from work with no pay. It was on the VECO computer network for employees to download, complete, and print. In the leave form, under the section that read, "Reason for leave request," Larsky typed the following:

"Due to personal pressures at home, I feel that I need some time to go away and reevaluate my life, my marriage, and my work. Please honor my request for a two week leave of absence."

Carmichael had authored the phony explanation. Larsky printed out the form at Todd's printer. He pressed Todd's signature ink stamp at the bottom of the leave form. He beautifully forged Todd Falco's initials beside the stamp and dated it the day that Todd disappeared. Larsky logged on Todd's computer and found his work itinerary for the week. Like the rest of VECO, Todd Falco and his marketing department was supposed to be busy preparing earnings reports from VECO subsidiary companies for the banquet. Larsky typed a fake memo from Todd with a list of the people he was to meet with that week. He printed the fake memo and took it to the reception area. He secretly placed it at the bottom of a stack of work in one of the secretaries' box. Larsky then gave Todd Falco's leave of absence form to that same secretary to file away in Todd's personnel file. She did as office manager Larsky had commanded, but not before she had read the entire leave request form herself. Later, she got to the fake memo and business list at the bottom of her work pile. She read the names of the people and then the memo:

"Please call these people for me and inform them that I'll be out of town for the next two weeks. Tell them it was unexpected, and that I apologize for any hassles this will cause them. This is a personal matter that I must take care of. Thanks. Todd."

As soon as she read the last word she went straight to the secretarial pool outside Carmichael's office. Like a dam bursting she immediately gushed all the information about Todd leaving town because of his bad marriage to Kay. The VECO secretaries buzzed about Todd and Kay and his leave of absence for the next ten minutes. Some wished that Todd would have opened up to them more. One who had fooled around with Todd complained about Kay Falco. She said that Todd told her how mean and unloving Kay was. Kay Falco didn't deserve Todd. The buzzing went on. Suddenly Ed Larsky was upon them all. He angrily rebuked them for gossiping when they should have been working. The secretaries, fearful of the hulking office manager, instantly scattered back to their desks and cubicles. Most of the VECO staff knew about Todd's leave by ten o'clock that morning. Carmichael and Larsky smiled about their whole cover up. It worked perfectly. They were ready for the police, now.

Tony Vero sped up Route 51 in his late father's '88 Mercedes convertible. He kept the rag top closed for his mental security. His first time out of his house in months was not going as badly as he'd expected. Once he pulled the car out of his garage and the sunlight bathed the interior, his fears were slightly allayed. The compact interior of the car was comforting, too. His stomach was still queasy, and his throbbing hangover symptoms pounded away at his senses. But that was just tough. He was on his way to the most important meeting of his life. He knew he had to overcome his pains and anxieties. He'd made several stops before his meeting with Carmichael at VECO. That gave him time to straighten himself out emotionally. Todd Falco's disappearance was the window of opportunity he needed. He knew he could corner the Family, though Carmichael and Larsky were going to hammer him hard. He'd have to take their shots and suck it up. Whatever it took to win, Tony would do it. Now he faced irrational fear, anxieties, cold sweats, and trembling hands that gripped the steering wheel for dear life. *Too bad,* he thought. *Gotta get over it.* He set his heart in the Mercedes as VECO loomed in the distance on Route 51: *Whatever it takes, Tony. Whatever it takes.*

Joseph Vero walked into Carmichael's office about 10:20. He wanted to be there when Tony arrived. He knew there was going to be a war between his nephew and Carmichael. Tony had ignored Carmichael those past two months just as he had ignored Joseph and his sister Gina. Now that this Todd Falco crisis had erupted, Carmichael would probably take out his anxiety on Tony. Tony was about to compound Carmichael's wrath, too. Joseph knew Tony was coming to force a deal with Carmichael. He tried to talk him out of it the night before, but Tony was a full-blooded, stubborn Vero. He was going to show up for the meeting with both barrels loaded. He told Joseph to stay out of it. Tony was the only Vero Joseph could think of who could take on Carmichael. Joseph realized that Tony and his great uncle were just alike: when both were focused on what they wanted, neither could be stopped.

Get ready to rumble, Joseph thought.

Larsky joined Carmichael and Joseph in the office. He closed the two oak doors behind him. He unlocked one of Carmichael's desk drawers and opened it. He pulled out a small meter with a metal wand attached to it. He switched on the meter and held the wand. He methodically began checking Carmichael's office for electronic bugs. Carmichael and Joseph knew the routine. They sat silently. A couple of minutes later Larsky was satisfied that the office was clean. When Tony got there they would be talking about Family business. That type of meticulous caution had kept the Family in business and them out of jail for nearly twenty years. Larsky went over and switched on the CD player. Once again music blasted from the outdoor speakers. Only on rare occasions had the Family met at VECO during work hours. The VECO employees had heard the loud outdoor speakers blaring before, but few would dare ask about it. They believed Carmichael was counteracting possible corporate spies. Larsky lowered the volume halfway, so the entire office staff wouldn't be shaken out of their seats. It was safe to talk.

"Did you visit Kay Falco?" Joseph asked Ed Larsky.

Larsky nodded. "Didn't go well. She's a complete wacko, like you said."

"She got mad and told Ed she was going to the police," Carmichael said.

"We may have other problems," Larsky said with arms folded. "Dalling Security called me this morning. The security guard came last night and let his dogs loose to run the property. He says they ran straight into the woods, like they were onto a scent or something. Well, the mutts came running back a few minutes later all freaked out in pain. He had to take them to a vet this morning."

"What happened?" Carmichael asked.

"The agent I talked to said they found traces of hot red pepper all over the dogs' snouts. Said their noses and mouths were full of hot spices. Dogs must've got a good snout full of it."

Carmichael and Joseph glanced at each other and then Larsky.

"Well," Larsky answered their unspoken question, "unless the raccoons and squirrels are all cookin' Cajun style back there, somebody put that stuff in our woods to throw them off. Dalling's gonna bring some more dogs out here at lunch time to do a thorough search of VECO's property. We'll see what they come up with."

"Somebody's been spying around VECO?" Joseph Vero asked.

"What would someone be doing back there with hot spices?" Carmichael asked.

"I dunno," Larsky chuckled, "but that agent sounded like those mutts were hurtin' pretty bad. Noses all burned up and all." He laughed, thinking about it.

"Someone's definitely been snooping here," Carmichael decided.

"This is just what we don't need right now," Joseph said, disgusted.

Carmichael's buzzer went off on his desk. He hit the intercom.

"Yes, Hilda?"

"Tony Vero is here to see you, Mr. Vero."

"Send him in please."

Larsky smirked and shook his head. "I see Mister Squirrelly decided to crawl out of his hole and actually show up for work today."

Out in the VECO lobby, one of the receptionists, Tamara "Tammi" Bannerman, watched Tony Vero out of the corner of her eye. She heard Hilda Jessup, the head secretary, tell him to go on back. She saw the handsome young man walk through the glass doors down the foyer between Carmichael's office and the lobby. She could hear the music playing outside Carmichael's office. Tammi, knew something big was brewing.

Tony Vero went to open the oak doors to Carmichael's office. His heart beat hard and he had butterflies in his stomach, like he was going into a high stakes football game. He was woozy, but wasn't going to show it. He had to keep his gameface. Any sign of weakness would be his undoing at the hands of his ruthless Great Uncle and Ed Larsky.

Tony entered. Carmichael stood up and looked him over, grim faced. Joseph Vero nodded approvingly at Tony. The Kid had shaved and gotten a hair cut. Though his black hair was a little longer than usual, it still looked neat and stylish. He wore a stylish dress shirt, a sharp pair of slacks, and dress shoes. This allayed some of Joseph's fears. The Kid was a least smart enough to clean up his act before he came to see Carmichael. Larsky stood to the side with his arms folded, chomping gum while looking out the window. His hatred for Tony Vero was so deep that moment he didn't even want to look at the young man.

Tony looked only at Carmichael. Carmichael stood behind his desk. Sunlight flooding through the window behind him gave him an ominous glow.

The trio was dead silent.

Out in the lobby Tammi Bannerman was dialing a phone number. The strikingly beautiful young black woman wore a headset with a microphone, like the other two receptionists. The phone she had dialed began to ring.

Carmichael and his great nephew eyed each other intensely. This was not a fond reunion. Tony realized that this was the first time he had ever been at odds with his two Vero uncles. It hurt, too. He loved them. He had truly had been the favored one in the Vero family. But after what he went through in Ft. Lauderdale, he was sure the Family would show him no sentimentality. He had to hit hard this morning.

The person Tammi Bannerman was phoning finally answered. Private detective Edgar Waters picked up the receiver. He was still in bed at 10:30 that morning, exhausted from the Dalling Security dog incident the night before.

"Yeah?" Edgar answered his phone in a gravelly voice.

"Have a seat, Tony."

"I'll sit down if everyone else will," Tony answered.

Carmichael's face darkened a shade. He slowly nodded to Joseph and Larsky to sit. Carmichael seated himself in his swivel chair. Tony sat directly in front of him, Joseph sat to Tony's left. Larsky shook his head, murmured under his breath for a moment, but defiantly remained standing off to the side.

Carmichael stared at Tony. "What do you think you've been doing for the last two months, Tony? Why haven't you returned my calls?"

Tony sat silent for a moment. Then he casually answered: "I didn't want to."

Tammi Bannerman spoke to Edgar Waters in a sugary sweet voice: "Mr. Rogers? This is Ms. Bannerman at VECO."

Edgar quickly snapped himself awake and grabbed for a pencil and pad of paper on the table beside his bed. He knew Tammi was about to give him important information about the Family at VECO. Tammi Bannerman was Edgar's only employee. They had successfully gotten her hired in the VECO secretarial pool about six months earlier. Since Tammi had infiltrated the office she had provided Edgar an inside picture of the comings and goings of Carmichael Vero. She was of little use to Edgar, otherwise. He dared not let her bug Carmichael's office or phone. Edgar knew the Family was too sophisticated not to watch after themselves. If the Family discovered a bug in Carmichael's office and found out who planted it, Tammi's very life would be in danger and the Family would clam up forever around VECO. No, Edgar needed Tammi's watchful eye. He needed Carmichael and the Family to be comfortable around VECO. People slip up when they're at ease.

Tammi spoke: "I'm calling to inform you, Mr. Rogers, of an important gathering that your client will want to know about. This gathering will include Mr. Clark, Mr. Lake, Mr. Jones, and a Mr. Thomas."

Edgar Waters swiftly scribbled on his pad: "Family meeting in Carmichael's office. Carmichael, Ed Larsky, Joe Vero and Tony Vero."

Tammi continued: "This gathering will be fully catered."

Edgar scribbled: "Office doors closed. Using outdoor speakers again. Top secret Family meeting."

"I'll notify you of its length later. I'm sure your client will be very pleased, Mr. Rogers. Thank you and have a great day!"

Edgar Waters hung up the phone. He jumped out of bed excited. Two Family meetings in less than fifteen hours. Both at VECO. This one was even during office hours! That was rare. The Family was having some sort of emergency. Tony Vero was VECO's in house private detective. Something serious was happening for him to be called in. This was the time for which Edgar had been waiting. The Family was scrambling. Now they would probably slip up. And Edgar would be there for it. He went to grab his portable tape recorder, but stopped. Usually Edgar recorded all of his notes about the Family and sent them in one package to his client at a later time. Not this time. He would have to call his client and personally give him this news. This could be the break they had been awaiting for years.

If Edgar could only get one little bug inside Carmichael's office.

Carmichael couldn't believe his ears. He leaned forward and gritted his teeth: "You didn't want to call me?"

Tony bluntly answered him. "If I wanted to talk to you, Uncle Carmichael, I would have called you. I didn't, so I didn't."

Joseph sighed and shook his head, ashamed of Tony's disrespect for Carmichael.

Larsky lumbered over to Tony ready to kill him.

"Who do you think you're talking to, Kid? Show your Uncle some respect!" Larsky yelled. He defiantly stood over Tony, ready to punch him. He wished the Kid would make a move.

Tony Vero wasn't going to let Ed Larsky destroy his one opportunity at freedom. Not intimidated, he simply looked at Carmichael and said, "Will you tell your watch dog to quit breathing down my neck?"

"I'll take care of this, Ed," Carmichael said.

Larsky remained behind Tony, his barrel chest heaving up and down.

Tony crossed one leg over the other and sighed patiently.

Carmichael came around from behind his desk and looked down on Tony. "You've disrespected me for the last month. Don't come in here today with a chip on your shoulders and act like I owe you something."

"I'm not here to disrespect you, Uncle Carmichael. I'm here to do business."

"Well, my first business today is to find out why you have been ignoring me, your own boss and blood relative!"

"What would I have to say to you after what you pulled on me in Fort Lauderdale?"

"Tony, you better watch what you say," Joseph warned his nephew.

Tony turned angrily at Joseph. "Watch what, Uncle Joe? The truth?"

"Shut up, Tony!" Carmichael commanded.

"You set me up in Florida!" Tony pointed at Carmichael.

"I did not set you up, Kid!"

"Everything fell perfectly into my lap when it was all over. You planned it that way."

"I did not. You overstepped yourself down there and got in our way."

Tony leaned forward on his seat. "I did the investigation like you hired me to!"

"You overstepped your investigation, Tony!"

"How?"

"You went beyond what I hired you to do. I hired you to find one man! You decided to meddle in our private business and play negotiator with him. I did not hire you to negotiate. You got in the way of our plans because you didn't keep in your place. When you overstepped your boundary and we executed our plans . . ."

"'Execute' is an excellent word choice, Uncle Carmichael . . ."

Carmichael ignored him. "When you overstepped your boundary and we executed our plans you had placed yourself right in the way. That's why you became the focal point of everything in Ft. Lauderdale, Tony. I didn't know that you had tried to negotiate, but you didn't stick to just being the private investigator like I had hired you to do. When we made our move you had put yourself in a bad position. I didn't find out until afterward. By then it was too late. The rest is history."

"Why didn't you tell me what your true plans were, Uncle Carmichael?"

Carmichael, Joseph, and Larsky all three groaned with disbelief.

"He doesn't get it!" Larsky waved a hand at Tony. "He's a little baby! I told you all that! Why didn't you all listen to me about him?"

"Tony, how could you ask such a stupid question like that?" Joseph chided.

"Kid," Carmichael explained with furious disbelief, "I'll tell you why I didn't tell you my plans. They were none of your business! I don't have to explain anything to you! Just do what you're hired to do and shut up!"

"But I didn't know that . . ."

"You shouldn't have to have known! You were just hired to find someone."

"Why didn't any of you listen to me about *him*?" Larsky asked again.

"Kid, what you've pulled since you got back from Florida has disappointed me almost as bad as your sister Gina and all this 'Christianity' babble she's into. In fact, Kid, you've disappointed me more than Gina. You know why?"

Tony just stared out the window.

"At least Gina's in Ohio with her head in the clouds, doing her holy mess. You're right here in my face! You, Tony, who chooses to disengage all contact with me and Joe, are a major employee of mine and a player in the Family! Do you know how serious of a mess we're in right now? Do you realize how much danger we face with Todd Falco scramming with our, *my* million dollars? Do you?"

"Yes. Uncle Joseph told me everything last night."

Carmichael leaned across his desk. "We are mega-players in this whole tri state area. We rule this region. We rule the action. And nobody knows we exist! I did that, Tony. The Family and VECO are *my* creations and *my* businesses and my whole life! This is all about *me*. Yeah, if this things blows up, your Uncle Joseph and Ed Larsky and the Zann's and Marv Lenstein all bite the dust with it, like me. And you do too! But I'm the one who created all this, Tony. This is all *my* risk. And I'll be the only one who'll ever control the Family and VECO. And I will control everything! I cannot deal with you acting like some kindergartner pouting because we didn't play like you wanted us to. I won't have that from anyone, not even you. You're not just my great nephew now, Tony. You're a Family member. That means I own you. And whether you like it or not, you will do what I tell you to do, you will answer when I call, and you will respect me with all the respect that is due me!" Carmichael put his hand under Tony's chin and pushed his head back a bit. "Do you understand me?"

His great nephew didn't answer. Tony felt numb. How could everything have deteriorated to this moment? His own uncle was telling him he was nothing more than chattel.

Carmichael snatched his hand away in disgust and started to turn away.

"You own me, huh Uncle Carmichael?"

Carmichael turned back. "Yes Tony. I have ever since you joined the Family. You've just been too naive to understand what we're all about here. When I was in La Cosa Nostra we had to take an actual blood vow to our family. That's how serious this Family is. You begged me to get in the Family. Great risks were taken to get you into the Family. You pushed your Uncle Joseph into influencing me to allow you in. You were a big risk. And just because your father was one of us didn't mean we were obligated to let you be. And now that you're in, you still don't get it. This is life and death. And yes, I do own you."

It was time.

"Then I want my freedom back," Tony said.

The room went dead silent for a moment again. "What?" Carmichael asked with disbelief.

"You're going to release me from the Family. You're going to set me free."

"I'll free you right now, you little fruit!" Larsky stepped toward Tony again.

"Stop it, Ed!" Carmichael commanded.

Larsky stopped and shouted, "Would you listen at him, Carmichael? He is so not like us it's not even funny! He doesn't get it. He's not a player. He's Mister Softy!"

"Tony," Joseph said, "I told you last night to forget this idea of 'getting out' of the Family."

"I want to trade for my freedom, Uncle Carmichael," Tony said.

"What are you talking about, Kid?"

Tony stood up. "I'm gonna find Todd Falco. I'm gonna get your money back for you. No one's going to know anything ever happened around here. I'll find Todd, I'll find your money. Life and business will go on for you as usual and this mess will all be over. Then you're going to let me go, and I'm going to disappear. And you're not going to come looking for me."

Carmichael was incensed. "No!"

"Yes!" Tony chuckled. "You don't have a choice!"

"No!" Carmichael repeated.

"I'm your only hope. I can trace Todd and that money with no problem. None of you can. You can't even hire someone else to do it. That would blow all this wonderful security you've built around your secret empire. You can't let an outsider handle Family business. Only a Family member can. Anyone else tracking down Todd runs the risk of bringing down the whole Family. I'm the only one who can find Todd Falco safely and end all this mess. And my fee for doing it is my freedom."

Carmichael stood speechless.

"You are in total control around here, Uncle Carmichael. But you've built this fortress so tight that if a Todd Falco slips up, this whole empire collapses. Well, I'm taking advantage of your one weakness. Once I straighten out this mess, you *will* let me go."

The weight of Tony's words pressed down hard on the senior Vero.

Tony read Carmichael's countenance. It was working! Carmichael showed it in his eyes. Tony pressed on. "I'm your only hope, Uncle Carmichael. You have no choice. You'll either do it my way and let me go, or we all go to jail. That's the only business deal I'm cutting with you today."

Like someone caught in checkmate, Carmichael desperately thought for a way out. Joseph and Larsky could only stare at him helplessly. It did seem that Tony had him.

"Time's wasting, Uncle Carmichael. It's been two days now. Your million and one hundred thousand dollars is out there somewhere. And you're losing more money every minute we spend here. Every minute Todd's not out there supplying more cocaine to his three dealers, you and the Family ain't makin' a dime."

Carmichael was angry, bewildered, betrayed, and defeated. He couldn't mask it, either.

Tony knew he had won. He didn't gloat, however. This victory was bitter. This deal would mean the severance of all ties with the only real family he knew. The only people on earth he loved.

After the silence, Carmichael angrily acquiesced. "How will you disappear, Tony?"

"I'll leave Pennsylvania for good. New identity. New everything. You'll never see or hear from me again. I'll just plain vanish."

"Until you turn us all over to the FBI," Larsky said. "Then we'll see you sittin' on the witness stand testifying against us."

"And go to jail myself? What kind of idiot would do something as stupid as that?"

"So Todd Falco disappears," Joseph said. "Then as soon as you find him, you disappear. How screwy is that, Tony? The cops would really come out of the woodwork after us. They'd give us the biggest rectal probe of our lives."

"And all you've gotta say is the truth: 'We don't know where he is!' You could even pass a lie detector test on that one because I'm sure not going to tell any of you where I'm going."

Carmichael glanced at Joseph, then spoke to Tony.

"Your Uncle Joe has been like your father since Pete died. He's the one who's watched after you and Gina. Is this how you're going to show gratitude and family loyalty to him after all he's done for you, Tony?"

Tony and Joseph Vero locked eyes.

"Uncle Joe knows I love him. He knows I could never repay him for all he's done for me. And he knows I'm a big boy now who has to make my own decisions. Is this a deal, Uncle Carmichael?"

Silence, except for the pounding of the music outside Carmichael's windows. Carmichael stared at his great nephew apalled. He could not believe Tony was doing this to him after all of the tremendous favor and support he and the entire Vero clan had poured on him over the years. He walked over to Tony and stood in his face.

"Ed's just about right, Tony. You're not much of a Vero."

"So it's a deal then, Uncle Carmichael? You hire me to find Todd Falco and your money. My fee is I'm out of the Family for good. And you let me disappear forever?" Tony could almost feel the intense hatred emanating from Carmichael.

"Find him, Tony. Then pack up and never show your face to me again."

Larsky yelled something unintelligible and stormed out of the office, slamming the two oak doors behind him. Everyone ignored his outburst. It was to be expected of Larsky.

"Where are you going to start your investigation?" Carmichael asked.

"I'm going to Todd's house and I'm gonna grill his wife. Then I'm going to his top dealer to find out what he knows about this Bernie Lowkowski Todd was dealing your money with. This Lokawski guy is the one causing us all this trouble. Either he and Todd Falco cut a deal or he's ripped Todd off in a bad way."

"You better not cross paths with the police and get them tangled up in your investigation," Carmichael warned.

"By the way, I'll report to you and Uncle Joe, only." Tony pointed toward the doors where Larsky had just exited. "Keep Larsky completely away from me. He'd kill me just for fun."

Tony Vero turned to leave Carmichael's office.

"Stop," Carmichael commanded. Tony turned back around to face him.

"You are the biggest disappointment ever to me, Tony. Your father tried my patience with his big mouth. And your sister with her Jesus freak act. But now you've exceeded them both, abandoning and using your own family in a time of crisis. We were all so proud of your football career and all you represented to us. You were a diamond in this family, Tony. Now you've turned into nothing more than a piece of coal in my shoe."

"Well, you're the one who tarnished me, Uncle Carmichael," Tony said, turning toward the doors. "I guess Ft. Lauderdale completely took away any reason for me to shine."

Joseph Vero stood by Carmichael's desk, numb.

"I'll call you this afternoon Uncle Joe and update you," Tony said.

Joseph could say nothing. Carmichael glared at him.

Good-byes would be morbid at that point. Tony Vero walked out, a winner once again.

Ed Larsky stood at the end of the foyer, arms folded, feet spread. The glass doors leading out to the secretarial station were closed. Tony looked at him and stopped. Larksy's eyes were red with hate.

"Hey, fruitcake," Larsky growled demonically.

What's he gonna do? Rip me apart in this hallway in full view of all of the VECO secretaries? Tony thought. He certainly didn't think Larsky was above that.

"Name-calling, Ed? In case you're too dumb to figure it out, you're pushing forty now. This is an office building, not the kindergarten playground. You have to make nice in front of all your employees, Office Manager Larsky."

"Carmichael may guarantee your safety when this is all over and you flit away like a butterfly," Larsky said. "But I don't."

"Well, Ed, I'd have thought you would love the idea of me disappearing from the face of the earth. Then you could finally try to take my place as the Vero's top Kid. That's what you've been so jealous about all these years. I was a Vero, and you weren't. I was a football star, and you definitely weren't. You're just a big, jealous baby. If you're so manly and tough and want to kill me, why don't you just go ahead and do it right here in this hall? Why wait to try and find me after I disappear?"

Larsky was so upset the veins in his forehead were pulsating. "You're not worthy to be a Vero, Tony. And I will find you. And you'll be afraid on the day that I do."

"Well, hopefully I'll find Todd Falco first, Ed. 'Cause if not, you're going to jail. And the way I feel these days, death would be a welcome surprise if I knew it meant you would wind up in jail for the rest of your life."

"Don't cross me on your way out of town."

Tony marched straight down the hall and up into Larsky's face.

"Don't cross me, period, Ed. You know I'm smart enough to find a way to put you in jail without endangering Uncle Joe or Carmichael."

Larsky leaned into Tony's face.

"You think you're that smart?"

"Of course I am, Ed," Tony said. "I'm a Vero!"

They eyed each other for a moment. Then Tony pushed past the hulking man and went out the glass doors.

The secretaries had all been watching, frozen in terror at the prospects of Ed Larsky becoming violent. Tony Vero walked past them and down the stairs. Suddenly they all realized Ed Larsky was now glaring back at them through the glass doors. They all scattered like mice back to their stations.

Larsky turned on his heals and stormed back into Carmichael's office.

Larsky slammed the oak doors behind him as he re-entered.

"Can't we do something about him, Carmichael?" he demanded.

After a moment of silence Carmichael spoke softly.

"The Kid's got us, Ed. He's right. He wins this one."

Larsky turned angrily on Joseph Vero.

"Okay, father-figure! Do your stuff to your nephew! Wake him up. He's playing us all like idiots and walkin' off into the sunset!"

"I don't like it any more than you do, Ed," Joseph said. "The Kid's right. The main thing right now is to get Falco and Carmichael's money. We can't do that. Tony can. And he's willing to use his position to blackmail us during our weakest moment."

"What kind of Vero is he, Joe?" Larksy asked.

"A Vero like the rest of us, Ed. When he smells blood, he pounces."

"Joseph," Carmichael turned slowly around.

"Yes?"

"You cooperate with Tony on this investigation. Tony can find Falco fast. Let's keep him happy so he doesn't get vindictive and try to make us sweat this out longer than we have to."

"Right," Joseph said, though he didn't think Tony would try something like that.

"How long can our drug operations stay in business without Todd contacting our dealers?"

"Todd and I would have stomped that cocaine from this buy over four or five times yesterday and delivered it to the three dealers today. We could have been raking in a fortune this weekend. But now . . ."

"Answer my question, Joseph."

"If those guys don't hear from Todd today they'll start snooping around for another supplier and then we'll be out millions by the end of next month."

"Those dealers . . ." Carmichael thought for a moment.

"What about them?" Joseph asked.

Carmichael turned to Larsky. "Can you locate our three dealers?"

"Yeah, no problem."

"We may need to eliminate them if Todd Falco doesn't show up. We can't have them around if the cops do investigate and catch on to what Todd does on the side. They're all potential witnesses against Todd and eventually us."

Larsky liked what he heard for the first time that morning. "Yeah, I could smoke 'em. I could make 'em all look like gang hits, no problem."

Carmichael nodded. "This may be a time for the Family to make a clean start with our narcotics branch. We could do things right from the beginning."

"That's a drastic step to take before we even know what's happened to Todd," Joseph protested. "He made us a fortune, Carmichael. No one else could have produced like he did for us. It was a risk. The whole Family's a risk. Beginning a new narcotics operation from scratch is going to be unbelievably difficult, especially if we have Larsky start a major gang war by killing all our dealers. I say we wait first and find out what happened to Todd."

"No," Carmichael sighed. "We need to act immediately. Tony was right. We gave too great a position to someone like Todd Falco. We can't operate like this again."

"Yeah, well, if Todd still is alive I'm gonna smoke him too for doing this to us," Larsky swore.

"Re-emphasize to Tony that he needs to stay away from the police, Joseph," Carmichael said, sitting back down at his desk. "I don't want him attracting their attention while he investigates. Now go call Marv and the Zanns and let them know Tony's on the case right now."

Joseph started to leave. Before he opened the oak doors he stopped and pointed at Larsky.

"Keep him away from Tony, Carmichael."

"Quit protecting the Kid, Joe!" Larsky yelled. "You ain't his daddy anymore! He's just stabbed you in the back, too. He's gonna be our end if he doesn't find Todd Falco."

"I mean it, Carmichael," Joseph respectfully warned his relative.

Carmichael calmly waved him off. "Go on, Joseph."

The oak doors closed, leaving Carmichael and Larsky alone. Larsky eyed Carmichael tensely. Carmichael glanced at him for a second, then looked away, irritated. After almost twenty years together he could read Ed's mind. He knew what Ed Larsky was going to say. Carmichael didn't want to hear it. Ed said it anyway:

"It's time to call him, Carmichael."

Carmichael looked up at Larsky, then looked at his desk and shuffled some papers. "I mean it! This is too serious, Carmichael. You've gotta call him. Now!"

Carmichael sighed. "It's been a long time since we've consulted him. I want to wait for Tony to come through."

"This is the worst I've seen things, Boss. This could be worse than your trial back in '81. Todd Falco's gonna cost us our heads. And Tony Vero sure ain't the answer to our problems. Only one person can help us now. And he's got power that Tony Vero and the Family don't got."

Carmichael stared at his telephone. Larsky leaned over his boss's desk and whispered: "Call the Magic Genie."

"Not yet, Ed!"

"The Magic Genie's the only reason we're still on top, Carmichael. We haven't gotten anywhere without him. He's gotten us out of every jam before. He'll get us out of this one, too."

"I'm in control, Ed. I run the Family. I don't want Cyrus Moreau involved right now."

"Why not, Carm? If you don't get Cyrus involved . . ."

"I want to handle this on my own! I've purposely not consulted him or used his services for the last couple of years."

"Then it's been a couple of years too long," Larsky said. He picked up the phone and held it to Carmichael's face.

"Ed," Carmichael said with irritation, "Cyrus Moreau costs you and me too much!"

Larsky knew Carmichael wasn't only talking about money. He didn't care. His eyes burned with fire.

"Then let's pay the price again!"

Ed pushed the phone up further into Carmichael's face. Carmichael shook his head defiantly.

"If we don't call the Magic Genie we lose *everything*!" Larsky growled in desperation.

There was no end to the madness of this day, Carmichael realized. He looked up at his henchman with a fierce glare and snatched the phone from his hand. Today was a day of many defeats for Carmichael Vero.

Larsky leaned back and breathed deeply, relieved. Carmichael pulled out his wallet and produced a card from inside.

"Now we'll be gettin' things done, Carmichael. The Magic Genie always comes through."

"Now well be paying hell, Ed," Carmichael said as he began to dial Cyrus Moreau's phone number. "I think that's where Cyrus lives."

Larsky laughed his evil chuckle. "Whatever it takes to stay on top, Carm. I'll do anything the Magic Genie wants. In fact, I'd pay the devil himself!"

"Ed, when you pay Cyrus Moreau, the 'Magic Genie', as you call him, you are paying the devil!"

TWELVE

Kay Falco struggled to get Dylon up the Beaver County Sheriff's Department's concrete steps. She was coming to file a missing person's report on her husband Todd. People coming and going stared curiously at her. This tiny, gorgeous woman, sobbing uncontrollably, was carrying her baby, his carrier seat, a bulky diaper bag, and her purse up those stairs like an ant determined to move a load ten times its weight. Kay knew everyone was watching her. She simply ignored them, working her way up the steps.

Am I hanging myself here today? she thought as she bumped the carrier and bags through the front doors. *When these policemen find out what Todd does for a living, will I go to jail? Will they take Dylon from me? What kind of mother will they think I am? Will Ed Larsky really come to get me?*

Ed Larsky's visit earlier that morning only sealed her stubborn determination to risk it all and go to the police. After she ran Larsky off she tried to make herself presentable. She'd showered, fixed her sandy hair, applied what little makeup she wore, and donned a light spring dress. She would have looked just fine (she never struggled with the fact that she was attractive), if only she could calm down and stop bawling. Her eyes were puffy and red. Her nose was chapped from constant wiping. She knew she was a spectacle enough without sobbing every other breath. But she just couldn't stop the crying. She feared she was having a nervous break down. Her nerves were just telling her that she'd had enough. She'd endured five years of hellish marriage to Todd Falco. The tears had gushed almost non-stop since Todd left her on Tuesday. Then, Todd disappeared. And as if that was not enough, Ed Larsky had to come by threatening her about not going to the cops. *He even had the nerve to threaten Dylon!* But she fixed him at the house, and she was going to fix him again this morning here at the police station.

The Beaver County Sheriff's Department was located in the heart of Beaver, Pennsylvania, just a few miles away from Beaver Falls. The department was a two story annex of the Beaver County Courthouse. Law enforcement agents and lawyers worked with the criminals being processed through the Beaver County justice system. Kay was grateful to find the main hall was not too busy. Several deputies wondered about. There was a deputy manning a receptionist's desk at the end of the hall. Kay spotted a dark wooden bench beside a water fountain. She gently sat Dylon's carrier and diaper bag down there. The boy was sound asleep. She could sit down for a moment and pull herself together before she went through with this. She pulled a mirror out of her purse. She examined her reddened eyes in the reflection. Nothing could be done about that, she conceded. She took a long, deep breath and slowly exhaled. There. That was better. She wasn't sobbing any more. She leaned up and sipped some water from the fountain. Momentarily feeling better, she picked up Dylon's carrier and walked over to the reception desk.

"Can I help you, Ma'am?" the deputy asked.

"Yes, you can," Kay said awkwardly. "My name's Kay Falco. I need to file a missing person's report. My husband's disappeared."

"Oh. I'm sorry." The deputy didn't seem too sincere. "How long has he been missing?"

"He left for . . . um . . . work, late Tuesday afternoon and I've not seen or heard from him since."

"Two days." The deputy thought for a moment. He picked up a phone and asked someone on another line about Kay's situation. He hung up. "I'll take you to a detective who'll help you," the deputy said.

Hope he's not a narcotics investigator, Kay thought.

The deputy led her down the hall into the Sheriff's Detective's office. It was a large, noisy room with about twenty desks, file cabinets, and computers. Plain clothed detectives manned many of the desks, some typing, some on the phone, three or so processing criminals. Phones rang, computer keyboards clickety-clacked, printers whined as they spat out reports. Wanted posters and ID photos decorated every wall. Deputies were coming and going, some escorting handcuffed suspects. It was a well lit room and that made Kay feel better. The deputy led her through the commotion over to a desk on the far side of the office. A large black man in a crisp tan suit sat at his desk with his back to them, typing on his computer.

"Detective Kirkland?" the deputy said above the noise of the room.

"Yes," Detective Ray Kirkland spun around in his swivel chair. He spotted the deputy standing next to a woman with a baby. Ray instantly recognized that this was the woman with the baby from his vision. Holy Spirit immediately confirmed this to him. He locked eyes with Kay Falco and wanted to grin real big. She was the reason for those stirrings during his prayer times the last several days. Once again, God revealed Himself. *Thank you, Jesus!* Ray thought, standing up to meet her. *Now I can find out what that vision was all about.*

The deputy introduced Kay, told Detective Kirkland about her missing husband, and Ray dismissed him.

"Mrs. Falco, I'm Detective Ray Kirkland," he said.

"Kay Falco," she tried to smile.

They shook hands, his big black hand engulfing her little white one. She thought, *This is the blackest man I've ever seen in my life!* Ray was very tall and muscular. His clear white eyes and milky white smile starkly contrasted his coal-colored skin color. Yet his sincere smile warmed Kay.

He held onto her hand. His gift of discerning of spirits kicked in. Holy Spirit helped him read people, to see by what spirit they operated. Kay Falco had a deeply wounded spirit. Her emotions were spent. As a law enforcement agent he came across many people in that condition.

She looked down at her hand in his, wondering what he was doing.

"M'am, you're trembling and your heart's beating a million miles a second," Ray said, finally letting go. "Why don't you set down that fine looking baby, sit down here, and relax."

Ray pulled a comfortable swivel chair around for Kay and got her to sit beside his desk. He then sat in his chair, put his computer to sleep, and turned to focus on Kay.

"You told the deputy your husband's missing. What's his name?"

"Todd Falco. We live over in New Galilee."

"When's the last time you saw Todd, Mrs. Falco?"

She felt her heart thumping in her throat. "Tuesday afternoon."

"Have you talked to him or heard from him at all since Tuesday?"

"No," she trembled as she nervously looked out the window behind the detective.

"Has anyone you know seen or heard from him, Ma'am?"

"No."

"And I'm assuming he's not severely ill or that he doesn't usually take off for a few days at a time without telling you he's leaving. That's not a normal occurrence in your marriage and this is why you're here to file a missing person's report."

"Yes," she said, barely audible.

Ray Kirkland felt compassion for her. He sensed Holy Spirit telling him to tread lightly. "Kay, I need you to tell me everything you know. Honesty's gonna be very important here. I need to tell you up front: we get all kinds of missing fathers and missing husbands reported to us around here. And those cases don't always get investigated because there's usually enough evidence to tell us these men have simply run away from their families. Another woman involved, didn't want to pay alimony or child support, you name the reason. The man just abandons his family. Sometimes he winds up contacting his family after a week or two. Those cases don't get a sheriff's department missing person's investigation, I'll tell you this right up front. To get an investigation you're going to have to convince us that there appears to have been some kind of foul play somewhere. You better have a special story to tell me about your husband so I can confidently walk into Sheriff DeBona's office this morning and get him to authorize a full scale investigation. Otherwise, he's gonna say, 'This is just another runaway husband. Not gonna spend department time or money on this one.' So Mrs. Falco, you're coming in here for help. You better tell me the whole story so I can help you."

Her lips trembled, her hands quivered. As hard as she fought it, Kay broke again.

"Todd . . ." she sobbed, ". . . he . . . I don't know . . . left Tuesday to go to a meeting . . . and . . ."

Ray handed her a Kleenex. "Who was he going to meet?"

Warning lights went off in her head. "A . . . um . . . client." She leaned over sobbing.

"What does he do for a living?"

"He works at VECO."

"So they'll know what he was up to that afternoon he disappeared?"

"No. Yes!" she tired to correct herself, but too late. She bent over her knees and wept.

Ray watched her sob for a moment. "Sit up, please, Kay." He was polite but firm. She obeyed, but still did not look at him.

"Look at me Kay. Look me in the eyes."

He had a very commanding yet reassuring voice. She slowly looked into his gaze.

Ray looked at her sternly. "Listen, now, Mrs. Falco. I don't know what's going on, but you're going to have to tell me the truth. I get all types in here, not saying you are one, but you're nervous and you already look like you have something to hide. If you want me to help you today, then don't play. You don't have to be afraid. I'm not here to get you. I'm here to see if we can find your husband. Okay?"

After a moment of sobbing she nodded her head. She looked down at sleeping Dylon.

"I have so much to lose . . ."

"Are you in any danger?"

She sobbed a moment, then finally nodded.

"Who? Why?"

"I don't want my baby taken away, but I do want someone to find Todd," she cried.

"No one wants to take your baby away, Kay," he reassured. He pointed toward her son in the carrier. "What's the big guy's name?"

"His name's Dylon," Kay said. "He's eight months old."

"Listen to me, Kay. You need to know I'll do all I can for you and Dylon. But you're gonna have to come clean with me. Who is threatening you?"

Kay looked around at the other detectives in the room. She made sure only Ray was listening. She leaned forward.

"Todd works for VECO, but he . . . he's . . ." she hesitated.

"Tell me the truth. Don't hold back. The truth will set you free here, Mrs. Falco."

She took a long breath. "Let's say that Todd is involved in some . . . illegal business. *He's* involved in it. I'm not!"

"Narcotics?" Detective Kirkland asked.

Kay nodded, deeply ashamed. "You probably think I'm a horrible mother, don't you?"

Ray smiled and shrugged. "Well, I don't know. Do you let him sell drugs out of Dylon's stroller?"

She looked up, then smiled a little when she realized it was a joke.

"He doesn't do anything from our house. Maybe some phone calls. I'd never let him." She didn't know why she was spilling her guts to this man so quickly, but boy did it feel good!

"Todd sells drugs?"

Kay paused to think. "I don't know how he's involved, or what exactly he does, I just know he is into drug money somehow."

"Does Todd have any prior arrests? For anything?"

"No. He's never been arrested."

"Does Todd use?"

"No. That's the funny thing."

"The real pros usually don't. Do you use?"

"No!"

"Does he work with anyone, I mean dealing? Is there anyone who worked with him?"

"I think so. I don't know who, though."

Ray leaned in toward her. "Honestly?"

"Yes. Todd never discussed his business with me. Ever. He kept me and Dylon out of it."

"So you can't give me any names of anyone who possibly sells drugs with Todd?"

She thought of that evil Ed Larsky threatening her that morning. Todd worked under him at VECO, but this morning was the first time she ever found out that Larsky knew that Todd was into more than VECO. This was her chance. *Give this cop Larsky's name!* But then she saw Dylon again.

Finally she said, "I . . . someone came by this morning, but I'm not going to say who."

"The person who's threatening you?"

Kay shook her head. "They didn't say anything about Todd selling drugs or acted like they knew he did. But they want to find him pretty bad. They have no idea where Todd went. They want to find him first. They told me . . ."

Ray waited. "They told you what, Mrs. Falco?"

"They told me not to come to you, or, I mean, the police. You know."

"Someone you can identify comes to you looking for Todd, tells you not to come see sweet little old me, and makes a threat against you, right?"

"Something like that."

"And you're not going to tell me who this person is?"

"They have nothing to do with Todd disappearing," Kay firmly explained.

"Maybe not directly, but they're serious enough about finding him that they may have some answers to help me find your husband. Which is what you want." Ray cocked his head and looked expectantly at Kay. "Give 'em over to me, Kay. Don't protect them."

She looked out the window again in thought. She thought about that cocky Ed Larsky getting up in her face in her living room with her innocent child right there . . .

"I'll tell you what, Detective Kirkland," she said. "You just need to go to VECO, where Todd works. Start there."

"Someone from Todd's real job is threatening you?"

"I didn't say that. I'm just telling you to go to VECO first."

"VECO?" Ray thought for a moment. "Carmichael Vero. That's his company, isn't it?"

"Yeah. What of him?"

"You never read about his trial and all that a long time ago? Mafia and what have you?"

"Yeah, but he's not like that now," Kay said.

"I didn't say he was. I just wondered if you remembered."

"I do."

"What's Todd do at VECO?'

"He's a marketing manager. He markets for their small companies. VECO buys and runs small companies and turns them into money makers. Todd makes sure they're properly marketed."

"Todd have any women on the side?"

Kay reddened again. She didn't like the way this man jumped around in his questioning. He was purposely trying to catch her off guard.

"Is Todd being unfaithful to you?"

Another sob. She looked down and nodded yes, biting her lip.

"What are the chances he's run off with this other woman?"

"Women," Kay corrected, humiliated.

"You know that for a fact?"

"Todd's had all kinds of bimbos over the years. I know it. I found out for myself."

"Mrs. Falco, have you been unfaithful? Is there another man who may be involved?"

She glared at Ray Kirkland.

He threw up his hands and said, "I gotta ask the tough questions, Mrs. Falco! If there was another man he would become a suspect if we decided there was any foul play."

"There's not now, never has been. I got enough to worry about with Todd. I don't want another man messing up my life!"

"Well could Todd be off with one of his other women?"

She sighed. "Could be. He packed a small overnight bag before he left the other day. Told me he was going to stay overnight in Pittsburgh, if his deal went well. He never said why he had to stay overnight there. He rarely has the nerve to run off completely with a woman. He's never run off for days at a time. He's good about coming home everyday. Todd's a hound. He loves 'em quick and I don't imagine he stays around sweet talking them. At least it's not been his pattern to do many overnights with his floozies. I do think he was getting ready to, this time, though."

"He packed an overnight bag and left. You said he might be going to Pittsburgh. Where in Pittsburgh?"

"I have no idea. I don't even know why he'd be going there. No idea at all."

"But how do you know he was going out on drug business?"

"He flat out told me. He said he had a big deal to make that day. He never goes any deeper than that, but he told me that much. He has this one old suitcase he usually takes with him on these big deals, too. He keeps his money in it at some point. He took his gun, too."

"Gun? What kind of gun? Is it registered?"

"I don't know. I think so. It's one of those 9 millimeters." She pointed at Ray's black gun in his holster. "Like yours. But a big, shiny silver thing like in the movies."

"And you don't know who he was going to see?"

"I already told you, I don't have any idea. Todd liked it that way."

"I'm guessing he drove himself?"

"He drove . . . Yes! I didn't think of that. Todd drives a white '96 Camaro. It's missing! You can have your police officers look for it! That would help, wouldn't it?"

Ray nodded as he wrote the information down on a note pad. Kay gave him the tag numbers.

"We can put out an APB on the car. You have a picture of Todd for me?"

Kay unzipped her purse and pulled out two photos. One was a portrait of Todd he used in his resume to get hired at VECO, and the other was a shot of him holding baby Dylon.

"You can keep those."

Ray looked at the pictures. Todd looked like a smarmy, selfish man. A man who didn't know what a blessing he had with such a beautiful wife, a healthy son, and a good job.

"Kay, besides a suitcase and a gun, what other evidence do you know of that proves Todd is involved in drugs? You can't name anyone he might deal with?"

"I can't name anyone. I've heard him on the telephone. I'd call the folks after Todd hung up and ask them questions, but they'd never tell me who they were and all."

"How'd you know who to call?"

"Todd never grasped the idea of re-dial or star 69. As soon as he'd hang up the phone and leave I'd hit the re-dial button or dial star 69 and find out who he was talking to. How do you think I found out about all the women? That's why I really was checking on him all the time. But in the process I'd catch him talking to strange men. Sometimes I'd catch them off guard and ask about buying drugs. They were never stupid enough to go into full detail, but sometimes they were dumb enough to start giving me a little bit of information."

Ray folded his arms with a smile and whistled. "Pretty smart, Sherlock Holmes."

"I'm not a fool! He was so self-absorbed he thought I was stupid . . ." Kay sobbed, ". . . but he was the stupid one."

Ray watched Kay, wondering whether or not she should be trusted. As a police officer he'd experienced so many liars who wouldn't know truth if it bit them. He'd seen people crying over spouses they'd personally killed to collect insurance money or to clear the way for a boyfriend or girlfriend. He'd arrested parents who shed crocodile tears over their children who they'd murdered with their own hands. Under any other circumstances he would have had no reason to trust Kay Falco. But Holy Spirit had prepared Ray for Kay that week. Ray sensed such a broken heart in her. She must feel some commitment to a man like Todd Falco if she hadn't ever divorced him. She was now willing to risk being implicated in an investigation of him, too.

Ray prayed silently: *Lord, order my footsteps in this case and protect my character. I believe it's your will for me to get involved in this, so You watch after me and shine Your light of truth on this investigation.*

Ray turned around and woke up his computer.

"I think we can get an investigation on this one, Mrs. Falco," he said.

"Thank you," Kay seemed genuinely pleased, beneath those tears. "I want Todd found. As much hell as he's put us through, even if he winds up in jail, I still want to know that Dylon has a daddy alive on this earth. Do you think I'm nuts wanting Todd to be okay, I mean after all he's put us through?"

"No. I don't think you're nuts at all. I think you're a woman who's expecting her husband to fulfill the promises of marriage that he made to you."

She paused. "I never thought of it like that. Do you wonder why I've stuck with him and not gotten rid of his sorry butt?"

"You originally fell head over heals in love with him. You found out that he's a criminal and you've always been afraid you'd go down with him if you didn't stick around to protect him. You're an honest citizen with a dishonest spouse and you're scared you'll lose everything, including your son."

Kay was flabbergasted. "That's so true! How'd you know that?"

"Seen a thousand like you, m'am," Ray smiled. "To be brutally honest, this is just another case of a selfish man destroying a good family with his sins."

Kay sat up. "'Sins'? You religious?"

"No. I'm not 'religious.' I have an intimate relationship with Jesus Christ. It has nothing to do with religion." It was that kind of talk that usually got Ray into trouble, but he didn't care. He knew Kay was hopeless without Christ, so he wasn't going to hold back the truth.

"What do you mean a 'relationship'?"

"When I accepted Jesus into my life He sent His Holy Spirit to live in me. You ever hear someone say, 'My body's a temple'?"

"Yes."

"Well, that's Biblical. God wants to live in you and me and make us His temple. And that's what I am. I'm a Christian. Holy Spirit speaks to me, teaches me about Jesus, lights up my way for me. That's why I can say that your husband's sinful lifestyle not only destroys you as a family but puts you into bondage with him."

After a moment's thought, Kay's demeanor softened. "You're kind of a straight shooter, detective," she said.

Ray pulled a tan Stetson cowboy hat off the top of his computer and donned it. One of his detective's badges was pinned to the front of it.

"I hit the target almost every time, Ma'am," he said in his best cowboy voice. She smiled a little. "Nice hat."

"My daughters gave it to me for Christmas several years ago. I'll wear it when they come to the office here. They think it makes me look like a real sheriff."

He handed Kay a framed family photo from his desk. "That's my family. My beautiful wife Shelly and Shaniqua and LaTonya."

"Great looking family."

"They're a blessing from the Lord Himself. He treats me real good like that."

Kay handed back the photo. "Do you think you can find Todd, Detective Kirkland?"

"I'm sure going to try, Mrs. Falco. Please keep in mind that these things take time and sometimes wind up fruitless. Especially if the missing person wants to be missing."

Kay understood.

"Let's get this report written up before your little man wakes up, there."

Kay sighed a long breath of relief. For the first time since Tuesday, she felt better. She felt fresh, like she'd been to confession. She had never before talked to anybody about Todd's drug business or his infidelity. It was like an incredible weight had been lifted off her shoulders. This Detective Kirkland was strange, the way he talked about God like He was right here living life with him, but for some reason she felt safe with him, like he could be trusted.

Kay Falco felt some hope. Not just about Todd, but deep inside she wanted to trust again, maybe even have faith she'd never had before. It was all a remote possibility at this moment, but at least to her it was a ray of hope inspiring her to go on.

The two men watched Family member Warren Zann as he emerged from his accounting office in New Castle, Pennsylvania. He walked to the parking lot and got into his BMW.

The stocky, bald man behind the wheel of the Bronco was Captain Leo Gandtz of the Pennsylvania State Bureau of Investigation. His SBI collegues called him "The Bull." Beside him was Lt. Saucier. Saucier, tall and laconic, mumbled through a cigarette:

"Betcha he's going to his porno parlor."

Gandtz started the Bronco's engine as Warren Zann pulled out of his parking space into New Castle's main drive. Lt. Saucier finished his cigarette and tossed it out the window. They followed Warren Zann's BMW out of New Castle to an adult book store on the outskirts of the city. Captain Gandtz drove past the place. Down the road they'd turn around and come park across the street at a diner and watch Zann from there.

As they drove past the book store, Gandtz commented:

"These places are soon going to be extinct. If people want porn, they're gonna get it off the internet from now on. Don't have to leave home, don't have to risk the embarrassment of being spotted entering some seedy building. That's why this yahoo is pressing our man to get those web-sites hooked up so fast."

"You really think Zann's gonna shut down these businesses that soon? This is a whole chain he's running we're talking about."

Gandtz nodded confidently. "He's gonna shut these down and put the money into the internet. That's where the real money is these days. Plus, he'll be able to push his child pornography products much more safely."

Saucier grunted. "If he doesn't catch on that the man he's hired to set up his internet business is an SBI agent."

The Bull grunted back. "I'm gonna break this weasel's back. He'll wish he'd never heard the words 'child pornography'."

THIRTEEN

K ay Falco was on her front stoop when Tony Vero drove up. She was cleaning up the glass she'd shattered earlier that morning when she threw her lamp at Ed Larsky. She had changed out of the dress she'd worn to see Detective Kirkland and back into her sweat pants and flannel shirt. She had Dylon playing in his play pen outside on the grassy front lawn. She was carelessly barefooted, crouched over picking up large shards of glass and placing them in a plastic bucket. The sun was out and shining to make a decent May afternoon.

Tony parked his pickup truck in the driveway behind her Mustang. Kay glanced at him as he pulled up but continued working. He could make out a disgusted look on her face like she didn't want to be bothered. Uncle Joseph Vero had warned him about her, and told the story of Larsky's encounter with her that morning. Tony didn't care. Finding this woman's husband was Tony's ticket to freedom. She better not get in the way.

Tony Vero and Kay Falco both had an attitude when they met that first time.

"What do you want?" Kay snarled without even turning to look at Tony while she picked up broken glass.

He walked right up and stood over her while she worked. "I'm a private investigator. My name's Tony Vero. I'm . . ."

"Vero?" she said with irritation. She smacked her hands together twice and stood up from her work. "You a Vero from VECO?" Kay said as she turned and squared off with him.

Tony was caught off guard, not by her rude attitude, but by her beauty. With all the talk of what a witch she was no one warned him that she was so pretty. Her brown fawn eyes. Her smooth, high cheek bones. She was so strikingly feminine and graceful, yet aggressive. It was like a switch was turned on inside Tony when he cast eyes her. Lost in his depression, anxiety and guilt over the last two months, Tony hadn't had time to operate in these types of feelings.

"Yes, I am a Vero from VECO," Tony said, trying to regain focus and concentration. "I'm investigating . . ."

"Get in your truck and leave here now! I already put up with one of your goons this morning, I'm certainly not going to put up with you!"

"I'm not here for you to put up with anything!" he shot back. "I'm out here to find . . ."

"Go back and tell that idiot friend of yours Ed Larsky that I went to the police and they're coming to question him!"

Tony realized that Larsky must have rattled Kay Falco pretty good. "You don't know what you're talking about, lady. Ed Larsky would rather kill me than call me friend. I'm not here because of him. VECO has hired me."

"You're a liar," Kay said. "You're here to give me that 'don't go to the police' message Mr. Larsky tried to give me this morning. Save your breath. I've already been. You and Ed Larsky and VECO are all in on this."

Tony turned red with anger. "Do not ever lump me in the same boat of human debris as Ed Larsky, again. Do you understand me? Larsky is nothing more than Carmichael Vero's one man goon squad. He hates me more than anything else on this earth. He didn't send me here and neither did Carmichael. I'm not here to give you any message. I've been hired to find your husband and put an end to all this. I'm here to get your help."

Kay's stared at Tony in disbelief. "Larsky came to threaten me this morning. Why should I believe you now?" she asked.

"About Larsky?"

"Yes. How do I know you're not just trying to get on my good side by acting like you really don't like Ed Larsky?"

Tony pointed at her shattered storm door. "Do you have a good side?"

"He came out here threatening me about not going to the police," Kay defended herself.

"He's an idiot. And he wants me dead. I have no reason to lie to you or butter you up. I'm here to find Todd, collect my fee for it, and let you and Todd and Larsky and Carmichael and everybody else get on with their happy lives. End of story. Now are you gonna work with me or just stand there and yell at me?"

Kay almost felt ashamed. She believed Tony. Sort of. He seemed sincere. Not like Larsky. She looked up into Tony's dark eyes.

"I've been through hell, Mister. I don't have to cooperate. I've got nothing to lose."

"Me too. I'm desperate. I want to find your husband and get on with my life."

Silence.

"Me too," Kay said softly. "I'm scared and I want Todd found."

"Then let's start this whole conversation over again and work with one another, okay Mrs. Falco?"

After a moment's thought she said, "Start by calling me Kay."

Tony breathed a sigh of relief. "All right, Kay. Did you really go to the police?"

"Yes. Larsky warned me that Dylon and I would pay for it if I did. I'm not gonna put up with threats against my boy. So I went this morning and filed a missing person's report with the Sheriff's Department."

Tony looked at young Dylon happily playing in his play pen in the afternoon sun and shook his head with disgust.

"Larsky's truly a moron. But he's dangerous. I'm telling you: don't mess with him anymore."

"I didn't want to mess with him in the first place," Kay said. "I tried to put him out of my misery," she pointed to the glassy debris all over her porch stoop. "I threw my lamp at him as hard a I could."

Tony chuckled. "I heard. Did it bounce off his big Fred Flintstone head?"

Kay laughed, now. "No. I missed. I did more damage to my house than him."

"What'd the police tell you about Todd?"

"This detective from the sheriff's department, Detective Kirkland his name is, he's going to investigate. He's going to VECO and he said he'd be coming here today, too."

Tony shook his head. "That doesn't help me. I can't afford to cross paths with the law on this."

"Why?" Kay asked.

Tony looked around cautiously. The Falco's lived out in the sticks, and the nearest neighbor was down the road, but you never knew who could be listening.

"Look, Kay. You and I both know what Todd really does for a living. You know his VECO job was his front."

"You're right," she said. "What of it?"

"Todd hasn't disappeared because of a business luncheon with a VECO client. He went to make a major cocaine deal on Tuesday. I need to know who he was dealing with so I can find him."

Kay's eyes teared up. She crossed her arms. "Do you think Todd's dead?"

"I don't know. All I know for sure is he's missing now because he had a whole bunch of money given to him Tuesday afternoon."

"How much?"

"Over a million dollars."

She was flabbergasted. "Are you joking?"

Tony shook his head.

"You mean that rotten jerk dealt with that kind of money?"

"He never told you?"

"He told me nothing, Mister. He kept me in the dark. You VECO people paid him that much?"

"VECO didn't pay anything for his drug dealing, but he made plenty over the years. I know he must have made a fortune."

"What has he been doing with all this money?" she anguished to know.

"I don't know your husband. I want to find him. Maybe I can clue you in later as to what he actually did for the drug business and how much he made. But right now we're racing the clock, here, if the sheriff's department's going to be investigating. Give me some information so I can track down Todd before they do."

"I don't have information. I told you that. Todd really never told me anything except to mind my own business. He paid for this house and my car, but he never gave me any clues as to who he dealt with."

"Is there anything here you can give to me to help me, Kay?" Tony asked.

She thought for a moment. Then she walked over and pulled Dylon out of the play pen.

"Follow me," she said.

Kay and Tony stood looking at the door of the third bedroom of her two story home. "Todd calls this his 'office,'" she said with disgust. She pointed to the deadbolt lock on the door. "I don't have a key."

"He never let you in here?" Tony asked.

"I've not seen the inside of that room since the first week we bought this house three years ago. Todd kept his lucky suitcase he used on his drug deals in there, but I don't know what else. So, go on" she commanded.

Tony looked at her, baffled by her command.

"That's his drug room, dummy!" she chided impatiently. "If you want information, break down the door and get it! 'Cause trust me, I've been up one side of this house and down the other, and Todd hasn't left any other evidence of his drug business around here. Anything you want'll be in there."

Tony looked at her, frustrated. How could someone so good looking be so mean?

"Step back," he ordered her.

He knew how to quickly get through a door. He learned at that California private detective's school. He leaned back on his left leg and kicked powerfully with his right foot between the doorknob and the deadbolt. The door exploded open. Splinters of wood and the twisted deadbolt landed on the floor, leaving a gaping hole in the door and a splintered crack in the wooden molding of the door frame.

"Bravo," Kay said, impressed.

She and Tony both entered Todd's "office." The room was dark and dreary. Tony switched on the overhead light and Kay pulled up the thick shades. Light flooded the bedroom for the first time in years. Dust caked everything. The room was almost empty. The only things Todd had in there were an old white desk and chair with a telephone, and a light blue file cabinet three drawers high. Tony tried the file cabinet. It was locked, of course. Kay looked in the desk drawer. There were some note pads and pencils, but nothing else of interest.

"You gotta key for this file cabinet, by any chance?" Tony asked.

"You kidding? You think Todd would give me one if he wouldn't even allow me in this room?"

"Just hoping."

Tony saw a closet. The door was open a crack. He pulled open the door and flicked on the light. It was a walk-in closet. On the floor were several large stacks of pornographic magazines and a couple of whiskey bottles. Kay walked in behind Tony. Her heart sank again as she saw the nude bodies on the magazine covers.

"More filthy women!" she gasped in disbelief. She began to redden and tear up again.

Tony picked up a magazine, glanced at it for a moment, tossed it down. Kay left the closet.

"'More,' you say?" he asked.

Kay tried not to sob, tried to calm down. She didn't want Tony Vero to see her break down. She walked over and sat down on the desk chair, shaking her head with disdain.

"Am I ugly?" she asked out loud.

Tony turned around and looked at her. "Hideous," he said sarcastically. She ignored him.

"Todd has chased after every woman he's ever seen. Now I find out he's been leering at porno magazines, too. Is something wrong with me?" She sighed and held her head. This was like finding out about one more affair Todd had been having.

"You didn't know about his 'collection' in the closet?"

"You kidding me? I would have ripped his eyeballs out if I'd known. Todd knows how I feel about this kind of trash in my home. Not with me and my son here."

Tony could see the heartache this was causing Kay and he felt a little ashamed, since he really didn't think twice about those kind of magazines. He had a few around his house, too.

"Look. I really need your help. Let's see if we can find a key for this file cabinet."

"Todd kept all his keys on his key chain. There's no key in this desk drawer. Unless those floozies in those magazines are hiding one, there is no spare in this room."

Tony looked on top of the closet shelves. Then he kicked over the magazine stacks and whiskey bottles to be sure there was nothing under them. He walked out of the closet and stood over the small file cabinet.

"This is some cheap K-Mart file cabinet. I could break into it pretty easily."

"Put it in your truck and get it out of here. If it has any information on his women, I want it. You understand me?"

"Todd have lots of affairs?" Tony asked.

"Yes, if that's any of your business."

"You got names for me?"

"Why? Looking for a cheap date?"

Tony was mad, now. "Listen to me! I am not playing! I'm trying to find your husband. Drop your little tough girl act long enough to keep your mouth shut and think for a minute. If Todd's been with some other woman, she may have information about who he was dealing with on Tuesday."

Kay sat up and put her hand on her chest while holding her mouth open in make believe shock. "Okay! Calm down. Sharon Lacello. She works for Brighton Analytical, one of VECO's chemical testing companies Todd markets for. She's Todd's bimbo of the month. Actually, she's lasted a bit longer than any other woman he's been with since he married me."

"Where's Todd like to hang out when he's not home with you?"

"Bars, clubs, any place with women. Sharon will know his current hang outs. He stopped telling me where he went years ago."

"Why you still married to him?" Tony really wanted to know.

"None of your business," she snapped.

Embarrassed, he bent down and picked up the file cabinet to take with him. It wasn't too heavy, but it did sound like it had quite a bit of material in it.

"I'll let you know if there's anything interesting in here," he said. He started out the bedroom door.

Kay stood up. "You listen to me. I'm cooperating with you for one reason, Tony: I want Todd found. I'm also cooperating fully with Detective Kirkland when he comes here. I'm not hiding anything from him. I'm going to tell him I had you break down this door and that I had you take that file cabinet so you could break into it. If the law comes looking for you, so be it."

"Thank you for all your hospitality, generosity, and congeniality today, Mrs. Falco," Tony said, then turned and calmly carried the file cabinet down the hall.

"Hey, I don't owe you anything!" She followed Tony. "This is my life, here, not yours. You Veros and your filthy money have destroyed our lives with this drug business. You've destroyed my Todd. I'm not going to go along just to make you Veros happy. I owe you nothing."

"And I don't owe you anything!" Tony remarked halfway down the stairs without pausing to stop. "I'd just like for you to muzzle your mouth long enough to help me, rather than verbally assault me."

Kay stood at the top of the stairs with her arms folded. She watched Tony's strong shoulders and back and looked over his backside. Tony was cute, strong, and funny. But she could tell something was haunting him. And he wasn't gung ho about VECO, like Todd had been, and Ed Larsky. He almost seemed hostile about it. It was almost like she could trust him.

When Tony reached the bottom of the stairs she shouted, "You find my Todd, Mr. Vero."

"I'll let myself out," he called back.

"I know," she said. Kay smiled a little smile. She whispered: "We'll see what kind of man you really are, Tony Vero."

FOURTEEN

Witchcraft. That was the word Holy Spirit spoke to Detective Ray Kirkland as he entered the VECO office building that afternoon. *Witchcraft?* Ray looked around the second floor while he walked up to the receptionists' area. He looked for occult symbols anywhere in the office. There were none. Carmichael Vero had the whole complex tastefully decorated in modern styles, with no occult overtones. Ray scanned the receptionists' desk areas and cubicles. He saw some crosses around people's necks, a strange shaped broach or pendant was worn here or there. Some ankle and shoulder tattoos on a few women. But there were no blatant symbols of witchcraft, satanism, or the occult anywhere.

What do you mean, "witchcraft," Holy Spirit? Ray prayed silently. Was he hearing correctly that day? He was. But he had no idea what Holy Spirit meant by it.

A secretary behind the counter stood up when she saw Detective Kirkland standing there. "I'm sorry," she said with a concerned look on her face. "I didn't see you. Can I help you, sir?"

"Yes, Ma'am," Detective Kirkland flashed his badge and a big smile.

Detective Kirkland walked down the foyer to Carmichael Vero's office. Ed Larsky opened the heavy double oak doors for him. He nodded at the tall detective as he entered the spacious executive office. Ray nodded back. This huge man did not look like the average company executive to Ray. His cold stare was too intimidating. Carmichael was seated at his desk doing paperwork. Larsky closed the doors and joined him in a chair at his side. He picked up a pen and wrote on a form. The two obviously had been working together. Ray scanned all over Carmichael's office, looking for any sign of the occult. He spotted none.

Carmichael did not stand up to greet the detective, nor did he offer him a seat. "How can I help you, sir?" he asked.

"Mr. Vero, I'm Detective Kirkland from the Beaver County Sheriff's Department. I'm here to get some information on an employee of yours."

Kay Falco did indeed go to the police, Carmichael easily deduced.

"Certainly, detective. Which employee would that be?" Carmichael asked as Larsky pretended to pay the visitor no mind while he worked on the papers.

"A Mister Todd Falco," Ray said, watching them both intently.

Neither Carmichael nor Larsky gave any reaction.

"What of him?" Carmichael asked.

"Has he shown up for work over the last couple of days?"

"No, sir."

"Have any of you here at VECO actually spoken to or heard from Todd Falco since Tuesday afternoon?"

"No, Detective."

"Mrs. Falco reports that Todd left the house Tuesday afternoon on a business deal and that's the last she's seen or heard from him. Did you or anyone here send him on any business trips or meetings Tuesday?"

"No, sir. Why do you ask?"

"Well, his wife came to see me this morning and filled out a missing person's report on him."

Larsky looked up at Detective Kirkland, now. "'Missing persons?'" he said with irritation. "Is that what she told you?"

Ray paused, staring at Larsky, then said, "Yes, Mister . . ." Ray did not know Larsky's name.

"I apologize, detective," Carmichael said. "This is Mr. Ed Larsky. He's VECO's office manager and Todd Falco's direct supervisor."

"Todd's not missing," Larsky said, matter of factly.

"He's not?" Ray asked with surprise. "You know where he is?"

"He ain't home with that wife of his and he's not coming to work for a while," Larsky said, standing up.

"Where is he, then?" Ray demanded.

"He told me he was heading south. But he's not disappeared. He filed a leave of absence form with me the other day, asking for a couple of weeks off. I granted it to him, but I wasn't happy about it. We got a lot of work to do here before next Tuesday."

"We're preparing a very important banquet for VECO stock holders, Tuesday," Carmichael explained.

Larsky's revelation was a surprise to Ray. "A leave of absence form?"

"Yeah," Larsky said. "He came to me Tuesday morning, handed me the leave form and told me he was going south for a few days."

"Where 'south' did he say he was going?" Ray asked.

"All he told me was that he was heading south for a few days. South where? I don't know."

"I'd like to see that leave of absence form right now, Mr. Larsky," Ray said.

"Sure," Larsky said coolly. He hit Carmichael's intercom button. "Hilda? Go to the personnel files and bring me Todd Falco's leave of absence form out of his folder. Now, please."

"Yes, sir," came the reply.

"Did he give a reason for the leave request?" Ray asked.

"Yeah. He wrote that he was having marital problems with that nutty wife of his and wanted to get out of town for a while."

"Pardon me?" Ray asked. "His 'nutty' wife? He said his wife was 'nutty?'"

"No. I did," Larsky said, disgusted. Carmichael stood up.

"Detective, we need to make you aware of something," Carmichael said with a somber expression. "I sent Mr. Larsky out to the Falco's home this morning to check on Todd's whereabouts. While he was there Kay Falco assaulted Mr. Larsky."

Ray stared at Larsky with disbelief. "Assaulted him? So Mr. Larsky, you went out at the Falco residence this morning?" Things were becoming clearer to Ray.

"She's a psycho woman," Ed said bluntly. "You see her front door?"

"Uh, no, Mr. Larsky. I've not been out to her home yet. I'm going there this afternoon."

"She cussed me up one side and down the other, yelled me out of her house, and then threw a lamp at me."

"She hit him in the leg with the lamp," Carmichael explained. "Shattered the glass on her front door . . ."

"Scared her little child, bruised my leg," Ed angrily interrupted Carmichael's account.

"Why?" Ray said, trying to contain a laugh that was about to erupt from his gut.

"I went out there to ask her what was going on. My top marketing executive decides he's just gonna leave town for a little while. Why? 'Cause he's having a bad marriage to that nut."

"That made her mad?"

"I told her I was thinking of tracking down Todd myself because I needed him to get his butt in here and give me some information on his clients. It's like he just ditched us all here at VECO. We not only got that banquet to get ready for, but Todd's in charge of marketing some of our biggest accounts. All the business he was involved in could go down the drain. But when I said we would find Todd, she freaked. She told me all of this was none of my business. Then she started threatening me like it was my fault Todd took off. She just plain freaked out on me."

Ray really wanted to belly laugh. "And she threw the lamp at you?"

"After I was out the door!"

Ray finally snickered out loud. He just couldn't help it.

Ed was clearly angry at Detective Kirkland, now. "And what's so funny?" he demanded.

Ray laughed and waved a hand at Larsky. "How much you weigh, Mr. Larsky? 250? 260?"

"What's that got to do with anything?" Ed was hot. Carmichael glared at Ray.

"Sir, you could be a linebacker for the Steelers. Kay Falco might weigh 90 pounds wet. I'm just trying to visualize that little woman intimidating you and throwing you out of her house."

"I was just trying to help her find her husband and she assaulted me!" Larsky shouted.

Carmichael interceded. "Detective Kirkland, my employee went out to the Falco's residence to offer VECO's assistance in what is surely a sordid and sticky marital situation, and in return Mrs. Falco verbally and physically assaulted him. She's lucky that I'm not having Mr. Larsky press charges against her. I would appreciate it if you would pay proper respect to this situation and withhold your laughter."

Ray humbly wiped the grin off his face. "My laughter was a bit inappropriate," Ray conceded. "I apologize. However, I'm going to tell you two right now that Mr. Larsky's story does not line up with the story Mrs. Falco told me about their encounter this morning."

"She's psycho!" Ed said, throwing a hand up in the air.

"She is an unstable woman, detective," Carmichael defended.

"Nonetheless, she feels vulnerable and threatened at present. She's filed a missing persons report and I'm here to investigate with Sheriff DeBona's blessing."

Someone knocked on the door.

Larsky opened it. A secretary handed him a piece of paper. Larsky snatched it and closed the door on her. He marched over to Ray and nearly threw the paper at him.

"Here's your missing persons report," Larsky snarled. "This idiot ain't missing. He's run away from his wife. I would, too."

Ray read the leave of absence form:

> "Due to personal pressure at home, I feel that I need some time to go away
> and reevaluate my life, my marriage, and my work. Please honor my request for
> a two week leave of absence."

Ray looked at Todd Falco's signature stamp at the bottom and examined Todd's initials.

"Well. I guess this is official, then. Todd has willfully left town and'll be returning in a week or so."

"That's right," Carmichael said confidently.

"But there is one thing that bothers me, gentlemen," Ray said. "If Todd planned on being away so long why did he only pack one tiny overnight bag?"

Carmichael and Ed stared confused at Detective Kirkland.

"What do you mean?" Carmichael asked.

"Mrs. Falco told me he only took one tiny overnight bag with only one change of clothes." Ray purposefully omitted the fact that Todd also took a large empty suitcase. "And maybe you two can answer another question for me then. Why didn't Todd Falco tell his wife he was taking a personal leave of absence? She told me he'd been doing nothing out of the ordinary this week."

"Did he take one of his chicks with him?" Larsky asked.

"Pardon me?" Ray played dumb.

"One of his chicks, his girlfriends. Did the lovely Mrs. Falco fail to tell you that her husband was so miserable with her that he constantly had women on the side?"

Ray wrote the information down on a small notepad, like this was the first time he'd heard it.

"Detective Kirkland, I'll be frank with you," Carmichael said. "Todd Falco is a valuable employee to us here at VECO. But his personal life is a mess. He's a notorious adulterer. His wife has mental and emotional problems. And then on Tuesday, he comes in here, files a leave of absence form, and takes off without even leaving a number for Ed to get a hold of him. He's made himself a liability to me."

"Oh?" Ray said, listening intently. "What's your point?"

"Do you know who I am, Detective Kirkland?" Carmichael asked Ray.

"Yes I do, Mr. Vero."

"Are you familiar with my arrest and trial and the false accusations my own government leveled against me back in 1981?"

"I know what you were charged with."

This was getting good! Ray wanted to find out where Carmichael Vero was heading with it all.

"Are you aware of VECO's impeccable record?"

"No, sir."

"You see, once I was freed from those phony charges, I started VECO with my own money, sweat and blood. I was determined to clear my good name and reputation of all charges of me being in La Cosa Nostra. This company has been unfairly audited four times in its nineteen year history by the IRS, yet all audits acquitted us of every unfair suspicion about my business transactions and financial dealings here at VECO. We received an impeccable report each audit. I run a tight ship here, Detective Kirkland. Because of the lies told against me by the federal government, I have to work twice as hard to maintain VECO's character and reputation among our clients and competitors. I demand excellence, quality, and clean living among my employees. I do not want to be under any public or governmental scrutiny ever again."

"Therefore?" Ray said with a smile.

"Therefore when an employee like Todd Falco and his wife live their lives as they do, especially as they have these last few days, I must swiftly deal with the situation to distance me and VECO from their unscrupulous lifestyles."

"You're going to fire Todd because he took off on you unexpectedly, and his wife assaulted your executive officer here," Ray deduced.

"Exactly, Detective!" Carmichael said. "Todd and his wife are now liabilities to VECO. What if she had seriously injured Mr. Larsky this morning?"

Ray snickered again, but then straightened up. Larsky glared at him.

"I've hired a private investigator to track down Mr. Falco, Detective Kirkland," Carmichael said.

"Why?" Ray asked, perplexed. "If he's not missing, as your leave of absence form here clearly proves, then Mrs. Falco's missing persons report is rendered null. All we have to do is find out where Todd Falco's vacationing and declare case closed. Why the private eye?"

"I want Todd found immediately, I want him to get in here quickly and tie up his loose ends with our VECO clients, and then make his resignation so I can replace him before our stockholder's banquet next Tuesday. Todd's been a valuable asset to VECO. But the longer he's gone, the worse things could get for us. I will no longer allow him to stay here and pose a risk to our reputation."

"So Todd's on the outs with you and his wife?"

"He is with us. I personally don't care what happens between him and his wife."

Ray nodded. "Who's this private investigator?"

"That's confidential information."

Ray's eyes widened. He pulled out a copy of Kay Falco's missing persons report and waved it at Carmichael and Larsky.

"It's not confidential now, gentlemen," Ray said, deadly serious. "Private investigators don't mean a thing to me. They're a cheap dime a dozen, and if this person you've hired crosses my path or even looks wrong at me, I'm going to hit him and you, Mr. Vero, with an obstruction of justice charge that will keep you both busy for quite a while."

"You can't just threaten us like that . . . !" Larsky started, but Carmichael raised a halting hand to his henchman.

"If it's such a touchy subject to you, Detective, even though your missing persons case will rightfully be closed now that you have this new information, I'll just go ahead and tell you our private investigator's name is Tony Vero."

Ray's eyes widened again. "The quarterback?"

"Yes."

"A relative?" Ray asked while he wrote down Tony's name.

Carmichael nodded. "We'll quickly find Todd Falco, we'll let you know where he is as soon as he's found, and you can go investigate something else, Detective Kirkland."

Ray grinned a big grin. "Looks like you gentlemen were able to wrap this case up quickly for me!" he said as he put away his notepad. "I'll let myself out. You'll be available if I have more questions, Mr. Vero?"

"Always," Carmichael nodded.

Larsky pointed at Ray. "You go out to her house and check out that front door. It's shattered to pieces. Ask her why she assaulted me. She's lying to you, Kirkland."

Ray opened the oak doors to leave, then turned around, his smile vanished.

"Oh, I'll judge who's lying here, Mr. Larsky. Good day, gentlemen."

Ray Kirkland disappeared behind the oak doors. Larsky went to make sure the detective was not listening on the other side. He turned around and looked at Carmichael.

"He's gonna be trouble! Call the Magic Genie," Larsky said.

"We've thrown him the only bone we needed to get him off our backs." Carmichael said. "He'll be gone about his business, now."

"Why'd you tell him we hired Tony to investigate?"

"In case he and Tony cross paths during their search. This way it won't be a surprise to Dick Tracy, there, and he won't come back to ask me why I'm having this investigated, too. I want you to start termination procedures against Todd, now, and start finding a replacement for him."

"You're going to completely fire him from VECO?"

"Ed, it's been two days. Todd's either run off with my money or he's dead. I want to make sure the story we've told Detective Kirkland looks legitimate. Fire Todd. Go through all the motions. Then begin finding his replacement."

"Call the Magic Genie again," Ed repeated.

"I spoke to his assistant, this morning. Cyrus Moreau will call me back. Quit worrying about him, Ed."

"We need him to set this mess straight. Only Cyrus can give us the kind of help we need. I'm starting to get worried, here. We need more action to cover ourselves."

Carmichael took a deep breath, held it for a moment, then let it out to relax. He sat back down at his desk. On a legal pad he took a pen and wrote a note. When he was finished he ripped it off the pad and handed it to his right hand man. Larsky read the note:

"Go to Joseph. Get the names of Todd Falco's three dealers from him. Go to Anthony Zann and get sixty thousand dollars of Family money. Then go smoke those three dealers. Make it look like three gang hits, a gang war. Hire your best man to do the job. That'll ease our problems some!"

Larsky read the note and smiled. Kill the top three men who make all the drug money for the Family. In one way it was hideously insane, killing three of their top cash cows. But in another way, it was hilariously evil, since Todd Falco held all the cards and their million and one hundred thousand dollars. If he was gone and the three dealers were gone, that would be two lines of defense to protect Carmichael and the Family.

Larsky chuckled. He put the legal paper in a paper shredder on top of the trash can and shredded it to minuscule bits. Carmichael smiled at him.

"This isn't over yet, Ed. Not yet. We're still players, here. We're still in control."

Ray Kirkland stepped back into the VECO office lobby. He still had Todd Falco's leave of absence form. He stepped back up to the receptionist's counter where three women were standing. He caught their attention.

"Excuse me," he said, smiling. "Who's Hilda?"

"I am," a woman in her fifties held up her hand. Her eyes widened with concern.

"Hilda, can you please make a copy of this leave of absence form for me? I think I'm going to keep the original for a few days. I'll return it when I'm finished."

"Sure." She took it and started toward the copy room.

"Hilda?" Ray stopped her.

"Yes?"

"Tell me, did you file that leave of absence form?"

"Yes, sir."

"Uh huh. And who gave you that form to file?"

"Mr. Larsky did, sir."

"Yeah. Tell me, when did Mr. Larsky first give you that form to file?"

"Just this morning, sir. A couple of hours ago."

"Really?" Ray thought for a second. "Did you ever see Todd Falco with this form at any time?"

"No sir."

"Miss Hilda, when did you first find out that Todd Falco had put in for a leave of absence?"

Hilda thought for a moment. "Why me and everyone else here, we didn't even know Todd was taking time off until Mr. Larsky asked me to file this form this morning. First we heard."

Ray broke into another sunshiny, happy day smile. "God bless you, Hilda!" he said.

FIFTEEN

Joseph Vero drove his Porsche around the back row of storage buildings at the Beaver Falls Storage Center on College Hill. His nephew Tony had called and told him to meet him at the small complex. The Kid wouldn't tell Joseph what he wanted over the phone. He saw Tony's blue pickup truck next to a storage room with its door rolled open to the top. Joseph parked and got out. Tony was inside. It was an eight by ten room. Tony had two large boxes and some furniture and weight equipment stored. He was standing over an open blue file cabinet. He had a tool box sitting open on top of it. He pointed to the file cabinet he'd broken into.

"This was Todd Falco's. I got it from his house."

Joseph walked into the storage room and looked at the file cabinet. Its top drawer was pulled open. Tony had a manila file folder in his hands.

"Check this out," Tony handed the manila folder to his Uncle Joseph. It had several papers in it. Joseph rifled the file. They were records kept by Todd Falco. Each record dated the time and amount of every drug transaction Todd ever made for the Family. He had Joseph Vero's name written for every large purchase, such as the one he was supposed to make on Tuesday. He also had the names of the Family's usual three customers, who would buy and deal the narcotics.

"Todd was a great record keeper, Uncle Joseph. Everything's documented. Every deal you and the Family ever paid him to arrange is recorded in that folder. If Todd ever went down it looks like he was ready to take you all with him."

Joseph remained emotionless as he read the files. "What else did you find in that file cabinet?"

"Just names and numbers. There's a complete record of Todd's women. I don't know about the rest of the names and numbers. I can go through them to see if any of these records match those in that manila folder."

"Just destroy that whole file cabinet and everything in it."

Tony shook his head no. "I can't do that. Kay Falco filed a missing persons report on Todd and says that as soon as the cops come to her house today she's going to tell them about me and this cabinet. She's not cutting us any slack. I want to get all the dangerous stuff out of here and hand the cops the rest like that's all Todd had in there."

Joseph, frustrated, took a breath and blew it out slowly. He stood for a moment staring into a corner, pondering this crisis. Tony noted his usual stoicism. Uncle Joseph was a pretty cool customer.

"It's the safest thing to do, Uncle Joe. I'll make sure there's not one incriminating thing in that file and I'll get it to the cops if they come looking for it. It'll look like I'm fully cooperating."

"They won't believe it. They'll come after you. They'll get a search warrant for everything you own. Will you be willing to sign a sworn affidavit for them saying that there was nothing else in that file?"

"Yeah. I'm ready. If they can find me."

"Because it may come to that once they found out you broke into it."

"Mrs. Falco gave me permission."

"So what? She can't be trusted, Tony. She blames Larsky and VECO for her husband's problems."

"Isn't she right?"

Joseph became animated. "What is your problem, Tony? Are you against us, too? After that stunt you pulled with Carmichael this morning I'm beginning to question whether I can even trust you."

Tony could have battled his Uncle Joseph on that comment, but did not. "I'm here to save you and Uncle Carmichael. I've promised I'm going to clean up all of this mess for you. I will."

"Well then do your job and quit pushing my buttons. Why did I ever listen to you and get you into the Family in the first place?" Joseph asked out loud.

"'Cause I was stupid and you believed in me."

Joseph glanced back at him. Slowly a smile formed on Joseph's face, a sly smile like a father might give to a son.

"Clean that file cabinet out right. Then take it back to your place. You better believe the cops are going to ask for it. You have it ready for them. I'm destroying this folder," he waved it. "Tony, you keep me constantly updated on your progress. And go find that Bernie Lokawski, whoever he is. He's the one behind all this."

Tony pulled out a sheet of paper from the file cabinet. He unfolded it and handed it to Joseph. The only thing written on it was "Bernie Lokawski-555-0896."

"My first and only lead on Bernie Lokawski, so far," Tony said.

"Then we're in trouble, Tony. This is getting pretty serious. I don't know if the Family . . . well, it doesn't matter." Joseph handed him back the paper and started back toward his Porsche, visibly worried. He got in and started the engine.

The Porsche disappeared around the corner. Guilt pierced Tony's heart as he watched his Uncle Joseph drive off. He now held the knife that could stab his Uncle Joseph in the back, for he had hidden one more file under the driver's seat of his truck. Tony knew he had to look out for himself first, even if it might hurt his uncle. So in his truck was a duplicate file to the one Joseph had taken to destroy. Tony had taken Todd Falco's original manila folder inside the storage center's office and paid the manager to let him copy it with the office copier. Tony would hold on to that file. If the Family wanted to double cross him when this was all over, he would be ready for the fight. They couldn't mess with him if he was holding Todd Falco's Family records.

Tony was getting out of the Family, one way or another.

The Beaver County Sheriff's K-9 van was parked outside Kay Falco's house. Two deputies had two German shepherds going through the Falco's home sniffing for any signs of drugs. Kay had okayed the search, wanting to cooperate with the missing person's investigation any way possible.

Detective Ray Kirkland stood by his police car on the Falco's driveway with Kay. He pointed to the frame of Kay Falco's front storm door. Shards of broken glass hung loosely around the edge of the frame. She was crimson with embarrassment. She had cleaned up all the broken glass from the ground by that point, but the empty door frame incriminated her.

"It sounds to me like there was a bit more to your mystery meeting this morning than you originally told me," Ray gently pressed her.

Kay shrugged, further embarrassed. "It's not like I was trying to hide this from you, Detective Kirkland. Remember, I didn't even tell you who was out here this morning, let alone what happened."

"Carmichael Vero says you're lucky he's not charging you for assaulting Ed Larsky."

"Ed Larsky ought to be grateful he's alive!"

"Mrs. Falco, Ed Larsky claims you were the trouble maker this morning." Ray pointed toward the remnant of the storm door. "It is apparent that you meant him physical harm. You better go on and tell me the truth right now."

Kay huffed, tapped her foot for a moment, and then told her story: "Ed Larsky was the one who came out here this morning. He knew that Todd was missing. He tried to act all concerned but I knew he was full of it. I was pretty wired at that point and I didn't give him any slack. Finally, he told me that he wanted to find Todd before anyone else did. He told me to let VECO find Todd and not to go to the police. I blew him out. Then he said that if I was really concerned for my son Dylon that I better not go to the police." She pointed toward the storm door. "And there's my reaction to that."

"Did Mr. Larsky say anything about drugs or Todd being some sort of dealer?"

"No. I did, though, and he just ignored me about it. He never let on like he knew about the drugs. He just wanted to get a hold of Todd for some reason."

"Have you ever, since Todd's worked at VECO, seen or heard or imagined any connection between Todd's drug dealing and VECO?"

"No. Never."

"There's no question in your mind?"

"This morning was the first time VECO and Todd's drug business even came anywhere close to being connected in my mind. Carmichael Vero runs a tight ship out there. He doesn't put up with any funny business. And up until Ed Larsky came out here this morning and threatened Dylon and me, I never even thought of making a connection."

"You trust Carmichael Vero that much?"

"Why shouldn't I? He's been very respectable. Especially to Todd."

Ray thought about VECO and Holy Spirit's warnings about witchcraft earlier that day.

"Was Todd involved in the occult at all?" Ray asked. He knew it was a stretch.

"The what?"

"The occult. You know, witchcraft, horoscopes . . ."

"You mean like devil worship?" Kay said with surprise.

"Sort of."

She laughed. "Todd didn't believe in any of that stuff. Shoot, Todd's an atheist, as far as I know. Like horror movies and things like that? He could've cared less about that stuff. He never brought it up. Now sex? He was obsessed, obviously. But not satan worship."

"So Todd never mentioned anything about the occult to you?"

"Never. Why do you ask?"

Ray smiled politely. "Oh, I just had some questions I was looking into."

Barking could be heard from inside the house.

"I do need to tell you something else," Kay confessed. At that point one of the deputies hollered out the front door for Detective Kirkland to join them upstairs.

Kay smiled, embarrassed again. "That's probably what I was going to tell you about."

Ray examined the broken bedroom door that Tony'd kicked in earlier that day.

"You kinda rough on your house, ain't ya?" he said to Kay. He did not look amused.

"I'm sorry! I wasn't thinking," she said.

"Well I don't understand, young lady," Ray said, irritated. "You come to us for our help, and then you let VECO's private investigator come in here and scoop all our evidence. Who knows what this guy has now that we'll never see? Do you trust this Tony Vero that much?"

"I don't even know him. Look, I honestly would've had you kick in this door the same way. Todd never gave me the key. There is no spare. There's no other way to get in here."

Ray sighed and walked into the bedroom to the closet where the deputies and their dogs waited. Ray noted with disgust all of Todd's porno magazines that Tony Vero had scattered about the closet. Both Starsky and Hutch were bent forward in the closet sniffing wildly with their haunches raised and hair standing on end. One of the deputies pointed to a rectangular indentation in the carpet in the back corner of the walk-in closet.

"This is the only spot in the entire house where these dogs have reacted, Detective," the deputy reported.

"What was in this spot, Mrs. Falco?" Ray asked.

Kay peaked in the crowded closet. "I have no idea. I told you, Todd never let me in this room." She examined the indentation in the carpet for a moment. "It might be the spot where Todd kept that old suitcase he used. I told you he went in here on Tuesday and got it. He took it with him when he left."

"And you say that he always used it when he was going on one of his deals?"

"Yes. I always knew what he was up to when I saw that suitcase."

Ray backed out of the crowded closet.

"Deputy Turner, see if you can get a good sample from that spot. Let's verify that these dogs are indeed smelling cocaine or whatever."

"Yes, sir," the deputy in charge of the canines said as he hauled Hutch out of the closet and out of the room.

Ray went over to the desk and chair in the bedroom. "You sure that private investigator didn't take anything out of here?" he asked Kay.

She walked over to the desk. "No. I went through there and the only thing in there is what you see. If I'd have found something I'd tell you."

Ray pointed at the indentation in the carpet in the bedroom where Todd's blue file cabinet once sat. "But that," he said angrily, "you let this Vero guy take from here with your blessing to break into it."

"Well, I specifically told him I was going to tell you that he had it," she defended herself.

"Oh!" Ray said, looking at the other deputy, who was shaking his head. "I'm sure, then, that if this Vero guy finds anything in it he'll hold it in good keeping for us until we get there to pick it up!"

Kay folded her arms and sighed. "Look, I want Todd found . . ." she began.

"Well if you do," Ray interrupted, "then from now on do not let anybody else near anything that might be evidence in this case. Do you remember our conversation about trust this morning at the station, Mrs. Falco?"

She nodded. Her eyes reddened.

"Then help me trust you by making wise choices from now on." He turned to the other deputy. "Deputy Simmons, I want you to find this Tony Vero guy. Locate him, hold him for questioning, and call me. I'll come to where you are as fast as I can. I want that file cabinet and everything that's in it."

Starsky lay flat on the floor and whimpered as Ray gave the orders. Ray sneered at the dog.

"You better shape up too, Starsky!" he said to the animal, and then leaned over and gave the shepherd's belly a good rubbing. "Call VECO, Deputy Simmons. Tell them I said I want Tony Vero right now. I want him found within the next hour. Tony Vero . . ." Ray paused, remembering. "Tony Vero, Beaver Falls football star. What ever happened to his college career, Simmons?"

"He went bust in college, Ray. Didn't make it for some reason."

Deputy Simmons left with Starsky. Kay Falco was nervous, now. She trusted Detective Kirkland and didn't want to upset him like she did. Why did she let Tony Vero do all that? For some reason she trusted him, too. Tears began to well up, again. The longer this went on the more frightened she felt. The realization was sinking in that Todd might be gone forever. And even though he was a horrible husband, Dylon at least had a father. And she did have tremendous financial security in Todd. She'd never really had to worry about money or support as long as they'd been married.

Ray saw the tears in her eyes again. She was trembling, too. He tried to calm down.

"We have an APB out on Todd and his car, Mrs. Falco. That nice white Camaro won't get far without being spotted. The newspapers and Pittsburgh TV stations will probably pick up the story, too. We'll run Todd's picture and publish a phone number people can call if they've spotted him or the car. We're doing all we can right now."

She didn't respond.

"You gave me his mother's name and address this morning. You said his father lives in California?"

"Yeah. He's a plastic surgeon out there. Todd hasn't seen or talked to him in years."

"Well, I'm going to talk to his mother and see what she knows."

"She won't know much. She's just as cold as Todd. She drinks her booze and lives off her alimony."

"That's sad," Ray said. "Those magazines Todd kept in this closet are sad, too."

"Everything's sad," Kay said, wiping her tears. "Our whole existence is sad."

The late afternoon sun shone brightly over the VECO office complex. It had turned out to be a spectacular early May day.

Carmichael and Larsky joined the Dalling Security agent and his German shepherd at the edge of the woods behind VECO, right below Carmichael's office. The Dalling Security agent handed Larsky a zip lock bag full of about ten ounces of hot red spices mixed with some dirt.

"Someone's been all over back there, according to Zeus, here," the agent reported, nodding at the German shepherd. He pointed to the bag of spices. "That's probably what they threw down last night that burned up our other two dogs so badly. Zeus and I followed that person's tracks from right back in these woods all the way out to Route 51. Zeus lost the scent on the side of the rode near some tire tracks, so whoever it was must have parked there and walked back through the woods to this spot. I'd say someone's been spying on you, Mr. Vero. Probably one of those corporate spies."

Larsky held up the bag full of the spices. "So they used the spices to stop the dogs?"

"It worked, too. Whoever it was must know guard dogs pretty well and came prepared."

Carmichael was visibly angry. This meant even more trouble for the Family because someone was hiring people to spy on his office. And they must have been there the previous evening when the Family members held their after hours meeting. All six Family members had been present, too, for this person to see and report to whomever hired them.

"I want guard dogs out here every night," Carmichael commanded the Dalling agent.

"That's gonna cost you quite a bit . . ."

"I don't care! Your one fat guard obviously isn't doing enough! I'll pay your money! But I want the dogs every night!"

"Yes sir," the agent said, shocked at Carmichael's outburst.

Carmichael composed himself. "Figure the payment and send the bill to Mr. Larsky here. I want the dogs here starting tonight."

Carmichael and Larsky were walking back toward the VECO building.

"Ed, check our vehicles for bugs. Check the outer office and secretarial pool for bugs after hours, tonight, too. Have you contacted Anthony Zann for that money yet?"

"Yeah."

"Well, be extra careful before you meet him and your other contact. Be absolutely sure you've not been followed before you meet with either one of them."

"Same as usual, Carmichael," Larsky said.

"No, Ed. Not same as usual. Someone caught us all here together last night. We have to do things better than usual."

"Do you think they got anything on us?"

"We debugged the office and blasted that music. I don't think so."

Larsky stopped him before he could open the door. "Carmichael . . ."

"Yeah, yeah. I know. Call the Magic Genie again."

"You got to!"

"I know," he said, irritated. "I will. I'll call Cyrus Moreau again right now."

"He's our only hope," Larsky said, "and I mean you and me, Carmichael. *Our* hope."

SIXTEEN

Mary Craven watched through the living room window as her children played out front. The Cravens lived on 6th Avenue in the College Hill district of Beaver Falls. It was supper time, but Mary's husband was a banker. He often didn't get home until after 6:30, so late suppers were normal for their family. Mary had just put supper in the oven and came to settle in on the living room couch. She watched her seven year old daughter and three year old son playing with two of the neighbor girls in the late afternoon sun. The little boy was wheeling around the sidewalk on a tricycle wearing a cowboy hat. The girls were jumping rope in the yard. All four were laughing and having fun. Mary smiled. It was a happy scene.

Until Frank Kranac drove up.

Mary Craven was terrified of her next door neighbor. The old black Ford Galaxie 500 pulled up along the sidewalk and parked where Mary's son played. As Frank Kranac emerged from his car, the hair stood up on the back of Mary Craven's neck. Frank Kranac stood at six feet, three inches. The fifty-two year old man was bald, except for some black and gray hair on the sides and back of his head. He had one gray, bushy eyebrow that grew across his forehead. His eyes were dark and sullen. His chin was pointed and covered in stubble. His long crooked nose hung like the stump of an old branch. He wore a red flannel shirt, ancient khaki pants and black work boots. Frank Kranac was lean in the legs and waist, but had arms thick like tree trunks. The four children didn't even notice him as he made his way around his car and lumbered up his front walk. But Mary certainly watched him like a hawk with every step he took. He walked with his face hung low. He had his sleeves rolled up, revealing his hairy, powerful forearms as they swung low across his hips. Frank Kranac reminded Mary of what bigfoot would look like. When he walked, Frank Kranac moved at a deliberate pace. To Mary, who had fearfully spied him many times, he lurked about like someone who thought they were under suspicion. Finally Frank Kranac moved slowly out of Mary's sight behind the Craven's tall shrubs that separated their two homes. Mary forced her husband to grow the shrubs so high so she wouldn't have to look at Frank Kranac. Or his yard, which was always a disgrace compared to the Craven's well manicured property. Now that he was out of sight Mary felt a little better about her children playing in the front yard. A little better, but not much.

Mary's husband usually teased her about her repulsion toward their strange neighbor. Mitch Craven always joked that Mary didn't like Frank Kranac because he was an unattractive, eccentric loner who let his house go to pot. That irritated her almost as much as Kranac frightened her. Mitch wouldn't believe that it was her woman's discernment picking up on something, well, just plain evil about Frank Kranac. Why couldn't Mitch see Kranac like she did? It wasn't just his unpleasant demeanor (he would not even acknowledge the Craven Family). It wasn't the fact that his house was run down with paint chipping from the wood siding, or that he only mowed his yard about once every summer. Her problem with Kranac ran deeper. His house was always dark. Even when he was home at night she rarely ever saw any lights on. He came and left at strange hours of the night. She had never seen the man with another human being. Never. She knew that he worked at the Standard Steel Factory a couple of blocks away in West Mayfield. Yet he never had any coworkers over, he never entertained lady friends, and no one ever visited Kranac during the holidays. And several times, Mary was just sure of it, she caught Kranac staring out his second story window into her daughter's bedroom. His head would vanish from view when he saw Mary. She had also seen him watching the little children playing on the sidewalk from his front windows. This frightened Mary. The man could not be trusted. To Mary Craven, Frank Kranac was either hiding something or hiding from someone. That was not a safe environment for raising two young children. God only knew what that man was doing in that creepy house.

Other ladies on the block had expressed the same concerns as Mary. They referred to Kranac as "the Thing." But because Frank Kranac kept a steady mill job and wasn't openly breaking the law, none of their husbands felt any threat about the man. They simply shrugged him off as being a penny-pinching tightwad miser that didn't want to be bothered with anybody. *He's a hard working mill hunky,* they would point out. *So he leers at you women from afar once in a while. He's harmless, leave him alone!* the men would tell their wives. *Men were so thick and insensitive to the obvious!* Mary thought. Mitch had so teased Mary that she couldn't even talk to him about her deep concerns over this potentially dangerous neighbor. He would just tell her that she read too many serial killer novels and watched too many murder movies. Mary was now to the point that she was so fearful that she wanted to move. Yet she knew Mitch would berate her if she told him why. She felt like she was going to explode, with all these frightening emotions bottled up inside her.

Mary Craven got up from the couch and went to a window on the side of her house that faced Frank Kranac's house. She pulled back the drapes a bit to peek through. She wanted to make sure Kranac had actually gone inside his house and wasn't watching the children through the shrubs. A cold sweat broke out on Mary's face and neck. She trembled as she peeped through her window at Kranac's run down old house. She didn't see him anywhere. He definitely wasn't outside snooping through the shrubs. Her stomach tensed as she thought about the man. Mary let the drapes drop back in place.

"Mitch Craven, you idiot!" she whispered, "Frank Kranac *is* evil!"

Frank Kranac locked his front door behind him. His house could have been the set of any horror movie ever made. The two story home had been built right after World War II, like many of the houses in Beaver Falls. However, most of the other homes had been routinely remodeled and updated with care over the years. Frank Kranac bought the house in the early 1980s and had never done a thing to it. The walls were cracked and coated with ancient cheap aqua green paint. Carpeting had been ripped out of the first floor and was never replaced. Thus the bare wood floors were marred with strips of torn carpet tape and tacks. The house was an asthmatic's worst nightmare. The air stank of mold and mildew. Filthy drab curtains covered every window. A gray coat of dust blanketed everything. The front door opened directly into a sparsely furnished living room. There an old couch was covered in a dingy floral bed sheet. A dilapidated coffee table was the pedestal for a 1980 Magnavox TV set with rabbit ears wrapped in tin foil. A murky, cracked mirror topped a badly chipped mantle over the fireplace. Yellowed stacks of newspapers cluttered each room. Many of the papers were dated before 1985. This was an abode of cobwebs, dust bunnies, outdated furniture and appliances. "Renovation" was obviously a word not found in Frank Kranac's vocabulary. He could afford renovation, if one judged by his Standard Steel factory salary. As a machinist he made decent money. He could have budgeted plenty for home repairs. But he obviously did not. Frank Kranac did not invest money in his house, clothes, or car. The truth was that Frank Kranac did not invest his money at all.

He did something else with his money.

Frank cautiously checked around his house that afternoon. His heart beat anxiously. His mouth salivated and his palms were cold with sweat. He had to go see his heart's desire. *Had to.* He went around to all of his windows on the first floor. He peaked suspiciously through the drapes of every room to ensure no one was spying on him. Especially that lady next door. He'd often seen Mary Craven gawking at his home trying to see what he was doing. She couldn't be trusted. The mailman couldn't be, either. The meter reader couldn't be trusted. *No one* could be trusted. Kranac checked the front windows again. He was semi-sure no one was watching him. He would never be one hundred percent sure, but for now things would have to do. Even though he rarely turned one on, Frank made sure all lights were off in the house. He double checked to be sure both the front and back doors were locked and bolted. At that point he went around the corner into his kitchen. The basement door was located in a nook between the kitchen and dining area. The only new, clean, shiny thing in Frank Kranac's entire house was the golden lock on that basement door. Frank pulled out a massive key-ring. The sinews in his powerful forearms danced and shuddered as he turned the key in the two-way lock. He opened the heavy wooden door, stepped down two steps, and shut the door behind him. Though it was pitch dark, he effortlessly used the key and locked the door behind him. He had plenty of practice walking around in the dark. He descended a rickety wooden staircase into the blackened basement. The hum of a dehumidifier was all that could be heard in the darkness. Frank Kranac maneuvered like a blind man in the blackness, turning right at the bottom of the stairs, walking five or six paces ahead. He then knowingly reached out his hand, grabbed a light string hanging from a ceiling fixture and yanked. One single sixty watt bulb lit up the dingy basement. The sweaty basement walls were painted white. Old wooden tool shelves lined the walls holding rusty implements. There were more newspaper stacks on the floors. The ground level cellar windows were covered with iron bars. Frank had painted all those windows black with thick coats of tar, so no one could see into his basement from the outside window wells. The middle of the basement had six stacks of crates and boxes resting on a ten by ten blood red rug. Frank methodically began to slide the heavy stacks off of the rug. In about ninety seconds the six stacks rested on the dingy gray cement and the rug was clear. Frank Kranac bent down and rolled up the red rug, revealing two four by eight sheets of plywood lying even at ground level. He pulled one sheet of wood back and leaned it against the crates on one side and then did the same with the remaining sheet. Frank Kranac stared down into a perfectly even eight by six feet wide, four feet deep pit that he had dug himself. The walls of the pit had been neatly finished with cinder blocks and concrete; the floor with cement. He pulled off several rows of two by fours that ran across the hole to support the plywood sheets and laid them aside.

Frank looked with adoring eyes upon his heart's desire. There in that pit, stacked wall to wall in perfect rows that ran almost two and a half feet high, was exactly twelve million, seven hundred and eighty-five thousand, nine hundred and twenty-two dollars. With seventy-eight cents neatly stacked in a corner of the hole. $12,785,922.78. Exactly. Frank had counted it all himself, many, many times.

Frank Kranac came as close to smiling as he ever would staring at his treasure. This filthy, verdant stack of American bills was his love, his hope, his inspiration, his very life. Everything he was rested in that twelve million dollar stash before him. Most of the bills were hundreds. There were some rare larger bills mixed here and there in the huge stack. Frank could have pointed out where they were, if asked. He knew the stacks that intimately. He did not have the total amount of the huge money pile written anywhere. No, the amount was burned into his brain cells. Some of that money came from whatever was left over from his monthly paychecks after he paid all his bills. He did not have a bank account anywhere. He never had. Banks could not be trusted. His co-workers at Standard Steel called him "Mr. Cash." He'd never used a checkbook or credit card in his life. He paid everything with cash, including his monthly bills. He'd even paid Jimmy and Greggy Richards with cash earlier that day at Grandview Cemetery. The only time he ever went to a bank was to cash his paychecks and exchange bulks of coins for bills. Frank Kranac eschewed coins. He loved paper money. And he wouldn't dare trust any of it to anyone in some bank where it could be stolen. So it all stayed here in his pit.

Tonight he was here to celebrate an addition to his fortune. If all had truly gone as planned, he would be adding greatly to his estate. For over in the corner of the basement, under a huge refrigerator box, another large chunk of money awaited. Tonight the new money would be counted, and the sum would be added to the already bulky stash that lined the pit. Truly, this was a night to celebrate.

Frank walked over to that corner, palms sweating and heart beating like a teenager about to kiss his first girl. Mouth drooling, he daintily raised the refrigerator box and set it aside.

Beneath it, sitting in that corner just as pretty as you please, was Todd Falco's wicker trimmed suitcase, plump with one million, one hundred thousand dollars.

And it was all Frank Kranac's now.

SEVENTEEN

Tony Vero steered his pickup truck out of the Reeves Bank parking lot and back onto 8th Avenue in downtown Beaver Falls. He had just deposited his copy of Todd Falco's manila folder containing Family secrets into his safe deposit box. He had purchased the safe box for his business, Vero Securities and Investigations, several months earlier. He kept it for safe storage of important client documents. Now he was storing a document that could fatally wound his biggest client, VECO, and its sinister alter ego, the Family. He felt like a traitor, knowing that most of the information would indict his Uncle Joseph Vero long before it incriminated Carmichael and Larsky. But so be it. He would be the betrayer only if they tried to double-cross him first.

He drove past Beaver Falls Senior High. The educational complex was illuminated by the bright May sun. A rock and roll song from his senior year pounded through his speakers. Glorious memories of friends, girls, sports victories and his spectacular football career flooded his mind. At Beaver Falls Senior High he was a winner above all. He was popular. The girls drooled over him. The guys were jealous of him. He had a loving father who adored him and he came from a family with money, money, money. He had college coaches from all over America scouting him, sweet talking him. In that high school he was like a king about to inherit the world. And when he graduated, he was firmly convinced he was going to leave Beaver Falls and rise straight to the top. He'd dreamt of being an NFL quarterback who'd break records. He'd dreamt of starting businesses with his NFL money, so that when he retired from the pros he could venture out and conquer the business world as an entrepreneur. Tony dreamt big when he was in high school. His life looked sweet from within that building.

So why was it that he was driving his pickup truck down 8th Avenue today, searching for some sleaze ball drug dealer, while working for family members who were nothing more than organized criminals?

"Some dreamer you turned out to be, Tony Vero," he mumbled to himself.

A beeper went off in his truck. It was a pager given to him by the Family. They all kept one for instant, safe contact. All the Family members knew that whenever it beeped they were to get to the nearest pay phone and call whatever number it showed. Cellular phones were too easily monitored, and you never knew when home and office phones might be bugged without Larsky to de-bug them. This beeper system was fail safe. He snatched the beeper out from under the driver's side visor and read the message. He pulled into the Dairy Queen on 8th Avenue and parked in front of the pay phone. Tony inserted a couple of quarters and dialed. His Uncle Joseph Vero answered on the other end. It was obvious from the background noise that he was at a pay phone, too.

"What's up?" Tony asked.

"Where are you?" Joseph asked.

"At the Dairy Queen. Why?"

"The Sheriff's Department is looking for you. They've called VECO three times. They want you to come in for questioning and they want Todd Falco's file cabinet. Where is it?"

"I have it right here in the back of my truck."

"You find anything else in it?"

"No. Just Todd's personal stuff."

"So it's all ready for the cops?"

"Yeah. It is."

"Good. Then let me give you their number and you go ahead and call . . ."

"You're nuts! I'm not calling them. Let them find me."

"Tony! Don't play games with them! Carmichael told them you were investigating Todd's disappearance for VECO. He had a leave of absence form from Todd saying he'd be away for a while. He told them that now he wants you to find Todd so he can fire him."

"That's Carmichael's great plan?" Tony said, incredulous.

"I don't know what he and Larsky are up to. All I know is Carmichael's now given you an open door to investigate this without butting heads with the cops. Just give them the file cabinet and . . ."

"You didn't hear me, did you? No cops! I'm not going to them. They're going to have to find me. I'm not putting myself into the line of fire."

"They are looking for you, Tony! You're wanted for questioning, now. They said they've even gone to your house to see if you were there. Don't mess around and make them mad."

Tony said nothing. He thought about the police interrogating him over this case. He thought about the events in Ft. Lauderdale, too. He had too much weighing on him. Right now he didn't think he could handle a police grilling.

"Tony, we cannot afford to raise the ire of the police at this moment in time."

"You let me worry about the police. This is my investigation. Good bye."

Tony hung up the phone. Uncle Joe would just have to get over it. The cops would surely find him soon enough. He'd crash somewhere for the night and work himself up for police questioning. In the meantime, he wanted to search for Todd in peace without anyone looking over his shoulder.

He looked at Todd's blue file cabinet in the back of his truck. He had to get rid of it.

"What better place for it to be than Todd Falco's house!" he said aloud. He went back to the pay phone to call Kay Falco. If the cops weren't setting up base at the Falco residence he would take it straight out there and drop it off. She could call them and let them know she had it. They'd come get it and that would give them something to chew on for a while. And Tony would at least have time to catch his breath.

Tammi Bannerman used the pay phone idea for safety, too. She'd left VECO at 4:35 and sped down Route 51 as fast as she could. She pulled into the Riverside Saloon in the Bridgewater Borough of Beaver County and practically ran inside to use the pay phone in the far corner of the bar. Only three people there, so she was safe. She punched in Edgar Water's number, her heart pounding with excitement. Today was certainly a day of breakthroughs for her and Edgar in his longtime investigation of Carmichael Vero.

"Yeah?" Edgar answered his phone.

"It's Todd Falco! He's what's going on!" Tammi said with glee.

"Who's he? What about the Family meeting this morning? What about Tony Vero?"

"Listen! The cops came in this afternoon. This huge brother named Detective Kirkland is investigating the disappearance of Todd Falco. Todd's VECO's marketing director and answers directly to Ed Larsky. He's a real cute guy, but he's married and he flirts with all of us and has affairs. Anyhow, he's not been to work for two days now, and suddenly this cop comes in questioning Carmichael and Ed Larsky and some of us about him . . ."

"Did the cop come in for the meeting they were having when you called me?"

"No, no. He came in after lunch this afternoon. That meeting was long over."

"Well, what happened with that meeting?"

"That's what I was getting too, Eddy!" "Eddy" was Tammi's nickname for Edgar. He hated it, but he was so fond of this fireball of a private detective that he never complained. Edgar Waters was twice Tammi Bannerman's age, but he had mixed feelings toward her. Half of him doted after her like a father, rightfully watching for her safety in a dangerous position. The other half of him wanted to sweep her off her feet and marry her. She was so energetic, yet disciplined and in control. She was perfect for this undercover position in VECO. But, for business reasons, Edgar kept things platonic. For starters, he didn't know if this gorgeous African American gal would even be interested in some white man twice her age. Second, he was generally shy with women and didn't even know if she was interested in him.

"When I called you this morning Tony had gone into Carmichael's office with Mr. Larsky and Joe Vero. They were blasting those outdoor speakers again."

"How long were they in there?"

"About twenty-five minutes. But Ed Larsky came slamming out of there steaming mad. He just hung around that foyer outside Carmichael's office, behind the glass door. He was so mad we were all like, terrified he might eat us! Then Tony came out and they had some words. We couldn't hear them, of course, but Tony left then and Ed Larsky went back into Carmichael's office again. The outside music stopped soon after that."

"Well, why was Tony there?"

"I saw a requisition form later sitting on Hilda's desk. It was a check request for Tony Vero Securities and Investigations labeled, 'Services Rendered'. So I believe Carmichael called Tony in this morning to hire him to look for Todd Falco."

"This Todd Falco's disappearance must have triggered all this panic within the Family," Edgar said. "How come I've never heard of him? He's never been a player in the Family business before, as far as we've known."

"He's never been in on any of the meetings, I can attest to that."

"Me too. But Todd Falco must have some Family connection, for them to have had two meetings and hire Tony Vero to look for him, all within forty eight hours of his disappearance."

"But that's not all Eddy! Just before I left VECO the cops had been ringing our phone off the hook looking for Tony Vero! They wanted to question him. I mean they must have called at least three times from 3:30 to 4:30 asking us to find him or have him call that detective."

"Find out why tomorrow. I wish you could have stayed late today to find out what else was going on . . ."

"I would have but you know that tightwad Larsky. The minute someone's not busting their butt near closing time he has us clock out to save VECO money. And I'm always the first to go! I don't think he likes black folk."

"Maybe we could sue VECO for discrimination," Edgar joked.

"After we crack this case," she giggled.

Edgar got excited thinking about the possibilities for Family slip-ups this situation was causing. "Man, this is great! Todd Falco must have stumbled onto Carmichael and the Family, or maybe he fills some gap for the Family. That can only be the reason for all this commotion with them over the past couple of days."

"Gotta be, Eddy" Tammi said, laughing. This was the first time in months Tammi had heard her employer so excited about this case. It warmed her heart to be the bearer of good news, for once. She cared for Edgar so much.

"See if you can track down Tony's whereabouts tomorrow. I need to start following him. I bet you I can get a sound bite on some of his conversations with my equipment. He's not going to be able to be so cautious if he's out in the field tracking down this Todd Falco. He'll slip up somewhere and I'll be able to get it on tape, just like I got his father Pete on tape talking about the 'Family' that supposedly never existed."

"I'll bet you Tony can lead you to some very interesting people, too, if Todd Falco is one of the Family members."

"Tony Vero could become a fountain of information for us. This is what we've been so patient for all this time, Tammi. You know what the Captain always says to me?"

"The Captain" was the only way that Edgar refered to the client who'd hired him to investigate Carmichael Vero. The man wanted anonymity. Edgar kept it.

"No. What's the Captain always say?"

"He says, 'Only the patient farmer gets to reap a crop.' That's us, baby. We're the patient farmer."

"Well then, Eddy, hand me a sickle and let me take off Carmichael Vero's head!"

Sheriff DeBona sat at his desk reading Detective Ray Kirkland's missing person's report on Todd Falco. Ray sat watching the Sheriff's expressionless face as the man read intently. The two were alone in the Sheriff's office. Sheriff DeBona was 52. He wore glasses and had spiked salt and pepper hair and shiny red skin. He was of average height with a large belly. He looked soft and gentle, but he had a will like a crowbar. He was known for his blunt speech and lack of patience for those he didn't like. Detective Ray Kirkland knew he was on that list. The Sheriff didn't have any garbage on Ray Kirkland, for he was a man of integrity. However, because of the complaints about Ray's open Christian faith over the years, the Sheriff did question whether or not Ray was a troublemaker. So Ray had to work hard for Sheriff DeBona. Ray had the respect of his coworkers, he wasn't on the take, and he kept a great attitude in the department. All of that was a plus. However, his love for Christ tested the hearts and attitudes of the many unbelievers around him. County bureaucrats who heard of his open faith in Christ often demanded that separation of church and state be enforced with Detective Kirkland. So when Sheriff DeBona removed him from his highly successful role as a homicide detective and placed him solely in charge of the very frustrating and tedious missing person's cases, Ray knew it was a demotion meant to send a message to him for opening his mouth about Jesus Christ in an unbelieving atmosphere. But instead of standing humiliated in the background of an aggressive investigative department, Ray worked even harder. He investigated and closed some "open" cases. He did tedious background checks on many missing people. He single-handedly cleaned up the missing person's department's messy cases and brought order to their files. Everyone openly commended him for his efforts and he gained more respect than ever. What the devil had meant for evil God turned into good.

Yet the Sheriff still seemed to keep Ray down when he could. While Ray was cleaning up some of those "open" missing person's cases, he found some with similar circumstances. These people were all reputed criminals who kept very low profiles. But they all vanished without a trace. Being a detective he formed a hypothesis about them, one that definitely linked the mysterious vanishings of the people in those files. Ray did a little leg work to backup his hypothesis, put a report together and submitted it to the Sheriff in order to launch a major investigation. DeBona inexplicably balked at Ray's report. He rejected Ray's hypothesis flat out. First, he said he couldn't trust Ray's hunches. Second, he declared he was not going to spend taxpayers' money launching major investigations into the disappearance of shady people who'd been missing for years. Some of these people had relatives and acquaintances who'd never even raised an outcry for them to be found. They were probably just criminals and deadbeats, drifters who'd fled when they got the chance. Ray was dumbfounded by the Sheriff's utter rejection, especially with the excellent track record Detective Kirkland had during his career. A fellow detective first mocked Ray's report by saying it sounded more like the "X Files" than a case that needed investigating. Sheriff DeBona then said a better name for Ray's report was "File 13," because that's where the report and the twelve missing men it named belonged. Since then Ray's report was officially known as "File 13." Though hurt, Ray handled the humiliation gracefully. He never could figure out why the Sheriff would treat him so shabbily on such a matter, but he had. He kept the report in his desk and pondered it occasionally. Ray knew the whole situation was one more kick from the Sheriff to keep him down. He understood the man was a politician who probably didn't like a detective who smelled of political incorrectness. DeBona didn't need wave makers stirring up criticism against the department. So Ray was still an uncompromising witness for Christ, but he had to tow a hard line around DeBona. He put it in Christ's hands and did.

Sheriff DeBona finished reading the Todd Falco report and sighed. He handed it back to Detective Kirkland, his face emotionless.

"How deeply do you think Mr. Falco is involved in drugs, Detective Kirkland?"

"The wife is certainly convinced of his narcotics business. As I told you, the canines found traces of something in one of the closets at his house. We'll know tomorrow morning what it was they found."

"This guy has no prior arrests. He's not listed in our criminal files anywhere. How do we know the wife isn't involved in his disappearance and is making up this drug story about her husband to cover herself?"

Holy Spirit told me she wasn't? Ray dared not verbalize that thought to the Sheriff. "She could be, but we have some circumstances occurring at Todd Falco's workplace that definitely aren't kosher."

The Sheriff leaned forward and rested his face in his hand. "Tell me."

"What do you know about Carmichael Vero, Sheriff?"

"His trial happened back before I was elected sheriff. They have an unsolved murder case on that witness who was going to testify against him. Carmichael supposedly reformed when he created his business. VECO is a rousing success and put Beaver County on the national business map. Carmichael Vero is hailed as a master businessman. Anything else?"

"I just wanted your take on him."

"I've met him at some local awards ceremonies. I don't really know him or like him. I think Carmichael Vero was a Mafia scumbag who had the only witness who could testify against him killed and got off Scott free. He has cleaned up his act, though. He's been watched like a hawk in the past by the FBI and the IRS and has a squeaky clean record since his arrest. Do you think he's involved in Todd Falco's disappearance?"

"Well, get this: Todd Falco leaves his house Tuesday for some sort of meeting. VECO says that they had not sent him to any meeting. He disappears. His wife files a missing persons report on him this morning. I go to VECO today. Suddenly Carmichael and an office manager named Ed Larsky produce this leave of absence request form from Todd Falco." Detective Kirkland pulled the form out of his coat jacket pocket and handed it to Sheriff DeBona.

"This was supposedly written, signed, and turned in to them by Todd Falco on Tuesday before he left work. The thing was, when I questioned the head secretary, she claims that she'd never seen the form until today, and that no one there even knew Todd Falco was taking a leave of absence. Then, I talked to Mrs. Falco this afternoon about whether Todd had been talking to her about taking a leave of absence."

"And?"

"It was news to her."

Sheriff DeBona laid the leave form out for Ray to see. "What do you notice about this form, Detective?"

"I see that it was typed and stamped, but nowhere did Todd Falco sign it. It only has his initials."

"Very good," the Sheriff nodded.

"Plus, Kay Falco says that Mr. Larsky went out to her house this morning and threatened her not to come to the police about Todd's disappearance."

"Why isn't she doing anything about that?"

"She attacked him! Yeah! You should see this tiny woman. She's a little girl, petite. Yet Mr. Larsky said he just went out there to offer VECO's assistance and she blew up on him and threw a lamp at him, hit him in the leg. But she said he threatened her. She chased him out of her house and threw the lamp at him through her front door."

"So there's no way of verifying the threat at this point," Sheriff DeBona surmised.

"No. It's he said, she said. I kind of believe Mrs. Falco, though. She's been like a woman coming to confession. It's like there's a load of sin being removed from her each time she's honest with me. And she's not afraid to speak the truth."

"So it looks like this is all pointing back to VECO and this office manager, this . . ."

"Ed Larsky. Something's up with him. Maybe Carmichael Vero, too. Plus I've got another problem with VECO. They've hired Tony Vero . . . you remember Tony Vero? Beaver Falls' quarterback? WVU?"

"Yes."

"Well, he's Carmichael's nephew or something, and he's VECO's private detective. But they've hired Tony Vero to look for Todd Falco, and Kay Falco went and gave him Todd's file cabinet he had locked up in some room in his house. I'm hunting him now, too, trying to get that cabinet."

"VECO's a step ahead of us, it sounds like," Sheriff DeBona noted.

Detective Kirkland nodded. "Can we get a narcotics investigation going? It would sure speed up this investigation. See if he really is a drug dealer. Turn up everything we can on Todd Falco before he disappears for good."

Sheriff DeBona thought for a minute. "Let's see how that sample from Todd Falco's house turns out. If it is positively identified as narcotics, we'll go ahead and launch a narcotics investigation, too. Meanwhile, you open this case wide up. Run APBs on Todd and his car, contact the Missing Person's Bureau and get them involved, and then call the media. Let's get Todd in all the local papers and see if we can't get his puss on all four major TV newscasts in Pittsburgh by six o'clock tomorrow night. I want the whole world to know who Todd Falco is and what he looks like. If he's still alive, someone will ID him. If he's dead, we'll need to start searching for a corpse."

"I'm on it," Ray said as he stood up to leave.

"One minute, detective," Sheriff DeBona stopped him.

"Yes?"

"This business of Todd's wife accusing him of drug dealing is the only evidence so far that he may be involved in drugs. He has no record whatsoever. You're not trying to work Todd Falco's disappearance into your 'File 13' theory, are you Ray?"

Ray looked down at Sheriff DeBona in his seat.

"Sheriff, the truth is the truth. If my hypothesis is true, it will become evident, eventually. I don't need to hype it up or try and support it myself. The truth will come out. I don't doctor cases to make me look better. I give my life to God everyday. He'll perfect that which concerns me. I don't have to try to perfect things myself. That would only mess them up. I believe in 'File 13.' I honestly haven't even related Todd Falco to it in my mind, though. I don't need to. I just want to find him and solve this case that grows more complicated and mysterious at every new turn. I know you're busy enough without having to try to deal with an employee with a personal agenda. Personal agendas destroy cases. Is that good enough, Sheriff?"

Sheriff DeBona crossed his arms and leaned back behind his desk. "That's plenty."

Tony Vero saw smoke pouring into the air from behind the Falco's house as he slowly drove his pickup down the rural street to Kay's New Galilee home. Tony did not want to run into the Beaver County Sheriff's Department there. When he called from the Dairy Queen Kay said the police hadn't been back by since they'd searched her house earlier. She could have been setting him up to for a police trap; he wasn't sure. Tony could only take the unpredictable woman at her word. From down the road he could see no police cars there. He would have turned and went the other way if he had.

He parked in the driveway and walked around the back of the house to see what was burning. There was Kay Falco standing over a burn pile at the edge of their back yard near the woods. She was weeping again, trembling as she clutched a rake she was using for the fire. She didn't notice Tony. He looked hard and realized that Kay was burning all those porno magazines they'd found in Todd's secret room upstairs. In the smoldering pile he could see their glossy images turning to ash in the flames.

Tony didn't bother her. It was a private moment of a wife destroying her husband's shame. He found the back screen door unlocked. He grabbed Todd's file cabinet from the back of his truck and set it in the kitchen. Kay met him as he was coming out the door, startling him.

"I . . . didn't want to bother you back there," Tony said.

She looked drastically different from the first time he'd seen her that day. She appeared to be in a grief-stricken trance. Her expression was sullen, her face red and sweaty from the heat of the fire, her eyes irritated by tears and smoke.

"You find anything in that file cabinet for me?" she demanded.

"In my truck," Tony said. He went to the front seat of his pickup and grabbed a manila folder with a black notebook in it. He took it back over and handed it to her.

"What is this?" she asked tersely.

"It's . . . you look at it, Mrs. Falco."

Kay held the folder low and away, like it might be ridden with anthrax. As she methodically paged through the black notebook a steady stream of tears poured down her face. She slowly shook her head in disgust and bit her bottom lip. The notebook was a memoir of all Todd's extramarital affairs. In it were the names, numbers, and very personal notes about all the women Todd had been with over the years, all hand written by Todd Falco himself.

"Leave," she commanded. She disappeared back around the corner of the house.

Tony stood alone, numb. "This is definitely a low point in your investigative career, Tony," he mumbled aloud. He reached in his pocket for his keys and turned to leave. But instead he found himself walking over to the corner of the house again to see Kay Falco. He watched the elegant woman for a moment. She stood over the fire. She was slowly ripping pages out of Todd's notebook, one by one. She would let each page flit and flutter into the fire, where it was instantly incinerated.

She was no longer trembling.

EIGHTEEN

Aleister Estate was a forty acre plot of land located in Great Neck, New York. The land formed into an almost perfect rectangle, all wooded and nestled on the water. The private property was heavily patrolled by armed guards, and the only entrance to the estate was secured with a powered gate. The estate was naturally divided into three sections, all joined by one long blacktop road. The far section was waterfront property with a twenty room mansion and two guest homes. On the water's edge was a large marina that was home to a speed boat and a luxury yacht. Between the three houses was a swimming pool, gymnasium, and tennis courts. A horse stable with three sorrel colored mares rested near the second guest home. The center section of Aleister Estate was a beautifully manicured private par 3 golf course. The eighteen hole course had been personally designed by a PGA champion for the owner of Aleister Estate. The course was wonderfully shaded by many elms, oaks, and maples. The front and final section of Aleister Estate was also the smallest. The property's entrance gate, a guard booth, and a two story office building with a paved parking lot occupied that plot of land. The two story office building had only two doors, a single heavy glass door on the front, and a metal emergency exit in the back. Beside the front door was what looked a small teller machine mounted on the wall. It had a keypad with a card slot. Everyone who wanted to enter had to own a security card and know the keypad combination. Inside the door was a twenty-four hour a day security unit. Intruders were doomed. A brass placard above the entrance of the building read "Moreau Enterprises" in raised letters.

Cyrus Moreau was the sole owner of Aleister Estate. He lived in the mansion and commanded his business empire from the Moreau Enterprises office building. Everything he needed was on the estate. There were many days of Cyrus's life that he never needed to leave his forty acres.

Cyrus Moreau was a master of witchcraft, and there lay his fortune. He set his heart on sorcery and pagan idolatry in his early teen years. His goal was to become a master of the occult world and have command over spirits and sorcerers alike. He achieved his goal before the age of thirty. Cyrus operated at the pinnacle of witchcraft ever since.

The Moreau Enterprises building was home to a chain of businesses all centered around sorcery and the occult, all founded and owned by Cyrus Moreau. Inside there was The Psychic Network of Power, a psychic telephone service. Cyrus established a 1-900 number, hired forty psychic consultants, many of whom were practicing witches and warlocks, and charged people ten bucks for the first five minutes and $2.50 per minute for every minute afterward to talk to his staff. The staff, who were extremely gifted at reading callers' mail, would impress them by telling them things about their lives no stranger could possibly know. Then they would give "spiritual advice" on how to handle personal affairs. In the process the so called psychics sent out demonic forces to the callers. These demons attached themselves to the lives of the callers, thus bringing further bondage. In many cases the spirits brought addictions to The Psychic Network of Power itself. Most callers were repeaters who called again and again trying to get insight and direction for their lives, or an easy answer to their problems. Cyrus Moreau ran half-hour "infomercials" about his network during prime viewing times on cable outlets all over America. Entertainment celebrities would host the half-hour advertisements and endorse the network wherever they went. By law all television and magazine advertisements had to run the disclaimer, "For entertainment purposes only." But the demonic activity generated in the lives of the customers hardly entertained. Instead it became one more destructive force in their lives, and a financial gold mine for Cyrus Moreau. His Psychic Network of Power was the third biggest money making psychic network in the world.

Moreau Enterprises also was home to a company Cyrus founded called New World Alchemists, Incorporated. New World Alchemists, Inc. produced herb, chemicals, ouija boards and paraphernalia required for occultists and new agers in common books of sorcery, enlightenment, and witchcraft. Cyrus then created the Enchanter's Nook, a chain of new age and occult stores that ran from New York down through Louisiana, which sold all of the products produced by New World Alchemists, Inc. He also advertised the products for mail order in the back of numerous tabloids, teen mags, and new age magazines. New World Alchemists, Inc. and the Enchanter's Nook chain were generating such tremendous revenue that Cyrus and his company heads were planning a major expansion out west and abroad. Kraken Software, Inc. was Cyrus' favorite company. He and other sorcerers hired out technology freaks and created high tech computer games embedded in heavily occult themes. The games featured sorcery, violence, and sex, and were becoming some of the hottest selling computer games in the nation. Cyrus and his imps would personally lay hands on each new piece of software that was going out and cast demonic spells over them. These so called "harmless" games were designed by Cyrus to open up the players to the demonic realm. Players were becoming addicted by the thousands. Many parental concern and Christian groups were up in arms over these atrocious games. Cyrus wore their criticism like a badge of honor. Smaller Moreau Enterprises moneymakers included an astrological internet service providing daily horoscopes for internet services in New York, Pennsylvania, New Jersey and Connecticut, an internet tarot card reading service, and catalogs and newsletters published for sale about Moreau Enterprises' occult companies. Cyrus Moreau made an obscene fortune through the occult. In fact, Moreau Enterprises netted record-breaking profits the previous year, and it was obvious from the first quarter numbers that they were going to break new records by the end of the current year. Cyrus envisioned selling shares and soon going global with his empire. The world was becoming enraptured with the occult as both a form of entertainment and religion. A visionary like Cyrus certainly could cash in on the public's lust for sorcery. He had a demonic anointing to operate in that gift. He knew it, too. He communicated with enough of the spirits who empowered his businesses to know that the spirit world was elated over his empire and their prospects for controlling more human lives.

Cyrus Moreau sat in his office in the Moreau Enterprises building. The forty-one year old man was bean-pole thin, about six feet tall, with curly black hair down to his shoulders. His face was gaunt. His cheeks, forehead and neck were brutally pockmarked from a merciless form of acne that plagued him in his adolescence. Cyrus adorned his body with the images of his pagan religions. Silver rings featuring human skulls, dragons, and occult characters glimmered on all ten fingers. Gargoyles and voodoo mojos hung from the ends of several neck chains. On his right earlobe was a tiny inverted cross, on his left earlobe was a crescent moon and inverted five point star. Beneath his drab designer clothing was a mosaic of occult tattoos that covered every limb and portion of his skinny body. Cyrus definitely lived out his faith.

Aside from many occult decorations, his office looked strikingly similar to Carmichael Vero's office. In fact, the entire VECO office building was very similar in design to Cyrus's. That's because Carmichael Vero was so deeply impressed by the layout of the Moreau Enterprises building when he had visited there in the early 1980's that he took Moreau's blueprints and doctored them to his own specifications. VECO's office building was like the daughter of the Moreau Enterprises' office.

Cyrus Moreau dialed Carmichael Vero's office phone number. Carmichael had phoned Cyrus twice that day, yet he purposely waited to call Carmichael back. Cyrus wanted him to sweat a bit. He already knew why Carmichael Vero called without even talking to him. Carmichael was a client of Cyrus Moreau's, but not as an addict of the Psychic Network of Power, or a patron of the Enchanter's Nook stores. Cyrus had yet one more business, one for which he did not advertise on television or in magazines. He was a "personal advisor." In short, people paid Cyrus Moreau to use his powers of witchcraft to further their careers. This was the original business that put him over the top and enabled him to spawn Moreau Enterprises. This was a secret business not affiliated with Moreau Enterprises. When it came to Moreau Enterprises, Cyrus wanted everything shouted from the rooftops. He kept impressive financial records of Moreau Enterprises and was a meticulous taxpayer, believe it or not. When it came to his "personal advisor" business, however, everything was whispered in the inner rooms. His fees were unregistered and the IRS knew nothing of them. In fact most of the clientele who'd become Cyrus's advisees over the years didn't want the public to know that they paid Cyrus Moreau for his unique but powerful services. The office walls around him were decorated with their celebrity photos. Featured were movie stars, singers, rock and roll, rap, and country bands, film and record producers, and sports stars from around the globe. All of the photos were personally autographed with thank yous and kudos to Cyrus Moreau, crediting him with voluminous successes in their lives. Though his picture did not hang on the wall, Carmichael Vero was among their ranks.

Cyrus waited as Carmichael's line rang. He switched the phone to the speaker feature and hung up the receiver when Hilda Jessup, Carmichael's secretary, answered.

Inside Carmichael Vero's office he and Larsky sat at his desk working on the reports he was to share at the annual stockholders dinner. As they worked Hilda Jessup buzzed him. Carmichael picked up his phone.

"Yes?" he said to Hilda.

"There's a Mr. Moreau on the phone for you, Mr. Vero," she said.

"Put him through," Carmichael told Hilda. He put his hand over the receiver and got Larsky's attention. "It's Cyrus," he whispered.

Larsky lit up for the first time since the entire Todd Falco ordeal began. "The Magic Genie!"

Carmichael's blood raced. Half of him dreaded talking to Cyrus Moreau. The man was so powerful that he gave Carmichael the creeps. His other half rejoiced that Cyrus called back, for if anyone could help solve Carmichael's problems, it was Cyrus Moreau.

Ed grabbed the receiver from Carmichael's hand and switched his phone over to speaker phone.

Suddenly, a pleasant, mellow voice filled Carmichael's office:

"Hello-oooo?"

Carmichael sat up. "Hello, Cyrus."

"Hello, Carmichael. Hello, Ed Larsky!"

Larsky sat up, almost shocked that Cyrus knew he was there. "Uh, hello Cyrus."

Cyrus leaned back at his desk and laughed. "Don't be so mystified that I knew you were there, Ed. I know wherever Carmichael goes, you go too." Cyrus pulled out two small sewing needles from a rubber skull on his desk. "You are all in quite a jam down there, aren't you, Carmichael?"

"Cyrus," Carmichael hesitated, "are we safe to talk like this over the phone here in my office?"

"Carmichael, you know that I am not careless, in the least. I know when we're safe to talk! We're not being monitored. Now, are you in a jam or not?"

"Well, maybe," Carmichael said, attempting to hide his anxiety.

"Maybe?" he said. Cyrus took one of the sewing pins between his thumb and index finger and touched the point to his desk. "Carmichael, you know I already know what's going on down there."

"You do?"

Cyrus stood the sewing pin up vertically on his desk. "I do. Your mediator between the Family and your business has vanished. Poof! Along with a large sum of your money. Am I correct?"

Carmichael could not speak. He could feel his heart pounding in his throat. Cyrus was amazing. Larsky's hair stood up on his neck and arms. He was spooked by the fact that Cyrus could somehow know this information.

"You know I'm correct, Carmichael. I don't have this guy's name yet, and the exact amount of money, but if you gave me some more time I could converse with the Dark Lords and they could get all that information for me. Along with this guy's address, and age, and . . ."

"His name's Todd Falco. He's vanished with a million and one hundred thousand dollars of mine, all meant for a deal."

"Tisk, tisk," Cyrus said, shaking his head but focusing on the sewing pin between his fingers. "Carmichael, why have you been trying to shut me out for the last two years?"

"What do you mean?"

"What do I mean? I mean you've purposely cut me off for two years now."

"It's . . . it's nothing personal. I just wanted . . . well . . ." Carmichael said. He was so ashamed of his awkwardness with Cyrus that he couldn't even look at Ed Larsky beside him.

"Go on," Cyrus gently commanded him.

"I guess I wanted to be at a place where I could run my businesses without your help and input."

Both Family members could hear a long, deep sigh coming from the speaker phone.

Cyrus Moreau, still focusing on the pin on his desk, slowly opened his thumb and finger away from the pin and lifted his hand off the desk. The sewing pin stood straight up now, all by itself, clearly defying gravity.

"Carmichael," Cyrus said patiently as he grabbed the other sewing pin, "who was it that got you off the ground after your trial all those years ago?"

"You did, Cyrus."

"Uh-huh. And who was it who built such an impenetrable wall of protection around your Family, Carmichael?"

"You did."

Cyrus took the other needle and carefully set its point on the top of the first needle as it stood mysteriously suspended on his desk.

"Carmichael, do you realize that I could commune with the Dark Lords who so secretly yet flawlessly protect the Family and command them to leave you all vulnerable?"
Silence.

"Do you realize, Mr. Vero, what a fragile existence the Family now lives, now that this Falco man has vanished with all your money?"

More silence. Carmichael could barely breath, he was becoming so frightened of Cyrus.

"Pride, Carmichael. Pride. That's what's operating in you when you cut me off. That urge to run everything without acknowledging my help. You want to be the man, all by yourself." Cyrus removed his hand from the second needle. Now both needles stood upright on his desk, one on top of the other, without any support.

"I've let you go these last two years, Carmichael. I knew what you were trying to do. I wanted you to get to the point where you thought you had broken out from underneath my powers and were standing on your on two feet. Then I wanted you to fall hard, like you have now, to teach you a lesson. You've never been standing on your own two feet, Carmichael. The Dark Lords I sent as sentinels have always been protecting you and the Family. You have just been deluding yourself. You thought you were the man, Carmichael, but you weren't."

Cyrus leaned over the two standing pins and twirled his left pointer finger around them. As he did, the two pins slowly started to spin around on the axis of the bottom pin.

"Who *is* the man, Mr. Larsky?" Cyrus yelled with enthusiasm.

Ed jumped, startled by the sudden rise in Cyrus's voice. "You're the man, Cyrus! I've always known it!"

"I know you have, Ed. I know your heart. You've always understood where your protection comes from and you've always been willing to do whatever it took to keep that protection strong for the Family." Cyrus leaned back in his swivel chair and watched the end on end sewing pins spinning all by themselves. They neither slowed down or toppling over on the desk. "What is it you always call me, Ed? 'The Magic Genie?' Is that it, Ed?" he asked gleefully.

Larsky didn't know what to say. For once he tried the truth. "Uh, yes, Mr. Moreau! But it's a compliment! I mean it as a compliment!" He wished he knew how Cyrus could know all these things.

"Carmichael?" Cyrus called out.

"What, Cyrus?"

"Why did you call me, today? What do you want me to do?"

After a few seconds of silence Carmichael said, "I want you to fix our problem."

"Then, Carmichael, you need to answer some questions for me first. For instance, are you done playing this dangerous game with the fate of the Family?"

"Yes."

"Are you willing to lay down that horrible pride of yours and acknowledge that I'm the source of all your success, and that I'm the only reason your shiny white butt isn't rotting in some jail cell somewhere?"

The two pins swirled endlessly on Cyrus's desk.

"Okay. I will."

"And most importantly, will you do whatever I ask you?"

Carmichael took a deep breath. He knew Cyrus could come up with some horrible things for him to do. But finally he said, "Yes, Cyrus."

"Well, then, Carmichael, I'm ready to fix your problem!" Cyrus smiled and put his hands on top of his head while watching the pins revolve like a silver tornado on his desk. "Let me start by telling you what I do know about your situation. Your missing money is being hidden right now. I perceive that it's buried somewhere. Someone doesn't want anyone to know they have it. It's not been split up. It's not been spent. I don't yet have the identification of the person who has it. There's something weird about them, about their situation. It's like they're identity is being hidden from me. I don't know if it's Falco, if he's involved or not, if he's double-crossed you. I just know someone's hiding the money underground somewhere. I'll get more information for you. It's gonna take some work in the spirit realm. But right now, you need to find the man who's robbed you. That's what this Falco disappearance is all about. The Family was set up to get your money. Now I've got to help you find who set you up, get your cash back, and cover all your tracks."

"Good!" Carmichael said, relieved. He looked at Larsky. "What's it going to take?"

"My fees have gone up quite a bit in the last two years, Carmichael. It's going to cost you seven hundred and fifty thousand, all deposited into my Swiss savings account."

"Seven hundred fifty thousand? Cyrus, I've already lost a million and a hundred thousand. Your charging me almost . . ."

"Whoa!" Cyrus commanded as he sat up. The swirling pins slowed a bit. "You better wake up! This is not just about finding your money and taking revenge on the one who stole it. This is about hedging you Family members back up so you're protected again. You see, I've also picked up on the fact that the police have already been by to see you about your missing man. Is that true?"

"It's true."

"Well, it seems to me that they suddenly have a lot of questions about your little playhouse that you call VECO. Do you want the police overturning every stone out there?"

Carmichael sighed. "No."

"Then you better express my fee straight to my account and let me get to work on this. Time's a wasting, Carmichael, and you're the one who's wasted it!"

Larsky glared at Carmichael, pointed to the speaker phone and nodded his head frantically in agreement to Cyrus Moreau.

After a moment, Carmichael gave in. "You're right. I will. I'll get on it right away."

The needles sped up, again.

"Good!" Cyrus said. "Oh, something else, Carmichael. What's going on there with your nephew?"

"Joseph?" Carmichael asked.

"No! You know I could care less about Joseph. I mean Tony."

Larsky rolled his eyes.

"We've hired him as our investigator on this Todd Falco matter."

"I've sensed some weird things have been going on with our little Tony Vero," Cyrus said, perplexed.

"He's been acting strangely, not himself. He's been very disappointing," Carmichael agreed.

"Sometime in the future I want a full update on him. Remember, Carmichael, you have promised Tony to me. He is mine. You watch out for him."

"I will," Carmichael promised. He could never figure out why Cyrus had always been so interested in Tony. But for years the "advisor" had an obsession with the young man.

"Carmichael, one more thing."

"What, Cyrus?"

"Do remember that you will never succeed without me and my Dark Lords that I control. Can you remember that from now on? Will you please have Mr. Larsky's faith in me and my powers? In fact, Carmichael, I want you to say it out loud."

"Huh?"

"Repeat after me, Carmichael Vero. Say, 'I . . .'"

Carmichael was humiliated. But he knew better than not to repeat after Cyrus: "I . . ."

"'Will never, ever succeed without Cyrus Moreau and his Dark Lords.' Go on. Say it!"

First there was silence, then Carmichael spoke. "I won't succeed without Cyrus Moreau and his Dark Lords."

"That's not what I said!" Cyrus corrected angrily. "I said, 'will *never, ever*, succeed . . .'"

"Okay!" Carmichael yelled in humiliation. "I will never, ever succeed."

"Without . . ." Cyrus prodded.

Carmichael shook his head slowly and closed his eyes. This was childish beyond his belief. "Without Cyrus Moreau and his Dark Lords. There. Are you happy, Cyrus?"

Cyrus leaned forward and blew the spinning needles off his desk with a blast of his breath.

"Immensely!"

NINETEEN

"You burned your husband's notebook?" Detective Ray Kirkland was at his wit's end with Kay Falco. The two of them and Deputy Simmons stood over Todd Falco's damaged file cabinet in Kay's kitchen. "What were you thinking?"

"I was hurt! I was angry," Kay explained helplessly. For the second time that day she was apologetic and embarrassed for her apparent thoughtlessness.

Ray was incredulous. "But did you have to burn it? Your husband wrote in it! It was a notebook full of the names of potential suspects in your husband's disappearance. A notebook that Tony Vero gave to you from this file cabinet. Your husband's file cabinet! The one you gave to Tony Vero and told him to break into before we could ever get our hands on it. You burned it!"

"I wasn't thinking! I was hurt!" Kay defended.

The big detective thumped his hands on his chest. "I'm hurt, Mrs. Falco! OUCH!" Deputy Simmons chuckled at Ray's theatrics.

"I'm hurt because of the way you keep sabotaging our investigation!" Ray said.

"I'm not sabotaging anything!"

"You let this Tony Vero steal prime evidence twice today. And then when he does return one important document that would be valuable to us, you destroy it! I've been trying to trust you all day, but you keep giving me reasons not to!"

"You look here, detective," Kay explained. "I told Tony Vero to give me anything he found in that file cabinet that might have anything to do with Todd's philandering. Tony gave me a black notebook full of Todd's personal memoirs about each and every bimbo he's been with over the last few years. I was so furious that do you know what the only thing was that went through my mind?"

Ray looked down at the petite woman. "Torture Detective Kirkland?"

"No! My only thought was," tears rolled down her cheeks, "I hope Todd is still alive so I can tell him that I'm the one who burned his little trophy book of conquests he was hiding from me."

Ray looked down at the floor and shook his head. He wanted to be understanding of the woman's raw emotions in the midst of this crisis, but she had destroyed major evidence.

"I wanted him to know that I knew all his little secrets, and that he was finished. So I burned it. It was stupid of me, it may have blown your case, but too bad. It's done and I'm not sorry!" She folded her arms, sniffled, and turned her head to cry silently. Ray walked over and gently put his hand on her back.

"I'm just very frustrated that on the first day of this case I've had several crucial pieces of evidence snatched from under me. Key evidence that I may never see now. Evidence that may have helped us find your husband. You have to admit that you've not helped the case one bit by your actions today. You've got to promise me that from now on you won't make even the slightest move concerning your husband without consulting me first."

Kay stood sobbing, unable to answer the detective. She was exhausted. She was embarrassed for her foolishness, humiliated by her husband. She almost wished that she'd never even gone to the police.

"Deputy Simmons," Ray commanded, "please take this file cabinet back to the lab and have it and everything in it dusted for fingerprints."

"Yes, sir," the deputy obeyed as he reached over to pick up the metal cabinet.

"And deputy," Ray pointed at the file cabinet Tony had broken into, "put out an all points bulletin for Tony Vero. He's now wanted for questioning for tampering with evidence and obstruction of justice!

Ed Larsky sat high up on a hillside bike trail overlooking Brady's Run Park. He was sitting on his Harley Davidson, puffing a cigarette. The sun had disappeared from the dusk sky. A cool early May breeze swept across the hillside and Larsky was feeling pretty good at the moment. Cyrus Moreau's phone call to Carmichael perked up his lagging spirits. The Magic Genie had straightened out Carmichael's bad attitude and promised to help them get out of this Todd Falco mess. Carmichael and Larsky were the only Family members that even knew the man existed. They purposefully kept Cyrus their secret. The day might come when the two of them may want to downsize the Family. One never knew the lengths one might need to take to stay at the very top. Cyrus's unearthly powers made things chillingly clear for Ed Larsky: with Cyrus they'd prospered secretly for seventeen years. This one time period Carmichael tried to operate without him caused them this Todd Falco crisis. The Family had to have the specter of Cyrus Moreau over it in order to survive.

Larsky stared up at the stars while he smoked. He heard the sound of a sister Harley cruising down the park road below. He instantly recognized the whine of the '68 classic. It was Tommy Wheeler.

Tommy Wheeler was the physical antithesis of Ed Larsky. He was a wiry man, only five foot, three, with straight brown hair in a pony tail and a baby smooth face. He was thirty-nine, like Larsky. They had been pack brothers together in the Plague biker gang. The Plague was nothing more than the strong arm for Mafia goons. But their reputation was insidious. They were greedy, bloodthirsty, modern day pirates on motorcycles. Larsky and Tommy joined when they were just out of high school. Their initiation into the Plague was a hit job in Ohio. They gleefully shot to death a man who had testified in court against a local mobster. Their murderous alliance had only grown since then. Tommy Wheeler was a master hitman. Larsky could get them both lots of work, thanks to the Family. The two were both firearms experts and keen marksmen. Together they were keen tacticians. They excelled at the logistics of a murder, confusing potential witnesses, and smoke screening police investigators off their trail. It was a match made in hell.

Larsky heard the bike slow to a low buzz right down the hill from him, then accelerate again as Tommy gunned it up the sometimes steep bike trail. Larsky looked at his watch. It was 9:05. The police who patrolled Brady's Run were surely sitting at the ice skating rink near the park entrance. They'd make their rounds in about fifteen minutes. He and Tommy could meet safely above. Larsky watched Tommy's headlight beam bounce violently up and down the treetops as he rode closer to the top of the trail. Larsky dismounted. He stretched his body hard. Tommy Wheeler finally appeared over the crest of the hill. He pulled along side Larsky, cut his engine and dismounted. The short Tommy Wheeler doffed his black helmet and unzipped his green army jacket as he stepped toward Larsky.

"Tommy Wheeler," Larsky acknowledged, his long blond hair blowing in the breeze.

"My brother," Tommy Wheeler greeted him.

The two struck hands and went through a lightning quick handshake routine that ended with one strike of a fist over their hearts. It was the Plague's secret handshake. Only blood members knew it or dared offer it.

"Bum a smoke?" Tommy asked.

"Always." Larsky produced another cigarette, lit it off his own, and passed it to the gang member.

"Let's see the jack" Tommy demanded.

Larsky went over to his Harley. Using a small key he unlocked the right leather side pouch over the back tire. He pulled out a canvas bag and tossed it to Tommy.

"Sixty grand," Larsky said.

Wheeler carefully inspected the contents of the bag. When he was satisfied he asked, "Who we doin' this time?"

Larsky finished a long, hard drag on his cigarette, then in one breath said: "Benny Miller, Stephen McClintlock, and Jermichael DeVries."

Tommy Wheeler choked and coughed on his smoke. "Why don't we do the President while we're at it?" he gasped as he caught his breath. "Those are three of the top players from here to Pittsburgh. Are you nuts?"

"They won't be after this weekend. We're takin' 'em all out. Gonna make it look like a gang war, too. Like they were all hittin' each other."

"If I had known who it was I wouldn't have agreed to twenty a piece, you Russian maniac. I would'a said more."

"Well, there's no bounty on their heads so you're gonna do it for twenty a piece. You've done worse for less."

"They're protected. No one knows who protects them, but it's like they're untouchable."

"I'll take care of their protection. But those three are goin' down."

"Okay, my brother. You got the jack, we'll do it." Tommy took a hard drag on his cigarette and let out a demonic snicker. "You're gonna rearrange the entire infrastructure of the drug world around here, aren't you, now?"

"Something like that," Larsky nodded. "Don't ask me no questions."

"You must work for some powerful mothers, Ed. No wonder you won't hang around us pikers in the Plague, anymore."

"I'm still a Plague at heart, Tommy. Always will be." He paused for a moment, then said, "Let me throw something else at you, unrelated."

"I'm all ears."

"How'd you like to score another big one, all by yourself? After we take out these three and finish this job?"

"Talk to me, brother!"

"This one would have to be our little secret. You couldn't go bragging about it. I don't even want any of our Plague brothers to know about it."

"I'm interested. But it's gonna cost you some hush-hush money. How much and who?"

"Fifty grand. Out of my own pocket."

Tommy's cigarette fell out of his mouth to the dirt path below. "Fifty grand? Who? Why?"

"This is going to be my pet project. My little baby. And I have to look squeaky clean when it's all said and done. Therefore I'm willing to pay you five times your price to do it secretly, without implicating me one bit."

"Okay! Who?"

Ed Larsky smiled like a shark: "Tony Vero."

Tommy Wheeler's eyes lit up. He burst forth in an uncontrollable hackle. He bent over holding his stomach for a moment, caught his breath, then straightened up again. "You want me to off Glory Boy? I might just do that one for free! Can I make it hurt?"

"I want you to make it done in absolute secret!"

"Count me in! When we gonna plan the job?"

"Soon. He's got to finish something he's working on for us at VECO, first. After that there'll probably be only a small window of opportunity for you to pull it off. I'll have to be highly visible with my folks at VECO during the job so I'll be pure as snow in their eyes. So you'll have to be on notice for me. I'll pay your contract in advance so you'll be all mine." Tommy shook his head smiling, almost not believing it. "Hoo! You are something else, Ed Larsky. I mean, you've always talked about how much you hated him and all, but I never thought you'd go this far. Kill Tony Vero. Count me in! You really are still one of us old Plaguesters at heart, aren't you!"

"Tommy Wheeler, I'm the worst!"

Tony Vero checked into the Holiday Inn near the Beaver Falls exit of the Pennsylvania Turnpike. He knew the Sheriff's Department would be in an uproar over Todd Falco's file cabinet. He didn't feel like he could handle dealing with them after this stress-filled day. So he had to hide out for the night. He took a shower and ordered a late night sub sandwich from the room service menu. He sat on the bed in a white tank top and boxer shorts, his black hair slick from the shower and green eyes red with fatigue. The jitters about being out of his house were coming back. He wished he could get drunk. But he vowed to stay sober so he could nail shut this Todd Falco case as fast he could.

He pulled out a small notebook from a heavy bookbag. From the notebook he produced the paper with the phone number he found in Falco's files: "Bernie Lokawski-555-0896." Beaver Falls phone number. There was no other record of Bernie Lokawski anywhere else in Todd's file cabinet. This was the only mention of him. Neither was the name listed anywhere. Either this number would produce for Tony or he'd have to start his investigation over again.

He picked up the telephone from the bedside table and dialed the number. It rang. Tony knew he had to be on his toes when whoever it was answered, be it Bernie Lokawski or someone else. He had to get as much information as he could before they got suspicious and hung up on him.

They answered:

"'Cherries'," a raspy voice said.

Tony recognized that name from something he had read earlier that day. In the background he could hear loud music, glasses tinkling, and loud conversation. Had to be a bar. Tony jotted down the name.

"Yeah, could you get Bernie for me?"

"Bernie who?"

"Bernie Lokawski. You know."

There was a pause.

"YO!" Tony heard the man on the phone scream to the patrons. "Is there a Bernie Lokawski here?"

None of the patrons acknowledged the man.

"There's no Bernie here." CLICK. Hung up.

"Don't hang up on me, punk!" Tony yelled. He pressed the button and punched in the numbers again. Busy signal. He slammed down the phone. He jumped off the bed wanting to kick something. Frustration clouded his mind. He knew it wouldn't help. He had to calm down.

He thought about that club's name: Cherries.

"I know I've seen that name somewhere else in Todd's junk, today." He thought out loud. He opened his bookbag on his bed again. This time he pulled out another manila folder. It was labeled "Todd's Journal" in Tony's handwriting. In the folder was an entire photocopied duplicate of Todd's black notebook that Tony had given over to Kay and watched her burn. She didn't realize the investigative use for it, but Tony clearly had. He was now the only person who had a copy of all of Todd Falco's personal documents from his file cabinet. Tony leafed through the white photocopied pages until he scanned what he was looking for. Bingo! There was "Cherries" mentioned in Todd's journal. He knew he'd seen that name. He pulled out several pages and read them carefully. Todd told quite a story about Cherries. Tony laid them on the bed when he finished and put the rest of the file back into the bookbag.

If he could find out where Cherries was he'd grab his pants and head straight there. He grabbed the phone book off the bedside table. He went all through the white and yellow pages. There was no Cherries listed anywhere in Beaver County. He picked up the phone and dialed Cherries' number again. Still busy. Nimrod must have taken the phone off the hook. Why? He dialed information and asked the operator if she had a listing for Cherries. Unlisted number. Using the phone book he began calling popular bars in Beaver Falls and asking the managers if they knew of a club named Cherries. The forth bar manager he phoned did. He believed it was a private club. He said it used to be the Elk's Club long ago when such things were fashionable. Tony knew the Elk's club. It was between 5th and 6th avenues near St. Mary's. Tony thanked him.

He got dressed.

Ray Kirkland and his wife Shelly embraced in bed. He came home mentally worn out after such a frustrating first day on the Todd Falco case. Latonya and Shaniqua were both in bed asleep when he came home. Shelly saw the look in Ray's eyes when he got out of the shower. It was an almost desperate stare, beckoning for intimacy. She obliged. Now as he tenderly held her strong, plump body under the sheets, Ray Kirkland began to open up to his wife about the Todd Falco case. Shelly never pressed her husband about his work. She prayerfully and patiently supported him all she could otherwise. The divorce rate for cops was out of this world. Shelly covenanted in her heart to be a submissive support to her man, never to nag him about what happened on the job. So when he did open up to her, it was often during a time of deep intimacy. Like now.

Ray revealed his vision earlier that week and how Holy Spirit had brought Kay Falco to him at work that morning. He methodically recounted every event of the day with Shelly. Her discernment exceeded his and he respected her opinion on his investigations.

"Something's up with that VECO place, baby," she said after hearing the day's events. "You be careful with those people who work there."

"I don't trust them. Not that Todd and Kay Falco are to be trusted, either. But like I said about Kay, she's one confessing woman! Honey, I could almost see the ton of weight being lifted off her as she kept opening up about her husband's life. They have a beautiful son. That man is a fool, doing them like he does."

"So Holy Spirit revealed her to you in a vision?"

"He sure did."

"And you believe she's trying to come clean?"

"Yup. No doubt whatsoever."

Shelly Kirkland sat up in the bed. "Then we need to pray for her."

Ray joined her upright. "I'm right with you!"

The two began to enter into fellowship with their Father, through Holy Spirit. They openly prayed in their prayer languages. They praised and worshipped their Savior. Between their passionate intercourse and lifelong dedication to the Lord, the Kirklands were quickly pressing into His presence in perfect heart unity. After timeless moments silent in His presence, Shelly began to pray:

"Lord Jesus, Precious Savior! We just stand as intercessors for this woman, this Kay Falco lady and her husband and baby. We thank you that her introduction to Raymond today was not a surprise, but You know all things, and showed her to Raymond in the vision beforehand. You wanted Ray ready for her, Father. So now we watch over her as watchmen on the tower and ask for Your love, favor, and mercy upon this woman! We ask that you put Your hand on her life and hedge her about. We plead the precious, righteous blood of Jesus over her life now, Father! Over her baby, Lord! Over her husband, God, in Jesus's precious name!"

"Father," Ray prayed, "Right now I want to lift up Todd Falco to You, in Christ's name. Father, You know all! You know where Todd Falco is. You know if he's alive or not. We petition You now, Abba, bring Todd Falco out into the open! If he's alive, flush him out and end this now, Father! If he's dead, expose his body so we'll find it and his wife and baby will be able to go on with their lives! Loose angels, Lord, to bring this man out into the light speedily. Do have mercy on his heartbroken wife, Father. Introduce her to Jesus and bless her with His righteousness. Redeem her, and adopt her into Your wonderful kingdom! Have mercy on that little woman, Lord, and save her soul!"

The intercessory prayers went on for a time. The two had so honored their heavenly Father that He was moving to answer their prayers as soon as the words, His words, His will, were leaving their mouths. The heavens were being shaken, and the power of Jesus Christ was being loosed to everyone involved in the Todd Falco case.

Tony drove his pickup down 7th Avenue. Beaver Falls had changed so much since when Tony and his family first moved there when he was a boy. Pete Vero moved them there in 1979. It was an urgent move for safety's sake. He wanted them out of Pittsburgh. Dangerous things were happening in the Pittsburgh Mafia family he and Joseph worked for under Carmichael. Pete did genuinely care about his family. He did worry for his wife and children's safety. Beaver Falls was a good choice in the late seventies. It was clean, the mills were still going strong, and the economy was good. Above all, it was a safe town.

"How things change!" Tony marveled. Since the mills shut down and the economy went bust the town had changed drastically. Gangs and violence now ruled the high school and downtown areas. Once a safe place to travel, from 7th Avenue down to the Beaver River was deteriorating into a danger zone. Drugs, especially the drugs the Family had been pushing in the region, were killing this city. Tony knew it.

The section of the downtown where Cherries was located was a prime example of degeneration. Tony had gone to St. Mary's school when he was in the elementary grades. St. Mary's was located across from what was then the Elk's Club. He remembered that area as a clean, friendly atmosphere. Now as he drove through he saw litter, loiterers, and trouble in the making along the way. Some people openly drank alcohol on the sidewalks and streets. The houses and buildings nearby were dilapidated.

As he turned off of 9th Street onto 6th Avenue he saw Cherries. The old Elk's Club sign that once hung out front was gone. There was no sign or billboard for the club anywhere. It was indeed a private club now. The old building rested over a steep, secluded alley between 6th and 5th Avenue. He and other boys from St. Mary's used to hang out back there when they were little.

Cherries' business must have been slowing for the evening. It was 11:00 o'clock on a Thursday night. Few cars were parked near the club.

Tony parked halfway up the block. The entrance to Cherries was on 6th Avenue. There was a concrete stairwell that ran from the street down to what looked like a basement door. Several men stood talking and smoking near the entrance to the stairwell. Tony squeezed by them and went down the steps. There was an old door at the bottom with a marred and grainy window. One could only see light and shadows through the thick glass. He went to open the door. It was locked. He pushed a lighted doorbell beside it and heard an ancient buzzer sound inside. The door opened quickly. A young bouncer with moussed hair stuck his head out. His arm muscles and belly bulged hard from beneath his white t-shirt. Tony could see a small foyer behind him with a similar door on the other side. He couldn't see inside the club.

"What?" the bouncer asked impatiently when he didn't recognize Tony.

"I want to get in," Tony declared.

"Get lost. This is a private establishment." He went to close the door.

Tony reached in his pocket and pulled out a hundred dollar bill.

"I want a membership."

The bouncer pondered the bait, staring at the bill. Yet after some hesitation he shook his head no. "You just can't go in here. Everyone knows each other. No one'll know you. They don't want no strangers in here."

Tony could have cared less about money at that point. He had to find Bernie Lokawski and Todd Falco. He pulled out another hundred.

"I want to get in this club *real bad*," he growled angrily. "You take these Bennies and I have more to give the manager inside."

The bouncer looked astonished. He couldn't resist this temptation any longer. He snatched the bills and said, "You follow me."

He lead Tony in through the foyer and opened the inner door. The club was nothing more than an old barroom. Steelers, Pirates, and Penguins paraphernalia hung everywhere. There was a long formica bar lined with metal stools. There were eight booths lining the walls, five tables, and a small runway and stage with a lighting system. Beside the stage was a large screen TV. A stack of pornographic videos was piled high on top of it. The ancient dark wood paneled walls were lined with autographed photos of strippers.

Oh great, Tony thought, *this is nothing more than a second rate strip bar for losers.*

There apparently was no show that night. There were only three men sitting at the bar and two more at a nearby table. They were all facing each other, laughing and drinking. Tony recognized none of them. They were all in their mid twenties to mid thirties. Some looked gruff, some looked geeky. No one looked impressive. They obviously had too much money to spend and no real woman to spend it on. Tony wondered if one of them was Bernie. One young, scruffy looking man tended bar.

They ignored Tony and the bouncer as they strolled by. The bouncer led Tony around the back of the bar to a closed door.

"Stay here," the burly man said to Tony, holding out his hand. He disappeared behind the black wooden door for a moment. Tony heard an angry voice. Then the bouncer reappeared.

"Danny'll see you now," he grunted at Tony and went toward the bar.

Tony walked into the office. On his way in he heard the bouncer tell the guys at the bar, "Look what that idiot paid me to get in here!" Tony heard a loud roar as the patrons all laughed about the money Tony'd spent. He ate his humiliation, gritted his teeth and pushed the door closed behind him.

The room was nothing but a tiny office space. A curly red-haired man sat at an old desk, crunching away on an old adding machine. He stopped, looked up, and pulled his glasses down his nose to check Tony out. He was lean, ruddy, in his early fifties. He didn't look happy with Tony.

"What's your story?" he said. "You that hard up to see naked women?"

"Not at all," Tony said. He pulled out his private investigator's license, the one that identified him as a VECO investigator.

Danny looked angrier now. "What do you want?"

"You know Todd Falco?"

"Yeah."

"How?"

"He's a member here."

"He been in this week?"

"He's not been in since last week. Why?"

"You know a Bernie Lokawski?"

"No."

"Bernie's not a member here?"

"No! I don't know any Bernies. What is your problem?"

"Todd Falco's missing."

"Missing?" Danny looked genuinely shocked. "Since when?"

"Since Tuesday. I think this Bernie Lokawski may know where Todd is. I believe Bernie Lokawski's been a patron here before."

"Well, you believe wrong. I told you I don't know a Bernie whatever his name is. And I don't let anybody in off the streets. You're lucky to be standing here. If you hadn't have paid off Fathead at the door you'd be outside, too."

"Oh yeah? That brings up a good question: why do you need such iron tight security for this place?"

"It's a rough neighborhood."

"Todd Falco come here often?"

"Once or twice a week, depending on if we have live entertainment. Now get out!"

"Not yet! Todd Falco's a highly successful businessman for an ultra successful company. He makes big contacts with big executives all over the region. Tell me, why's he hanging out at some hole like this watching cheap girlie shows and dirty movies? There's all kinds of high class expensive strip joints and sports bars out near the Pittsburgh airport where people like Todd usually hang out. What's the attraction here?"

"I don't know and I don't care. Get out!"

Tony pointed out toward the bar area. "Why would he be hanging out with that bunch of losers out there? Why's Todd patronize this place so faithfully?"

"Who do you think you are?"

"Answer my question!"

"We're the only strip club in downtown Beaver Falls! We are a licensed after hours club. Our members are mostly middle to upper-class whites who aren't here for the atmosphere. They want to see babes. I provide babes. They want to remain anonymous and they are all guaranteed privacy. Privacy that I have to protect! To top it all off we have the best strippers on the circuit performing here. He's just like them out there, looking for a good time . . ."

"Todd Falco's getting more than just a good time here!"

"That's it! I've had it with you." Danny went to open the door to call the bouncer. Tony pushed it shut with his foot and shoved him back toward his desk. Danny's eyes widened. Tony squared off with him. He pulled out several photocopied sheets of paper from his pocket and threw them at Danny. They floated and landed on top of the owner's feet.

"So what are those?" Danny pointed down.

"Something I copied from Todd Falco's journal. Several long, detailed accounts of some interesting on-stage activities he and several other members here performed with your so-called 'strippers.' He wrote that this type of activity occurs at 'private shows' for 'premium members' who pay ridiculously high 'bonus fees' to you. Todd was a very thorough journalist, I've found. Full names, dates, details . . ."

Danny was dumbfounded, his face bright red. He did not reach over to pick up the papers.

"Does the police know what goes on here, Danny? Huh?"

Danny said nothing.

"How about the health department, Danny Boy? I bet they'd revoke your license real fast if they knew what went on with these girls you hire in here. They'd shut you down instantly, wouldn't they?"

"You're messing with the wrong man!"

"What would the police do if they knew you're a pimp, your strippers are prostitutes, and this bar is a brothel?"

"Get out and never show your face in here again!"

"Let's find out!" Tony picked up the phone on Danny's desk and punched in 911. The line rang. Danny watched with terror in his eyes for several seconds. He then reached over pushed the receiver down on the phone. Tony hung up. They locked eyes, both their chests heaving.

"I could go to the police with this and shut you down," Tony said.

Danny said nothing. His glaring eyes and face matched his crimson hair.

The phone rang. Tony picked it up. Danny went for the door again, but Tony put his hand on his chest and stopped him a second time.

"Hello! Cherries!" Tony answered with mock friendliness. "No one dialed you here . . . This is Cherries, m'am. We're a bar down near St. Mary's . . . Maybe one of the patrons came in here goofing off. You know how drunks are . . . We'll, yes you can send a car if you want to but we're all fine here . . . Look, I'm just a patron. Why don't you talk to the owner? He's standing right here!"

Tony pushed the phone into Danny's chest. Danny took hold of it and slowly put it up to his face. He spoke calmly to the police dispatcher. He confirmed everything Tony said. Finally, the dispatcher was convinced nothing was wrong and told Danny no police car would be dispatched. He hung up, trembling.

Tony stared him down in disgust. "Todd's here for the prostitutes. You know it. I know it. I'm a respected member of this community. I could let this secret be known real quick and you'd be out of business and in jail. You have a bunch of low-lifes patronizing this rat hole for the same reasons Todd did. One of them came in here and made a business contact with Todd. Bernie Lokawski. Todd had his name with your phone number here written down."

"I told you I don't know a Bernie Lokawski!" Danny repeated. "I've never heard that name until you came in here tonight. I'm not lying to you!"

"That may be true, but Todd's missing because of him, and his files link him to this place. I need to find him to find Todd. You had better cooperate with me or I'll be the biggest trouble you ever saw! I want your list of all your members here."

Danny slowly walked around behind his desk. He went to open the top drawer. Tony quickly leaned over his desk and snatched him by the arm. He yanked him around the other side and went back around the desk himself.

"I trust you as far as I could throw you. Which drawer is it in?" Tony demanded.

"Bottom," Danny growled.

Tony reached first into the top drawer. He pulled out a black .45 caliber pistol.

"Figured you had something for me in that top drawer!" He ejected the bullet cartridge and pocketed it. He tossed the gun back in the drawer. He then pulled a leather record book from the bottom drawer. In it was a listing of all Cherries' members. There were about two hundred or so names. About twenty of the names had stars beside them, Including Todd's. Tony deduced they were the "premium members" Todd had written about. He looked for Bernie Lokawski's name. It was nowhere on the list.

Tony held up the book. "I'm taking this. I'll bring it back tomorrow." He pointed at the office door toward the bar. "I'm going to question those members out there. I'm gonna come back and question more tomorrow night. You're gonna let me, Danny Boy. You're also going to let me come back in here any time I want. I'm a lifetime member now! If you ever hinder me or mess with me I'll immediately go to the police. I just want Bernie Lokawski and Todd Falco. I'm not here to get you. You let me do what I need to do and you'll be fine. I'll be a lot nicer to your patrons than I was with you. By the way, I want my two hundred bucks back from your pit bull out there."

"What?"

"My two hundred bucks I had to pay so I could get in here tonight. Get it back for me right now."

"This is blackmail!" Danny gasped.

"No, it's extortion. Do it now!"

Danny angrily yanked open his office door. "Randy!" He hollered. "In here, now!"

Randy the beer-bellied, mousse-haired bouncer strolled in with a smile and a beer.

"Yeah, boss?" he said innocently.

Danny pointed his thumb at Tony. "His two hundred bucks. Give it back to him now!"

Randy looked angry. "No way!"

Tony crossed his arms. "Danny, if he doesn't give it to me, fire him."

"Shut up!" Danny told Tony. "Randy, give him the money now or leave here for good! This is your fault anyway! What kind of bouncer do I want who's gonna take payoffs from bums off the street?"

Randy stood speechless for a moment, mouth gaping in silent protest.

Danny glared at him and grumbled, "Now!"

Finally, the bouncer slammed down his beer and pulled out Tony's two hundred dollars. "I'll get you for this!" he mumbled to Tony as he handed him the money.

Tony laughed. "You'll have to get in line, fatso. By the way, Congratulate me! I'm a lifetime member now! Explain it to him, Danny." He left the office with the leather record book under his arm, replacing the two hundred dollars in his wallet. Danny berated his careless bouncer, his voice echoing through the bar.

Tony looked over the five patrons laughing around the bar. They were all white. Two at the bar looked like young businessmen, in nice slacks and ties. The other three looked like working class types. One was tall and husky, like an old ball player who'd gotten fat. Two of them looked like brothers. They both had crewcuts, wore identical blue t-shirts, khaki shorts and muddied boots. They were Jimmy and Greggy Richards, and they were buying all the drinks that night. Tony went and stood in the midst of them to catch their attention. They completely ignored him. Finally he interrupted their banter.

"Yo!" he said. They all looked at him like he was some weirdo. He hoped someone would recognize him now that they could see his face.

"Hey," the oldest looking one at the bar said. "You're Tony Vero!"

They all reacted favorably to him at that point, save Jimmy Richards. He suddenly straightened up on his barstool and looked highly offended at Tony's presence. Tony saw the angry reaction in his eyes, yet he did not recognize him. The others began to smile and wanted to know what ever happened to Tony at West Virginia University. Some offered to buy him a beer. They even started talking about his high school career. Even though all of them looked older than Tony and some out-weighed him, he was by no means intimidated by this crowd. They were almost like a bunch of kids. Almost pitiable. Tony wanted to ask them if their mommies knew they were hanging out at a place like this.

Tony smiled at the one who made him. "How'd you recognize me?"

"I work for Brighton Analytical. I helped sign all the paperwork with Carmichael Vero so he could get us off the ground three years ago."

A bull's eye already! "Well then," Tony went on smiling big, "You know Todd Falco!"

The quintet erupted. They began chanting Todd's name and high fiving each other, all talking about Todd's way with women. The adulterous Todd Falco was a god to this sex starved group. Tony waited for the Todd Falco-inspired revelry to die down. He noticed that Jimmy Richards was still giving him the evil eye. He obviously had a big beef with Tony about something. Tony looked over at the other guy who looked like him. He was not upset with Tony, for whatever that was worth. Their blue t-shirts read "Grandview Cemetery Groundsman." They had to be brothers, they favored one another so much. He ignored the surly one and continued working the crowd.

"I know Todd really was key to getting that deal with VECO off the ground. You know a Sharon Lacello at Brighton Analytical?"

"Yeah! And so does Todd. Real well!" They all began to hoot and holler. Tony suddenly pictured poor Kay Falco, trembling, crying, in deep agony because of Todd's philandering. He felt shameful for letting this bunch dishonor her with their disgusting display. He needed them, though, and tried to bite his tongue.

The older patron extended his hand to shake with Tony. Tony obliged. "My name's Phil Carboni. I know Todd real well. In fact I'm the one who turned Todd onto this place about a year ago. He loves the girls here."

Snickers broke out among the men.

"Boy does he ever!" the largest of the crowd blurted out. They all burst out in laughter. Kay Falco haunted Tony's mind, her beautiful face humiliated and broken. He felt offended that they were honoring such a jerk as Todd Falco when he mistreated his wife like he did. Why did he even feel that way? He didn't know where those feelings were coming from. He wanted to shut these louts up on behalf of Kay.

"Do any of you know Todd Falco's wife, Kay? The woman he cheats on all the time? Anyone here ever met her?"

The smiles quickly waned, the cheeriness died down. Tony noticed several wedding rings around that circle of men. There may have even been a moment of shame for one or two of them.

"I've met her," Phil Carboni said, staring at Tony with a leery expression. "What's up with her? And what's up with *you* now? I though you were cool?"

"What about her?" one of them asked angrily.

You're losing them, Tony! He thought. *Real 'em back in!*

"Kay Falco filed a missing person's report with the police today. Todd's missing."

Their jaws all dropped; all but the one who had looked upset to see him. Jimmy Richards was too busy shooting laser eyes at Tony to care.

"What do you mean?" someone asked.

"Todd's disappeared. Gone. Any of you seen or heard from him?"

"Doesn't anyone know where he is?" Phil Carboni asked.

"No. That's why I'm here. That's why I'm asking some respect for his wife."

Their faces softened, but just a little.

Tony continued. "I think that there's another man involved with Todd's disappearance. A man by the name of Bernie Lokawski. Anyone here know a Bernie Lokawski?"

They all shook their heads and grunted.

"That's strange," Tony said. "'cause I have some information that links Bernie to this place. No one recognizes that name?"

"I do," the bartender said. Tony recognized his raspy voice. He was the one who'd answered and hung up on Tony earlier. "Someone called here tonight looking for him. But he wasn't here."

"That was me," Tony confessed. "That's why I'm here now."

The one who had been eyeing him angrily finally spoke up: "We don't know no Bernie! Why you so nosy?"

Tony looked him over. Jimmy Richards was a homely, stocky guy. He was obviously a weightlifter and he obviously had a big gripe with Tony.

"I'm trying to find . . ." Tony started.

"Who are you to stand their and try to make us feel bad about Todd Falco's sex life? You a preacher?"

"No," Tony defended. "But I do know Todd and I know his wife and his baby. And I just can't stand here and laugh and disrespect the woman under her current circumstances."

"We're not disrespecting anyone! Todd's just the man when it comes to the ladies, and that's too bad for his wife." The stocky aggressor hopped down off his barstool and squared off with Tony. Jimmy Richards was easily a half foot shorter than Tony. "Do you even know who I am?"

Tony looked down in his face. He was close to Tony's age. "Should I?"

Jimmy pushed his chest up into Tony's. "What business is it of yours to be comin' in here asking about Todd or that other guy or anyone?"

"Knock it off, Jimmy," Greggy Richards said. He too was stocky, homely and had a crew cut. With a slight smile he casually limped over to Jimmy, put his hand on his chest and pushed him back toward his barstool.

"You'll have to excuse my brother, Your Holiness," he said to Tony. "Jimmy's pretty tough when he's been drinking." He whispered something in Jimmy's ear. Jimmy's countenance fell a little.

"All right, Greggy," Jimmy said, wincing. He took his place back on the barstool, but continued his angry gaze at Tony. Greggy returned to his seat, still smiling but shaking his head.

Phil Carboni spoke up again. "Why are you looking for Todd?"

"I've been hired to find him, that's all. Look, I'm not here to bust anyone's chops. I just figured you'd all want to help find Todd, being that you're his friends and all." Tony was really pouring it on. He wished he could grab a drink at the bar to help calm his nerves. "The person I really need is Bernie Lokawski."

Jimmy lit into Tony from his barstool: "Well, there ain't no Bernie here, none of us knows the guy, and you've wasted a bunch of money. So why don't you take your nosy self and get out of here! Gonna come strolling in here like you own this place, too!"

"Jimmy, hush!" his brother Greggy commanded again.

"What is your problem, little man?" Tony asked Jimmy. "What'd I ever do to you?"

"It's time for you to go, Mr. Vero," Danny said from his office door behind the bar. Tony turned to see the manager standing in his doorway. Randy the bouncer was marching dutifully over to Tony. Tony gave Danny a dirty look to warn him not to mess with him.

"I know you're a member, now," Danny said, "but you've asked your questions and you're just irritating my customers, now." Randy the bouncer stood defensively in front of Jimmy and folded his meaty arms, trying to intimidate Tony.

"I'm honestly not trying to irritate anyone," Tony sighed. "Look, men, Todd's gone, I need to find him, and it's just been a long day. I don't mean anyone any harm. I do need your help and I know Todd would deeply appreciate any help you all could be to him in this situation. I need to find Bernie Lokawski." He reached into his pocket for his wallet. He laid a twenty on the bar and pulled out a business card. He handed it to the bartender. "The twenty's for beers on me. To make up for if I upset you all tonight. That's my card he has now. If any of you think of anything that might lead me to Todd or Bernie Lokawski, please get that card and call me. I'll be back in sometime over the next couple of days. We cool now?"

They all hesitated, but then softened up. Except for Jimmy, who was still fuming. Tony didn't expect any concessions from him.

Phil Carboni, being the oldest of the bunch, acted as their spokesman. "Yeah, Tony, we're cool now." He put out his hand to Tony once more.

Tony shook it, wanting to vomit. He'd really put on quite a disgusting display for all these degenerates, all in the name of finding that chief lowlife, Todd Falco. Each new turn in this Todd Falco case turned out to be a deeper descent into sleaziness. As he left the bar he murmured:

"If I ever do find Todd Falco, I'm gonna punch him right in the mouth!"

Standard Steel's graveyard shift was going great guns at midnight. Standard Steel was located in the West Mayfield district of Beaver Falls, right past College Hill. The May moon illuminated the small sheet metal plant and the long trains that sat outside her shipping bays, trains that would soon snake through Beaver County with their shiny cargo. This mill had always been micro-managed. Therefore, it had successfully survived the regional plant shutdowns and twenty year long depression that had made Beaver County a part of the notorious north eastern Rust Belt. So the eleven to seven shift was fully manned that early Friday morning.

Inside, a plant foreman tracked down one of Standard Steel's top machinists: Frank Kranac. Frank Kranac worked straight midnight shifts at his request. His work was excellent but his creepy demeanor could make the graveyard shift quite unpleasant. In fact, the foreman hated having to work night shifts with Kranac. Frank Kranac was so repulsive and foreboding he was like a vampire that one needed to watch over one's shoulder. He was an unfriendly loner. He did not respond to common pleasantries. He droned lifelessly when he did speak. The only people Kranac mildly associated with were a crew of profane sheet metalists that worked swing shifts. A few of them, like Kranac, were Vietnam War vets. They were his only bizarre fellowship at the mill. The little foreman hated to admit it but Frank Kranac intimidated him. His face was as though someone had put a mask on a evil spirit; like someone had tried to paint a mock stoicism over a bitter evil. His eyes were like a doll's eyes, dark and void of humanity. He had a massive frame yet he could slink silently like a panther. The only good thing about him was his quality of work. They could put him on a project by himself and leave him alone to do a good job. Other than that . . .

The foreman found him at the end of a dark row of dead machinery. Hunched over, Frank Kranac worked a socket wrench under the belly of a small press. The foreman stopped a few feet short of the machinist. For a few seconds he watched the man's powerful arms at work. He wished he could just leave the man alone and forget he was looking for him.

"What do you want?" Frank Kranac droned from under his goggles and hard hat without even looking up.

The foreman jumped, startled. "Mr. Kranac?" he shouted over the din of plant machinery, pretending he wasn't sure if he'd found the right man. "You have a phone call in the office." His voice squeaked with intimidation. "The caller said it was an emergency."

Frank stood up within two feet of the foreman and towered over the little man. He liked frightening that foreman. With piercing eyes he stared a hole through him. The man had to steady his knees from shaking.

"I'll be right there," Kranac finally said, after he was satisfied he'd frightened the man enough.

Frank Kranac entered a filthy office. The phone on the wall was blinking on hold. He looked around and closed the door. He was alone. With a massive hand he picked up the receiver and punched the button.

"What?"

Jimmy and Greggy Richards had just left Cherries and were cruising up Seventh Avenue. Jimmy was driving and holding a cellular phone.

"Hey Frankie, this is Jimmy. We got trouble. Some guy came into Cherries tonight looking for Bernie Lokawski."

"Did you tell him he's out of town?"

"No, I . . ."

"Well, you know Bernie's gonna be out of town until things cool down here. It's too soon to start planning another deal

"Frankie! That's not what I'm talking about! This guy wasn't looking for Bernie to make a deal with him! This guy's looking for Todd Falco. He says Todd's been missing and he thinks Bernie Lokawski had something to do with it!"

There was silence on the line. Greggy wanted to know what Frank was saying. Jimmy shrugged his shoulders and shook his head anxiously at his brother. He was afraid of Frank's possible reaction to all this.

Finally Frank Kranac broke his silence: "Who is this guy?"

"Tony Vero. His name's Tony Vero. He was the big quarterback for the Tigers a few . . ."

"What did he say about Bernie?" Frank said with irritation rising in his voice.

Jimmy was getting flustered. "Well, he said . . . he wanted . . ."

Greggy impatiently snatched the cell-phone from his brother. Frank heard them arguing over it.

"Frankie, this is Greggy!" the eldest brother announced, out of breath.

Frank was upset, now. "What is you two's problem? Just tell me what this guy said!"

"Frankie, this guy could be trouble. He wants to know all about Bernie Lokawski and Todd Falco. He asked everyone there questions, but no one had even heard of Bernie, and Jimmy and I sure didn't let on like we knew who he was. But this guy's a snoopy one. He paid to get into . . ."

"How does he know Bernie and Todd are linked? You two been shooting off your mouths at one of those girlie shows there?"

Fear overcame Greggy. "N . . . n . . . no! No Frankie! Honest! We haven't said a thing!"

Jimmy peered over at his older brother's frightened eyes. His hands trembled on the steering wheel.

"Well if you two birdbrains haven't been shooting off your big mouths then the only explanation is that this Tony . . . what's his last name?"

"Vero, Frankie. Tony Vero."

"Then this Tony Vero must have some pretty big connections to Todd Falco. Only Todd would know Bernie."

"W . . . w . . . what'll we do, Frankie?" Greggy asked.

"You listen to me good: You two act ignorant, as usual. You don't know no Bernie. Bernie has to stay gone for a good while now, until this completely blows over. In the mean time, I want you two to find out what this Tony Vero's gig is. Find out why he's looking so hard for Bernie and Todd."

"How do we find out, Frankie?"

Frank Kranac sighed with impatience. "He'll be back into Cherries again, stupid. He'll be back for more questions. He's not going to find a trace of Todd Falco or Bernie Lokawski. So he'll come back. And when he does come back, I want you two to follow him, find out what his story is, and keep watch over him for me. You got that, stupid?"

"Yeah, Frankie! We got it."

Frank Kranac's twisted mind was burning with a plan: "You find out what the deal is with Tony Vero. Then I'll take care of him myself!"

TWENTY

In Columbus, Ohio, Gina Vero woke up around 2:00 a.m. with a heavy burden for her brother Tony. She obediently sat up in bed to pray for him. She was groggy with sleep, yet felt an overwhelming sensation that something was up with Tony. The dark haired woman really wanted to be faithful in her intercession, but it was a battle this night.

"Lord . . . I don't know . . . do something with Tony!" she desperately cried out. "Save him, Lord Jesus! Don't let my brother die and go to hell!"

She continue to pray for several more minutes. Her prayer was rambling and sometimes detached because of sleeplessness, yet it was heartfelt. And a lot of it was according to the Word. Therefore it was acceptable before God. It brought her peace and it moved the spirit realm.

In Great Neck, New York, scrawny, long haired Cyrus Moreau was awake praying, too. But he was praying to demons. He sat on the floor in the middle of a completely black room in his mansion. He had blanked his mind and begun to summon the Dark Lords that he was so sure he controlled. He chanted his chants with fervent determination, for he was a disciplined man. Soon the hard work paid off. He felt the icy cold presence of the spiritual entities begin to fill the room. Then he felt his soul being crowded by these forces. He began chanting again, but this time it was a different chant, one that only arose when he was channeling the Dark Lords. He communicated with the spirits, telling them he wanted to know more about the Todd Falco case for Carmichael Vero. He wanted to procure new information so he could impress Carmichael and get more money out of the filthy-rich hoodlum. They weren't interested in hearing about it. The spirits began to speak to Cyrus. They began bothering him with their concerns. Their desires welled up in his belly until Cyrus had to speak them forth. These cursed spirits would only focus on one thing anytime Cyrus brought up Carmichael Vero's name to them. Cyrus began to give voice to what they wanted. Over and over he repeated in a raspy, moaning voice the focus of their evil desire:

"Tony Vero! Tony Vero! Tony Vero! Tony Vero! Tony Vero!"

Tony Vero woke up screaming.

He bolted upright in his hotel bed, drenched with sweat, panting heavily. He stumbled out of the bed and then nearly jumped out of his sheet-white flesh: he thought someone else was standing in the room with him. There wasn't. It was only his reflection in a full length mirror. Legs shaking, the frightened young man went over to the sink and downed four cups of water one right after another. How he wished he had some alcohol! Something to quickly dull his nerves.

That same horrible nightmare woke him up. He was so wrapped up in the events of the day he'd forgotten about the reoccurring dream. He'd done nothing to defend himself against it. He was exhausted, hadn't drunk at all, and passed out asleep, foolishly unprepared. So the apparition returned to haunt his subconscious. That same dreadful nightmare:

Gus Savage in Ft. Lauderdale, skin sweaty, pallid; trembling on his knees before Tony. Tears of fear in his bulging, bloodshot eyes. Begging Tony, pleading to him-

"Tony! Help me! Don't let them get me! You can stop this! Please! Don't let them do this to me, Tony! Please make them stop! Please! Pleeeese! To-neeeeeeeee!"

Then came the horrible screaming. The unbearable helplessness. Then the blood.

Alone in the hotel room, Tony Vero wondered how he could ever bear that vision again.

TWENTY-ONE

VECO was rocking at six o'clock that Friday morning. The outdoor speakers were blaring noisy music at dangerous decibels. Ed Larsky had completely swept Carmichael's office for bugs and dismissed the Dalling Security Unit. Inside the Family was meeting for their second emergency meeting in three days. They had to meet early so none of the other VECO employees would be around to get suspicious.

Carmichael and Joseph Vero, Anthony and Warren Zann, Marv Lenstein and Ed Larsky, all dressed in crisp business suits, were gathered around Carmichael's desk for the meeting.

"You've got to be kidding!" Anthony Zann said, astounded at what Joseph Vero had just told them.

"We are gravely serious, gentlemen," Joseph replied. "The police seem to be pushing their investigation for Todd Falco pretty hard. Carmichael and Ed believe the only way to safely buffer us from Todd's narcotics operation is to put our three main contacts to rest."

"By Monday morning," Ed Larsky announced, "Benny Miller, Stephen McClintlock, Jermichael DeVries, and anyone standing next to them, will be history."

"So, that's what the sixty grand was for yesterday," Anthony Zann, The Family accountant realized.

"We're shutting down our entire narcotics operations indefinitely," Carmichael explained. "When this episode is over, the Family will reunite and begin planning a newer, broader, and more efficient network of buyers, sellers, and dealers with which to make money. This new model will be built fail-safe. We'll not endure another Todd Falco incident in the future."

Marv Lenstein was aghast, along with the Zanns. "But the fortune we're going to lose in the mean time!"

"Millions, this year alone," Anthony Zann protested.

"The police will never get anything on Falco. They'll never trace those three dealers back to us," Warren Zann whined. "Can't we keep them and have Joseph sell to them in the mean time like he used to do for us?"

142

Carmichael looked down and shook his head. "We'll not be taking that risk, gentlemen. The Falco operation, though it has been most profitable for us up until now, is terminated."

Larsky smiled. "Next week they'll be burying the entire operation for us!"

Ray and Shelly Kirkland were interceding together again. Ray was getting ready for work and Shelly was about to get Latonya and Shaniqua up for breakfast. Ray had been in the study, worshipping, praying as always. He brought his intercession into the bedroom when it was time to get ready for work. There he asked Shelly to join him, as they'd prayed together the previous evening.

"It's Kay Falco again, Honey," Ray explained. "She really needs Christ. She really needs God's hand to touch her in this situation. I just can't get past this."

Together they prayed for the peace of Jesus Christ to come upon Kay Falco. They broke the curse of depression that Ray sensed was overcoming her. They stood for her strength to face whatever Todd's situation was bringing. They asked God Himself to step into this woman's life, convict her heart of sin, and bring her to the revelation of Christ the Savior. Heaven and earth were both moved on behalf of the Kirklands' prayers that morning. Kay was affected.

At 9:05 AM, VECO was bustling with the full day's activities. The Family left without a trace. No one suspected anyone had met there earlier.

Tammi Bannerman answered a phone call at her receptionist's station. She spoke into her headset: "Good morning! VECO. Tammi speaking. How may I direct your call?"

"Is Joseph Vero in this morning?" a young male voice asked.

Tony Vero! Tammi thought. "Yes he is. May I ask who's calling?"

Silence for a moment. "Just patch me through to him, please, young lady."

"Yes, sir," she dutifully replied. Definitely Tony. *Young lady.* Indeed! She was his age. He still must not want the police to track him down, she realized. She pressed the button to Carmichael's office where Joseph was meeting. Carmichael identified himself and she asked to patch through a call for Joseph. She muted the speaker on her headset and patched Tony through to Carmichael's office. She then rerouted the call through her phone and heard Joseph speaking to Tony.

"Where have you been, Kid?" Joseph asked. "I've called you at home last night and this morning. You're still not on this 'I'm not going to answer my phone,' binge, are you?"

"No! I'm not staying at home right now," Tony said. "I don't want the cops messing with me."

"Tony, why are you causing all this trouble with the police? Why haven't you contacted them yet? The Sheriff's Department called here all yesterday afternoon and evening . . ."

"I took the file cabinet back out to the Falco's last night right after you called me, Uncle Joe."

"You did? Did you take care of everything?"

"Oh, yeah," Tony said ironically, thinking of Todd's incriminating files in his safe deposit box at Reeves Bank. "But that should keep the Sheriff's Department busy for a while."

Tammi Bannerman could not believe what she was hearing.

"Where are you staying?" Joseph asked. "What have you been doing since I've talked to you?"

"I've been investigating! Like you've hired me to do. I'm on it. And what does it matter where I'm staying? You would have told the police where I was yesterday if I'd told you. You're not listening to me, so . . ."

"Tony, I will not tell them where you are staying!" Joseph assured. "But Carmichael has been running interference for you with the Sheriff's department and wants this to stop now. He wants you and I to keep close tabs. Now tell me where you are so I can get a hold of you!"

"I'm at the Holiday Inn. Room 211."

Tammi was furiously writing notes.

"Where are you going today?"

"Chasing leads. I got a good one last night. Let's meet for lunch today at one at the Hot Dog Shoppe in Chippewa, if you can. I'll have dug up more details by then. I'll fill you in."

Joseph agreed. The two said their good-bye's and hung up.

Tammi was electrified. That was the most she'd heard two Family members divulge during a VECO phone conversation the whole time she'd been there. Edgar Waters was right. The Family was desperate. This was the kind of slip up he predicted from them. She dialed Edgar's number.

In his trailer, Edgar Waters sat at a table with some electronics equipment. He had one of VECO's standard business pens. He had gutted it and was installing a tiny surveillance microphone in the tip of it with a pair of tweezers. His phone rang. He pressed his speaker button.

"Yeah, Tammi?" he said calmly as he planted the microphone.

"Mr. Rogers?" she said with excited smile. "Get your shoes on. You're not going to believe what I have for you today!"

In an interrogation room at the Beaver County Sheriff's Department, Detective Kirkland and a Deputy Simmons stood over a table spread thick with the contents of Todd Falco's file cabinet. The damaged file cabinet sat empty nearby. The two had just finished going over the last of the documents. Ray Kirkland was disappointed, to say the least.

"Mmm, mm, mmmm," he shook his head with irritation. "Todd's VECO files from business deals, some files for taxes and benefits, and some files from college. Not exactly secret documents that need to be kept locked in a file cabinet locked in a room where even your wife is forbidden."

"Definitely not," Deputy Simmons agreed. "I'll guarantee you there was more than just this junk locked away in that cabinet."

"We do know from Kay Falco that Todd's secret diary was in here, too. She burned the thing! God bless her, anyway. That could have presented a possible reason for the tight security. But most guys would have just tucked secret sex files away in a box in the attic or something. Why deadbolt a bedroom door, and lock it away in a file cabinet? That would only draw my wife's attention to it that much more! I've busted some sloppy criminals before, with evidence openly scattered all over their home for all to see. But they were usually druggies and drunks too smashed to be cautious or even care. Todd Falco's case seems to be the opposite. He's double locked something important so the first obvious place anyone would point to would be the locked room."

"And that's exactly what Kay Falco did for Tony Vero, yesterday," Simmons said. "She's definitely either so torn up she's not thinking at all or she's trying to obstruct justice."

"I truly believe it's the former with her. Now Tony Vero, there's one person who seems to be tampering with evidence and obstructing justice. I'm flat ready to slam him with a warrant . . ."

Sheriff DeBona entered the room at that point with a folder in his hand. He walked over to Ray Kirkland.

Ray smiled. "Why Sheriff, this is a surprise visit."

"Yes, Detective. But you're the one who gets the surprise today." He handed Ray the folder. "The lab just finished the results of that sample from Todd Falco's closet yesterday. Cocaine. Pure grade. And I mean pure! It's not been stomped or cut with anything. The lab says it's like stuff they haven't seen in twenty years. Impressive sample."

"Well, Hallelujah!" Ray grinned big, reading the report. "Thank you Jesus for confirmation to Kay Falco's word."

"It looks like she could be right, Detective. Now I'm going to keep my word to you. I'm having the narcotics department launch an investigation into Todd Falco's drug life. I would say with a sample of this grade he wasn't a user just looking for a fix now or then. I've commanded the narc squad to hit the streets and gather all information they can on Todd Falco from the dealers and players in the county. Let's see what they have on him. He has no record or listing on the computer files. What are you doing with the missing person's investigation?"

"I'm having an eleven o'clock news conference to get Todd's case information out. I have channels 2, 4, 11, and 53 from Pittsburgh coming in, and the Beaver County Times and the Pittsburgh Post-Gazette. I'm putting all the information on our website and several others around the country. By six o'clock tonight Todd Falco will be a household name and his picture will be everywhere. Let's see if we can't force him out into the open."

"Good," Sheriff DeBona said. "I want you to go back to VECO today and put pressure on Carmichael Vero. Let's rattle him good. Maybe with some negative press about one of his employees he'll give us some cooperation to nail this case shut fast, since he's so worried about VECO's image. What else can I do for you?"

Ray grinned big again. "Well, I've got a big problem with Tony Vero."

"Tampering with evidence?" the Sheriff asked.

"Yes, sir. Maybe obstruction of justice, too. But we don't have enough on him to do anything, right now. I do have a plan on how to deal with him, though, and would like your blessing on it."

"I'm all ears," the Sheriff smiled back.

Prayer warrior Audra Dutton was in a spiritual battle once again. She was walking through her home calling forth righteousness into the lives of the people who had hurt her the most. She prayed that the Father would show great mercy to them, that their sins would be cleansed by Christ's blood.

Holy Spirit had once again interrupted the widow's schedule. "Daytime talk's gonna have to wait," Audra said at about nine that morning as she was preparing to watch television and have coffee. She felt the impulse of Holy Spirit all over her again and went to warring. She prayed in the spirit. She sang and danced before Jesus. She read from the Bible and spoke the Word of God out loud. She was faithful over her burden to pray over the people responsible for her son's death. Her son, Orlando Dutton, died of a drug overdose seven years earlier. Orlando would have been 29. At 22 he was hooked on crack cocaine. He ran with some tough crowds in Beaver Falls. He lost his senses. He even neglected his construction job at times in order to party. Audra prayed for his deliverance. Orlando showed up at Audra's church one Sunday morning without warning and gave his heart to Jesus during an altar call. Audra rejoiced that day. Yet eight days later Orlando was found dead in his car outside a club in downtown Beaver Falls. He had died of an overdose of crack laced with dangerous amphetamines. Bitterly disappointed, Audra thought her heart would break in two. Her anger toward the drug dealers who fed upon Orlando's weakness was unbearable. She found herself becoming an embittered woman instead of the salt and light of the world Jesus Christ had called her to be. It was an understandable lapse of faith by a grief-stricken mother. Then, a month after Orlando's funeral, having lost the second and only man in her life, Holy Spirit stopped her cold in the midst of a raging fit in her house. He exposed her heart that day and forced her to admit with Whom she was really angry. Audra and God had it out, for she blamed Him for Orlando's death.

"If You hadn't have taken his father when he was so young he may have become something! Instead of a crack head! That was my boy those motherless animals killed!" She shouted at Him. "Didn't he give his life to You a week before he died? Why? Why did You allow this to happen? Why did You allow the devil to win?" He let her go on and get it all out.

As she lay grief-stricken on her living room floor Father God sought to console her wounded spirit. He first reminded her that a broken and contrite heart He would not reject. If she would stop the anger and only worship Him in her brokenness, He would be able to reach into her broken heart and begin to minister His healing balm to her. But she had to enter into His holy presence; He could not fellowship in the midst of her anger and cursing. At the end of her rope, she obeyed and began praising Him and His goodness. She soon found Holy Spirit's anointing on her to worship. That day Audra Dutton gave up the most expensive worship she had ever given unto the Lord: true worship given from a broken heart. It was so sweet to Him, a sweet perfume in His nostrils. She felt His presence envelop her like never before. Time began to stand still. He was completely sensitive to her debilitating pain. It was as though in the spirit realm He took her up into his mighty arms and loved on her as a precious Father. He ministered to her the hurt and pain He felt the day the sinful world killed His precious Son. But He also ministered the glorious victory His Son won that day on the cross over death and hell, and He reminded her that Jesus forgave all who had crucified Him. After an unknown time in His presence He gave Audra Dutton the key to overcoming her pain and anger: "Forgive and pray for those who killed your son. I love them as much as I love you and your son. Allow Me to place My burden for them on you. It is light. I will lift your heavy burden of anger." A revelation came over Audra. Her grief was only being compounded by her deadly anger. She said, "Yes, Lord! Yes, heavenly Father! I will forgive! I will receive Your loving burden for those people who killed my son. I will lift them up to you in intercession! I will pray for their souls, their salvation! I will pray for their children to be saved and blessed! I will fill this void in my heart left by my son's loss with Your precious burden of love! I will, heavenly Father! I will! I will, I will, I will . . ."

Her heavenly Father then spoke the most life-changing word to Audra He'd ever spoken before. It was almost with an audible voice like thundering waters that He spoke to Audra Dutton: "Daughter, you weep and your heart is broken over the death of your son. But remember My Word where it says you should not grieve as those who have no hope. For Orlando is with Me now. He stands in My presence, amidst the throngs of My saints in glory. He did give his heart to Me. And I called him home before he slid away from Me into darkness forever. He is now and forever in the light and you will see him and rejoice with him one day."

Audra leapt from the floor in ecstasy. Sorrow became joy. Grief, laughter. Mourning turned into dancing. She could almost envision Orlando in the arms of the Mighty Savior. Hours after an embittered, broken woman had begun to wallow in anger, a newly resurrected Audra Dutton arose from the floor of her home, from the direct presence of God, a new woman with a mighty mission: She was going to spend the rest of her life praying for those drug dealers who brought her Orlando to his death. Under Holy Spirit's burden and direction, she would pray until every single one of them was saved. And she had no idea who they even were! She was just going to pray until Holy Spirit said, "There, you've done it! You've seen them all into My Glory!" The devil had meant to destroy this woman of faith by killing her son. But God turned his evil intentions for His almighty will. And He was going to make satan sorry he had ever lifted a finger against His precious daughter, a woman of great faith.

And the lives of the people who killed her son were being changed daily by her prayers.

Tony Vero sat on his bed in room 211 of the Holiday Inn. He was reading over Danny O'Hurley's leather membership book from Cherries. He was tired from lack of sleep. He had dozed on and off several times after his nightmare woke him up. But after that horror his unconscious was hard-pressed to kick in. He got up at 8:00, showered and dressed. His stomach was in knots, not being in the safety of his own house. He wanted to just go home, lock the doors, and get hammered. But . . .

He was looking at Jimmy and Greggy Richards' names in the leather book. He was flogging his mind for information on Jimmy Richards. Who was that little creep? Why was he so angry and offended at Tony? Tony didn't remember ever meeting him anywhere. He picked up the phone book and looked up their names. Sure enough, they lived together out near Wampum, just up Rt. 18 from the Holiday Inn. Grandview Cemetery, where they worked, was just up the road over the hill from the Holiday Inn, too. He would go check them out, first thing, to see if he could jog his memory. Jimmy Richards sure did remember him, for some reason.

Tony reached into his bookbag and pulled out a slip of paper from a notebook. On the paper three names were written: Jermichael DeVries, Stephen McClintlock, and Benny Miller: the three top drug lords in the tri-state area. Their addresses were written beside their names. Tony knew Todd Falco supplied Family bought narcotics directly to those three men. Tony wanted to track them down to see if they knew Bernie Lokawski. Getting close to DeVries and McClintlock would be tough. They were major players who were under the Family's secret protection. For Tony to get close to them would be a big risk. If he was spotted with them, he could expose VECO's big Family secret. It would be tough. Now Benny Miller, he was another case. Tony could go to see him and not risk anything. Benny Miller was not just a drug dealer: he had also been Tony's number one running back and receiver for the Beaver Falls Tigers. Benny was selling while he was in high school. He dropped out of college and went on to take over the largest gang in Beaver County. Benny would be accessible. Tony would see him.

The telephone rang next to Tony. He wondered if his Uncle Joseph was calling him back about something so soon.

"Hello?" Tony said.

Click. The caller hung up.

"Same to you," Tony said, hanging up. He wondered what that was all about.

Downstairs in the Holiday Inn lobby private investigator Edgar Waters hung up the desk phone. That confirmed what Tammi Bannerman had told him. Tony Vero was there. Edgar would wait and follow him the rest of the day.

TWENTY-TWO

L arsky walked into Carmichael's office when the executive was alone. He handed the eldest Vero a folded sheet of paper. Carmichael unraveled it and read: "You remember those two witnesses we called the Magic Genie about a few years ago?" the note said.

Carmichael looked up, perplexed, and nodded.

Larsky grabbed a pen off Carmichael's desk and wrote: "We paid Cyrus Moreau to kill them. They died of heart attacks in custody. Cyrus said it was part of our protection." Carmichael read. Completely puzzled, he said out loud, "So?"

Larsky wrote: "Benny Miller, Stephen McClintlock, and Jermichael DeVries are under our protection AND Cyrus's too. Cyrus warned you and me before that if we ever wanted to off one of our underlings we better call him first so he can remove their protection. Otherwise, he said our plans might backfire on us 'in the spirit world'. We ain't got room for any backfires right now."

Carmichael nodded again, finally getting Ed's point. He wrote: "I'll call Cyrus immediately."

Larsky smiled, relieved. He took the sheet of paper and ran it through the shredder.

Tony Vero drove his pickup truck up a steep hill to Old Route18, just outside the Beaver Falls city limits. Off to the left was a tall, steep hill with an old dirt road woven into it. At the mouth of the road was a sign: Grandview Cemetery. Grandview was one of the oldest cemeteries in Beaver County. It occupied a level plane on a hillside overlooking the Beaver River valley. Tony donned a Pirates ballcap and cheap sunglasses to hide his face. He steered his dark blue Ford around the winding curves until he reached the cemetery at the top. Grandview reminded Tony of a graveyard scene from one of those locally produced zombie movies. The road wound around the hill-top cemetery in a figure eight. Tilted tombstones and twisting, gnarled trees filled out the landscape. An old cement block building stood near the entrance at the top of the hill. Half of it was an office with an old wooden door, the other half a double door garage. It was surrounded by cement coffin cases, old landscaping implements, and a yellow tractor. A Chevy pickup and a Dodge Neon car were parked beside the garage. Tony hoped those two vehicles belonged to Jimmy and Greggy Richards from Cherries. The t-shirts they both wore the previous evening indicated they worked at Grandview as the groundskeepers. Tony stopped his truck near the garage and scanned the landscape: sure enough he saw a stocky, blond-headed figure on a riding mower near the far edge of the cemetery. That had to be Jimmy, the younger brother who was so irate at Tony's presence at Cherries. Tony drove slowly around the road, watching Jimmy straddling the riding mower. Off to the right Tony suddenly noticed the reason they named the graveyard "Grandview." He slowed the truck. From that hillside one could see the whole way up the valley north toward Koppel. As he then looked south down the valley he could see the point where the Beaver River twisted over toward New Brighton. Definitely a grand view. As he made another curve past a huge tree Greggy Richards suddenly stepped out from behind the tree in front of him. The eldest Richards was holding a gas-powered weed eater and wearing goggles and soundproof earmuffs. Tony slammed on brakes. Gravel crunched under the tires. Greggy jumped, startled from his work. He was so engrossed in his weed eating he didn't see Tony's truck coming. He looked directly into the windshield at Tony. Tony prayed the ballcap and glasses would work. Greggy waved a hand apologetically at Tony and then limped back off the road, returning to his weed eating. He didn't make Tony. Tony drove past him. Greggy had almost seemed downright friendly toward Tony the night before. Much the opposite of Jimmy. Finally Tony made the outer curve of the figure eight loop. There was Jimmy, mindlessly driving that mower, crew-cut hair, blank stare. He paid Tony no attention as the truck drove by him. Tony desperately tried to place Jimmy Richards somewhere in his memory. Why did that sad little man hate him so? What had Tony ever done to him? He shrugged his shoulders, coming up with no answers. However, he would not give up. He'd find out what little Jimmy's beef with him was. But in the meantime he'd have to keep an eye on him as he kept up the investigation at Cherries.

"Cyrus Moreau," the mellow voice finally came over the line.

"Cyrus, this is Carmichael Vero."

"Why, it's a pleasure to hear from you so soon, Carmichael! I'm afraid I don't yet have any new leads for you, but I assure you I'm work . . ."

"No, no, Cyrus. I trust you're doing all you can," Carmichael lied. He resented paying this man a three quarters of a million of his own dollars for work he'd never actually see being done. It made no sense to such a pragmatic business man. "I'm calling to make you aware of something so you can help us. Is it safe to talk?"

There was silence for about twenty seconds. "I think we're safe, Carmichael. What is it?"

"Ed came to me this morning and reminded me of something. We're going to eliminate three of the Family's top 'employees' this weekend."

"They all work for your missing man, huh?"

"Yes, Cyrus. Exactly! Since he's gone we need them to be gone, too."

"You didn't want me to take care of them for you?"

"Well . . . it's just cheaper to do it ourselves. You understand the money this crisis has already cost us."

"Spoken like a true tightwad, Carmichael! So your man Larsky reminded you of my warning of the dangers of trying to take out someone under my magical protection. He truly is a man after my own heart. Too bad he's so stupid. I'd try to train him up in the dark powers . . ."

"But can you do it for us? Can you assure me these three men will not be under your protection when we go to do the jobs?"

"I'll get on it immediately, Carmichael! They'll be exposed and vulnerable."

"Thank you! But wait . . . uh . . ." he hesitated. He wanted to ask to be sure . . .

"The answer is 'no', Carmichael. You won't have to pay me extra for this!"

Though Benny Miller was a top cocaine dealer in the tri-state area and the leader of the Beaver Valley's most notorious gang, he was never hard to locate. He did not live in secrecy. He had a very large home on 4th Avenue in Beaver Falls. He dressed in high-priced, fashionable clothing and drove a Mercedes Benz. He was a home-grown product of Beaver Falls. Like Tony Vero, twenty-four year old Benny was highly intelligent, and like Tony Vero, Benny was a football hero. He held rushing records for Beaver Falls Senior High and ran up some impressive reception statistics, too. Benny was a natural leader and businessman. After two years as an accounting major and mediocre running back at Slippery Rock University, Benny quit college. It was only interfering with his ever expanding drug businesses. He had one group selling in Beaver Falls for the two years he was in college. Meanwhile, he ran a lucrative business from his apartment in Slippery Rock, and even branched out into steroids and other illegal athletic enhancing drugs for the jocks at the Rock. He was very involved in smoking marijuana on the side, however, so that affected his grades and athletic performance. Quitting school was an acceptable option. He moved back to his hometown, bought and remodeled the huge home on 4th Avenue, hired a contract killer to smoke the local gang leader of Beaver Falls' most powerful drug gang, and took over the gang himself. He set up protection for his drug business, made peace with smaller rival gangs, and became a legitimate landscaping and construction contractor to front his illegal activities. He was smooth, like a small scaled version of Carmichael Vero. He met Todd Falco through fellow dealer Jermichael DeVries and was recruited for the Family because of his ability to pay large sums of cash for Todd's narcotics. He didn't know there was a Family, of course, and that he was protected by the Family itself. Likewise, he didn't know that he was protected by very powerful demonic forces assigned to him by Cyrus Moreau. The demonic hordes built large strongholds around him and his gang, almost rendering them invincible. Benny lived under the delusion he was untouchable. He'd been living like a king for four years, amazingly undetected by law enforcement. So he lived large, out in the open for all to see. Therefore it was not hard for Tony Vero to locate Benny Miller that Friday morning at ten. Tony parked his pickup truck in front of the "Miller Mansion," as many locals jokingly called the spacious, spotless house.

As Tony came up the walkway running through Benny's yard, a hard-looking young man with dreadlocked hair came out the front door to stop him. He couldn't have been more than seventeen. He had on a Cincinnati Red's baseball jersey, red Nikes, and blue jeans with one pant leg rolled up. He puffed hard on a cigarette. Tony noticed another older man stood inside the front door, hiding his left hand behind his back, looking him over.

"You not wearin' colors, whitey," the gang banger who came out to "greet" him, said.

"I probably never will, either," Tony remarked. "I'm Tony Vero. I'm an old friend of Benny's. He in?"

"That's none of your business! I do know one thing: you got nerve comin' on our turf like you own it. Why don't you show some respect?"

Tony smiled an unfriendly smile. "Look kid, you've done your job real well. I'm scared! Now go inside and ask Benny if I can have a word with him. I'm Tony Vero. I'm legit. He'll know me when you tell him my name."

The young gang banger went back to the house, purposefully taking all the time he could. He conferenced with the man in the door. The man disappeared for a minute, then returned and nodded at the young "greeter."

The youth came back to Tony. "Let's go, big mouth."

Benny Miller sat at a desk in a large master bedroom on the second floor. He was still lean and strong, like Tony remembered, but had grown his afro out to a giant black puff. Two well-dressed accountants sat with him, going over figures. When the young gangster and Tony Vero appeared in the doorway of his bedroom, Benny was yelling on the phone, angry as a hornet. Tony suddenly realized who and what Benny was talking about and eavesdropped intently:

"Don't cry to me about how much money *you're* going to lose this week! *I'm* the dealer, punk! I'm the one who's going to lose the fortune! . . . I can't help it that my supplier cut my throat this week, crack head! You act like I wanted him to! Don't you think I'd load you up to sell if I had it? . . . I told you, he didn't show up for our deal! I can't locate him! It's not my . . . You . . . Shut up! . . . I said SHUT UP! Now you listen to Benny Miller one last time, crack head! You work for me! Me dealer! You pusher! Get over yourself! If you ever call me up again to fuss me out, my boys are gonna come after you so fast you're not even gonna have time to wet your pants!"

He slammed the phone down, shaking the table violently. Both accountants looked up at him, calm but seemingly perplexed by Benny's anger. "Pushers!" he yelled at them. "Self-centered morons. They think the whole world revolves around them."

Benny turned, looked up at Tony and laughed with joy. "Tony Tiger!" he said with his trademark raspy voice.

"Benny M!" Tony grinned. Benny got up and the two banged their fists together several times and gave a quick shoulder to shoulder hug.

Tony stepped back and looked at the drug lord's hair. "You got that major seventies' 'fro going there, Benny."

"It's in style, you know," he smiled. "Sit down and talk to me, Tony Tiger."

The duo sat in two expensive hardback smoking chairs off to the side of the bedroom near a fireplace. Benny pulled out a fat joint and lit it up.

"Toke one like the old days?" he offered Tony.

"Nah, man, I'm on duty!" Tony joked.

"You a cop, now, Tony Tiger?" Benny joked back. "You didn't get too good for weed, did you?"

"Haven't had much, lately. I've been sticking to booze, I guess. Quite a set up you got going for yourself, here, Benny! I think I could get into the White House to see the President easier than I got in here to see you today. Didn't expect a strip search and a prison inspection!"

Benny giggled. "It's not that bad, now. I got to watch out for myself, you know. I'm on top now."

"Yes I know. That's why I'm here."

"What do you need, QB?"

"I need the run down on a certain supplier here in town. This dude has some A-1 coke and is supposedly selling it. A client's hired me to find him. I need to know if you can ID him for me."

"Name?"

"Bernie Lokawski."

Benny shook his head. "Ain't never heard of no 'Bernie Lokawski.' He don't deal 'round here."

Tony shook his head in disgust. "Man," he said, "No one's heard of this guy. Yet he's passed around some fine cocaine. Pure stuff. Looks real fine, according to my client."

Benny shrugged, inhaled another puff of his joint, held it, released it. "I know all the players around here. I'm the number-one G. I don't let anyone come into the Beaver Valley to undermine my business. You ain't sitting in the finest house in Beaver Falls for no reason, you know."

"I do know, Benny. That's why I'm starting here at the top."

"Can't help today, man. But I'll tell you what I'll do. Gimme your card. I'll have the boys put the word out on the street for this cat. If he's around I'll find out real quick for you. Come back and see me if you get any more low down on him. The more information I have the quicker I can get something on him."

"I will," Tony said as he started to get up. "I appreciate your help on this."

He knew Benny had been talking about Todd Falco to that pusher on the phone. Tony knew Todd used different aliases with all the dealers he sold to for the Family, in order to protect his identity and buffer the Family even further. He wanted to pump Benny for some information on Todd Falco, even though Benny didn't think Tony knew Todd. That phone conversation would be a great lead-in.

"You sound like you got troubles of your own, from what I heard you saying on the phone."

"What big ears you got there, granny! If you must know my top supplier cut my throat big time this week. He stood me up without even a phone call. He's been good to me for four years. But now I've lost a fortune because of him."

"What happened to him?"

"No one knows! I went to our usual rendezvous on Wednesday. Same bat time, same bat channel. But no bat! He hasn't shown up and I can't locate his stinky carcass anywhere. That's why that baboon pusher I sell to called me to complain. Like it's my fault! I called my man Jermichael DeVries in Alliquipa. My supplier hooks up Jermichael's operation, too. Jermichael says the same thing: homeboy cut his throat. Didn't show up with the goodies this week."

"Doesn't anyone know where he is?" Tony asked naively.

"No. Hey!" Benny's face lit up. "Maybe I could hire you to find him for me!"

If he wasn't feeling so horrible, Tony would have had to bite his tongue almost clean off to keep from laughing. He was having a hard enough time locating Todd for the Family.

"Can't do it, Benny. I just can't believe he's disappeared like that, though. With no one able to trace him."

"Black widow," one of the accountants said aloud from behind them, not even looking up from his work.

"Shut up, Marcus," Benny said, holding his hand up at the accountant. "I'm tired of your 'black widow' stories."

"What's he talking about?" Tony asked.

"Marcus here's a Penn State honors graduate. He's a remarkable bookkeeper and counselor to me. But all the sudden he's got a Twilight Zone imagination this week since my man split on me, rambling on about the 'black widow' of the Beaver Valley instead of giving me the wise counsel I need."

Tony was intrigued. "What's the 'black widow,' Marcus?"

Marcus looked up at Benny for permission to speak. Benny sighed impatiently. "You might as well go on, Marcus," he said. "You got this white man's ears perkin' up like a dog."

"My uncle was a player in Beaver County," Marcus explained. "Major dealer. Then one day ten years ago, he just plain vanished. Without a trace. His apartment, cars, belongings, everything he had was left untouched. But he was gone. Cops wouldn't do much. A black drug dealer disappearing wasn't a problem to them. When our family started to look into it we found out that Uncle Charles wasn't the first drug dealer to disappear like that around here. There were others. Some of the local gang bangers told us about a 'black widow' they thought was systematically preying on dealers for their drugs and money. But no one can identify this cat . . ."

"Who lives in a coffin, comes out during the full moon, and can only be killed with a silver bullet," Benny joked sarcastically. He pointed his thumb at Marcus. "I'm afraid Marcus is the product of this *X Files* generation we live in, Tony Tiger." He cocked his head toward the accountant. "Your uncle took the money and ran, Marcus, far as I'm concerned. He's probably sitting on some Caribbean beach with a shorty and a forty . . ."

Tony interrupted Benny, not affording to be skeptical: "You sure other dealers have disappeared like that, Marcus?"

"Lots of local players believe so."

"How come we don't ever hear about it?"

"Listen, the police are not going to spend one minute searching for a missing drug dealer, especially a minority. Where Benny's supply man is, I don't know. But I ask you this: would you pass up at least two business meetings where you could rake in over a million dollars and not even call to explain why or reschedule? 'Cause that's what Benny's man did this week."

Benny winked, nodded, and slapped Tony on the back. "Marcus's got me there, Tony Tiger. I can't argue that logic. Now you need to go. I got business to attend to."

Tony stood digesting it all, pondering the validity of Marcus's 'black widow' hypothesis, wondering whether to shrug it off as just some local urban legend. He wasn't feeling too hot.

"Thanks for lettin' me into this fortress, Benny. Remember Bernie Lokawski for me."

"I'm all over it, Quarterback." Benny vowed as he watched Tony head down the staircase. A question nagged him. He called out: "Hey, Tony?"

Tony stopped on the steps and turned to Benny.

"You and me, Tony Tiger, we was some hot stuff in high school football. We *were* the Beaver Falls Tigers. Back then, you know where I thought we'd both be by now?"

"Playing in the NFL," Tony nodded, not even hesitating.

Benny nodded his head, too. "Why aren't we in the NFL, Tony Vero?"

Tony didn't know if he could handle any deep conversations, the way he felt. "You want the lie to make you feel better or the truth to smack you upside your head?"

"I want the truth."

"I won't wind up standing in cement shoes on the bottom of the Beaver River?"

Benny smiled again, giggled. "Tell me the truth."

Tony sighed. "You're a pothead and I wasn't ambitious enough. Your weed killed your ambition. I didn't want it bad enough to overcome all the odds against me. It's your fault and my fault we aren't anything more standing here than a felon and a private detective."

Benny raised a finger: "A private detective who's probably *working* for a felon, Tony Tiger."

Tony nodded. Benny smiled.

"You just remember who made you look so good on that gridiron, Tony Tiger! I could have dropped a few passes just to keep your stats down and humble you!"

"You're lucky I even threw to you, Benny Miller."

TWENTY-THREE

Cyrus Moreau was in a frenzy. He was frantically trying to call off the Dark Lords who were protecting the Family's drug empire. However, the demonic forces were protesting. Never before had he felt such a vehement negative response from the spirit realm after he had given a command. Something was going on in the spirit world over Beaver County. Some rumblings, some chaos. Perhaps Godly people were praying. But Cyrus didn't care about that. He knew as long as there were Christ-focused believers in the world there would be occasional spiritual clashes. But he was Cyrus Moreau. He was a master of the spirit realm. Most so-called "Christians" didn't even believe sorcerers like him existed. So he wasn't going to let this little spiritual tremor stop his wishes. Those Dark Lords would have to obey his commands!

He and two of his apprentices were in the black room of his mansion. He was training the gifted young man and woman in the dark arts, raising them up to assist him in his vast occult empire. For this lesson he instructed them on how to call off spiritual protection over a human being. It was a reverse spell, since the purpose of the original spell he cast was for their protection. It should have been a breeze for the apprentices. But when they informed him they were meeting with much resistance, impatient Cyrus became angry with them. He rebuked them for their spiritual weakness and then commanded them to watch a master in action. Twenty minutes later, he'd reached no resolution, either, and was having a screaming fit. His apprentices dared not laugh in front of him, though they would later mock him in private over his dysfunctional witchcraft.

Cyrus had to honor Carmichael Vero's wishes to have the protection pulled from Stephen McClintlock, Jermichael DeVries, and Benny Miller. Granting the wishes of the obscenely rich was how he made a living. He would lose a fortune and be humiliated if he could not produce results. In a final, desperate act, Cyrus summoned one of the chief demonic forces he lorded over. He demanded the presence of the fiend. An icy chill filled the black room. The two apprentices even cowered in fear as they felt such a mighty, dark force enter the very space where they stood. Cyrus commanded the demon to give up protection over the three drug lords.

"No! Warfare! Angels! Not safe!" was the growling response.

Enraged, Cyrus delved deep into his sorcerer's arsenal. He shouted a lengthy command he'd learned from an ancient book of witchcraft. He'd paid a fortune to a dying witch in Europe for that spell book. The demon roared in protest. It was working. Cyrus repeated the command again, slowly and with authority. The icy presence moaned an agonizing acquiescence. It began to leave. For some reason it and the other Dark Lords had to obey the command of this puny human.

"You don't know what you've just done!" it growled as its presence vacated the room.

Cyrus stood for a moment, sweaty, chest heaving, exhausted from the fierce wrangling. He looked at his two apprentices. Wanting to save face, he sneered at the two of them and said, "That's how it's done!" They weren't impressed.

In the spirit realm over Beaver County, Pennsylvania, those demonic forces gave up their strongholds around Stephen McClintlock, Jermichael DeVries, and Benny Miller. The priceless protection that had made those drug lords what they were was gone. But the voids left behind were instantly claimed by angelic warriors from the throne of Jesus himself. When the demons tried to regain the ground they'd just given up, a major battle broke out. Covered in the prayers of the saints, the hosts of heaven pushed back the demonic hordes much further than Cyrus had ever wanted. More than just those three drug dealers were exposed. A huge hole suddenly ripped in all of the Family's protective covering. A hole that the Dark Lords instantly recognized would probably never be filled again.

Tony Vero didn't know why he was on his way to Kay Falco's house again. Oh, he knew the lame-o reason he'd tell her he was there. But in his logical mind he couldn't explain why he was driving back there, except that he wanted to see her again. But why? Especially after yesterday's visits with the wild woman. Then she was cantankerous, angry and abusive. But beneath that fortress of defenses Tony knew there was a beautiful, strong, even funny woman.

"And married," he soberly reminded himself out loud as he turned down the final New Galilee road toward her house.

He was exhausted from lack of sleep. He knew seeing Kay Falco would wake him up. At the least she might shock him into alertness.

Kay Falco didn't know why she was thinking about Tony Vero all morning. She was married to Todd, though each new revelation about his secret life lowered him deeper into the bowels of creepdom. But he was missing. She didn't know what she was going to do if he had left her. Or worse yet, what if he was . . . ? She couldn't even entertain those thoughts at the moment. The point was, she should have been worrying. She should have been depressed. She should have been concerned for Dylon. Instead, she wasn't worrying at all! She had peace for some reason this Friday morning. She didn't know that Ray and

Shelly Kirkland had been praying for her, of course. She had no idea Christ had honored their intercession and was Himself upholding her that day. She only knew there was an unidentified peace and strength that she was going on. It felt multiplied times better than the fear, anger, depression, and resentment she felt yesterday. But she filled that void with thoughts of Tony Vero. Why? He was handsome, rugged, had gorgeous eyes, and had a great sense of humor. But he was haunted. She sensed something deeply disturbing him. And he wasn't her husband! But she couldn't stop thinking about him. So when she saw his blue truck pulling into her driveway, she wasn't disappointed.

They greeted, both pretending they weren't really happy to see the other. Tony entertained baby Dylon for a moment or two. They made small talk about him. She then coaxed Tony into the dining room to show him something. On the dining room table she had three high school yearbooks laid out. She had her Beaver Falls yearbooks from her junior and senior years, and Todd Falco's Blackhawk High School yearbook from his senior year.

She pointed to the two Tiger yearbooks. "Look who I found in here," she said, directing his attention to the open pages. Both yearbooks were open to Tony's football photographs from his freshman and sophomore years as a Tiger. He leaned over the table and perused them.

"That Detective Kirkland was talking about you playing football in college and all, yesterday. It jogged my memory," she explained.

Tony looked up at her. "He finally get Todd's file cabinet?"

"Oh yeah. He was not happy with you or me."

"Too bad for him." Tony looked back down at the pages, pretending to be interested.

"You and I had a relationship before," she smiled. "Sort of."

"Then you weren't too memorable, I'm afraid," he joked.

"I cheered for you back then," she giggled.

"What was your name back then?"

"Kay."

"Thanks! Last name?"

"Foley."

He looked at his team photo. "Man, I was gorgeous!"

"For a pimply-faced, overconfident, prima donna who thought he was God's gift to the game of football and every girl on the earth!"

"Hey, now!" he mugged. "I didn't have pimples!"

She smiled and opened the Blackhawk High School yearbook to several pages featuring their state championship basketball team. There was Todd Falco, eighteen years old, leading the Cougars to victory.

"I remember when he played," Tony said. "He was wicked from the foul line."

"He rarely missed a shot. His coach had him draw fouls to get points on the board."

"They had a great team that year. Todd could jam on that court."

Kay's heart was pounding like a jackhammer. For some reason she trusted Tony. She saw something precious in him. She needed to talk. She wanted to open up to him. She feared rejection, though. She watched him reading. He seemed so strong . . .

"He was everything to me," she suddenly blurted out. "That's why I've stayed with him."

"What?" Tony looked up, completely perplexed.

She blushed, much to both their surprise. "I've stayed with Todd despite who he's turned out to be because he's all I ever had."

Silence.

"I'm answering the question you asked me yesterday. You asked why I don't I leave him, since he's been with every floozy around."

Tony nodded, smiled. "Oh. You also told me it wasn't any of my business."

"It wasn't then. I've decided to make it your business, now!"

He laughed. "What a difference twenty-four hours makes."

"I'm not stupid and I'm not desperate for a man. But when I met Todd He was incredible. He was tall, gorgeous, outgoing. He had big dreams and the confidence and determination to make them come true. He treated me like I was the only lady on earth. He took care of my every need. In a way, he still does, financially. Do you know I've never had to worry about paying a bill? Doing the bank account? Dylon and I've never wanted for a thing?"

"Material things, maybe," he pointed out.

"Yeah, but that's important to a woman. He was shrewd with me, though. He knew I was vulnerable."

"Like a shark."

"Ha, ha. He made me build my entire life around him. He was my everything, and he wanted it that way. My parents retired and moved to Florida. I'm an only child and so were they, so I didn't have any relatives or anything. He gave me a social life. He wined me, dined me, took me out everywhere. He knew so many people, had so many connections."

"Drug connections?"

"He dealt, some. I knew he did. I was into pot, pretty much. Once in a while we'd do a line or two. But he made a lot of money buying and selling on a small scale. I was stupid. I thought it was romantic. He was like a rogue. He could whirl us away on expensive vacations, he could always get us anything we needed . . . it was an eighteen year old girl's dream come true. Two years later, we were married."

"Don't tell me: the dream turned into a nightmare when VECO came along," Tony surmised.

"Yeah! How'd you know?"

"Those folks have a way of making sweet things sour," he said somberly.

"Like you?"

Tony's eyes flashed a "back off!" look at her. "We're talking about you, I thought."
"So we are. You're right. VECO was the beginning of the end. The deeper he got involved over there the more distant he grew from me. Then, over the last few years, the other women started. By that point he had sheltered me from real relationships with other people. I had no one to trust, no friends to turn to. I was afraid to. His drug dealing isolated me. I've been afraid we'd go to jail and leave Dylon to be raised in foster homes. 'What's your husband do?'" she said in a mocking, dim-witted voice. "'Sells drugs. Has affairs.' I never knew how bad it was, though, until Todd disappeared this week. I thought I had caught all his extramarital activities, but after his notebook you brought me last night . . ." She closed the Blackhawk yearbook. "I never dreamed he'd be making million dollar drug deals. Is it VECO that has him selling so much cocaine?"

Tony thought for a minute. "No," he didn't lie. "VECO's not the one behind his drug business."

"What about that Larsky?" she asked. "He's a major creep."

"Ed Larsky is not one to be messed with."

"Is he the one? Should I go confront him? 'Cause I have half a mind to go over to VECO and blow him out in front of everyone Todd worked with . . ."

Tony became animated: "Do not mess with Ed Larsky! I mean it. You stay away from him. If you see him coming, get out of his way. In fact, run!"

"Is he that bad?"

"You don't want to know."

"Is Todd involved with killers? Is Larsky that dangerous? What's the truth?"

"The truth?" Tony did his best Jack Nicholson impersonation: "You can't handle the truth!"

Kay laughed. Genuinely laughed. It felt good. She calmed herself and then gracefully straightened up her body. "I can," she smiled, looking him dead in his cool green eyes.

Tony's heart melted. This woman was something else! She was beautiful. She was hungry for heart to heart conversation. She was volatile. He let his guard down at that moment. He would regret it later, of course.

"I want to know. How is Larsky involved with Todd's cocaine business?"

"I need some water."

"Get it yourself. Tell me what's going on, Tony Vero!"

He went into her kitchen and gulped back a long, cool drink from the faucet.

She didn't enjoy being ignored. "Tell me the truth!"

He set down the glass on the counter. He didn't look at her. "You'll put yourself in more danger by knowing."

"I don't care anymore! I think I deserve to know the truth about the people who've turned my Todd into a complete monster and destroyed my family. Ed Larsky's the one who's connected with Todd's cocaine business, isn't he?"

Tony stared out her kitchen window. Why was he protecting the Family? What had they done for him that now merited his protection of their secrets? His father was ruined by them. His mother all but committed suicide because she couldn't handle Pete's Family lifestyle. Then there was Ft. Lauderdale . . .

"Sit down," he finally said. "It'll take a while."

She sat at the kitchen table, crossed her legs, and rested her face in her hand, index finger up on her cheek.

"I got time!"

Tony told the story:

"My Uncle Carmichael was in the Mafia. My dad and Uncle Joseph were too. They worked for some family that had ties from Pittsburgh to Philly. Carmichael got arrested in a huge FBI sting back in 1981. My dad told us that there was this one Mafia lieutenant the Feds had busted. This guy was their silver bullet. He was turning over testimony and evidence on all these hoods, nailing convictions for prosecutors all across the state. They completely put away the family Dad and Uncle Carmichael belonged to. Uncle Carmichael's trial was one of the last. My dad had moved us down here and they had done some racketeering in this area. That lieutenant turned over evidence about their crimes in Beaver County. So Uncle Carmichael's trial was held here at the Beaver County Courthouse. That was a bonus for the Feds, since Beaver was just a blue collar town off of the beaten path. They had this firecracker of a DA here named Michael Davis. He's Pennsylvania's attorney general, now. That guy was something else. He was a decorated Vietnam officer who'd won every trial he'd personally tried. He put a lot of men behind bars. The newspaper ran a big article about him right before Carmichael's trial. They talked about his religious conversion while he was in Vietnam, how he was active in his church, how he was so into the Bible and all. He was a religious guy, but a real pistol of a DA. Anyhow, he and the Feds didn't have anything on Uncle Carmichael except the testimony of that one Mafia lieutenant. His testimony was to be the centerpiece of the trial, just like all the other wiseguy's trials he was testifying in. Uncle Carmichael's only hope against a conviction was if he could nail that lieutenant. From jail he put out a two hundred and fifty thousand dollar bounty on that guy's head. He was protected around the clock by Feds. The only time he'd be out in the open was the day he arrived at the courthouse to testify. That would be the only shot anyone could get at him. Enter Ed Larsky. He was a biker for the Plague and a mill hunky out at Crucible Steel in Midland. The Plague were Mafia enforcers around here. Ed got word of the bounty. He was and still is an expert marksman and weapons nut. He knew all the guns and how to use them with deadly accuracy. He wanted the bounty. He wanted to make a name for himself. He was crazy, and only nineteen at the time. He went to Beaver, studied all the buildings surrounding the courthouse, and made a plan. The day of the Mafia lieutenant's testimony in Uncle Carmichael's trial, Ed Larsky was a block and a half away, up in the attic room of some old lady's house. She was out volunteering everyday. He broke in. He sat near that upper window overlooking the courthouse down the street. He had a semi-automatic carbine rifle with a silencer and a high-tech hunting scope. The police caravan pulled up with that lieutenant, their silver bullet. Larsky had a bullet for him. They had that guy all beefed up with bullet-proof armor, and they tried to surround him. But Dad said with all the convictions this guy had won up until that point both he and the Feds were a little too confident. Being cocky and wanting to show the guy off to the press, they escorted him from the van into the courthouse a little too slowly. They gave Larsky one whole second of a free shot at the guy's head. One second Larsky shouldn't have had. But Dad said it was their fault. They were just too cocky. Larsky squeezed off two rounds. One of them went right through that lieutenant's head. The cops went ballistic. They instantly sealed off all of Beaver, all of that neighborhood. Suddenly, one extra cop was out sealing off the street where that old lady's house was. Larsky was a real monster back then. Muscular, huge, like an Arnold Swartzennegger. Dressed up in that Pennsylvania State Trooper's outfit that day and shouting orders to all the citizens trying to leave their houses, no one dared question his authority or ask for his identification. Not during the pandemonium that assassination caused. He patrolled that street for almost twenty-five minutes, just as cool as a cucumber. He even talked to other police officers who were roaming up and down the street. Ed had on a flack jacket, just like all the other officers. Hidden inside that flack jacket was that carbine rifle, broken down into its various parts. When he had finally cleared a getaway for himself he hopped into a 'borrowed' car, donned an overcoat to hide his police uniform, and calmly drove off into the sunset. He went to work at Crucible Steel that night, as scheduled. He had a sack under his work jacket, filled with that carbine rifle and his police uniform. During a break time, he stepped dangerously close behind the huge crucible full of white hot molten steel and flung that sack right up over the top. Two points! All evidence of his crime was incinerated forever. With the state's key witness dead, Uncle Carmichael was acquitted, of course. That DA, Michael Davis, was humiliated. His key witness was shot dead right underneath his nose and they couldn't find one clue on the killer anywhere. Uncle Carmichael put on a great act about that dead lieutenant. His lawyers put out a statement from him saying how 'grieved' he was over the loss of 'an old friend,' and that he would contribute to all efforts to bring his dear friend's assassins to justice. Yada, yada, yada. Ed claimed the two hundred and fifty thousand dollar bounty through the leader of the Plague. Word got back to Uncle Carmichael. He sent word to Ed to look him up in the future, after the outcry over the trial blew over. Uncle Carmichael, finally free from all charges against him, started VECO. He eventually met Ed Larsky face to face. Carmichael wanted his protection and loyalty. Ed wanted to give it. He sent Ed to a two year business school. Ed graduated with a worthless management degree. Carmichael hired him to become the office manager for his new VECO office building, and Larsky became his personal body guard and secret enforcer. And they lived happily ever after . . ."

Kay threw up her hands, frustrated. "But how does Todd fit into all that? He was still a boy when all that happened. I thought you said the FBI put that Mafia family out of business?"

Tony leaned forward toward her. "This is where it becomes dangerous for you to know more about these two."

"Like I'm not in danger with that psycho Larsky already? Tell me!"

"Carmichael's Mafia family was gone. Carmichael even renounced his blood oath to the Mafia, and had Dad and my Uncle Joseph do the same. He wanted to completely distance himself from the mob. Lots of small-time wiseguys came along afterward trying to rebuild the family organization. Carmichael had Larsky chase them all off. If not worse. You see, Uncle Carmichael had vision. He was going to start over. But this time, he was going to make it fool-proof. No more old country Mafia organizations for him. He was much more subtle than that. He built VECO up over five years, recreating himself from a Mafia bookkeeper and counselor into a dynamic entrepreneur. And he was. But behind that money-making facade Uncle Carmichael started a new crime organization. With my Dad and my Uncle Joseph he organized a criminal network of drugs and other businesses in this region. Larsky brutally enforced. But it wasn't Mafia. No ties to La Cosa Nostra this time. No dons, no lieutenants. No glamour. No bragging. No more bribing judges and officials. There was now no need to, if everything is done secretly with buffers protecting him. This was Uncle Carmichael's secret creation, and he wanted to make a fortune without the wiseguy trappings and folly that went with the mob. To show his disdain for the Mafia, Carmichael named their new organization 'The Family,' keying on the similarity of business but refusing the blood ties. The Family is built directly into VECO. VECO is the front. No one knows it! The government's been mad at Uncle Carmichael since the trial in '81. Three times the IRS has audited VECO. The Feds were sure VECO was an organized crime set-up. But all three audits turned up nothing but a legitimate business. And a generous one at that. Uncle Carmichael has VECO give to charities and local organizations. He has strict 'morality' policies for all his employees. In fact, since you went to the police yesterday, he's talked to them, told them all about you 'assaulting' Ed Larsky . . ."

"Hardly," she interrupted.

"Well, they've sure made you and Todd out to be kooks to the Sheriff's Department, 'cause they've told them I've been hired to track down Todd so they can close out his business and fire him."

Kay's face reddened. Her eyes watered. Her lips quivered. "Fire him? But . . ." she was speechless. "That's not fair! Todd's risked his life for them . . . How'd they get Todd into this?"

"Sometime before or after Todd was hired at VECO Uncle Joseph caught wind that he dealt in narcotics. He offered him the position as the Family's buffer at VECO. He would live a double life. He'd work as VECO's faithful marketing manager and deal in the drugs with Family money, taking a quality cut for himself. Of course he dove at the position. Uncle Joe hooked Todd up with one major supplier somewhere near Pittsburgh. This guy drives across state several times a month and gets South American shipments from some Philadelphia dock. Todd takes Family money and buys bulk wholesale from this guy. Then Todd and Uncle Joe stomp on their stash, get them where they want them in quality. Todd turns and sells the stash to three local dealers. Everyone makes a fortune. Todd included."

"So this drug wholesaler from Pittsburgh is responsible for Todd's disappearance?"

"No. Some new guy Todd somehow got mixed up with. A local guy, supposedly. He passed himself off as some sort of smuggler. He gave Todd a cocaine sample a couple of weeks ago. The Family loved the quality. They told Todd to set up a deal and buy from this guy. That's where Todd went Tuesday."

"What's this smuggler's name?"

"Bernie Lokawski. It's him I'm trying to find right now. With no luck. No one around here's seemed to have heard of the guy. He set Todd up, it looks like."

Kay crumbled emotionally. "He's probably killed my Todd, hasn't he? He's killed my baby's father . . ." Tears and sobbing instantly poured out of the little woman. She buried her face in her hands. She was frightened, again. She wondered how she would get along alone with Dylon.

Tony went over to her and crouched down by her side. *Now you've gone and done it, moron!* he said to himself. He didn't know how to comfort her. He wished he'd just kept his big mouth shut and not told her anything. He put a hand on her shoulder. She reached back and held it tight. It wasn't much security for Kay Falco.

"Got you!"

In the woods about fifty yards from the Falco's kitchen door, private investigator Edgar Waters was in a state of rapture.

"We got you!" he growled again, not allowing himself to scream aloud. "We got you! We got you! WE GOT YOU, CARMICHAEL VERO!"

He'd dropped his parabolic dish to the ground and was shaking his fists in the air in a frenzied victory dance.

He'd recorded every word of Tony Vero's account to Kay Falco. He'd not missed a syllable. Five years! That's how long it took to get something like this. Five years of hard surveillance, fruitless investigation, and three dead witnesses. Five years of frustration. It had all seemed vain and hopeless. Until now.

Tony Vero had just completely spilled the beans. And Edgar was there the catch it all on tape.

He had to tell the Captain about this right away. But how could he leave Tony? Once he lost his trail today the elusive Vero might never be tracked again . . .

He had a sudden flash of brilliance. "I'll call that Detective Kirkland and tell him where you are, Tony Vero!"

That would hold Tony for a while. The Captain had to be phoned and allowed the pleasure of listening to Tony Vero's testimony. The man had been so disappointed all these years.

But the tide had just turned. And this would be the Captain's first payoff.

TWENTY-FOUR

Tony Vero pulled out of the Falco's driveway and slowly started down the narrow rural road. He would have spent the time driving chastising himself for being so stupid with Kay Falco. He'd given away the Family secret and caused her another nervous breakdown, all in one conversation. That would have preoccupied him for a while. Instead, a Beaver County Sheriff's Department squad car was waiting for him in the middle of the road up ahead. And the police lights were flashing.

"We've been looking for you since yesterday, Mr. Vero," Deputy Simmons said as he handed back Tony's drivers license.

"What can I do for you, officer?"

The deputy held up a cellular phone. Tony just stared at it.

"Go ahead and take it," Deputy Simmons ordered with a devilish grin. "It's for you!"

Tony reluctantly took the phone. Sighing, he wondered what this was all about.

"Hello?"

"Hi there! This is Detective Ray Kirkland of the Beaver County Sheriff's Department. I'm the one in charge of the Todd Falco case. How are you today?"

Tony didn't know what to make of the chipper voice on the line. He played along.

"Oh, I'm okay, I guess. How are you?"

"I'm blessed! I been looking hard for you the last twenty-four hours. Thought maybe I'd have to start a missing persons investigation on you!"

"Uh, no sir. I'm here."

"I know! That's why I sent the deputy out there to retrieve you. You're gonna come have lunch with me!"

"Oh, that's very generous of you, but no thank you! I already have a lunch date today."

"You don't now! Just call whoever she is on that cell phone and tell her you can't make it. You're going to come have lunch with me. We got a lot of catching up to do!"

"Am I under arrest?" Tony asked bluntly.

"Would you like to be? Look up at the deputy, Mr. Vero."

Tony did. Deputy Simmons held up an arrest warrant. Tony saw his name and address on it. He read obstruction of justice and tampering with evidence charges. The bottom was folded under so he couldn't see that it hadn't been signed by a judge.

Detective Kirkland told him, "You can meet me in the slammer in 'cuffs, or at the Eat and Park downtown Beaver Falls, for lunch on me. Which is your preference?"

Silence.

"Wise choice!" Detective Kirkland said. "See you at lunch! Please follow the deputy."

Pennsylvania State Attorney General Michael Davis sat dutifully in an honors ceremony. The Harrisburg board room was filled with executives, police officers, and reporters. The fifty-three year old state attorney general played a key role in equipping many of Philadelphia's finest with a new bullet-proof body armor. A police association was honoring him and the armor company for their efforts, complete with a press conference. Youthful and fit, Michael Davis sat upright in his chair, posture perfect. He was politely trying to focus on the corporate executive making a speech from the podium when his cell phone rang. He quickly retrieved it from his suit jacket pocket, not wanting the ringing to distract the speaker. He got up and stepped to the back of the boardroom, placing his free hand over his other ear as he spoke.

"This is Michael Davis," he answered softly.

"Captain, this is Edgar Waters. Can you get to a regular phone and call me back?"

"You'll have to give me an hour or so, Sergeant . . ."

"I'm not trying to be rude, Captain, but what I have you'll want to hear right now."

Michael Davis stepped out into the hall. There were some empty cubicles down from the board room with desks and telephones.

"Call you right back."

Michael Davis sat stoically in that cubicle chair as he listened to Edgar Waters' raw surveillance recording of Tony Vero's account to Kay Falco. Every unanswered question the former Beaver County District Attorney had for almost two decades was answered in that one recording: Carmichael Vero, Ed Larsky, that Mafia lieutenant's assassination in 1981, VECO, the Family, everything. While stoic on the outside, inside the Attorney General was electrified. His heart thumped in his throat and his hands grew cold as he absorbed every word of Tony Vero's history of the Family.

When it was over Edgar Waters heard nothing on the other end of the line.

"Sir? You still with me?"

Davis finally spoke. "I am, Sergeant Waters. I have so much to do, now. I'm thinking."

Edgar smiled. He could picture the man's face. He remembered Captain Davis's stoic, logical, yet genteel demeanor from the three years he served under him in the Marine Corp as a communications and surveillance specialist. Edgar trusted that the Captain was already formulating the next three to four steps to take with the Tony Vero recording.

"Okay, Edgar. Here's what's needed. Can you get to your engineering studio and clean up the quality of that tape?"

"In less than an hour."

"Excellent, as always. I want you to make one digital copy and three cassette copies. Put the digital copy in safe keeping. Back it up on your hard drive, too. I want the other three copies expressed to my office and in my hands tomorrow morning."

"Done, sir."

"Get back on Tony Vero, if you can. He's obviously an open well of information. How is your agent getting along undercover at VECO?"

"Very well, sir. Tammi's a pistol. She's one of a kind."

"Good. Keep her under wraps there and in good standing. We're about to need her in a big way." He leaned back and let out a long sigh. "It's been nineteen years for me, Edgar. The last five for you. What you've played for me today is going to mark the beginning of the end for our long investigation. Carmichael Vero's not going to escape me this time. No Ed Larsky, no assassin's bullet, nothing is going to keep me from seeing him to justice for all of the lives he's destroyed. You've made it possible for me. And I appreciate how tedious this has been on you and your social life over the years. But Edgar, the patient farmer . . ."

". . . gets to reap the harvest," Edgar grinned. "Yes, sir! And I'm proud to be reaping this with you!"

When they hung up, State Attorney General Davis did not move from his chair. This whole development was such a shock to him. He felt dual emotions. The exhilaration of finally catching one of the Family members on tape primed his adrenaline. But the horror of actually confirming that Carmichael Vero truly had been getting away with murder and vice for years was sickening. The thought of the lives and families Carmichael had destroyed for his own profit was too much to take. He couldn't afford to feel overwhelmed by this revelation. Davis needed to be focused, sharp, and wise in order to bring Carmichael Vero's empire down forever. He needed help and he knew where his only true help would come: he turned around in the cubicle, got down on his knees with his hands folded on the seat, and prayed. Michael Davis was a praying man. He prayed often, he prayed in faith, and God heard the dedicated Baptist when he called upon His name. The Father was most pleased to uphold this Godly man's causes. Michael Davis set this entire development at the feet of his Savior, trusting in Him for all the wisdom, patience, and power he would need to see this through to the end. Things started happening immediately in the spirit realm on behalf of Michael Davis.

Eat and Park restaurant in Beaver Falls was packed and noisy with its lunch time crowd. Inside, Tony spotted the tall, powerfully built black man Deputy Simmons had described he would find. He waded through the crowd to Ray Kirkland's booth. He was apprehensive about what the detective might want. Ft. Lauderdale raged in the back of his mind. *Surely, this cop couldn't know about that, could he?*

"Detective Ray Kirkland?" Tony asked.

"Tony Vero?" Ray flashed his big grin.

Tony slid in the booth across from him. Ray reached his hand over for Tony to shake. "The quarterback?" Ray asked.

Tony shook his powerful hand and nodded.

"Tony Vero, the quarterback for the Beaver Falls Tigers, one of the most heavily recruited high school quarterbacks in America. Went to West Virginia University, didn't you?"

"Yeah."

"What ever happened to you?" Ray was genuinely interested.

"Tore my rotator cuff in my throwing shoulder. Ended my career."

Ray's jaw dropped, his eyes got as big as eggs. "No!"

"Yes. My sophomore year. I left college all together."

"And that was one of the most frustrating, disappointing, and helpless times of your life, wasn't it?" Ray asked solemnly.

"It was," Tony said in almost a whisper. He didn't know how to read this strange man. Was Detective Kirkland genuinely sympathetic or mocking him?

Ray knew Tony doubted his sincerity. "I'm serious, Tony. You probably thought you were in hell when that happened."

Tony just stared at him with a confused look.

"You don't understand, Tony. I know just how it was. I was there myself."

"How?"

"Same thing happened to me when I played for the Steelers."

Tony looked skeptical. "You played for the Steelers?"

"That's right! Our beloved Pittsburgh Steelers. I was a linebacker drafted out of Kent State by the Baltimore Colts back in 1978. The Colts traded me and two other players in the pre-season to the Steelers. Now I was fodder to the Steeler management, mind you. They knew they were just going to get rid of me. I mean, I was playing for the same positions held by Jack Lambert and Jack Hamm, or maybe a defensive end position. I was trying to become a member of the infamous Steel Curtain Defense. But at summer camp in Latrobe I went in there with one goal: I was going to do what ever it took to be signed on the Steeler's roster. I was going to hit harder, work harder, do harder than any other man on that team. I prayed to the Lord to strengthen me. I was not only going to endure, but I was going to make it shining brightly. These were the Superbowl champion Steelers, now! This was the Steeler Dynasty team. Bradshaw, Franco Harris, Lynn Swann, John Stallworth, Joe Green. They'd won two Superbowls by that point, mind you, so I had to impress them. I said to myself, 'Get ready for the toughest month of your life, Ray Kirkland, 'cause this is your one shot at your dream.' I went out there those first two weeks and I gave them all I had. It was incredible. They were all over me. They tried to bust me, to break me, but they couldn't. I was shining brightly on that field. And I was starting to get noticed. But then . . ."

The waitress came and took their order.

"Where was I?" Ray wondered as she walked off. "Oh yeah! But then, the first day of the third week of camp they put me in at Lambert's position for a play. By this point they were expecting me to excel, I'd done so well. Everyone was watching me. They called a blitz. Terry Hanratti was in at quarterback. I don't even know where Bradshaw was. It was a pass. I busted through the hole, being double teamed, mind you, and when I got past them Rocky Blier came at me to block. When he hit me I slowed up, the two guys I'd busted through fell back on my right leg and snapped my anterior cruciate ligament."

"ACL. Same injury that Rod Woodson and Greg Lloyd had a few years ago," Tony said.

"Exactly!" Rays eyes lit up. "And both of them just had to sit out one season after their operation. Both of them returned, thanks to modern medicine. But in 1978, a torn anterior cruciate ligament was a career ending injury. Indeed it was."

"And that ended your career?"

"Ended it on that very play. I was laid up in the hospital after the operation for healing and therapy. The Steelers didn't even tell me in person. The general manager of the team called an agent I was working with to tell him they couldn't hold onto a severely injured last round traded draft pick. And that was it. By the time the next season started I wasn't running at one hundred percent and no NFL team would even consider letting me try out after that injury. It was over. That was the end. And I felt my life was over."

"I do know that feeling," Tony commented.

"And I was mad at God!"

"Mad at God?"

"Mad at God! Boy was I mad at Him! Man, I was twenty-two years old. I'd been serving Jesus Christ since I was seven years old. I'd lived right, I was a virgin . . ."

"A virgin?"

"A virgin! I was a virgin."

Tony noticed the guy in the booth across from them perk up and look at Ray like he was a nut.

Ray went on. "God gave me a revelation when I was in high school. He told me if He didn't give me the girl to marry, don't touch her. Don't even kiss her, 'cause she ain't mine to use for my lust. Romans chapter thirteen says, 'Put on Christ Jesus and make no provision for the flesh to fulfill its lusts.' And I understood it and did it!"

Tony looked over at the eavesdropper, who had a queer look on his face. Surely this Detective Kirkland was insane.

"But anyhow, I was mad at God. I had served him and thought I was such a holy man and all. I was prideful about it, too. But I was lying in that hospital bed, thinking my life was over when Holy Spirit began to speak to me about suffering and the will of God. He took me to the Bible to the story of Joseph in Genesis, and Job. Both of them suffered greatly and thought they were out of His will. But they weren't. In the midst of their suffering and what seemed to be the end of their lives they were right in the middle of His will, being led to the next phase of their lives, the glory phase. He showed me that I had to die completely so He could use me. That injury broke that self-righteous pride I had about having served Him all those years. Knowing I could no longer play football really humbled me."

"So you're saying that you were stuck up on yourself 'cause you served God, and he broke you by ending your NFL career right out of college?"

"That's right."

"You think God really cares about football?"

"Of course He does! He cares about all the things we care about. He loves us. Now, he doesn't care about which team wins or loses or anything. But He cares about the people who play. He created every one of us in His very likeness and image and put us on this earth. He sent his only begotten Son to die for us so we could be saved. His blood can cleanse our every sin and stain. So yes, He did care about whether or not I made it onto the Pittsburgh Steelers. And He didn't want me to."

"He told you He didn't want you to?"

"He let me know that what I was going through was for His purposes. When I couldn't even get an NFL tryout the next year, He reminded me of something I'd wanted to be since I was a child."

"Which was?"

"A cop. I'd always wanted to be a cop. And I believed He wanted me to be a cop. But when I started playing football, I lost sight of my original destiny. He changed that."

"Sounds kind of harsh of Him."

"Not really. He doesn't play when it comes to fulfilling our personal destinies. And in the back of my mind regarding my NFL career, it was all flesh. I just wanted the fame and fortune."

"And you're saying He stripped those goals from you."

"Exactly. False goals that were preventing me from doing what He really wanted me to do. When I was finished, I took my criminology degree from Kent State and applied to become a police officer in Pittsburgh. My original goal! My rookie year they sent me off to school to prepare for getting my detective's badge. I met Shelly, my wife, that year. We got married . . ."

"So you finally lost your virginity?" Tony smiled.

Ray smiled back. "I'm pure and undefiled this day, young man. God blessed me with a woman who is the desire of my heart fulfilled. I bet our sex life is better than anyone else's, 'cause we did it God's way, not ours."

Tony nodded. "May be."

"Is!" Ray smiled. "But that year I made detective. Five years later I heard about the opening in the sheriff's department down here, and the rest is history. This is my ministry. I've been able to minister to more people through my law enforcement career than I could ever have guessed. I've been blessed beyond measure. I don't know how an NFL career would have gone. But, God had a plan. What I thought was the end of my life was really the beginning. I live out everyday with excitement and joy, knowing that I'm now truly living out God's destiny for me. He knows the end from the beginning."

"He does, huh?" This man's crazy faith about God suddenly seemed real for some reason. Tony's heart pounded like a jackhammer.

"Sure He does! He knows everything about us. He knows the thoughts and intents of our hearts. He knows our every action. He even knows what was in Todd Falco's file cabinet when you found it." Ray grinned slyly.

Oh, Tony realized, *that's why he wanted to meet.* He knew how to throw him off.

"Well, my torn rotator cuff has not been the beginning of anything for me but hell and heartache. I'm glad your God's been so good to you."

"He can be good to you, too, Tony, if you'll get to know Him." Ray smiled lovingly.

The waitress brought their lunches at that point, so Tony was able to avoid the subject. It made him very uncomfortable to even think about it. Ray felt such an anointing of Holy Spirit on him. He knew he was digging up hard ground in Tony's heart with his testimony. He knew the word of God was being planted. Tony was a man dying inside. He sensed him sucking it all up like a sponge. The waitress left.

"Pass the ketchup . . ." Tony started, but he noticed Ray had his head bowed. *Oh no,* Tony thought. *He's gonna say grace . . .*

Detective Kirkland blessed his food loudly: "Jesus, I'm grateful for this meal and this time with Tony Vero. Bless the food, bless him. Show him Your love and mercy and greatness. And I pray You would help us build a relationship now, in Your name. Amen."

The guy in the other booth was staring at them again. Tony just shrugged and smiled with embarrassment.

"I embarrassing you?" Ray asked as he bit into his burger.

"A little. But you don't seem to care."

"'I'm not ashamed of the Gospel of Jesus Christ, for it's the power of God unto salvation.'"

"So my sister tells me," Tony said.

"Your sister knows the Lord?" Ray asked with pleasant surprise.

"For the past year or so."

"Why don't you?"

Tony bit into his burger. "I don't know." He knew the man wasn't going to give up, so he did ponder the question. "I guess I don't think He'd be interested in someone like me."

"Well, I told you already, you're wrong. He's very interested in you. So am I."

"I can tell you are. What do you want from me?"

"I want to give you one chance to come clean with me before I have to find out the truth myself. I want to know what was in Todd Falco's file cabinet. I want to know about your investigation and anything you may have uncovered in the last twenty-four hours. This is your one shot at coming clean with me, Tony Vero."

"Come clean with what?" Tony asked, trying to act offended at the accusation.

"Oh, don't even go there. I see right through you. It's not even a challenge for me. You're as transparent as glass."

Tony paused. He knew he had to give him something. "Look, the main thing I found in that file cabinet was a journal Todd kept. I gave it back to Kay Falco 'cause it pertained to Todd's sex life. And he had a big sex life outside his home. But trust me, that's all that was in it."

"But I can't trust you. She burned it before I could see it." Ray stared him down.

"That's not my fault!"

"Oh, but it is. You've been a step or two ahead of me since she filed her report yesterday. Then you've been like a ghost yourself. You've purposely scooped me, purposely avoided me. You been in my way since square one. I could have you in the clink now. I'm being merciful in giving you this opportunity to come clean yourself. Now tell me the truth!"

Tony threw down his fries in frustration. "I've been doing my job! That's the truth!"

Detective Kirkland leaned over the table. There was no trace of a smile now. "Let me tell you something, Tony Vero," he said deadly serious. "I can be as nice as can be, but I play no games! You've just blown your one chance. I'm gonna be all over you, now. If I prove you're lying to me, or if I prove you've been involved in obstruction of justice, I'm going to haul you in and you won't see daylight again 'til you're forty years old. You understand me, Tony Vero?"

"Yeah," Tony grunted.

"And if I find out your lying has impeded my investigation, I'll do all I can to not only see you locked up, but to make sure you never privately detect anywhere in this country again. You got that?"

Tony stared angrily. "Yes."

"Good. Now Let me give you one more word of warning."

"Like you haven't threatened me enough already?"

"This is not a threat. Someone does not like you . . ."

"Listen, the list gets longer by the day . . ." Tony said.

"Shut up and listen! The reason we knew to find you out at Kay Falco's house this morning is that we got an anonymous phone call that you were out there. The person called from a pay phone at some store in Big Beaver. Someone tipped us off about you. Not that I'm ungrateful . . ."

"I'm sure you're not," Tony chided. His mind raced, trying to figure out who'd be following him.

"You are not making many friends with your investigation, Tony. Watch your back."

"Like you care!"

"Oh, I told you already, I do care! Now go about your business, young man. I'm sure we'll cross paths again during the course of our investigations. Maybe we'll chat some more. I bless you to have a good day."

Tony smiled sarcastically, "I'm sure you do." He slid out of the booth and turned to leave.

"Oh, one more thing," Ray stopped him. Tony turned and went back to the table, rolling his eyes. "I know it's Carmichael and Mr. Larsky you're covering for. But they would just as soon see you tossed to the lions and your scraps fed to the birds before they'd lift a finger to protect your butt."

He leaned over to Ray. "You're probably right," he said. "But what you don't know is I'm not doing this for them." He tossed a five dollar bill for a tip on the table and left the restaurant.

Ray leaned back and smiled, watching the strong young man walk past the outside window. "I like him, Lord!" he said aloud. "He's all right! Protect him for me and watch over the seed I planted today."

Ray caught the man in the other booth staring at him again.

"What you looking at?" Ray asked him loudly. "Don't you ever talk to God?"

Startled and intimidated, the man turned back to his lunch.

Ray bit his lip so he wouldn't laugh out loud.

TWENTY-FIVE

Joseph Vero's Family beeper went off at one o'clock as he waited for Tony at the Hot Dog Shoppe. Joseph went into the restaurant to the pay phone in the foyer. He dialed the number on the beeper. It was Tony.

"Where are you, Tony? You're supposed to be here. I'm busy today, you know."

"Oh, I ate already," Tony said, nonchalantly.

"You what? Why didn't you . . ."

"Guess who bought me lunch today, Uncle Joe."

"Tony, I don't have time for this . . ."

"Detective Ray Kirkland from the Beaver County Sheriff's Department."

"What did he want?"

"What do you think? He wants Todd's garbage from his file cabinet. He wants me in jail. He gave me my final warning. He's onto me. He already has an arrest warrant with my name."

"Why didn't he bust you, then, if he's got so much on you?"

"I don't know. He's one of those Christians like Gina. He talked about God one half of the time and how he was gonna bust me the other half. But you all better batten down the hatches at VECO. This guy's coming at us. And he's for real."

Detective Ray Kirkland pulled into Tony Vero's driveway. He parked behind another sheriff's cruiser and a lab van. Deputy Simmons stood in the front door of Tony's house. The search warrant was in his pocket. Several deputies and some lab boys were freely making their way in and out. They were just about done with their search of Tony's house.

Ray noticed the front picture window was smashed. A large piece of cardboard that was used to cover it lay on the ground outside.

"I guess getting in wasn't a problem," Ray remarked, looking at the open window.

"Glass man's on his way, according to the answering machine," the deputy smiled.

"What is it with these VECO people and broken windows?" Ray said. "Looks like Kay Falco's been visiting. Find anything important in there?"

"Not a thing. Yet. Doesn't look like he keeps any important documents here. That window's not all that's smashed up, though. Look in here."

Ray entered Tony's foyer and saw the demolished trophy case. He examined Tony's copious athletic awards, beaten into worthless debris by the bat that lay on top.

"There's been some sort of trouble here, Ray. But we can't figure it out. Brick thrown through the picture window. Display case all smashed to bitty bits. But the rest of the house is spotless. I can't figure it."

Ray shook his head sadly, picking up the picture of Tony and his father with Joe Namath. The beaming Tony Vero in that picture was not the Tony Vero who showed up for lunch that afternoon. "I don't know about the window," he said, "but I do know who smashed this trophy case."

"Who?" Deputy Simmons asked.

Ray held up the photo for the deputy. "He did."

"Joe Namath smashed this trophy case?" Deputy Simmons asked with a silly grin.

"Ha, ha. No. Tony did it himself."

"How do you know that?"

Ray thought about Tony at lunch. "He hates himself. Horribly. Guilt is killing him."

Cyrus Moreau sat at his office desk, flanked by the young witch and warlock he was training. They were waiting for Carmichael Vero to answer his line. In the mean time, Cyrus was lecturing the two.

". . . and this is the type of warfare that evolves from their prayers. This is the warfare causing me all this trouble in Carmichael's case. Those people live their lives sold out to their God, like we to our craft. And when they do, they're almost unstoppable. That's where we come in. We have to curse them at their weakest points. Their marriages, their homes, their health, their secret habits, et cetera. If our spirit forces can pinpoint an open door in their lives, we can send out warfare against these Christians who constantly interfere with the dawning of our master's New Age . . ."

"This is Carmichael Vero," the voice interrupted over the speaker phone.

"Hello again, old friend. Hey listen, we need to talk."

"Is it safe?"

"Of course! Listen, things are much worse than I first diagnosed . . ."

"Aw, Cyrus!" Carmichael said with impatience. "You sound like my car mechanic! What's wrong, now?"

Cyrus sat up. "Now listen, Carmichael! You are the one who's tempted fate here in the last two years, trying to push me out of the picture. All I'm doing now is taking the spiritual readings of the Family for you. I'm trying to find out what damage has been done. And I'm calling to tell you there's bad karma around the Family and VECO. Weird things are happening in the spirit world around you. I can tell you this: If you don't follow my instructions implicitly, I cannot guarantee you the safety of the Family and your empire. There's a dangerous shaking going on all around your operation. It's a warfare that I run up against at times. And your side's losing. That's why your boy Todd Falco disappeared. If you'd have been consulting me regularly like you should have been, none of this . . ."

"Yes, doctor! Thank you! But I haven't, I've apologized, and all I want now is for you to fix things. What needs to be done? What can we do to make your work go better for us?"

"There's a full moon Sunday night."

Carmichael's heart fluttered at those words. His body chilled. He knew what was about to be asked of him.

"Cyrus . . . I can't . . ."

"You know what I'll be doing here Sunday night, Carmichael. And there's a bonus."

"We have our stock holders banquet next week, Cyrus! We'll be working all through the weekend . . ."

"I'll also be having a workshop here at Aleister, after the black mass. I'm inviting all my clients. I want you and Larsky to come, too. My best sorcerers will be assembled, operating in full mode after the sacrifice. You'll get instant troubleshooting, instant solutions for this seemingly impenetrable malaise overshadowing the Family. You have my guarantee."

Carmichael and Larsky had been to several of Cyrus's black masses and workshops. Carmichael, a man who could order the murder of any human without remorse, couldn't shake the memories of the disturbing events he witnessed those nights. He couldn't do it again.

"I won't be able to, Cyrus. That's why I pay you the money I do. You handle the 'spiritual' stuff for me. I reap the benefits. You make a healthy profit in the meantime."

"All right, Carmichael. I'll try to ward off the trouble for you. For now. I'll try and locate the money and Todd Falco in the spirit realm. But there's real trouble out there right now. I'll not let this rest. Your best option is to hear from the Dark Lords yourself Sunday night."

"I trust you to accomplish that for me with great success, Cyrus. I do believe in you. That's why Ed calls you the 'Magic Genie.'"

"That's lovely, Carmichael. But do you know where the greatest source of trouble is emanating from amid the Family? Who has become a lightning rod for spiritual warfare?"

"No. Who?"

"Tony Vero."

An exhausted Tony Vero sauntered into Brighton Analytical's lobby. The successful VECO subsidiary employed Sharon Lacello, whom Kay Falco deemed to be Todd's current mistress. A little placard on her secretary's desk identified her. Sharon was not the babe Tony expected. She had pale skin and curly bleached hair with auburn roots.

She wore way too much makeup and a revealing green dress. She looked cheap to Tony.

Actually, Tony thought, *knowing Todd Falco's style, she's probably exactly what I should have expected.*

"Can I help you?" she asked in a soft voice as he approached her desk.

"Actually, I'm here to see you, Ms. Lacello," he said, showing her his VECO investigator's identification.

"Pertaining to what?"

"Todd Falco."

Tony couldn't believe it: she turned even whiter.

"I thought VECO was investigating our affair and you came here to fire me," Sharon said, blowing cigarette smoke. She and Tony were talking in a trashy, vine covered lot behind Brighton Analytical.

"Well, I could report it," Tony said to get her attention.

"Go right ahead," she said cooly, puffing on the cigarette. "I can't help it Todd and I are soul mates."

Tony snickered. "Is that the line he used on you?"

"It's the truth, not a line. He spent more time with me than that nasty wife of his." Her soft voice floated lamely in the breeze. Tony was really unimpressed with her.

"Do you know who I am?"

"You're a nosy private investigator. Who do you think you are?"

"I'm Carmichael Vero's nephew. I could have you fired for your relationship with Todd. He's married. There are morality standards for VECO and all their companies. It's in your contract."

"What do you want from me?" she asked angrily, in her soft, monotone voice.

"All you can give me on Todd Falco."

"I don't know where he is or why he's disappeared. He cut my throat Tuesday. That's the last I've seen or heard of him."

"So take me back to Tuesday, then. That'll be a great start."

"Todd was supposed to pick me up at seven o'clock. We were going to a concert in Pittsburgh, and then to the Airport Ramada. We had a room with a whirlpool bath we . . ."

"Please spare me any details," Tony pleaded. "Why didn't you go?"

"Todd didn't show. Didn't even phone."

"He ever do that to you before?"

"Once in a while. When his wife would interfere."

"When's the last time you actually did talk to him?"

"He called me at work Tuesday morning to finalize our plans and let me know he was ditching his wife for the night." She puffed the remainder of her cigarette and tossed it into some bushes.

"You know where Todd was going Tuesday afternoon?"

"No." She looked blankly out over the lot. Tony watched her. She was lying. Tired and at the end of his rope, his patience snapped.

"You know Uncle Carmichael's gonna fire Todd because he deals drugs? Did you know that? He'd fire you, too, if he knew you were fooling around with a married VECO employee who deals drugs. If you don't level with me, if I'm not happy when I leave here, you may never work here again!"

"I've had enough of you . . ." she started to open the door.

"Not yet!" Tony pushed the door shut. "You two were such 'soul mates.' Did Todd ever talk to you about his drug deals?"

She clammed up and stared into the distance again.

"I'll take that as a 'yes.' Listen, space cadet, your 'soul mate' might be on ice for all eternity because of his drug deal on Tuesday. I need you to tell me about who he was dealing with. All I need is a name. Give me one name and then I'll get out of your face forever. Deal?"

She looked up, pursed her lips, then mumbled, "Deal."

"Tell me the name of the man Todd Falco was buying from on Tuesday."

"Is this safe? Will I be in danger?"

Tony held up his hands and twisted around in a circle. "You see anyone else out here? Give me the name!"

She took a deep breath. "Bernie Lokawski."

Bingo! "'Bernie Lokawski,' you said?" Tony was getting excited again.

"Yes."

"You know that for a fact? You've heard Todd mention 'Bernie Lokawski'?"

"Yes! You deaf?"

"What do you know about him?"

"Not much. Todd met him at Cherries. The man smuggled in some sweet powder from South America. Todd was going to score big with him Tuesday night, then we were going to celebrate."

"That's all you know?" he demanded.

"That's all I know!"

"You ever seen or met Bernie Lokawski?"

"Never. I don't work with Todd. But I can get him to tell me anything! Now let me go, unless you're about to kidnap me. I've got to get back to work now!"

Tony stepped away from the door and pointed his finger in her face: "Don't ever tell the cops you know anything about Todd and Bernie Lokawski! Go!"

She opened the old metal door, but turned back to Tony. "I get the idea you're looking down your nose at me because of my affair with Todd. You probably don't know what it is to have a love like ours!"

Tony laughed out loud. "You and a hundred other women Todd's been with! You're delusional. I know his wife. I feel bad for her and their baby. You're just Todd's flavor of the month. You need to have more respect for yourself, Sharon."

"So do you, Tony!"

She slammed the door, leaving Tony alone in the lot.

Tony headed back around Brighton Analytical to get to his truck. He was elated that Sharon Lacello confirmed there was indeed someone calling himself "Bernie Lokawski" at Cherries. At least that corroborated the slip of paper Tony'd found in Todd's file cabinet. Bernie, whoever he was, wrote down Cherries number for a contact point for Todd Falco. But Tony remembered Danny O'Hurley's membership list for Cherries. Definitely no Bernie Lokawski written in there. Bernie was either an alias, or he was somebody who could safely get into the club without being a member. Much to his chagrin, Tony was going to have to hang out at Cherries that night and maybe even Saturday night so he could uncover Bernie's identity. The thought of hanging out with that crowd of creeps at Cherries was . . .

"Hello again, Tony Vero!"

There was Detective Ray Kirkland, tall, arms folded, beaming ear to ear, leaning up against Tony's pickup truck. Deputy Simmons stood beside him. Ray's police car was double parked behind Tony's truck. This was the first time Tony'd seen Ray standing up. He could not get over his intimidating stature.

"Fancy meeting you here! Looks like you scooped me again! I came out here to question Sharon Lacello, and when I went inside, they told me you were already outside with her! Like I said at lunch, you always remain one step ahead of me, Tony Vero. Deputy Simmons and I have been pretty busy, though. We just finished doing a house search at . . . um . . ." Ray turned to Deputy Simmons, "What was that address?"

Simmons tried to hide his smile. "Uh . . . wait a minute!" He pulled out the search warrant they'd used. "I have it right here!" He unfolded the paper. "Oh, yes! 2235 McKinley Drive!"

Tony's jaw dropped. Ray smiled cheerfully.

"Didn't find anything. Yet! Beautiful house though. Wasn't it, Deputy?"

The two began bantering back and forth, describing different parts of Tony's home. Tony turned crimson with anger.

"That can't be legal. You couldn't just do that!"

"Yes we could," Ray said. "We had a warrant! Searched it from top to bottom. Took some file cabinets out, too! We'll let you know if we find anything important in any of them. Same as, I'm sure, you would have done if you'd found anything in Todd Falco's file cabinet!"

"You're not funny!" Tony said as he went to his truck and plunged his key into the lock.

"Your house has some battle scars. What happened to your front window? Kay Falco been by to see you?"

"You're still not funny," Tony said coolly.

"And why'd you destroy your own trophy case like that, Tony?"

Tony froze. His expression betrayed him. Ray saw it. It was all he needed. He leaned and whispered to him over the hood of the truck: "One day, when you want to talk about all the guilt and anger that's eating you up on the inside, you come talk to ol' Detective Kirkland. I know the remedy for a guilty soul."

"That right? I suppose you're gonna tell me 'confession is good for the soul.'"

"Not necessarily. Only if the confession you're making is to Jesus Christ in repentance for your sins. Otherwise, you're just blowin' air. I do know you're battling depression, and that you hate yourself. You seem to blame yourself for something. Christ can set you free from that, Tony. Till then, you're going to be the haunted, miserable, fearful soul you are now. I think working with Carmichael and Mr. Larsky has done you in. You're not like them."

Tony didn't know how Ray Kirkland could read his mail like he did. He was intrigued, though, and wished he could talk to Detective Kirkland some more. But his only priority was to finish this job and get out of Pennsylvania forever. Maybe then he could mull over what Ray Kirkland and his sister Gina had been saying about Jesus and God.

"You done with me now?"

"Nope! You're going to come back to VECO with us. You, me, Carmichael, Larsky, we all gonna have a long talk!" He smiled and pulled out another search warrant. This one had VECO's name and address on it. "And while we're talking, our boys are gonna be searching VECO with a fine tooth comb!"

TWENTY-SIX

The Beaver County Sheriff's Department invaded VECO at 2:45 that afternoon. Despite an angry protest by Ed Larsky, Detective Kirkland served the search warrant to Carmichael Vero himself. The eldest Vero was livid with the intrusion. He argued that he would have gladly let the police search Todd's workspace, files, and records without the warrant. Detective Kirkland explained he had the warrant and was going to use it to his fullest extent. The police carried out Todd's computer, all his files, and everything in his desk. Detective Kirkland made head secretary Hilda Jessup hand over all files on Todd Falco, his clients, and all the VECO companies Todd marketed. The Sheriff's Department filled the back of a van with all the materials they took. During the search Carmichael called Joseph Vero, who was at his office with Marv Lenstein. Joseph arrived at VECO in record time. Tammi Bannerman, pumped with adrenaline, dialed Edgar Waters and let him know in their own code what was happening. A Pittsburgh news crew who had followed Detective Kirkland to VECO filmed the search to use in their Todd Falco coverage. Larsky refused them entrance to the building so they filmed from outside. A perky female reporter did a take by the VECO entrance sign, and later recorded a statement from Joseph Vero. The story and footage ran that evening.

Detective Kirkland brought Tony Vero into the VECO offices with him. Carmichael and Larsky glared at the young private detective nonstop during the search. He didn't bother trying to explain. Part of him even secretly enjoyed watching his great uncle and Larsky sweat out the search. He wondered why they were so jittery. If Todd was the Family professional he was supposed to have been, he wouldn't have been so thoughtless as to leave any traces of incriminating evidence at VECO. And Tony had personally taken care of the evidence at Todd's house, so they were safe.

Once the search was completed, Detective Kirkland asked to speak with Carmichael privately in his office. Joseph and Larsky demanded to be present. Ray made Tony join them all.

Carmichael forgot it was Ray who wanted to speak to him. He stood face to face with Detective Kirkland in the middle of his office, pointing his finger up at him. Ray towered over the executive, but Carmichael was not one to be intimidated.

"If you knew how long I've struggled to build my character and reputation, you'd realize why this arrogant stunt you've just pulled is so demeaning to me and this company!"

Joseph stepped forward. "As VECO's attorney I can tell you that this was nothing more than an act of harassment by your department meant to intimidate us."

Ray stood silent, knowing they weren't going to shut up. He'd get his word in.

"What you've just done only puts us in a bad light and casts further doubt on our character," Joseph protested.

Ray suddenly squinted as though something started to bother him. He slowly began to look around the office. Joseph went on:

"We've been battling this same ugly stereotype for twenty years because of those false charges against Carmichael."

Ray sniffed at the air with a sour look on his face. Carmichael, Tony and Larsky began to look around the room to see what he was sniffing. Joseph went on:

"You could have come in here quietly and removed all that information yourself . . ."

Ray was wincing now, and sniffing with his nose up in the air like a canine. They looked at him like he was nuts.

". . . but you chose to humiliate us with this media stunt and propagate a negative paradigm about Carmichael and this legitimate business he's . . ."

At that point Ray was fanning his hand underneath his nose while slowly shaking his head. The others were looking all over. Ray lifted his feet, one at a time, and inspected the bottom of his shoes like he was looking for the source of whatever he was smelling. Totally distracted and irritated, both Carmichael and Joseph asked him what in the world he was doing.

"Shoo-oo! Don't you all smell that?" Ray asked them incredulously.

"Smell what?" Carmichael yelled, fraught with irritation at the detective's theatrics.

"That smell! Can't you smell that odor? That horrible stench? It reeks in this office!"

Carmichael and Larsky both looked all around them.

"We don't smell anything! What smell are you talking about?"

"That stench! It smells like . . . smells like . . ." he looked up as though he were trying to come up with a description. "I know!" his face suddenly lit up. "It smells like obstruction of justice in here!"

He caught them off guard with that one. Their reactions betrayed it.

"Yes! Obstruction of justice is what I smell. And intimidation and threats against a witness. And tampering with evidence. That's what I smell!" His face turned to stone. He walked around the room, starring them in the eyes one by one as he roamed. "You see everyone, I have a missing man named Todd Falco. His wife filed a report. She's told me that she believes her husband is a drug dealer. I have neither evidence to refute or verify her story. But I do have lots of suspicions that run right back here to this office! I have Mrs. Falco telling me that Mr. Larsky here personally went out to her house yesterday and threatened her not to go to the police. Next I have a leave of absence form that's as queer as a football bat, which was supposedly filled out by Mr. Falco himself. Someone initialed it, but we're going to match some of Mr. Falco's initials in the files we took from here today against the ones on that leave of absence request. Next I find out you've all hired Tony Vero here to investigate on behalf of VECO so you 'can find Todd to fire him' because he's such a lousy human being and he's endangering your reputation." He turned and stood next to Tony. "Now Tony beats me to Todd Falco's house and breaks into Todd's private room and takes his file cabinet. He doesn't offer me the chance to examine its contents . . ."

"Mrs. Falco told me to take it . . ." Tony tried, but was abruptly cut off.

". . . but Tony breaks into the file cabinet, and when we finally do get it there's nothing in it but Todd's basic, worthless personal files. Of course, when Mrs. Falco has us come to her house to pick it up, she does tell us that Tony discovered a private journal of Todd's. But she burned that before we could see it. Then we spend all afternoon and evening trying to hunt down super detective here, but *he* disappears!"

Tony shrugged his shoulders.

"Now he won't come clean with me on who he's talked to, what evidence he's examined, and where his investigation has led up to this point."

Joseph spoke up: "All of your accusations are circumstantial! You have no evidence to back any of that in court."

Ray ignored Joseph and stepped back over to Carmichael. "Mr. Vero, there is mounting evidence of obstruction of justice in this case on the part of your employees standing in this room. And as in all cases of obstruction, the question is not really 'how,' but 'why?'" He stepped back over to Tony. "Why are you hiding evidence from me, Tony Vero? Why are you one to two steps ahead of me all the time, and leaving me no evidence in your wake?" He turned and stood toe to toe with the hulking Ed Larsky. "Why did you really go out to see Kay Falco yesterday morning, Mr. Larsky, when, according to you, that ninety pound woman physically assaulted you and kicked you out of her home?"

Tony snickered. Larsky glared a hole through his head.

"Therefore, since the obstruction allegations clearly substantiate themselves over and over again, Sheriff DeBona had me swear out two search warrants today. I had my deputy and a crew search Tony's house this afternoon, and you all know what we just did here." He faced Joseph Vero. "I don't care about VECO, or Carmichael's past, or his reputation, or anybody's 'paradigm' of this business, Mr. VECO Attorney." He finally stepped back over to the door. "Gentlemen, you all reek! You stink! You look like millionaire executives, but you smell like criminals! And I don't even know what the connection is between you and Todd Falco's disappearance, but you are making it perfectly clear to me that there is one! And I don't care how successful and powerful you are: if you are interfering with my missing person's investigation of a possible drug dealer, I am going to take you all down! And no money and power will stop me!" He stared them all in the eyes one by one, one last time. "You are all officially on notice. Don't act so surprised and offended the next time I show up here. Good day!"

Ray exited and closed the oak doors behind him. Carmichael, Larsky, and Joseph all turned and looked angrily at Tony.

"What'd I do?" he asked defensively.

"Be more careful!" Joseph yelled.

"I'm doing all I can! I haven't even let you all know what I'm up to or where I've been. The only reason he caught up with me is because someone tipped him off this morning when I was out at Kay Falco's house. Someone's been watching me."

"Who?" Joseph asked.

"I'll tell you," Carmichael sneered. "The same person who was out here snooping around VECO Wednesday night. The same person who injured those Dalling Security dogs. We are being assaulted on several fronts."

"Maybe by the same people," Tony said.

"This is turning into a real mess," Larsky whined. He pointed to Tony and warned: "And you better not be the cause of our downfall!"

"You moron!" Tony chided. "Why would I want . . ."

"Both of you shut up!" Carmichael shouted. "This is exactly what we don't need now! We've got to remain unified and focused, or that cop and whoever else is going to see us all to jail!"

"I don't get that Detective Kirkland," Joseph said. "He just showed his entire hand! He just got in our face and laid out all he has. But it's like he's not afraid."

"That's what I was trying to tell you on the phone today," Tony said. "He's a wacko, and he's not afraid of anything."

"Well, cop or no cop," Larsky snarled, "that Detective Kirkland's just made himself some bad enemies!"

"Watch him," Tony cautioned. "That guy's like a locomotive. You hear him coming from a long ways off, but when he finally gets to you there's nothing you can do to stop him. He's for real, man."

"Well, I'm for real now," Carmichael growled at Tony. "You better find Falco! I don't know what you've been doing, but you better do it in double time! And without running into that Detective Kirkland! We are depending on you. And time has just about run out for us!"

TWENTY-SEVEN

Tony sped down 7th Avenue to Cherries in his father's Mercedes. He hoped the Mercedes might throw off the police if they tried to hunt him down again. He knew they'd searched it when they were at his house that afternoon, but they were used to seeing him in his blue pickup. It was 5:45 of what turned out to be a beautiful late May afternoon. Tony had left VECO after their encounter with Detective Kirkland and returned home to see what the police had done to his house. Everything looked all right. His computer and file cabinets were gone, as Ray Kirkland said. Some drawers and closets were mussed up a bit, but nothing Lula couldn't clean when she got there. The window man had been by and replaced the picture window Uncle Joseph broke. His house survived.

Earlier, exhausted after little sleep and a frantic day, Tony lay out on his patio lounge chair and slept in the sun for an hour and a half. He had no nightmares of Gus Savage and Ft. Lauderdale. He awoke at 5:30 refreshed. He had a long night ahead of him. Heading back to Cherries he hoped to get some help locating Bernie Lokawski. Todd claimed in his journal that he went to Cherries almost every Friday after work. He also named some of the regulars he knew there whom he considered friends. Those clowns Tony met there the previous evening were useless. These other guys Tony read about might be just who he needed.

Tony knew he wasn't going to get the royal welcome at Cherries.

Randy, the beer-bellied bouncer, answered the door. He tried to refuse Tony entrance. Tony held up Danny O'Hurley's leather membership book and said: "Don't start with me. I got the goods on Danny. I'm about to return his little book to him. Besides, I'm now a lifetime member to this hell-hole, remember? Now get out of my way before I force Danny to fire you or lose his business."

Randy poked his finger hard into Tony's chest. "I'm gunning for you!" he said as he let Tony by. "First chance I get, you're mine!"

"Sorry, big boy. I'm already taken!" Tony smiled as he went inside.

In Danny's tiny office the owner reached out to take his membership book back from Tony. Tony snatched it away before he could grab it.

"Now what?" Danny protested.

"I need you to do something else for me."

"Do something else for you?" Danny's face reddened with rage. "You're lucky you're still alive! You don't know who you're messing with!"

Tony shook his head and laughed. "Look, all I have to do is hand the cops Todd Falco's journal and you'll be in jail and this place'll be nothing more than a rat infested basement. Now quit whining and do what I tell you."

Danny huffed impatiently. "What?"

Tony handed him the membership book. "Go out and turn on that large screen TV to Channel 4. I want everyone out there to see Todd Falco on the news."

There were about twenty patrons in the bar for happy hour. The "entertainment" didn't start until eight, but Danny sold cheap beers to get people early. Tony recognized no one from the previous evening. He ordered a Coke and sat at a table in the midst of the crowd, listening to their conversation. Danny turned on the news, to much protest from the customers. Tony heard one big fellow named Mick ask where Todd was. No one knew. Tony remembered Mick from Todd's journal. Mick was also a "premium member" who attended Danny's "special shows."

The Todd Falco story was the fourth piece on the newscast. When Tony saw Todd's picture superimposed on the screen beside the news anchor, he shushed everyone in the bar.

". . . Beaver County man. Thirty year old Todd Falco, of Beaver Falls, has been missing since Tuesday of this week."

Mick yelled out, "There's Todd!" and many people in the bar began to perk up with concern. He and Tony silenced everyone again.

". . . He is a respected employee of Vero Company Industries, and as Anna Lundgren reports, this case has the Beaver County Sheriff's Department baffled."

The reporter's voice spoke over a video feed of Detective Ray Kirkland speaking at the press conference he held that morning. Finally, his voice was heard:

"As of yet we have no leads or witnesses. Not even his car has been located. We suspect foul play, and we need the help of anyone who may have seen Mr. Falco anytime since Tuesday."

"I can't believe this!" Mick shouted, genuinely concerned.

Kay Falco's face suddenly lit up the screen. "What a babe!" someone yelled, and a few lust-filled men chortled and howled. Her face and hair were done up, and she was wearing a golden necklace and large golden-hoop earrings. Even Tony was taken aback by her beauty, though she looked so distraught. It was sad. She held baby Dylon as she was interviewed. Her segment was brief and Tony couldn't make out a whole lot of what she said because of the cat calls. Mick was still trying to shut everybody up. Next Joseph Vero appeared on screen, lamenting Todd's disappearance but complaining about the Sheriff's Department's extensive search of VECO.

"I can assure everyone that the police search of VECO was unfounded and that they'll uncover no evidence of Todd Falco's vanishing from here."

"Go get 'em, Uncle Joe," Tony muttered. The news anchor flashed the number for the Beaver County Sheriff's Department and the Missing Person's Bureau. She urged any viewers with information about Todd to call. When the station cut to a commercial break, a commotion broke out. Big Mick started asking people if anyone knew what was up. That was Tony's cue. He shut off the TV, hopped up on the stripper's stage, and got everyone's attention.

"Hey, Tony Vero!" someone remarked. Another person yelled that they didn't want to see Tony strip. Laughter broke out.

"I am Tony Vero," he spoke loudly. "I've been hired by Vero Company Enterprises to find Todd Falco. I have a lot of information about Todd Falco that those reporters don't. I have some big leads regarding his disappearance, and they all lead back here. I really need your help." He looked at Mick. "And as Todd's friends, I'm asking you to cooperate so we can find him together."

Tony saw Danny O'Hurley rolling his eyes behind the bar.

"I asked some of the guys here last night," Tony continued, "and I'm going to ask you. Does anyone in here know a man named Bernie Lokawski?"

No one motioned that they did.

"I have reason to believe Todd was with Bernie Lokawski when he disappeared on Tuesday. And I have evidence that this Bernie has been to Cherries before. No one ever heard of him?"

Nothing.

"Well let me ask this, then: Do any of you remember seeing Todd talking with someone strange here, maybe someone that you didn't recognize?"

Now there was some commotion. Mick was talking to some of the folks around him.

"Yeah!" Tony heard him saying to them. "That big ugly guy . . ."

Tony stepped off the stage and went and stood in their midst. He looked at Mick. "You remember Todd talking to someone you usually don't recognize here?"

"Well, I've seen the guy before," Mick said, "but he's new. This big goon that started coming in recently. He's only been here a few times. Ugly creep. Bigger than me, bald on top, one big unibrow running across his face. Arms like tree trunks. Doesn't hardly say a word. But he sure chewed Todd's ear off one night a few weeks ago. And he had Todd's full attention."

Tony looked around and shouted, "Can anyone identify this guy he's talking about?"

"Those two geeks brought him in a couple of times," someone commented.

"You mean Jimmy and Greggy Richards?" Tony asked. Everyone laughed.

Mick spoke up again. "Yeah, they called him some cutesy-pie name. Billy . . . Freddie . . ."

"Frankie!" someone yelled.

Everyone yelled in agreement. Tony pulled out his photocopy of Danny's membership roster. The only Frank on the list was one of Cherries' newest customers: Frank Kranac.

"'Frank Kranac'?" Tony asked. They didn't know.

He looked at the roster again. There was no address or telephone number beside Frank Kranac's name. Tony noticed he'd paid his membership fee in cash in April. From what Tony could make from the list, Danny didn't seem to demand personal information from those who paid lump sums of cash.

"Danny," Tony yelled to the owner behind the bar, "What do you know about Frank Kranac?"

Danny shrugged his shoulders. "Jimmy and Greggy dragged him in with them three or four times. He's never been here alone. He don't talk to nobody. He's just some weirdo."

Tony pointed to Mick and his crew. "These guys say they saw Frank Kranac chewing Todd Falco's ear for a while one night. Did you see them talking together?"

"No," Danny said, shaking his head.

"I did," the raspy-voiced bartender spoke up beside Danny.

"You did?" Tony walked over to the bar.

The bartender nodded his head, slowly and surely. He pointed at Mick. "Just like Mick said. They sat over at that table by the door, off to themselves, and yakked for about a half an hour one night."

"When?"

The bartender shrugged. "About two weeks or so ago. Maybe a little longer. And you know, come to think of it, that guy's not been back here since then."

"That right?" Tony looked around at everybody. "Anybody seen this Frankie guy here in the last couple of weeks?"

Everyone shook their heads no.

"Anyone here know those Richards brothers very well? Jimmy and Greggy?"

Everyone moaned and made rude comments.

"Greggy's an all right dude," Mick commented, "but his brother's an idiot. Brags and acts like he's all big and bad. He was just some chubby little runt in high school. Started taking steroids a few years back and got some muscles. Now he thinks he's Jean Claude Van Damme or someone."

"They usually come in on Friday nights?"

Everyone burst out laughing.

"They come here *every* night," the bartender explained. "They practically live here. They couldn't see a live naked lady any other way."

Everyone burst into hysterics and went back to their own conversations. Danny leaned across the bar, grabbed Tony by the shirt and whispered, "You listen to me: you got your information. Now it's time for you to disappear and leave me alone!"

Tony snatched himself from Danny's grip. Danny latched onto his forearm. He was about to go off on Tony.

"Hey!" Tony shouted. Everyone looked at him and Danny. He pointed at the owner and in a loud, cheery voice yelled, "Danny's been a real help to me and my investigation here at Cherries, everybody! Why don't you all give him a round of applause for all he's done to help locate Todd Falco!" The patrons gave Danny thunderous applause and a roar of approval. He looked at Tony like he could shoot him. Tony fake-smiled at him and leaned back over the bar.

"You listen to *me*, Danny Boy!" he whispered angrily. "I don't have any information on Todd Falco or Bernie Lokawski. All I got is some question mark named Frank Kranac. You hear me: if you want me to disappear forever, you help me shake down Jimmy and Greggy Richards when they get here tonight. Help me pump them for all I can get about this Frankie guy. Then, I promise you, I'll leave here and you'll never see me again!"

Benny Miller and his well-dressed crew sat in his living room, eating Chinese. Benny happily scooped low mein up out of a box with chop sticks. Jaws churning like a machine, he would happily moan "mmmmmmm!" with each bite. Childish as it was, no one ever dared mention it. All eyes were glued to the television, watching the six o'clock news, as usual. One of his accountants started to ask him a question when Benny saw a picture on the news and almost choked on his noodles. They all looked at him and then at the screen. There was Todd Falco's picture.

Benny threw down his take out box and shouted, "That's my connection! That's my man!"

"That guy?" one of his gang members asked.

"Yeah! He's been my supplier for years, now. He's the one who stood me up this week and cost me all my money!"

They listened to some of the details of the story.

"His name ain't Todd Falco," Benny began. "Well . . . it looks like he's been using an alias with me. But that missing joker right there on the TV is my man. He better not just be missing, he better be dead for all the money he's lost me this week!"

They showed the young reporter standing in front of VECO, doing her story about the police search that afternoon.

Benny suddenly whistled loudly and his afro almost straightened out. "'Vero Company Enterprises,'" he said with wide eyes. "Todd Falco worked there. Bim!"

"What's up, Benny?"

Benny grinned smugly: "I just figured out what Tony Tiger was up to here today!"

Tommy Wheeler prepared for murder in a dirty basement of a rural Beaver County home. Like a soldier he moved with assurance and expertise. He methodically loaded 9-mm pistols, a shotgun, and a machine gun, all unregistered. They snick-snicked and click-clicked as he'd open them, oil them, and load the magazines, cartridges, and shells. He stuffed each one into a suitcase and duffel bag when he finished with it.

Ed Larsky descended the rickety wooden steps and dropped a briefcase at Tommy's feet. The lanky hit man picked it up and opened it. He grinned ear to ear.

"That's the full fifty thousand," Larsky said. "No down payments. You're contracted to me, now. Once I give you the word, you take out Tony Vero. Quick and secret-like. I'm never involved, you act like you never done it."

"As you want it," Tommy nodded. "Now I got something for you!" He opened a brief case and pulled out a long rod stuffed with plastic explosives and rigged with an electronic receiver. He held it up for Larsky's approval.

Ed whistled with delight. "That's a beauty! Sleek and compact!"

Tommy held up an transmitter in his other hand. "This rig could demobilize a tank."

"I want nothing left of Jermichael DeVries but tiny pieces," Larsky commanded.

"They won't even be able to take fingerprints!" Tommy promised. He handed Larsky the duffel bag. The powerfully built man pulled out the 9-mm and inspected the machine gun inside.

"You got the sawed-off ready?" he asked as he unzipped his jacket to get to his holster.

Tommy patted the suitcase. "Ready enough to turn someone into a sieve."

"That'll take care of Mr. McClintlock," Ed said, zipping up his jacket over his gun. "Are the babes ready?"

"Ready to rendezvous. Car and truck's ready, too. I got it all under control, Russian!"

Ed smacked both hands on Wheeler's shoulders. "Let's rock and roll!"

TWENTY-EIGHT

Tony Vero spent a long hour and a half in Cherries' foyer, waiting for Jimmy and Greggy Richards. He wanted to catch them alone. Randy the bouncer resented that he had to have Tony sitting beside him in the cramped space for that long. He made rude comments about Tony to customers as they came in. Tony endured the ridicule. He just sat there imagining what his new life would be like when he left Beaver Falls and put all this madness behind him.

Finally, the Richards brothers buzzed the door at 8:15. Randy looked at Tony and let them in. They were chatting away as they walked into the foyer, until they saw Tony Vero sitting there waiting for them.

"Oh, it's Superstar," Jimmy moaned with disgust.

Tony looked at his watch. "You two are late! The show started fifteen minutes ago."

They both made sure they bumped into him as they tried to get to the inner door. Tony slammed his foot up on the door, blocking them.

"You're not going in there, yet," he told them.

Jimmy got angry, fast. He kicked Tony's leg and yelled, "You better move now, if you know what's good for you!"

Tony stood up in front of the door and stared down at Jimmy. "You're gonna have to answer my questions, first. Then you'll get in to see the skin."

Greggy turned to Randy for help. "Randy! What is this? Do something . . ."

Randy reluctantly shook his head. "As much as I hate this guy and would love to see you two kick his brains out, I gotta stop you and ask you to wait here for Danny."

They were flabbergasted. As they protested, Randy called Danny on a walky-talky.

"Is this how you treat paying members?" Greggy whined to Danny.

The four of them stood outside Cherries under an awning overlooking 6th Avenue. Danny leaned against the rail overlooking the entrance steps. He told the Richards brothers, "Lookit! I don't want the cops coming around here questioning my members about Todd Falco." He pointed his thumb at Tony. "This so-called 'investigator' here thinks he can find Todd fast. Plus he and everyone else inside thinks you two might know what's up with his disappearance. So if you want to come in here tonight, fellows, you're gonna have to cooperate with him, first."

Greggy was highly offended. "I can't believe you, Danny! You're going to listen to this guy's wick-wack and not believe us?"

Tony ended their pity party: "Who's Frank Kranac?"

"Who?" Jimmy feigned ignorance, not too convincingly.

Tony leaned into his face: "Frank Kranac! You two do know him. You're the ones who brought him here, according to Danny and all the others."

"What about Frankie?" Greggy asked.

"Why was he here talking to Todd Falco a couple of weeks ago?"

Jimmy shrugged, irritated. "How are we supposed to know who Frankie talks to and why?"

"Does he know Bernie Lokawski?"

"How am I supposed to know?" Greggy barked.

"Where can I find Frankie?" Tony asked.

Greggy leaned back against the rail and grunted. "You listen, hotshot. You don't know Frank Kranac. He ain't someone you want to mess with."

"Frankie'll break your neck, creepo!" Jimmy snarled. "He trained with the Special Forces in Vietnam . . ."

"Frankie doesn't want to be bothered with people," Greggy interrupted his brother, wanting to tone down the conversation about Kranac. "He served his country in Vietnam, he's come home from the war and worked in the steel mill ever since. And he works hard. Not many people can get to know him. For good reason. He just wants to work and be left alone. So if I were you, I wouldn't go messing with him."

"You're not me." Tony glared at him. "I want to find Todd Falco. Frank Kranac is now the missing link. And you two are protecting him. Now where's he work and where's he live?"

"I'm telling you," Greggy said, smiling nervously and shaking his head. "If you go messing with him he's gonna . . ."

Tony angrily deferred to Danny. "Owner and manager, these two are not cooperating."

"Now this is nothing but harassment, Danny!" Greggy protested. "Drilling us and wanting to drill Frankie just because he sat down with Todd Falco one night a couple of weeks ago is totally out of line!"

Danny shook his head. "I think this moron's right, fellows. You do seem to know something. I do not want the cops here at all! Now tell him what he wants so we can all get this behind us!"

"I could just take all this information I have to the police right now," Tony warned. "Then you can all bypass me and deal straight with the law."

Greggy folded his arms and shook his head in disgust. His heart beat double-time. Jimmy looked up helplessly at his older brother, wanting him to do something. They both feared Kranac and the police. Neither could quickly think up a way to throw Tony off Frankie's trail.

"Where can I find Kranac?" Tony asked Greggy, again.

Greggy spat over the rail and stared out at the street. Tony had him. He realized he had to give up Frank Kranac. He would just have to tell him what happened and let him deal with Tony.

"Personally, I could care less if you want to go poke your head in the lion's mouth," he told Tony. "You just go find Frankie and start asking him all these stupid questions you're asking us and see if he puts up with you."

"You really want me to go to the police, don't you? Where does he *live*?" Tony growled.

Greggy was silent. Jimmy pushed him on the shoulder. "Tell this moron so he'll get lost!"

Greggy heaved a big sigh. "6th Avenue, College Hill."

Jimmy was mortified.

"Address."

"I don't know his address. He lives across from the church near the ball field. I've never really been to his house. I've just dropped him off there before."

"Where's he work?"

"Standard Steel in West Mayfield."

"How do you two know him?"

"Our dad worked with him at Standard Steel for a few years. That's how we met him. When Dad died, Jimmy and I kept up with him."

"Why'd you start bringing him here to Cherries?"

Greggy looked at him like he was an idiot. "To see the babes! Why else?"

Tony stepped back and stared down the two of them. Jimmy made a sour face back at him, still full of hatred for Tony. Tony slowly shook his head.

"You," he said to him, "I still don't know what your problem is with me, but I can tell you both one thing: you two know a whole lot more about all this than you're telling me. And when I find out, I'm gonna take you both down with Frank Kranac, and Bernie Lokawski, and anyone else involved in Todd's death."

"'Death'?" Greggy sneered, rolling his eyes. "I thought he was just 'missing'."

"I'm beginning to smell one big set-up, here." He turned to Danny. "And Danny Boy, you better hope I'm wrong, or the cops will be crawling all over this place, thanks to these two and Frank Kranac."

Jermichael DeVries' red Corvette gleamed under a street light in front of an apartment building in Aliquippa. He was inside with one of his many mistresses. His number two man and closest confidant stood guard outside the car. He was faithful to watch up and down the street the whole time, making sure he saw no vehicles pull up and park anywhere within his sight. Jermichael's man was an ex-gangster. He knew all the gang bangers drive-by tricks and how to be alert for them.

Things were quiet at 8:35 this Friday night. Cars came and went without problems. Jermichael would soon finish up inside and the two would head to Pittsburgh and hit the high-priced clubs. After a lull in passing traffic, a huge red Dodge Ram suddenly turned a far corner and slowed to a crawl as it approached Jermichael's Corvette. The guard held his vision steady on the cab, looking for any suspicious movement. There was none. He put his hand inside his jacket and fondled the butt of his Beretta in its holster, ready to produce it, barrel blazing. When the Ram stopped in front of the Corvette, he saw no need to panic. In the cab were two extremely loud and drunk young women. They began to compliment him on the Corvette and call him over to them. They were pretty, built, and barely dressed. They had a bottle of whiskey and cigars and were blaring loud music. He glanced up and down the street, ensuring that they were not sent to be a decoy. He saw no suspicious activity anywhere. They seductively called him up to their vehicle in the street, asking if he wanted to party with them. They looked good and were obviously ready for action. Jermichael DeVries was always looking for more women to satisfy his insatiable appetite. His guard figured he could make a connection and score points with his boss. He stepped out past the Corvette and up to the truck. He immediately identified the two women as biker chicks from their Plague tattoos and regalia. But they weren't bad at all. The driver's shirt was unbuttoned down to her torso, revealing her bra. After several minutes of filthy conversation and innuendo the driver quickly unsnapped her bra. The passenger cackled and Jermichael's number two man climbed halfway into the window to get at them. They all laughed and howled. Tommy Wheeler slid out from under the back of the Ram pickup, attached his bomb to the bottom of the Corvette's gas tank, and disappeared back under the truck, all in less then seven seconds. A moment later Jermichael's guard stepped down off the side of the Ram. He and the girls set a rendezvous time for later, and away the Ram sped. He scanned up and down the street again, noting no changes. He looked up at the apartment building, wiped those girls' lipstick from his mouth, and sighed with delight. Jermichael would be quite pleased with him for this awesome set-up he'd made.

Jermichael DeVries emerged from the apartment building twenty minutes later. He quick-stepped out to the 'Vette. His guard watched up and down the street with his gun drawn. He circled the vehicle as Jermichael hopped into the passenger side. He opened the driver's door and joined Jermichael inside. He cranked the fine engine and gunned the gas. The two talked about women. Jermichael liked his girlfriend back inside the apartment. His guard was eager to tell him about the chicks in the Ram. Jermichael listened intently as they sped down the block. When his guard told him about what the driver had done in the cab and how they wanted to meet him and Jermichael later on, Jermichael suddenly got antsy.

"You never met 'em before? They just pulled up and wanted to start partying with you like that?" Jermichael asked, getting agitated at what he'd heard.

Tommy Wheeler sat in an old, gray Toyota up the street, watching the 'Vette head in his direction at high speed.

"It was this car, G!" the guard said, smiling uneasy. He hoped he didn't make Jermichael mad, hooking up with those crazy biker chicks. "What of it, G? They cool."

Tommy Wheeler held up his electronic transmitter as Jermichael's 'Vette flew by his car. He waited until it was another block up the street from him.

"I don't know," Jermichael said uneasy. "Sound too much like a set-up to m . . ."

Tommy pressed the button and sent the signal to the receiver on the bomb under Jermichael's Corvette. He saw the flash under the Corvette lift the entire vehicle about a foot or two off the pavement. Before gravity pulled the car back to earth a holocaust engulfed the body and cab, blowing out all the windows and sending balls of fire skyrocketing from the interior of the cab. The smoldering 'Vette slammed back down on the pavement and lifelessly veered left into the other lane. It smacked into an older car parked in front of a house, bounced up in the air on impact one more time, and crashed down to rest on the sidewalk.

Before the 'Vette even stopped rocking, Tommy Wheeler was speeding down a side street. He knew Jermichael DeVries and his number two man were already incinerated down to their bones. He'd done this before.

He watched through his rear-view mirror and whispered, "One down, two to go."

Detective Kirkland couldn't believe he was pulling into Kay Falco's driveway with his entire family in the car. He never, *never* mixed his family up with his cases and suspects. This world was far too dangerous to even consider pulling such a stunt. But here he was at 8:30 on a Friday night doing just that.

He and his family watched Ray on all three Pittsburgh six o'clock news broadcasts. Shaniqua and LaTonya switched back and forth between two channels, proudly watching their father. Ray videotaped the channel he thought had done the best job at his press conference. To help them celebrate his television spots (he could have cared less), he took them all to Pizza Hut for supper, and then to Hank's Ice Cream in New Brighton for dessert. On the way home, between vanilla ice cream slurps and crunching cones, Ray explained to Shelly how he had begun to pick up some new signals from Holy Spirit that afternoon after he'd confronted the Veros in Carmichael's office at VECO.

"Actually, it started after I had lunch with Tony Vero and then went to his house for the search," he confided.

"You mean you're picking up on things about Tony Vero?" Shelly asked.

"Well . . . yeah. Like that vision I had of Kay Falco this week before I even met her. There's some spiritual battle going on here in this Todd Falco case. And I'm beginning to see there are things, spiritually, I mean, that I'm not getting about Tony Vero."

"Like what?"

"I don't know! That's what I'm saying. He's a mess! I believe he's got an even bigger load of sin and depression on him than Kay Falco does. I do feel like we need to pray for Kay Falco some more, though. She seems ripe for the harvesting, if you ask me. She's really at a place where she needs Jesus."

"Raymond," Shelly said. Ray didn't like it when she called him "Raymond" like that. That usually meant she was about to get him to do something he didn't like. "We need to go see Kay Falco and minister to her in person."

"No way . . ." Ray was about to put his foot down and become adamant. But his wife and daughters all immediately stepped on that adamant foot of his.

"Yeah, Daddy!" eldest Shaniqua chided. "We want to go see that baby of hers." The girls swooned over little baby Dylon when they saw him and Kay on the news.

"You all do not know what you're talking about," Ray said. "We are *not* going to go to the house of . . ."

"Raymond," Shelly repeated in *that* tone of voice, "That little woman I saw on the news tonight is about the most broken thing I've ever seen on two feet. I mean she is just plain *hopeless*."

"We wanna see the baby!" LaTonya spoke up. "Now, Daddy! Do what Mommy says!"

"Yeah!" Shaniqua joined in. "Mommy's right! You need to go pray for that lady in person!"

"And see the baby!" LaTonya laughed.

"What is this?" Ray protested. "Three women against one man!" He looked up, "That's why I wanted a son, God! You three need to listen to the head of the household, here . . ."

Shelly chuckled. "You know that's not going to work in this case. You're trying to be disobedient to Holy Spirit!"

"I am *not* going to take my family to the home of a suspected drug dealer! And Kay Falco's a possible suspect in her husband's disappearance!"

"I thought you said you believed her and that she was telling you the truth?" Shelly said.

"Well, I do . . . but I could be wrong! I've missed it before. I'm not a perfect prophet."

"You aren't missing it!" Shelly upbraided him.

"If Sheriff DeBona found out I was taking my family to suspect's homes and praying with them . . ."

"Since when have you cared about what Sheriff DeBona thought about your ministering to people? What's he gonna do, put you in charge of Missing Persons? He's already done that!"

"Well . . ." Ray could think of no other protest; they had him cornered. Shelly's idea about personally visiting Kay Falco must have been the Lord, and he was indeed bucking it.

"You sound like a pharisee, Raymond, worrying about what people might think if you went to minister to a lost person in one of your cases. Would Jesus care about that?"

"W. W. J. D., Daddy!" Shaniqua said. "W. W. J. D.! What would Jesus do?"

Instantly, Shaniqua and LaTonya were both chanting "W. W. J. D." non-stop.

"Okay! Enough!" Ray raised his voice, but laughed a bit, too. "I'm gonna W. W. J. D. you!"

"I know we need to go see her, Ray. Right now."

He knew she was right. He was still uncomfortable about the situation, though.

"If you weren't so beautiful . . ." he laughed. "I just don't won't my family getting around these criminal types in my cases. I worry about you all . . ."

"'Let your light shine before men, that they may see your good works and glorify your Father in heaven,'" Shelly quoted Jesus from the Sermon on the Mount. "You got a whole family full of light. Now let's go shine it on Kay Falco's darkness and let God worry about all that other mess you're talking about."

Ray and Shelly locked their brown eyes. He reached over and held her hand. They gazed lovingly at each other as he drove.

"Well, kiss her, Daddy!" LaTonya commanded.

Through her curtains Kay Falco saw headlights pulling into her driveway. She didn't know who would be coming to her house at 8:30 at night. A frightening thought suddenly dropped into her mind:

"That better not be Larsky!" she whispered, trying to psych herself up in case it was. She went to the living room window, baby Dylon in hand, and peeked out the curtains. She saw a gray Taurus station wagon parked there with its lights still on. She could make out figures inside. It looked like a black family. Kay then recognized the tall powerhouse who stepped out of the driver's side.

She ran to the front door. She saw Mrs. Kirkland getting out of the car too, and heard Ray telling his daughters to stay in the car until he said it was all right. Kay met Ray and Shelly on her front porch stoop.

"Mrs. Falco?" Ray said, uncharacteristically nervous. "I hope we're not bothering you tonight . . ."

"No. Not at all," Kay said. Her heart was thumping, she was so glad to see somebody. She wondered what he was doing bringing his whole family to her house.

Ray guided Shelly up to Kay. "This is my wife Shelly," he introduced. Shelly and Kay shook hands politely. "We were driving around tonight . . . and got to talking . . ."

Shelly took over. "Mrs. Falco, when we were driving I just felt the urging of Holy Spirit to come see you and spend some time with you tonight. Would it be all right if we did?"

Tears instantly rolled down Kay's face. "Yes," she sobbed. "I can't believe this!"

"Can't believe what?" Ray asked.

"I . . . I don't pray at all, but tonight, for some reason, I told God that if He could hear me, that I just couldn't bare to be alone tonight," she was barely able to get it out.

"Well He relayed your message to us!" Shelly said with a warm smile.

Kay was trembling. Shelly leaned up and hugged her. Kay rested her head on Shelly's strong shoulder. Shelly could feel the horrible weight of oppression she was bearing from all the trauma of the week. In her strength she took up Kay's burden.

"Uh, my girls were wondering . . ." Ray started, but the next thing he knew Shaniqua and LaTonya slid up from behind him, hands held out to baby Dylon, smiles on their faces. Kay grinned through her tears.

"Would it be all right if the girls took care of your little man?" Ray asked, but Kay was already giving up Dylon to their tender arms.

"Take him to the couch, please," Kay requested with a smile. She put her hands on the Kirkland girls' heads. "They are so beautiful," she remarked.

Inside, Shelly and Ray let Kay download on them. All her hurts, all her pains, all her fears. Todd had never physically harmed her, but his shameless lifestyle had obviously left Kay an isolated, emotional cripple. Meanwhile, the girls fed and played with Dylon, even getting him to giggle once or twice.

After a long while of just listening to Kay pour out her wounded heart, Shelly asked if they could pray for her. Kay was reluctant, but only for a moment. She explained that she just wasn't used to any "God stuff." They laughed and Ray told her they'd break her into it slowly. They laid hands on her, prayed over her, ministered the word to her. They shared their testimonies of God's glorious healing and blessings with her. Finally, Ray shared what salvation was with her and asked her if she wanted to invite Jesus Christ into her heart. She frankly told them she didn't think she was ready to make Christ her Lord, but she did agree to come to church with them on Sunday.

When the Kirklands left an hour later, Kay Falco was deeply touched and encouraged to go on, the Kirklands were blessed for their obedience to Holy Spirit, and God had an open door into the life of one more person. And He wasn't finished yet.

TWENTY-NINE

At 10:25 that Friday night Frank Kranac was packing his lunch box and thermos, preparing to go in for the eleven to seven shift at Standard Steel.

Tony Vero sat in his Mercedes half a block down the street from Kranac's 6th Avenue College Hill home. The house was pitch dark for most of the night as Tony observed him. Occasionally a light would flick on momentarily in one room, then in another, as Kranac went room to room about whatever business he was up to. But mostly the house was black inside.

"Kranac's a bat!" Tony muttered with disgust at one point. He didn't want to knock on Kranac's door and start questioning the man at his house, in his element. He wanted to follow him to some well-lit area, and confront him there. The Richards brothers told Tony that Kranac worked graveyard shifts. Tony figured the man would have to emerge soon to get into his old black Galaxie 500 out front and go to work.

Around the corner and parked on a side-street from Tony Vero sat Jimmy and Greggy Richards in Greggy's Neon. They were watching Tony watching Frank Kranac's house. They had left Cherries in a huff, got into their car, and followed Tony from far behind when he left. When he drove straight to the College Hill district of Beaver Falls, the Richards brothers knew right away he was heading for Frank's house. They knew Frank's routine: Kranac left for work at 10:35 nightly, like clockwork. Therefore they watched Tony right up until 10:30 and then speed-dialed Frank's number on their car phone. They wanted to put off having to tell him the bad news and incurring his wrath until the last possible moment.

Inside, Frank Kranac's ancient kitchen phone rang as he made a bologna sandwich.

"What," he answered.

"Frankie, listen." It was Greggy Richards. "You're gonna need to go out your back door and meet us in the alley. We'll take you to work tonight. Tony Vero's right now sitting in a gray Mercedes Benz a few houses up from yours waiting for you."

"What?" Frank yelled furiously. "What's he doing looking for *me*?" He slammed down the receiver on the kitchen counter and went into his darkened living room. Peering through the curtains of a front window, Frank Kranac did indeed see someone sitting in a gray Mercedes several houses up 6th Avenue. He stormed back into the kitchen, picked the receiver back up and shouted, "How does he know where I live?"

In the alley behind his house, Frank made Jimmy get out of the passenger's seat and into the back of Greggy's Neon. When the mammoth Kranac plopped into the shot-gun seat, the entire car rocked from his immense weight. Greggy and Jimmy's stomach's did cartwheels. Kranac gazed furiously at Greggy. Jimmy slunk down far in the back. Greggy put the car in gear and sped down the alley with his lights out, so Tony Vero wouldn't see them between the houses. Greggy could feel Frank's dark, soulless eyes burning the side of his head as he stared at him. The eldest brother was terrified, for he was the one who ratted Frank to Tony.

"Tell me right now," Frank growled through gritted teeth, "how that punk knows where I live."

"He . . . he's onto us, Frankie!" Greggy whined as he sped across a street and up into the next alleyway of College Hill. He wanted to get Kranac to work as fast as he could to get him off his back.

Frank brought his mighty right arm down on the Neon's dashboard, his huge fist and meaty forearm connecting with full force. The grates of the defrost vents popped out and bounced around the dash board as the car trembled from the impact. Greggy and Jimmy almost jumped through the roof.

"How could he be onto us?" Frank roared.

Greggy's hands shook on the wheel as he explained. "He's been into Cherries, Frankie! Everyone there told him that you were with Todd Falco that one night, and he somehow knows Bernie Lokawski's involved with Todd. He thinks he's dead." He turned the Neon left onto 37th street and headed north toward West Mayfield, which was just up the road.

"Dead?" Frank asked.

"He told us tonight that he thinks Todd's dead!" Jimmy blurted out. Greggy turned and glared at him for daring to speak. Jimmy continued anyway. "He says he knows he was set up!"

"You two moron's were talking to him about Todd Falco?" Frank yelled.

If Greggy had been flying at light speed they couldn't have gotten to West Mayfield quick enough. "Look, Frankie!" he said. "Tony Vero was waiting for us tonight when we got to Cherries. He'd put all that information together himself just by talking to all those big mouths inside! He knew all this stuff before we ever got there."

"He thinks Todd was set up by you and Bernie Lokawski!" Jimmy said, voice quivering. "And he knows Greggy and I are the ones who got you into Cherries to buy a membership."

"But he's still looking for Bernie!" Greggy explained. "He thinks you're the only one who knows Bernie Lokawski. He wants you to lead him to Bernie. That's why he's sittin' outside your house right now."

"That's what I keep askin' y'ins," Frank said, his bear chest heaving up and down like a giant bellows. "How does that little Vero punk know where I live?"

There was the Corner Tavern bar on the right. Greggy turned the Neon left again, tires squealing from the speed at which he was driving. He could see Standard Steel down the road on the left.

"Answer me!" Frank yelled again.

Neither of the Richards would. Frank Kranac turned completely around in his seat, looking ready to pounce on Jimmy. He looked down at the youngest Richards with the evil eye. Jimmy's knees were shaking violently. He held his trembling hands up to his throat, trying to protect himself from Frank's wrath.

"Did you tell Tony Vero where I live, you little cockroach?" Frankie whispered demonically. "Did you rat me out to him?"

Jimmy cowered as deeply into the seat as he could and shook his head back and forth.

"N-n-n-no!" he barely whispered.

Kranac turned his entire body in slow motion back over toward Greggy. Greggy gripped the steering wheel like a vice. His hands still trembled.

"So it was *you*!" Frank Kranac snarled in Greggy's right ear as he drove. "You ratted me out to him!" Greggy could feel his hot breath on his face, could taste its very stench in his mouth and nose.

Greggy quickly steered his car into Standard Steel's parking lot, tires spitting out gravel as he drove as quickly as he could up to the check-point gate and slammed on brakes to let Frank out. He hoped whoever was in the guard booth would be visible enough to keep Frank from hurting him there in the car. An elderly man sat in the booth, looking at a portable television. He paid Greggy's Neon no attention.

"Look, Frankie!" Greggy explained, voice breaking with exasperation. "He said he was going to take all that information he'd gotten from those pukes in Cherries straight to the police if I didn't tell him! He said he'd just let the law handle all us! I had no choice! I knew you were smart enough to handle Tony Vero! I knew we could all take him and get him out of the way just like we did all the . . . well, you know! So I just bought you a little time! Jimmy and I will help you do what needs to be done! And, of course, we'll do it for free this time since . . ."

Frank held his left hand up in the air, signaling for Greggy to shut up. Greggy did. Frank looked straight ahead into the dark of night. He appeared to be calming down some, his chest was heaving with less ferocity than before. He sat pensive for a moment, as though he was working out a plan. He finally broke his silence, sounding the calmest he had since he answered the phone when they first called him a few minutes earlier:

"You two get back to that bone yard as fast as you can this weekend and get things ready for Tony Vero." He turned and looked at Greggy. "Hear me, and hear me good: you keep tabs on him for the rest of the weekend. Don't let him get out of this town. Do you understand me?"

They both yes-yessed him with reverent fear.

"We're gonna have to take care of him fast. But we need to get all our mess in order, first."

Jimmy asked, "But what about Bernie Lokawski? Tony's after him pretty bad."

"Bernie's tracks are well covered. He'll never find him. You let me worry about that. Now, do you both understand what I've told you to do? Or do I need to tear out one of your hearts just to ensure that the other moron will do exactly what I'm telling you to do right now?"

They both no-noed him.

"Then get things ready. The next time I call you this weekend, you better be ready to take Tony Vero for me. You got that, morons?"

They assured him they did. Both of them felt relieved, especially Greggy. They escaped what surely would have been Frank's angriest burst of wrath they'd ever seen.

Frank cracked his door open an inch and bent down to get his lunch box and thermos. Greggy's stomach muscles relaxed. Frank was finally going to get out of his car. The guard in the booth suddenly stood up and limped into Standard Steel's main building.

In less than a second Frank dropped both lunch box and thermos back to the floor, and like lightning rammed his right forearm up under Greggy's chin, slamming his head back against the driver's side window. Frank's elbow connected with the window and cracked it into a giant spider's web. Greggy's windpipe was instantly closed off. His eyes bulged and his face turned red from lack of oxygen. Jimmy froze in horror, cowering in the back seat.

Frank's face was right up into Greggy's. But, unable to breath now, Greggy could not smell his breath this time. Frank Kranac's blackened eyes bulged with rage. "I warned you ten years ago never to cross me," he growled. "I told you that you better not ever rat me out."

Greggy was beginning to see stars. Unconsciousness was approaching. But Kranac was far too powerful for him to do anything about it.

Frank finished his warning: "If I do go down because of you, if Tony Vero gets to me and tries to do me in for all this, *you* Greggy Richards, *you* will be the one I kill first. Even before I kill Tony Vero!"

Frank swung his forearm up under Greggy's chin, releasing his throat, but knocking his head back against the window. Greggy fell forward over his steering wheel, gulping air, chest heaving. Jimmy gasped, too, relieved that Frankie hadn't killed his older brother. Kranac exited the car before they knew it, the Neon bouncing up and down from the release of his great weight. When Jimmy saw that Kranac was inside the mill, he got out of the back seat and jumped up front with Greggy.

"Wow! Jimmy said relieved, slamming the door. "That was close!"

Greggy, massaging his throat and panting for his life, glared at Jimmy. "Close?" he wheezed. "You idiot! Did you see what he just did to me?"

"Well, yeah," Jimmy said. "But I was afraid he was going to do it to me!"

"If I have any more coffee I'm gonna be up all night!" prayer warrior Audra Dutton laughed as her hostess filled her cup one more time.

The pastor's wife of St. John's A.M.E. Church of Beaver Falls liked to have the over-forty-single and widowed ladies of her church over several Friday nights a month for food and fellowship. They had share times, Bible studies, prayer, whatever these precious women needed for encouragement and nurturing. Pastor Cole Jenkins and his wife Janette were atypical shepherds for St. John's, a church used to traditional, dry preachers. They were full of passion, compassion, and truly longed to see Christ's kingdom established on the earth. So Janette Jenkins was pleased to open up her house the second and forth Friday of the month for fun and ministry. The older singles all looked forward to it. Especially widowed Audra Dutton, and her divorced friend and committed prayer partner Sharon Harrison.

It was almost a quarter to eleven, and Janette Jenkins realized they'd chatted and laughed so much that they'd not even gotten to any prayer requests. So, desiring to send them all home soon, Janette spoke up.

"Ladies. Ladies! I would like us to end in prayer tonight. Are there any prayer re . . ."

"Right here!" Audra Dutton stood up, waving her hand. The other ladies all laughed. Audra always had prayer requests. She always wanted them to pray with her, to be in agreement with her. And the other women already knew what she was going to ask for:

"I need you all to pray in agreement for my burden!"

Audra had shared the details of her burden before with these fine women. They knew it was for those people responsible for her son's death. They knew she didn't even know for whom she was praying, since no one ever found out who Orlando was buying drugs from when he died. Some of the women believed in her burden. Some did not. Some believed her but thought she took it too far. Many judged her, but were either patient with her or too afraid to dispute her. So they often prayed with her despite what they thought.

Soon the room full of women were praising and glorifying the Father. They all quickly felt the presence of Holy Spirit fill the room. The anointing poured heavily over them, preparing them for intercession. Janette, Audra and Sharon Harrison quickly sensed Christ equipping them to lift up Audra's burden. Then they all burst forth. Some prayed in tongues. Some prayed protection and blessing over those drug lords and dealers. Some prayed God's grace and mercy over them, while others spoke words of knowledge and prophetic utterances. Audra prayed for the sons and daughters of those people who were directly responsible for the death of her son. Though they didn't know for whom they were praying, their intercession moved the spirit realm mightily. Their faithful prayers broke through in the lives of two specific people: Benny Miller, the man who personally supplied crack cocaine to Orlando Dutton, and Tony Vero, the son of those men responsible for the distribution of those drugs.

At eleven o'clock Ed Larsky and Tommy Wheeler rendezvoused on a secluded rural road near the Pittsburgh International Airport in Hopewell Township. Larsky left his Ram behind some trees and got into an ancient lime-green Vega with mag-wheels, tinted windows, and runner lights.

"Where in the world did you get this disaster?" he asked Tommy Wheeler as he joined the hit man inside the car.

"This belongs to one of Jermichael DeVries' top enforcers," Tommy grinned proudly as he drove them back to the main highway. "Conspicuous, ain't it?"

"It's perfect," Larsky said, perusing the crusty interior. "Every witness to Stephen McClintlock's drive-by shooting will definitely remember this piece of junk. The cops will have a description in a heartbeat."

"You paid to have all this mayhem look like a gang war. By the time we finish off Benny Miller tomorrow night, it'll look like Stephen McClintlock took out Jermichael DeVries, and DeVries hit McClintlock and Miller. That oughtta keep the cops so confused they'll be chasing their own tail for months."

"I heard on the scanner that DeVries and his number two G were found dead on the scene, crisp and toasty in his car. Beautiful."

"A walk in the park. I could've done all three of them the same way if you hadn't wanted to make it look like a gang war. But Mr. McClintlock's gonna be the easiest of the three. DeVries and Miller are gang bangers. Tough, protected. But McClintlock's one of those tree-hugging environmentalist fruitcakes. He deals drugs and he deals big, but he's more concerned with the rain forests and endangered species than he is with being a gang banger. He donates a lot of his profits to Green Peace and other radical animal rights organizations. He's so self-righteous. He sells drugs, but uses the money to save Mother Earth."

"He must think he's some sort of Peter Pan," Larsky commented.

Tommy Wheeler stared over at him. "You mean Robin Hood."

"Whoever," Larsky snarled. "He's about to become extinct."

"Bees always go for the honey," Tommy said in a low voice. "When you wanna get to the man, always use their women."

Larsky and Wheeler were watching Stephen McClintlock's guard, standing next to McClintlock's Ford Explorer, smoking a cigarette. They were in the ugly Vega down the road from McClintlock's Hopewell Township farmhouse, located off a long country road far from civilization. About thirty cars lined both sides of the road in front of the farmhouse and packed an open lot beside it where the Explorer was parked and being guarded. A barn out back was well lit with noisy grunge music blasting into the night air. The rumbling bass shook the entire area. It reminded Larsky of a Family meeting.

"That's quite a gig McClintlock has going. He does this every Friday?" Larsky asked.

"Just about. Inside you'll find weed, coke, beer and booze, and an assortment of all the sweetest lookin' college chicks from Pitt, Duquesne, Point Park, Carlow, you name it. Stephen's a major supplier to the campuses of Pittsburgh, and one of those suave, older men the younger chicks all swoon over. He's Mr. Environmentalist do-gooder, gives the chicks his collegiate lines, hooks them with his esoteric philosophies, then gets them under his charming spell. He lures them out here on Friday nights to party with him and his friends. But he's picky; we couldn't have gotten any of our Plague sisters in here. If McClintlock doesn't okay the babe, she don't come in."

"You've done your homework," Larsky commented.

"You didn't mark three pikers for death this weekend, my brother. Miller, DeVries, and McClintlock are the big boys of the region. Everybody who's somebody in the underworld knows their MOs. Didn't even take me four phone calls to nail this one. You ready to put out the honey for this bee?"

"I'm with you. This one's your baby."

Tommy Wheeler pulled out a cellular phone and hit the speed-dial. One of the two Plague women who distracted DeVries' number two man earlier that evening answered.

"Now," is all Wheeler had to say. He hung up. "This bee we're trying to sting doesn't want his old lady to know that he pollinates here on the weekends. He's convinced her that he makes drug runs on Friday nights. Our girl is right now dialing his cell phone. His guard there is holdin' it for him and he's gonna answer it. She's gonna act like his old lady and fuss that Nimrod out, wanting to know why Stephen didn't answer his own phone. The guard'll tell her they're at a rest stop or some nonsense and that Stephen's in the John or something. Then he's gonna run into that barn as fast as he can and get McClintlock. He's gonna want to answer her immediately, so she doesn't get suspicious. He'll come to the parking lot so she can't hear all that noise. That's what's gonna get him out into the driveway for us to nail him."

They watched McClintlock's guard standing by the Explorer. Suddenly, he jumped, threw down his cigarette, opened the door. McClintlock's phone was on the front seat. A few seconds later, he was jumping back out of the truck and running fast to the barn.

Larsky shook his head. "I'm impressed! You've definitely earned your sixty grand!"

"Get ready, brother," he told Larsky.

The two donned identical masks of a horror movie character and drew their weapons: Tommy had the two 9 mm handguns; Larsky had the machine gun and the sawed-off shot gun.

Tommy cranked the engine and steered the car slowly out onto the road with no lights. They watched some people standing around the cars in the lot beside the house. He let the car crawl slowly down the rural road, hidden behind the line of cars on the side. He stopped the Vega right beside the last car near the entrance of the driveway. Larsky pushed open the Vega's poorly made custom sun roof and rolled down his passenger's window. He stood up through the roof, shotgun in his left hand, machine gun in his right. His gut barely fit through the tight hole.

Stephen McClintlock, his guard, and one of his top pushers emerged from the shadows between the house and the barn into the lot. McClintlock looked more like a grungy college student than a high priced drug dealer. He had a bleached blond Julius Caesar haircut, a gotee beard, and a thick silver necklace around his throat. He wore jeans, a white T-shirt with an environmentalist message, and a flannel shirt he had tied around his waist. His guard and pusher dressed similarly.

"Three tree-huggers," Larsky sneered.

They were heading toward the Ford Explorer, not fifteen yards from the Vega.

"Bee coming for the honey!" Tommy reported with glee.

"Wait for my signal!" Larsky spoke down into the Vega.

McClintlock pointed his key chain toward the Explorer. The alarm system "BLEEP-BLEEPED" loudly. He and his boys were about ten steps from the truck when Larsky growled, "Now!"

The waiting Vega suddenly exploded with sight and sound. High beam lights, runner lights, and hip-hop music suddenly split the air as Tommy stomped the gas pedal and squealed into the lot as fast as he could. McClintlock and his men were startled by the spectacle of the Vega suddenly blaring onto his property. Tommy steered the Vega directly at the trio. Blinded in the high beams, McClintlock and his guard caught on fast. They each drew handguns, but they were too late. Larsky pointed the shotgun at the trio and pulled both triggers. The hail storm of penetrating shot pellets left McClintlock and his two men bewildered. Before they could stagger for cover, the machine gun and both 9 mm pistols were frantically tearing them up, along with the Explorer and the earth around them. The party-goers in the lot screamed and scrambled for cover. Larsky and Wheeler fired non-stop at McClintlock until they were satisfied by the looks of the carnage that he was dead. Before they were through, though, they turned their gunfire upon others in the parking lot, sadistically wounding five other people, and decommissioning as many vehicles as they could. Satisfied with their wrath, Larsky disappeared back inside the Vega, Wheeler flung the vehicle back around in a doughnut, and steered the screeching car back onto the road. They laughed, demonically charged, as the funky Vega sped back toward the main highway.

So in less than three hours that Friday night, the Family had rewarded two of its three biggest money makers by snuffing out their lives. All because Todd Falco had disappeared.

The next morning the news media would report that an apparent gang war had broken out in Beaver County.

"One suspected drug leader and his associate were killed by a car bomb explosion in Aliquippa. His rival and his two associates were killed in a drive-by shooting attack in Hopewell that left five bystanders wounded. The police believe both suspects had targeted one another."

Later that morning, the police would arrest the owner of the green Vega for the shooting death of Stephen McClintlock. They would learn that he was a gang enforcer for Jermichael DeVries, the suspect killed by the car bomb. And even though that gang enforcer would vehemently deny having anything to do with the drive-by murder of Stephen McClintlock and his men, they would still search for his accomplice and the motives behind the apparent drug war that had broken out.

Larsky would grin like a shark and tell Carmichael Vero: "Two down, Benny Miller to go."

THIRTY

That night, back in his home, Tony Vero dreamt of a mangled and decaying Gus Savage in Ft. Lauderdale. Eyes wide with terror, the phantasm pointed his bloody, accusing finger at Tony, saying: "Why did you do this to me? Why? You did this to me, Tony! This was your fault! You did it, Tony! Toneeeeeeeee . . ."

Tony awoke, trembling, sweaty, wishing what the apparition told him wasn't true.

At a quarter past one Saturday morning in Columbus, Ohio, Gina Vero was on a mission from God. For real. She was heading to her car to drive two and half hours to Beaver Falls, Pennsylvania. There she was going to see her brother Tony and tell him all about Jesus Christ. And she wasn't even going to let hell stop her. She had just got off work at the popular Italian restaurant where she waitressed for high tips. There her boss had just blown her out for asking him for Saturday night off. He was furious, reminding her that was their biggest business night of the week, and if she couldn't be available, then she could just find another job. But she didn't let that stop her. She would just have to go and be back in Columbus for work by five. She wasn't going to let his hot temper discourage her. Too wired to sleep, she went straight to her car and left immediately.

She prayed as she started toward the turnpike: "Heavenly Father, I ask you to be with me as I go to minister to Tony. Please, Father, dig up the hard, stony ground of his heart right now to prepare him to hear the words that I speak to him about Your Son Jesus. Holy Spirit, anoint me to say what the Father wants me to say regarding the Gospel of salvation. Stop the devil who will come to try and steal the good seed that I'm going to plant in Tony's heart. Send angels to surround me and protect us as we speak. Prepare Tony, now, Father, to hear me and receive Your Spirit. Thank You Father!"

Gina Vero was ready for anything.

Detective Ray Kirkland had a dream that night, too:

He saw Tony Vero lying in the middle of a darkened room, on his back, eyes closed, hands folded together on his chest. He appeared to be breathing peacefully, but was unmoving. Above him the hand of God was descending, as though the Lord wanted to touch Tony. From the darkness around him, the enemy suddenly appeared in the form of grotesque human figures, dark and oozing evil. These figures were all holding swords, guns, knives, and spears, seeking to kill Tony. So there lay Tony Vero, breathing but still, with both the Creator trying to lay hold of him, and the enemy trying to kill him, but neither one having reached him yet. To Ray it looked like some sort of spiritual race to see who would get Tony first, Heaven or hell. Suddenly, in the dream, Ray heard Holy Spirit speak to him: "Who will get Tony?"

God's voice woke Ray up. He slid out of bed, got down on his knees and listened to the ever present voice of His Father:

"Who will get Tony?" He asked again. "Will I get him or will satan? Who will get him?"

Ray had to be honest. "I don't know, Lord. Who will get him?"

"The one of us who gets our people to him first. If My intercessors and witnesses get to him first, I get him. If satan's people do first, he gets him. Tony Vero is My chosen vessel. I anointed him with My purpose and potential when I formed him in his mother's womb. My call on him is great, yet remains buried and uncultivated. The enemy wants to uncover it and warp it for his desires and purposes. The enemy sees the potential I create within all people. He either gets to people first and usurps that potential for himself, or destroys them all together.

"You've only seen Tony Vero as a hindrance to your case; someone who is standing between you and the truth. I do not see him this way. He is a life that I created for My purposes. I want to bring Tony Vero into My kingdom. I want to bless him to fulfill My destiny and purpose for his life. He is not just a barrier to your police work. He is of my choosing. Yet the enemy literally seeks to kill him. Tony's very life is in danger. If my people do not intercede for him and reach him for Me, he and My destiny for his life may be lost forever, and the enemy will successfully destroy My word that I spoke over him in his mother's womb. Quit looking at him with your carnal eyes, seeing him only as a lawbreaker. Pray that you may see him as I do. Be My ambassador to him, and trust Me with him and your case."

Ray was floored by what he heard. He was ashamed of his selfishness and ignorance toward the Father's heart for Tony Vero. Yet God encouraged his faithful son:

"Ray: who gets Tony?"

Ray nodded his head. "If I have anything to do with it, You do."

THIRTY-ONE

In the darkness of Saturday morning, Tony Vero sat in his recliner, lights and television on, batting a paddle ball up and down in perfect rhythm. He could not get back to sleep after his latest Gus Savage nightmare hours earlier. So he sat sleepily in his living room, watching the tube, hoping for the daylight to shine soon so he could crash on his couch and catch a few hours sleep before he went back after Frank Kranac. The Family would soon demand concrete results in his search for Todd Falco and their money. Kranac was his primary link. He was all that stood between him and Falco. Tony was going to get him.

His thoughts drifted to Kay Falco. How he wished they didn't. But he couldn't get her fawn-ish brown eyes out of his head, the arch of her neck, her sandy blond hair, her wedding ring . . .

Even though Todd Falco was missing, she was still married to him. He sat upright in his chair to jolt himself out of those pleasant visions. He'd been with many women, but never a married one. For some reason, that bothered him.

He thought about the police removing his file cabinets and computer from his house. They wouldn't find any incriminating evidence. He was always cautious about not keeping any trace of the Family in his personal files. Same with VECO. The police carted all that material out of the VECO office buildings the day before, but Carmichael was too smart for the police. They'd get nothing. That Detective Kirkland was a trip. His white, flashing smile. His infectious joy. His genuine faith in Jesus. Was that guy for real? He and Tony's sister Gina needed to get together, the way they acted like God was real. Then a thought blindsided the tired young man: What if God is real?

That sobered him. He safely went back to thinking about Kay Falco.

Suddenly, headlights illuminated his living room curtains. A car was pulling into his driveway. He looked at the clock: 3:55 am. Who'd be coming to see him at this time of the morning? The cops to arrest him? Larsky to strangle him? He threw down the paddle ball. Carefully avoiding the broken glass that still littered the living room floor, he stepped over to the window to see if he could get a glimpse of who it was. It was Gina.

"Well speak of the devil. Or angel."

Gina's knees were shaking as she got out of the car, carrying an overnight bag. Why was she so nervous? This was only Tony. She never got along with her Dad or Uncle Carmichael, but she and Tony and Uncle Joseph had always been close. So what was making her so jittery? *Help me, Lord!* she prayed. She was glad all the lights were on in the house. At least it appeared Tony was home. She stepped up onto the front porch. Before she could ring the doorbell, the front door swung open.

"Hey, Sis," Tony greeted her.

She was elated to see Tony. She stepped up and gave her younger brother a long hug. "Thank you, Jesus," she whispered.

"No, I'm Tony," he said into her ear. She giggled, then stepped back and guffawed when she looked at his messy, puffed up hair.

"Nice bed head, little brother," she laughed as she tried to pat it down.

"I was just thinking about you," Tony told her as he took her bag and led her inside.

"That's funny," Gina said, "'Cause I've been thinking about you for weeks!"

"It's like you're the walking dead, now, Tony," Gina said as they sat on his couch, drinking coffee in the pre-dawn hours.

"It's just bed head!" he joked, patting his wild hair as he gulped some coffee.

She wasn't amused. "You know what I'm talking about! You've been someone else since you came back from Ft. Lauderdale. Uncle Joseph told me you've been locking yourself in here, refusing to talk or see anyone, never leaving. I'm worried about you, Bro."

"Worried about what?" He wanted to distract her, desperately not wanting to discuss Ft. Lauderdale and his breakdown. "Look, I don't know if you're aware of it or not, but I've been out of the house since Thursday morning. In fact I didn't even sleep here Thursday night. I can come and go when I want. I just wanted some time to myself to think . . ."

"Oh, can it, Tony! You can't lie to me. I'm your sister! I know you. You are not a 'hide in the house and get drunk' kind of guy! Now what did Uncle Carmichael do to you in Ft. Lauderdale?"

"What are you, a shrink all the sudden? Carmichael didn't do anything. Don't you worry about Ft. Lauderdale. That was Family business and it's over and finished."

"When Dad talked about 'Family business' it usually meant felony crimes, if not murder itself!"

"Get off it!"

"No, Tony, I won't! I came here for a reason! I never did understand your decision to go to work for Uncle Carmichael when you quit college. Carmichael's our uncle, and I love him as family, but he's the reason Pop had a heart attack in his mid fifties. The Family and all it represents is what drove Mom to anti-depressants and booze for the last six years of her life, until she finally killed herself . . ."

"No one knows if Mom killed herself or not, Gina! She left no notes and the doctors all said it could have been an accident . . ."

"Do you remember that burned out shell of a hag Mom became at the end of her life? Huh, Tony? You were fifteen when she died. Don't tell me you don't remember what she became, what she was like then. Well, Tony, that same zombie stare she had in her eyes toward the end, that's what's in your eyes, now! It's the Family stare!"

"Comments like that aren't going to win friends, Sissy."

"Stop joking! This is serious, Tony! This is your life, your soul we're talking about!"

"That's just it, Gina!" he shouted, getting up from the couch, "I don't want to talk about it!"

She stood up too. "Well you're going to! That's why I'm here. Uncle Carmichael and the Family are killing you. You are in trouble, Tony. You are dying on the inside and it shows all over! My outgoing, happy, athletic, fun-loving little brother is dead, now." She pointed her hands at Tony. "And this . . . this lifeless, cynical zombie-man I'm looking at is all that's left. And I blame Uncle Carmichael and the Family. All they know is sin. Sin kills! This is the same thing that happened to Pop, same thing that happened to Mom. Death! The only thing left now is for you to physically lay down and give up the ghost."

Tony felt like he was awake in the middle of a major surgery. Gina was grabbing him at the root of all that was destroying him. He knew she was right, but saw no solution to the problem. He just wanted to find Falco and the Family's money and disappear forever.

Gina saw the hopelessness in his eyes. She put her hand on his shoulder to stop him from leaving the living room. "It's one thing to be dead, Tony. But I know Someone who has the power to cleanse you of all your sins and bring you back to life."

Frank Kranac got home from work at 7:20 that Saturday morning. He double checked to make sure the house doors were locked, tossed his lunch box and thermos onto the kitchen counter and headed straight for the cellar. He unlocked the door, descended the stairs, and turned on the light. There was no time for sleep.

He had to see his money. In his basement, he began to move the large crates that covered the carpet that hid his buried fourteen million dollar fortune. He pulled back the carpeting and wood, exposing the huge stacks of cash. He sat down at the edge of the pit and pored his eyes over all that money. Frank Kranac was possessed of a miserly spirit. He didn't know it, but that's what gripped his soul, a demonic spirit of avarice. All Frank Kranac knew to do with money was hoard it. People who saw him thought him to be either quite poor or at best eccentric. Most of his clothes were at least ten years old. He had the same boots and shoes that he'd worn since the seventies. He would pay cheap cobblers to replace their souls when they wore out. He lived with ancient appliances because to buy new ones would cost him some of his money. If they broke, he repaired them. In all his years of accumulating that money in his pit, he never once spent one dime of it. He paid his meager bills and bought what little groceries he ate with his machinist's pay from Standard Steel. His electric bills were ridiculously low. In the winter, he never turned his thermostat above fifty degrees. He wore heavy clothes to keep him warm. He lived to his detriment so he never had to touch the money. He had no long term plans for what to do with the money. He had no investment schemes for it, no laundering ventures, no plans or goals for it whatsoever. That miser spirit wouldn't allow it. Instead, he lived in complete fear and bondage to his money. They only thing that registered in his warped spirit regarding that fourteen million dollar fortune hidden in his house was one constant, angst-ridden question: *What if I lose it all?* He thought it was great to sit there and stare at it for hours. But his primary feelings toward it were merely: *What if I lose it?* Therefore, it never brought him happiness, it never brought him joy, and it surely never brought him contentment. Frank Kranac's fortune only brought him fear and bondage. If he were to spend it, some of it would be gone, and he'd have less. Then soon he'd spend more of it, and there would be even less. And eventually, if he started to spend it, it would all be gone. And that would kill him, for all he had was this money. It was his security. And that miser spirit that bound his soul would take him round and round and round with these feelings of elation and fear, elation and fear. That's all that Frank Kranac was.

So in his isolation at work, Kranac had spent the entire night planning to protect his buried treasure. He needed to deal with Greggy and Jimmy Richards, but most of all, he needed to take care of Tony Vero. Tony Vero was the number one threat to Frank Kranac's hidden fortune. He was the real trouble maker. He represented the people who would come gunning for them if the whole truth about Todd Falco was ever uncovered. He was the enemy of all that Frank Kranac believed to be security. He figured Tony Vero was working for the people who supplied Todd Falco the money to buy those drugs. Kranac had been in the criminal world long enough to spot a middle man, and he smelled Todd Falco a mile away. That white collar pretty boy didn't have millions of dollars lying around to buy cocaine. He figured Todd bought and sold for a powerful organization. In turn, these same people hired Tony Vero to hunt down Todd and the money. And that Vero was pretty good, to have already somehow traced Falco to Bernie Lokawski and Frank. He had to deal with Tony Vero swiftly.

After minutes of just staring at his fortune, with his mouth cottony and his hands clammy, Frank Kranac sighed and slid down into the money pit. And slowly, ever so slowly, he meticulously began the long accounting process that drove his tormented soul. He had to count every bill to ensure he hadn't lost even the slightest amount of his fortune.

He *had* to.

At 9:25 that Saturday morning, Pennsylvania State Attorney General Michael Davis sat in his Harrisburg office listening to Edgar Waters' recording. He listened to Tony Vero's dissertation to Kay Falco about his Great Uncle Carmichael. In that one speech, Tony revealed every truth Michael Davis had sought after all those years since Carmichael Vero's infamous trial and acquittal back in Beaver County, Pennsylvania. The tape was excruciating for Davis to hear. Tony Vero's account of Ed Larsky's assassination of the prosecutor's star witness was like having an ancient wound suddenly torn open and exposed all over again. The humiliation, the defeat, the helplessness, all those negative feelings were suddenly dredged up within the powerful state attorney general.

When the tape was over, Davis hit the stop button, leaned back in his swivel chair, and took inventory of his heart. He knew he had to be right before the Lord before he could take on Carmichael Vero again after all these years. God had taken him too far, worked too much in the man to let him fall now to a character flaw like revenge.

"'Vengeance is mine, saith the Lord,'" Davis spoke the scripture aloud. "'Pride goeth before a fall' . . . 'The Lord is my strength and my shield, I will trust in God my defender,' 'He will uphold me, He will be my defender,' 'He will perfect that which concerns me.'" Davis spun his chair around and looked out the window at the beautiful May morning. If it weren't for Edgar Waters' phone call and recording the day before, Davis would have been spending this day at home with his wife in their lush garden. Instead he was in his office contemplating how to put away Carmichael Vero, a criminal so powerful that he could threaten the peace and safety of Michael Davis and his family. All the old bitter feelings of animosity that God had tried to work out of Davis from all those years past had to be put to death before he ever attempted to tackle Carmichael Vero again. Building a winnable, legally sound case against such a man was going to take so much time, patience and work.

Michael Davis had wanted to reopen the criminal investigations of Carmichael Vero for years. But at every level of his public service he was met with queer resistance. Every law enforcement leader and government official would discourage his every attempt at trying to uncover the truth about Carmichael Vero. "Why?" "You lost your only chance back in 1981." "He's a legitimate business man, now." "VECO's survived three IRS audits, and have come out smelling like a rose, they're so legitimate." "Carmichael Vero's obviously not only reformed himself, but he's been an asset to Pennsylvania's state economy. Opening some new investigation against him now will only look like a bitter political move on your part, Mike." Those were the reactions to his every request, much to his bewilderment. His biggest opponent in recent years had been the chief of the State Bureau of Investigations. The man would no longer even talk to Michael Davis regarding Carmichael Vero. Davis had become sure that there was a major conspiracy in the state government to protect Carmichael at any cost. He became so sure that he secretly launched investigations to expose those ties. But no ties were uncovered between Carmichael Vero and any government employee. There were no ties in the natural. The conspiracy that Michael Davis thought he'd uncovered was in the spirit realm. What Michael Davis had no way of knowing was that all refusals to investigate Carmichael Vero were the direct fruits of Cyrus Moreau's work. Moreau had sent out spells of blindness, confusion, and distraction on government and law enforcement officials all over Pennsylvania, and had effectively built an impenetrable "cloak" of protection around Carmichael Vero and the Family, as Edgar Waters once put it. It was especially effective on the chief of the State Bureau of Investigations. He'd become Carmichael's primary defender, and didn't even know it. Davis' frustration with everyone's lack of desire to investigate the man was reasonable. But it was demonically being challenged. That, Davis could not see. But he did get a major break with Tony Vero's recording. Now he had grounds to launch an investigation.

First his heart had to be pure in the sight of God. "'Commit to the Lord whatever you do and your plans will succeed.' 'The steps of the righteous are ordered of God.'" He meditated on all those scriptures and then prayed: "Father, You have exalted me to this position. I do not wield it lightly. I will vehemently pursue justice. Yet I refuse to allow the works of my flesh to get in the way." He put his hand on his chest. "So I declare that bitterness, unforgiveness, hatred, malice, and all the thoughts and feelings of my flesh toward Carmichael Vero are this day crucified on the cross of Jesus Christ with your Son, and today I am resurrected with Him in life, peace, joy, and victory. You will see me through this case, Heavenly Father. You will be my guide, and as always, Lord, I want to have clean hands and a pure heart before You. Have mercy on me, Lord, for my weak nature, but build me up by Your Holy Spirit to be a man of truth and righteousness, to execute judgment by the laws of this state, and to walk in Your wisdom and guidance. I pray Your protection over my wife and family as I begin to build this case against Carmichael Vero. And I commit all my ways to Your merciful and sovereign hands. I pray all this, Lord, in the name of Christ Jesus Your Son. Amen."

The phone buzzed on his desk. He punched the button.

"Yes, Melanie," he answered his secretary.

"The Governor is on the line, sir, returning your call."

He sat up. "Thank you. I'll take it." He reached down and opened a drawer and pulled out a manila envelope with the name "Harvey Kitner" written on it. He opened it, ejected the "Tony Vero" tape from the recorder, and dropped it into the manila folder with the contents within it. He wondered how the Governor was going to react to all this information.

As he went to push the button for the Governor's line, Michael Davis sighed, thinking about how many years this case against Carmichael Vero was going to take to build. Little did he know, that because he was a humble man in God's sight, and hungered and thirsted after righteousness, that God was going to lay the whole case in his lap within a week.

Cyrus Moreau had spent all night in his mansion with his occult apprentices trying to locate Todd Falco and the Family's million and one hundred thousand dollars. They spoke spells and incantations. They used various occult tools to retrieve information from the spirit realm to break the case for Carmichael Vero. However, he and his cohorts came up fruitless. Cyrus did have a peculiar vision, but it wasn't noteworthy in the Falco case. They'd come against such warfare and spiritual blockades that there could only be one explanation for his failure to meet Carmichael's needs up to this point:

"Christians," Cyrus moaned aloud. "Serious Christians. Praying."

He was still overwhelmed by resistance he met the day before when he was trying to call off his spells of protection over Jermichael DeVries, Stephen McClintlock, and Benny Miller. Rarely had the spirit realm which he "controlled" so vehemently opposed his wishes and commands. And all that night it was as though he and the young male and female sorcerers he was training were running up against one brick wall after another in the case. This would not do. He had too much invested in Carmichael Vero to fail on his behalf now. The Dark Lords were too interested in the Family and their criminal interests for Cyrus to just shrug his shoulders and declare defeat. He needed to get serious. He needed to break this case. He needed . . .

"Blood!" He pulled out a cellular phone and dialed Carmichael's home phone number. Carmichael finally answered. "What?"

"This is Cyrus, Carmichael! What ever happened to a 'Good Morning'?"

"You locate Falco and my money, yet, Cyrus?" Carmichael asked, irritated.

"Well, not exactly . . ."

"Then it's not a good morning. What can I do for you, anyhow, my friend?"

"Tomorrow is the full moon, Carmichael. I keep sensing over and over again that you are in one seriously bad spot right now. I cannot overemphasize how important it would be for you to be here at Alleister Estate tomorrow evening for our 'workshop.' You and Larsky. We'll get the best results for you then."

"Cyrus," Carmichael whined, "I . . . I told you that we have this stockholder's meeting on Tuesday night that we've got to get ready for. Larsky and Joseph and the Zanns are all gonna meet me at VECO today and tomorrow to work on our reports . . . it's just too much to ask . . ."

"So are convictions and jail terms, Carmichael! You are in deep doo-doo right now . . ."

Carmichael snapped: "What am I paying you for, then, Cyrus? I'm sending you a lifetime fortune to take care of all this for me and yet you still want me to clear my slate and fly all the way to New York to see you put on your Halloween costume and . . ."

Both were silent for a moment.

"Cyrus . . . I . . ."

"Fear not, old friend!" Cyrus tried to hide his rage. "I'm gonna chalk that outburst up to plain old fashioned stress and fatigue due to your current situation."

"Th-thank you, because . . ."

"But let me tell you this: you don't pay the doctor to tell him how you want the illness cured. You pay him and he cures the problem however he sees fit! And I, Doctor Cyrus Moreau, Master of the Spirit Realm, am telling you that if you want to see all this mess cleaned up, you better have your shiny behind here tomorrow night for the workshop! Or else, regardless how much money you've paid me, I cannot guarantee your future. And it is a future that you have jeopardized yourself by stubbornly trying to cut me out of the picture these last two years! Now if you want to see a closure to all this, clear your slate and get here tomorrow! Capice?"

"I do," came the humble reply.

"Good!" Cyrus said, much calmer. "And one more thing: Gina Vero has come to Beaver Falls to see Tony. She's come to spread her Gospel of poison in him."

"Gina? How do you know that?"

"I saw her."

"You saw her?" There was silence for a moment as Carmichael was perplexed. "You in Pennsylvania?"

Cyrus groaned with impatience at Carmichael's stupidity. "No, dummy! I am not in Pennsylvania! I am in New York! Where I live! The Dark Lords showed me the vision last night! I saw her in the spirit realm driving to see him! Wake up to the powers I have, please! At least I know Ed Larsky believes in me."

Carmichael, the atheist, still didn't know what to make of all this witchcraft. It still didn't fit into his empirical thinking. He just knew Cyrus produced amazing results.

"You are in charge of watching over my little Tony Vero," Cyrus reminded him. "Don't let his sister get to him and poison him with her sappy Christianity. The Dark Lords lost her to Christianity. Don't let them lose Tony!"

Benny Miller and his well-dressed crew sat in his living room eating breakfast, watching cartoons. Benny happily slurped a bowl of Fruit Loops. Jaws churning and milk dripping down his chin, Benny would "mmmm-mmmm!" with every bite. As usual, his faithful flunkies pretended it wasn't so. A cell phone rang. It was Marcus's. Benny's accountant and advisor laid down his bagel and answered the call. A few seconds later he stood straight up, eyes wide as eggs, and yelled out loud in disbelief.

Benny looked up at his right hand man and yelled, "What up with you?"

Marcus was deeply shocked. He tried to calm down for Benny. "It's Jermichael, Benny. He's dead!"

Benny's countenance plummeted. Every one who worked and stayed with Benny Miller knew that Jermichael DeVries had been the closest thing to a mentor Benny ever had. All eyes fixed on their boss.

"How?" Benny asked with fire in his eyes.

"He . . . he was blown up in his car last night, Benny."

They all watched Benny's bottom lip quiver and his chest heave faster and faster. The drug lord jumped up and threw his cereal bowl against the wall as hard as he could. The explosion of glass, milk, and cereal splattered over some of his gang members and their girls.

"Who did him?" Benny shouted.

"Police are saying it was Stephen McClintlock . . ." Marcus began.

"Then he's mine! Call out a hit on that . . ."

"Benny!" Marcus held up his hand. "Someone smoked Stephen McClintlock last night, too."

"They was both killed last night?" Benny asked.

Marcus nodded. Benny and Marcus stared at each other silently, each reading the other's mind. All eyes were on them.

"You're now the number one G north of Pittsburgh, Benny," Marcus spoke out loud what they both were thinking.

Benny was stunned, but he was still capable of leading his operation. "I want everyone battle ready. Now!" He commanded. The room exploded with action, everyone running to and fro. "All girlfriends, out of here! Load your pieces, call in all our boys off the streets, get all our products off the streets, go to your holes and crawl in 'em!"

Benny and Marcus left the living room to go up stairs. On the way Benny looked out his front door: no guard. Benny furiously ran up the steps. He looked up and down the hallway. In one of the guest bedrooms down the hall he saw a pair of Jordans hanging off the side of a bed. Benny turned on his heals and stomped down to that room, knowing full well who was in there. He kicked open the door the rest of the way and found the seventeen year old named Horace Weston passed out on the bed. It was Horace's turn for guard duty in front of Benny's house.

Marcus came in behind Benny. He shook his head with disgust at Horace, who was derelict in his duties. They'd had this problem with him twice before. "Want me to wake him up?" he asked Benny.

"Nah," Benny said, "don't wake him up. He has a job and family as long as he's asleep!"

Still enraged from the news about Jermichael DeVries, Benny went over and snatched the young gang banger up off the bed by his red shirt. Horace awoke with a start. Fear came over him when he realized what was happening. Benny could see by his reddened eyes that he'd been smoking their crack again. He smacked him three times hard across his face.

"This how you guard my house when we're at war, crackhead?" Benny shouted.

Horace Weston moaned and tried to explain he didn't know they were on alert. Benny took him by the shirt, escorted him down the hall, and pushed him hard down the stairs. The young man rolled down one flight and banged his head and shoulders against the wall. Bewildered and frightened, he struggled to get up as fast as he could. He knew he'd blown his last chance with Benny. As he hurried out the front door in shame he heard Benny yelling:

"We'll see how well you survive a war out on your own, dead crackhead man!"

THIRTY-TWO

Gina Vero talked to Tony about Jesus Christ for almost an hour and a half before sun-up that Saturday morning. She was very pleased with how it went. At first Tony listened to her testimony emotionlessly, and she thought maybe she wasn't getting through to him. But after a while he suddenly began to ask direct questions about Jesus, the Bible, and how He'd affected her life. He didn't open up to her about what happened in Ft. Lauderdale, but he asked questions about God's forgiveness that led her to understand he felt horribly guilty about something. He didn't want to pray the sinner's prayer of salvation with her, but he did let her put her hands on him and pray for him. She boldly prayed that Jesus would open Tony's eyes to the Gospel of salvation, that Holy Spirit would enlighten to Tony his need for repentance and to receive Jesus as Savior, and that God would send His angels to protect Tony and lead him to other saints of God to be a witness to him of God's salvation. Tony never said a word as she prayed. He just sat on the couch and stared at the television, but he didn't protest or reject anything she declared, either. By six that morning, Gina was at peace with the results of her mission. She'd said and done everything she'd set out to accomplish in the Lord. Tony felt a little better too, and even was bold enough to tell her so. At that point, the sun was peeking over the horizon and light began to flood the living room. Tiredness overtook them both. Gina went upstairs to her old bedroom, and Tony crashed on the couch, both of them content. Peace had overtaken the Vero house.

Until Uncle Carmichael and Ed Larsky showed up.

Carmichael heeded Cyrus Moreau's warning about Gina. Larsky came to his house that morning for them to have breakfast and then go meet Joseph and the Zanns at VECO. They decided they better check out Tony's house on the way to see if Gina was indeed visiting. If so, she was blatantly disobeying Carmichael's orders to stay away from Beaver Falls forever. They took VECO's limousine so they could have it cleaned later in preparation for VECO's big shareholder's banquet on Tuesday. As Larsky steered the long vehicle into Tony's driveway, Carmichael instantly spotted Gina's car. Amazingly, Cyrus was right again. But Carmichael was too infuriated with Gina's disobedience for him to spend any time in awe of Cyrus's witchcraft.

Tony had been asleep five hours on his living room couch in the warmth of the morning sunlight. There, horrifying dreams of Gus Savage and Ft. Lauderdale were held at bay, and the young man slept in peace. The already angry Carmichael had to ring the door bell for two minutes before Tony was stirred from his slumber. Disoriented, Tony staggered from the couch to the window to see who it was. There sat Uncle Carmichael's limo behind Gina's car.

"I'm pretty popular today," Tony droned. He reluctantly went to the foyer on wobbly legs. He looked out the peephole and saw Carmichael and Larsky both standing there, dressed in expensive leisure outfits. Tony opened the door, knowing full well he was opening it to trouble.

Carmichael stood there, filled with rage. Larsky stood behind him, muscular arms folded, eyes full of contempt for Tony.

"Why, this is a surprise! Good morning, you two!" Tony said, squinting from the bright sunlight.

"What are you doing here?" Carmichael yelled. "It's eleven o'clock and you're here asleep! Why aren't you out looking for Falco?"

"I have been looking for . . ."

"And what's Jesus Freak doing here?" Carmichael demanded to know.

Upstairs in her old bedroom, Gina heard the shouting and woke straight up. She knew it was Carmichael. Frightened, she began to pray. She grabbed her purse and pulled out an address book. She found Uncle Joseph's cell phone number and dialed him quickly.

Tony pointed at Carmichael: "You can come in here," he said. Then pointing to Larsky he said: "But he can't."

"You're not going to tell us who's gonna come into Pete's house and who's not!" Carmichael protested.

"Pete's house?" Tony laughed. "My name's on this deed, now. I pay the taxes. This is my house! And fat head there is not stepping one foot across this threshold."

Larsky growled something unintelligible at Tony. Tony paid him no attention.

"This house was built on Family money!" Carmichael said.

"By Pete, who willed this house to me when he died, so now it's mine, and if you want to come in here, Larsky stays out!"

Joseph spoke to his niece from his car: "I'm on Route 51 near VECO, Gina. I'll be there in two minutes."

Larsky was yelling at Tony from the porch: "The only reason you don't want me in there is because you know I'm gonna break your neck when you tell us you haven't found Falco yet!"

"I don't think they heard you out on Route 51, moron!" Tony yelled at Larsky, who was storming back to the limo. "Why don't you tell everyone what we're doing!"

Carmichael stepped into the foyer, his eyes widening like saucers when he saw the demolished trophy case. "What have you been doing in here, Tony?" he said with disgust, pointing at the mangled debris.

"Oh, I thought I saw a snake in there," Tony quipped. He went into the living room.

Carmichael went to follow him. "You did that? You know, I'm beginning to think Larsky has been more right about you than . . ."

Tony turned on him. "You know, I don't care to hear Larsky's opinions from his own mouth, let alone to hear them second hand from yours."

"What are you doing with your investigation? Why aren't you out working right now? And what is Gina doing here, when I've demanded that she never show her face around us again?"

"She didn't come to see you. She came to see me."

"What for?"

"She is my sister!"

"She's trying to lay that holy roller mess about Jesus on you, isn't she?"

"What we talk about is none of your business."

"Oh, yeah?" Carmichael stormed over to the foot of the staircase and looked upstairs. "Your Holiness!" he shouted. "Holy Jane?" he roared. "Why don't you come down here and let me remind you what I commanded you to do when you decided you were too good for us?"

Tony went over to Carmichael. "Leave her alone!"

"You and your fake religion aren't going to brain wash any of *us*!"

"That's it, Carmichael!" Tony warned him.

"Who do you think you are now, Gina? Your father was right about you all the time: you are a good for nothing tramp!"

Tony stepped over and grabbed Carmichael by the shoulder of his shirt. As soon as he did he realized it was a grave step to take. Carmichael turned on him like a lion who had been snatched by his tail during a kill. Definitely intimidated, Tony still stood his ground. Carmichael smacked his hand off his shirt.

"Do you realize what you just did, Kid?" Carmichael whispered, eyes filled with maddened disbelief. "If Larsky was in here . . ."

"This is my house!" Tony said. "Gina is my sister. You will not humiliate her in my house."

"You do not tell me what to do! I rule the Veros!"

"Once I find Falco and your filthy money, you don't rule me anymore."

"You impudent punk!" Carmichael raised his hand in the air. "I oughtta . . ."

"That's enough Uncle Carmichael!" Gina shouted from the top of the stairs. "Here I am! Don't take your hatred for me out on Tony."

Carmichael and Gina locked eyes. Looking at him, she couldn't believe the utter contempt he held for her.

"Gina, leave us alone," Tony commanded.

"Why are you here?" Carmichael asked her.

"I ask you the same question," Gina replied as she started down the stairs with confidence.

"I am Carmichael Vero. I'll come and go as I please! I give the commands in this family. And I told you to never show your trashy face in Beaver Falls again!"

"Tony is my brother," she said calmly. "If I want to visit him, I have the right. I didn't come to your house, Uncle Carmichael. I came to Tony's."

Carmichael pointed a finger at her as she reached the bottom step. "You disgraced this family, your father, the Vero name itself. You are a disgrace, Gina, and . . ."

Tony put his hand back on Carmichael's shoulder. "I warned you not to talk to my sister like that . . ."

He glared up at Tony, but continued after Gina: ". . . and no silly religious conversion is going to erase this one fact: you are a good-for-nothing, drug-addicted slut!"

Gina did not break. She did not whimper or tear up. Instead she held up her head and with passion said: "I was a drug-addicted slut. But Jesus has washed me in His blood. Now I'm the likeness and image of God Himself. Now the only disgraceful thing is the fact that you'd rather curse me and Him and go to hell, than love me as your niece and get to know the changes He's made in my life. If you did that, you'd have to acknowledge He is real, you are a sinner, the Family is a sham, and you need Christ."

Carmichael looked rabid. Tony stood in front of him to keep him back from Gina.

"Those are just words, you little slut!" the elder Vero growled. "You're exactly what you used to be. You are still a little tramp and nothing can change that . . ."

Gina very calmly shook her head and with conviction proclaimed again, "No. You are lying, Carmichael Vero." Still there was peace and strength in her voice. In the past Carmichael's words would have had her broken to bawling by that point. But not any more. She felt the strength of Holy Spirit welling up from within her heart to stand her ground. "I am not those things anymore. What I said is true. It's real. It's grace. God's grace through Jesus His Son. And your hatred for Him and for me doesn't make your lame words true. So you are lying about me now, Uncle Carmichael."

Carmichael completely lost it. "No one calls Carmichael Vero a liar!" He lunged wide-eyed at Gina. Tony grabbed him in a bear hug to restrain him. He spewed obscene curses at Gina over Tony's shoulder. Gina took two steps back up the stairs and stood stoically. Tony was frightened, never even imagining his Great Uncle Carmichael was capable of such a guttural rage. Carmichael then began to turn his anger on Tony: "And you, you little . . ." Tony saw Carmichael's right fist swing upward at him. He quickly grabbed Carmichael's arm, twisted it backward, spinning the older man around, and brought it up high into Carmichael's back. Just as Tony was carefully laying Carmichael face down on his floor, Joseph Vero came through the front door. When Joseph saw Tony kneel down on Carmichael's back to restrain him, he quickly slammed the door shut to prevent Larsky from seeing what was happening.

"Tony! Carmichael! What on earth are you two doing?"

"Uncle Joe! Why, it's a Vero family reunion at my house today," Tony panted from atop Carmichael. "Unfortunately, Uncle Carmichael doesn't like our guest of honor."

"Tony," Joseph said, grabbing Tony under his arm to raise him up off his great uncle, "if Larsky had seen this you'd be dead right now. He wouldn't have thought twice, Kid."

Carmichael ordered Tony to get off him. Joseph pulled Tony up out of the way and Carmichael slid out from underneath him and sprung to his feet with surprising agility. Chest heaving, he stared at Tony with hellish offense. Locking his angered gaze on Tony he pointed at Gina and softly growled:

"You would choose the black sheep of the family over the ones who've loved you and nurtured you, Tony? You would choose her over the ones who gave you a second chance at life after Pete died and your football injury ended your career? You'd choose to disobey me to favor this traitor to the Vero name? To the point of physically dishonoring me like you just did? Do you understand what you're becoming, Tony? How ashamed your father would be of you right now?"

Tony stared back at Carmichael and said, "Do you understand how ashamed I am of you and my father, Uncle Carmichael?"

Carmichael smacked Tony hard across his cheek. Gina gasped at the dreadful cracking sound the harsh blow made. Tony took the searing, stinging slap, not flinching one bit, his steely green eyes still locked on Carmichael's. A raspberry red hand print instantly began to swell on his cheek. Joseph shook his head, not wanting to believe this whole surrealistic event.

"That's what your problem is, Tony," Carmichael breathed through gritted teeth: "Pete didn't smack you around enough to straighten you out. Maybe if he had you'd have sense enough to side with us instead of your outcast sister."

"Both of you stop!" Joseph commanded. "I cannot believe what I'm witnessing!" He looked at Gina standing halfway up the staircase. "Gina, honey, please go back up stairs and close the door so we can get this straightened out."

Though she wanted to be a part of any family conversation, Gina knew it would be better to obey. "I will, Uncle Joseph." She went to her room. There she watched Larsky out her window and prayed for peace over the trio downstairs.

Joseph turned to his uncle and nephew. "Carmichael, Tony, you two are blood! You are on the same side. There is a common enemy against us, and Carmichael: I don't think it's Gina! She has obeyed you and stayed out of your face for a year. Tony, Carmichael's not your main problem. He's done all he could for you. Our enemy is whoever it was out there who robbed us blind this week. That's who's causing all this frustration. But you two are taking it out on the wrong people, your own family members. Carmichael, you know that our very lives are at stake right now. We could all wind up in prison for life if Tony doesn't get to the bottom of this."

"That was my original question to Tony this morning," Carmichael said, much calmer under the sway of Joseph's reasoning. "Why was he here asleep and not out finding Falco?"

Joseph looked at Tony. "What's up with that, Kid?"

Tony looked to Joseph. "I tried to tell him. I'm onto the person who I believe is one of the ones directly responsible for Todd Falco's disappearance. I went to this guy's house, but he was working. I know where he is, and all I need to do this weekend is nail him down to get the information I need. There are no other leads. This guy is it, I'm telling you."

"And then you'll have the money?" Joseph asked.

"I'll at least know who does and then you all can go get it yourselves. Uncle Carmichael, I've been working my butt off the last two days, non-stop. I've barely slept. That's why I was here asleep this morning. Gina came by on her own. But I don't apologize for not kicking her out. She is my sister and my last closest relative since Pop died. I . . ."

"You'll have my money and the people who stole it by Monday morning?" Carmichael interrupted coldly.

"Yes." He stared at Carmichael. "Do you still *want* me to finish?"

Carmichael was reeling from his raging fit and the humiliation of having been physically subdued by Tony. He stared off angrily into the distance.

Joseph looked at him. "The Kid's asking a legitimate question, Uncle Carmichael. Do you want him to finish or do you want him to pack up and disappear right now?"

Carmichael still looked away from them both.

"Everything you are hangs in the balance, Carmichael. Now the Kid says he's on the verge of wrapping this up and you'll be able to get everything back the way we had it before. Do you want him to finish or not?"

"I'm still your best hope in recovering all your losses and getting the Family back in order," Tony said. "I told you I could do it and I'm about to produce."

Blank stare, no acknowledgment from Carmichael.

"Everything that happened here today, this isn't what I wanted . . ."

Carmichael turned on Tony and said: "I want your finished investigation in my lap at VECO on Monday morning. If you don't have the money, I want the name and address of whoever does so I can get it all back by Monday night. Then you better not ever show you're face in Beaver Falls again. I'll consider you and Gina as dead. In fact, if either one of you ever does show up around here again after Monday you will be as good as dead. Tell her I said so."

Carmichael pushed through Joseph and Tony. He disappeared quietly out the front door.

Tony looked at his Uncle Joseph. "This was a total disaster. The cops would've called this a 'domestic dispute' and arrested us."

"You're lucky you're not dead!"

"That's why I didn't let Jughead into my house. He might have killed us all, the way Carmichael reacted to Gina."

Gina quietly made her way down the stairs again. "I saw the limo leave. I see you're still alive, Tony."

"For how long is the question."

"Neither of you realizes how badly you're pushing it around here. With Gina coming to town like this, and with you, Tony, showing off your worst attitude with Carmichael and Larsky. You both remind me of your old man making him mad. You do as you please around Carmichael."

"What are you talking about? How'd Pop tick him off?"

"Pete and that Gus Savage used to run off and spend fortunes at Atlantic City on the weekends. All flash and show. Well, you know how Carmichael put the kibbutz on that kind of activity. He didn't want Family members to attract attention to ourselves by hot-dogging like we did in La Cosa Nostra. Carmichael's a stoic. Pete was an Epicurean. The two clashed over it pretty often the last few months before Pete's death. Carmichael told him to knock it off. Every time Pete would return with more stories, Uncle Carmichael would blow him out over it. Pete never did learn to fear him the way Carmichael expected him to. You two haven't, either."

Tony stuck his tongue out and arrogantly blew a raspberry. "That's what I think of Uncle Carmichael now."

"I'm not in bondage to Carmichael Vero any more," Gina shrugged. "The Lord's set me free from his intimidating spirit. But I'll prophesy this to you both: the day is coming that Ed Larsky is no longer going to be at Carmichael's side. And on that day, Carmichael Vero's going to be like a pit bull missing his bottom jaw."

"I gotta go," Joseph sighed.

"Are you really going to spend the day with them at VECO?" Gina asked.

"I have no choice. We have a lot of work to do for Tuesday's shareholders banquet. I have to do my job."

Gina looked concerned for her Uncle Joseph. "Won't they . . . ?"

Joseph shook his head and smiled. "I've been handling Carmichael and Larsky for almost twenty years. They haven't gotten the best of me yet. I don't plan on letting them today, either."

He surprised Gina by hugging her tight and giving her a kiss on the forehead. She squeezed her uncle back gratefully, teary-eyed over his support and affection. He left.

"Are you all right, Sissy?" Tony asked Gina as she wiped her eyes.

"Are you all right, is the question. Look at your face!" She went to touch his swollen cheek. He winced and pulled away from her. "I need some ice on it, that's all."

She followed him into the kitchen.

"I'm thinking of a Bible verse that Jesus said," she thought aloud.

"Which is?"

"Jesus said that He didn't come to make peace, but to divide. He was explaining how faith in Him would go so far as to even divide families. The Veros aren't exempt from that scripture, as Uncle Carmichael proved to us today."

Tony wrapped some ice in a paper towel and daubed his cheek gingerly. "I can't believe he acted like that, trying to physically attack you. I never would have expected that from him."

"It was demonic. The evil spirits in him were furious at Jesus in me. He was controlled by demons that wanted to kill me."

Tony looked at her skeptically. "I don't believe in demons."

"Well, you ought to now," she said. "You just saw some in action."

As Joseph Vero's silver Porche disappeared down the road toward Route 51, private investigator Edgar Waters lowered his surveillance gun and turned off his tape recorder. He came to Tony's house at 7:30 that morning, hoping to follow him as he continued his investigation. Edgar hoped to get a great lead on whatever Tony and the Family was up to. Instead, he got the jackpot. From the woods across the road from Tony's property, Edgar watched stunned as Carmichael and Larsky pulled into Tony's driveway in their limo around eleven o'clock. He was able to quickly break out all his gear from his bag. He caught the entire exchange between Carmichael, Larsky, and Tony on the front porch. He caught most of what was said inside the house, up until the time Joseph went in and shut the door. Then he was only able to get about a quarter of what was said behind the closed doors. But that was all right! He'd caught quite enough! The Family had indeed hired Tony Vero to track down Todd Falco and some of their money. Edgar had them all on tape talking about it.

"That's strike two, Carmichael," Edgar said out loud as he packed his gear in the woods. "The next one I get, you're out!"

Benny Miller's ex-guard trudged hopelessly across 7th Avenue. The seventeen year old Horace Weston, whom Benny had just kicked out of his gang for sleeping on the job, was tired, hungry, thirsty, and wanting another fix. He had no money, and now no friends. He'd worked so hard to get into Benny's gang so he'd belong somewhere, have a surrogate family. Now, all his sacrifice was for nothing. Once Benny kicked someone out, which was rare, that person was marked for violence, if not death. Once Benny's crew saw him out in public they would hunt him down and beat him mercilessly. Once any rivals who feared Benny Miller saw him they would more than likely smoke him on the spot, now that he was unprotected by the number one gang in Beaver County. He was a marked man, strung out, hopeless and desperate.

Across 7th Avenue was a convenience store. There were two vehicles parked outside: an old Nissan pick-up truck and a shiny, white, 1970s Cadillac. Horace was slowly making his way through the parking lot when he saw something that snapped him alert: the white Caddie looked like it was running! Horace's blood began to fill with adrenaline. He looked into the store window. There was a tall man in his forties, and an ancient old white woman at the counter with the clerk. No one else! That car had to belong to the old lady! Horace had a cousin in Pittsburgh who could take him and the Caddie to a chop shop for big bucks! Looking around the parking lot, Horace suddenly had hope. The old lady was paying the clerk. Horace suddenly bolted to her car. It was indeed running! He grabbed the door handle: unlocked! How could that old white woman be so stupid! Just as he slammed the door and was putting the car in reverse, the big guy who was in the store came bursting through the door yelling at Horace. The man quickly had a handle on the Caddie's door as Horace slammed the gas pedal. The door flew open and out of the man's grasp as the Caddie accelerated backward in an arc. Horace's reflexes still weren't all they should have been and he miscalculated his speed: the Caddie slammed backward into the wall of the building next door. Horace's neck snapped back and from the impact, stunning him long enough for the man to run upon the car and snatch out the youth by his Cincinnati Reds baseball shirt. The man threw Horace to the ground, shouting angrily. Horace tried to reach for his knife in his pocket, but the man was on him again. He twisted Horace around and slammed the skinny youth face-first onto the pavement. Police sirens wailed in the background, for the store clerk had instantly phoned 911. A Beaver Falls squad car was already on it's way down 7th Avenue, heading in the direction of the convenience store. Horace was flat busted. The police arrested him, the elderly woman demanded to press charges, and the tall man was commended for intervening and apprehending a car thief. What had looked to Horace like a criminal's dream come true was actually a Divinely appointed set-up for the hopeless young man's arrest. Horace simply took the bait and got caught, as was Divinely intended.

So fell the first domino in the chain that ended with Carmichael Vero and the Family.

THIRTY-THREE

E d Larsky left VECO at three that Saturday afternoon to meet Tommy Wheeler so they could prepare for the Benny Miller hit. After servicing the VECO limousine and getting his pickup truck, he went out to Wheeler's secluded rural home. In his filthy basement Wheeler had equipped both an AK-47 and a .458 Magnum rifle with laser scopes. As Larsky descended the stairs, a red laser dot shone on his forehead. Wheeler stood at the bottom of the steps with the .458 aimed at Larsky.

"Save that for Tony Vero," Larsky grumbled. "What's with the .458? You gonna assassinate an elephant?"

"No," Tommy said, lowering the rifle as Larsky reached the bottom. "You're gonna assassinate that arrogant clown Benny Miller." He patted the .458. "With this you're gonna blow his heart clean out the back of his body, after I torch his house and spray it with the AK-47."

"Why don't you just call in an F-16 air strike? What kind of plan is this you come up with?"

"The only kind I can come up with to get Benny Miller right now. My source on the streets says Benny found out about Jermichael DeVries and Stephen McClintlock and he thinks he's next on the hit list."

"Well, he must not be too stupid, 'cause he is next!"

"But he doesn't know what's really up. He's just paranoid. He and his boys have hit the mattresses. They're in war mode. He's called in all his street vendors and holed himself up in his house, battle-ready. The only way I know to get to him now is to burn him out, like you would a wasp's nest."

"Can't you get us a grenade launcher, Wheeler? We'll just level the whole house?"

"I could, and we'd kill a whole bunch of 'em, but that wouldn't guarantee we'd kill Benny Miller. Don't get sloppy on me. You've paid me twenty grand to kill him. I'm a professional. I have a reputation to maintain. When we're finished tonight, we're gonna know Benny Miller's dead. So I gotta get him out of the house to do it. He's only got a front door and a back door. I'm gonna toss some Molotov cocktails through the upstairs windows, they'll come running out, guns blazing, you'll be waiting in the tree of the abandoned house across the alley, I'll come around the front. Whoever of us sees him first plugs him and anyone else with him. Then we disappear."

"This is gonna be a war on 4th Avenue tonight."

"You paid me to have him killed by Monday morning. I'm gonna. We're gonna take the risk. But my source told me he's definitely expecting an attack. He knows he's the number one G, now."

"Well, I want you to be ready to go after Tony Vero first thing Monday. He's told my boss he's gonna be done Monday with the little assignment we need him to carry out for us. Once we're finished with him on Monday, he's all yours."

Tommy Wheeler cocked the .458 bolt action with a loud click. "Tony Vero'll be dead before sundown Monday night."

Audra Dutton sat lazily on her back porch, soaking in the beautiful weather. She started to wonder about what she would do for supper that night. Sharon Harrison wasn't going to be available to eat with her. Her stomach still registered full to capacity from a large submarine and salad she devoured at lunch. As she ignored it and contemplated supper, she got a quick flash in her spirit from Holy Spirit. It was, "Fast."

"'Fast'?" she laughed aloud. "You mean like, 'fast food?'"

"Fast," came to her again, loudly and clearly. She was to go on a food fast. It had been a while since she fasted. As she shook her head, upset and unready for such a call from the Lord, something happened to Audra Dutton that had never happened before. An open vision appeared before her eyes in the yard. She knew it wasn't in her mind's eye, but a vision before her, like a hologram. She knew it was of the Lord. She looked forward and saw the forms of two very handsome young men standing in her yard. One was black, one was white. Both were in their mid-twenties, both were athletically built, striking to the sight. After five seconds the open vision vanished. She trembled with the fear of the Lord. Then, from within her, His voice very clearly said:

"Fast for those two men. They need your faithful intercession. Fast and pray over them. Pray for their lives, their very souls. They need protection."

Audra's heart was beating rapidly. Her palms were sweating, her fingers and legs tingling from the power of Holy Spirit breaking forth on her. She began to wonder why He was commissioning her with such intensity. The answer came instantly within her heart:

"I yearn jealously for you! You have been faithful over the little things I've given you. Now receive the greater level of commissioning. Fast. Drink water and juice only. Sanctify yourself to Me. Set your mind on the things of My kingdom. And be in prayer for these two men."

Audra fell to her knees as the powerful presence of God lifted. Panting, she looked around excitedly to see if anyone was watching. She was alone. She thought about those two young men. The images of their faces were etched into her mind.

Audra Dutton didn't know who Tony Vero and Benny Miller were, but now she clearly knew their faces.

"You gotta hear this one, Chief," a detective told the Beaver Falls Chief of Police. The mustachioed, burly chief slowly got up from his desk and followed the detective to a tiny interrogation room near the jail cells of the police station. In the interrogation room sat a lanky seventeen year old black male, with corn-rowed hair, wearing gang reds. A tall state-appointed lawyer stood behind Benny Miller's ex-guard, with an arrogant smile on his face.

"This here's Horace Weston," the detective told the chief as he closed the door behind them. "Busted today at the Seven Eleven for grand theft auto. But after talking to his attorney here, Mr. Weston turned around and told me quite an interesting story about where he's been staying and what's been going on around there." The detective walked over to Horace and stood right beside him. "Tell the Chief what you know."

Horace sat stone-faced, looking straight at the wall. "I been one o' Benny Miller's enforcers the last six months. Been guardin' his house for him."

The chief stood with his hands in his pocket, poker-eyed, chomping gum.

Horace continued: "Everyone in this room know Benny's the number one G around the county. Don't none o' you cops ever mess with him. Well, this week his connection didn't come through for him. Benny's been out new supplies."

"What kind of supplies?" the chief asked.

"Do I gotta spell it out for you?" Horace sneered at him. "Coke, man," he said, impatiently shaking his head. "Benny's supplier cut his throat. Benny's been on the warpath about it all week. Takin' his anger out on the rest of us, like it our fault . . ."

"Benny ejected Horace from his gang, this morning, Chief," the detective moved the story along for Horace. "Horace was asleep at his post. That's why he tried to steal a car from an eighty-three year old woman. He's on the outs with his homeboys."

"Man! I wasn't . . ."

"Oh!" the Chief interrupted him and came to life. "So I'm talking to a dead man, here! Why am I wasting my time even listening to this dead man?" He started to turn on his heels to leave.

"Stop trying to frighten my client," the attorney warned.

"What client? This is a dead man," the Chief said, pointing to Horace and opening the door to leave.

"Man, cop, what you want from me?" Horace sat forward and pleaded.

"What do I want? You told my detective here some sort of story, but I haven't heard it and I am becoming less interested in it by the second."

"I just want a promise that you'll cut a deal with the DA for me! One that's cool with my lawyer. Then I'll give you something you ain't gonna be able to get anywhere else but from me!"

The chief leaned over into Horace's face. "You gotta tell me what you have for me before we even talk about cutting any deal. Right now I got a seventeen year old gang banger on a felony charge of grand theft auto. You gonna do us better than that, Horace? 'Cause if not, I'm walking out this door and you're not gonna see any of us again until your first court date."

"Tell him, now!" the attorney commanded Horace.

Horace looked out the open door. He could hear people in the jail cells talking. "Close that door," he whispered. The chief did. Horace took a deep breath. "Benny Miller got everyone on the warpath 'cause Jermichael DeVries and that Stephen McClintlock both got wasted last night. Benny think someone comin' after him now. Thing is this: Benny's called in all his stuff off the streets. He's called in all his pushers and sellers, from the top to the bottom. They all bringing their stash to his house today and he guardin' it down in his basement. He'll have the junk stockpiled there. He think you afraid of him. He'll have any coke and Mary Jane he hasn't sold from the last time his connection loaded him up. They'll probably be several grand worth of stuff sittin' in his house tonight. All you gotta do is show up at the right time."

The chief scratched his head. "You gonna draw me a diagram of his house? Where he keeps his stuff? Where his muscles are hiding so my boys don't get their heads blown off in a fire fight?"

Horace thumped his finger on the table emphatically. "I'll give you everything, cop. 'Cause the fact of the matter is this: if you don't get Benny Miller and his gang, they gonna get me!"

THIRTY-FOUR

Tony Vero sat in his blue pickup truck and watched Frank Kranac's house all afternoon. He parked on a side street a block in the opposite direction from where he kept surveillance the night before. Kranac's black Galaxie 500 sat out front. There were no signs of life all day from within the house. Tony wondered if he was at work again. He knew he'd been home for a while the night before, but somehow must have slipped out the back door for work without Tony seeing him. He didn't take his car. Maybe he walked or carpooled with someone. But that Saturday Tony was going to wait until he emerged, if it took all day.

Gina left for Ohio around one. They had lunch together at the house, but Tony was too quiet and pensive for her liking. He couldn't get past the fact that this might be the last time she ever saw him. After his run-in with Carmichael that morning, he was more ready than ever to wrap up the Falco case and disappear for good. He knew he could live without seeing Gina, though he'd miss her fiercely. She openly loved him, especially since she gave her heart to Christ. So he felt guilty, knowing she was about to be robbed of her brother. It was like he was about to commit suicide or something. In effect, he was about to eliminate Tony Vero all together. He just wished there was a way Gina didn't have to suffer. Maybe he could contact her safely sometime down the road. He'd have to see.

Over lunch she doted relentlessly about his sore face from where Carmichael had cracked him. Tony told her to quit fussing about it and forget it. He allowed her to pray for him again before she left. She prayed a powerfully anointed prayer over Tony, calling forth both God's protection over her brother and His holy conviction to overtake his heart regarding Christ. She told him she knew something was terribly wrong with him, but that back in Ohio she'd continue praying for him daily. She reminded him one more time that Jesus truly did love him and died for his sins so he could live in Him. Then she got into her car and left. Tony wanted to cry. But to avoid wallowing around in self pity, he instead got into his truck and went after Frank Kranac.

Tony passed the hours of sitting in that truck waiting for Kranac to come out thinking about the only thing that made him feel good: Kay Falco.

"You're infatuated like some school boy, Kid," he muttered aloud. He had to admit it. But it was a dangerous infatuation. She was married (if Todd was indeed still alive), she had a kid, and she could raise fiery hell at the drop of a hat. But Tony loved that in her, for some reason. Everything about her was wild and exciting. Her eyes, her hair, her . . . everything! He shook his head in disgust with himself. "The last thing you need to do, Tony Vero, is to get mixed up with the likes of Kay Falco. She has enough problems. She *is* a problem! So are you . . ."

Frank Kranac suddenly emerged from his front door, snapping Tony out of his romantic dream world. The fifty-two year old man lumbered down the cement steps to his car. He wore a faded pocket t-shirt, blue pants, black work boots and white socks. Between that outfit, that run-down house with ankle high grass, and the ancient Ford Galaxie, Tony had to gasp at the man's eccentricity. That huge, ugly man was a card and a half. The Galaxie sunk low and bounced up and down from Kranac's weight as he plopped into it. Tony slid down in his front seat so he wouldn't be spotted. Kranac slowly steered the car out into the street and made his way up 6th Avenue. When he was a block up, Tony popped up, cranked his engine, and took pursuit.

Less than a minute later, Kranac pulled into the parking lot of the Corner Tavern, in the West Mayfield section of Beaver Falls, right up 37th Street from College Hill. Tony used to frequent that bar himself. The Corner Tavern was owned by a man named Eddie Malinski. Eddie was a deathly gaunt man, with sandy hair, squinting blue eyes hidden behind thick glasses, and a big bushy mustache. He was a Vietnam vet, not known for his friendly demeanor, yet he ran a well-liked establishment. Tony saw Kranac disappear into the front door as he pulled his truck into the parking lot. Tony quickly gathered his thoughts. He had a plan for confronting Kranac. He was determined to make it a worthwhile confrontation. He got out and went into the tavern.

He stood in the door way and looked around. Some folks sat in the adjoining dining room, where spaghetti dinners or burger platters could be ordered on Fridays and Saturdays. But the barroom was conspicuously empty. A Pittsburgh Pirates pre-game show was loudly demanding attention on an overhead television set. There was an elderly couple sitting in a booth at the one end of the bar, and two men in their forties sitting at a table at the other end. Both pairs were silent, sipping beers and watching the television. Eddie's son, whom everyone called, "Red", sat at a round table off in the corner. He was a brute. Tall, bulky, with fiery-red hair, he was about thirty. To Tony, he looked like he was dressed as a hillbilly oaf. He wore overalls, a flannel shirt with the sleeves chopped off to reveal huge triceps, and a black ball cap backwards on his head. He was chewing a huge chaw of tobacco and spitting the brown juice into a beer bottle. But Eddie, Kranac, and those other five were it as far as patrons went. That was good for Tony.

Frank Kranac was alone at the bar, drinking a frosted mug of beer, watching the Pirates warm up show. He looked monstrous from behind, his shoulders and back were so broad. Yet Tony commanded himself not to fear this man: Kranac was the only obstacle between him and his freedom. Tony knew this guy was going to clam up. His only hope was to catch him off guard and nail him unaware. Slowly Tony sauntered up to the bar near Kranac. He stood about four feet behind him, pretending to be listening to the television. Kranac instinctively tilted his head and glanced over his shoulder with one eye. Tony didn't register in his mind, so he turned his attention back to the pre-game. Tony waited until the lanky bartender was occupied at the far end of the counter, then he made his move on Frank Kranac. He swiftly sat down at the barstool beside him. Kranac tilted his head only enough to investigate who it was. He recognized Tony only as the one who had been standing behind him. He sighed, irritated that the whole bar was free but this pest decided to invade the space right next to him. He turned his attention back to the TV. Tony made sure the bartender was well occupied with something at that far end of the bar. Heart pounding in his chest, hands almost trembling, he leaned over within inches of Kranac and said loudly enough for only him to hear:

"Where's Todd Falco and the money?"

In what seemed to Tony like slow motion, Frank Kranac cocked his head around and locked his dark, soulless eyes on Tony with virulent contempt. Now, Tony Vero had never personally seen satan before. But after seeing Kranac's face in reaction to his question, he imagined that's just what satan would look like.

You've struck paydirt, Tony, he thought with glee. His heart thumped like a freight engine in his chest.

They stared each other down, nearly nose to nose; neither flinching. Kranac realized this pest in his face must be Tony Vero. His first wish was to palm one of his massive hands over Tony's face and snap his neck like a dry branch. But he quickly squelched that obscene desire. He had to be much more subtle. He knew Tony had been slinking after him like a cat for the past several days. Frank had to play like a cornered rattler, now, and turn the tables on this brash meddler. With his eyes still venomously locked on Tony's, Kranac simply said:

"I don't know what you're talkin' about." He twisted his head back around, slow motion again, and took another deep gulp from his frosted mug.

Tony stayed right at his side. In a dull whisper he said: "I think you do. You and that Bernie Lokawski, and that Jimmy and Greggy Richards, you all know exactly what I'm talking about. You know where Todd Falco is." Tony watched for some reaction, but Kranac had none that time. "You set him up. You all got his money. All the cops in Beaver County can't find him. They probably don't even know that you exist. But I do, 'Frankie,'" he imitated Jimmy's Richard's annoying voice. "I know you trapped Todd Falco like an animal and you stole all his money. And I've come to expose you all."

Kranac was still poker faced. Wanting to rile the giant of a man, Tony leaned even closer to him. Like a defiant madman tempting fate near the jaws of a ferocious beast, Tony whispered into Kranac's ear, "Know how I know, Frankie? Jimmy and Greggy told me *everything!*"

Kranac's brow furrowed into a contortion. Fury filled his eyes. Tony relished it. "They told me all about you and Bernie Lokawski," he lied to Frank. "They turned you right over to me . . ."

Kranac suddenly sat up in his stool and yelled for the bartender: "Hey, Eddie!" he jabbed his left thumb toward Tony. "This punk, here, is harassing me!"

Eddie stood up at the end of the bar and instantly bounced his skinny frame over to Frank and Tony. Anger blaring through his thick glasses, he asked Tony, "What's your problem?"

Kranac didn't give Tony a chance to respond. "He just comes up to me and starts making accusations about people I don't even know who he's talkin' about. I don't even know this punk and he's bothering me for no reason. I just wanna drink my beer and relax in your bar, and I'm bein' harassed."

Eddie turned red. Tony stood up from the barstool and pulled out his wallet. He hung it open so his private investigator's license shown. Eddie leaned down and briefly examined it.

"I'm a private investigator," Tony explained. "I need to question Mr. Kranac, here, regarding some serious allegations about Todd Falco's disappearance . . ."

Eddie suddenly scowled and backhanded the wallet hard out of Tony's hand. It flipped through the air and banged off one of the large picture windows all the way by the door.

Tony began to protest, but Eddie snapped his fingers and tersely called, "Red!" Suddenly his beefy son shot across the barroom and stood right behind Tony. Tony could see the massive Red out of the corner of his eye, but didn't turn to confront him. Kranac emotionlessly looked straight ahead and took another swallow of his beer. Though he could have personally mangled Tony, he coolly sat back to let Eddie and Red handle him.

Eddie leaned across the bar and pointed a finger in Tony's face. "I don't care about your stupid investigation. This is my bar! I'm tired of your generation! Always coming in here bothering my good patrons! Frank Kranac is a Vietnam vet, you spoiled punk! He's served his country, and now he works hard for a living. In a real job, in a real mill! I bought this place so people like him could come in and unwind and enjoy a cold beer. This place is for people who have to work for a living, not for spoiled, has-been superstars who flunk out of college and live off their family fortune!"

Tony looked at him, offended. Eddie nodded emphatically. "Yeah! I know who you are! And the Vero name don't mean a thing to me. You're just a bunch of crooked, Mafia hoodlums! Look at you," Eddie pointed to the huge red hand print Carmichael planted on Tony's face. "You look like you already been beat around today. You were probably causing trouble somewhere else like you are here. Now, you have exactly no seconds to get out of my establishment!"

Tony looked over at Kranac. Kranac calmly stared ahead and took another quaff of beer. Disappointment flooded the young man. He leaned over to give Kranac one final warning, but Red didn't like Tony lingering after his dad had commanded him to get out. Eddie's hulking son snatched Tony by his left arm and slung him around toward the door. Tony caught his balance and stopped himself before he tumbled to the ground. Defiantly, he turned back toward them and said,

"Nice trick, Frankie! But having them kick me out of here isn't gonna make me disappear! You will see me again."

He walked over to where his wallet lay, with Red hot on his heals. He bent down to pick it up, defiantly slow as a turtle. Red impatiently stood over him, chest out, fists clenched.

"I'm leavin'," Tony grunted at him, irritated. Tony had to bury the urge to attack Red. He felt he could have overtaken the bigger man with several quick kicks to the groin and abdomen and a right cross to break his fat nose. But he figured they'd just call the police, press charges, and have him thrown in jail. That would even further stifle his investigation and delay his freedom from the Family. He choked down his pride and walked out the front door, humiliated by Red and Eddie, and headed to his truck. Frustration and rage were rising within him. He was upset that he didn't get a better shot at breaking down Kranac. The closer he got to the truth about Todd Falco, the more out of control the whole case seemed to be spinning. It was like it was getting further and further out of his hands. He was starting to worry he'd have nothing worthwhile to give to Carmichael on Monday morning. Nothing concrete to even bargain with, if necessary. He unlocked the door of his truck and climbed in. Red stood in the open doorway and sneered at him. From his truck he saw Kranac shake Eddie's hand in gratitude. Eddie patted Frank on the arm, in assurance of his support for his old comrade. Tony could almost hear him say, "*Semper Fi*." Eddie poured Kranac another beer. Tony cranked his pickup and took off. As he drove past the door he said out loud:

"Drink up now, Frankie, 'cause you won't be drinkin' up too much longer!"

Ed Larsky, wearing all black, steered a brown Duster off 7th Avenue and headed down 11th Street toward Benny Miller's 4th Avenue residence. Tommy Wheeler procured the unregistered car from a hack shop to use for the Benny Miller hit that Saturday night. The .458 with the laser scope lay disassembled in the tire well of the trunk, until needed later when Larsky would take his position in a huge tree across the alley from Miller's house. The plan was, after Wheeler had driven Miller's gang out of his house with fire, Larsky would have a clear shot at Miller while he tried to flee to his Mercedes in his garage out back. Of course Miller's boys would open fire on whoever shot their boss. But Wheeler would hopefully have an open shot to mow them all down with his AK-47, spooking the rest of their gang back into the house, giving both of them enough time to flee.

Larsky spat out the window in disgust. "This is insane," he said. "This is gonna turn into a major military conflict in downtown Beaver Falls." He wasn't afraid of gunfire and action. He just didn't want to get caught. The Family had enough problems as it was.

Beside him on the seat lay a thick ski mask and a police walky-talky, set to an obscure frequency. He was to give Wheeler the signal when he was in place and ready for action.

A block away from 4th Avenue, Larsky spotted what looked like neon lightning flashes coming from around the corner. The dancing light beams got brighter and more animated the closer Larsky got to 4th Avenue. *Around the corner*, he thought, *that's where Miller's house is.*

"Abort," came Tommy Wheeler's voice, monotone, over the walky-talky.

As Larsky got to the corner of 4th Avenue he snatched up his walky-talky and barked impatiently, "Abort? Why!"

The flashing lights grew more colorful in the street ahead, and Larsky could see many of them were spinning. He stopped at the corner, and nudged his car up far enough to see Miller's house at the far corner of the block. There was the source of all the flashing lights: Benny Miller's house was surrounded by police vans and cars. There were both Beaver Falls police and Beaver County Sheriff's vans. About ten vehicles in all. Larsky could see swift silhouetted figures dashing about amid the flashing of strobe lights. Well armed and armored police officers and deputies were escorting a long parade of handcuffed gang members from Miller's house out into the vans and police cars. A police car was parked in the middle of the road to the left of Larsky, blocking his passage. An officer in riot gear walked over to the Duster and shined a flashlight beam in his face. Larsky squinted. With his right hand he turned off the walky-talky and stuffed it and the ski mask under his leg.

"What's going on, officer?" he asked politely.

"Drug raid, sir," the officer answered. "You'll have to go down the block and detour the other way."

Larsky nodded slowly, sorely disappointed and angry over the fact that Benny Miller was about to escape death and continue to be a major threat to the Family's security. As he drove straight ahead at the officer's bidding, Larsky watched the parade of suspects being led away. Somewhere in the midst of those shadowy figures, Benny Miller was escaping judgment.

"Abort," Larsky sighed.

THIRTY-FIVE

D etective Ray Kirkland finished a long, frustrating day at the Beaver County Sheriff's Department. He and Deputy Simmons combed through Tony Vero's belongings, and all the confiscated materials from VECO. They meticulously went through file cabinets, through computer programs, discs, and the memory space on their computers. They could find no signs of anything belonging to Todd Falco in Tony Vero's materials, and there was absolutely nothing consequential in Todd Falco's VECO files and computers. They did find some interesting quirks regarding Todd Falco's attendance records at VECO.

"Everyone else's comings and goings at VECO seems to be monitored quite rigidly by Mr. Larsky," Ray noted about the personnel attendance records. "Secretaries are paid hourly, not salary wise, and must keep meticulous sign-in sheets. Records are tightly kept on salaried executives, sales executives, and secondary bookkeeper's office hours, to keep them accountable. But when it comes to Mr. Todd Falco, there appears to be a double standard."

"Comes and go as he pleases?"

"According to all these records. He doesn't seem to have to answer to Ed Larsky about his comings and goings. The dates he's actually been in the office are recorded, but there's no written accounts of his meetings, no travel records or mileage kept. Not like the others."

"We found no records like that in any of his personal files from his home file cabinet."

"We sure didn't," Ray agreed. "Mr. Tony Vero may be keeping some of those for us," he said sarcastically. "But as far as his daily attendance hours at VECO, it appears Todd Falco got to be a free spirit. But that's all we got in any of this stuff."

"Aside from some girly pictures Todd has on file on his hard drive, there appears to be nothing illegal or even remotely controversial on his VECO computer," Deputy Simmons remarked with disappointment. "Two warrants, two searches. Was this all a waste?"

Ray pursed his lips and shook his head. "No. Our time wasn't wasted." He pulled out a piece of paper he'd set aside earlier. It was a bank statement of Tony Vero's from Reeves Bank. "I found another lead that I think will be important."

Simmons pointed to the bank statement. "How's that a lead?"

Ray waved it in the air. "This bank statement says Mr. Vero has a safe deposit box. He has no goodies in his house, careful man that he is. But come Monday, I'll have me a warrant for that safe deposit box of his, and I'll bet you it's gonna turn out to be like a treasure chest for us!"

Ed Larsky waited for the light in his red Ram at the intersection of 37th Street and Route 18 in the College Hill district of Beaver Falls. He and Tommy Wheeler had quickly rendezvoused after the aborted Benny Miller hit attempt. Tommy took the .458 and the Duster off of Larsky's hands, and Larsky got his truck back.

"Now what?" Wheeler asked him.

"We can't do a jailhouse hit. We're not ready for that. I guess for the time being Benny Miller gets away."

"What about the twenty grand you paid me for the job?"

Larsky thought for a moment. "We can't pay you for something you haven't done."

"But it's not my fault the cops raided his home today . . ."

Larsky angrily put his hand up signaling for Wheeler to shut up. "You still owe me a job for Monday. Just keep this twenty grand and I'll square it away somehow. Get ready for my call on Monday."

With that he left, angry and frustrated. He phoned Carmichael and in code language broke the bad news to him about Benny Miller. He then drove around and smoked for a while to gather his thoughts and figure out what to do next. It was at that point that Larsky was at the 37th Street and Route 18 intersection, waiting to turn in the right hand lane. And it was at that point that he spotted Tony Vero driving north up Route 18 in his little blue pickup truck.

Larsky was infuriated just seeing Tony. "Where's he think he's going to? And why isn't that spoiled little brat out looking for our money and that good for nothing Todd Falco?"

The light changed. Tony's truck sped out of sight. Larsky switched his blinker over to the left hand turn signal. The guy behind him blew his horn impatiently. Larsky, angry as a hornet to start with, yelled at him through the window. He pulled out in front of a car in the left hand lane. That person honked at him, but Larsky was too busy stomping the gas peddle and cutting across both lanes to worry about him. He pulled onto Route 18 north and began to search for Tony's truck. He finally caught up to him, staying about five cars behind. Grumpy and irritable, Larsky found something through which he could take out his frustrations. He decided he'd find out what Tony Vero had been wasting his time on instead of doing what the Family was ordering him to do.

"I'll fix you tonight, Tony Vero."

When Ray went to leave the Sheriff's Department at 9:00 o'clock that night, he felt the need to go check up on Kay Falco. He wanted to make sure she was still going to go to church with them in the morning. Sometimes it's harder for people to say no in person than it is over the phone. He'd try to cement her final word on it. Shelly had the girls at her sisters in Butler for the day. They wouldn't be back until sometime after ten. So he felt free to grab a burger and pay her a visit. He hopped in his squad car and headed out.

Tony went to knock on Kay Falco's kitchen door, then hesitated. What in the world was he even doing there?

He was devastated after not being able to break Frank Kranac as he wanted to, and being humiliated at the Corner Tavern. Now he needed to swing around and tackle Kranac from another angle, and that was going to take some work. When he drove away from the bar, he was suddenly overtaken by the depression and anxiety that had been plaguing him. He became highly aware of the huge void in his heart, and the guilt that hung on him over Gus Savage. He needed something to quell all the disappointment and frustration and hopelessness. Amazingly, Jesus Christ was the first thing that came to his mind. It was an overwhelming thought of, "Let Him fill that void that's always been there and wash away your guilt." He didn't know where it came from. It definitely wasn't a natural thought to him. And it wasn't scary or freaky or anything negative, either. Actually, the prospect of the thought was quite peaceful and comforting. Of course he didn't realize it was Holy Spirit Himself giving him a personal invitation to invite Christ into his heart as Savior. The anointed prayers of intercessors like Gina Vero and Audra Dutton had cleared the pathway for God to actually plant such a seed of invitation in Tony's heart. But Tony, being spiritually dead, only allowed the thought to comfort him for a minute, feeling it was "cool," but something he was still unsure of. Therefore, he turned his heart back toward the things of the flesh, things with which he was comfortable: his overwhelming feelings for Kay Falco. Endorphins flooded his mind and testosterone filled his system as Kay Falco's natural beauty captivated his thoughts. Soon he found himself driving out to her house uninvited, with no real reason to show up there other than he simply wanted to see her and be with her. As he parked in her driveway, he admitted those feelings he had for her were insane. He knew it was dangerous to even be out there at night with her alone. He even remembered one of his instructors at the private investigator's school in California lecturing his class about such matters one day:

"Never, NEVER get involved with a client or a suspect or someone involved in one of your investigations. Such involvements are not only unprofessional, but dangerous. They could jeopardize your entire case, your practice, your very life."

He knocked on her kitchen door anyway. Holy Spirit pricked his conscience deep within, crying out for him to get back into his truck and go home. He stood struggling for a moment, a war raging between his fleshly will and the will of God that wanted him to check his hormones and keep from defiling the Falco marriage.

But in the end, the will of man once again rejected the will of God. Tony choked off that voice of reason within his heart, quickly lifted his fist, and banged on Kay Falco's kitchen door once more. Kay Falco appeared to be in a daze as she first walked into the kitchen. But Tony noted her gorgeous eyes lit up when she saw him through the screen door. Even in her grief, she was a vision to Tony. Her hair was up in a spout on top of her head. She wore a white T-shirt with an unbuttoned flannel shirt over it, hanging loosely over her tight blue jeans. She didn't smile at Tony, yet she was clearly pleased to see him.

"Hello," she said softly through the screen door.

"Hi."

Neither showed any signs of excitement, both worn out emotionally. Somewhere in the house Dylon could be heard crying.

"You find Todd yet?" she asked through the screen door.

He shook his head. "No. But I'm an inch away from him."

"Then why are you here if you're that close?"

"I just blew a lead. I'm giving him time to cool off before I go back at him again. I'll have everything sewed up by Monday morning. I'm that close.

"You mean you'll have my Todd then?"

"No . . . uh . . ."

Dylon was still wailing off in the distance.

"Do you need to go check on Dylon?" Tony asked, concerned.

"No. He's just fussing 'cause I put him to bed early. You won't have Todd by Monday morning?"

"Um . . . can I come in?"

She thought for a moment with a blank expression. He could tell she was in a dark place. The unbearable stress was clearly taking its toll on her.

Finally she said, "Why not?" and let Tony in.

Tony explained to Kay that he didn't know where Todd was, or if he was alive or not. He said he couldn't give her any details about the case until he knew all the facts. She didn't cry or even tear up, but she did sigh an awful sigh, like one who was breathing their last breath. Tony's heart sank for her. Hopelessness seemed to hang about her. He wanted to encourage her that it was going to be all right, but knew better than to make such a impotent statement. Todd Falco was a drug supplier who worked for the Family. Chances were, he wasn't okay, and life for Kay and Dylon was not going to get better soon.

"I wish there was something I could say."

Kay leaned back against the kitchen counter. "I wish there was, too." Suddenly, she noticed the big raspberry hand print on the side of his face. She gasped and quickly stepped toward him to examine it closer.

"What happened to you?" She gently laid a soft hand on Tony's cheek. Her touch gave him butterflies in his stomach.

"Hazardous duty," he replied.

"Who did this to you?"

"Some old lady at the grocery store. I got fresh with her . . ."

"Did this happen because of Todd's case?"

"Um . . . semi. Look, it's nothing, really. I'm just fine. I . . ."

"How much is VECO paying you to find my Todd?"

Tony grunted. "More than you know!"

"Look at you! That's horrible! Those people out there at VECO ought to be ashamed. They're the ones who've destroyed Todd. Now they're destroying *you*."

"Just because I have a red mark on my face? Leave me out of this . . ."

"I'm not talking about your outside, Tony. I'm talking about your inside. They're killing you, just like they seem to kill everything they touch. It shows all over you."

"Listen! I don't want to talk about me. I came out here to see how you're doing. You're the one who needs some support right now."

"Ha! You're just as fouled up and isolated and lonely as me, Tony Vero. You didn't come out here yesterday morning for your investigation. Same as you didn't come here tonight for any good reason."

"I came out here to check on you!"

"You're a private eye on a case. Why should you care about me?"

He stumbled around for words. None came to him.

"I'll tell you what the deal with you is: you want a friend as bad as I do. You're broken. You're like a shell of someone who used to exist. Like a haunted house. The only thing left on the inside of the wrecked exterior is a ghost of what used to be . . ."

"Beautifully poetic," Tony stopped her. "But I don't need your psycho analysis. You have no idea who I was or who I am . . ."

"You got a girlfriend?"

"What's that got to do with anything?"

"Shut up and answer my question! You seeing anyone?"

"No, for your information! I've not had a steady girlfriend since Christmas. I've been dating different girls here or there, but recently . . ."

"Recently you've been too much of a shattered human being to maintain a dating relationship! And I'll bet you VECO's behind whatever's made you like this."

"I don't . . ."

"Want to talk about it. You've told me! You don't want to talk about anything. So why are you here with me, Tony Vero?"

Why was he? He stood frozen. She sure never beat around the bush. She was pinning him against the wall demanding an explanation. He felt humiliated again. His pride commanded him to leave, but his feelings for Kay were gluing him in place. They gazed into each other's eyes long and hard. Her beauty was stirring his passions for her more than ever. Kay's passions were rising, too. Tony's admiring gaze, his attractive mixture of vulnerability and strength, and his genuine concern for Kay and Dylon stirred her heart for him.

"You're broken," she whispered, tears in her eyes. "You need someone. That's why you came here tonight. You have no other reason. You need someone."

"Why are you pressing me on this?"

"I hate pretentiousness." She gazed deeply, longingly, into his green eyes. "And I'm tired of hurting. I want something to make all this pain go away. Something to make me feel better."

Their hearts almost thumped loud enough for the other to hear. Slowly, he reached his hand out and stroked her left cheek. She closed her eyes and cradled her head against his masculine touch. He luxuriated in her beauty. After the pain and disappointment of the day, Kay Falco was positively intoxicating to him.

"You're incredible," he breathed, barely audible.

They could feel each other trembling. They were so drawn to each other. She opened her eyes and looked up again into his. Their souls locked tight. Ever so slowly, Tony began to lean his face toward her. In response, she slowly raised herself up on her toes and gently put her face up to meet his. They stopped for but a second, staring into each other's eyes, then continued on their path. They closed their eyes. With their lips only a fraction of an inch away from meeting . . .

Ed Larsky popped his big head up outside her screen door and said loudly: "Awwww! Isn't this sweet! The private eye we hired to find Todd Falco is out at his house making moves on his wife!"

Tony and Kay simultaneously jumped, startled, and quickly backed away from each other in shame. Their "magic moment" was shattered. Larsky boldly yanked open the light kitchen screen door and invaded Kay's house. Tony pushed Kay back to the corner of her kitchen counter and stepped in front of her. He didn't know what a psychopathic killer like Larsky might do.

"What do *you* want?" Tony yelled.

"Who said you could come into my house?" Kay stepped from behind Tony. "And why are you spying on me on my property?"

Larsky stared into Tony's eyes with deep contempt. "The big question is, why are you here with her when you should be out looking for Falco?" He then turned his glare on Kay. "And aren't you just the 'grieving wife'? Oh, you're so upset about Todd! Yet here I catch you making out with another man, you little hypocrite!"

Kay let into him, but Tony's mind was racing furiously. Larsky was a true animal. He wouldn't let this opportunity to corner Tony like a bug go by without stomping him. Tony knew he wasn't going to get out of this one in one piece. As his mind frantically searched for a safe way out for him and Kay, Tony suddenly saw the glory of God: behind Larsky, through the kitchen screen door, Tony saw the silhouette of a police car pulling into Kay's driveway. Relieved beyond words, he instantly re-focused his thoughts to much more than just getting Larsky out of their hair: he quickly figured out a way to bait this beast.

As a red-faced Kay was screeching at Larsky, Tony suddenly stepped back in front of her and said: "Leave her alone, Larsky! It's me you want, not her!"

Larsky straightened up and mockingly put his hand on his cheek. "Ahhhhhh! Ain't you gallant! Sticking up for the married woman you're puttin' the moves on! She'll always remember how you got your head ripped off defending her." He salaciously looked Kay up and down. "But don't worry, Baby. I'll comfort you real good once I take care of Tinkerbell, here."

Tony had to play him for a few more seconds. Timing was of the essence. "You're trespassing on her property, Dopey!" In a theatrical move, Tony put his arms behind him on Kay's hips, as though he was valiantly rising to her defense. "I'm warning you one last time, leave her alone!"

"Why?" Larsky growled, stepping into Tony. "Ain't I good enough to put my hands on your whore?"

That's just what Tony was hoping for: Larsky to give him an open excuse. Larsky had taken the bait. Tony set the hook: the smaller but agile young man socked Larsky square in the mouth with a lightning quick right. Larsky stepped back once, eyes wild. He daubed his mouth with the back of his hand and examined the blood. With that, Larsky descended upon Tony with a guttural scream. Tony saw his hands go up as he charged. Superb reflexes intact, he instinctively ducked up under Larsky so only his back would be open for the oncoming blows, protecting his face and chest. With Tony's head down into his stomach, Larsky tried to knee him in his face. Tony crossed both forearms over his face and managed to absorb most of the blow of Larsky's tree-trunk sized thigh coming up at him. Larsky latched onto him with his left arm, locking it like an iron vice around Tony's torso. With his right arm Larsky brought down punch after punch onto Tony's back. Kay cringed at each nauseating "THUMP!" of Larsky's fist into Tony's lower back. With all his strength, Tony pumped his legs up hard, lifting Larsky up off his feet. He forced him backward, carrying the huge man on his shoulder and slamming him against Kay's kitchen table. The table crunched against the wall behind it and toppled onto it's side. Larsky tumbled backward over the table, his head denting the wall behind him, and Tony slid out from under his grip. Larsky stumbled to his feet, lip busted, blood dripping down his chin. Tony noted the menacing rage in Larsky's eyes and stepped backward. Larsky charged him again, screeching with primordial rage. He swung a hard right, connecting with Tony's forehead. Tony rolled with the punch, spun around, and tried to bring a counter punch with his right on the rebound. But Larsky latched onto his arm, stopped him cold, and kicked him in his side. Tony tried to head butt him with the back of his head, but Larsky knocked him off his feet and drove him to the floor. He quickly pinned Tony face down to the ground. He raised his cement-like fist high into the air and brought it down six times on the back of Tony's head like a sledge hammer. Frustrated with that, he focused his eyes on the back of Tony's neck, concentrating on that vital, vulnerable point at the base of his skull. Trapped under Larsky's huge body and fully aware of Larsky's hellish hatred for him, Tony truly believed this was the end. Screaming wildly, Larsky brought down his fist toward the back of Tony's neck. But Detective Ray Kirkland dove through the air and knocked Larsky clean off of Tony before his punch connected. Ray landed on top of Larsky and put a mighty choke hold on him. Tony rolled up onto his feet to see Detective Kirkland struggling to hold Larsky to the floor.

"Stop now!" Detective Kirkland commanded the frenzied Larsky.

But Larsky became like a wild bull. He managed to get up onto his knees under Ray's tremendous weight and began to buck and kick and swing his elbows, cursing uncontrollably.

"You are under arrest! Stop now!" Ray commanded again. But hearing Larsky rant, he began to realize that there was something more than just Larsky energized beneath him.

With Ray's full weight on his back, Larsky mightily forced them both up to their feet and turned on Ray. Before Larsky could grab Detective Kirkland, Tony rushed forward and blind-sided Larsky, body slamming him against the wall.

"Get out of my way!" Ray yelled at Tony and rushed upon Larsky himself. Both men weighed the same, but Ray was clearly a head taller than Larsky, and used this advantage. He drove his right forearm deep into Larsky's throat and pinned him against the wall. Larsky grasped Ray's huge arms by the triceps and tried to pry himself loose. Ray was beginning to realize the futility of trying to use his own strength to overpower a man clearly driven by demonic rage. He turned his heart to God and forcefully spoke into Larsky's ear, not addressing Larsky, but the spirit realm:

"I bind you and command you to stop in Jesus's name!"

Larsky gulped, eyes wide, and froze for a moment. Ray was nearly stunned by the results it got, but then Larsky continued his struggle.

"Use your gun on him!" Kay yelled.

Ray ignored her. In a speedy word of knowledge, Holy Spirit identified the spirits at work in Larsky. Ray slammed him back against the wall again and this time shouted at the exposed entities:

"Murder! Violence! Rage! I bind you in the name of Jesus!"

Larsky's eyes bulged with confusion and shock. Those demons working within him calmed momentarily, but suddenly his eyes glossed over with hatred again. Trying to rebound, he pushed himself off the wall at Ray and growled:

"Get off me, you stinkin' . . . !"

Kay gasped at the racial slur Larsky spewed at Ray. Unfazed, Ray once again slammed Larsky back against the wall and this time shouted:

"I command you spirits of murder and violence to cease and be bound, right now IN JESUS'S NAME!"

Christ's authority from Heaven manifested right there in that kitchen, binding those demons. Tony and Kay watched blown away as Larsky's entire demeanor suddenly transformed from that of a frenzied beast to a yet angered, but subdued human being. Ray's prayer worked. Larsky looked up at Detective Kirkland, around at Tony and Kay, chest heaving, unable to believe he was defeated. His physical demeanor even changed. As though in a fog, Larsky dropped his arms and let his taut shoulders relax. Ray watched him on guard, ready for another wave of attack, but could clearly sense the powerful man had given up the fight. Relieved beyond measure, Ray twisted him around and pressed him up against the wall, arms spread eagle.

"You are under arrest, Mr. Larsky," Ray panted as he began to frisk him. He read his rights to him, frisked him thoroughly, and then cuffed his hands behind his back.

Larsky sat cuffed and locked in the back seat of Ray's police car. Two deputies quickly responded for backup. Ray took separate statements from Kay and Tony regarding what caused the violent outburst Ray stumbled upon. Their stories, though similar, didn't exactly jibe. Ray became suspicious at that point.

He went back into Kay's kitchen. Kay was pleading for Tony to go to the hospital.

"I'm fine!" Tony found himself explaining away his injuries to a concerned woman for the second time that day.

"He's got some bad lumps on the back of his head, and look at his lower back," she pushed Tony around and yanked up his shirt for Detective Kirkland. Tony's lower back was one swollen splotch of blue and yellow bruises from Larsky's vicious kidney punches.

"Where else are you injured, Mr. Vero?" Ray asked.

"Nowhere," Tony shook his head, irritated. "I said I'm okay. He just bruised me up, some, but I'm not dying here."

"He acts like his side is hurting from where that animal kicked him," Kay added, "and his head is a mess."

"Sit down in that chair there," Ray said.

Tony started to refuse.

"I said to sit down in that chair!" Ray commanded. "Do what I say!"

Disgruntled, Tony obeyed. Ray examined his face, noticing the welt where Carmichael had cracked him earlier that day.

"He got you pretty good, there," Ray commented. Neither Tony nor Kay bothered to explain that it wasn't Larsky who'd left that wound on Tony.

Ray pulled out a tiny penlight from his jacket pocket and flicked it on.

"Open your eyes and look up at the top of the wall over there."

Tony sighed and lifted his eyes. Ray shined the flashlight beam into Tony's right eye, then pulled it away. His left eye, then pulled it away. Tony's eyes contracted and dilated normally.

"No sign of a concussion," Ray reported. He ran his massive but gentle hand over the top and back of Tony's scalp, feeling for lumps. "You do have some pretty big knots back there. But I think you've proven your head is indeed pretty hard," he joked.

"Make him go to the emergency room!" Kay commanded Ray.

"No!" Tony snapped.

Detective Kirkland shook his head. "He doesn't seem severely injured anywhere. If his ribs are broken, the doctors can't do anything for that. If he's not cut or bleeding I can't force him to go anywhere. He may have internal injuries that we couldn't diagnose here . . ."

"I don't! I'm fine."

"You are hard headed!" she scolded Tony.

"Look who's talking!"

"Stop, now!" Ray commanded. They did. He stared them both down. "You two listen to me. You're versions of what happened here tonight are quite interesting. 'Interesting,' I say, but not exactly the same. Would you care to tell me what really happened?"

They both looked away from Ray. Kay felt ashamed, knowing what was about to happen with Tony before Larsky interrupted. Ironically, she was grateful now that Larsky did interrupt them. She could still say she'd at least remained faithful to Todd and their marriage. Thanks to Larsky! She never would have believed she'd have Ed Larsky to thank for anything.

Ray looked at them, waiting for an answer. "Well? Mr. Vero, I thought you and Mr. Larsky were VECO partners. On the same side."

Tony laughed sarcastically. "I am on VECO's side. So's he. But Ed Larsky's hated me for years."

"Why's he hate you?"

"Why's anyone hate anyone?"

Ray got impatient. "It was not a philosophical question! Did you steal his wife or girlfriend from him? Do you owe him money? Did you run over his dog . . ."

"I've never done anything personally to Ed Larsky. Never. I don't know why he hates me." Tony did know why Larsky hated him. But Ed Larsky's virulent jealousy of him wasn't any of Detective Kirkland's business.

He looked at them one more time. "For the last time, do you two want to tell me what really happened?"

Tony shook his head adamantly. "I stick to my statement."

Kay reluctantly nodded. "Me too."

Ray shook his head with disgust. He looked at Tony: "Breached, violated evidence," he looked at Kay: "Destroyed evidence. Now you two have given discrepant accounts of what happened here tonight. I don't think any of you people have told me the truth all week." He turned and walked out the door.

Detective Kirkland told the two deputies to stay with Kay and watch after her for a few hours outside her house. He went back into the house and told Tony to wait outside. Tony looked Kay in the eyes, trying to elicit some sort of look from her before he left. She looked down and wouldn't meet his gaze. He understood the embarrassment she was probably feeling at the moment. If Larsky hadn't shown up, who knows what they might be doing alone in her house at that point. In *Todd's* house. Tony sauntered out the door, feeling the sting of shame.

Ray went to Kay.

"I've asked the deputies to stick around here and keep an eye on you until you get settled in. They'll be outside."

"Thank you," she said. "But it's not necessary."

"My wife Shelly and I want to know if you're still going to come to church with us in the morning, like you said last night?"

She hesitated. "I . . . I don't know. It's so late now, and after all this garbage that happened here with that awful Ed Larsky, I just don't know . . ."

Ray put his hands on her shoulders. "Listen: You were really hip on the idea of coming to church with us last night when we had the opportunity to pray with you. I'll tell you a harsh fact: anytime anyone takes a positive step towards the Lord, the first thing the devil's gonna do is try and bring discouragement and confusion. He doesn't want you to come into the holy presence of God, because he knows if you do, God's gonna love you and get you. That's all most of this was about tonight with Mr. Larsky and Tony Vero. A distraction and a discouragement."

She looked up at him. "You still want me to come? Aren't you mad at me?"

Ray smiled. "No! I'm not mad. I just don't know who to believe, right now. If you can handle that, my wife and I would really love for you to come to church in the morning and be ministered to. And Shaniqua and LaTonya would love to see Dylon."

Kay nodded her head and smiled weakly. "All right. I'll come."

"Can I get a handshake on that, Ma'am?"

She giggled lightly. "You sure can."

They shook.

Ray went outside and told Tony to get in his truck and meet him at the station.

"What for?" Tony asked.

Ray opened the door of his car. "Mr. Larsky here wants to press charges against you."

"What? You were here! That's preposterous!"

Ray climbed into the driver's seat. "Well, since I can't get a straight answer from anybody tonight, he might just be right."

"Yeah, right," Tony grumbled.

Ray cranked his car to leave, Larsky sat silently sulking in the back seat. As Detective Kirkland backed the car out of the driveway, Tony walked over to where Larsky could see him. When Larsky locked eyes with him, Tony tapped his forefinger up to his temple and mouthed, "I'm smart!" Larsky suddenly remembered their conversation at VECO two days earlier. More hatred flooded Larsky's soul. He'd been one-upped by Tony Vero once again.

"Last time ever!" he growled in that back seat.

In the wee hours of Sunday morning, a very somber Carmichael and Joseph Vero came to the Beaver County Sheriff's Department to bail out Larsky. Tony immediately phoned them after Larsky was hauled away. He told them what happened, laying all the blame on Larsky's hot head.

"He freaked out on me!" Tony whined to the elder Veros.

"But did you have to get him arrested?" Joseph chided him.

"Me get him arrested?" Tony lied. "Are you nuts? I can't help it he assaulted a sheriff's detective and then called him the 'n' word. That prejudiced moron!"

Detective Kirkland charged Larsky with assaulting an officer. A magistrate set his bail at five thousand dollars. Carmichael paid the bail, Joseph acted as his attorney and heard the charges from Detective Kirkland. Joseph commanded Larsky to drop any ideas about pressing charges against Tony, by Carmichael's decree. Tony was standing there with Carmichael and Joseph when a deputy led a scowling Ed Larsky out of the jail annex in handcuffs. His bottom lip was cut and swollen from Tony's punch. He wouldn't even look at Tony. He was uncuffed, processed, and commanded not to leave the county until his hearing in several weeks. He said nothing. Joseph impatiently told the deputy they knew the procedure and took the paper work. The four of them turned quickly to leave, Larsky sulking in the lead, Tony slowly taking up the rear. They were just about to the exit when Detective Kirkland appeared coming from the opposite direction. He put his hands up and ordered the quartet to stop.

"Now what?" Joseph asked angrily. "We've already been through due process and now we'd like . . ."

Ray interrupted the attorney. "I have some questions for you regarding the Todd Falco case."

"It's very late, Detective!" Joseph spoke on behalf of the quartet. "It's been an extremely long and frustrating evening. Can your questions not wait?"

Ray smiled and shook his head. "No! They cannot. This will only take a few moments of your time and we can do this right here." He pulled out VECO's attendance records from a folder he held. He asked Larsky and Carmichael, "Regarding employees comings and goings at VECO, how come everyone's work hours are so meticulously recorded except for Todd Falco's?"

"What?" Carmichael asked with rude impatience. Larsky completely turned away from Detective Kirkland in disgust.

Ray held up the records. "Attendance is meticulously kept on all employees at VECO. Hourly wage earners mostly, of course, but even most of your sales executives and salaried employees work schedules are recorded to monitor their hours. Everyone except for Todd Falco. His daily attendance is marked, but that's as far as it goes. Unlike all your other employees, he comes and goes without record during the day."

Carmichael snatched the folder from Detective Kirkland, brow deeply furrowed. He pretended to scan through it, as though he were trying to figure out what the detective meant. He already had the pat answer for that question memorized. He turned to Larsky like he was looking for help. "Ed, this is your work. What's going on with this?"

Larsky, staring at the wall, sighed impatiently. He knew the drill, too. "Todd Falco is our marketing manager and he spends most of his time away from the office dealing with all our companies," Larsky droned mindlessly.

"Oh, yeah," Carmichael acted like his memory was jogged, but still answered Detective Kirkland with indignation. "Falco's in charge of all our companies' marketing schemes. He's to come and go as he pleases, since most of his work is done out of the office. I told Larsky years ago not to keep track of Falco's time at VECO, since most of it is inconsequential to what he does for us. Can we all go now?"

"You trusted him that much?"

"We're not number one in the tri-state region for nothing, Detective. Todd Falco was one of my top men."

"Yet you want to fire him, you said the other day."

Carmichael became riled. "I told you! His home life does not meet up to VECO's expectations any more! I cannot tolerate controversial figures ruining VECO's reputation . . ."

Ray turned and gawked at Ed Larsky with a look of deep confusion on his face. Carmichael noticed his gaze and became even more indignant.

"Ed's a different story!"

"Oh?" Detective Kirkland laughed questioningly. "A violent racist is not a 'controversial figure' over at your business?"

Joseph stepped in front of Carmichael and stopped him before he said something to get himself in trouble, too. "Detective Kirkland," Joseph said authoritatively, "I think this conversation has gone far enough."

"How about transit records for tax purposes?" Ray asked. "Why don't I find any transit records in your files or in Mr. Falco's personal files, with all the traveling he supposedly does?"

"That's Falco's business," Larsky droned to the wall again. "He's to keep track of that."

"Well, he hasn't."

"Who cares?"

"Well, I do, right now, Mr. Larsky. Mr. Vero, will VECO's satellite companies where Mr. Falco spends so much time have records of his hours at their offices?"

Joseph interrupted him again. "Sir! It is going on one o'clock in the morning! From your lame line of questioning I gather that you really don't have many plausible leads on Mr. Falco's disappearance, do you?"

Ray folded his arms and looked up at the ceiling, trying to be patient with Joseph Vero.

"Answer me, please?"

"No, Mr. Vero, I don't. I've not one trace of Todd Falco anywhere. All of the APBs I've put out on him and his Camaro have turned up nothing. It's like he's completely vanished into thin air. Meanwhile, one thing I definitely do have is all of you over at VECO apparently self-destructing, as was demonstrated tonight by Mr. Larsky and Mr. Vero here."

"You unfairly ransacked our offices, yesterday, Detective," Carmichael said. "You took everything regarding Mr. Falco you could get your hands on. You have drilled us, twice now. You have all you could get from VECO, with no hindrance whatsoever from us. So if you have any more questions about anything, I'm afraid you're just going to have to figure it out yourself. We're not making any further comments to you about anything at VECO."

Ray laughed. "You don't have to! Everything there seems to be unraveling quite quickly before our eyes. Falco's case keeps pointing right back to VECO, right back to you four. You're scrambling like cockroaches in the light. And unfortunately for you all, I happen to be around to watch it all."

Joseph put his hand up. "You've already needlessly harassed our company enough. We know you're out to get us . . ."

Ray chuckled and shook his head at Joseph's worthless self-pity.

"We know that the law enforcement agencies in this region are all prejudiced against Carmichael Vero because of false charges against him that he not only beat, but are ancient history."

"I'm not interested in ancient history, Mr. Vero. I'm interested in the ugly present. And things keep getting uglier and murkier around you four every minute. I'm turning the focus of my investigation on you all, now. And I don't leave any stones unturned. I just wanted you to know that you're going to be seeing a whole lot more of me over the next few days, and I expect you all to be smiling and cooperative."

Carmichael walked on, brushing arrogantly past Detective Kirkland. Joseph and Larsky followed him. However, as Tony tried to rush by, Ray snatched the youngest Vero by his shoulder.

"You're comin' with me!" Ray smiled.

Carmichael and Joseph both turned around fuming. "Now what do you want?"

"This doesn't concern you two, gentlemen!" Ray snapped. "I just need to talk to your boy here for a minute. He'll be right out!"

Tony sighed, exhausted, but compliant. He waved at the other three. "Go on."

In an empty office Detective Kirkland looked Tony straight in the eyes.

"Mr. Larsky says that when he came to the house, you were inside making out with Mrs. Falco. That true?"

Tony shook his head. "No," he said calmly. "Larsky's a liar. He's lied to you probably every time he's spoken to you this week. He's lying tonight."

"You weren't kissing on Kay Falco in her house tonight? Being romantic? You weren't taking advantage of a crushed and broken woman who's desperately vulnerable at the moment?"

Tony could only look out the window, unwilling to match Ray's gaze.

Ray pointed his huge finger right between Tony's eyes. "You listen to me, Tony Vero: You stay completely away from Kay Falco from now on. You understand me? She has enough worries on her soul right now with her husband vanishing like he has. You two don't need to add the sin of adultery to her baggage at this dangerous point in her life. You *both* will get burned by that sin. You got that, Romeo?"

"I'm not 'Romeo'!" Tony growled.

"Well then, show some common sense and stay away from a vulnerable woman who's just dying for something to fill that awful void in her life! You don't need to be going out to see her in person anymore. If you need anything else from her, phone her! You got that?"

"What business is it of yours?"

"I'm going to protect people from trouble any chance I get! In fact, I'll tell you this, too: You're crazy for trusting those three men from VECO. Mr. Larsky does indeed hate you, and Carmichael and Joseph don't seem to be real thrilled with you at the moment, either. Don't trust them."

"Oh, yeah? Well tell me, Mr. Know-It-All, who should I trust?"

Ray grinned ear to ear and patted Tony on the shoulder. "Jesus Christ! The only One we can trust."

Tony smiled faintly and shook his head. "I deserved that one, didn't I?"

"Set yourself right up for it!"

"Well, there must be something to it. You're the second person today to tell me that."

As Joseph pulled out of the Sheriff's department parking lot in his Porsche, Carmichael and Larsky plopped into Carmichael's Cadillac. Inside, Larsky punched the dashboard with a furious blow.

"I hate Tony Vero!" he screamed. He turned toward Carmichael. "Everything's falling apart! Benny Miller got away alive! That cop in there is onto us! Tony's makin' a fool of us. We're gonna lose it *all* if we don't do somethin'!"

Carmichael was speechless. He knew Larsky was right. Things were deteriorating more rapidly every hour.

"Did you hear me?" Larsky yelled. "We're gonna lose everything. What are we gonna do? No! You're the boss. What are *you* gonna do, Carmichael?"

Carmichael looked out the windshield up at the sky. The moon was a sliver away from being full. After a long, pensive silence, Carmicheal proclaimed:

"You and I are going to fly to New York tomorrow."

Larsky couldn't believe his ears. "What did you say?"

"You heard me."

"We're going to see the Magic Genie?"

Carmichael's eyes burned with hellish determination. That lust for power and control rose within him like a poisoned wellspring. He was overtaken by his impulse to fight for survival at the top no matter what the cost.

"We're not gonna lose one thing. We're not going to allow Todd Falco or Tony or that stinkin' detective in there to jeopardize our future. We're going to fight and pay whatever price it takes to stay on top. You and I are going to Cyrus Moreau's workshop tomorrow night. Cyrus promises he can fix everything for you and me then. We're going to do whatever he says and let him work whatever magic he has to keep us on top and alive and living how *we* want to live, Ed!"

"Just us?"

"Just you and me."

Larsky smiled with evil glee. "It's about time you and I take control of everything."

"And we will now, my friend. It's our destiny!"

THIRTY-SIX

A t 6:30 am, an exhausted Carmichael Vero was climbing the stairs of his Lear
jet at the Beaver County Airport. Ed Larsky was packing their luggage and
golf clubs into the cargo bay under the belly of the plane. Larsky was delighted to be
going to Great Neck, New York, to participate in Cyrus Moreau's black mass and workshop.
The witchcraft and savagery of the event would be well worth the trouble to Ed. He knew
Cyrus would be able to solve their problems for them if they'd give themselves over to
his desires that night. Carmichael was just plain nervous. He knew Cyrus was going to
make him pay in person for having rejected his services the past few years. Who knew
what Cyrus was going to make Carmichael do at that horrible black mass. But down
inside, like Larsky, he knew that once they'd heeded Cyrus's dark predilections, their
situation would change. The Todd Falco ordeal would be dissolved, put behind them,
and they'd be on top again.

Once they paid the devil in full . . .

The governor's mansion in Harrisburg, Pennsylvania, was in its glory at 9:30 that
Sunday morning. The morning sunshine was hot, creating a light haze of moisture
hovering above the misty lawn. All the flowers were in bloom, the lawn was trimmed;
birds and squirrels chirped and played. The American and state flags, high on their poles,
hung limp in the breezeless morning air. Below in the flower garden, the Governor of
Pennsylvania and Pennsylvania State Attorney General Michael Davis sat at a white iron
garden table, drinking coffee. There was an empty third chair between them. On the
table, near a steaming coffee pot, a cassette player was playing Edgar Waters' recording
of Tony Vero's account of the Family he'd told to Kay Falco, two days earlier. Michael
Davis had come to meet the Governor with a very strategic agenda. He tried to appear
stoic, careful not to watch the Governor's face while he listened to the revelatory tape.
But in fact, Davis was very apprehensive about this meeting. He'd had so many perplexing
disappointments over the years every time he tried to launch any investigation of
Carmichael Vero. Would he now find the Governor would behave the same as all the
others, rejecting his notions too? He knew Carmichael Vero was a powerful kingpin,

255

using the misery of human bondage to make an illegal fortune. But any time he tried to go after the man, that intangible "cloak" would manifest, rendering Carmichael's criminal empire seemingly impenetrable. It was the most disconcerting situation Michael Davis had ever faced. He was the Attorney General of Pennsylvania! He had the legal authority to investigate and prosecute on behalf of the state of Pennsylvania. Yet every time he tried to move against Carmichael, his power and authority seemed rendered impotent. He didn't understand how Carmichael could win every time. Davis had led combat missions in Vietnam, trained grunts as a Marine captain, fought to put dangerous criminals away in courtrooms, and waged fierce political fights as the state attorney general. Warfare was a way of life to him. But Carmichael Vero represented a war fought and lost on every level. The government now even seemed to side with the vile man, with so many politicians and law enforcement leaders blocking and discouraging Michael's every attempt at prosecutions. So here he was again, risking rejection once more. This time, however, he was taking his case to the top. The Governor seemed eager to hear Edgar Waters' recordings and listen to Davis' case. The Governor did indeed listen intently to the Tony Vero recording. When it was over, Michael Davis turned off the cassette player. The Governor had a grave look of concern on his face. Good! Davis wanted to add fuel to the fire.

"I have more, if you're willing to hear it."

The Governor lifted his coffee cup to his mouth and nodded. "I want to hear everything you have for me."

Davis went to press the play button. "This is Tony Vero's father, Peter Vero, recorded in his home about five years ago."

The husky voice of the late Pete Vero could be heard on a static-ridden recording: ". . . if it wasn't for the way Carmichael set things up, if it wasn't for the Family, me and Joe and Carmichael would either be second rate pencil pushers, or we'd all be in jail. Any garbage we as a family gotta put up with is well worth the security and cash the Family affords us . . ."

The sound of a truck going by could be heard, more static. Michael stopped the tape.

"Who was he speaking to?" the Governor asked.

"He was speaking to his wife and his son."

"He was talking to his own family about the Family?" the Governor asked.

"Yes, sir. I have one more recording that was captured by my investigator yesterday. The quality is pretty poor. He recorded it long distance, same as the others, then I had to record it over my answering machine as he played it for me last night. You can still make out what they're saying, though." He pressed the play button again. The Saturday morning argument between Tony and Carmichael and Larsky on Tony's front porch could be heard. Carmichael mentioned the Family by name. They all argued about Tony's investigation of Todd Falco's disappearance. Some of what was said was intelligible; other parts were not. When the conversation moved from the porch into the house the quality became so bad they could no longer make out who was saying what. Davis turned off the cassette player again.

"Who's this 'Todd Falco' they're looking for?" the Governor asked.

"He's a VECO employee. He's been missing since Tuesday. The police have been investigating his disappearance. VECO has also hired their private investigator Tony Vero to find him. Tony Vero was explaining all that Family information about Carmichael and Ed Larsky to Todd Falco's wife. My investigator believes this Todd Falco to be a key Family member. From all he can gather, Falco disappeared with a whole lot of Family money. They've been scrambling like chickens with their heads cut off ever since. That's how we've suddenly been able to capture so many sensitive conversations on tape after years of nearly nothing. In their apparent panic over their missing cash, they've dropped their guard."

"They certainly sound divided on that last recording."

"You know what the Bible says about a house divided, sir."

"Tell me about this Edgar Waters who's been investigating Carmichael Vero."

"Sergeant Waters was the communications specialist in the unit I trained at Camp Pendleton back in the early seventies, sir. He was a corporal, then, an electronics and surveillance expert, a dedicated soldier, and one tough Marine. He was a fellow Pennsylvanian and my most loyal soldier. He served with honor in Desert Storm, and then retired. I met up with him in Philly back in '94. He'd put in his twenty in the Marines, retired, and started his own private investigations agency. When everyone else in this state refused my wishes to launch an investigation on Vero, I hired Sergeant Waters. He moved to Beaver Falls and has been onto Carmichael and VECO every since. He has since hired a young woman fresh from police academy and got her hired at VECO as a secretary. So we also have an undercover agent keeping watch over Carmichael and VECO."

"And you're paying her salary, too?"

"I am fully funding this entire private investigation out of my own pocket. Yes."

"But Mike, that's the thing that I'm concerned about. You're the Attorney General of Pennsylvania, yet you've personally hired an investigator to look into the life of a private citizen, as suspicious as Carmichael Vero might be."

"President Clinton hired private investigators to dig up dirt on law abiding citizens, sir. Look, I've tried for years to open up a new investigation on Carmichael Vero, but I've met nothing but resistance on all sides."

"Mike, you're the State Attorney General! You call the shots. You open the investigations."

"But no one will hear me out on it. I've . . . I've never been able to talk to anyone but my wife about this, so I'll lay this on you. Go easy on me! I know I'm about to sound like a paranoid, conspiracy-theory nut. But every time I've tried to launch a major investigation, no one, and I mean no one, will cooperate with me. I've had lieutenant governors block me. I've had both state and U.S. senators come to advise me against it. I've had leaders of law enforcement agencies turn me down, flat cold, refusing me. No one has been willing to climb on board this issue with me. The FBI refuses to investigate because Carmichael Vero and VECO have had three IRS audits in nineteen years, and came up clean as a baby out of the bathtub every time. The FBI says they'd have nothing to build their case on. People immediately complain of lack of evidence, they accuse me of a 'witch hunt,' or a personal vendetta because of his original Mafia trial back in Beaver County. I mean this has been going on for years."

"And what about the SBI?"

"The SBI's who I need the most and Harvey Kitner's blocked me every step of the way." Harvey Kitner was the Director of the State Bureau of Investigations. No SBI investigation could be launched without his authorization. "The man won't even hear the name 'Carmichael Vero' anymore."

The Governor shook his head. "Have you ever thought of launching a racketeering or corruption investigation on any of these officials . . ."

"I've already had them investigated secretly. I've turned up nothing. No links between Carmichael Vero and any of these guys, pre or post Carmichael's Mafia days. As far as I could find out, Harvey Kitner and Carmichael Vero have never even met. Yet the man has defiantly, even arrogantly at times, blocked my every request."

The Governor took another sip of his coffee. He rewound the tape for a few seconds and then let the last part of Tony's story play over again.

"But this changes everything now, doesn't it Mike?"

"Very compelling, to say the least. On one loop we have the entire story of Carmichael's triumph over the legal system via assassination of a witness, and on the other loop we have three of VECO's top dogs and Tony Vero running scared about a missing employee and missing money. All criticisms of me aside, I'd say we should have the complete backing of any law enforcement agency on this one."

"And you need the SBI."

"And Harvey Kitner will stand right in my way, for some unknown reason."

The Governor sighed. "You really want to go through with this?"

"We'll give him the benefit of the doubt. Play the tape for him, offer him the chance to launch the investigation himself. If he does, we'll go soft on him."

"If he refuses you this time?"

"I'm gonna cut his legs out from underneath him, sir. He'll never forget that he purposefully refused me for no good reason."

"You believe Carmichael Vero's that guilty?"

"He represents everything unjust and sinful. He should have been convicted in '81. He's still free and operating today, preying on our sick society." He pointed to the tape recorder: "Now we know why. It's a travesty."

"I'll call in Harvey," the Governor said. He called over a state trooper standing guard nearby and told him to bring out Harvey Kitner to join them.

Harvey Kitner was a stout, balding white man, in his fifties like the Governor and Michael Davis. He strolled confidently out of the mansion into the garden, chewing gum. He rolled his eyes when he spotted Attorney General Davis. An aloof man, he never hid his disdain for Michael Davis. Kitner had a record as a tough law enforcer his entire career. The two had never clashed on any issues other than the Carmichael Vero investigation requests while holding their government positions. However, Kitner was a political liberal, and he disliked Michael Davis's conservative views and Christian beliefs. He shook the Governor's hand as he joined them at the table, and politely but limply shook Davis's hand without even looking at him.

"Gentlemen," he said carefree, "what can I do for you this morning?"

"Harvey, Mike and I want you to listen to something to get your opinion on it."

Kitner nodded in agreement. "Sure. Fire away."

Davis reached over and pressed the play button on the cassette player. Tony Vero once again told his story about Larsky's assassination of the Mafia witness in '81. Once Kitner realized what the tape was about he glanced away from Davis and muttered, "Figures." For the rest of the recording he sat bored, eyes glossed over. Once Davis stopped the recording at the end, Kitner looked over at him and sighed, "You never give up, do you?"

Davis shook his head slowly but deliberately. "No, Mr. Kitner. I do not."

Harvey Kitner looked at the Governor of Pennsylvania. "I suppose you've heard his recording of Pete Vero, too."

"I have."

"And we're all supposed to be moved by all this? This suddenly makes Carmichael Vero a criminal?"

"No," Michael Davis leaned over the table. "This doesn't 'suddenly' make him one. He's been one all along." He pointed to the cassette player. "And now we have proof . . ."

Kitner looked over at the Governor. "Carmichael Vero may or may not have been in the Mafia way back when. But since '81, he's run a legitimate business, VECO has survived not one, not two, but three IRS audits. Their record stands impeccable . . ."

"And it appears that there is now new evidence that would merit a criminal investigation," Davis asserted.

Kitner pointed at the Attorney General and addressed the Governor. "He's been after Vero since the assassination, even though there's not been one shred of evidence suggesting Vero is into anything illegal. There have been no signs of any evil-doing on his part and definitely none at VECO. I believe Michael Davis's judgment is clouded by his hatred and lust for vengeance against Carmichael Vero for a humiliation that's never been solved and certainly has never been linked to Vero himself."

"His own flesh and blood relative implicates both him and his henchman on this tape," Davis said.

"That brings up another good question: Where did you get this recording?" Kitner asked.

"That's my business."

"You're investigating Vero yourself, aren't you?" Kitner's face was turning red. "I should have guessed you would."

The spells of protection Cyrus Moreau had sent out to cloak Carmichael Vero and the Family were firmly implanted into Kitner's psyche. Harvey Kitner was faithfully performing the function of those spells. Now, Kitner didn't know he was under the influence of a demonic spell. He didn't even know someone named Cyrus Moreau existed. But the spells worked well, regardless.

"Will you have the SBI launch an investigation with this new evidence?" Davis asked.

Kitner slammed his fist on the iron table, bouncing over the coffee pot. "Absolutely not! I will not take a part in the railroading of a citizen of this state!"

Davis and the Governor looked at each other. They knew something was queer about Kitner's blind refusal, but neither knew anything about witchcraft spells.

"You see what I mean, sir?" Davis asked him.

The Governor sat, eyes wide, perplexed at what he just witnessed. "I do." He looked over at Harvey Kitner. "You're going to ignore a prime piece of evidence like this Tony Vero's testimony and completely turn down the opportunity to investigate?"

Kitner sat up, nervously. "You don't understand, Governor." He pointed at Davis. "This man's judgment is clouded by his past humiliation. I can't let a state official sworn to uphold the law use his position to harass a seemingly innocent citizen without just cause."

"You see no 'just cause' in investigating a powerful businessman like Vero for criminal activities testified to by his own relative, caught on tape?"

Kitner's forehead broke out into a sweat. The curse was trying to work through him, but the light of truth was beginning to breed confusion in his entranced mind. "I . . . I . . ." was all he could get out.

"Harvey, I'm afraid it's your judgment that appears to be clouded."

"What . . . what are you talking about, Governor?" Harvey asked with glazed eyes.

The Governor nodded at Michael Davis. He leaned down to get a briefcase from under the table. He opened it, pulled out a manila envelope, and slid it across the table to Harvey Kitner.

Kitner wouldn't open it. "What's this about?" he pointed angrily at the envelope.

"Your secretary of eight years," Michael Davis said.

Kitner's eyes lit up with shock. "What of her?" he demanded angrily.

"Twelve thousand dollars of embezzlement. That's what. A few hundred here, a few hundred there, but a steady stream taken over a five year period."

"What are you talking about?" Kitner nervously feigned ignorance.

"You found out about it three years ago. You covered it up."

Kitner straightened up, indignant. "What an accusation!"

Davis pointed to the envelope. "It's all right there, Harvey. Three years ago, a two thousand dollar discrepancy occurred in the books regarding the Widows and Orphans Charity Foundation you very nobly started twelve years ago. Your secretary had her hands in the pot, over the years had accumulated twelve thousand in embezzled funds from your charity, and you caught her subtracting two grand from your fund into her banking account. When you caught her, you covered it up by replacing the money with two thousand of your own dollars. Then you signed the treasury statements like nothing had happened. The embezzlement stopped at that point." Davis picked up his coffee cup and looked away from Kitner, out over the gardens. "But the sexual affair you had been carrying on with her for four years didn't. It continues today, without your wife and four daughters knowing anything about it."

Harvey Kitner sat with his shoulders slumped, his chest heaving hard. His posture was that of a parade float with a bad leak. He stared at Davis, face crimson, hands shaking.

"What do you have to say, Harvey?" the Governor asked him sternly.

Kitner looked back and forth at the two, wide-eyed and trembling. "This is blackmail!" he rasped.

"By no means," Michael Davis coolly assured him. "But what your secretary did was blackmail. When you caught her dipping into your charity pot, you then realized the magnitude of how much she'd actually taken over the years. You threatened to have her arrested and press charges. But she threatened to tell your wife and children all about your sexual relationship if you didn't fix the problem for her. You forked over the two grand, letting her keep the two she took. But you swiftly gave control of the Widows and Orphans Charity over to an SBI captain to ensure that your mistress's greed would never land you that close to scandal again. To show her gratefulness for your 'mercy,' she poured out her love and affection on you more than ever, always with the unwritten threat that she'd spill the beans about your affair to your wife and family if you even got any ideas about bringing up her embezzlements again."

Harvey Kitner was sheet white. Michael Davis was shining the light of truth on the core sin that opened the door for Cyrus Moreau's spell to lay hold of Harvey Kitner. The iniquity of sexual lust was the door for the witchcraft to enter his life. The spell attached itself to that oozing sore of adultery that infested his soul. From that point on, it was as though a fog entered Harvey Kitner's mind every time Carmichael Vero's name was brought up. Carmichael suddenly had a spot in Harvey's heart, for no known reason to him. And any time somebody mentioned a "Carmichael Vero investigation," that demonic influence assigned over him would rise up and cause Harvey to immediately defend the criminal back in Beaver County.

"You want me to start an investigation of Carmichael Vero?" he tried to throw out a line of hope for himself.

Michael Davis pursed his lips and shook his head vehemently. "Nope. I want you to step down as Director of SBI."

"S . . . s . . . step down?"

The Governor nodded in agreement. "You're a year and a half from retirement. Retire early. We'll grant you full pension. No penalties. But step down from your office immediately."

"And get out of my way," Michael Davis stared him down.

"But I . . ."

Davis put his hand up. "I know what you're going to say, and I agree with some of it. You didn't embezzle any money. You're not a thief. Your mistress is. Therefore, I'm willing to look away from the whole sleazy mess, if you'll just step down, get out of my way, and let justice prevail in this state again."

Kitner angrily slid his chair back away from the table and stood up, knees wobbling. He pointed an accusing finger at Davis. "You! You love this, don't you? You've always been a judgmental, finger pointing, religious hypocrite. Why don't you remember those oh-so-important words of that Savior of yours: 'He who is without sin, cast the first stone'?"

Davis shook his head firmly. "Not true, sir. I've held that 'stone' you accuse me of throwing for three years now. I'm still not throwing it. I've covered your sin. If I was everything you accuse me of being I would have openly pressed charges against you and your secretary and seen you both publicly humiliated and jailed. Instead, I've covered your sin. That's what my God says to do in His word. 'Love covers a multitude of sins,' and 'It's a good thing to cover the sins of a brother.' I'm letting you leave office in honor, not shame. So is the Governor. He's gone to bat for you. You ought to thank him."

"Your resignation is effective immediately. I want you to hold a press conference and make it official first thing in the morning," the Governor commanded.

Harvey Kitner swayed woozily in the warm, still spring air. Stripped of his authority as Director of SBI, the spell that had plagued him for years was instantly rendered impotent within him. Suddenly, a thought occurred to him: *Why have I been defending Carmicheal Vero so, a man I don't even know?* He realized if he had not defended him, maybe this scene wouldn't have been played out today.

The Governor and Davis both looked up at him from their seats with deep concern. He looked wan and weak.

"Harvey, do you need me to call in a doctor for you?" the Governor asked.

Kitner shook his head. He stared out over the lush gardens, quite bewildered, then turned on his heals to leave.

"Harvey?" Michael Davis called out.

Kitner turned around, eyes dull and lifeless.

"I know . . . I know you probably don't care much to hear this, but if you need help straightening out some of your personal problems, I am very willing to stand by you."

Kitner didn't acknowledge him. He turned and left.

The Governor turned to Michael Davis. "That was the strangest thing I've ever witnessed."

"You saw the way he mindlessly defended Carmichael Vero?" Davis asked.

"It was like he wasn't even aware of it. Like he was under a spell or something."

The truth of his statement still didn't sink in to them.

"I have a question for you, now," Davis announced. "What if the next SBI director reacts the same way?"

The Governor shook his head and picked up the overturned coffee pot. "He won't. You're going to personally launch this investigation. I'm ordering the interim SBI director to put you in charge of whatever resources of the SBI you'll need. You'll launch the Carmichael Vero investigation immediately."

The stoic Davis was excited, but held his emotion. "Thank you, sir. I want Leo Gandtz to head my investigation."

"Gandtz? 'The Bull'? What case are you going to pry his jaws off to get him on the Vero investigation?"

"Believe it or not, he's already on it. He just doesn't know it."

Davis got up to leave. He shook the Governor's hand firmly.

"Thank you, sir, for your support."

The Governor remained in his chair, but squeezed Davis's hand tighter, not letting it go. "Don't thank me. Just get Carmicheal Vero this time."

Davis nodded. "Him and his empire."

Kay Falco could not believe what she was experiencing at Beaver Valley Covenant Church. The congregation had broken through to the throne of Christ Himself with their abandoned Sunday worship. Holy Spirit had overtaken the place. The Presence of God was incredible. People were raising their hands, singing new songs to the Lord, worshipping Him freely. And He was touching hearts and lives, including Kay Falco's. She was weeping again. But this time, it was not so much over the sorrow and heartache of her broken life. These tears were cleansing tears. In the manifest Presence of God, Kay Falco was convicted that she was lost without Christ. The worship leader spoke at one point about asking "Jesus into your heart." Kay knew she needed to. She knew she wanted to. Her life was in shambles. She wanted the forgiveness and love this man sang of. She had never felt anything like this before. She didn't know God could seem so real.

Ray Kirkland watched Kay intently during the worship service. He was ushering that month, so he observed her from the section of the church to which he was assigned. He saw his wife Shelly rubbing Kay's back gently while Kay was broken. Ray prayed in his Spirit language for her the whole time. He and Shelly wanted with all their hearts for Kay Falco to be saved that Sunday. They had brought many visitors to Covenant Church over the years, and left disappointed many times as those did not leave with Christ in their hearts. The Kirklands prayed before the service that this Sunday would be different. Kay Falco was ripe for salvation. She needed Jesus in the worst way. They would accept nothing less than for her to be saved today during a salvation altar call.

Just when things were really picking up, Ray's pager went off.

Irritated, he almost wanting to ignore it. But he knew it was the Sheriff's Department. Greatly disappointed, Ray went into the lobby and speed dialed Sheriff DeBona's number on his cell phone.

Sheriff DeBona answered and told Ray, "We need you over here now. There's an important development here that you need to be a part of."

Ray could have argued and asked to be excused for a while, but didn't. Displeased as he was to have to leave the church service this day, he complied.

"I'll be right there, Sir."

He went back in and whispered what was going on to Shelly. She stopped praying long enough to kiss him, and then turned her attention back to Kay.

"Save Kay today, Lord," Ray whispered the prayer once more as he exited the building.

The other Family members were incredulous at Joseph Vero's announcement.

"What do you mean Carmichael and Larsky left town for the day?" Warren Zann demanded an explanation.

Anthony and Warren Zann, Marv Lenstein, and Joseph Vero were gathered in Carmichael Vero's office at VECO. Joseph had the outside speakers blasting that loud music. Carmichael and Larsky were to be there with them, so they could all put the finishing touches on VECO's reports for Tuesday's stockholders banquet. However, Joseph had just informed them of their Family head's abrupt change of plans.

"Carmichael phoned me at 5:30 this morning and told me he had to go out of town for the day and was taking Larsky." He showed no emotions.

"Where did they go?" Anthony Zann asked, uncharacteristically impatient.

"They didn't inform me," Joseph answered calmly.

"What kind of scam do they have going?" Anthony asked.

"Will they tell us where they went when they get back?" Marv Lenstein asked his legal partner.

"That's Carmichael's business, not mine," Joseph shook his head.

"This is way too fishy!" Warren Zann said, paranoid as usual.

"And why did Larsky have to go with him?" Marv Lenstein asked. "I saw that he smoked Stephen McClintlock and Jermichael DeVries for us. But what about Benny Miller? I haven't seen his dead face on the news. I hope he's cooling off down at the morgue too, by now."

Joseph shook his head grimly. "Benny Miller's alive and in police custody."

The Family members were growing furious.

"Why? How?"

"Benny Miller's whole operation was raided last night before Larsky could get to him. The cops have him cooling off in jail. He's alive, and heavily guarded."

Anthony Zann shook his head: "This is not good."

Warren began to whine again, then Marv Lenstein joined him. Just as the cacophony of complaining reached a crescendo, Joseph Vero slammed his fist on Carmichael's desk.

"Gentlemen!" he said gravely. "We are the Family! We rule this whole region! We do not act this way! We've never lost it during a crisis before. And we're not going to start now! Carmichael and Larsky are off taking care of our problem even as we speak, I'm sure. I don't know where they are, but they're not the type to abandon ship. This type of behavior will not solve even the least of our problems. We are still on top! And when this is all said and done, we will still find ourselves on top. We must act like we're there, in the meantime!" He looked around at them authoritatively. "Do I make myself clear, Gentlemen?"

After a moment's hesitation, the other remaining Family members slowly began to concede that Joseph was right. Yes, they admitted. This wasn't over yet.

"Good!" he said. "Now, there's not thing we can do about Carmichael and Larsky. We need to attend to this work before us to make sure VECO shines brilliantly on Tuesday."

The Zanns and Marv Lenstein finally relaxed a bit and began to focus on their reports. Joseph was pleased that his speech loosened them up. Oh, he didn't believe one word of it. But he needed them to so he could implement his own safeguards over the next day or so. As he watched them settle into their VECO reports, Joseph Vero thought: "Rome is *surely* burning, now."

Holy Spirit's conviction was all over Kay Falco.

Pastor Dave came up toward the end of the worship service at Covenant Church and began to speak while the musicians played. He spoke a message of hope in Christ. He explained that through Jesus the curse of Adam and Eve that brought sin into the world was broken. That all of our sins were broken at the cross, but we must accept Christ into our heart as Lord and Savior to receive the benefits of His forgiveness. God bore witness to Pastor Dave's words by His Spirit. The hearts of several lost souls were pricked. Kay Falco was one of them. Holy Spirit suddenly gave her revelation of just Who and What Jesus Christ really was. She saw for the first time why she needed Him, now more than ever. The path had been laid that day for Kay's salvation. The breakthrough worship of righteous men and women of God had ushered in His very Presence. The prayers of Ray and Shelly Kirkland focused His revelation and conviction on Kay. And finally, Pastor Dave's words summarized all of what was happening in her heart, almost like he was reading her mind and talking to no one else but her. Before he could even invite an altar call, Pastor Dave suddenly saw a sobbing, broken Kay Falco, trembling as she made her way down the isle toward the front of the church. Shelly Kirkland, who'd been praying with her eyes closed beside Kay, suddenly realized what Kay was doing. Her heart overflowing with joy, Shelly made her way up the isle behind Kay Falco. Kay got to the altar and fell to her knees, broken, sobbing. She didn't need anyone to have her repeat a sinner's prayer to Salvation.

Kay Falco had already asked Jesus Christ into her heart to save her.

"There's a break in the Todd Falco case," Sheriff DeBona told Detective Kirkland when he arrived at the Sheriff's Department. "We need to go over to the annex." The Sheriff led the tall detective down the hall. "You ever heard of a 'Benny Miller'?"

Ray ran the name through his groggy mind. "No, sir."

"He's a dealer from Beaver Falls. Been running a big operation there for the last few years. He's apparently been quite a player. We raided his house on a tip last night. He and his boys were sitting on three hundred grand worth of stash, mostly marijuana; some blow. They were armed to the gills, like they were ready for war. Miller thought someone was coming for him. Only when he realized that we had his house surrounded did he give up, rather than hold a major fire-fight with us."

"Anyone link 'em to that DeVries or McClintlock that got killed Friday night?"

"We've linked him to Jermichael DeVries as an acquaintance. But they each had their own separate outfits."

They breezed through the hallway that led to the jail annex.

"Anyhow, Mr. Miller's got quite a story to tell. So good, in fact, that he went and hired himself Mustafa Kaazim as an attorney."

"Oh, boy!" Ray chuckled. "Mr. Miller must be an African American."

"He is," DeBona said. "You know of Mr. Kaazim, I presume."

"He and I attended the Baptist Church in Beaver Falls for about five years. Nine years ago he converted to Nation of Islam. He's been fighting the Jihad against all you white devils ever since. So Miller's got something for us about Todd Falco?"

DeBona stopped and knocked on a door. A deputy let them into an interrogation room. Inside there were two young assistant district attorneys. Standing beside a table was Mustafa Kaazim, a bespectacled, lean, bald black man in his late forties, dressed in an expensive, crisp olive-colored suit. And sitting smugly in center ring was none other than Benny Miller.

"Gentlemen," DeBona greeted all the players in the room. He then turned to Benny Miller and said, "Mr. Miller, this is Detective Ray Kirkland. Detective Kirkland is in charge of the Missing Persons department for the county. He's the one I want you to tell your story to."

Benny Miller looked up at Detective Kirkland unimpressed; said nothing. Finally he leaned his head back confidently toward Mustafa Kaazim and said, "Moose!"

Kaazim burst to life. "My client has not yet heard an agreeable offer from the DA's office!"

The assistant DA's both huffed and groaned. "Mr. Kaazim," one of them exclaimed in exasperation, "there's nothing here to offer! Mr. Miller was caught last night in his home, not only with three hundred and fifty thousand dollars worth of crack, cocaine, marijuana, and heroin, but also with an array of illegal and unregistered firearms. There were over sixty felonious charges pressed against Mr. Miller and his twenty-three gang members in one bust. The deal we offered him in return for his testimony is the best we can do with so many federal laws having been broken by this man. Besides, he still hasn't convinced me that he even has any worthwhile information."

"'Trafficking' is absolutely unacceptable for my client when he can put away a dangerous supplier of the magnitude of the one he's ready to testify against. Give us a possession charge for the firearms and marijuana, drop the heroin, cocaine and crack charges, and my client will talk! There's a much bigger fish out there for you all to catch!"

The other assistant district attorney stood up and waved a hand at Benny Miller. "We busted a major drug trafficker last night, one of the biggest this county has ever seen! He *is* the big fish . . ."

Kaazim held up one finger and interrupted: "But he can give you a *bigger* fish! Deal with us! This man's still going to be locked away for years, anyway. For a few more years of his freedom, he can give you a whale!"

Ray sighed impatiently. "Tell me what you got, Mr. Miller, then we can decide what we're going to do with it."

"No!" Mustafa Kaazim put up his hand toward Ray. "He will not talk until we cut a deal." Kaazim stood upright, adjusted his expensive gold-framed glasses on his face. "I think I'm beginning to understand what your hesitation is, gentlemen."

"You do?" one of the DA's asked. Sheriff DeBona braced himself. He knew what was coming next from Kaazim.

"Yes," Kaazim stated sadly, beginning to pace back and forth behind Benny Miller like he was trying a case in court. "You see, we've been talking about fish here. As I see it, you're happy that you've caught a big *black* fish." From the table he picked up a missing person's flyer with Todd Falco's face on it. "But now that my client can offer you an even bigger *white* fish, you're not interested in anything he has to say!"

Benny grinned and nodded. "Get 'em, Moose!"

"Mr. Kaazim," the Sheriff broke in, "I'd advise you not to play a dangerous game of racism regarding your client at this stage of his negotiations. We could just drop all this nonsense right now and . . ."

"You'd be doing exactly what I said you'd be doing! Protecting a powerful white man at the expense of this black man seated at this table."

Benny mockingly made sad puppy dog eyes.

"That's it!" a weary Ray Kirkland had enough of Kaazim's display. He walked angrily to the table where Benny Miller was seated and leaned over into Benny's surprised face. "You listen to me, little man," Ray bellowed. "I'm blacker than you and Kaazim combined. You ain't gonna waste my time talkin' about skin color! I'm interested in criminals."

Kaazim stepped forward. "Are you also going to allow yourself to be caught up in this whirlwind of racial injustice at the hands of the White Man, Detective? Very sad! You know, they have a name for people like you, my brother."

Ray stepped forward with fire in his eyes and pointed his long finger directly at Mustafa Kaazim's face. "Mr. Kaazim," he rasped, "Let me just warn you right now. It's only been several hours since one man tried to call me the 'n-word.' So help me, if you call me an 'Uncle Tom,' I'm gonna take you out, right here in front of the Sheriff!"

Kaazim timidly took a step backward and shielded himself with one arm. Before he could reply Ray focused again on Benny. He grabbed the flier of Todd Falco and waved it in the drug lord's face. "Let me tell you about this 'white fish' your attorney's harping about: he's floating belly up somewhere!"

Miller and Kaazim looked confused. Ray clarified for them: "He's dead! No longer alive! He's gone to the big tuna factory in the sky! You dig, little man?"

Benny Miller was dumbfounded, a rare event in his flamboyant life.

Ray got within inches of his face. "My missing person's investigation is about to turn into a murder investigation. Todd Falco's shown up *nowhere*. No one's been able to even trace his vehicle! I been doing this for years and I'll tell you what this all means: he's dead!" Ray pointed at Miller and Kaazim. "Your fish is *dead*. You two have nothing to bargain with. So drop it." He turned toward the Sheriff and the assistant district attorneys. "Drop all these plea bargains and let's go. You got a major trafficker here. Charge him and forget his worthless testimony." He headed for the door. "Let's go, Sheriff."

DeBona was enjoying Ray's theatrics. He played along and followed him to the door.

"Hey!" Benny protested, perplexed that they were walking out on him.

Kaazim burst out angrily: "This is clearly another case of racial injustice! This is just one more black man gonna go down while some much more important white man gets off Scott free!"

Ray opened the door. "A *dead* white man. Who ain't going anywhere!"

Benny Miller was beginning to fear for his hide.

"Fine!" Kaazim shouted. "You'll not get a conviction with these trumped up charges! My client's not afraid to . . ."

"Shut up, Moose!" Benny yelled at his attorney. He stood up and yelled at Ray: "This isn't the first time a major drug mover has disappeared in Beaver County! Do you know there's other drug suppliers like him who've disappeared? Never seen again?"

Ray and DeBona stopped in their tracks. Ray's ears perked up. Benny tried mightily to recall the story his accountant and counselor Marcus told Tony Vero the other day about his drug dealing uncle who disappeared ten years earlier.

"'The black widow,'" Benny remembered out loud.

Ray closed the interrogation room door again. "What of him?" he said, surprised. "You know about all those 'black widow' stories?"

"Yeah," Benny answered, much more humbly. He could see he had Ray and the Sheriff's full attention, now. "Drug dealers in this county, they'd set up a deal with someone, then they'd wind up disappearing for good."

"Yes," Ray nodded in agreement. He was shocked that Miller knew what he was talking about. Ray nodded back toward the Sheriff. "I wrote an entire report on this. Sheriff DeBona's seen it. My colleagues call it 'File 13.' They say if it's true, that's just where all those criminals belong-in the trash."

Benny sat wide-eyed, thinking. He turned around and motioned Kaazim over to him, then whispered in his ear. Kaazim's eyes lit up like gold, then he nodded happily at the young man. He looked at the assistant district attorneys: "My client can give you not only Todd Falco, but the people Falco's been running drugs for, and now, the 'black widow' himself!"

Ray, DeBona, and the assistant district attorney's all stared at one another in shock. Sheriff DeBona spoke up: "We want names! Not myths, urban legends, and ghost stories! We want names!"

"I'll give you names!" Miller replied confidently.

"I want the trafficking and possession of heroin, crack, and cocaine charges dropped," Kaazim pointed at the two assistant district attorneys.

They whispered to one another for a moment. One of them finally spoke up: "He tells us all he has, first. Then, if he can give us all he's just promised us, we'll only charge him on possession of marijuana and illegal firearms, and he'll plead 'guilty'."

Kaazim grinned a huge grin. "Done!" He patted Benny on the shoulder, "Go, son!"

Ray bellowed: "Start with Falco!"

Benny nodded. "That Todd Falco who you all're looking for. He ain't no business executive. He's been supplying me cocaine every other week for the last four years."

Ray held up the flier of Todd Falco. "This guy?"

"He's the one. I saw him and you on the news the other day."

"He's been selling you coke?"

"For the last four years I said."

Ray was excited. This indeed was a break. "How much do you usually buy from him?"

Benny shrugged. "Anywhere from three to five pounds, every other Wednesday. But he didn't go by the name 'Todd Falco.' He been given me an alias."

"Where's he get his stash to sell?"

"I asked him no questions, he told me no lies. 'Bout four and a half years ago I was hunting around for a supplier. He sent word my way he was interested. The rest is history."

"Your attorney just said you could give me who he's been running drugs for!"

"I can! But I don't know where he gets his stash from."

"Then tell me who he runs for."

Benny took a deep, confident breath. "VECO."

Ray wanted to shout "hallelujah!" The Sheriff had to lean back against the wall to stabilize himself. One of the district attorneys whistled loud and shrill.

"You know that for a fact?" Ray wanted reassurance.

"Tell me this? Why was Tony Vero, a VECO private investigator and the relative of Carmichael Vero himself, over at my house the other day, looking so hard for another drug dealer?"

Ray lit up even more. "Tony Vero was at your house? You know him?"

"Of course I know him! We played football together! I was the star of the team when he played."

Ray guffawed at Miller's arrogance. "Right. Now, did Tony Vero tell you he was looking for Todd Falco?"

Benny shook his head no. "He never once mentioned Todd Falco."

"Well then, who was the drug dealer Tony Vero was looking for?"

Benny looked at the assistant district attorneys. "I'm about to keep the second part of the deal we just made." He looked back at Ray. "Tony Vero was looking for some cat he'd never heard of. Said he was dealin' some sweet powder."

"Name?"

"'Bernie Lokawski.' And I believe this Bernie Lokawski is the 'black widow' I promised you."

"Why? Because Tony Vero was looking for him?"

"Not just that. When Tony was at my house, we got to talking about how my supplier, Todd Falco, though I never said his name, had vanished without contacting me. Tony Vero was real interested in that little story. Then my main man Marcus Clark starts tellin' his 'black widow' stories about his uncle and Tony Vero perked up like a doggy smellin' a bone."

"Who was Marcus Clark's uncle?"

"I think his name was 'Otis Bridges.' Disappeared the same way Todd Falco did ten years ago."

Ray turned and looked at Sheriff DeBona. "Otis Bridges is in my 'File 13' report. Got a whole section devoted to his case."

DeBona turned red with embarrassment.

"And you think that all this fits together?" Ray asked Benny Miller.

"In the same week, you got Todd Falco of VECO disappearing, and then Tony Vero of VECO asking around for Bernie Lokawski, another suspected drug dealer. The two go side by side in my book. And they're all tied together in a three-way knot: Todd Falco runs for VECO, Tony Vero tries to track him down on behalf of VECO, and Bernie Lokawski, whoever he is, is the one who's playing invasion of the body snatchers with local drug dealers and their cash."

Ray and the district attorneys all eyed each other. They called him aside. Sheriff DeBona joined them.

"He hasn't given us anything, really!" the first assistant claimed.

"You think this guy's for real?" the other asked Ray.

Ray looked at Sheriff DeBona and nodded. "I do. I actually believe what he's telling us."

"But he has no real evidence to give us! Just a great story."

Ray laughed. "The only new thing here is that Tony Vero has been over to Miller's house looking for a drug dealer. But I believe he's onto something. I think his story's worth investigating."

"But Benny Miller has nothing really substantial to offer us in return for a plea," one of the district attorneys whispered again.

"Just a fantastic lead we can check on," Sheriff DeBona said. "But for all legal purposes he has nothing on VECO. He's given us nothing he can legally bargain with."

Their huddle broke. Kaazim and Miller were confidently beaming at them. The first assistant district attorney asked outright: "Where's your hard evidence?"

Miller's smile vanished. Kaazim was outright flabbergasted. "What do you mean?" "We can't solve a case or win a conviction on this drug dealer's stories alone. We're asking, do you have anything concrete we can run with that will lead us down the road to convictions for Todd Falco, if he's indeed even alive, or anyone at VECO, or this Bernie Lokawski you alluded to?"

"We . . . ! I don't . . ."

"How about something on Carmichael Vero? Can you give us something there?"

"I . . . !"

Ray and Sheriff DeBona opened the door to leave. "We'll see if we can get anything with this information," Ray honestly informed them.

The assistant district attorney's gathered their belongings. "In the meantime, Mr. Miller, if you can come up with any more information for us that will get us closer to some convictions, we'd sure count it toward your case."

The deputy went to cuff Benny Miller. Benny stood up, mouth gaping, helpless. "You can't do this to me! I'm dealin' with you!" he protested.

"Oh, if we can substantiate any of this story you've told us and make any convictions, the deal we made is yours," Sheriff DeBona said. "But not until we get arrests and convictions. Until then, I'm sure Mr. Kaazim will find some way out of this for you. He's one of the most brilliant lawyers in Beaver County."

"Thanks for your help!" Ray smiled curtly.

As Miller and Kaazim both opened their mouths to protest, Ray slammed the door shut from outside. As he and DeBona headed back down the hall he waved his hand under his nose and winced.

"It stinks in that room!"

THIRTY-SEVEN

A leister Estate of Great Neck, New York, was glorious that Sunday afternoon. The brilliant spring sunlight and crystal blue skies sharply accented Cyrus Moreau's artistic landscape designs for his tripartite property. The land was so pristine that one could easily be distracted by the beauty of God's creation and forget what blatantly defiant acts of evil were going to be carried out there later that evening by the light of the full moon.

But Carmichael Vero wasn't distracted enough to forget.

He was so uncomfortable with the evening's prospects that Ed Larsky eventually had to tell him to lighten up. Larsky, who would willingly participate in any activity that would put him over the top, was elated with the obscene carnival-like atmosphere on Moreau's property. Familiar and unfamiliar faces from the corporate and entertainment world were present that weekend for the festivities and demon worship. Their spouses, mistresses and lovers, entourages and attendants either followed them dutifully or were dragged behind in the frenzy of activities. The best foods and alcoholic beverages were being offered at every venue, along with many assorted illegal narcotics. No expenses were spared for the guests who came to participate in Cyrus Moreau's black mass and "workshop" celebration. They came for one reason: they knew their participation in these abominable rituals would give their careers the "push" they needed. Cyrus' clients who participated in those occult rituals would quickly see success and the accomplishing of personal goals. Many of them gave testimonies to one another about how Cyrus and his coven members had altered their destinies forever via gross manipulation of the spirit realm. At pool-side a Hollywood movie star told bikini clad girls how after a fast and successful launch to his career in the 1970's, his popularity burned out unexpectedly in the eighties. It was in 1992, he explained, after a decade of being called a has-been, that he was invited to have Cyrus consult for him. After participating in one of these black mass/workshop weekends, the actor's career suddenly skyrocketed again. His portrayal of a violent criminal in a bloody black comedy earned him an Oscar nomination and instantly skyrocketed him back to the top of Hollywood's "A" list of stars. To date he was commanding fifteen million per picture. He told all who were listening that he had

Cyrus and his magic to thank for the revitalization of his career. On the golf course a European soccer star testified how Cyrus manipulated a team owner and "pushed" the athlete to the pinnacle of the soccer world in Europe and South America. All over the estate such stories were being traded. Nervous newcomers were assured of the same guarantees for their willingness to participate that weekend. Despite the repulsive and illegal activities they would have to partake of, the bottom line was this: it would be worth every bit of it when success rolled around for them.

After Carmichael and Larsky settled their belongings into one of the spacious rooms of Cyrus' mansion, they took their golf paraphernalia to the clubhouse. There they were told that Cyrus wanted them to join him and his partner out on the thirteenth hole. Larsky steered their golf cart out onto the par three golf course from the clubhouse and lounge. He was uncharacteristically starstruck and giddy as he recognized famous faces of executives, producers, media reporters, entertainers and athletes. Carmichael was less impressed and by no means giddy. He had a leaden lump in his stomach and a knot in his throat. He wished to be anywhere else but here. He'd spent two years trying to rid himself of the specter of Cyrus Moreau over VECO and the Family. Now he was about to entrench the menace even deeper into both of his businesses, thanks to Todd Falco's untimely vanishing act. So as Larsky gushed and awed and pointed fingers at well-known people, Carmichael merely grunted with a distant affirmation. He rued the day the name "Cyrus Moreau" first rang in his eardrums:

It was 1979. Carmichael was the consigliari to Martino Barrato. On a business trip to Atlantic City Carmichael Vero met a famous recording artist and some-time movie star. The man had four gold records and his performances at the gambling resorts were perpetual sell-outs. He had Carmichael up to his penthouse after a show for a huge party. There the two got to talking about investments and hit it off immediately. Both were of kindred spirit, gifted with business savvy. Demonic spirits of greed ruled them. They were more interested in the moneymaking aspects of their professions than the lustful trappings that went with them. Martino Barrato, the crime boss, liked this singer too, and the Barrato Family would often book weekends at the resorts where this man was performing so they could all party together. So Carmichael's camaraderie with this glamorous entertainer was quickly cultivated. About three months into their friendship, Carmichael wanted to hear all about his success story. At pool-side of a famous New York City hotel one weekend, he spilled the beans to Carmichael.

"Man, I couldn't get anywhere in the business. I lived like a mutt for years, just trying to land gigs. I landed an occasional backup gig as a session man in the studios. But that was it. I'd hit a brick wall and couldn't get no farther. It was then that I had my eyes opened to the fact that I could get someone to break down that brick wall for me."

"What are you talking about?" Carmichael asked him.

"I'd been consulting with this groovy astrologer. My horoscopes kept spelling out success for me, but said that there was one vital piece missing to the puzzle of my destiny. That was when she turned me on to a cat named 'Cyrus Moreau.'"

"'Cyrus Moreau?'"

"Yeah! What a moniker, huh? This cat's unreal! It turned out that she worked for him and set up a meeting for me. When I met this guy the first time, he was levitating two feet off the ground!"

"Huh?" Carmichael the atheist immediately wanted to disbelieve anything that conflicted with his empirical mind. But this famous singer continued:

"I know, you don't believe me, but I swear on my mother's grave it's true. The man was floating on air in a trance. But when he came down, he put his finger right here on my heart. He told me exactly what I wanted and how to get it. He's a wizard. Really! Like Merlin was in the old stories. This guy can control outcomes. He did it for me."

"What'd he do for you?" the skeptical Vero's curiosity was aroused.

"The record company I been with all these years, it was the one I always wanted to sign with. They produce my style of music and I knew I'd fit in there like a glove if I could ever land a contract. But back when I was a struggling bum waiting tables and singing in cheap speakeasies, this label wouldn't sign me on 'cause of one man. The executive there hated my guts for some reason. I never did anything to him. I don't know what his problem was. Everyone else there was hot for me, but that one executive treated me like trash. Then I started consulting with Cyrus Moreau. He told me if I'd come to his place for a weekend and participate in some of his magic rituals with him, he'd get me that contract. He quoted me a price it would cost. I told him I didn't have that kind of money. He said that for twenty percent of my contract and first-years earnings, he'd let me come participate and he'd fix my problem. Well, I was game then! I went, he did one of those black masses like you see in those satanist movies, then he and a couple of witches got together and in front of my eyes cast a spell against that studio executive. Carmichael, I kid you not, three days later that executive suffered a major stroke, he spent three months in one of those convalescence homes, then he died! He croaked! As soon as that guy had the stroke, the new executive immediately signed me up on that label. On the day they were having a funeral for that old man who'd caused me all that trouble, I was wrapping up my first album in the studio. That record went gold. It was all a rocket ride to the top after that!"

Carmichael leaned over his lounge chair, captivated, and put his hand on the singer's knee. "You're telling me that this Moreau fellow whacked that record executive without using a hit man?"

"No hit man! No bullets, no poison. Magic! The obituary read 'natural causes.' No police investigation, no suspicion. I was Scott free to reap all the benefits."

"This Moreau guy can whack people without a hit man?"

"He doesn't need a hitter. He has invisible hitters! I can hook you up with him if you'd like."

Carmichael never followed through on the singer's offer in 1979. A year and a half later the feds busted the Barrato Family and Carmichael. In jail awaiting his trial he remembered the story about Cyrus Moreau. He tried to get that entertainer-friend to contact Cyrus for him. But the man abandoned Carmichael when all the negative publicity about his Mafia arrest hit the papers. Carmichael was unable to contact Cyrus Moreau for help. Instead he put the contract out on that rat Mafia lieutenant, Ed Larsky assassinated him, and their destiny together was sealed.

It was after he was freed and began his plans to create VECO and the Family that Carmichael tracked down Cyrus Moreau. Moreau was not yet the marketing giant that he later became; he was still on his rise to power at that point. The Dark Lords had already shown Cyrus that Carmichael Vero was coming to him. They told him one was coming who was going to make Cyrus lots of money over the years. Cyrus didn't have his name, but he had a clear imprint of Vero's "aura," as the Dark Lords had taught him to discern. Upon their meeting, Carmichael was initially disillusioned with Cyrus Moreau. Cyrus was young, very long-haired, and covered with tattoos. He looked more like some impudent rock star than a master of the spirit realm. He even had a constant entourage, a coven of witches and warlocks who followed him everywhere. They catered to his every beck and whim. Cyrus was instantly awed by Carmichael Vero, though. He clearly saw Carmichael as a man of uncanny vision. He was one who could plant deep foundations and build an incredible moneymaking empire. He knew he could make a fortune from this Vero. In 1981, in Cyrus's newly completed offices in Great Neck, Carmichael and Cyrus sat down and planned out the strategy for creating a wildly successful VECO to hide a new Family enterprise. Carmichael explained how he wanted to build a new criminal empire, while the whole time appearing to be a legitimate businessman. He didn't want any Mafia ties or lifestyles. He explained that he had his nephews Joseph and Pete Vero and a pair of accountants named Anthony and Warren Zann who would all be invaluable assets to his new creation. Both agreed it would be best for Carmichael if those others never even knew Cyrus Moreau existed. Cyrus explained what powers he wielded and how he could help Carmichael build a supernatural wall of protection right into the very foundations of VECO and the Family. He promised Carmichael that if he paid him a fortune up front, VECO and the Family could prosper for years under his supernatural protection. Carmichael would not have to buy out cops and politicians for his protection, in fact the opposite would be true: he could avoid them forever. Carmichael lit up. That's exactly what he was looking for. Cyrus explained how he had set up his own legal spiritual advisory business, which he intended to vastly expand over the years, and used it to front all his spiritual moneymaking efforts for which he didn't want to be taxed. Carmichael's plan was similar, and they mapped it out for him together. Cyrus explained how Carmichael's blood oath to the Mafia would always come back to haunt him if he didn't renounce it. It gave the Mafia legal authority in the spirit realm over him, Cyrus explained. Carmichael agreed to renounce that blood oath. Cyrus lead him in his renunciation, laid hands on him, and declared them broken forever. Carmichael Vero was no longer a made man. With that, Carmichael and Larsky participated in their first "workshop" in 1982. There he and Larsky made a new oath, an oath to the Dark Lords, promising them their allegiance through their relationship with Cyrus Moreau. They promised them their very souls in exchange for the prosperity and protection of their businesses. Neither Carmichael and Larsky believed any spirits actually would ever have control over their souls. That was fine to Cyrus and perfect to the Dark Lords. Demons love when humans don't believe in them. Cyrus and company cast their first spells, sending out demonic hordes the size and power of which they'd never "commanded" before to protect Carmichael's legal and illegal endeavors. Cyrus' pride told him that it was his extraordinary powers over the supernatural realms that moved such mighty demonic armies on behalf of Carmichael and the Family. The truth was, the demonic principalities over the regions of Pennsylvania were elated with the scope of Carmichael's vision and wanted to have such an oppressor under their control. He was a human so bent on the destruction of his fellow man for his own gain that he would launch such an ambitious enterprise as VECO and the Family. Carmichael used the twenty million dollars he'd made with the Mafia to launch VECO. He financed savvy entrepreneurs with great dreams and inventions, but no resources through which to launch them. Within months VECO was up and rolling, and the Family was in operation. First hundreds, then thousands of people were getting hooked on sinful vices that quickly became demonic strongholds in their lives. Families were destroyed. Children were abused and scarred. Marriages broke up. And Carmichael and the Family made a fortune from it. The demonic princes over the region were ecstatic that they were gaining so much access into the lives of people. Cyrus knew the spirit realm was tremendously pleased with his venture with Carmichael, but he had no idea how much. Hell was expanding on the earth and the kingdom of God was being hindered with each drug deal that went down and porn video or magazine sold. All thanks to Family money.

Carmichael gained great favor in peoples' eyes because of VECO's astounding success. It thrived on a squeaky clean image, built up the economy of Western Pennsylvania, and put Beaver County on the corporate map. To many Carmichael was completely rehabilitated from any possible past Mafia ties. Just what he wanted. It fronted the Family so well, no one suspected a thing.

In the mid nineties, two separate people caught onto the fact that a "Family"-type organization might exist under Carmichael. Both of these individuals, white collar criminals themselves, eventually were arrested for separate crimes. When in custody and questioned, they both began to spill the beans about a possible criminal empire located at VECO. State Attorney General Michael Davis caught wind of both cases. He secretly got Edgar Waters involved to get a deposition from each man. Each time, however, the Family caught wind of both men before they could ever give depositions to anyone. Both times Carmichael and Larsky turned to Cyrus. Both men wound up dead of natural causes while in custody. That kind of hellish protection, and the constant undetected, uninhibited activity of the Family and its drug and pornography businesses made all involved believe they were invincible.

For years Carmichael was grateful for Cyrus' intervention. But as time went by Cyrus's fees increased, highly irritating the greedy Vero. Along with the increased fees came deeper demands from the Dark Lords. The few "workshops" that Carmichael and Larsky did attend became increasingly more diabolical in nature as time went on. Rituals that originally resembled a harmless horror movie to Carmichael in the eighties had degenerated in horrifying orgies of depravity, even repulsing the hardened ex-Mafioso. Then pride began to kick in. Carmichael began to doubt Cyrus Moreau's input into his two empires. Wasn't he Carmichael Vero? Couldn't he have built VECO and the Family on his own? Did he jump the gun in his zeal to found his own crime conglomerate in 1981 when he turned first to Cyrus Moreau for help? The big question was the one Cyrus put to him on the phone a few days earlier: Who was the man? Was is Carmichael, or was it really Cyrus who put his empire over the top? It was at that point that Carmichael purposefully shoved Cyrus Moreau and his maddening occultism out of the picture. For two years the Family thrived, supposedly on its own (the demonic walls of protection were still in operation the whole time). Carmichael and Larsky slowly were forgetting about the specter of Cyrus Moreau-until Todd Falco vanished. Now Carmichael found himself back at Aleister Estate, submitting himself once again to Cyrus, delving even further into his dark world.

Larsky gleefully bounced the golf cart across greens and fairways, rudely cutting in front of fellow guests in mid-strokes and chips, even running over two balls in play. He didn't care. Let someone try to stop him. He and his boss were the guests of honor of the host himself by personal invitation. Carmichael, in an increasing funk, didn't have the gumption to even rebuke his henchman about the rude behavior. As they rolled over the crest of the hill near the twelfth hole, below in another golf cart at the thirteenth tee sat Cyrus Moreau and a rising pop music star who was becoming the raging fad in America at the moment. They were waiting patiently for their team partners to arrive. Cyrus, long hair, golf hat, and designer sunglasses, grinned ear to ear at the sight of Carmichael Vero and Ed Larsky. "Gentlemen!" Cyrus roared gregariously. "Welcome to Aleister Estate! It's certainly been a while, hasn't it, Carmichael?"

Carmichael merely nodded silently as Larsky pulled their cart alongside Cyrus's.

Cyrus waved a hand at the young pop star sitting next to him in the cart. "Do you two recognize Mr. Rodriguez? His first song is still number one on the pop chart. His second release is currently at number eleven and rising. All thanks to me!" Cyrus beamed. Cyrus studied Carmichael.

"Carmichael, Carmichael!" Cyrus shook his head slowly, still smiling. "You're supposed to be here to unwind and have fun this afternoon, and yet I sense . . . fear! Yes, it's fear!"

Carmichael Vero angrily turned three shades of red beneath the sunglasses.

"Don't be afraid, Carmichael," Cyrus flashed white teeth. "Save the fear for tonight!" His mocking laughter pierced the beautiful spring air all across the par three course.

THIRTY-EIGHT

Tony Vero's last bastion of serenity was shattered to pieces that Sunday afternoon. He'd spent the late morning and early afternoon in his Mercedes scoping out Frank Kranac's place on Sixth Avenue. There was no sign of life from the creepy recluse. It was hot in the car, even with the windows down. Too many people were passing by him staring at him, and he was getting sleepy from the heat. He had little sleep that early Sunday morning when he got back in from the Sheriff's Department. His mind was a whirlwind from the events of that Saturday: the beautiful Kay Falco and the kiss that never was; the raging bull Ed Larsky pounding on him and then being hauled off to jail; and the words of Life Gina spoke and prayed over him. Between his lusts, his fears, and the Lord, it was a near sleepless night. So the fruitless stakeout in the Mercedes got old real fast. He began to nod off. It was a brilliant day, the light would be flooding his living room just right. His sofa was calling him. He cranked the engine and went home. He settled on the couch, hot bare feet instantly soothed on the soft, cool sofa fabric. He settled his head into one of the huge puffy pillows and quickly dozed, confident of his peace of mind with all those safe rays of sunlight shining through. This was the only place he'd known peace since Ft. Lauderdale.

But there in the sun light Tony suffered his most vivid, horrific Ft. Lauderdale nightmare of all. Demonically inspired to further drag him into the bondage of dread and depression, this dream spawned quickly and took him by surprise. In his mind's eye he was in a sunny, safe place, a beach setting of white sand and blinding light. He spotted a table laden with cool drinks near a stucco-walled bungalow. He stepped over to take one of the enticing glasses dripping with condensation in the heat. As he neared the table, he saw the sliding glass door of the bungalow was open. Immediately he was compelled to walk into the stucco hut. Through the door he saw the interior of a bedroom, still well lit but musty with a smell of . . . what was that smell that was so pungent in the dream? . . . the smell of . . . smell of

Death.

Gus Savage leaped upon him in the dream, knocking Tony back onto a filthy bed. The mangled, bloody man quickly overpowered Tony and held him flat. Tony's sleeping body convulsed on his couch as though the dreadful scene was actually occurring. In the dream Gus pinned Tony so he was unable to move. A self-induced paralysis overtook his sleeping body, and he was literally held fast to the couch unable to move a muscle.

In the dream Gus Savage sunk his head down nose to nose with Tony's face. The apparition of the man who used to be screamed a cry of desperation that made Tony cringe with guilt. Trembling with terror, Tony's gaze was locked on Gus's bloodshot eyes, knowing full well the question the man was about to ask:

"WHY, TONY?"

Tony struggled to free his wrists from Savage's grip, but it was futile. Gus repeated the now expected, "WHY? WHY? WHY TONY!" Each time Tony cringed with helpless guilt, shamefully unable to answer the pitiful man's question, desperately struggling to be free from the ice cold specter of Gus Savage. Tony was alone in this hellish vortex. No one shared the unbearable load on his soul. He had no one to rescue him. No one could help him, and that overwhelming sensation made the dream even more terrifying. He was now at his lowest point ever: alone, isolated, lonely, blood-guilty for another man's life; he was in hell on earth. The demonic forces who were inducing these nightmares whispered to his soul that no one could help him. They told him he would have to die and spend eternity in this hopeless guilt. He acknowledged their despairing message of doom and could only believe it to be true.

But then, from somewhere within Tony's spirit, a distant yet powerful voice suddenly pierced the hopelessness of the situation. It was Gina's voice, softly saying: ". . . the Power of Jesus can set you free . . ." And then he heard Ray's sure, powerful voice saying: ". . . Jesus Christ is your only hope . . ." And in the midst of his personal hell a powerful revelation came to Tony Vero: he did have Someone he could call upon.

In his dream Tony looked up into Gus Savage's accusing stare as the living corpse held him fast on his back. Tony fruitlessly tried to speak. Even in reality on his couch, his lips only quivered, his lungs merely gasped and fluttered because of the torment. But he thought again about his ever present Help, the One who had probably always been there, but he had foolishly ignored. This revelation suddenly sparked a flicker of hope that energized him in his unconscious state. This time, in the dream and in the real world, Tony Vero took a deep breath and shouted out loud: "JESUS HELP ME!"

He did. His Presence filled Tony's living room, breaking the spell of the demonic trance he was under.

In his mind's eye Tony watched Gus Savage's eye's bulge with terror. He felt the icy, demonic grip of the man loose his body in the dream as the apparition had to flee from a Presence infinitely more mighty than he. The curse and the paralysis of the tormenting slumber was instantly broken . . .

He was free!

Tony instantly awoke. Suddenly free to move, he leapt from the couch, drenched in sweat, and took wild swings at the air as though Gus Savage might still be lingering about in the natural. In his frenzy he connected with a lamp, demolishing the lampshade and shattering the light bulb. Looking around in the light of day he realized what had just happened. He still had the creeps so he ran to the front door and went outside, panting in the warm sunlight. He sat in the grass next to his driveway, stunned by what just took place. How could he have had the nightmare in the middle of a sunny afternoon? That's why he slept in the day, so he wouldn't have those dreams. And this one was the worst yet!

He smeared the sweat off his forehead. Quickly forgetting the deliverance Christ had just given him, he focused on this one fact: he would never have peace again, as long as he knew what had happened in Ft. Lauderdale. He looked up at his house. That place sure wasn't the answer to his troubles. No, he'd go after Frank Kranac, solve the Todd Falco case, and run away from this house, the Family, Beaver Falls, and everything that reminded him of Ft. Lauderdale forever.

But was there any place on earth far enough away where he could out run the torment of another man's blood?

A shaken Tony was driving through College Hill preparing to go face off with Frank Kranac again when his Family beeper went off in his truck. He snatched it out of the visor, read the number, and pulled his blue Ford pickup into the Sheetz parking lot. He dropped thirty-five cents into the outside pay phone and dialed the number. It had to be his Uncle Joseph, for Carmichael and Larsky flew out of town for the day. As he waited for the other line to ring, he realized that the first three numbers he dialed were one of the combinations designated for local cellular phones. He heard the familiar pause and light background beeping noises of a cell phone call before the other line finally rang. He wondered what was going on, for that sure wasn't Joseph or Carmichael's cell numbers

Tony about jumped out of his skin when Detective Ray Kirkland answered on the other end: "Good Day! This is Detective Ray Kirkland," his cheery voice rang.

"Uh . . ." Tony didn't know what to do. Should he hang up? How did Kirkland get his private Family beeper number? No one had access to it except the Family members.

"Is this Tony Vero already?" Ray's warm voice boomed. "Don't hang up!"

Tony looked up at the spectacular Sunday afternoon sky. He wanted to hang up, hop in his truck, and scram. Instead, against his gut feelings, he was compelled to answer the man. "This is he."

"Tony! That was fast! I didn't think you'd respond that quickly. Where are you, my friend?"

"I'm . . . I'm in town."

"Good! Drop whatever you're doing and meet me over at the Stop 'n' Sock driving range. I'll have two buckets of balls ready for us."

Tony sighed, irritated. "Sorry! I'm a working man. I don't have time to come play with you today, Detective . . ."

"Oh, I think you'll make time for me, especially once I tell you who we got cookin' in a jail cell at the county clink!"

Long pause. "Who?"

"Benny Miller! And what a story Benny told me about *you* this afternoon!"
Tony's heart sank deep into his belly.

Ray let the impact of his words find a deep root in the silence. Then, in a very authoritative voice he said: "You meet me here in fifteen minutes for questioning, or I'm gonna come get you and haul you in myself."

Stop 'n' Sock was a combination putter golf, par three, batting cages, driving range, and ice cream stand. All venues of the recreational center were not surprisingly packed that gorgeous Sunday afternoon; especially the popular driving range, built over a grassy valley. Every spot on the long wooden deck was filled with both avid and amateur golfers trying to perfect their swings.

Tony spotted the tall, athletic detective out in the middle of the long driving range platform. Ray noticed Tony approaching and smiled like he was truly glad to see him.

"Tony Vero! You sure been on my heart a lot these days," he said as he teed up a shot.

"How'd you get my pager number?" Tony asked as he walked over to the empty space on the driving range beside Ray Kirkland.

The huge Ray Kirkland ignored Tony's question to concentrate on his drive. With a graceful swing he swatted a golf ball mercilessly with a giant three iron. The ball arced silently into the sky, across the grassy valley below, and landed hundreds of yards away near the property fence.

"Bad shot," Ray remarked about the drive, still in his follow-through stance.

"Looked fantastic, to me," Tony said. "I wish I could drive 'em that far."

"It's not the distance I'm looking for. I want that!" Ray pointed at the lone telephone pole standing high in the middle of the driving range. Mounted at the top was an old metal Coca Cola sign, dented and dinged over the years by numerous golf balls. "Hit the Coke sign and win a free, icy cold bottle of Coke! I've been trying for twenty years. Never once hit the thing."

"I hit it twice when I was in high school," Tony commented as his stepped up onto the driving platform next to Ray, taking up the club and basket of golf balls that were waiting there for him.

"Twice? Bless God, Tony Vero! But that doesn't really surprise me any. I could tell the moment I met you that you were the consummate athlete. Probably isn't much you can't do athletically once you set your mind to it. That golf club the right size?"

Tony held it down in front of him, got into the driver's stance, and took a hard slice. "Perfect. Good choice." His back was still sore from the pounding Ed Larsky'd laid on it the night before. He took several more swings to loosen it up. He then poured his bucket of balls down a hole in the platform, stepped on a metal pedal, and up popped a tee with his first ball mounted and ready to be socked to the moon. "Now answer my question: how'd you get that pager number?"

Ray lined up his club head with the ball for the next shot. "I'm a veteran cop. How hard you think it is for me to get a silly pager number?"

Tony hauled off an impressive shot. "That's not a business pager. It's for private use, only. How'd you get the number? I need to know so I can correct the leak in privacy."

Ray wacked the ball hard into the air. It missed the Coke sign by ten feet. "It's not much of a mystery, private detective. We emptied out every important document from your house two days ago, remember? Deputy Simmons and I had a little 'Let's Get to Know Tony Vero' party all day yesterday at the station. I can even tell you your grade point averages from high school and college. You had one old bill from the pager company in your file cabinet, that's all."

Pokerfaced on the outside, Tony breathed a deep sigh of relief. At least Family security hadn't been breached like he thought.

"I couldn't reach you at your house today, and I didn't feel like trying to track you down. I'm kind'a tired today from our little party we had with Ed Larsky last night. So I gave the pager number a shot. That's all there is to it. Cool?"

"Yeah." Tony lined up his next shot and swung the driver.

"Good! Now tell me who Bernie Lokawski is."

Tony pulled hard, flubbed the shot. The ball corkscrewed far off to the left.

Ray watched it disappear over the hillside. "Sliced it." He turned around and looked Tony right in the eyes. "Who's Bernie Lokawski?"

Lying to this man was too hard. Tony gave up. "I don't know who he is."

"Benny Miller sure says you do. He's willing to testify to it to knock years off his sentence for the major drug bust he went down with at his house last night."

Tony snickered as he depressed the tee pedal. "They finally busted Benny M after all these years?"

"He had a lot to tell us about you. In fact, he's using your entire visit to his house the other day as his bargaining leverage with the district attorneys."

"So why'd you drag me out here to drive golf balls with you? You obviously think Benny knows everything."

"'Cause I need you to fill in the minor puzzle pieces for me that he can't. So don't stand there and deny that you don't know who Bernie Lokawski is. It's time to come clean. It's too late to lie to me."

Tony impatiently slung his driver up over his shoulder. "I didn't lie to you. I don't know who Bernie Lokawski is."

"But you know he exists?"

"Yes I do. But I sure haven't found one trace of the man. Todd Falco disappears completely, and the one suspect I have is even more untraceable than him." He set his driver in position and knocked a three-hundred yard shot.

"Why'd you go see a drug lord like Benny Miller the other day?"

Tony wanted to strategically feed the detective information. Enough to come clean with, too little to indict himself. "You were right about Todd Falco. He's a drug dealer. According to Todd's mistress over at Brighten Analytical, Todd was about to make some sort of major buy from a supplier named Bernie Lokawski. Thing is, I can't find any sign of a Bernie Lokawski anywhere in Beaver County. Benny Miller, Todd's friends, nobody's ever heard of the guy."

"He doesn't exist," Ray said as he teed up another ball. "We ran his name today as soon as Benny mentioned him to us. There's no Bernie Lokawski anywhere in the USA with a criminal record. No one uses that name as an alias, either. Unless he snuck over from Poland this week to deal cocaine in Beaver County, Pennsylvania, there is no Bernie Lokawski."

"Yeah, well, you ever heard of those 'black widow of Beaver County' legends the drug dealers all talk about?"

Ray slung his club up over his shoulder, this time, chuckling for the irony of the question. He turned around to face Tony again. "I wrote the entire police report on the 'black widow' legends, praise God."

"You did?"

Ray flashed his infectious white grin. "'File 13,' my colleagues named it."

"They didn't believe it? They didn't believe *you*?"

"All I started with was twelve unsolved missing persons cases from the last fifteen years. All of 'em were drug dealers, pushers, suppliers. Everyone knew it. It was obvious. A lot of criminals like that bounce here and there, use aliases, 'disappear,' as it were. But these twelve people all vanished instantly and completely. I mean, they didn't pack anything, they didn't tell any of their family members, they just vanished from the radar screen and have never shown up anywhere else on any police or FBI files. Lots of time vanishing criminals like that pop up somewhere. Lotta times in jails in other parts of the country. Not these twelve. They're gone. Even some of their cars vanished . . ."

"Like Todd's."

"Exactly! Homeboy's Camaro hasn't been spotted anywhere. And I have him and it all over the police and internet services. Eight of the twelve missing had their cars vanish, too. So I have twelve county residents who happen to be drug dealers all vaporizing into thin air."

"But you couldn't prove that? The Sheriff's Department couldn't prove that?"

Ray held up his index finger. "The Sheriff's Department didn't *want* to prove it! The Sheriff himself wanted nothing to do with my report. He's the one who named it 'File 13'. He told me in no uncertain terms to bury it. He said that the citizens of this county would hang him from the highest branch if he ever used taxpayer's money to investigate the disappearance of twelve criminals whom the average citizens would be just as glad to know had vanished. 'Every one of 'em belong in a trash can, anyhow, like your report,' he told me."

"Hence the name 'File 13'," Tony caught on.

"Twenty points for you, Tony Vero! Sheriff DeBona doesn't exactly value their lives. And if someone is secretly offing our local drug dealers, that's just fine with him. Keeps drugs off the streets and saves voting taxpayers the money for investigating, prosecuting, and keeping pushers and dealers alive in our jails once they're convicted. So it's a moot issue with him."

Tony remembered the racial issue's Benny Miller's accountant Marcus brought up about the 'black widow' legend. "Plus, some of those people who disappeared were probably middle to lower class black people."

"Thirty points for that one! I've been a law enforcement officer for over twenty years now, and I'll tell you this: a black man's still twice as guilty as a white man, and half the time guilty until proven innocent. I'm grateful for the strides we've made in civil rights. But the hearts of men are still deceitful and wicked, and prejudice is a specter I still even have to battle. Yes. The department is not going to spend money investigating the disappearance of some minority figures who are probably major drug dealers, too. That's my opinion."

"So they just made fun of your report?"

"Yeah, kind of. But I know I'm right, and God knows the truth, too. He'll reveal it in His time. Twelve people He loves, regardless of who they were, vanishing like that over a fifteen year period." Ray shook his head sadly. "He knows where they are. He'll uncover the truth for all to see, one day. Twelve souls . . ."

"Thirteen, now, if Todd Falco's the latest victim of this 'black widow.'"

"So why'd you go to Benny Miller's the other day?"

"I've always known Benny's been a major drug mover in Beaver Falls. Even when we were playing championship high school football together he was selling all over the place. Now that he's the biggest druggie around I figured he'd know all the other players in the county. But he never heard of Bernie Lokawski."

"So how's Carmichael Vero involved in this drug scandal of Todd Falco's?"

"He's not," Tony lied.

"He's obviously paying you to find one of his employees who's a drug dealer. Why's he want him found?"

"Carmichael's guilty until proven innocent, too, because of the past. He's gotta work twice as hard to keep his reputation as a legitimate businessman. He won't stand for any bad press about VECO. It could hurt his business. So your news piece about Falco that they did at VECO the other night was devastating to Carmichael. Especially since the story ran the weekend before his big stockholder's banquet this Tuesday."

"I'm not a reporter! I didn't run that piece."

"Yeah, but your theatrics out at VECO certainly guaranteed attention. You brought a search warrant when it wasn't necessary. You guys all hauled out file cabinets and computers and office boxes for the news people to videotape. You grilled everyone like Todd's body might be buried somewhere on VECO's property or something. That sure impugned VECO to everyone in the Pittsburgh area. Like Uncle Carmichael had something to do with Todd Falco's disappearance."

"And him hiring you to sneak around and hang out with drug dealers doesn't look bad?"

"He wants evidence gathered so he can have Falco publicly exposed and fired to make sure he looks like an honest, concerned, law abiding citizen and VECO's reputation remains untarnished. If that requires some dirty work by one of his employees on the side, then so be it. But he'll come out smelling like a rose, just as he should. He's a Vero."

"Speaking of which—you own that big house and I saw in your records that you have close to a five hundred thousand dollars in CDs, stocks, and savings. That all your Father left you when he died?"

"Me? Yes." Tony wondered where in the world Detective Kirkland was heading with this question.

"And you have a sister. He leave her anything?"

"She got a hundred grand. Blew most of it quickly, though. She was a wild one before she 'met the Lord.'"

"And that was all the money he saved over the years? That was his estate?"

Tony straightened up at that question. "What's all this got to do with Todd Falco's case? I don't think this is any of your business."

"It's just something Holy Spirit pointed out to me when I was going through all your personal records yesterday. Answer my question: that money your Father left you, was it his net worth accumulated over the years?"

"What do you mean 'Holy Spirit' pointed this out to you?"

Ray looked at him. "He did! He always talks to me. He's supposed to. Answer the question! Was that your father's estate?"

"No, it was not. He left me a half-million dollar life insurance policy and the house, and he left Gina a hundred thousand dollar policy."

"So what happened to the rest of Pete Vero's estate?"

"I have no idea!" Tony said, irritated with Ray's nosy probe. Ray knew this question would throw the young man into a tizzy. Holy Spirit had indeed prompted him to ask Tony the question. And Ray liked the results it was getting.

"Your father was obviously successful at something. VECO, the Mafia with Carmichael, maybe, whatever. He lived in that nice big house, drove expensive cars, yet when he died you never thought to look into his estate? Grant it, that half-million dollar life insurance policy was icy cool. But hey, the man had to have more stashed somewhere."

"His brother, my Uncle Joseph, had full power of attorney over Pete's estate. Dad never talked to me about his finances. All I knew was that when he died, he had a policy to cover his funeral expenses, and he left Gina and me the insurance benefits."

"What about your mother's assets from her death?"

"Mom didn't have much. I got mine from her as soon as she died. I spent most of that in high school and college. Why am I even talking to you about this? You an investor looking for another client?"

"You're sitting on half a million in assets. That house and land you live in gotta be worth almost three-hundred thousand. You're almost a millionaire at age . . . what? twenty-three?"

"Twenty-four."

"Twenty-four. Yet you work as a private detective for your Father's old family company. You could be anywhere, doing anything you wanted to, starting your own company . . ."

"'Vero Securities and Investigations' is my company! It does well and I happen to be a great investigator."

"Yeah, but VSI is owned by VECO! Your Uncle Carmichael ultimately controls it. VSI is a VECO subsidiary, like Brighten Analytical, McThomas Fiberoptics, HealthCorp Software Designs, and all the other VECO spawned companies. I saw all the paperwork on Vero Securities yesterday. You didn't even start your company, and Carmichael controls it! So why you wasting time nosing around for your Great Uncle when you could be doing anything else on earth? You let your attorney uncle take all your father's assets, and you let your rich great uncle start a business up for you so he can order you to get your hands dirty to protect his reputation. Weren't you the next Joe Namath, according to *Sports Illustrated*? Weren't you an 'A' student in high school? You're smart. You're athletic. So why are you nothing more than a third rate flunky in a million dollar business? And why do they all want you around?"

Silence, save for the constant cracking sound of wood and metal striking golf balls. Even though Tony had been asking himself the same question recently, he didn't want to face the truth that Ray Kirkland was bearing down on him.

"I'll tell you why, Tony Vero: you're being primed to be the next head of the Vero Family La Cosa Nostra."

"There is no Vero Family Mafia!" Tony lied again.

"I suspect there sure is one, and I suspect that it's somehow all tied to VECO, and I suspect that Todd Falco was a huge part of it. That's why Carmichael has you looking for him. I think Carmichael Vero is a crime boss. I've told him so to his face, in so many words. He's the crime boss, he has no sons to pass it on to, Joseph has no sons to pass it onto, and they're priming you to take over the empire one day when they're ready to retire and you're ripe enough to handle their Mafia Family. That's how La Cosa Nostra works."

"Rubbish!" Tony stepped across the platform to square off with Ray Kirkland. "What do you know about La Cosa Nostra, 'missing persons detective?'"

Ray gladly met Tony face to face. He thought of the prophetic dream he'd had several nights earlier. He remembered Jesus's great love for Tony. Staring down into the young man's eyes, he boldly proclaimed: "I know this: you're treading on thin ice with this case."

"What are you talking about?"

"I told you that you been on my heart the last few days. The Spirit's been speaking to me concerning you. I believe your life's in danger."

"By whom?" Tony truly wanted to know.

"Who've you crossed, lately? You been around some salty cats these past couple of days. Fist fighting Ed Larsky last night. Need I say more about him? How 'bout Benny

Miller? Do you know how many illegal firearms the deputies pulled out of his house last night? He obviously doesn't play around with people. How 'bout this Bernie Lokawski?"

"I thought you just said he doesn't exist?"

"The name doesn't exist in any of our files or local and national registers. But that doesn't completely rule the man out of existence. And here you are all over town with your semi-famous self looking for the guy. If he does exist and catches wind of you, you could be in danger. And what about the Veros? You are the chosen one to take over your family's accursed criminal empire. But I could tell by their reactions to you last night you aren't exactly in their graces right now. Especially Larsky. And if you don't play like they want you to, and become who they want you to become to take over the reigns of their business, they'll turn on you. They'll 'abort' you, as it were, if you don't fall in line with their wishes. 'Cause they need an heir, and you're it."

Tony's chest heaved up and down; his hands trembled. He hated hearing what Ray said, but was flabbergasted at the man's pinpoint accuracy in describing his life.

"You're in a deadly catch twenty-two, and you truly are damned if you do and damned if you don't. You only have One Hope on this earth of ever getting out of this trap."

Tony stared out over the range as golf balls sailed endlessly in all directions. Holy Spirit was all over him. He knew the answer was Jesus. Jesus had "saved" him from that latest nightmare only an hour or so before. Ray was only confirming what he knew to be true. But to acknowledge anything Detective Kirkland was saying as truth would be to indict himself and the Family. Despite how much Tony felt a longing to really know Jesus right then, he wasn't ready to put himself and the Family in that predicament.

"Kay Falco came to church with us this morning."

Tony perked up a little. "Kay did?"

"Yes. She gave her heart to Jesus."

Kay got saved? he thought. In a strange juxtaposition of emotions, Tony's heart felt warmth and joy for Kay's decision, and at the same time emptiness and dark depression for himself.

"Tony," the formidable man said gently, "Jesus Christ is the only Hope you have. I know you're not going to come out and admit all of the ties to crime and sin you have. I understand that. But I know by the Spirit that they do exist, that all I've said is true, and that you need Jesus. You're feeling His presence right now, aren't you? Right here on this driving range. He's everywhere, Tony, yet He longs to live in your heart. The only way He can get in there is if you invite Him in. You must confess your sins to Jesus. You must ask Him to come into your heart. You must make Him your Lord, and allow Holy Spirit to save you. He wants to save you, Tony. That's why Jesus came to earth: to die on the cross for you, to pay your price for your sins, to cleanse you, and bring you into the presence of His heavenly Father."

Tony still said nothing, though he was deeply stirred. It was as though his soul was dry chaff, and Ray's words were fire igniting it.

"Listen, Tony. You're in a quandary right now. Your position seems hopeless. But Jesus' title is the 'Christ.' That means 'yoke breaker.' He's the only One who can set you free from all the bondage and oppression you're under. He can set you free from that depression, that fear and anxiety, that hopelessness that's made a once energetic and lively superstar into a dark, sullen loner. He's the only One Who can protect your life. He can handle this horribly complex situation with your family members. It won't happen overnight, and you may have to bear some more scars and bruises to your soul like those on your face right now. But He can turn you around, if you'll only repent, invite him in, and trust Him only with your life. Do you understand what I'm saying?"

Tony slowly nodded. "Yes. I do. It's the same thing my sister's been telling me."

"Do you want to pray with me right now, Tony? To make Jesus your Savior?"

Tony stood motionless. He could pray the prayer right then, and trust his shattered life to Christ for Him to fix. This thought was pressing so hard on his will. Yet the enemy of his soul was right there to try to sow confusion and snatch away the mighty seeds that Holy Spirit had planted. Fleshly complacency rose up in him. Tony thought of Carmichael and Larsky again. The Family. His vow to find Todd Falco. He thought of how close he was to closing this case and how he was going to disappear and start all over someplace else. A new life, new identity. *Yeah!* the thought played in his mind. *Then you could postpone inviting Jesus into your heart now, you won't have to have this detective pray the sinner's prayer with you, and you can do it all by yourself when you've gotten your own new identity and settled down in some other state! You can get right with God and not face the music for all you've done being a Family member!* That new thought sounded wonderful to Tony. His conscience could now bare the blow of rejecting this personal invitation from God Himself to know Him as Savior. At the same time he could continue living like he wanted, feeling placated by the thought that he could ask Jesus to be his Lord and Savior at a later time. That's what got this God-ordained pressure off his back. He'd just answer to God another time. Tony was falling into one of the devil's greatest traps: postponing Salvation for another day. Procrastination is a door to hell.

The devil won that round.

Tony declined. Ray Kirkland sensed the atmosphere around Tony change as Tony declined his invitation. He could almost see Holy Spirit grievously lifting off Tony's soul. Ray was disappointed but not moved by Tony's rejection. He was a fighter, and knew that endurance was key to victory in the Kingdom of God.

"All right, Tony," Ray conceded graciously. "You don't have to pray for Jesus' salvation now. But anytime you wish, *you* are the one who can invite Him in. You don't need big old Ray Kirkland to lead you. Holy Spirit will do it, if you'll let Him. You got that?"

Tony nodded, eyes vacant and dim. His flesh was relieved that he didn't let Detective Kirkland pray with him, but that painful void in his spirit stung even more now. Depression seemed to wash over his heart again. He wondered why he felt so bad about what seemed to be a good choice.

Ray looked down at his watch. "I've got to get going. I need to spend time with my family." He looked up at the Coca-Cola sign. "I'll give it one more shot." He set up another ball and readied his stance. Tony stepped back. Ray swung hard, connected with the ball, followed through completely. The ball lurched upward, arced, and came down well past the prized metal sign atop the telephone pole. He turned, and smiling a glorious smile, said to Tony: "Another day, maybe!"

As Ray leaned over to pick up the empty ball bucket, Tony sarcastically said, "Hey, I want to know when I'm suddenly going to be detained for questioning again so I can mark it down on my calendar."

"That depends."

"On what?"

"How much you've told me so far is the truth. I still think you're withholding evidence from me. I still think you have a lot more to come clean on. Everything's going to remain stuck here at this impasse of lies you've built until the truth is revealed. I'll just send a deputy to haul you in next time I need you, Tony Vero." Ray put his hand out for Tony to shake. Tony did, hard.

"Thanks for your concern," Tony sincerely added. He hesitated, then added, "Pray for me, man." He couldn't believe he actually said it.

Ray winked, gathered his things, and walked around the side of the facilities.

Tony breathed a sigh of relief.

They were both satisfied with the results of their meeting. Both still had vital pieces that the other did not. Ray had Tony's safe deposit box account number. Tomorrow he would get a warrant and have Reeves Bank open it for him. Tony still had Frank Kranac and the Richards brothers, and the Family was still secure. Tonight he was going to break this case, at any cost. Tomorrow he would lay the Todd Falco mystery to rest in Carmichael's lap, then he would disappear forever.

Tony stood watching the spot where Ray disappeared around the corner. It was so strange: for all the trouble and pressure Detective Kirkland was bearing down on him, he still was very fond of the man and very glad that he'd met him. He laughed: a police grilling on a driving range.

He teed up another ball. Looking out over the range he eyed the Coke sign and hesitated. *Why not?*

Confidently, he lined up his shot. His focused on his goal with uncanny determination. He readied every fiber of his body. His entire being was centered on that shot. When he knew all was ready, he let the club rip.

The ball clanged off the Coke sign, almost dead center.

Everyone suddenly took notice of what Tony had just done. Amid the thunderous cheers and shouts of disbelief from all the other patrons on the driving range, Tony calmly put his club over his shoulder and picked up the empty ball bucket.

He never mentioned the shot to Ray and he didn't bother to collect his free bottle of Coke.

Edgar Waters watched Ray Kirkland hop into his car in the Stop 'n' Sock parking lot. In his van, Edgar finished putting away his surveillance gun and checked his recording of Ray and Tony's conversation in the van's cassette player. The parabolic dish worked quite well. You could hear every word they said, crisp and clear. The Captain's plane was due at the Beaver County airport at 5:30. Edgar rewound the tape to the beginning and ejected it. He would personally greet State Attorney General Michael Davis with this special present. He would also find out more about this Detective Ray Kirkland of the Beaver County Sheriff's Department. This guy seemed to have the whole vision for what was happening at VECO.

Michael Davis would surely want to meet this Ray Kirkland.

THIRTY-NINE

Frank Kranac waded through filthy stacks of cash in his money pit. Drenched with sweat, he'd spent the day locked in his cellar counting his fortune, as was his ritual. He was interrupted again by the sound of pounding at his front door upstairs. He froze still in the dim light of the musty basement. Next, the doorbell rang and rang. He knew it was Tony Vero.

It was the third time in less than an hour and a half that meddler came calling at the door. He wouldn't dare go upstairs to chase him off, though. Not while his money pit was wide open. He knew if he just stood still for a few moments Vero would leave. While waiting his kitchen telephone rang for the third time, too. That had to be the Richard brothers, calling to inform him that it was Tony Vero banging on his front door again. *Those morons!*

He slowly turned his head and gazed over his prized treasure. Fourteen million dollars. Never in his wildest imagination in his poverty stricken youth would he have believed he'd ever be sitting on such a stash. And it was *all* his. He didn't have to share it with a wife or children. Nor any partners. No one could lay claim to it. The government couldn't tax it away. Neither would he let that cretin Tony Vero banging on his door get hold of if, either.

Frank Kranac sat perfectly still and let Tony grow weary of knocking.

"Freak!" Tony mumbled out loud as he kicked Frank Kranac's front door in frustration. He knew the weirdo had to be in there. Kranac's car was out front. The man wasn't up at the corner Tavern or down at Cherries. Tony'd called Standard Steel and they confirmed that Frank Kranac was indeed off that Sunday. And he'd caught Jimmy and Greggy Richards following him in their car around College Hill an hour earlier. When Tony turned to cut them off and confront them they lost him, mindlessly imperiling other drivers during their getaway. But Tony could see Kranac wasn't in their car with them. No, the man was locked in his house, and he was probably well aware of who it was knocking at his door. And it was most frustrating to Tony: his one link to breaking the

Falco case and winning him freedom was hiding out only a few feet behind that door. And there wasn't one thing he could do about it.

A sudden dizziness overtook him. He turned and sat down on the cracked front stoop. Despite the sun and the heat he was breaking out in a cold sweat on his forehead. His breath was getting short as anxiety began to pour over his soul. He was overwhelmed by the wide open space around him. He felt intensely exposed out there in the open. He needed to go lock himself away in his home. There he could hide, drink himself into oblivion, and shut out the world. But not *now.* Not when he was so close! He put his head down between his knees hoping to get some blood pumping into his brain to snap him out of it. The Family was not going to let him leave town and disappear if he didn't produce Todd Falco and their money in the morning. He couldn't go near Kay Falco for comfort. And what was probably the worst of it, he'd turned away the only man who seemed like he truly cared about him when he refused Ray Kirkland's prayers and help that afternoon. Perhaps he'd even turned down God Himself by refusing His salvation when Gina and Ray both offered it to him this weekend. That thought struck him hard: two different people who don't even know one another tried to lead him in prayer to know Jesus. What was that all about? Could that have been God really trying to reach out and get hold of him?

Does God give you a second chance if you flat out refuse Him? the thought overtook him. He felt even worse, now, if that was possible.

"Help me," he whispered to no one in particular, his head down near his ankles.

Suddenly the sound of laughing children filled the air from somewhere behind the house next door. The voices were coming from behind the huge hedges that divided the two properties. They got closer and closer as the unseen children made their way from the neighbor's back yard to the front, still cloaked by the shrubs. Tony looked down to the sidewalk as the chirping voices floated in that direction. Instantly three little children appeared from behind the end of the hedges, two girls and a boy. The little boy had gooey chocolate all over his hands and was chasing the two older girls, who were both squealing with delight at the chase that was on. Tony sat up and watched them. Amazingly, their innocent play brought a slight smile to his face.

"David James Craven!" a mother's voice called to the little boy from behind the hedges. Tony couldn't see her. "Don't you dare get that chocolate on Sarah and Nicole's clean dresses!" The mother's drill sergeant shouting didn't even slow little David's messy pursuit. The girls squealed even louder.

Tony could hear a man's laughter from behind the hedges. The mother chided her son again. The man laughed even harder as the boy refused to halt his chase.

"Mitch, stop him!" the wife commanded her husband.

"What's the big deal, Mary? It'll wash out. It's only chocolate."

"But Nicole's mother may not want her dress all dirty! David! Stop it!"

Mary Craven stepped down her front yard to the sidewalk where the kids were running. Tony still couldn't see her. She grabbed little David. As she was pulling him aside from the girls she took notice of Tony's truck parked behind Kranac's black Galaxie.

"Mitch!" Tony heard her half whisper. He could almost see her now. "Someone's visiting 'the thing' next door!"

Tony smiled at her apt description of Frank Kranac. Suddenly Mary Craven peaked from around the hedges near the sidewalk to see who was visiting Kranac. She spotted Tony and jolted, startled to find someone sitting on Kranac's front porch. Tony sat up, surprised at the sight of her. The nagging voice was deceptive: "Mary" was a very attractive blond in her late thirties.

"Mitch! There's a man sitting on his porch!" she cried out alarmed to her husband. She held David to her side. Any visitor of Kranac's was surely as suspect as he. Tony looked like death warmed over, too. He was sickly, wan. From around the hedges Mitch appeared, a pudgy white collar type also in his late thirties. He took quick notice of Tony's pallid, weak condition.

"Can I help you?" Mitch said with a mixture of compassion for Tony and concern for his family.

"Maybe," Tony said weakly. He slowly forced himself to stand up.

"You look awful," Mary remarked. "Do you want us to call an ambulance for you?"

Tony shook his head and slowly walked down the steps toward the sidewalk. "No," he said. "I'm all right. I guess I'm just having a spell of some sort. I got light headed and had to sit down back there."

Mary looked over his forearms. There were no needle marks. Tony was well-dressed, in decent shape, and he had a nice pickup truck. She decided he wasn't a dangerous junky. "Are you a friend of Mr. Kranac?"

Tony shook his head once more and pulled out his wallet. He showed them his private investigator's license. "My name's Tony Vero . . ."

Mitch Craven's eyes lit up. "I thought that's who you were! I didn't want to say anything! How's your shoulder since the injury?"

"You're that quarterback!" Mary remembered. "We went to all your games."

They shook his hand and introduced themselves. Tony had to recount his injury and the end of his football career. He recited the lame, memorized speech that he gave to all the strangers who recognized him.

Mary leaned over and looked up at Kranac's door. "So what are you doing here at Mr. Creepy's house?"

"Mary!" Mitch rebuked her. "Maybe this is a family member of his that you just insulted!"

Tony grinned and shook his head. "No way! I've been here on business all weekend. I'm trying to get some information from Mr. Kranac, that's all. I think he's home but he won't come to the door. He is a genuine weirdo."

"Is that so?" Mary looked angrily at Mitch. "Let's see what Mr. Vero's impression of Frank Kranac is, wise guy!"

Mitch waved her off, irritated. "Mary acts like he's Mr. Serial Killer with a basement full of decapitated bodies."

Tony's eyes lit up and his face went sheet white again. Mary Craven gasped and put her hand up to her face when she saw Tony's reaction.

"You do know something bad about him!"

Tony looked at their cute little boy and the sweet little girls all playing behind them. He got bad visions of what Kranac might be capable of. "No, it's just that . . . well . . . I'd keep an eye on things around here. Especially with the children . . ."

Mary Craven hauled off and smacked Mitch hard on his arm. Mitch "Owww!"-ed and stepped away from her in shock. Tony was taken aback, wondering what can of worms he'd just opened for this couple.

"See!" She yelled at her husband. "All these years you've been telling me I'm 'crazy' and just 'overreacting' to this freako next door and here *this* man confirms everything I've been telling you, Mitch Craven! You never listen to me!"

"I didn't mean . . ." Tony wanted to quickly smooth over any argument his careless comment may have started, but was interrupted.

"What do you know about Mr. Kranac?" Mitch asked. "Why are you questioning him?"

Excitement was defogging Tony's mind. "I . . . that's private information."

Mary started to tell Mitch that they needed to call the police and have them come to check out Kranac. She mentioned that maybe Tony could give them information they didn't have. It was then that the fog of anxiety and confusion in Tony's head was instantly blown away by a dreadful revelation: this is the same way things went down in Ft. Lauderdale!

What are you doing here talking to these people, Tony? the alarm sounded in his mind.

Here he was hanging out at Frank Kranac's house in broad daylight, talking to the man's neighbors when he knew full well he'd probably be giving Carmichael and Larsky this guy's name and address the next morning. It could turn out just like Ft. Lauderdale! And worse yet, Tony had actually just shown *this* couple his identification card!

Stupid! Tony thought to himself.

Mary was asking Tony if he'd stay a minute at their house until the police could get there, and Mitch was telling her to leave him alone. It was at that point that Tony made a b-line to his truck. Both Mary and Mitch Craven called for him to stay, but he jumped into the truck and took off as fast as he could. The Cravens were left staring at each other in confusion.

As he sped down 6th Avenue on College Hill, Tony couldn't shake the horrific thoughts of Ft. Lauderdale that had been reawakened in him that afternoon. That haunting malaise was upon him once more. Suddenly he had only one thing on his mind: why did things in Florida go down as they did? Why did the Family have to operate like *that*? He wanted answers and he wanted them now. Tony knew of only one person who could or would give him a straight answer about Lauderdale.

He squealed rubber left onto 37th Street and headed straight to his Uncle Joseph's house.

Edgar Waters arrived at the Beaver County Airport at 5:30 in a rented navy-colored club wagon. He got out of the van and scanned the small airport parking lot in the late afternoon sunshine. He spotted two stone faced men with luggage standing near the fence by the runway. They were both staring him down coldly from across the lot. One was tall, lanky, in his late thirties, wearing a long brown trench coat, sucking on a cigarette. His dark brown hair was slicked back away from his leathery face; his piercing eagle eyes scanned right through Edgar. The man beside him was shaved bald like a cue ball, much shorter, but stocky like a wrestler. He wore a black leather jacket over a plain white dress shirt with a black tie. He chewed gum mechanically and stared Edgar down like he was a worthless housefly. Both wore black cowboy boots. Neither spoke. Neither smiled. These two salty characters had to be the SBI agents Attorney General Michael Davis described would rendezvous with them at the airport. Edgar slowly made his way toward them, hands in his jeans pockets. They both eyed him suspiciously as he approached them.

"Captain Gandtz of the SBI?" Edgar asked the bald one. The man looked at him, but didn't answer. "Edgar Waters," he extended his hand to the man.

The strong fellow took Edgar's hand and squeezed it hard. "Leo Gandtz," he introduced himself emotionlessly. He thumbed over at the tall man in the brown trench coat. "That's Lt. Saucier."

Saucier nodded and grunted impolitely. He didn't look at Waters, nor did he extend his hand. Edgar just nodded and grunted back at him.

"You're the special investigator Mike Davis told us about," Gandtz confirmed.

"Yes, sir," Edgar replied. They sure weren't interested in being friendly.

"So you got some hot stuff for us all, 'investigator'?" Gandtz remarked with harsh skepticism in his voice.

Waters played along. "Hotter by the minute. I just picked up another stinger of an audio on one of our suspects this afternoon. Another eye-opener."

"Better be," Saucier growled, staring out over the runway and sucking on his smoke.

"'Better be?'" Waters scowled at him. He'd had enough of John Wayne and Dirty Harry's condescending attitudes. "What if it's not up to your standards, Hot Shot? What's gonna happen?"

Gandtz pointed at him: "You listen: Mike Davis just pulled us off a costly stakeout in New Castle this morning. We were on the verge of a major sting. He made us drop everything, lay down our case and come to this washed up steel town because of some so-called 'important' recordings you've made over the past few days. So what Lt. Saucier means is you had better have something important or we're going to be very upset about this interruption in our investigation. We don't have time to play."

"'Play?' I don't think Attorney General Michael Davis ever plays, men." Edgar pointed to a roaring Lear jet that was floating in for a landing behind them: "But you'll have to take that up with him personally, since you don't seem to trust his judgment."

Michael Davis got off the jet alone, as was his fashion. He was the anti-politician, eschewing entourages and the gratuitous trappings that supposedly went with his position. He shook Edgar's hand with a small grin, openly acknowledging his gratitude for the faithful investigator. He hadn't seen him face to face in months. Neither tried to speak near the roar of the jet engines. Edgar went to the luggage compartment of the Leer and grabbed Davis' two pieces of luggage. Davis grabbed a huge cardboard box. On their way toward the parking lot Edgar nodded at Gandtz and Saucier, who chose to keep their position near the runway fence while Waters went to greet the State Attorney General.

"Captain Happy and Lt. Happier ain't so glad to be here, Captain Davis."

"They giving you a hard time, Sergeant?" Davis smiled.

"They're upset that you pulled them off whatever case they're working on."

"They've not been pulled. I didn't have time to explain anything to them. Don't take it personally, Edgar. You're about to find out why they're the best in the state. You have us a war room ready?"

"I got us a conference room at the Holiday Inn near the Turn Pike. Told 'em that we didn't want it cleaned or serviced. Told 'em they better not step one foot in it. Got you and Frick and Frack there your own rooms, too. And I have us that club wagon you wanted."

"Excellent."

"Got another loop of Tony Vero today, too."

Davis' eyes lit up. "Another one? Is he getting stupider by the day, or what?"

"This is a real interesting one. He was meeting with some detective who's in charge of the Todd Falco investigation. You gotta hear it in the van."

They stepped through the fence and went over to Gandtz and Saucier. Davis laid down his box to greet the two grumpy SBI agents.

"Captain Gandtz. Lt. Saucier," the Attorney General shook both their hands with a smile of gratitude. They showed more enthusiasm for him than they had Edgar Waters. "Sorry about the sudden change of plans on a few hours notice."

Gandtz spoke bluntly: "Mike, I have more respect for you than anyone I know in Harrisburg. You know that. You know I support your work. But I do not understand what you've done to us today. What are we doing here?"

"Leo, they tell you about Harvey Kitner resigning as SBI head today?"

"Yeah. Harv was methodical and reliable, but he had no character. Good-bye to him. But what's that got to do with all this?"

"A whole lot. Let's get into the van. I'll brief you on everything."

Edgar drove the club wagon. Davis rode shot gun. Gandtz and Saucier sat in the seat behind them. They finished listening to Edgar's latest recording of Tony Vero talking to Detective Ray Kirkland at the driving range hours earlier. Edgar ejected the cassette tape.

"I like that Detective Kirkland," Davis said. "He's a straight shooter."

Gandtz piped up skeptically from behind them. "What kind of cop gives a suspect an altar call?"

Davis chuckled. "One who cares for the spiritual well-being of the suspect, Leo."

Edgar looked at the two SBI agents in the rear view mirror as he drove. "I hope that recording was important enough to meet your standards, gentlemen," he said with mock concern.

Davis looked over at Waters. "These two cowboys giving you a hard time, Sergeant?" He pulled down his sun visor, opened the vanity mirror on it, and looked back at Gandtz and Saucier. "Back off, fellows. What Sergeant Waters has for us dovetails directly into your case."

"How?" Gandtz asked. "Would you please tell us what's going on and why we're involved?"

"What *are* they working on?" Edgar asked Davis.

"You certainly know who Warren Zann is, don't you Sergeant Waters?"

"Sure do. One of VECO's accountants and one of Carmichael Vero's six remaining original Family members."

Gandtz and Saucier both looked at each other in confusion when Edgar Waters mentioned Carmicheal Vero and the Family. They had no idea what he was talking about.

"Right. Well, Captain Gandtz and Lt. Saucier have been secretly investigating Mr. Zann for about seven months now on child pornography charges."

Gandtz piped up. "That's what we were doing today when Attorney General Davis called us in New Castle. Warren Zann runs one of the biggest child pornography networks in the state. But nobody seems to know it except us. We have an undercover man who's going to make contact with him either tomorrow or Tuesday. We've worked this agent up right. Zann thinks he's been in the business for years and is about to make a major investment. That's why we need to be back in New Castle. Our boy is green and needs our constant supervision and coaching on this."

"You'll be able to give it to him, Leo," Davis assured him. "But since Harvey Kitner's resignation this morning, the Governor's given me the okay to take out Warren Zann's boss."

"Zann has a boss?" Saucier asked. "He *is* the boss."

"No. He isn't. That's why I summoned you two to meet me here. Warren Zann is not the head. He's a part of something much bigger than that atrocious child pornography business he runs."

"There's bigger than Zann?" Leo Gandtz was flabbergasted.

"Sgt. Waters, do you know why I personally called in Captain Gandtz and Lt. Saucier? These are two of the best racketeering and vice investigators Pennsylvania has. Captain Gandtz is known as 'The Bull.' He's taken down three of the most powerful rings in Pennsylvania." Attorney General Davis spun around in his seat. "And what he doesn't realize is that I'm now assigning him to take out the biggest and the most heinous organized criminal this state has probably ever seen."

Gandtz was intrigued, now. "Brief me, boss."

"Harvey Kitner was removed as head of the SBI today, Leo. The Governor gave him no choice. Harv was standing in my way on investigating and prosecuting the man who single-handedly runs one of the most expansive and twisted conglomerates I've ever seen. Leo, I'm putting you in charge of bringing to justice once and for all a kingpin named Carmichael Vero. A kingpin so powerful that Warren Zann even answers to him. You think you're up for that, Leo?"

Gandtz's eyes sparkled. "You want me to bring down a kingpin of kingpins?" He looked over at Saucier, furled his lips and nodded. Saucier nodded too, now satisfied with the reason for the interruption of their investigation. Gandtz looked back at Davis. "Yeah, boss. You can count me in on this one. I'll guarantee you I can bring down a sleaze ball like Carmichael Vero. In fact, I'd love to."

Michael Davis also nodded, grateful to hear Gandtz sign on. "Excellent, gentlemen. And I guarantee you'll still be in complete charge of taking down Warren Zann this week. It's directly related to our Carmichael Vero case. In fact, I have a feeling we'll be working on a whole lot of related cases at one time. Edgar?"

"Yes, sir?"

"I want you to get hold of Sheriff DeBona. From that tape you just played for me it sounds like we can get the cooperation of local law enforcers, too. I want you to find the Sheriff and have him get me that Detective Ray Kirkland. He's got his nose in Carmichael's trash pretty deep himself with that Todd Falco investigation he's running. I think he and we could all benefit from an alliance to bring down Carmichael Vero."

"Yes, sir."

Michael Davis stared out at the beautiful setting sun on the horizon. He thought about Ray Kirkland. He was obviously a Godly man. A man of character. A man who's heart was right. "I want Detective Kirkland on board with us, Sergeant. We need him."

"You got him, Captain. You got him."

FORTY

Audra Dutton was very faithful to God's commission for her to intercede over the lives of the two young men she'd seen in the vision on Saturday. Therefore, Tony Vero and Benny Miller were kept well under the word of the Lord by Audra that Sunday. She had spent the second day of her fast in deep intercession. Having never experienced a vision like that before, she phoned Pastor Jenkins and his wife Saturday evening and submitted what happened to them. After a few moments of prayer over the phone, Pastor Jenkins told Audra that God often did speak to intercessors through dreams and visions. Pastor told her to keep the vision to herself for the time being, but that if she knew God had spoken to her in the vision, that she definitely should be faithful to it until further instructions from Holy Spirit.

So Audra went to war. It was a powerful day of church, then coming home and experiencing the sweet, holy presence of Jesus Christ in an intimate fashion.

At six o'clock Sunday evening she took a break from the intercession. She flicked on the television and went into the kitchen to fix a glass of tomato juice. The news had just come on, but she wasn't paying it any attention. She returned the juice can to the refrigerator. When Audra Dutton came singing into the living room she was totally unprepared for what she would see on the television set. She turned the corner and there on the large screen she saw Benny Miller's face on the news. Like someone who had just seen a ghost Audra jolted and screamed. Her glass of tomato juice shattered on the bare hard wood floor beneath her as she clasped her hands to her face in shock. The anchor woman was detailing Benny Miller's arrest and charges the previous evening. Audra learned his name, that he was the leader of a major drug gang, and that he too lived in Beaver Falls. At that point the revelation came to Audra, one that she doubted she'd ever receive: this was probably the man who sold her son Orlando the drugs that killed him. And Benny Miller truly was that man. This was the face of the anonymous person for whom she had been interceding all these years. This was the fruit of her prayers. After all this time, now that her heart was right, her Father was showing her the face of her son's killer. And Audra's response? She stepped away from the broken glass on the ground beneath her, fell on her face before Him, praising Him for His great mercy, and calling down that same mercy upon the head of this Benny Miller.

"Oh gracious and merciful Father! Have mercy upon this blind man who would sell deadly drugs to one of your children and snuff out his life! Forgive this man for what he did to my Orlando! Forgive him and SAVE him now, Father! Save this Benny Miller! Bring your servants to him in that jail they're holding him in. Bring in the righteous preachers who can effectively minister the gospel of salvation to this lost soul and bring his heart to repentance before Jesus! Save this Benny Miller, Lord! Save Benny Miller! Save him, Lord! Save him!"

Tony Vero banged on his Uncle Joseph's front door. Joseph Vero lived in an exclusive section of Patterson Heights on the hill overlooking Beaver Falls. Like Carmichael he lived single in a house big enough for ten people. Like Carmichael he'd been married several times, each marriage lasting no longer than a year and a half or so. Like Carmichael he was a workaholic who put money above everything, including women. Joseph played the field when he had the time, often dating thirty and forty year old business executive types. Joseph was talking to his current flame on his portable phone. He smiled as he let Tony into his house.

Tony blurted out to his Uncle: "I need to talk to you *now*." When he quickly realized Joseph was sweet talking his latest woman, Tony growled, "Tell her good-bye and hang up!"

The smile slid off Joseph's face like wet cement. He glared at Tony. Tony could hear the woman on the phone ask what in the world was going on. Joseph calmly spoke to his girlfriend. "Connie," he said tenderly, "I'm afraid my nephew is being rude at the moment. I apologize on his behalf. I'll say good-bye now, and I promise you that if Tony survives this night, he'll never interrupt us again."

Joseph let Tony in and closed the door. He watched Tony while he hung up the phone. The Kid was frantic. He looked wide-eyed around the living room like he was searching for a comfortable seat, but he never sat down. Joseph knew he was at his wit's end; angry, unstable, insecure. He was a man violated by a revelation he wasn't prepared to experience. Tony wanted to talk to his uncle. Joseph was the closest thing to a father he had. He paced wildly back and forth, rubbing the back of his neck, unable to find a place where he could begin to express himself. But he didn't need to say anything. Joseph knew what was vexing him. He knew why the Kid was there. He didn't let Tony struggle about for the words to express himself:

"It's your Father's fault, Tony," Joseph began the conversation for him.

Tony looked at him in shock, then got offended, angrier. "What do you mean it's Pop's fault? What are you talking about?"

"It's Pete's fault you've been exposed to the Family and now you're living in such torment. If Pete would have guarded his mouth like he was supposed to, you wouldn't

VIOLENT MEN

301

even know the Family exists. You *shouldn't* know the Family exists, let alone have been devastated by what you perceive the Family did to you in Ft. Lauderdale."

Tony took it all in, eyes watering; frazzled.

"All you ever saw was the glamour and glitz. Pete took you to Atlantic City. You got to wine and dine with him, surrounded by women and lots of celebrities. He'd show off his prized athletic son proudly to them. Maybe give you a couple hundred dollars to go play the slots and games while he talked business with other wiseguys. All he ever showed you was the glitter. Well, at age twenty-four, you've learned the hard lesson: all that glitters is not gold."

"No. In the Family it turns out to be blood! How can you live with yourself, Uncle Joseph? How could Pop?"

"Your Dad loved the vice, Tony. He loved the money. He loved being a wiseguy. He loved the worldly trappings that went with the lifestyle, the respect a made man can get among the wealthy and successful. It was his high, his rush. That's how Pete got off. Me, I'm more like Carmichael. I'm not in it for the trappings. Carmichael and I weren't ever a 'Charlie Goodtime' like Pete was. Carm and I aren't even in this for the money, though we've both made a substantial fortune off it. No, Carmichael and I, we're in it for the 'juice.' It's the electricity of this rogue lifestyle that allures us. To do what we do but still look like respectful executives and career men. To be the envy of all, yet outsmart those in authority. To sit at a meeting with corporate executives one minute, and then load up Todd Falco with a million dollars for a buy the next; that's the juice. Then to watch the millions come rolling in later. I can only get that from the Family. If someone gets run over because they're in our way, well, that's just the way things go. Sorry for them. I'd die if someone locked me up in jail. I've got to be in control of my life, this juice. Lock me up, and I'm finished."

"What about those who actually have died, Joseph? What about them?"

"What can I say? Unfortunately, the nature of our lifestyles, Tony, requires that some people are going to lose their lives."

The veins bulged on Tony's neck and forehead. "And you're just fine with that?"

Joseph stepped toward him and soberly replied: "That's the nature of this business! We're not missionaries out to save people. We're intense business men who do whatever's necessary to gain the juice and keep the power and money. We *can't* know any other way. It would kill us. We can't go legit. It was never even an option to Carmichael. I'd rather have a million in the Family business than fifty million working only at VECO. We're not legit, Kid. We're winners who take *all*, and we'll take down anyone who stands against us."

"So Gus Savage stood against you? That frightened, worn out, old skeleton of a . . ."

Joseph reddened a shade and stepped closer to the Kid. "Gus Savage was your father's fault, too, if you have to know the truth, Tony! And yes, he did stand in our way by ripping us off!"

"You're gonna blame Pop for Gus?" Tony was incredulous.

"Pete should have broken *all* ties to La Cosa Nostra when Carmichael told him to. But he held onto Gus Savage. Now *he* was a thorn in all our sides. And your father was more loyal to *him* than to the Family. And unfortunately, Gus ultimately paid for your Pop's mistake. You act so shocked and disgusted with what happened in Ft. Lauderdale, but it was your father's ill-ties and loose lips that caused that whole incident, Kid, the incident that you think's shattered your whole life."

"You're gonna blame your dead brother for something that happened four years after his death? Your sick!"

"No, I'm not. What I'm telling you is the truth. Pete is responsible for the whole situation. It was his refusal to do what Carmichael knew was the right thing that set up everything that happened in Ft. Lauderdale. And Ed Larsky was right about *you*, not that I'm a big promoter of Ed Larsky's correct calls. But you are not Family material, Tony. You have too much of your mother in you and not enough of your father. I always knew a Ft. Lauderdale experience would shake the life out of you when it occurred. And look at you: you *are* shaken."

"Yeah, well, should I apologize for having a conscience, Uncle Joseph?"

"No. But you should definitely get out of this business."

A single tear rolled down Tony's face. "I'm sure trying with all my might, Uncle Joseph. I'm trying."

Joseph walked over to Tony and put his hand on his shoulder. Tony didn't respond, but he didn't pull away, either. Joseph pointed at a bottle of wine he had out. "Kid, you're a mess. Why don't you have a drink and relax a little bit?"

Tony shook his head. "I can't. If I get started I'll just be drunk for days. I've gotta have this Falco case wrapped up and on Carmichael's desk by the morning, or he and Larsky'll have my head."

"What's happened to Falco? Who has the money?"

"I think Falco's dead. I think I know who did it. But I don't have it all figured out yet. I will before sun-up, though. I don't think this is the first time this has happened to someone like Todd around here. I have one more person to find and then some big puzzle pieces to fill in by the morning. You'll all know what happened to Todd and your money then."

Tony walked over to the sofa and sat down. That question Detective Kirkland asked him earlier was bugging him badly. He looked up at Joseph. He had to know.

"What happened to all of Pop's money when he died?"

The question caught Joseph off guard, and Tony noted it. Joseph's eyes widened. His mouth opened but no words came out.

"Uh-oh," Tony said. "This is gonna be good."

Joseph sat down on the recliner across from the couch and leaned forward, his elbows on his knees. "Why are you asking this all these years after Pete's death?"

"That Detective Kirkland asked me about Pop's estate this afternoon."

"Why's he bringing it up? How's he know anything about Pete's estate?"

"The Sheriff's Department cleaned out my entire house on Friday. The got all my records and transactions. He went through all my records looking for info on Todd Falco. In the process he wanted to know why Pete only left me an insurance policy . . ."

"'Only left you an insurance policy'? He left you a half million dollars!"

"In *insurance*. Detective Kirkland made a good point. Besides my house, what happened to all of Pop's assets? His bank accounts? I think you know, judging by your reaction to the question. What happened to all Pop's money from the mob and the Family? I know he was loaded."

Joseph looked ashamed for the first time Tony could remember. He reached over, picked up his wine glass and knocked off its contents. Tony glared at him, waiting for an answer.

"What happened to Pete's money? Mine and Gina's inheritance?"

Joseph picked up the wine bottle and poured himself another glass. He had a grave expression. "The Family got it."

Tony leaned forward, jaw agape. He couldn't believe what he just heard. "The Family got it?"

Joseph poured the wine down his throat and nodded, eyes shut. "All of it."

"Why?" Tony raised his voice.

Joseph sighed. "That's the agreement you make when you join the Family. If one of us croaks, the other Family members get all their assets."

"How much was he worth?"

"You don't want to know!"

"You blood suckers! That was our money! Gina and me."

Joseph leaned forward. "No! That money was made by Pete while working for the Family and earlier in La Cosa Nostra. That's *our* money. Pete knew it and he made no bones about having it all signed over to our accounts when he died. That's why he arranged for insurance money for you and Gina."

"How much? Tell me!"

Joseph closed his eyes and rubbed his right temple. "twelve million," he whispered.

Tony gasped and turned sheet white. "Pop had twelve million . . . Well how much are you and Carmichael and Larsky and the rest worth?"

"Like I'm going to run down the list for you? It's our money and our business what each of us is worth. But like I said, we all made it with Carmichael and we'll all kick it back to one another if we start dropping dead. That's the Family way."

"Yeah, but so much for Pete and Dorothy Vero's family! Gina's money's all gone to the wind from her partying. She could sure use some of that twelve mill!"

"She didn't make it. She doesn't get a cent. That's Carmichael's policy. I'll loan her some if she needs . . ."

ERIC FLORE

"Where do you keep it all? How's the government not know about it?"

"Anthony Zann sets up Swiss and offshore accounts for us all. The government doesn't know it exists and they can't touch it."

Tony shook his head in disgust. "You are bloodsuckers."

"And you're working for us!" Joseph leaned forward from the recliner far enough to get his finger into Tony's face. "So don't get a holier-than-thou attitude toward me. You're one of us, Tony! Whether you're man enough to admit it or not!"

"I'm *not* one of you!" he roared back at his Uncle.

"You'll do anything to win. I guarantee it. It's a Vero trait. You're one of us. Put in a pinch, you'll come to our level of play. And it's a bloody level, boy!"

"I won't!"

"You say you won't, but I'll prove it to you right now. How bad do you really want to get out of the Family, Tony? What will you do to win your freedom? Huh?"

Tony looked at him puzzled, uncertain of where he was going.

"What's the deal you made with Carmichael on Wednesday to get out of the Family?"

Tony started to realize what he was getting at. He didn't answer. Another wave of shock began to overtake him in the realization of what Joseph was implying.

"You won't repeat it? Let me repeat it for you: If you find Bernie Lokawski or whoever set up Todd Falco and you turn them over to Carmichael, he'll let you leave the Family and our lives forever. Isn't that correct?"

Tony was too stunned to answer.

"What do you think Carmichael and Larsky are going to do tomorrow when you turn over those people who wacked Todd Falco and stole our money?"

The thought staggered Tony's mind. Joseph saw it.

"Yeah, Kid, that's right! You think they're going to give them some sort of holy absolution to pardon their sins against the Family? No, you know what Carmichael's going to have Larsky do. Yet, even though you know what they're really going to do to these losers, I guarantee that you're still going to turn them over to Carmichael and Larsky in the morning. Why? Because you're that hungry to get out of the Family!"

"Shut up!"

"And because you're just like us you're more than willing to win your freedom tomorrow by getting someone else's blood spilled! And then you'll have another Ft. Lauderdale type guilt-trip to deal with. Except this time, you won't be able to blame it on the Family and your own naivet•. This time, *you'll* be the one who shed the blood!"

"No!" Tony's mind couldn't handle it all. The truth of what Joseph was saying was blowing away any hope of redemption he held in the back of his mind. The trap he was living in as a Family member tightened even harder around him. Because Joseph was right: to get out of this nightmare, someone else had to die, and then the nightmare wouldn't be over, it would only get worse. Tony Vero was truly as Ray Kirkland had described him earlier that afternoon: damned if he did, damned if he didn't.

Tony cursed the Family out loud in a desperately pained voice and ran up out of Joseph's living room toward the door. Joseph walked after him and shouted:

"I don't care if the truth hurts you, Tony! You're going to know when you leave here tonight that you don't have any right to point a finger at me or any Family member! You are a Family member, too! You are a Vero! And everything you're doing now is just proving what's been true all along! And I'll tell you something else . . ."

Tony tore open the front door. It banged loudly against the foyer wall beside it, the doorknob leaving a hole in the drywall.

Joseph continued: ". . . Tony Vero—you're being primed to become a Family member for life! Carmichael considers you to be the next head of the Family when he's gone! Not me or the Zanns or Larsky. You, Kid! He's priming *you*. And you're turning into one of us faster than you'll ever admit!"

Tony remembered Ray Kirkland's same warning to him earlier that day. He sobbed violently, staggered out to his truck, and opened the door. Joseph appeared in the doorway and yelled:

"You couldn't even handle Ft. Lauderdale, Kid! How you gonna handle what you'll set in motion tomorrow?"

Tony peeled out of Joseph's driveway leaving smoke in the air from the burnt rubber. He pounded on the steering wheel hard, with a primitive roar of anguish, and actually bent it in his guttural rage. Joseph's words of truth echoed in his head:

You couldn't even handle Ft. Lauderdale! How you going to handle this?

Tony sobbed with guilt, pain, and anger. He sobbed like a baby, broken-hearted beyond what he believed could ever be repaired; his spirit crushed by the awful truth of a demonic family curse.

Ft. Lauderdale. The whole ugly incident began to replay in his head as he sped down Darlington Road. *Ft. Lauderdale.* The nightmarish visions danced and leapt to life within; almost mocking him with the torment they brought.

How could his life have ever taken such a horrible twist? he wondered.

A ghastly twist like Ft. Lauderdale . . .

FT. LAUDERDALE

February 28

VECO was bustling with productivity that cold winter morning. But the chill in the office was warmed by a sunny, smiling Tony Vero who appeared at the top of the stairs near Hilda Jessup's secretary's station. Many of the young receptionists and secretaries nudged one another and swooned at the sight of the handsome, confident young Vero. His hair was crisply styled, accenting his ethnic features and green eyes. He donned a black leather jacket, gray and black slacks, and black cowboy boots. He flashed his gregarious smile at Hilda and humbly introduced himself to her like no one would know who he was:

"Hi! I'm Tony Vero. I have a ten o'clock appointment to see Carmichael Vero."

Hilda smiled back and waved him over to the waiting area off to the left. "Oh, listen to you, acting like I don't even know who you are! I'll buzz Mr. Vero and let him know you're right on time."

Tony stood patiently over by one of the couches. He studied the tasteful paintings on the wall like it was the first time he'd seen them. He was merely hiding his excitement. Tony Vero was on fire inside. He felt alive and full of purpose for the first time in the four years since Pete died and he left college. He had graduated from the fifteen month private investigator/body guard school in California, top of his class. He loved LA and the whole West Coast scene, and he made lots of friends and contacts out there. Upon his return Carmichael set up Vero Securities and Investigations, a VECO subsidiary run by Tony himself. VECO and the Family would be his primary clients, but Carmichael and Joseph both encouraged him to pick up outside business on the side so it would all look legit. The best thing about VSI was that Carmichael fronted the money to launch the business. Tony didn't have to touch the insurance fortune his father left him. This was a win/win situation for him and VECO and the Family. VECO hired him for five cases. Three were to investigate the transactions of several VECO subsidiary companies and confirm that everything at those businesses was legitimate. The two others were court case investigations for Joseph and Marv Lenstein regarding VECO lawsuits. These were complicated lawsuits, with legal issues that Marv Lenstein feared Tony wouldn't be able to properly discern. But Tony went to the Geneva College library, got law books and looked up all the legalese that plagued those cases, and surprised everyone by digging up information against the opponents that he wasn't even hired to find. He blew away all five assignments, accomplishing above and beyond what Carmichael and the Vero/ Lenstein law firm had wanted him to do. They acclaimed him as a go-getter who could tackle the toughest challenges with ease, once he put his sharp mind and unwavering determination to them. He was the Kid again! Not some injured, washed out college drop out who'd wasted great potential. His future shone brightly, once again. He walked with his head high, confident and proud, like he did when he was on the playing field.

And on that fateful February day, Carmichael was going to give him his first Family assignment. An assignment he knew he'd be able to blow away, whatever it was. He didn't realize, of course, who would really be blown away when it was all over.

Carmichael's office was spy-proofed when Tony Vero came jaunting through the oak doors. Larsky had checked for bugs and rock and roll music blasted from the speakers outside to ward off spies.

"They got Gotti on tape. They'll never get us," Larsky always vowed when the office was ready for Family meetings.

Larsky and Joseph leaned on either end of Carmichael's desk as the excited young man came bounding in. A chair awaited him. He shed his leather jacket and took the seat, nodding and smiling at his two uncles and the perpetually unfriendly Larsky.

"Uncle Carm. Uncle Joe. Ed!" He tried to get Larsky to smile at him, but was once again disappointed. He never knew why the hulking Larsky had to be so hostile. But Tony was one who would never give up the quest for Larsky's friendship. Larsky, on the other hand, simply wanted to kill Tony Vero and dump his body in the Beaver River. Such were their natures.

Joseph smiled proudly and winked at Tony. Carmichael looked him square in the eyes and slid a folder over to him on his desk.

"We have a Family case for you, Tony. This is strictly Family business. It is to be handled discreetly, with top security and caution on your part. You got that before we begin?"

Tony stopped smiling and nodded confidently, going along with Carmichael's officiousness. "Yes, I got it. And I will."

Carmichael nodded in agreement. "Good! Because this case is important to me personally and to the safety of the Family. I need this one to be top priority with you. And Tony?"

"Yes?"

"We're testing you with this case. None of us have been able to crack this one. It's not going to be a breeze like some of these others you've handled for us. This one's an almost impossible task."

Without hesitation Tony piped up: "I'll crack it. I know I will. I want it." Tony's face hardened, his eyes glowed with conviction.

Carmichael nodded at Joseph. Joseph Vero straightened up from Carmichael's desk, took his hands out of his pockets. He picked the folder up off the desk and handed it to Tony.

"There is some old business from our days in La Cosa Nostra, Kid, business that should have been cleared up long ago but has now come back to haunt us."

Tony opened the folder. Inside was a single paged bank statement from a West Virginia banking and investment firm. Carmichael's name was on the account.

"Look at the balance, Kid."

He did. "Zero-point-zero-zero. As of October eighteenth of last year." Then Tony looked up at the previous balance: $356,783 and 56 cents. His eyes lit up with shock as he looked up at Carmichael. "I take it you're not the one who emptied this account."

Carmichael sat stone faced.

"When we were with Barrato," Joseph explained, "we had an associate named Gus Savage."

Tony nodded. "Pop's buddy. Used to meet us in Atlantic City sometimes when Pop took me there. Bawled real bad at his funeral."

"He's the one," Joseph said. "Gus was one of Barrato's wiseguys. He was deep into vice and gambling. Always got Pete involved with his schemes. He and Pete were always real tight. Probably the best friend Pete ever had." Joseph pointed at the folder. "That money was actually about eight hundred grand back in the mid-seventies. Carmichael made it when he was with Barrato."

"Selling vacuum cleaners?" Tony quipped. Carmichael did not smile.

"He had Pete and Gus launder that money by buying a cement business with it. They then sold the company, took the money to that little town in West Virginia, and opened that account for Carmichael. Carmichael had accounts like that all over Podunk towns in West Virginia, Ohio and here in PA. Less chance of feds finding out about them and questioning us about the origins of the cash. Anyhow, that account's been there since 1978. Carmichael used five hundred grand of it to help launch VECO. When Carmichael split ties with the Barratos and founded VECO, we had to take a lot of the money we made in La Cosa Nostra and transfer it into Family holdings. Anthony Zann took good care of that for us. A year or so before your father died Carmichael had him and Zann begin to gather all those small-town bank accounts and consolidate them into one of our Family off-shore accounts in the Caymans Islands. We'd been slowly working through that process, account by account, but this old account that you're looking at is one of the ones that we hadn't attended to yet. It was never transferred. You follow?"

"It was never transferred, then wound up empty in October."

"Exactly. Tony, we got right on this as soon as that bank account came up with a zero balance. Anthony Zann went back to this bank in West Virginia to investigate. In fact he's been to every one of our old banks that we used from our Barrato days. And it seems that for the last two years a certain man has been going to our old banks trying to gain access to several of our accounts. His description has been matched impeccably by all the different bankers. Some of those accounts Zann had transferred over to Family accounts and funds, according to his plan. This person couldn't get access to them. But this one, he could, since it hadn't been transferred."

"But how?"

"The only way anyone could get into this account was to have the proper access numbers and documentation originally given by the bank."

Carmichael spoke up: "And I only gave two men that money and the authority to open my account for me."

"And Pop's dead," Tony said.

Carmichael and Joseph nodded gravely, acknowledging Tony's realization of whom they were accusing.

"Gus Savage has been living in Beaver Falls here with all of us since the feds busted Carmichael. He's owned an Italian restaurant out on Rt. 18 for a long time. He was still tight with your father. But it looks like Gus held onto all his old Barrato documents, including these bank accounts he opened for us. Then he decided to help himself to some of Carmichael's money."

"If he was that tight with all of you, especially my father, and a brother from the Barrato clan, how come he never became a Family member?"

Joseph looked to Carmichael for help.

"Tony," the elder Vero spoke, "Gus Savage was what made-men refer to as 'expendable.' He was dependable to a certain level, and he could get the job done for you. But he was a weasel at heart. What he's done to us now is something I always figured he might do."

"Why'd he get as far as he did with Barrato, then, if he was such a weasel?"

"He married Barrato's niece," Carmichael answered. "Treated her well for a few years, too, before they divorced. By that time he was pretty tight with Barrato himself. He's quite a brown-noser."

Joseph spoke up. "Barrato was a muscleman. He had firepower like no one else and could intimidate an angry grizzly. But some of his choices for clan-members were questionable. Gus Savage being one of them." He pointed at Larsky. "Ed, tell him the deal about Gus Savage last October."

Larsky didn't bother to look at Tony. "He fled town the same week our money disappeared. And I mean homeboy fled town! He packed his travel gear and hit the ground running, leaving an old house, his old car, everything. But first he signed his restaurant over to his sister that same week."

"And the guy all those bankers described fits Gus Savage's description perfectly," Carmichael explained. "This was a no-brainer for us to piece together, Kid. Gus Savage ripped me off. He still had all his original access material from 1978 and used it to steal my money."

"And you want me to find him now," Tony grinned.

Carmichael laughed, well pleased with Tony. "That's why you're the Kid!" He leaned over toward him. "We can't locate him. We haven't even been able to trace him out of Beaver Falls since the night he disappeared last October."

"I can," Tony crowed.

"I know," Carmichael nodded. "But I'm serious. We don't even have a starting point for you. All we know is he went to that West Virginia Bank, withdrew my money, and now he's run off with my cash. And I want him found. Now!"

"We've got to close all our doors to the past, Tony. Gus Savage will always be Carmichael's last open door to La Cosa Nostra."

Tony laid the folder back on Carmichael's desk. "He's not magic. He can't make himself disappear. I'll find him for you. I'll get your money back for you. Gus Savage is a good as caught."

Tony went after Gus Savage's sister first. He found her at Gus's old restaurant later that afternoon. In her late fifties, wearied and haggard from her affiliations with her mobster brother, Cora Savage Nanbrook had only a broken marriage and Gus's Italian restaurant to show for anything. Gus did manage to put the business in her name before he took off in October, that much Tony did get out of the woman. But once she saw the Vero name on Tony's investigator's license, she clammed up real fast. She acted like she hated Gus and didn't care where he was. Tony could tell she was pretending. She finally grew offended at Tony's non-stop questions and had two big fellows show him to the door. Tony knew he'd get nothing more from her like this.

As employees left the restaurant at the end of their night shifts, Tony tried to get them to answer questions about Gus in the parking lot on the way to their cars. Most had been hired after October and didn't even know the man. The ones who did either told Tony to get lost or had no relevant information for him. Finally, one of them went back in and told Cora that Tony was still hanging around questioning people. Cora's two big bouncers chased him completely off the property at that point.

"You win round one, Gus," Tony muttered as he drove off down Rt. 18. He knew the man would win the first couple of rounds. "But my round's coming."

March 1

Tony spent the next morning looking for more of Gus's former associates. Many of them were dead or in jail. Typical in the underworld. Good health and long life were not usual traits of Mafioso. Gus had no real ties in the Beaver Valley who could help Tony. As gregarious as Tony remembered Gus Savage as being, it turned out he was quite isolated and lonely in these latter years of his life. After Pete died, Gus had no real tight friends. Maybe that's why the man cried so uncontrollably at Pete's funeral.

Tony exhausted all his leads fast that day. He realized what a great job Gus had done of vanishing. He left no traces, no leads. He better have, if he was going to scam Carmichael

Vero out of his three-hundred fifty thousand dollars. Everyone who worked with Carmichael in Barrato's clan knew that he was dangerously shrewd and capable of getting to anyone who crossed him. Gus ensured he left Beaver Falls with no leads to where he might be.

Tony decided to create his own lead to the man who'd ripped off Carmichael Vero.

March 2

Allison Mehall was an ex-girlfriend of Tony's. She was one of the few, however, that remained good friends with him. She was a receptionist at the Beaver Valley Health Associates Clinic in Beaver, PA. Tony needed to use her in his scheme to ferret Gus Savage out into the open. He walked into the office first thing that morning with a friendly grin and a wink for Allison. She was grumpy and busy and didn't reciprocate. He waited patiently in the waiting area for ten minutes while the lithe receptionist went from phone call to paperwork and back again until she finally blurted out:

"Okay, Tony. What do you need?"

He rushed to her station. "What a way to greet the best man you've ever been with!"

She rolled her eyes and stuck her finger down her throat. "What? What do you want? Can't you see we're busy this morning?"

"You want to make an easy two hundred dollars?"

She looked skeptically at him. "How? Is it something perverted and disgusting?"

"I need your help finding someone," he explained. "For a case I'm working on."

"How do I help?"

"Well, you work here at this health clinic. The person I'm trying to find is a criminal. He's hiding. I need to flush him out. His sister lives in Beaver Falls. I want to call his sister and scare him out of hiding. I'm going to say I'm Doctor What's-his-face here with the Beaver Valley Clinic . . ."

Allison held up her hands to halt him. "You have got to be kidding! Get out of here before you get me fired . . ."

"Five hundred dollars," he raised the ante, desperate. "No one will know."

Allison froze.

"He's a criminal, Allison. The guy's a menace and I've been hired to root him out of his hiding place. I really need your help and I'll pay you five hundred dollars to do it."

Deep in credit card debt, she certainly needed the money. The Vero's were loaded. She looked around to be sure no one was listening. She leaned into him, an almost pained looked on her face, and whispered somberly: "Six hundred and I'll do it. But you get me fired and you'll owe me a whole year's salary! You got that?"

"You're not going to get fired!"

She pointed fiercely at him, reiterating the point.

"I got it," Tony conceded.

Allison lightened up a bit. "So you just want to use our office name?"

"Yes and no. I need you to call his sister from here in case she has the caller ID junk on her phone. You'll talk to her and tell her that you're looking for her brother's address and that it's an emergency. When she takes the bait let her talk to me, 'the Doctor.'"

"What if she doesn't cooperate?"

"Then I'll need you to let me talk to her. I'll get her to break one way or another. I'll just hang out in your waiting area until you can get her on the phone."

"We'll get caught, you know! I'll get fired!"

"You won't get caught! Once she gives up the man's address you'll never hear from her again. Or me."

"That a promise?"

"Your loss, Babe," Tony grinned.

She still looked apprehensive.

"$600 for your troubles. For working with me."

Silence.

"Couldn't six hundred go a long way for you?"

She pointed her finger in his face. "You better stay out of my hair while you're here! And the first time one of the attending doctors or nurses asks about you I'm kicking you out of here and we call this whole thing off!"

"It'll never get that far, but it's a deal."

Tony had Allison use an alias when she called Cora Savage Nanbrook. Who would know the names of the receptionists at that place? Cora was very skeptical at first. This was the second time in two days someone had come to her looking for Gus. She told Allison she'd have to call her back. Cora grabbed a phone book and looked up the Beaver Valley Health Associates Clinic in the yellow pages to verify that the place was real. She then dialed the number and Allison answered.

"I want to speak with Doctor Reider, please." That was the doctor Allison told her was handling the developments of the HIV case. Allison put her on hold and quickly handed the phone to Tony. After making her wait ninety seconds, Tony had Allison patch him through.

"Doctor Reider," he announced in a silky smooth voice.

Allison sat amazed at the transformation that took place in him. He didn't even sound like Tony. He very officiously told Cora a story about one of Gus's ex-girlfriends. He said blood work came back HIV positive. She was concerned for all her ex lovers. He even used accurate medical terms and knew the procedures in dealing with such a discovery. He then explained that he wanted Gus to come to the office and sign an affidavit declaring he personally received the information regarding the results of the test. Cora said that was impossible. She said she'd just notify Gus herself and let him know one of his ex-girlfriends was HIV positive.

Tony lied. "You don't understand any of these legal regulations, do you? That is confidential information. This patient has a legal right to notify her ex-lovers privately and confidentially. For me to divulge her name would be a violation of the law. The only reason I even had you called by our receptionist is because no one can seem to locate your brother. You are the next of kin this woman referred to on her legal work, and you are now responsible to help us locate him for her."

"'Responsible'?"

"Yes! Legally! This woman can contact the AIDS Advocacy Commission and have their lawyers deal with you publicly for not cooperating with this legal document I have in my possession." He was making this all up, of course. "And the AAC has won cases in seven states against people like you."

"You are rude, Doctor!"

"You brother's life is in danger, a compassionate woman is seeking to help him by notifying him, you are refusing to cooperate, and you are calling me 'rude'? Listen, you can hang up right now and forget this. I won't ever call you back again. But I cannot guarantee some AAC lawyers won't be subpoenaing you one day at your house. Or that your brother won't infect someone else."

He heard her gasp on the other end and curse Gus. He took a long breath like he was trying to patiently reason with her.

"Look: we simply need to notify your brother. All you have to do is tell him to come here to our office in Beaver. You will never be bothered with this again once that happens. We truly don't mean to harass you. But you must understand our concern in the midst of a world-wide epidemic. And you will be legally responsible."

Allison sat back in her chair, arms folded, shaking her head with disdain for the way Tony could come up with such horrific lies at the drop of a hat. She stuck her finger down her throat again. Tony put his hand in her face and turned his back to her so he could concentrate.

After a long pause, Cora took the bait. She announced with frustration, "Gus doesn't even live in Pennsylvania anymore. He can't come to your office."

"That's not a problem, either. Just give us his home address and we can send a certified letter to Gus through the U. S. mail. Once he signs it, it's legally binding, he's officially notified, you and I are off the hook, and life goes on quietly for all."

"He doesn't have a home address. He has a post office box."

Tony wanted to curse; checked himself, quickly calmed himself down. "That'll work," he said as pleasantly as he could. "They can just put a note in his box and he can sign it at the desk of that post office."

"Well . . . wait a minute. Let me get his address. This is all confidential on his part, too, right?"

Tony tried to contain his smile. "Absolutely!"

Cora rummaged through her purse. He got his paper and pen ready.

"Here it is: PO Box 18879, Ft. Lauderdale, Florida, 33346."

Tony scribbled the last numbers down with delight. "Thank you, Mrs. Nanbrook."

"Some people value privacy, you know, Doctor Reider!"

"I understand that, Ma'am. And I promise this is all confidential. I'm simply going to put this notification in the mail today on behalf of my patient, and that will be the end of it for you and me."

"It better be, Doctor!" She hung up.

Tony handed Allison the phone. His victorious smile drained when he saw the shame, shock, and disappointment on her face.

"What?" he asked defensively.

"You just scared me."

"What are you talking about? I just nabbed the guy I was after!"

"You're not the Tony Vero I know. Paying me so you could harass some old lady with lies."

Tony grew angry. "You don't know what a scum bag this guy is I'm after!"

"You don't know what a scum bag I just saw on the phone with that poor woman! The Tony Vero I knew would never do such a horrible thing. What kind of people do you work for who would turn you into such a creep?"

Tony pulled out his wallet and produced six one hundred dollar bills. "The kind of people who can pay me to pay people like you to help me. Don't get all saintly on me, Allison. You agreed to this."

He stuck the money out for her to take. She just stared at it.

"Seriously, Allison! Don't act all holy around me. You earned this. Now take it and get off your high horse. I catch criminals. It's my job. The end."

She slowly reached up and shamefully took his money. "You're right about that: this is the end. Don't you ever come near me again."

"What is your problem, girl?"

"You just set me up, baited me, and used me like a cheap whore, Tony Vero!" She shook her head slowly, a tear forming in her eye. "If you don't feel the shame and disgrace I feel right now after what you just made me a party to, then you are in sad, sad shape, Tony. Maybe even beyond hope. You're definitely not the man I used to know."

Allison stood up, put a tissue to her eyes. "I was glad to see you at first." She started down the hall. "Now I wish you had never even come here. This is like a nightmare. What kind of man are you, now?" She disappeared into a ladies room.

Tony stood there alone, looking around perplexed. He just got the one link to the man he'd been after for several days with no leads whatsoever! *Shame? What's she talking about?* he thought. *It was sweet victory! Used her? She just made six hundred dollars off me!*

"What just happened?" he said aloud to nobody.

March 3

Tony took a morning flight out of Pittsburgh. The Family was much more jubilant about Tony's breakthrough than Allison Mehall was. They loaded him up with four grand worth of Family cash so he could rent lodging and vehicles, and get himself a flight home. They loved his plan to flush out Gus Savage, too: Tony sent Gus a certified letter from a false source. Gus would have to sign for it at his post office during the daily nine to five hours. Tony would stake-out the post office during the day until he spotted Savage. The Family was impressed with his ingenuity. Tony was secretly stoked to be going to Ft. Lauderdale during Spring Break. He'd miss the ice and snow of Pennsylvania and check out all the babes baking in the sun.

He had exchanged all of his identification and credit cards in his wallet for bogus ones with an alias. He even had a California driver's license with his photo and alias. Someone at his investigator's school had hooked him up with an illegal organization that created designer credit cards at top dollar prices for aliases. Therefore, he left all traces of Tony Vero in Pennsylvania. He was now "Mark Guider," according to all the bogus information he had on him.

At high altitudes the brilliant rays of sunlight illuminated the interior of the 737. Tony stared out the window at the crystal blue skies above and the billowy, pristine clouds beneath. His thoughts were not on the beauty of creation, however. Tony couldn't shake the stinging words of Allison Mehall the day before. *What kind of man are you?* He'd rarely ever heard anyone speak of him so. Usually when a negative word was aimed in his direction it was out of jealousy, and he'd write it off as such. But Allison Mehall's words shook him to his very core. For the first time in his life the golden boy actually had to stop and think about that question she asked:

What kind of man am I?

He didn't know quite what to think on that jet. But Holy Spirit was definitely about to reveal to Tony Vero who he really was. And He knew Tony would be completely devastated by the answer.

Spring Break at Ft. Lauderdale was the Dionysian orgy Tony knew it would be.

Frolicking college students were everywhere. The streets were packed, the sunny beaches couldn't hold one more beach towel, and the hotels, bars, and clubs were all crammed. Tony smiled the whole time, feeling right at home in the midst of the wall to wall partying.

After he arrived, he spent the rest of the time securing a hotel room, which was almost impossible, and then renting a car. He had to use the bogus credit card he'd bought for the first time. He feared it wouldn't work. It did. *Great investment!* he thought, relieved.

By the time he was settled in a room the post offices were closed for the day. But that was all right. Gus wouldn't receive the certified letter he sent until at least the next day. He drove to find the 33346 Post Office anyway, and understood immediately why Gus Savage set up his PO box there: it was as obscure as a post office could be. Settled in an old building at the end of a street near a wooded area, it definitely wasn't the most convenient or frequented locale in Ft. Lauderdale.

"Chalk another one up for you, Gussie!"

Hungry and ready for supper, Tony found a great restaurant and bar on the beach. He ate well, charmed his way into a group of five beautiful college girls from Iowa, and partied the night away with them. He struck up quite a spark with the only brunette in the group. They made out on the beach, though she wouldn't let him get too far with her sexually. But she did exchange phone numbers with him and agreed she'd like to party with him again the next night.

Drunk and electrified by the revelry, Tony finally made his way back to the hotel before sunrise.

March 4

His alarm shocked him out of his half drunken stupor at 7:45 that morning. He tried to shower and dress as quickly as possible. He had to get over to that post office to spy in case Gus Savage showed up. With his mouth stuffed full of an onion bagel and visions of black-haired Natalie from Iowa dancing around in his brain, Tony staggered into the post office just as it opened. He located the Gus's PO box. He found a bench in a corner, and settled down for the long stake-out. He pulled out a sketch pad and charcoal pencil from a knapsack. He would be posing as an art student doing sketches all week in case a postal employee questioned him.

Tony's only regret was that he couldn't spend time on the beaches during the day because of the stakeout. But he definitely had the nights to chase babes in the crowded bars.

The stakeout was painfully monotonous and fruitless the first several days. Not only was there no sign of Gus Savage, but Tony spent every night drinking and playing with little sleep. So trying to stay awake and alert in that post office while watching the parade of humanity march through all day was most tedious. When he would catch himself dozing he'd suddenly see Ed Larsky's bulldog face giving him the stern warning: "Don't fall asleep and miss him!"

"I'd hate to face Larsky if I did sleep and never find Gus," he droned. He'd sit up, slap himself in the face, and hum to arouse himself from grogginess.

Ft. Lauderdale went into a frenzy at the end of the week. The weekend was a welcome relief to Tony from the monotony of the stake out. The post office closed at noon Saturday, allowing him the rest of that day and all day Sunday to frequent the beaches, go on rogue hunts for girls, and catch up on his sleep.

He'd spent another night with Natalie from Iowa, then moved on to Lauren from Kentucky, and then to Anisa from Long Island. He let Natalie and her friends hang the third night, not meeting them at an agreed upon rendezvous. When he was with Anisa at a jam-packed club, Natalie and the delegates from Iowa suddenly showed up and cussed him out, causing a most unpleasant scene. Luckily, Tony thought later, pretty Anisa was so drunk she barely paid the outburst any mind and still wanted to go back to Tony's hotel room with him.

The weird thing about all the partying for Tony was the fact that it was leaving him with confused feelings. He began to sense these were empty experiences for him. It wasn't like when he was eighteen, nineteen, or twenty and played football. He was constantly busy with practices, games, workouts, schooling, and a load of hard work. The partying and carousing with his friends was like the icing on the cake of a perfect life. Now that he was twenty-four and not anywhere near as active, the same type of partying was much less gratifying. It was almost to the point of being sickening and pointless. He had to admit it.

"Wow," he observed. "What's the deal, Tony? You're not growing up are you?"

The twinge of conscience and maturity didn't slow his pursuit of the wild life, though. He acted as though chasing more of it might actually begin to satisfy him again. It didn't.

March 9

Somehow Tony missed Gus Savage when he entered the post office at 10:50 that morning. He must have been daydreaming while he stared out the window and Gus entered from the opposite door from where he was watching. But on that morning when the post office was as bustling with traffic as Tony had seen it, he suddenly looked up at the long line to the clerks' windows and there in line, slouched over and reading a certified mail notice in his hand, was none other than Gus Savage. Tony shot upright on the bench. Adrenaline squirted violently into his blood stream and his heart pumped it through double-time. He stared at Gus. The man took no notice of Tony sitting on the corner bench. He looked like he had aged twenty years from the time Tony last saw him at Pete's funeral. His hair, which had always been salt and pepper, was mostly salt, now. Gus was bald on the top with a horseshoe puff of longer hair running around the back and sides of his head. He had a big gray bushy mustache and huge bags under his eyes. He wore a bright Hawaiian shirt, black shorts, and flip flop sandals. His shirt was half buttoned down the front with a huge mat of gray chest hair sticking out. He wore a golden pendant that bounced around in all that hair. His legs were stocky and just as hairy. The sight of him made Tony laugh. Gus looked more like an aging disco freak turned beach bum than a once dangerous wiseguy.

Definitely no plastic surgery or disguises for this guy, Tony thought. *He just decided to dress badly to throw us all off.*

Tony gathered his things into his knapsack and quietly sneaked out the door without Gus seeing him. He went and got into his rental car and waited. Gus emerged about ten minutes later. He donned black sunglasses and looked around at all the cars and people. Tony figured the empty package he mailed him via certified mail probably spooked him. He still didn't spot Tony, who was also wearing sunglasses as he slouched down in the front seat. Gus got into an old tan BMW and drove back toward the main avenue. Many cars were coming and going from the post office so he didn't notice Tony pulling out and following from three cars behind.

Tony was grateful to be leaving that post office behind forever. "I'll never send a letter again!" he mugged as he glanced at the old building in his rear view mirror for the last time. He followed Gus across town.

Gus lived in a quiet but affluent neighborhood about ten minutes outside the Ft. Lauderdale city limits. It was a smaller home, with a well-manicured centipede lawn, several palm trees, and huge pine and willow trees shading the entire property. Gus's BMW disappeared in the garage as the automatic door closed behind him. Tony sat at a stop sign a block away and gave Gus time to settle inside and forget his problems before he confronted him. He parked across the street from Gus's home and nonchalantly made his way up the sidewalk to his front door. The shrubbery around the house was meticulously trimmed. Tony guessed a lawn maintenance crew showed up weekly. Gus was keeping a low profile, to be sure.

Tony's heart pounded violently. He wasn't really afraid, for he was the hunter and knew it well. Gus was running hard, trying to escape the wrath of Carmichael Vero. Tony meditated on that for a moment before he confidently raised his hand and rang Gus Savage's doorbell.

"Gotcha, Gus," he muttered triumphantly as he waited.

Gus looked out a peephole through his front door. He didn't recognize the young man in sunglasses. He didn't look armed, whoever it was. He didn't know what to think and stood and watched him for a moment.

"Hello?" Tony said when he heard someone on the other side of the door.

Gus reluctantly unlocked the dead bolt, but left the chain locked at the top. He opened the door as far as the chain would permit.

"What?"

"Gus Savage?" Tony asked friendly-like. Gus didn't reply. "Open the door, Gus."

Gus still didn't recognize who it was, but feared the worst. He opened the door anyway.

Tony finally removed his sunglasses when he stood face to face with him. Gus Savage's eyes lit up with happy recognition of a familiar face.

"Tony!" he said with joy, but for only a second, for Gus instantly remembered who Tony's great uncle was and quickly made the connection.

Tony grinned as he saw the smile drain from his visage. "Hey, Gus! Long time no see!"

Gus's shoulders slumped. "Yeah, and I wish it was a little longer!"

"You're not packin' a piece, are you Gus?"

"If I was I'd a put daylight through you already. You carryin'?"

"Nah. Don't like 'em."

Gus's eyes darted all about the neighborhood and over Tony's rental car. "You don't have company with you, do you?"

Tony flashed his teeth and shook his head. "Nope! I'm all by my lonesome."

"Good!" Gus sighed with relief. "For a moment I thought maybe you had that animal Larsky with you."

"No. He's chained up back in his dog house in Beaver Falls."

Gus laughed a weak laugh and tried to read Tony. Tony wouldn't give him time to.

"Aren't you gonna ask me into your nice expensive new home, Gus? That air conditioning feels real good from here."

Gus hesitated, then stepped aside from the doorway. "I guess I will Tony. I guess I will."

Gus offered Tony a drink. Tony refused, not putting a poisoning past Gus Savage's possible reactions to seeing him. He had Tony sit on a couch. Gus started toward his dining room.

Tony kept his guard up. "Step back in here please, Gus!" Tony warned. "If you try to leave my sight again I'm going to go off on you in your own house."

He looked at Tony like he was off his rocker. He pointed toward the thermostat on the dining room wall. "Do you mind if I turn up the air conditioning in *my* house? I'm a little warm right now, don't you know!"

"I'm telling you, *I'll* cool you off if you take one more step toward a door out of here."

"Listen at you!" Gus said angrily. "Is that how you speak to a family member?"

"My last name ain't Savage."

"Yeah, but your father and I were like brothers. And you know it! He was closer to me than he was to that stuffed-shirt brother Joseph of his."

Tony nodded. "You and Pop were tight."

"Closer than brothers! I was like your uncle! I knew you when you was poopin' your diapers. And I was always your biggest supporter when you were on that field playing. I was just as proud of you as Pete was. I went to *all* your games. You were in Atlantic City with Pete and me a couple of times. I treated your mother with respect. I *am* a family member to you! And now you're gonna waltz into here and show your butt just 'cause you think you got somethin' on me?"

Tony laughed at how Gus was exaggerating his connection to Tony to save his butt. He was close to Pete, but not to Tony. He rarely ever came around the house, may have been to a game or two of Tony's, but paid Tony little attention on the Atlantic City excursions Tony took with Pete. "I do have something on you, Gus: about three hundred and fifty-six thousand dollars."

Gus turned sheet white. His knees wobbled and he had to grab hold of the wall to stay upright.

"That's right. I know everything. Don't deny it, now."

Gus stood dumbfounded. He looked around, wishing for a way of escape. Tony waved him back over to the living room.

"Why don't you come in here and have a seat with me, 'Uncle Gus'?"

Gus's hand trembled as he smoked and sipped a whiskey over ice. He wanted to throw Tony off track with small talk about Pete, but Tony kept him focused.

"So what were you thinking, Gus? Did you think you could drain Carmichael of hundreds of thousands of dollars without him knowing it or doing something about it?"

Gus grunted sarcastically. "That penny-pincher not knowing about it? He'd know if I borrowed a cent from his piggy bank."

"Yeah, but you didn't 'borrow' anything. You snatched three hundred and sixty grand that wasn't one bit of yours."

Gus looked at Tony. "Wrong!"

Tony's eyes lit up. "'Wrong'?"

"I deserved that money! I earned it!"

"Carmichael never said it was yours . . ."

"You know what I mean! I was just as much a part of Carmichael and the Veros as anyone else. When Carmichael dumped the Barrato's and set up VECO he dumped me, too! After I was so faithful to him all those years! He set up Pete and Joseph, hooked up those obnoxious Zann brothers in his new scam, but he stabbed ol' Gus Savage right in the back! I know he's got more going at VECO than American capitalism! I know your Pop and Joseph and the Zanns have all been a part of it with him. They all got their piece of the action. But what about my piece of the pie? Huh? What about my years of service? I'm one of the primary reasons all those bank accounts sat around building interest for Carmichael in all those little hillbilly towns all those years. When the Feds put the screws to Carmichael's finances after they arrested him, I'm one of the main reasons that he had any cash left afterward to create VECO! Was I thanked? No! Was I rewarded and honored in any way whatsoever? No! I was cut completely out of the deal and treated like a leper." He took a swig of whiskey and a long, shaky draw off his cigarette. He lowered his tone to almost a whisper. "I was humiliated. I sat around for months waitin' for Carmichael to ask me on board. Seein' all that was going on at VECO. Waitin' for some recognition." He took another sip, sighed, looked down at the floor. "When I realized he was never going to contact me I did the most humiliating thing of my life: I went to your Pop, Tony, and practically begged him to go to Carmichael and ask him to give me some sort of job at his company. Carmichael had that Larsky corner me one day. He told me to never to contact Carmichael again. He told me to pretend like I never even knew him. He said if I didn't he'd . . ." Gus took another drag off his smoke. His bloodshot, jaundiced eyes watered lightly. "That was Carmichael Vero's answer to my years of loyalty and service. He threatened my life. Disowned me."

Tony should have suspected the tears and sorrow were contrived to save Gus's hide, generated by Gus to elicit Tony's sympathy and mercy; instead Tony sensed that Gus's pain was genuine.

Gus straightened up a bit; his self-pity turned to vengeful anger. "So when I sat around all these years working my fingers to the bone at my restaurant while Carmichael and all my ex-cronies were making a fortune, I started to get a little resentful, to be honest. And when things got a little tough last year I just decided to help myself to what I rightfully consider to be mine!"

Tony chuckled. "You can try to say that it's 'rightfully' yours if you want. But it was Carmichael's money, he made it, and the only reason you even knew it was there was because he had you and Pop set up that account for him. And according to all the bankers they talked to, you didn't just try to rob that account. You went around to all of those 'hillbilly' towns and tried to drain all Carmichael's accounts dry. This just happened to be one that still had some cash in it."

Gus's face turned red.

"And you were probably a little disappointed when you found out the account that originally had eight hundred grand in it twenty years ago only had three hundred and sixty in it now."

Gus's face soured. He angrily turned on Tony. "Well what would you have done? Huh? If everyone you knew was either locked up in jail or had turned their backs on you? You gonna sit here and put me down for trying to get what was coming to me? You who had everything handed to him on a golden platter by his generous father?" He quickly downed the half glass of whiskey that was left. "I had to work for my money, Tony! And what I lost, no one tried to replace for me!"

"You made your own bed, Gus."

"Maybe so, but here you are to put your foot on my neck while I'm down! At least your father had some class about him! He was the only person who still remembered me, still treated me with any dignity. He remembered we were made men together in La Cosa Nostra and treated me like a brother even though Carmichael warned him to never be seen with me again. Your father showed character!" Gus began to tear up again. He shook violently all over. "He chose loyalty over Carmichael's money. You're turning out to be less like your father than I thought. Coming down here 'cause of Carmichael's money, gonna kill the one man who was tight with your Pop and faithfully honored you and your family." He sobbed, put his hands over his face.

Tony was flabbergasted. "'Kill'? Who said anything about killing you?"

Gus had completely lost it by then. He was sobbing like a baby, head cradled in his hands, rocking backward and forward over and over again, to Tony's horror. Gus used to be a strong, proud man. Here he was now, reduced to a blubbering wreck. Tony could hear him bemoaning Pete's death, weeping about how badly he missed Pete, who was the only true friend he'd ever had. Tony's heart rent a bit more. Gus sobbed about how lonely he was and how he didn't want to die alone. He went on about the pain and emptiness in his heart, just crying, shaking, and rocking back and forth, crying about dying a lonely man. Tony could barely believe what a sad, pathetic man Gus Savage turned out to be. After a minute or so of the display, he could take no more.

"Hey!" he shouted, trying to break Gus out of his spell of self-pity. Gus continued, unhindered. Tony got up and went over to him. He leaned over him and grasped Gus's shoulders, trying to steady him from his rocking motion. "Gus! Knock it off! That's enough. No one's here to kill you."

With that Gus did stop rocking, but he continued to tremble, sobbing violently. He put a hand up on Tony's arm and leaned his head against Tony's hip, soaking Tony's jeans with his tears. Tony broke away, went into the kitchen, grabbed some paper towels, and returned to Gus.

"Here," Tony handed him the paper towels. "Dry up. Calm down."

Gus took them, blew his nose several times, honking like a goose, and dried his eyes. Tony went and poured him another whiskey, straight to the top of the glass. He handed it back to Gus, who took a deep breath to steady himself, and guzzled three quarters of the glass's contents in one long drink. In a moment, Gus was steady again, lighting another cigarette, catching his trembling breath, thanking Tony profusely for helping him snap out of it.

"You don't n-n-n-know . . ." Gus breathed deeply, ". . . how l-l-lonely I've been since . . . I got down here. I thought it would be like when . . . like when I was younger. I ran down here to start a new life. Thought I'd hook up with the right folks like I had in Pennsylvania. Hook up with a young babe to be my steady. Be popular again. But no one's accepted me, really. No one's interested in some old washed up wiseguy. Maybe a person here or there. But I really have no one. I've been terribly lonely, especially since your Pop died, Tony. Coming to Ft. Lauderdale didn't turn out to be what I thought it would be. It's been one long, lonely hell for me." He snorted, took a drag on his cigarette, another gulp of whiskey, and a long deep sigh. He looked up at Tony. An embarrassed smile broke out on his face. "Thanks, Kid! I sure feel better now. I guess I needed a good blubberin' to get over my sorrows." He stared at Tony for a minute. "Now what, Kid? You gonna turn me over to the executioners?"

"Why do you keep saying that? What do you think I'm here for?"

Gus shook his head and shrugged his shoulders nervously.

"Hey, I'm not heartless, Gus. I do remember how close you were to Pop and all. I haven't forgotten how much you were a part of his life. I'm not here to get you. You stole Carmichael's money. I'm here on his behalf. You're gonna give it back to me, I'm going to return it to him, and you're going to run away to Timbuktu and never be seen here again."

Gus's eye lit bright with hope. "'Give it back'?" Gus still disbelieved. "And that'll be it?"

"That's how it's gonna have to be! I'm the one down here doing the business. Now, what have you done with the money? You still got it all?"

Gus looked at him like he was a rube.

"Well, then, how much of it do you have left?"

"About two hundred grand."

"That won't do with Carmichael. Well, then, we gotta figure a way for you to get the rest back so you can give it to me. What'd you do with the other hundred and sixty?" Tony looked around Gus's posh house. "I bet this place cost you a fortune."

Gus shook his head and crunched some ice between his teeth. "Uh-uh," he grunted. "Rented."

"You're renting this place?" Tony tsk-tsked and shook his head with disappointment. "Renting is a poor investment choice. You're just throwing your money away! You get no return."

"Thanks, Charles Schwab!"

"Well, what have you done with one hundred and sixty thousand dollars in less than five months?"

"What are you talkin' about? I've lived!"

"Not like a normal Joe, you haven't, if you've blown a hundred and sixty grand!"

"I practically did nothing but work at that restaurant for fifteen years. I took that money so I could go have some fun, and I did. I been to Vegas a few times and I like to bet a game or two every week."

"Well, you've obviously been losing big, if you're down that much in five months. Where's the other two hundred grand?"

"I got it stashed in a safe deposit box at a securities firm."

"You can get to it when you want it?"

"Yeah."

"Then we're gonna go get it all this afternoon."

Gus nodded sadly.

"You're also gonna go to your new goombahs down here and hit them up for a loan for the rest."

Gus looked offended. "What makes you think I'm mixed up with wiseguys?"

Tony gave him a droll stare, now.

Gus sighed and conceded. "All right. My bookies know some loan sharks who might front it me."

"One hundred and eighty thousand."

"No, one hundred and *sixty* thousand."

Tony shook his head defiantly. "One hundred and *eighty* thousand. The one sixty plus the price for your head as a goodwill gesture toward Carmichael. Maybe then he'll leave you alone once he gets his money back."

"Do you know how long it'll take me to pay back a hundred and eighty grand to some goon?"

"Do you know how long eternity'll be if Carmichael has you smoked? You did this all to yourself. I really don't care what happens between you and the loan sharks. I'm saving your carcass now, when it's really not a part of my job description. Quit whining, get your things, and let's go get this three hundred and eighty thousand together so I can have it back in Carmichael's lap by supper time tomorrow night."

Gus swallowed hard, trembling. "All right. Let's do it."

Tony drove Gus around Ft. Lauderdale in his rental car. Gus was grim, but cooperative at first. But as the day wore on, he grew more chatty, grateful to finally have someone to talk to, even if it was someone Carmichael sent to nail him. Tony's amiable ways loosened him up even more; that and the fact that he was the son of Gus's longtime friend. Tony began to actually enjoy their conversations, especially as Gus started recounting tales about Tony's father. Tony actually even began to prod and poke Gus to tell him more about Pete Vero. And Gus was more than happy to oblige. Tony soaked up stories about Pete that he'd never heard before, and particularly liked the Mafia tales about him and Gus when they were with the Barratos.

They had the remaining two hundred thousand dollars out of Gus's safe deposit box by two that afternoon. Gus had it stored in an old briefcase, the bills all in hundreds. Tony breathed a sigh of relief when he actually saw the money. He'd feared Gus was lying to him about having any left over and that he'd spent every bit of it. That would surely have sealed Gus's death warrant by Carmichael. Gus also had a folder full of documents that he went through. To Tony's surprise he produced two deeds to undeveloped properties near Pittsburgh, worth about seventy thousand dollars total. He told Tony he'd bought the lands back in the seventies when he was with Barrato. Gus took the deeds with him in the briefcase.

"What're those for?" Tony asked.

"Collateral."

"For what?"

He looked at Tony like he was an idiot. "The loan sharks! What do you think? They're just going to loan me a hundred and eighty grand out of the goodness of their hearts?"

Gus's bookies were three men, forty-ish, from New York. They held court in an empty hotel lounge. They sat at a corner table drinking, watching sports networks, talking on cell phones, making book for gambling addicted people. Gus made Tony sit at the bar while he went to talk to them. Tony observed: Gus acted very glad to see them. They paid him little attention at first, either staring at the television or talking on their phones. Finally one of them attended to the broken man, talking to him cordially. After a long conversation, the man dialed someone on his cell phone. He talked to the other party for about three minutes then hung up. He pulled out a piece of scrap paper, wrote something on it, then slid it across the table over to Gus. Gus thanked him profusely, kissed the paper, and waved good-bye to the three of them. They didn't acknowledge his departure.

"Got it!" Gus waved the slip of paper in the air victoriously at Tony.

"What is that?"

"It's the address for a man my bookie says might be able to loan me all the money with my properties as collateral."

Tony shook his head in acknowledgment, but wondered why Gus would be so happy about the fact that he had to borrow a hundred and eighty grand from someone who in all probability would kill him if he didn't pay it back. Then Tony remembered: Gus Savage had also stolen a fortune from Carmichael Vero last October. Cautious living was not one of his traits.

Tony wound up waiting two hours for Gus outside some Ft. Lauderdale high-rise apartment. Gus called up the apartment of the "loan officer" from the lobby. They told him to come up alone. Tony sat for a while in his rental car, then at an outdoor bar at the foot of the complex. For a while toward the end Tony thought for sure Gus had split out the back, called a cab, gone home to get his car and belongings, and split town.

"Carmichael will kill me," Tony repeated every once in a while, growing both impatient and nervous. Just when he was ready to storm the place searching for Gus, out the front door he appeared, practically bounding and skipping like a kindergartner.

"I did it!" he yelled to Tony triumphantly. "I got the money! They're ordering me the money right now!"

"What took you so long?" Tony snapped impatiently.

"They didn't speak English. It took me a while to get through to them. My Spanish is very rusty. But we finally worked out a deal!"

"They're just giving you the cash like that?"

"No, man! I had to put up everything I own. They took my deeds, the title to my Beemer, and my Gold Mastercard." His eyes lit up like an enamored schoolboy. "But I got a job with them! They're gonna let me do some work for them!"

"You're kidding me."

"No, man! We talked business and they're gonna let me work off some of the cash I'll owe them. It's the exact kind of set-up I was looking for. I'm just the guy to fill a slot in their business they need tightened up. This was the break I was looking for, Kid!" He laughed and smacked Tony upside his arm. "This morning I thought you was the Angel of Death standin' on my doorstep. Here you turn out to be Lady Luck . . . or Lord Luck! Whoever! All I know is these cats are gonna be the hook-up I've wanted ever since I left the Barratos. The hook-up Carmichael wouldn't be for me. I'm in!"

Tony chuckled and steered the excited man back toward his car. "Glad I could help out," he said sarcastically. "What kind of crew is that up there?"

"You should see the set-up they got in that apartment! They have those little electronic bank computers that can access accounts anywhere in the world. Then they had some lackey in Pittsburgh actually get access to the records of my deeds to verify them in only about twenty-five minutes! These bozos are like the CIA up there. They're for real, man."

"Probably the local front for some South American cocaine cartel."

"Who cares! I got a job and we can go pick up the money right now."

"Is it gonna take two more hours, Gus?"

"So whiny all the sudden! I'm goin' in the hole to pay off your boss and you're complaining about the time it's taking. Ungrateful and spoiled. Not at all like your father."

"That may be a compliment, Gussie."

Gus picked up his cash at a "financial institution" in a run-down, nearly abandoned shopping outlet on the outskirts of Ft. Lauderdale. The lending association was completely run by Latinos, who neither spoke nor wrote in English. The loan sharks from the high rise had faxed over all the information and paperwork on Gus so the "lending officer" inside was ready with a stack of already prepared forms for Gus to sign. Armed and uniformed sentinels guarded the place. They watched Gus like hawks. He

ERIC FLORE

struggled to communicate with the lender in order to correctly fill out and sign all the paper work. They took Gus to a heavily guarded vault in the back. A grim looking fellow ran old, rumpled hundred dollar bills through a money counting machine, and the cash was loaded by stacks into a cotton sack. The money counter and the lender heavily suggested to Gus in Spanish that he not recommend their "institucion" to anyone else. The did not wish for word of mouth advertising, they sternly explained to him. Gus "yeah-yeahed" them and hit the door running.

He hopped into Tony's car excited with sweat beading his face. "I got it all right here." He opened the sack full of bills.

Tony was flabbergasted by the sight of the filthy cash. "Man! What have we gotten into!"

"What are you talkin' about?" Gus was perplexed by Tony's trepidation.

"Where do you think these yahoos are getting this kind of cash to just give out? I'm telling you, this is nothing but a money laundering scam for some major cartel somewhere. That's probably money they made in some screwy CIA deal in some Colombian jungle."

Gus looked at him like he was an absolute rube. "Who cares? All I know is I got your money for Carmichael and my neck is officially off the Vero chopping block! I don't care who fronts all this." He smiled. "In fact, I'll be working for them, indirectly."

Tony opened the briefcase with the two hundred thousand on his lap. "Count it out for me and put it in here."

Gus counted out the remaining hundred and eighty thousand Tony had demanded from him, placing it in the briefcase as he went along. When he was finished counting, Tony noticed there were still several stacks of money left in the sack.

"What's that in there?"

"This is *my* money."

"Huh?"

"Kid, you're taking all I have to my name! I borrowed two hundred grand from these hombres so I'd have twenty thousand to live off of until I can get back on my own two feet. Which I don't know when that'll be now that I owe these people so much."

Tony snapped the briefcase shut, put it in the seat behind him, and cranked the engine. "That's your fault and your problem, Gus! Meanwhile, I'm starving! Where we gonna eat?"

"Eat? You want to eat with me?" Gus was both shocked and honored.

"My treat! I'm celebrating the successful end to my biggest case ever!"

"Yeah," Gus laughed weakly. He cursed Tony. "You don't know how proud I am of you, Kid," he moaned sarcastically. "Dioni's."

"'Dioni's?' What's that?"

"That's where we're gonna eat."

"I want to hear more about my father. Tell me more over supper."

Gus smiled at him genuinely. "Love to. Your Pop's one of my favorite subjects."

Their dinner together was surprisingly enjoyable for them both. Dioni's, an authentic brick oven Italian restaurant done up in rustic olive colors, provided a perfect atmosphere for fellowship. They shared a pricey bottle of imported Italian wine, which Gus was getting the better of, and shared a huge salad. Tony engulfed Gus's stories about his father, laughing hysterically at the funny ones, ooing and oh-ing at the surprising ones. It was like getting to know his father over again four years after his death. For Gus the whole time was therapeutic. He had the weight of worrying about being caught by Carmichael off his shoulders: he officially had been. And instead of wrath, he was given the second chance by Tony. That was a marvelous relief. Plus it was great to have civil, friendly conversation with a familiar face after months of isolation. He reminisced candidly about his glory days with the Barrotos and Pete Vero. Tears formed in Gus's eyes as the memories flooded him. At one point he even sobbed, then choked the emotions back. He looked up at Tony, glaring at him.

"You think crying makes me a weak man?"

Tony shrugged incredulously. "Nah. Not really. I'm a sensitive guy of the nineties."

"Yeah, well, you'd be cryin' too if you hadn't seen a friendly face in months. I went from having Pete and our old lifestyle to next to nothing when he died, then to all this for the past five months. It's been hell. I sure miss your Pop."

"And all his money you spent at Atlantic City."

Gus chuckled, smiled. Lightened up again.

"My Mom never would have missed you, though" Tony said, scooping more salad.

Gus almost choked on his lettuce snickering. They both burst into laughter. Gus straitened up.

"Your Mom was a saint, Tony. She didn't appreciate my friendship to Pete at all, for sure. But she married a wiseguy. Wiseguy's ain't known for good marriages. Your Pop was one of the few I knew who maintained a long lasting relationship. That's why he had so much respect from the other men. They knew Pete was devoted to your Mom, his family. I was married twice. Neither lasted two years. Wiseguy's like to play too much."

"You played a lot in Atlantic City, I remember."

"Yeah! So did your Pop," Gus said matter-of-factly, cramming another gob of salad into his mouth.

The smile on Tony's face weakened a bit. "Wait a minute, wait a minute." He was genuinely shocked. "You're telling me Pop played around?"

Gus suddenly looked irritated with Tony. "What is it with you, Kid? You know, for someone who acts so worldly you sure are green. Green as an apple in April. Yes, your father played around, Tony. He had women on the side. Not as much as the rest of us, but over the years he had his share."

Stunned, Tony thought out loud: "I never knew!"

"What do you mean you never knew? That's what wiseguys do! Why do you think we're in this business?"

"I thought it was the money!"

"What do you think the money brings, moron? Broads! We want broads with our money!" Gus laughed hysterically. Tony felt his stomach beginning to tighten. He never thought of his doting father as an adulterer.

"Did Mom know that Pop had affairs? I mean, I never heard them arguing over women . . ."

"Tony, it's like an unwritten rule with Mafia wives: your man's gonna play. You can try to cause waves about it. Some Mafia wives do. Cat fights ensue. Nasty ones between Mafia wives and their husband's honeys. But if you're a Mafia wife and you want peace and a lasting relationship with one man, you shut your big mouth and turn your head the other way. That's what your Mom did."

Tony suddenly remembered his Mom's face: dull, lifeless, eyes glazed. She was perpetually zonked on Valium or drunk on wine. Now it all made sense. How could he have been so blind to the truth, he wondered.

Gus saw the hurt on Tony's face and tried to make him feel better. "Kid," he said, laughing and shaking his head, "Pete was good to your Mom. He never flaunted his broads in her face. He was always careful to keep them far from her. That's why he spent so much time in Atlantic City. That's where our hook-ups were. Pete loved your Ma, and never wanted to disgrace her."

"So that's why he took me to Atlantic City when I got older," Tony quickly realized. "I gave a good report to Mom when we returned. He never played when I was with you two."

Gus tapped the side of his forehead and winked at Tony. "The green apple has ripened quickly!"

Tony's face soured. "So Pop was using me all those times. He never paired up with a woman when I was with you two in Atlantic City. When I'd get home, I'd tell Mom all about the trip, never making any mention of strange women, of course; there were none. Pop would look great." He paused, disappointed. "He used me." His shoulders slumped from the weight of the revelation.

Gus tried to perk him up. "Nah, Kid! You got it all wrong! Pete loved you. He adored you. Everyone knew all about you everywhere he went. You're all he talked about."

Tony couldn't hide his disappointment. "But still, he was playin' on the side, and he used me to cover it up."

"Tony . . ." Gus began, but the waitress brought their entrees. She gave Gus his spaghetti with Italian sausage, and Tony his ravioli. Gus dug in, but noticed Tony was just poking his food with his fork. He was deeply wounded by the revelation of his father's infidelity and could not hide it.

"Aw, come on, Kid! Give Pete some credit. He did all he could to shield your mother and you two kids from all the trash that went with the Barratos. He even moved you out of Pittsburgh to Beaver Falls when you were a little kid 'cause he wanted you all out of the line of fire. He wanted a good family and he maintained it. He protected you all."

"He dishonored Mom."

"No," Gus said, shoveling spaghetti into his mouth. "He protected her from what would have hurt her."

"She lived most of her life in depression. He didn't care if she was hurt or not."

Gus dropped his fork and pointed his stubby finger at Tony. "Not true! Pete even used drastic measures to protect your Mom from getting hurt. He proved he'd do anything to protect his marriage."

Tony finished a gulp of wine. "What are you talking about now?"

Gus looked around slyly to be sure no one was listening. "Probably one of the hottest broads your Pop ever saw on the side was this twenty-nine year old stewardess from New York. He met her in Atlantic City with me about twelve years ago. She was a looker, and she was a wild one. But she had a husband. Still lived with him. She worked routes to Atlantic City to play with folks like us on the weekends. She and your Pop hit it off. They fell hard and fast for each other. They were together quite a few months. She was one of the few he'd actually contact from Beaver Falls during the week to maintain his relationship with her. And it was mutual. But after a few months, she started getting real pushy with Pete. She went ahead and left her husband and she started telling Pete to leave Dot. He refused, of course, and told her to cool it for a while. Well she would have no parts of that. A month later she showed up at VECO looking for Pete. Here she'd moved to Pittsburgh. Transferred to the old Pittsburgh airport so she could see Pete more often. Thing was, she never even talked to Pete about it. He was angry as a wasp. He told her never to show herself around him again, at VECO or anywhere in Pennsylvania. He let her know that he was married and that he was not going to dissolve his marriage for her. She still didn't have your home phone number yet, but your Pop got wind of the fact that she was calling VECO and me and Joseph trying to get the number. Then she kept houndin' him, telling him she had given up everything for him and wasn't going to be scorned. One day she cornered him in the parking lot at VECO and completely freaked out on him. He told me later she had a gun and was going to kill him and herself right there. He finally talked her down from it and didn't hear from her for a while."

"Had Mom found out?"

"Not that I know of. But then things got real ugly."

"Oh! Only then?"

"Listen: this broad's husband moved to Pittsburgh hunting her down. Somehow they got back together. Then he and her both started calling Pete at VECO. They threatened to harass him and Dot if Pete didn't start putting up some hush money every month."

"They tried to blackmail a Mafioso," Tony rolled his eyes at their stupidity. Then he sarcastically asked with a naive smile, "So what'd Pop do, have them both killed?" Tony went to take a fork-full of ravioli, but realized that Gus had neither answered his sarcastic question, nor was he even moving. Tony froze with horrific disclosure, then slowly lifted his eyes to meet Gus's dark gaze. Gus's grim countenance said it all. Tony's mouth slowly dropped open and his face drained to pallid. He looked at Gus, then shook his head slowly, only able to mouth the word "no".

But Gus nodded implacably, wanting to force Tony to see the lengths at which Pete had gone to protect his marriage and his family.

"Yes, Tony," he said softly but sternly. "Drastic measures. That's how far Pete was willing to go for you all."

Sheet white, Tony finally was barely able to blurt out a forceful: "No! Pop couldn't have done something like that."

"He had to, Tony! They gave him no choice."

Tony could barely whisper. "He didn't! That's not like him. You're just making this all up to get back at me for finding you here in Ft. Lauderdale!"

"You're crazy! You, Mr. Private Detective, can go investigate it for yourself. I'll even give you her name. She and her husband were living up in Avalon, in an apartment off of Ohio River Boulevard. When Pete realized that he had to take care of them once and for all he went and hired . . ."

"Don't say it . . ." Tony squinted as though it would stop up his ears.

". . . Ed Larsky to do the job."

Tony put his face in his hands. He felt as though his guts were slowly oozing out of him.

"What? Why are you acting like you are so surprised by all this? Larsky rigged a natural gas explosion in their apartment. The cause was untraceable. She died instantly. Her husband died a week later in the hospital; never gained consciousness. It looked like some accident. But they never bothered Pete or your family again! Tony! What are you getting so bent out of shape over? It was twelve years ago and Pete's gone, now! I'm telling you, he did it for you all . . ."

Tony pounded hard on the table, rattling all the china and utensils, and then pointed at Gus. "Don't you blame Mom and Gina and me for that! We never would have asked him to kill anyone! I wouldn't have wanted someone's life snuffed out just so I could feel better! Mom wouldn't either. You two may have been like that, but we aren't!"

Gus leaned back and winced at Tony. "You know, I don't get you at all! What did you think your father was? Huh? He was a wiseguy! You think he wasn't involved with hits when we were with the Barratos?"

Tony leaned forward, eyes watering. "Well, *he* didn't kill anyone himself!"

"No, but he was involved! You are so naive it's pathetic. You think your Pop was some saint or something. We were made men in a bloody business. I'll tell you where Pete went wrong with you, Tony: he protected you from all the blood and dirt he was involved in, but spoiled you with all the glamour. You got to see all the fun and the trappings and the money and the famous people Pete knew, but you never got one glimpse of the rip-offs, robberies, scams, cons, and violence that goes with La Cosa Nostra. And because of that you grew up with this sissy-boy mentality about it all. This business is blood, Tony! It's pain! Toil! Graft!" His voice cracked, face reddened. He sat back and took a swig of wine. Then he leaned forward again, and whispered, "It's death, Tony. Death. That what your father was in. A deadly business. And so is Carmichael, now. Get your head out of the sand."

Tony leaned back and sighed sadly. Everything seemed to be whirling around him. His whole perception of life had just been unraveled in a matter of a few moments of conversation. He knew nothing would ever seem the same to him again.

"Don't worry. You just yanked it out for me."

Tony began to drink heavily with Gus to try and numb the pain. A drunken Gus desperately tried to get Tony's mind off the revelation about his father, but it wasn't working. He got Tony to leave Dioni's and take them to another club he frequented nearby. There Gus was the life of the party, buying drinks for everyone since the place wasn't crowded yet at only 8:00 p.m. Tony attempted to act like he was having fun. Hey, he kept trying to tell himself, he'd just cracked Carmichael's uncrackable case and had even gotten all of Carmichael's money back with interest. The Family will be proud. He could put on a smile and enjoy life for a while. But deep inside he was a violated man, his very paradigm of life suddenly shattered.

He went to the bar and asked the bartender about a pay phone. He directed him to one in the corner. Tony got about ten dollars in quarters and pulled a chair up to the phone. He directly dialed his Uncle Joseph's pager number in Pennsylvania. The computer operator chimed in and told him how much to deposit. He did, got the pager, and dialed in that pay phone number. He drank a whiskey as he waited by the phone. He could hear Gus belting out songs at the top of his lungs. Fifteen minutes later the phone rang. It was Joseph, calling from a pay phone near his home in Patterson Township.

"Kid! Where have you been? It's almost been a week now! What's going on down there? Carmichael's about to have a conniption over you!"

"Uncle Joe! Be quiet for a minute. I got the money back."

"You did what?"

"I found Gus Savage and I got all Carmichael's money back. Plus an extra twenty-thousand for interest."

Joseph was silent on the other end. "Well . . . that's great, Kid. I'm impressed. So you know where Gus Savage is?"

"Right now he's here with me at this bar getting hammered."

"But you know where he lives?"

Tony, both drunk and still reeling over the news of his father's secret life, couldn't compute why Joseph was even asking such a question. "Yes. I know where he lives."

"Good! Give me the address."

"What? Why?"

"Carmichael wants it! That's why we sent you down there, Kid. To locate Gus. Now the job will be complete. Give me his address."

In his fog Tony couldn't figure what was going on. He felt funny about it, but he gave Joseph Gus's home address in Ft. Lauderdale. He couldn't figure Joseph's angle since he'd gotten Carmichael's money back. No problem, though. He'd tell Gus to go on and move out of the place and relocate where no one could find him, just in case.

Joseph finished scratching down the address. "Great, Kid! Man! I'm really proud of you! You've done a great job! Listen, I'll be getting an airline ticket to Pittsburgh to you. Don't question it when you get it. Just take the ticket and go to the airport and catch that flight."

Tony was completely confused, now. "What are you talking about? What's going on? How are you going to get it to me?"

Joseph was growing impatient. "Kid! You work for *us*. A good soldier just does what he's told. Now shut up, stop asking questions, and be looking for an airline ticket. You got that?"

"Yeah," Tony droned, more confused than ever. "I got it." He hung up the phone.

He waded back into the crowd and tried to steer clear of Gus, who refused to call him by the alias he was using. He couldn't figure why Joseph was so dead set on getting Gus's home address. The Family didn't have any contacts in Ft. Lauderdale who might hurt him. Then thoughts of his father and murder raced through his mind. Head smarting, Tony ordered another drink and tried to settle himself.

At nine-thirty he'd had enough of Gus and that club. He told Gus it was time to get him home. He dragged him out of the bar, Gus singing sixties' songs at the top of his lungs. Even though Tony was fairly drunk, he selfishly got behind the wheel of his car to drive anyway. He drove the chatty Gus back to his house and helped the sloppy-drunk man to his door.

"Tony . . ." Gus slurred as he held onto Tony's meaty shoulder. "Kid . . . I don't know how to thank you . . . you did me right by not having me killed."

Tony shook his head impatiently. "I don't know why you keep saying that! I didn't come here to kill you. I came to get Carmichael's money back!"

Gus laughed hysterically as he fumbled with his keys to unlock his front door. "You are so greeeeeeen!" he giggled. "I'm sorry, Kid, but you ain't wiseguy material. Not one bit."

Tony snatched the keys angrily from him and found the front door key himself. "No one said I'm trying to be a wiseguy, moron!" he barked as he unlocked Gus's front door.

He pushed Gus into the foyer, Gus crooning happily again. Gus stumbled, Tony snatched him and pulled him up, shaky himself. Gus laughed heartily, but suddenly got dead silent.

"Tony!" Gus moaned with horror.

Startled, Tony looked up toward the living room. There, standing at the edge of the foyer, was both Ed Larsky, with his arms folded patiently across his barrel chest, and short little long-haired Tommy Wheeler, who was pointing a 9 mm pistol at Gus.

"Hiya, Twinkie!" Larsky sneered at Tony. "Close that door behind you."

"Ahhh, no!" Gus whimpered.

Dreadful realization flooded Tony's drunken mind. Terrified himself, he pushed Gus behind him to the floor and began yelling. "What are you doing here, Ed? I got the money! I took care of everything!"

"I gave him everything back!" Gus squeaked with fear from behind Tony.

Larsky reached to a table behind him, produced a heavy ax handle and pointed it at Tony. "I told you to shut that door!"

Tommy Wheeler pointed the gun at Tony. "Do it now!"

Tony held up a hand to them and obediently shut it. "There! It's done! Now what are you two doing here? Carmichael sent me down here to get the money, and I got the money. It's in the trunk of my car." He pulled out his keys for them. "Here! Go out and get it yourself! You'll see . . ."

"I gave it all back to him and more!" Gus reported, clutching Tony's legs for safety.

Larsky shook his head with disdain for Tony. "You are such an idiot! No one hired you to get any money back! We just hired you to find this weasel!" Larsky waved the ax handle at Tony. "Move out of the way now so we can see our little thief."

Gus wrapped himself around Tony's legs even tighter. Tony couldn't move an inch.

"Let him go, Larsky!" Tony said.

Larsky looked dumbfounded. "What? You have got to be kidding me!"

Tommy Wheeler pointed the gun at Tony again. "The man said to move out of the way so we can see Savage! Now step aside!"

"Help me Tony!" Gus whimpered from between his legs. "Please!"

Tony held up his hand to halt them. "Wait! Gus has twenty thousand dollars, the price for his head! He'll pay you both ten grand each for this hit if you'll just let him go! He'll disappear tonight and you and Carmichael will never even know he's alive on the earth again!"

"Yeh-heh-hesssss!" Gus screeched. "I got it out in the car! Ten thousand each I'll give you! Just please let me go . . ."

Larsky shook his head with absolute certainty. "No way. Gus ripped off the Family. He's been a splinter in the Family's butt for years. Carmichael wants him taken care of once and for all. And besides! Tommy and I don't hire out to weasels!"

"Please, Tony!" came the plea again.

Tony tried to move again, but Gus wouldn't budge off him. "Ed! This is so senseless! I got all the money back! He will be gone! It'll be like he's dead! He'll never bother Carmichael or the Family again! Just let him go!"

"Tony! Save me! Please!"

"MOVE AWAY FROM HIM, NOW!" Wheeler shouted, startling both Tony and Gus.

"I won't! You've got to leave him alone! There's no sense in killing him!" Tony knew he was pushing it hard against these two soulless beasts. He started to fear for his own life.

Wheeler aimed his gun right between Tony's eyes. "Want me to pop him too and put him out of our misery?" he asked Larsky.

Larsky thought for a moment. "No. His Uncle Joseph would probably get me in trouble with Carmichael if we killed the Twinkie, too."

Gus was trembling so hard he was making Tony's body shake. "I'm beggin' you for mercy, Tony! Please stop them from doing this!"

Wheeler continued scheming. "We could make it look like he popped Gus then popped himself. A murder-suicide kind of deal."

Larsky still shook his head skeptically. "Nah. Wouldn't work for me. Carmichael and Joseph would still have my head over it." He put his hand out toward Wheeler. "I'll handle this." He walked over to Tony in the foyer. "You are choosing this weasel over the Family. When I get back I'm gonna report this to Carmichael, how you interfered with my business." Tony was frazzled beyond reasoning. He could barely think.

Gus reached up and grabbed Tony's shirt at the stomach. Tony looked down into the pitiful man's horrified, childlike eyes. "Tony!" Gus squalled. "As your father's lifelong friend, I'm beggin' you, pleading with you: save me! Don't let them do this to me! You can stop them!"

Larsky leaned over and breathed his cigarette breath in Tony's face: "You're so pathetic! You don't get none of this, do you? This is why we hired you! To find Savage so I could get ahold of him. You did it. You're finished here. I'm here to do the rest of the job."

Gus shook Tony's shirt hard to get his attention back. "You can stop them, Tony! Please! Help me! Don't let me die alone like this!"

"This is how we handle guys like him," Larsky said. "This is what Family life's all about, Twinkie." He brought the ax handle up to rest on his shoulder. "Now get out of my way and quit interfering with Family business."

Tony glanced at the thick ax handle in Larsky's powerful hands; then over at Tommy Wheeler's 9 mm, which was still pointed right at his face. Despite all his physical training at the private detective school, there was no way he could disarm Larsky and dodge a hitman's bullets. Not in that little foyer, and especially not with Gus death-locked around his legs. The finality of it all overtook Tony: this situation was hopeless. He couldn't help Gus if he wanted to. He'd just wind up getting killed with him in the process. And Tony Vero was too terrified of death to get killed on Gus Savage's behalf. Larsky and Wheeler were going to get their way. The Family would get what they wanted from the start. Once again, they had won.

He looked down at Gus, made his final, gut-wrenching decision, then turned back to Larsky: "I can't get him off me." His voice squeaked like a child's. He couldn't believe he was even making such a barbaric pronouncement of judgment against someone. The whole scene was horrifyingly surreal.

Gus looked up at Tony with profound betrayal. "Nooooo! Don't do this to me, Tony! Don't sell me down the river like this!"

Larsky nodded and sneered at Tony. "Good choice." He reached into his jacket pocket and produced an airline ticket folder. "Here. You're going to catch this flight over in Miami tomorrow afternoon at 3:00. You'll be back in Pittsburgh by 5:30. You can't fly out of Ft. Lauderdale. Someone might make you."

"Tony!" Gus screeched.

Tony took the ticket. Everything was moving in slow motion. Dazed, he looked around the house. "But my finger prints are all over the place."

Larsky shrugged indifferently. "Not for long."

Gus jerked at Tony one more time. "Please, Tony . . . !"

With that Larsky swung the ax handle down on top of Gus's head. The man dropped limp to the hard floor, loosing Tony's legs, but rolling under them. Tony tripped backward over Gus and slammed hard against the wall. Larsky and Wheeler laughed gleefully at the scene. Their inhumanity tore at Tony's insides even more. Tony struggled to get up, wishing to God there was something he could do to stop this insanity. Gus rolled around on the ground holding his head, crying scared like a five year old being abused by a pack of bullies. Larsky leaned over with a grin and snatched Gus by the back of his collar. He began to drag him out of the foyer like some worthless animal. Tony's heart ripped in two as he watched Gus Savage being dragged to his doom. Gus looked up at Tony for the last time, his hands stretched out taut, pleading to the young man:

"Stop them! Don't let them kill me like this! I don't want to die alone, Tony! Save me, please! You can still save me! Please! I don't want to die alooooooooooone . . ."

And with that, Larsky dragged Gus around the corner and Tony never saw him again.

Tony stood helpless, his back against the door. Wheeler snickered at him and grinned like satan himself. "A human being can withstand hours of pain. Don't you want to stick around and join in on the fun?" When Tony didn't answer, Tommy pointed his gun at him once more and yelled, "Get out of here, little girl!"

Feeling like a cowardly traitor, Tony fumbled for the door knob, yanked it hard, and bolted outside. As he slammed the door shut behind him, he heard a nauseating thumping noise, followed by Gus Savage screeching with pain. His imagination raced, conjuring dark images of what twisted things they would do to that helpless, pitiful man.

And it was *his* fault!

Despondent, Tony raced back to his motel. He would ditch his rental car and take a bus over to Miami immediately. But he would leave Ft. Lauderdale forever.

He was frantic with guilt. He had never hurt inside as badly as his did now. Not even when his mother or father died. The Family had willingly used him to help kill a man! He was a betrayer, now; a Judas. He'd turned someone over to their death for money.

But I didn't know that's what they wanted! Why didn't I? How could I have been so blind not to see this whole set-up from the beginning!

Carmichael and Joseph knowingly used him. He remembered back to his first meeting with Carmichael about coming to find Gus. He strained to recall their exact words at that VECO meeting. They came back to him crystal clear:

"We've got to close all our doors to the past, Tony. Gus Savage will always be Carmichael's last open door to La Cosa Nostra."

That was their whole point.

Tony! Save me, please!

He thought about what those monsters Larsky and Wheeler were doing to poor Gus.

You can stop them, Tony! Please!

Maybe it would have been better to die there with Gus, Tony thought, *at least trying to save the poor wretch.*

At his hotel Tony got out of his rental car and ran as fast as his shaken, drunken legs would carry him. He bolted up the outside steps to the second floor to his room. As he stumbled quickly down the outside corridor he saw a black silhouetted figure sitting outside his door. He slowed cautiously, watching the person stand up into the light.

"Mark Guider?" The familiar voice called him by his alias he'd been using.

He got close enough to identify her. It was Anisa, the girl from Long Island he'd fornicated with several nights earlier. She was obviously drunk, too. He wondered what she wanted. He didn't have time to romance her. He had to get rid of her quickly.

"Anisa? What are you doing here? I have to get going . . ."

"Who do you think I am, Mark?" she asked him, deep offense evident in her voice.

He got his room card ready in his hand to open the door. He just wanted to get past her. "Anisa, I don't have time . . ."

She pushed him back away from the door. "No! You will make time for me!" She reeked of beer. "I will not be treated like some slut!" She pointed her long finger hard into his chest. "Who do you think you are? You sweet-talked me like I was special, then used me for sex! Then I met up with Natalie tonight, that girl from Iowa who yelled at you the other night. Remember her? We spent some time together . . . had some drinks. We started trading notes about you. And we didn't like what we were finding out about our 'mutual experiences' we had with you!"

This night was a genuine living nightmare for Tony. Anisa obviously had some serious issues that were challenging her outlook on reality. "Look!" he said. "I've got to go! Now! I'll give you my address! Write me a letter, let me know how rotten you think I am, but get out of my . . ."

She smacked him across his face, connecting her hand with his flesh as hard as she could. He swayed backward a bit, completely caught off guard. The physical pain and humiliation of the assault still didn't eclipse his anguish inside. It was as though he'd been raped by the Family, used by them to spill Gus Savage's blood.

"How dare you use me like that!" she screamed. "Acting so sweet, so gentle and innocent, telling me how special I was just so you could land me in bed!" She sobbed a drunken sob. "At least Natalie had sense enough to say no to you and not sleep with you! And you lied to me! You said I was the only one you'd been with down here. But Natalie says she found out you were even with someone else other than she and I!"

Tony held his hand over the side of his head to stop the smarting. He yelled, "This is Spring Break at Ft. Lauderdale! Do you know how many people are down here having sex with strangers they just met? You didn't put up a fight or need much encouragement, girl!"

"I'm not like that! Usually! I don't hop into bed with anyone who comes along! You used me! I'm a living, breathing, human being! Not some piece of meat to be used! You made me feel like you were in love with me! I was having feelings for you!"

"And we had a great night together and it's over! Now get out of my way!"

"You will show me respect!" she screeched.

He figured that either God or the devil himself had sent her to torment him for what he had just done to Gus Savage.

An elderly man stepped out of his room a few doors down and observed them carefully. "Are you okay young lady?" the old man asked. "Do you want me to call for help?"

Tony was indignant. "*I'm* the one who needs help, Mister! She's freaking out on me!"

The old man disappeared back into his room without a word. Anisa pushed Tony hard against the railing.

"You will respect me, Mark Guider!" she sobbed. "I want to be treated as a somebody. You acted all good and right. But you're nothing but a hypocrite."

He was speechless, frazzled. She looked him square in the eyes, tears pouring down her face. "What kind of a man are you?" she growled.

His eyes bulged. *That question again!*

"What kind of man are you?" She repeated, stepping back away from him. "You act like you're a golden boy. But you ain't much of anything!" She shook her head and slowly began to stagger back toward the steps. "What kind of man are you?" she mumbled again, disappearing down the stairs.

Tony rubbed his stinging face. He took his card and swiped it through the lock, her words echoing in his head.

March 10

The next two days were only more hell for Tony.

He made it out of Ft. Lauderdale on a bus to Miami at half past midnight. But a bad storm front moved in the next day canceling all the flights out of Miami International Airport. Tony's next flight would be at 9:00 the following morning. So he sat alone in an airport bar drinking all day. When it shut down at 11:00 p.m., a drunken Tony laid down across some hard seats in an airport waiting area and slept for about four hours. He woke up in the middle of the night, despondent, needing a bath, and desperate about his future. He never went back to sleep.

March 11

Groggy, hung over, he sat waiting near the boarding area for his flight, staring out at the rainy Florida morning. He'd watched the Miami news that morning on an airport TV. There were no reports of a murdered Gus Savage from Ft. Lauderdale. Poor Gus! Would anyone even take notice that he was gone? Would anyone miss him? What a sad man! And what a horrible way to die.

And it's all your fault that he's dead, Tony Vero!

The 9:00 a.m. flight to Pittsburgh was definitely on, despite the continued rain. A voice on the loudspeaker announced it was boarding. He boarded sadly, not daring to look anyone in the eyes.

In his aisle seat in coach twenty-five minutes later, Tony sat in a daze, just staring at the rain out a window across the aisle. Therefore he never saw Ed Larsky coming down the aisle toward him. The bulky man whapped that morning's Ft. Lauderdale newspaper into Tony's lap, startling him terribly. Before Tony could respond, Larsky leaned over and whispered to him:

"Looks like you been a bad boy in Ft. Lauderdale, Twinkie!" He then disappeared toward the front of the plane.

Now what? Tony unfolded the Ft. Lauderdale paper on his lap. He scanned all over the front page. Down at the bottom right corner, there was a headline that read: "Brutal Murder Shakes Pine Knolls Heights." Tony's heart began to thump. Pine Knolls Heights was the housing development where Gus Savage lived. He began to read the article:

> The sleepy community of Pine Knolls Heights is reeling today after the brutal murder of one of its residents. The unusually safe retirement development is shaken by the death of Gus Savage, 54, in his home, the victim of a beating. His body was discovered early yesterday morning by a cleaning crew used by the owner of the rental house.

Tears formed in Tony's eyes as he continued to read. On the front page the article went on to explain that Gus's former residence wasn't known. The Ft. Lauderdale police explained that he was apparently tortured to death by someone with a baseball bat or some other blunt wooden object.

> "Mr. Savage's body was gruesomely disfigured. It appears that the man was kept alive and continually tortured for quite some time," Detective Ernesto Martinez was quoted. He said there were no apparent motives for the senseless act. "There were no signs of robbery anywhere on the premises."

Tony tried to dry up his eyes. But his heart was breaking to pieces over Gus. He continued to the bottom of the page, and his anguish quickly turned to fear:

> The police are searching for a dark haired man in his mid twenties who answers to the name "Mark" (article continued on page A-6).

Heart pounding, he quickly flipped over to that page, and to his shock, there was a police sketch and a written description of the "suspect" that both came dangerously close to capturing Tony's likeness.

> The suspect was seen together with the victim several places the day of the murder. The identity of this suspect is unknown, but witnesses say the two were

together as late as the evening of the murder. Anyone with information about this man should contact . . ."

Tony's face turned sheet white. He looked up the aisle to find both Ed Larsky and Tommy Wheeler's heads peering out from behind their seats, both giggling at Tony like devilish high schoolers. Larsky slid one pointer finger down over the other at Tony with the "shame! shame!" gesture. Tony's face turned crimson with rage. They laughed even harder and both disappeared back in their seats.

He laid his throbbing head back in his seat, and squeezed his eyes shut tightly. He had no idea how he was going to handle all this trauma.

Tony marched into VECO late that afternoon. He had Gus Savage's briefcase with the three hundred and eighty thousand and the cotton moneybag with the remaining twenty grand. Pale, bitter, he stormed right past the receptionists desk-

"Can we help you Mr. Vero? Mr. Vero? Uh . . . you can't go into Carmichael's office . . . ! Please, Mr. Vero . . . he's on an important conference call . . . !"

-and straight through the glass doors into the foyer to Carmichael's office. He plowed loudly through the heavy oak doors. Both Carmichael and Hilda Jessup jumped. Carmichael was on the phone, Hilda was working on a laptop computer. Hilda asked the young man to stop and wait a minute. Tony ignored her and charged up to his desk anyway. Carmichael couldn't hang up on the important business call, but smiled awkwardly at his great nephew. He could tell the Kid was miffed about something. He'd never seen that look on Tony's face before. Tony said nothing. When he got to Carmichael's desk he tossed both the briefcase and the bag at his uncle. They bounced off the table, hit Carmichael . . .

"My Heavens!" Hilda reacted to the rude outburst . . . and bounced to the floor behind his desk amid a flurry of business papers. Carmichael sat up, indignant, rage in his eyes, but kept the phone call going. He and Tony locked red eyes. They stared through one another for several moments, silent, but each reading the other's thoughts with perfect clarity. Carmichael figured what was in the baggage. He just pushed the briefcase and sack under his desk while Hilda was in there and continued with his phone conversation. He wasn't going to play along with Tony's tantrum.

When he was finished glaring at Carmichael, Tony turned on his heals and left VECO in the same manner he arrived. He went home to his house and remained there drunk. There he soured like an infected wound. And evil spirits thrived in his soul. Despair and fatalism overtook him. The nightmares about Gus started. The agoraphobia set in. He tried to wash it all away with heavy drinking, but that merely fertilized the demonic breeding ground in his heart. Torment increased.

God had allowed "the golden boy" to be taken apart in Ft. Lauderdale. Now that his hard heart of sin was smashed, Tony had to face the truth about his true spiritual state. Despite the pain, brokenness is often the mercy of God readying someone to hear His message of true salvation.

Broken and desperate, Tony was as ready for God as he'd ever be . . .

FORTY-ONE

Aleister Estate, in Great Neck, New York, was a beacon for all evil that Sunday evening of the full moon.

Cyrus Moreau's black mass was an orgy of depravity, inhumanity, and abominations expressly forbidden in the Bible. He held the event in the ballroom of his mansion. Evil pierced the darkness of the huge room, along with dim candlelight and guttural noises from both humans and inhumans alike. Cyrus and his coven of witches dressed in their traditional black hooded robes. All that could be seen of him beneath the darkness of his hood was his nose and chin, with his long black curly hair flowing out from the opening around his pockmarked jowls. He conducted the ceremony with a contempt toward everything good. Every act, every word spoken was vile and unclean, spawning an atmosphere conducive to demonic activity, which was the whole point of this black mass in the first place. Cyrus wanted undeniable demonic manifestation at its pinnacle for his workshop. When the carnal degradation of the black mass reached its frenzy, he ordered his coven of witches, warlocks, psychics, readers, and mediums to set up their "work stations." Occult paraphernalia, spell books, and objects of magic and voodoo were spread out all over the room for Cyrus Moreau's high paying and influential customers. He invited them to come partake of the "wisdom of the dark lords." Cyrus promised his patrons guidance and supernatural powers to fulfill their wildest desires and most sinister schemes. He had several share "testimonies" of supernatural help they'd received from past workshops. Then they all paired up with his coven members and dispersed throughout the room to the various stations of witchcraft.

Cyrus took Carmichael and Larsky aside and told them to wait for him. He said that after he assured that all his other guests were taken care of, he was going to handle them himself. Cyrus had carefully kept Carmichael under his wing all day long. During the black mass he forced the reluctant participant to perform some of the most atrocious of abominations committed during the obscene ceremony. Every time Carmichael hesitated, Cyrus reminded him of the danger the Family was in. Carmichael would reluctantly comply, but shuddered at times at the utter wickedness of the acts. The bottom line was he was willing to do anything to maintain his throne over his sinister Western Pennsylvania empire.

After assuring the many famous and powerful people were all being "ministered to" at various stations, Cyrus made his way back over to the two Family members. Carmichael's eyes were wide with both expectancy and apprehension. Larsky's were wide with glee. He reveled in this madness.

Cyrus walked up into Carmichael's face. With a contemptuous voice he said, "Carmichael, I've been waiting for this moment for two years, now. You want your problems solved. But first the dark lords want retribution for your impudence."

Carmichael's heart beat with fear.

"Come here," Cyrus commanded.

Carmichael and Larsky followed him through the haze. Cyrus spoke along the way.

"By trying to push me and the dark lords out of the picture you've caused quite a disturbance in the atmosphere around VECO and even over the region you rule. The dark lords assigned to your empire are facing quite a battle over it these days."

"Battle? What kind of battle?"

"The kind of battle where the enemies of our darkness try to force their 'righteousness' into the situations we've created. They try and turn our power and influence to naught. You're selfishness and pride have caused quite a gap in the spirit realm over the Family. You all are in quite a bit of trouble, now."

"Can you locate my money and Falco?"

"I probably won't need to. Tony Vero will. He's close, the dark lords have reported to me. He'll handle it. You've got a bigger problem that we need to deal with."

They stopped at Cyrus's personal station. There he opened a book of incantations and curses. It was a huge, thick, dusty volume that creaked when it opened. Carmichael and Larsky had seen the ancient tome before, and recognized it quickly.

"Now we're talking!" Larsky grinned, pointing at the book. "This one's the terminator! This is the book you used to get rid of our other 'problems.'"

Cyrus nodded under his hood. "Yes, Ed Larsky. You have a good memory." He turned to Carmichael. "This book holds mixed feelings in your heart, though, doesn't it, Mr. Vero? From the last time you paid me to open it four years ago?"

Carmicheal tried to hid his true emotions. "I . . . I don't regret anyone I've had you kill with your powers."

"Hm-mmm," Cyrus snickered skeptically. "That's what you say, but I see through you. Your heart holds some regret over our last venture into this book of death."

Larsky laughed. "I don't regret it one bit! Pete Vero was a big mouthed . . ."

"Silence, you oaf!" Cyrus snapped at him. Larsky, who outweighed Moreau almost three to one, was startled. Cyrus so enjoyed intimidating men who were physically bigger than he. He pointed his long finger in Larsky's face. "We are not here for your amusement! You speak only when you're spoken to for the rest of this evening! Do you understand me?"

Larsky nodded with fear. "Yes, sir!"

Cyrus turned the tome to a certain page. "You two have an enemy worse than who ever's killed Falco and robbed your money. Who's this black man I keep seeing in the spirit realm? This black cop who's plaguing you?"

"Kirkland!" Carmichael gasped. "Detective Ray Kirkland! He's all over Tony and us. He certainly has been a sore spot."

Cyrus turned on Carmichael impatiently. "'Sore spot'? You fool! This man has determined in his heart that he's able to bring you and VECO down, along with whatever secret you're hiding from him!"

"The Family!" Larsky whispered with concern.

"Yes!" Cyrus nodded. "A 'sore spot,' indeed! Do you realize who this Ray Kirkland is? I've seen him in the spirit realm. He's a disciple of the Living God, sold out to his Christian beliefs. The Light radiates around him like a double-edged sword. This man could be your very end!" He scanned through the spell book and stopped on a page marked with blood.

Carmichael hesitated, looking at the book. "Can you . . . can you kill him? Kill Kirkland? I mean, with *that*?"

"If I don't, I'll lose one of my best clients!" Cyrus raised his hands and positioned himself over the book. "Yes, I'm going to snuff out his life, just like all the others you've had me snuff out. But he's going to be a challenge."

"'A challenge'?"

"Cursing these sold-out Christians is difficult. Our Enemy in the spirit world protects people like Mr. Kirkland. He's well fortified. He's one of those people who believes that Jesus was the Christ and can perform all things."

"But you think you can do it?" Carmichael double-checked, wanting Ray Kirkland out of the picture. "I mean, I could try to get Larsky to whack him. But he's a cop. It would be difficult. We'd probably get caught . . ."

"I can do it!" Cyrus snapped. "The powers of darkness are going to start overtaking the powers of Light at some point! I'm sure of it! And I believe that I, Cyrus Moreau! Master of the Universe! am the one who will start the tide turning against the Light! I'll be the catalyst to turn the tide against people like Kirkland. There's not many like Kirkland out there, but when we encounter them, victory has been nearly impossible. Until today! I hold all elements of nature and the spirit world at my command, and I'll not let Anyone stop me from taking any life I wish!" He positioned himself over the spell book and raised his hands high in the air. Poised to command a spirit on an assignment of death, he arrogantly proclaimed:

"I *will* kill Ray Kirkland! And the kingdom of light will not stop me!"

Audra Dutton and Gina Vero were both praying for Tony at the same time. Audra was on a roll during her fast. Gina was just off work and very tired from her long weekend. Audra was highly animated, shouting, proclaiming, declaring the Word of God over this "white boy's" life, this young man from her vision she could not identify. Gina was lying in bed, desperately wanting to be passionate in her prayers for her brother, but finding herself struggling like the disciples of Jesus did in the Garden of Gethsemane. She forced herself to at least sit up until she could touch the heart of her Father regarding Tony. After a while, she did catch onto a Spirit anointing and prayed powerfully for Tony's life, safety, and salvation.

Because of the intercession of these two Godly women, mighty warfare was breaking out in the air over Tony. And what a war it was!

Frank Kranac had just finished his final accounting of his sweaty fortune in his basement when his telephone began to ring off the hook. Feeling safe about his money, he left his pit open and ascended his stairs to his kitchen to take the call.

"What?" he barked into the receiver.

It was Greggy Richards. "Frankie! We lost Tony Vero again! Is he back at your place?"

Kranac envisioned snapping Greggy's neck like a dried reed. "You idiots. No. He's not been here for hours. Do you at least have everything ready for him?"

"Yes. We're all set. And we got a call tonight! A plot owner croaked this morning! We have to have his plot prepared for burial on Wednesday!"

Kranac nodded in approval. "That'll work perfect. Meanwhile, you two dummies catch back up with Vero tomorrow. And this time, if you lose him, I'm gonna catch up with *you*!"

Greggy hung up the phone trembling. He turned to Jimmy. "If we can't find Vero tomorrow, I'm outta here!"

Jimmy's eyes bulged. "Not on your life, Greggy! You ain't leavin' me to face that psycho by myself!"

"If Vero gets Frankie caught, Frankie'll kill me first! We gotta catch that twerp fast and hand him over to Frankie, or we're dead!"

Jimmy shook his head in disgust. "I *hate* that Tony Vero! I thought I'd seen the last of him in high school! Here he is torturing me again!"

"What'd he ever do to you in high school?"

"Don't you remember?"

"No! You've been out of high school for almost ten years now. What was it?"

Jimmy turned with impatience and grabbed the keys to his truck. "I can't talk about it now. It'll spoil my appetite."

"Where do you think you're goin'?" Greggy asked frantically.

Jimmy opened the door to leave. "Cherries. I gotta see some babes to get my mind off all this stress!"

Cyrus Moreau had never experienced such turmoil in the spirit realm. He commanded the death curse out on Ray Kirkland, but he again sensed great reluctance by the spirits concerning his order. The demon he was summoning to the task was practically kicking and screaming not to do it. Cyrus knew it was because Ray Kirkland was so well-protected in the spirit world. Cyrus had seen God's hand of protection on Christians

ERIC FLORE

before. It was like an impenetrable shield of His Glory and His angels. The demons hated even nearing believers like that. Some "so-called" Christians weren't a problem for Cyrus and his witchcraft. They declared their faith in Christ but lived according to their own carnal wills, leaving themselves no real covenant for their God to work with. He'd cursed plenty of them successfully. But people like this Ray Kirkland, Christians who had a relationship with their God and were sold-out to Him and His word, these Christians were dangerous. And almost impossible to overcome. Actually seeing this curse to completion and killing Ray Kirkland was going to be quite a tall order. But prideful as ever, Cyrus would not take no as an answer. This spirit was stubbornly refusing the assignment, but Cyrus once again forced the issue.

Carmichael and Larsky began to grow restless watching him. The last three times they paid Cyrus Moreau to put a death curse on someone, he quickly dispatched the "dark lord" and within a day or so the subject of their curse was dead of "natural" causes. But tonight they could see Cyrus was in a power struggle to set this in motion. And Cyrus was growing impatient, even in front of all his guests.

"What . . . what's taking so long, Cyrus?" Carmichael asked, nervous about the prospects of Ray Kirkland investigating him and VECO. "It never took this long before."

"Shut up!" the sorcerer growled impatiently. Hands held up high, he began commanding the stubborn spirit with angry incantations. The spirit continued its resistance, but Cyrus persisted. Soon, many of his clients at the workshop began to take notice of the frustrated sorcerer. He could see them watching him out of the corner of their eyes. As their attention on Cyrus increased, so did his pride. Realizing that he had to save face or lose their confidence (and money!), he was going to accept no other answer but "yes" from this spirit. He groaned and gave high satanic orders to the spirit. However, this spirit of death he was locking wills with was most uncooperative. Cyrus perceived what it was telling him:

NO! Warfare! The Hosts of Heaven have amassed a great army! A great cry has gone up from the people of the Living God! A great wave of His Glory! This man is too powerful in Him to attack and win! Your curse could be our very doom!

Some of the other witches in the coven began to sense the outcry of this demon, too. They cautiously tried to worm their way over to Cyrus to warn him of the doom the dark lords were declaring over the spell. Cyrus was incensed at them all.

"I am Cyrus Moreau! I am the Master of the dark arts! As *I* will it, so it will be! I control the dark lords! They listen to *me* and do my bidding as I command! I will not be denied my will!" He turned toward the spell book pointing frantically, "And I adjure you, spirit of death, by the ultimate powers of darkness, do my bidding! GO FORTH and KILL RAY KIRKLAND!"

There was an angry acquiescence in the spirit world that ripped a tear in the atmosphere inside Cyrus's home. As the unwilling demon finally obeyed and fled the house to carry out his assignment, an audible "whoosh" broke the air violently, followed by a flash of blue light in the air for all to see, and then a loud, inhuman groan that sent shivers down every spine present. The whole place fell dead silent as everyone looked around. The coven looked at one another with concern, as though something wrong had just happened. Cyrus glared at them all like he was just daring one of them to try and say something to him. For he had just won, hadn't he?

After everyone had turned back to their work stations, Cyrus joined Carmichael and Larsky, smiling with satisfaction at his "win," but breathing heavily, clearly winded by it.

"Now, Carmichael, you truly see who's in charge of the spirit world," he bragged.

Carmichael looked at him wide-eyed. "Now what, Cyrus?"

"We await word of Detective Kirkland suddenly dropping dead! That's what! But right now *you* must answer to the dark lords for your impudence these last few years. First, I want you to tell me all about your nephew Tony. I sense that we've lost him from the destiny we planned for him."

As Larsky snarled jealously, Carmichael reluctantly recounted the tales about Tony over the last two months since Ft. Lauderdale. Cyrus was most disappointed to hear about him.

"I sense the hand of our Enemy on him strongly now, and the interference of Christians in his life."

"I know his sister has been trying to convert him for a year now."

"I thought I told you to keep her away from him?"

"I did, but she's been sneaking back around, like you saw 'in the spirit realm' yesterday."

Larsky spoke up with disappointment: "We should have taken care of her when we took care of her father."

Cyrus addressed Carmichael. "Regardless of who's been influencing him, you have failed concerning Tony! You were to raise him up as an heir to take over the throne for the Family! The dark lords had deemed it to be so! They work in generations! They always want the latter generation prepared to take over for the former. Since you have no children they chose Tony to be your heir. You were to disciple Tony to be your heir! You have botched your assignment! Now there'll be no heir prepared!"

Larsky looked frantically back and forth at them, hoping for their attention. His heart was about to burst within him. "I'll be the heir!" he blurted out. "I'll take over the Family!"

They looked at him, shocked at his outburst.

"It's all I ever wanted! That's why I've known Tony couldn't handle it! Carmichael! All I've ever wanted was your confidence that I would take your place when that day comes!"

They stared at him silently for a moment. Suddenly Cyrus Moreau cackled once. Then he reared his head back and roared with mocking laughter.

"You're too stupid to take over the Family, Larsky!" he laughed. "You were never considered a competent heir before, and you're definitely not a suitable replacement to the dark lords, now! You are nothing but a flunky. A well paid one, at that. You're a great watchdog for Carmichael, but you'll never be deemed fit to rule over a kingdom in the dark realm." He chuckled again. "You've been quite a bit of entertainment to me, though, Ed, the way you seethe with hatred toward Tony. You act like he's the worst thing on earth. But deep down in your heart you actually wish you were him! You've always wanted his place in the Vero family."

Larsky could only stand dumbfounded, mortified that Cyrus was accurately revealing his heart for all to hear. Cyrus reached out and put a comforting hand on Larsky's shoulder. "But don't feel bad, though, Ed. Your jealousy over Tony Vero has been well merited: he's ten times the man you'll ever wish to be!" He roared hideously again. Larsky nearly shrunk from humiliation, but dared not rise up against the powerful sorcerer.

Cyrus turned back toward Carmichael. "But we digress! Again I say that Tony's ultimate downfall from our original scheme must fall on your shoulders, Carmichael."

"But Cyrus!" Carmichael persisted. "It's not my fault Tony isn't cut out for this! I've tried to disciple him. I brought him on board the Family, invested the money to send him to that school in California, and have given him every chance to shine. When we sent him to Ft. Lauderdale, though, we found out what he was really made out of. He doesn't have the mettle to make the Family. He's not like us, for some reason."

Cyrus sighed. "You are correct on that point. He's too much like his mother. Tony inherited all her compassion and got none of the cold, hard instincts that drove Pete to such a life of darkness. But regardless of his inherent weaknesses, you still have to contend with this . . ." Cyrus reached up under his robe and pulled out a wrinkled, torn, black and orange football jersey. Carmichael recognized it. It was Tony's Beaver Falls Tigers game jersey, stained with Tony's own blood. Cyrus had Larsky steal from Pete's trophy case six years earlier. Cyrus held it up to his face. "Remember this, Carmichael?"

Trembling, Carmichael nodded.

"Remember the blood ritual we performed together with this? Using Tony's blood from this shirt to seal an oath with the dark lords that *you* would be the one to raise him up to take over the Family empire and serve the dark lords? That you would give him over to them to do their bidding?"

"Yes," he whispered weakly.

"You swore with an oath that you would be responsible for Tony, no matter what."

Carmichael had no reply.

Cyrus tossed the jersey onto Carmichael's head. "You've made too many mistakes. You must make amends. It's reckoning time between you and the dark lords, Carmichael Vero!" Carmichael snatched the shirt off and dropped it to the floor, his heart pounding with anxiety.

Cyrus led them over to a section where a young woman was seated at a Ouija board. She was in her early twenties. She had long, stringy hair and looked like she was in a drug-induced fog. Cyrus began to stroke her hair gently. It took her a moment to respond to his touch, but when she realized who it was loving on her, she smiled faintly.

"This is Lucinda, gentlemen. The powers she wields to converse with the dark lords are uncanny. She is a master of the board, having been working it since she was eleven years old. Lucinda and her board are like one. Her abilities have been priceless to me. I think of her as one of my most valuable protegees." He turned and stood over her. "Lucinda! This man is a very important client of mine. However, he has made selfish mistakes these past two years, and his very empire of power may crumble at any time. He must make atonement to the dark lords. He's going to ask you a question. I want you to answer it for him."

She closed her eyes lightly, nodded slightly, and placed her hands on her board.

"Carmichael, call Lucinda by name. Confess to her your high pride that has diluted you enough to believe that you and the Family could survive without the guidance of the dark lords. Then ask her what you should do to pay atonement to them." He pointed to a black chalkboard and a piece of chalk lying on the ground beside Lucinda. "Pick those up and write down all the letters the board spells out so you'll see the very clear message the dark lords will have for you."

Carmichael was reluctant. It showed in his countenance.

"I am not exaggerating, Carmichael Vero! The fate of your very empire rests on how well you'll meet the demands for atonement the dark lords ask of you! Do it!"

Carmichael slowly leaned over and picked up the chalkboard and chalk. He stood up and faced Lucinda. Looking down on her, he called out: "Lucinda! I have wronged the dark lords. What do they want me to do to make atonement for my pride against them?"

Lucinda stirred like a half dead woman getting a small dose of electricity. She began to rock back and forth, slowly at first, then gradually building up her pace. A victim of sexual abuse as a child, she'd turned to the occult for an escape and a sense of control in her life. Now, this poor soul was completely under the bondage of demons. The line between her will and theirs was blurred. Cyrus called her a "master of the board." But they controlled her, not she the spirits of the board.

The principality that Cyrus unwittingly served heard Carmichael's question and quickly emitted its response to the spirits behind the Ouija board. They began to compel Lucinda to move the dial and spell out the chief demon's message for Carmichael Vero. Lucinda's rocking motion became more frantic, but her hands remained steady in their motion. As she moved the pointer from letter to letter, Carmichael wrote each letter down on the chalkboard. After only several letters the message became quite clear to the four of them. Larsky grinned; Cyrus nodded with pompous approval. Lucinda was violently swaying as she finished the last two letters. Carmichael wrote them with a heavy heart, but also with the determination to carry out the wishes of the dark lords. As Lucinda's hands left the board, her rocking slowed. Carmichael dropped the chalk and slapped the board to the ground. He stood up and they all stared at its message:

KILL TONY

Carmichael took it all in for a moment, sweat forming on his brow.

"It's about time," Larsky mumbled with relief. At least the evil spirits were on his side.

Cyrus turned toward Carmichael. "You have the atonement the dark lords are calling for. If you want the Family to be saved, you must kill Tony."

Carmichael turned and looked back to the spell book Cyrus had used to send the death curse out on Ray Kirkland. "Why don't we just go ahead and hire you to curse Tony right now?"

Cyrus shook his head slowly under his hood. "No."

"But . . . you did it for us last time, four years ago!"

Cyrus still refused. "*You* hired me to put that death curse on Pete Vero four years ago because you felt he was jeopardizing the security of the Family. I gladly did it. But it was your doing. This situation with Tony is different. This time, you have sinned against the dark lords. You must spill Tony's blood yourself. It must be done under your orders. When his blood is on your head, you'll be atoned in the sight of the dark lords who protect you. But you must do it!"

Larsky stepped forward. "Consider it done!" he sneered.

Carmichael glared at him, quickly comprehending Larsky's innuendo.

"I already have the contract out on him. Tommy Wheeler's gonna carry it out as soon as I give him the word. I did it with my own money, too."

Carmichael was flabbergasted that Larsky would do such a thing without his orders. Cyrus was amused:

"That's what I like about you, Ed: you are as ice water-cold to the core as any human I've ever met!" He laughed heartily. "Going to kill the Vero's golden child without even telling the Veros. That's rich!" Cyrus shook his head, giggling uncontrollably at the whole affair.

Carmichael looked away from Larsky and down to the blackboard again.

KILL TONY

He guessed it was only inevitable. Tony had brought it on himself.

FORTY-TWO

T ony Vero descended upon Cherries like a raging fireball.
          After several hours of driving around, frantically trying to forget the episode at his Uncle Joseph's house, he swung past Cherries around 11:00 PM and spotted Jimmy Richards' truck out front. He screeched to a stop, squealed into a nearby parking space, and ran down Cherries's cement stairs. He rang the bell and pounded on the locked entrance door for two minutes. The music pounded from within. Randy the bouncer didn't answer. Tony figured that they couldn't hear or were in the middle of one of their raunchy performances. He punched the bottom of the door, turned around and leaned back against the wall, panting from frustration and anger. He felt like the world was closing in on him. He had never suffered from claustrophobia before, but down in that musty pit of an entrance he could feel it coming on. It was all wearing on him: days of being out of the safety of his home, along with the supreme disappointment of being so close to finding Bernie Lokawski and whoever nailed Todd Falco, but then having every door seemingly slammed shut in his face. He was losing it, knew it, but felt helpless to do anything about it. If he could get inside Cherries, he was going to take it all out on that creep Jimmy Richards. He walked up the steps about three quarters of the way to get his head out into the open, when suddenly the door below opened. A young couple stepped out drunk, laughing . . .

"Hold that door!" Tony yelled as he leapt down half the flight of stairs.

The man mindlessly held the door for him and Tony bolted through the foyer into the bar.

The place was dim and smoky. The only lights shining were the ones pointed at the small stage. The girls had just finished their last set and were walking toward a back room in their robes. There were only about eleven people there, including Danny O'Hurley the owner, Randy the bouncer, and Jimmy Richards. They were all yucking it up over at the bar when Danny spotted Tony charging toward them like a bull. He saw the rage in Tony's eyes.

"Randy!" the owner shouted and pointed at Tony.

Randy hopped off a barstool and cut Tony off. Tony was obviously heading straight for Jimmy Richards. Jimmy hopped off his stool and stood behind two other guys. Randy wrapped Tony up in a vicious bear hug and lifted his feet up off the ground.

349

"Where do you think you're goin', big shot?"

"Richards!" Tony snarled as Randy swung him backwards through the air. "Where's Bernie Lokawski? Where's Frank Kranac?"

Jimmy cowered. "Some one stop him!"

Tony looked sideways at Randy, who was now walking him back toward the foyer. "Get off me!" he roared.

But burly Randy forcefully carried Tony off, despite his incredible struggle. The patrons all roared and whooped with glee at the spectacle.

"Teach him a lesson, Randy!" Danny shouted from behind the bar. "Fix it so he never comes in here again!"

"Glad to," Randy huffed, obviously laboring with all his might to contain the wild Vero.

The patrons shouted and cheered Randy on. Some of them went to follow them into the foyer to see what they expected to be a massacre. But Tony had worked himself sideways when Randy got him into the foyer, and managed to kick that inner door shut, blocking any patrons from joining them. They could see Tony breaking free of Randy's death hold and dropping to the floor just as the door shut on them.

Tony looked up at Randy with demon eyes. Randy quickly realized Tony wasn't all there.

A moment later, brutal sounds of skirmishing could be heard from within. The patrons all saw two shadows grappling through the grainy glass window. One was obviously overpowering the other. Like animals smelling blood they tried to get the door open to watch, but it was jammed shut.

Jimmy looked fearfully at Danny behind the bar. "You got a back door? I gotta get out of here! Can I use your fire exit?"

"No!" Danny said. "You aren't gonna need it. He'll be beaten to a pulp and gone by the time you leave here tonight."

The group was all "ooh!"ing over at the foyer door. From the shadows inside one of the combatants had clearly overtaken the other. They could see the shadow of a fist viciously rising and then descending like lightning down onto the other person, followed each time by the nauseating sound of flesh and bone pounding on flesh and bone. The fracas was clearly a one-sided slaughter now.

"Randy's goin' to town on the pretty-boy prima donna!" one of them giggled.

"He's gonna kill him!" someone said with uneasiness.

"I would have never thought Randy was that quick with his fists," another thought aloud.

The brutal beating continued for another few seconds.

Danny and Jimmy watched with anticipation.

"Danny!" one of them by the door finally spoke up, concerned, "You might need to get out there and stop Randy! That Vero's gonna be a dead man!"

The beating quickly stopped, and the shadows disappeared. All eyes were on the door.

Silence for a moment.

"Randy?" someone shouted through the door? "Come on out!"

The door suddenly flew open from a hard kick, the grainy glass shattering everywhere. Tony Vero furiously emerged from the foyer. Everyone gasped. They could see Randy's unconscious body behind him, slumped on the foyer floor. Tony looked like an enraged lunatic. He made eye-contact with Jimmy Richards, who groaned uncontrollably.

"Enough games, Jimmy!" Tony roared as he marched over toward Jimmy Richards. "Where's Bernie Lokawski?"

Danny shot instantly from behind the bar and disappeared into his office.

Jimmy stepped backwards, eyes wide a saucers. Once Tony got past several of the frightened patrons, they ran for the door, jumping over Randy and fleeing from the bar. The strippers, dressed now, ran out of their room and followed them out too. Jimmy was backing up against the far wall, flanked by five other patrons. He was shaking from head to toe, terrified to face Tony.

"Answer me!" Tony shouted.

Jimmy nearly hit the ceiling, startled. "I . . . I . . . I . . . d-d-don't know! Ask Frankie!" he said, cowering near the jukebox. Tony got to the edge of the bar, beside the entrance to Danny's office. Danny suddenly came bounding out with his .45 in hand. Before he knew it, Tony had ducked back toward the bar like a flash of light. When Danny turned the corner Tony leaped up and body slammed the short red-headed man, grabbing Danny by his gun wrist at the same time. The .45 fired, blasting a hole in the ceiling. Everyone screamed with fright and hit the deck as dust and debris floated through the air. Tony followed through perfectly on his hit and laid Danny out on the ground. He grabbed the gun out of Danny's hand with his left, and cracked Danny across his jaw with a right. He stood up and everyone saw he now had the gun.

"Stop messin' with me!" Tony shouted.

"Someone help me!" Jimmy Richards screamed from the floor.

Defenseless on the ground, Danny held his hands up over his face and begged for mercy, but Tony ignored him and turned toward Jimmy, who was crawling like a snake along the wall toward the row of booths. Tony quickly went and stood over the frightened man. Blinded in his rage, he cocked the .45 without even considering what he was doing and pointed it down at Jimmy's face.

"Please don't kill me!" Jimmy screamed with terror.

Tony shouted, "You've messed around with me for days now! Not giving me what I've wanted. This is your last chance! Where's Bernie Lokawski?"

"Ask Frankie! Please! He knows everything!"

"What did you psychos do with Todd Falco?"

"Please don't!"

"Would you answer my questions!" Tony roared impatiently, the gun shaking in Jimmy's direction.

"Frankie'll kill me if I say anything!" Jimmy whimpered.

Tony reached down and snatched Jimmy up by the shirt . . .

"Aaaahhhhh!" Jimmy closed his eyes and held his hands up helplessly.

. . . and Tony stood him up against the wall, sticking the gun right up to the bridge of Jimmy's nose:

"Me first!"

Frank Kranac finished covering his money pit with the wood, the rug, and the boxes. He was as satisfied as he could be that his money was all there and accounted for, safe for the time being. Sweating profusely, he wanted to wrap up his work, take a shower, and find something to eat. He would stay up all night, since he worked steady graveyard shifts and was due back exactly twenty-four hours later. As he made his way back toward the cellar steps his Marine trunk from his service in Vietnam caught his eye. He stared at if for a minute, contemplating opening it. Then he waved at it and grunted, deciding against it. Trying to sort that whole experience out in his head caused him great frustration. Plus, it would only serve to distract him from his fortune, and he couldn't bare any more distractions than what he'd had recently. That might somehow jeopardize all his money. It was better to just leave that trunk and his whole Vietnam experiences alone these days. But as he went to turn off the basement light near the foot of the stairs, he quickly changed his mind and went back to the trunk, drawn to it like a magnet. The contents of Frank's Marine trunk represented the conflict that had gone on over his soul in the 1960s and early '70s. He didn't call it the "conflict," or even recognize it as such. He was not perceptive enough to make such a connection. To him the contents of the trunk represented a mere choice he had made that somehow eventually landed him there in his basement with a fortune.

He leaned over and slid the trunk out away from the wall. He kept it locked at all times, like everything else he owned. He pulled out his key chain, a ringing, jangling conglomeration of over thirty different keys for the locks in his home and at his job. He could point out any of the keys, even the ancient, worn ones, and instantly identify what locks they opened. He singled out the tarnished military key from the center of the huge ring and unlocked the Marine trunk. Inside were his uniforms, records, and regalia from his Marine stint during the war. Intermingled with those memories were photographs, letters and trinkets from that time period. Everything was meticulously folded and positioned in the trunk. On top of it all lay a framed photograph and a dog tag. There lay the conflict. The photograph was of one Darlene Rivenbark, the only woman he'd ever loved, and who ever loved him. He stared at her eyes and callously wondered where she was today, what she might be doing. The fact that she wasn't with him didn't shake him, though. It's better that she wasn't. He probably wouldn't have his fortune today if she were around. After a flash of Darlene memories, he picked up the dog tag and fondled it in his thick, stained fingers. He looked over the engraved name on the dingy silver tag: Bernie Lokawski. The little metal plate conjured images of their experiences together during the war. Bernie Lokawski was a Marine sergeant. He was short with an athletic frame, his crew-cut hair jet black. He wore thick black sunglasses and a perpetual fox-like grin. Frank Kranac considered Bernie Lokawski to be his best friend ever. He never had more in common with another human. Bernie knew what the deal was. He knew what was truly important in life: living large and making money. Bernie was the brains of the duo, a schemer and a fast talker who could charm a jungle tiger from his prey. Frank was the brawn, tall, laconic, not very learned nor perceptive. He couldn't get far past his own needs, like eating and earning cash. Everyone called them George and Lenny. Bernie would laugh in recognition. Frank had no idea who George and Lenny were, so he couldn't understand what people were laughing at.

He pushed the trunk back and sighed. Darlene Rivenbark and Bernie Lokawski. Frank had to choose which of those two people would win his soul back there in the early seventies. He chose Bernie Lokawski.

Frank met them both during his stay at Camp Lejeune, North Carolina, when he was nineteen. Darlene was a secretary in town. A year older than Frank, but openly smitten by the huge, strapping, silent Marine. She was the beauty that tamed the beast. The uncultured Kranac was raised in the Beaver Valley by an alcoholic father and mousy mother, both of whom were eccentrics and misers who pinched every penny dry. Frank never left Western Pennsylvania as he grew up, and had no exposure to anything but school and work. When he enlisted in '68 and met Darlene a year and a half later he had much to learn. But Darlene was rich with patience. She completely melted at the way Frank struggled to work so hard at always trying to do the right things at the right time for her, when he obviously had no idea how to do anything romantic or normal. In a military town full of hot shot Marines, she felt safe at Frank's side. The huge man was intimidated by no one and would chase off the toughest of pests from the beautiful brunette. He doted lovingly over her during the first few months of their courtship, and she was in heaven. There was only one thing stopping her from discussing marriage with the man: he was an absolute heathen, and she was a Born Again Christian. Darlene had been a lifelong Baptist who loved Jesus with her whole heart. To her own folly she ignored scriptural warnings about being unequally joined to an unbeliever. She desperately tried to get Frank saved, but his empirical, practical upbringing allowed no room for faith or a God. She was a strong witness, though; a woman of character and integrity. Frank couldn't help but sense there was a Goodness hovering about the dear woman.

But just as Darlene was making headway concerning Frank's salvation, along came Bernie Lokawski. Bernie was an ungodly man from Milwaukee, a man of vice and sin, but an intelligent man. He had already made sergeant when he first met Frank Kranac. He had never seen such a specimen of a man, before: without ever lifting a weight in the gym, Kranac was naturally huge and powerful. His arms, chest and thighs were massive, and there was little he couldn't do. They met in a bar after Lokawski watched him make short work of four huge Marines in a row in an arm wrestling contest. Kranac sent each opponent away in pain, while he didn't even appear to break a sweat. Bernie introduced himself to Frank, told him he was a martial arts instructor for the Marines. As time went by, Bernie got Frank transferred from a warehouse job to his instructor's camp. Frank took naturally to the combat classes, easily defeating everyone he sparred. The two became inseparable. As they paled around, Darlene could begin to see the struggle going on for Frank's soul. She would tell him what a bad influence Bernie was, but Frank wouldn't hear of it. Bernie knew what the deal was, what was important in life. Satan used Bernie to steal Frank from Darlene and Jesus, and Frank gladly went along with them.

Bernie taught Frank basic martial arts moves used by the special forces of the military. He liked to use Bernie for sparring with some of his best grunts. If they could successfully tangle with a Frank Kranac, they could handle anybody.

Frank remembered the first time Bernie taught him how to kill someone in hand to hand combat.

"You're like a moose, Frankie-boy. This won't be difficult for you at all. Once you strike the right points, your enemy won't even know what hit him."

He instructed Frank on how to break a human neck from the front and behind. Frank learned quickly on dummies, and mock practices with other Marines. Bernie would train Frank's opponents on how to defend themselves, but if Frank got close enough to grab them, it was all over. He would swiftly pull the opponent to himself, wrap his tree-trunk arms around them, lay his weight on them, and work them into a headlock from behind, so he would have his elbow joint up under their jaws. With that, Bernie would whistle the opponent dead.

"One tug of your arm at that point, one twist of their head, and Mister Opponent is a dead man. You'll snap his neck like a twig."

Bernie's hold on Frank perverted into a death lock of manipulation. He was so charismatic he could get Frank to do nearly anything in order to please him. Darlene Rivenbark sensed it and saw Frank drifting further and further away from her and the Gospel she'd been planting. Bernie didn't just indulge in heavy drinking. He loved to carouse with the wildest of women. It was this that lead to the end of Frank and Darlene's relationship, and not because she became jealous. One group of ladies Bernie and Frank became attached to started leading them to a palm reader in the city. This strange woman would do readings of all their lives. They began to frequent her regularly for kicks. They participated in spiritually dangerous activities God expressly forbids in the Bible (the visitation of psychics, witches, and seers) to protect his magnificent human creation from the destruction and curses of the devil. Those who blatantly ignore His warnings invite demonic manifestations and future destruction. It was during these readings that powerful demonic forces began to attach themselves to Frank Kranac's soul. These unclean spirits were sent to undo all of the seeds of the Gospel Darlene had planted. The distance between Darlene and Frank widened even more.

Spiritually she sensed something terribly wrong with Frank. Finally, she confronted him, telling him how she wished he would give his heart to the Lord, and settle down. She said she wanted him to forget his relationship with Bernie Lokawski, and marry her. Frank had never been so torn in all his life. He felt such a peace around Darlene, and she definitely brought out the best in him with her powerful Christian influence. He had even considered giving his heart to Jesus at one point. The fact that he was even considering it was miraculous in itself. But the palm reader put an end to that. One evening, when the "girls" rendezvoused with Bernie and Frank at their favorite bar, they took them back to Madame Sophia. That night, influenced by the demons she constantly communed with, Madame Sophia singled out Frank and offered to do a "free reading," since the miserly man didn't like spending money on such frivolous activities. Frank agreed, and she began her calculated reading:

"Oh!" she said stroking his hand tenderly and flattering him. "You are such a *strong* man! So powerful! What hands! What muscles! Such a specimen of manhood!"

Bernie and the girls all agreed heartily with the witch. Frank's ego swelled.

Madame Sophia suddenly leaned over his hand and stared at it with concern. "But what is this Madame Sophia senses about you? What is this weak religion that I see that young lady you've been dating has been trying to push you into?"

"You mean 'Holly Holy Roller'? Miss Darlene 'Can I Pray for You?'" Bernie said sarcastically. The girls all snickered and mocked Darlene along with Bernie.

"Who is this girl that's trying to weaken such a strong man as you?" Madame Sophia asked Frank.

Terribly confused as the spirits there were tugging to uproot the Gospel from his heart, he explained who Darlene Rivenbark was.

"What does such a strong a man as you want with such a weak religion? Christianity will only make you weak! This woman will take such a powerful man as you and make you a pushover! She'll run your life and make you a sap! I see it very clearly before you! Her religion of 'forgiveness' and 'kindness,' it will only sap your strength and destroy the very masculinity that makes you so virile! Do you want to be lead around by the nose like some mousy wimp by this Christian woman? Do you really want to become weak? Such a strong man as you?"

The demons discovered areas of his soul that his father had built up with false notions of masculinity. Frank was suddenly terrified at the scenario of becoming weakened by Jesus. He surely didn't want to be weak. His pride demanded strength. Once that weakness was uncovered by the spirits, they were able to begin building a stronghold there, one that would drive the Gospel out from Frank Kranac once and for all.

Madame Sophia pronounced a death curse over him, disguised as a blessing: "Stay far away from this woman, her Christianity and her Jesus! And you will be blessed with even greater strength, and eventually, wealth! You do not need weakness! Such a masculine man as you needs to build his prowess! Be who you are *destined* to be! Be a *man!*"

In his basement in Beaver Falls, Frank Kranac sadly reminisced about the day Darlene Rivenbark broke up with him once and for all. He could still see her standing before him with tears in her eyes, hands trembling.

"You don't mean this, do you Frank? You wouldn't force me to make such a choice. You couldn't."

Like a zombie in stature, demonically influenced, Frank mindlessly repeated what had become his mantra:

"I am a strong man, Darlene. Your Jesus is just going to make me weak. You're not going to be able to have both of us. You need to decide once and for all which one of us you want in your life. And you can't marry Him!"

She bowed her head sadly and slowly held up her right hand. She removed an expensive friendship ring Frank bought for her during happier, carefree times in their relationship. She held it out to him.

"That's where you've made the biggest mistake, Frank. I'm already married to Him. I won't choose you over Him. But you need to know this: you can't marry Bernie Lokawski."

She sweetly laid the ring in Frank's giant hand, and laying both her hands over his, she closed his fist over it.

Frank never saw her walk away. After a dazed moment, he just suddenly realized she wasn't there anymore.

Frank Kranac lost his soul forever in Vietnam. The war itself isn't what tainted him. He didn't lose what little faith he had due to battle-scarred emotions, or questioning man's inhumanity to man. No, he lost his soul because of Bernie Lokawski and his wicked ways.

Frank had been in Nam for nine months, but had seen little action. A talented mechanic and machinist, he was usually kept in the safety of some base working on jeeps and helicopters. Bernie Lokawski pulled strings and got Frank transferred to Saigon in '71. He wanted "Lenny" back at his side. Bernie got him another warehouse job, similar to the one he had in Camp Lejeune. By that time Bernie Lokawski had slithered his way into the drug trade in Saigon. He worked with drug lords from the city to move shipments throughout the country, and even to U.S. troops fighting the war. He was cunning and shrewd, and mixed well with both the Vietnamese and the Americans fighting the conflict. He was also quite a con artist in the Marines, and could easily manipulate the system during the madness of war. Bernie had gone rotten to the core.

Frank Kranac had become a black hole of a human being by that point. He was completely self-consumed, did nothing for anyone else, nor did he even consider his fellow man. Any light that had even remotely influenced him during his relationship with Darlene had now been driven completely from him. He was consumed with narcissistic darkness. Self-worship had become his god. That and money. That miserly spirit that had been passed down to him by his parents had been built up into a massive demonic stronghold in his soul. He began hoarding all he could. Those demons began spawning a paranoia that often cripples and isolates a man. Everyone around Frank became suspect: he believed everyone was after his money. He was sure that anyone who tried to get close to him was just out to somehow steal his cash from him. That's all he knew. Therefore friendships and relationships disappeared rapidly. His Marine comrades began to tire of his brooding. He withdrew himself from the unit to which he belonged. When Bernie got him that transfer to Saigon, he gladly took it. He and Bernie hit if off again, immediately. Their penchant for immorality had grown exponentially during their time apart. Prostitutes and hard drinking fast became a way of life for them. As soon as Bernie gave Frank an eyeful of the money he was making moving illegal narcotics, the spirits of greed immediately whet Frank's appetite for that kind of cash. It wasn't long before Bernie was leading Frank on his drug escapades at night. Bernie taught him all there was to know about the wartime drug trade, and Frank caught on fast. He learned the ins and outs quickly, and was strictly mercenary about the whole scenario; there were no notions of conscience or right and wrong about it. It was a quick moneymaker. It was illegal, human lives were the cost, but there was a fortune to be made. He remembered the words of Madame Sophia, how he'd be a masculine man and one day make a fortune. This life of crime was the key to wealth. He just knew it.

The two of them were preparing to run a shipment of heroin one night in a sweaty Saigon warehouse. They were packing the plastic bags of heroin into coffee crates marked for the front lines of combat for the troops. As they were sealing the crates, Frank noticed he was suddenly doing all the work and Bernie was standing there catching a smoke, watching him with a queer expression on his face.

"What's wrong with you?" Frank stood up, sweating, and glared at his crony.

Bernie took a long drag off his smoke. "You know, Frank, I was thinking about something."

"What?"

"These yahoos we're gonna trade with tonight. These Vietnamese. We've dealt with them before. They're gonna be loaded. There'll be three of them. One of them will have a rifle ready on us. The other two will open the crate and inspect our goods. Then they'll hand us the money in their leather bags."

"Same as usual, Bernie."

Bernie took another drag from his cigarette and looked up at Frank Kranac with a sinister stare. "You know, we could double our money tonight, Frank!"

Frank didn't follow him at all, but was definitely interested in the sound of extra money. "How?"

Bernie took another long drag from his smoke. Then, matter-of-factly, he asked, "You ever kill anyone, Frankie-boy?"

A chill ran up then down Frank's spine. He cocked his head and looked queerly at Bernie Lokawski. "You know I haven't. Why you askin' me that?"

"Well, you're the biggest guy in Saigon. Those Vietnamese we're gonna deal with are like mini-people compared to you. You know all that combat training I taught you?"

Frank just stared at him silently, trying to follow along.

"Like how to kill your enemy with your bare hands?"

"Neck breakin', Bernie? You talkin' about neck breakin'?"

"We couldn't shoot these little guys. The authorities would hear the shots and be all over us like white on rice. But if you could take out the guy with the rifle, and then both of us take out the other two, we'd come away from tonight's deal with a fortune of money in our pockets *and* this heroin that we could still sell later!"

Frank looked uncertain.

Sweat poured off of Lokawski's face. He blew smoke at Kranac. "Doublin' our money, I'm tellin' you, Frankie-boy! That's what we'd be doin'!"

Frank looked worried for a moment. "What if . . ."

"What if nothin', Frankie! I've seen you incapacitate three of my toughest Marines at one time! You broke one of their arms, the other's ribs, and took out all three of them fair and square, one against three! What could you do to those tiny walkin' toothpicks we been dealin' with if you just put your mind to it!"

Frank hesitated to answer him, the seeds of murder not yet finding root in him.

"Oh come on, man! You are the toughest, strongest cat in all South Vietnam! You alone could take out all three! It'll be quiet, we'll dump off the bodies where no one will ever find them, and we'll be thousands of dollars richer in one night!"

Frank still didn't sign on for the vicious gig.

Bernie walked up and whopped Frank over his huge shoulders with both hands. "Think of it! You are the strongest man around, and tonight you can be the richest, too!"

Frank envisioned his cash coffer overflowing, then sending it stateside into a high yielding account. He could have quite a bit of money saved up by the time he returned to the states.

Bernie read his face, saw his eyes beginning to light up. He smacked Frank lightly on his right cheek and got real happy. "That's it, Frankie-boy! I knew I could count on you!"

"We split the cash, right?"

Bernie put his hand out and shook the hulking man's huge fist. "Fifty-fifty!" He put the cigarette back in his mouth. "We'll call this 'The Bernie Lokawski Special!"

Murder hovered chaotically around Frank Kranac's heart at that point, waiting to see if he'd actually partake of this spirit.

Their demonically inspired plan went off without incident late that evening. A spirit of blood and murder came over Frank Kranac and enabled him to carry out Bernie's plan. Bernie struggled with the one man he was supposed to overtake, so

Frank wound up killing all three of the Vietnamese dealers himself. He blacked out for some reason when he took out the rifleman. It was a textbook attack on his part, he snapped the man's neck so quickly the guy never knew what hit him, but Frank blacked out for about five seconds while he did it. When it was over, though, Frank felt like cold cement was being poured down into his soul. The demonic strongholds within him were built even higher, now that he had openly added cold-blooded murder for cash to his repertoire of sins.

"Like stealin' candy from a baby!" Bernie smirked after they deposited the three bodies into a nearby reservoir.

Frank nodded and smiled slightly. "We can make a ton of money doin' this, can't we?"

"You wanna do more like this?"

"Well, we can't keep killing off our money sources. How will we make any money later?"

"You kiddin'? We do this a few more times and sell off this heroin when it's all over, and we'll never have to worry about workin' again! 'The Bernie Lokawski Special' can make us millionaires!" Frank grinned genuinely for the first time in two years. It was a cold, lifeless grin.

"The Bernie Lokawski Special" became Frank and Bernie's modus operandi.

Over the next two months wily Bernie used the heroin to lure three more big money buyers into their death-trap. Frank would overpower them quickly and take them out without a sound. Seven more bodies were disposed of. Through satanic eyes, their lives meant nothing to Frank. He could only see the money he was accumulating. And that became the problem, for his tunnel vision left him blind to the fact that Bernie Lokawski had been using him. Frank was the one doing all the killing. Bernie had killed no one. Frank was also blind to a scheme Bernie had been pulling on him regarding the split of their profits. But Bernie's pride blinded him to the fact that Frank Kranac had carefully been watching how to lure and trap all those yo-yo's they had murdered. He caught onto the workings of "The Bernie Lokawski Special" quite fast. He was not the "Lenny" Bernie had been calling him. In fact, he even found out what that meant. One day in Saigon another soldier explained to Frank who "George" and "Lenny" were. When he picked up a copy of Steinbeck's *Of Mice and Men* and read it because it was so short, he quickly became incensed that Bernie and others had been referring to him in such a manner. Frank knew he was not retarded in the least. And when he finally found out that Bernie Lokawski had been ripping him off where the profits of their crimes were concerned, he decided to show Bernie just how smart he really was.

Bernie Lokawski had been secretly selling off portions of their heroin stash behind Frank's back. Frank found out one day when he decided to check the contents of their supply. Almost a quarter of it was missing. He checked back a week later. It was down to about sixty percent of the original supply. He knew Lokawski wasn't a smack head. He also knew Bernie had been sneaking around suspiciously in his off time. The demons in his soul screamed for Frank's indignation regarding this injustice. *He* was the one getting his hands dirty, and in the process Bernie was ripping him off with *their* heroin behind his back! Frank was devastated by the weight of the betrayal. He not only thought of Bernie as a business partner, but his best friend ever. After a moment of shock, he coldly waved off the insult and betrayal as nothing more than a business move on Bernie's part. One Frank would have to pay him back for. Inspired by the unclean spirits that influenced him, Frank Kranac devised a plan to turn the tables on Bernie Lokawski, the one who'd stabbed him in the back.

Bernie Lokawski slyly made his way down the darkened Saigon ally, looking over his shoulder, making sure no one was following him. He cut into a back doorway to a filthy butcher shop. The door was unlocked, as promised. His contact, some interested buyer named "Lo Sin," would be awaiting him inside. He pulled his .45 out, just in case. The back section of the shop smelled of blood and offal. There was little light, save what candlelight shone through the doorway and cracks in the wall from two candles lit in the front of the shop. Bernie pointed his pistol in front of him, trying to see in the darkness. When he reached the doorway into the front of the shop he whispered: "Lo Sin!" He stuck the gun through the door before him, about to enter. A sudden heavy and sharp blow to his wrist dropped the .45 to the ground. It was followed instantly by a hard fist to his lower jaw, and Bernie Lokawski, a hand to hand combat trainer for the United States Marines, quickly found himself incapacitated and defenseless on the ground. A lone light bulb flicked on above and there standing over him was the last person he expected to see: Frank Kranac. Frank had a hard look in his eye. He was steady and cool. He was a man on a mission and Bernie could see it clearly in his countenance. He'd picked up Lokawski's gun and aimed it down at him.

Bernie looked up at him and tried to speak, his bottom jaw paralyzed and aching: "I trained you well, Franky-boy. But you make a bad Vietnamese. You're too big."

"There is no 'Lo Sin,' if you haven't figured it out, yet. I paid a local to pretend to be interested in what you were selling." He cocked the gun. "Hand over the smack."

Bernie hesitated as if he didn't know what Frank was talking about, but then gave up the idea of the charade. "Can I get up?"

"No."

He rolled over on the ground, stuck his hand down the back of his pants, and produced a cellophane roll full of several ounces of the heroin. He tossed it to Frank's feet.

Frank looked down on it and shook his head. "You really do believe I'm that stupid, don't you Bernie? You really do think of me as 'Lenny.' Like I'm gonna bend over to grab that bag and give you the opportunity to pounce forward and pull my feet out from under me so you can get a hold of me and your gun. Well, I ain't that stupid! And if you haven't noticed yet, you're the one lying on the ground with a busted jaw. You're the one in the

trap, now. Bernie Lokawski has been lured into his very own 'Bernie Lokawski Special.'"
He leaned over just a bit and growled, "By me!"

"You're not gonna frag me, Corporal Kranac. I've written down all that we've done
and secured it in a place where if I'm ever killed, the letter will immediately be sent to the
Colonel. You'll be hanging from a gallows within six months of my death."

"Like I'm gonna believe that one." Frank held the .45 with both hands, and returned
the trigger to it's "safe" position. Then he put the pistol down the back of his khakis.

The dazed Bernie Lokawski stumbled to his feet quickly. He tried to take an attack
stance, but Frank put him squarely back down on the floor with a vicious kick.

"It's kinda ironic, Bernie," Frank said as he stood over his nearly incapacitated
comrade like he was wounded prey. "You taught me how to do people in with my hands,
silently, and now here I am havin' to do you in, too. I wish you hadn't o' stabbed me in the
back like you did. I really thought you was my friend."

He reached down and snatched Sergeant Bernie Lokawski's dog tags from his throat.
In Frank's mind, he truly wanted something tangible with which to remember his partner,
his friend, his soul mate.

There in the basement of his Beaver Falls home, Frank Kranac sat by his footlocker
and fondled Bernie Lokawski's dog tags from almost thirty years ago. He didn't remember
Bernie as the one who'd stabbed him in the back. He didn't remember him as someone he
had to murder. He simply remembered him as his friend and mentor. To Frank Kranac it
was the ultimate homage to his old comrade that when he moved back to Beaver County
in the early 1980s he began running "Bernie Lokawski Specials" with all the local drug
dealers. It was also an honor that he used the alias of "Bernie Lokawski," the man who
taught him all he knew about luring drug dealers, taking their lives, and robbing them of
their high fortunes. Frank laid the dog tags back into the trunk, and locked it up, thinking
of another irony: when he snapped Todd Falco's neck a week earlier during their
rendezvous, Todd Falco knew him only as Bernie Lokawski. It was like the guy who'd
been dead almost thirty years now could reach through time, in the embodiment of Frank
Kranac, and still pull such a beautiful rip-off. Frank was a million and a quarter richer,
but Bernie was getting the credit.

As he shut off his basement light he said out loud with all sincerity, "What an honor."

Tony had Jimmy Richards and all of Cherries in a panic.

With the gun in Jimmy's face and the other patrons and Danny all cowering on the
floor, Tony backed Jimmy up to one of the wooden booths.

"I know you and your brother are all wrapped up with Frank Kranac and Bernie
Lowkawski, little creep! What did you do with Todd Falco and the money?"

"I . . . I didn't do anything with him or the money! I'm telling you, ask Frankie!"

Tony pushed him back into the seat of the booth. Jimmy suddenly found himself
sitting, with Tony standing over him waving the gun.

"Answer my questions!"

"I can't! Frankie'll kill me! You don't understand!"

Tony shoved Jimmy backward, his head falling back onto the seat. Insane with determination, Tony pushed his hand down into Jimmy's chest and put the gun in his face.

"Answer me, or I'll pull this trigger!"

Several of the patrons pleaded for Tony to stop.

"Who has the money?" Tony growled.

"I can't tell you!"

Tony quickly pointed the gun off to the side of Jimmy's head and pulled the trigger. The .45 roared, blasting a blackened hole into the seat of the booth an inch away from Jimmy's ear. Jimmy screeched with terror, then quickly realized he was still alive. His left ear was ringing so loudly and deeply, however, he couldn't hear from it. He quickly remembered the question Tony just asked.

"Frankie has the money! Frankie does!"

"Who's Bernie Lokawski? Where is he? Who is he?"

Jimmy whimpered again and slowly shook his head, tears of fear in his eyes. "Please don't make me tell you this! I can't! Frankie will kill me if . . ."

Once again, Tony pointed the gun away from Jimmy in a flash and pulled the trigger, this time blowing a rat-hole into the seat on the other side of Jimmy's head. Jimmy jumped and squealed again, but Tony held him down, slammed the hot gun barrel between his eyes and cocked the hammer. Jimmy could no longer hear, both his ears were clanging so loudly, but he could see that Tony was speaking again and read his lips:

"The next one is going through your head! Who is Bernie Lokawski?"

This time, hearing temporarily gone, with powder burns on each side of his face, Jimmy finally gave Tony the answer to his question:

"Frankie *is* Bernie!" he blurted out. "Frank Kranac is Bernie Lokawski! That's the name Frankie uses when he sets up his drug deals, when he's settin' up those dealers for a kill! Frankie killed Todd Falco and took all his money! Frankie is Bernie Lokawski!"

It was as though Tony was instantly snapped out of his spell. Gun trembling in his hand, the rage on his face quickly melted away; his eyes turned lucid again. He looked down at Jimmy, who was shaking violently with fear there beneath Tony's grip. Tears were pouring out of Jimmy's eyes and streaming through the gun-powder stains on both sides of his head. There for just a moment, in Jimmy's horrified expression, Tony saw the pathetic face of Gus Savage. He realized that he was the reason Jimmy currently looked the way he did. Mortified at what he'd just done, Tony stood upright and let Jimmy loose. He looked around at Danny and the patrons all cowering on the floor behind him. Someone was near the door helping Randy the bouncer, who had come to. Randy looked bad, but he was alert. After looking around at everyone, Tony stepped back, undid the clip of the .45, and removed it. His face was turning sheet white, he was sweating profusely; he frightened himself. He was a different Tony than the one who had arrived. He turned and staggered across the bar to the door. He threw the ammo clip behind the bar, cracking a whiskey bottle. He looked one by one at all of the patrons as he made his leave. They were beginning to get up off the floor, slowly, cautiously eyeing this lunatic to see if he would freak out on them again. As he got to the door, Mick stood up, looking tremendously disappointed in Tony. He bravely asked:

"What kind of person are you?"

There was that question again! It floored Tony to hear it one more time. He stopped, but didn't turn to look at him. He looked down at Danny O'Hurley's .45 in his hand, which was still smoking. He tossed it aside into one of the booths. He answered loud enough for no one to really hear him:

"I'm a Vero."

He staggered out the door and disappeared.

FORTY-THREE

Carmichael Vero's Lear jet arrived back at the Beaver County Airport at 4:45 am that Monday morning. Carmichael and State Attorney General Michael Davis were both at the same airport within hours of one another, a situation they both would have found quite ironic.

Carmichael left Aleister Estate shamefaced. It had been a long flight home from New York, especially for Larsky. He felt downright jubilant that demon spirits had actually ordered the cold blooded murder of Tony Vero. But Carmichael brooded in a tense fog the entire journey. He would not speak. He looked like a schoolboy who'd been spanked for misbehaving. He had been, as far as Larsky was concerned. Carmichael had turned his back on Cyrus and the Dark Lords on purpose. Now he was paying the piper. Served him right. Why brood? But brood the elder Vero did. Larsky didn't dare try to speak to him.

The sun was barely a spark on the horizon as they left the plane. Larsky grabbed their luggage and golf bags and pulled them on a cart behind them as they headed toward the parking lot. While they were still within the roar of the Lear's jet engines, Carmichael turned and spoke to Larsky for the first time in hours, still not looking him in the eye.

"I want you to get a hold of Tommy Wheeler first thing when you get home. Explain that upon your signal today, he's to follow through with the hit on Tony. How much have you paid him?"

"Fifty grand."

"Tell him to dispose of Tony's body so it'll never be found. I'm going to reimburse you the fifty you paid him for the job."

"But Carmichael, I've already taken care of . . ."

"I'm not doing this out of the goodness of my heart. You heard Cyrus tonight. I am to be the one who sees to Tony's death if we ever want things to return to normal for the Family. Fifty grand, no one ever finds Tony's body, and I'll pay you back your money. That's how it's going to be. You got that?"

"Yeah. I got it."

Carmichael stopped Ed, grabbed his own luggage and golf clubs off the cart, and headed toward his car. Larsky was truly surprised by that. Carmichael Vero hadn't carried his own bags anywhere in years. Though the man seemed angry, Larsky sensed there was great frustration and sadness somewhere beneath all that anger. The cold hearted Russian couldn't figure out why. Why would Carmichael be upset about having to take out his pea-brained great nephew, who'd caused him so much heartache? Especially if it was for the cause of saving the empires he'd built?

A heartless man can't fathom one that has even a smidgen of love remaining.

Audra Dutton's alarm clanged her out of her slumber at 5:00 AM. She had vowed the night before to get up early and spend more special time in God's Presence, worshipping Him and interceding on behalf of Benny Miller and that young white boy. She kept her vow and moved the heavens on behalf of Benny and Tony.

Cyrus Moreau awoke with a start after only two hours sleep. He sat up and looked out the window at the sun barely rising. He was shocked because he hadn't been thinking about the tremendous success of the "workshop" that weekend. Nor was he tuning into the power of the Dark Lords who were buzzing freely about his property. No, he was so shocked because he had been dreaming about Brother Maynard again. How could that have happened when he was sure that he had purged his soul of all those old memories? That part of his life should now have been like looking at some stranger's life and not his own. But somehow, his memories of Brother Maynard and the true love that man exhibited remained. Why was he thinking of that special love, again? Where'd that kind of love come from? Surely the Spirit of the Enemy couldn't possibly still be trying to reach *him*! Or could He? Surely, Cyrus Moreau was too far gone for that!

He lay back on his bed, thinking of St. Thomas's Prep Academy in upstate New York. The dread of those memories of humiliation! But Brother Maynard was truly a beacon of light and goodness in those days of torment and shame. Brother Maynard, the man who wore that red rose pin on his frocks and shirts. Cyrus recalled those two days of his junior year that he got to spend with Brother Maynard, that amazing Catholic Priest and literature teacher at St. Thomas's. Cyrus Moreau, the Master of the Spirit Realm, did not exist then. At that time he was only known by his real name, Johnny Cirello. Johnny's father was Xavier Cirello, the great New York shipping magnate of the 1950's and sixties. The man was a millionaire and a business wizard, but he cared little for his only son. There was always business, booze, and golf to attend to. He had no time for his insecure and frail boy. When Johnny reached the ninth grade his father shipped him off to St. Thomas's to board his four years of high school. The scrawny Johnny Cirello weighed only ninety-five pounds and suffered from severe acne. Awkward and uncoordinated, he quickly became the fodder of all ridicule and teasing. He was severely beaten to a bloody pulp several times over his four years at St. Thomas's, and was tormented mercilessly on a daily basis with hateful words and pranks. His only solitude was a hidden corner of either the St. Thomas Library or the local town library. Having no father to turn to and too few friends, young Johnny Cirello took solace in books. Knowledge first became the brilliant student's friend; later, his god.

That fateful weekend of his junior year began late on a Friday afternoon when Brother Maynard paid a surprise visit to the third floor bathroom of the Monsignor Sullivan Dormitory. There were three students who lived to make Johnny's life at St. Thomas a living hell. Mitchell Roush, a senior, was a huge jock. He loathed the skinny, acne-plagued Johnny Cirello. He lead two juniors named Billy Cardigan and Adam Coates on continual Johnny Cirello assaults. That Friday afternoon, the three of them, along with three underclassmen, snatched Johnny from his room, "Hey, Pizza Face! Are you a woman trapped in a man's body?" and carried him off to the restroom. Several moments later, Big Brother Maynard, with his dark brown hair and droopy eyes, burst through that bathroom door like a hurricane. Inside he found Mitchell Roush, Billy Cardigan and Adam Coates standing over Johnny Cirello, who was trembling and crying uncontrollably. They had forced a dress on his skinny body again, and were smearing lipstick all over his face. The three underclassman were laughing and cheering the trio along. Brother Maynard, usually a gentle soul, exploded with indignation when he saw what they were doing to Johnny. He snatched up Mitchell Roush under his arm and tossed him bodily out into the hall. Then he turned on Billy Cardigan and Adam Coates: "What do ya think your heads will sound like when I bop them together like coconuts?" They both ducked around him in terror and bolted out the door, followed by the three underclassmen.

Cyrus remembered the great dignity with which Brother Maynard treated him while they were alone in that bathroom. He gently washed Johnny's face off. Then he angrily tore the dress off his back and tucked it up under his frock to keep for evidence. This incident was the last straw in a huge haystack of abuse and mistreatment Mitchell Roush had caused not only Johnny Cirello, but others, too. Mitchell was sent before the school's board and expelled because of Brother Maynard's testimony. Billy Cardigan and Adam Coates were suspended for the rest of the quarter, and the three underclassmen were all disciplined lightly for taking part in the incident. Of course, Cyrus remembered that others rose up to take Mitchell's place as tormentors after he was gone. But none were as cruel and demented as Mitchell had been. And even Billy and Adam finally laid off him for the most part, during their last year and a half at St. Thomas's.

Brother Maynard couldn't get Johnny to calm down that night. Cyrus remembered how he made him wait outside his office while he called his father, Xavier Cirello, and pleaded with the man to come pick up his son and take him home for the weekend. But even after explaining what humiliation those thugs had just put Johnny through, Xavier Cirello refused to leave his weekend at the Hamptons to come fetch his son. He even refused Brother Maynard's request to send a hired hand to take him home. Cyrus never forgot Brother Maynard's reply to his father on the phone that night:

"You know, Mr. Cirello, it's a shame that a wonderful son like Johnny is wasted on such a lousy father as you! You have such a gift from God in this young man, and you've squandered it on your own selfish ambition!"

The thing that always impressed Cyrus about that gutsy statement was that his father had clout with the New York diocese and could have easily made life rough for Brother Maynard because of that one remark. Xavier Cirello was also the leading donor to St. Thomas's Prep Academy. But Brother Maynard didn't allow the man's wealth and influence to keep him from telling the truth. Cyrus always respected that.

Brother Maynard didn't want to throw Johnny back to the wolves in that dormitory, so he set Johnny up in the rectory guest room for the weekend. That's why that weekend had always been so special: Brother Maynard befriended Johnny and ministered love and acceptance to him. It was one of the few times anyone ever showed him unconditional love. One of the main things Cyrus remembered about Brother Maynard was the way that he would look at him. The majority of people who talked to Johnny never knew how to react to the severe strains of acne that disfigured him. Most people could not hide their repulsion. But Brother Maynard looked at Johnny with love and dignity, not with disgust. (Brother Maynard also took Johnny to several dermatologists during his last year and a half at St. Thomas's and had his acne treated. And he paid for it out of his own pocket.) And he just plain *talked* to Johnny Cirello, and listened to what the boy had to say, making him feel special. And Johnny was genuinely impressed because to his surprise Brother Maynard actually knew what he enjoyed. He didn't think anyone knew or cared about the things he liked. Yet Brother Maynard remembered Johnny and his interests from his literature classes. He remembered the stacks of books the boy read. He remembered the brilliant debates the boy could hold about all types of literature they studied in his classes. That night he ordered them a pizza. He drank red wine, and served Johnny Pepsi. Over dinner Brother Maynard purposefully struck up a literary debate he knew would distract Johnny from that afternoon's degradation . . .

". . . but Goethe was showing us through Faust's destruction that knowledge for the sake of selfish ambition is vain and prideful, ultimately leading to our downfall . . ."

Johnny threw down the anchovy he was about to eat and rebutted: "But Faust wasn't torn to bits and dragged away by his knowledge, but by the demons he sold his soul to! If he had searched for knowledge with a pure heart, instead of copping out and selling his soul for it, he would have begun his journey on the right foot . . ."

"But what does the book of Wisdom in the Bible tell us? 'The fear of the Lord is the beginning of knowledge!' Goethe was telling us that all other paths to knowledge are destructive and vain. Take your studies over the last three years, for example."

"What about my studies? What do you know about what I've studied?"

Brother Maynard leaned back and folded his arms comfortably. "You started in my ninth grade lit class reading Nietzsche, Machiavelli, and Voltaire."

Johnny froze. "How do you know that?"

"I notice the books my students read. Most of them read nothing more than Mad magazine and auto books. You actually read literature! But those types of authors you were reading were Faustian in their search for truth and reality: knowledge for the sake of selfish empowerment. And from there you moved straight on until you now carry around stacks of books about witchcraft and sorcery."

Johnny's eyes lit up with shock that he would know that, too.

"So your 'pure hearted' search for knowledge started with Nietzsche and has lead you to Anton Levay's *Satanic Bible*. Hasn't your quest for knowledge lead you straight down the path to destruction and vanity?"

Nothing but silence and shock from Johnny. Although he was convicted by Brother Maynard's words, he was flattered and excited that the man knew so much about his studies.

"For instance, Johnny, I know that you've checked out *The Exorcist* five times in the last school year."

Johnny's mouth dropped. "How do you know that?"

"I saw you bring it to class several times. Then I saw you checking it out of the library again, one day. So I checked the library card and saw how many times. Why are you so obsessed with such a book?"

"Oh, it's awesome! And I read that they're making a movie version of it!"

"But why, Johnny?" the Brother asked as he gulped some more wine. "That's my point. Your search for knowledge has been as selfish as Faust's. From the selection of books you've been reading, you're obviously searching for the kind of knowledge you can wield for personal power."

Johnny felt free to be honest with Brother Maynard, knowing the man would not condemn him, no matter how he felt. "Well, I won't deny that, Brother Maynard. I've been searching for real power. I've not seen it anywhere else on earth. But I can see it in magic."

"You can't see real power in the God of the Universe we've taught you about for almost three years now?"

"I can't see *Him*. Period! But I can see the things I'm learning in these books coming to pass in my life. You got something against witchcraft?"

"The Bible does. And so does the Vatican. I don't like it's negative influence."

"Oh! But I see it as true power!"

"True power for what?"

Johnny looked down timidly at his pizza, unable to meet Brother Maynard's gaze for the shame and humiliation that filled him. "You saw what they did to me today," he said almost inaudibly. "You know what I go through every day of my life. How's a Schlep like me going to make it through life without power? I see sorcery as a true source of power to help me overcome all these cretins who seek nothing but my daily torment. Sorcery will be my true power!"

Brother Maynard shook his head and chuckled. "Sorcery? What kind of power is sorcery? What about real power?"

Johnny sat up confused. "'Real power'? What's your idea of 'real power'?"

Brother Maynard smiled sincerely. "Forgiveness."

Johnny became indignant. "Forgiveness? Forgiveness! What kind of power is that? There's no power in forgiveness! Do you not see how horribly people treat me? Did you not see what those fools were doing to me in the bathroom tonight? Can't you see how my father doesn't want me? If the whole world seeks to destroy me, what possible good does forgiveness hold for me? Doesn't my very survival dictate that I use any means necessary to overcome them all and have my revenge against them?"

Brother Maynard put his head back and laughed aloud. "Dear Jesus!" he looked heavenward and prayed, "Do open this misguided young man's eyes!" He looked back down at Johnny. "Look, Johnny, do you think you're greater than Jesus?"

Johnny hesitated. "What if I were to tell you that I don't believe in Jesus?"

Brother Maynard shook his head. "I didn't ask you that! I'm well aware that you don't. But just for a moment, in your mind, pretend that Jesus truly is the perfect, guiltless Son of God. You wouldn't be greater than *Him*, would you?"

Johnny rolled his eyeballs and got real sarcastic. "No. I wouldn't. Because I'm under *original sin* and He's not!"

Brother Maynard's eyes lit up and he smiled real big. "Precisely! He was born perfect! So while you're a sinful man like the rest of us, yet you're tormented unfairly, He was not sinful, but Holy, yet he was mercilessly tormented, mocked, spit upon, rejected, scourged, and then nailed to a coarse, splintered cross beam! And while you think you're rejected by your father, His Father had to turn His back on Him while he hung on the cross because . . ."

"'. . . All our sins were upon Him at that point.'" More eyeball rolling.

"Exactly! And while you think you're all alone, His crowds of thousands all turned on Him, demanded His death, and in His dying hour He had only one friend who was brave enough to stand by His side."

"Your point being, Brother Maynard?"

Brother Maynard leaned over the supper table toward Johnny. His smile vanished, but the twinkle in his eye didn't. "My point is this: you are sinful and tormented, yet you seek revenge. Jesus was Holy and tormented, without reason," he held up a finger to accent the point, "yet what did He do on the cross?"

Johnny couldn't answer.

"He said, 'Father, *forgive* them! Not, 'Father, destroy them!' And who in history would have blamed Him if He had uttered such a response? But he forgave everyone who had mistreated Him. Yet here we have Master Johnny Cirello, who's searching for 'power,' not to do good, but to get over on all the people who have so unfairly harmed him. What good is that power, Master Cirello?"

Johnny looked around, searching his heart for an answer. His eyes lit up: "'Revenge is a dish best served cold!'"

Brother Maynard scratched his head in mock thought and said, "Didn't the Klingons say that?"

"No! It was a famous line from Russian literature! The Klingons lived to rip off the best of human elements and . . ."

Brother Maynard put both hands up and grinned. "I'm just kidding! I know all that." Brother Maynard thought for a moment. "You know, Johnny, revenge may be a dish that works best served cold. But the true cold of revenge is the chill it causes the heart. Jesus told us to love one another. He said 'the eye for an eye' deal doesn't cut it, now that He's been manifested. That will only lead to your own destruction. Love is what counts. Love and forgiveness, because He first forgave us. Even Mitchell Roush!" He winked at Johnny.

Johnny swallowed his Pepsi. "It's a good thing He forgave Mitchell. 'Cause I sure can't!"

Brother Maynard leaned back in his chair and sighed a true sigh of frustration. Shaking his head he told Johnny Cirello, "I do pray that one day, Master Cirello, you will see that revenge is not the way to go. And neither is witchcraft."

Johnny chugged his Pepsi and belched.

"Amen!" Brother Maynard said with a grin.

Johnny laughed so hard the Pepsi spurted out his nostrils.

Later that weekend, Johnny was looking at the red rose pin Brother Maynard wore on his frocks.

"Hey, Brother Maynard? What gives with the red rose?"

Brother Maynard fondled the pin on his brown outfit. "'I am not my own but I was bought with a price.'"

"Huh?"

"St. Paul wrote that. Jesus had to shed his blood in death to save me. The red rose is my symbol of Christ's blood, the greatest commodity in the universe. It's that blood, Johnny, that He shed to redeem us. I wear this pin to constantly remind me Who it is I'm living for and serving: the Redeemer Who had to shed His blood in order for me to be redeemed. When I'm reminded of His great price for me, I remember that I'm His and that I need to live for Him. That's what gives with this red rose."

Johnny thought hard about it for a moment. Then he shyly replied, "Well, I don't think He's real. But if He is, you do an excellent job of living like Him."

Years later Johnny Cirello no longer existed. He had been erased and replaced by Cyrus Moreau, Master of the Occult. Cyrus was fast working his way up in the New York coven to which he belonged. He began enacting his revenge on some of the faces from the past who had tormented him when he was defenseless. Billy Cardigan was killed in a freak elevator accident. Adam Coates was suffering in a mental institution from some unknown, tormenting psychosis. But Cyrus Moreau saved the cruelest of torture for Mitchell Roush. Slowly, bit by bit, beginning with his reproductive organs, Mitchell Roush was experiencing what doctors could only diagnose as some rare form of leprosy. With each stage Mitchell would receive anonymous letters in the mail, containing messages that cruelly mocked each new condition (Like, "How's your love life?" when his privates reached their critical stages). Cyrus wanted to believe this revenge was so sweet, so perfect; that he was getting those cretins back with these vicious curses he was casting upon them. But deep in the recesses of his soul, he felt cold. Bitter cold. And Brother Maynard would rise up so crystalline in his memory to bring conviction, never fully allowing Cyrus to enjoy his pursuit of revenge.

"Forgiveness," Cyrus would hear the words loudly and clearly. "Forgiveness." The very concept of it was so foreign to him, yet deep within his heart there was a curious longing to search out what the word truly meant. He knew that longing was planted there by Brother Maynard.

"Forgiveness."

Cyrus had to work hard to purge his soul from past memories and influences. Serving satan quickly hardens the heart. Self-worship, which is what true satanism is, is one of the most expedient methods of becoming desensitized. Cyrus Moreau was making his meteoric rise to the top of the occult world. He wanted all traces of conscience and past memories to be erased by his wicked pursuits of the dark arts. They did help. But never enough to completely purge him. Brother Maynard and his Christ were always hiding deep in the recesses of his soul.

Xavier Cirello died early in 1981. Cyrus Moreau read the news of his father's death on the front page of the New York Times. The article said that his estate was looking for his only son, Johnny Cirello, the sole heir to Xavier's fortune. Upon finishing the article in the Times, he promptly tossed the newspaper into the fireplace and watched it incinerate. Cyrus made sure that no one knew he was Johnny Cirello. Neither did he contact Xavier's estate to claim even a penny of the Cirello fortune. And he kept his busy schedule that week and went nowhere near his father's funeral.

In 1986 Cyrus Moreau was searching the obituaries of the Times to see if someone he had been paid to curse with cancer had died yet. In the obits he saw the notice announcing the death of Father Maynard Pascal. Something rose suddenly within Cyrus's heart. Just what were those feelings? He hadn't felt anything like them in years. Sweet memories of the unconditional love that man had poured on him during his years at St. Thomas Prep Academy flooded his soul. Suddenly, he missed Brother Maynard. He wished he could talk to him one last time. Those feelings were warm and sweet. He couldn't help it, though he wished he could.

Cyrus Moreau canceled all of his appointments for the day of Maynard Pascal's funeral.

An open casket funeral service for Father Maynard was held in St. Mary's Cathedral in New York City. The church was packed with over a thousand people. The atmosphere was so strange everyone took notice of it. People were joyful, smiling, not in the least bit morose or worried about where the spirit of Father Maynard might be. Who could morn the death of such a beloved man who sacrificed himself daily and lived the Life of Jesus Christ to the fullest?

Several noticed a black leather-clad, long haired mourner who sneaked in quietly and joined the service. The man looked more like Alice Cooper than someone who'd be paying last respects to a Catholic Priest.

Several of Maynard Pascal's friends and fellow priests paid respect to him in the pulpit. These words, spoken by one of them, summed up the feelings of all present:

"I cannot mourn over the death of such a man as Father Maynard. For one thing can be said of him on which we'd all agree: Father Maynard Pascal exuded the Spirit of Jesus Christ."

Everyone agreed out loud with a smile. Even Cyrus Moreau had to acknowledge the truth of the statement.

When the mass portion of the service ended, Cyrus joined the funeral line that snaked throughout the church to walk past the casket. Though hundreds stood in the long line to see Father Maynard one last time, everyone was patient, kindhearted, joyous, just as Maynard Pascal had been in his life. As people got to his body to either sprinkle holy water on him or whisper a prayer over him, everyone noted how good he looked. Even embalmed and gray headed, his face held the same peaceful, loving countenance it always had. Cyrus Moreau spoke to no one in line, but in his heart agreed with all the nice things the people around him were saying about the man in the casket. When he reached Brother Maynard, Cyrus neither prayed or sprinkled holy water on him. He simply laid a single red rose on his chest, in honor of the Christ for whom Brother Maynard lived, loved, and served on a daily basis.

If Christ was for real, the warlock had to acknowledge, then Brother Maynard did Him great credit.

Cyrus Moreau felt strange sitting on his bed in Aleister Estate, watching the sun rise, thinking about Brother Maynard. He felt that piercing Presence again, the Presence that he had set himself against as an enemy. Yet that Presence, the same that hovered about Brother Maynard, continued to come back from time to time, seemingly to haunt Cyrus with a call of true love, mercy, grace and righteousness. Why would his Enemy do that? It couldn't be true! He was wicked! Pursued wickedness with all his heart! Yet this God seemed to pursue him with that same love that Brother Maynard had for him. Why? Cyrus suddenly got a revelation sitting there on his bed: the fact that he even had the honor to know Brother Maynard was perhaps the way that God chose to show Himself to him as real.

"No!" he yelled, standing up beside his bed, pulling his covers back so he could climb back in. He *had* to deny that! For not to and to continue to live out his life as the Master of the Spirit Realm would be the ultimate indictment of himself.

But as he jumped back under his covers, there was the smiling face of Brother Maynard, deep in the recesses of his heart . . .

FORTY-FOUR

Frank Kranac was reading a machinists manual from work at 5:55 that Monday morning when his kitchen phone rang.

"What?"

"Uh . . . Frankie?" Frank recognized it was Greggy Richards' cowardly voice. "Um . . . you awake? I didn't wake you up, did I?"

"What do you want?" Frank snarled impatiently.

"Uh . . . Jimmy's here, and he's drunk as a dog. He's been drinking all night . . ."

"What do I care about that?" Frank shouted.

"Ummmm . . . well, he's drunk because he's been spilling his guts to me about something that happened to him last night."

"What?" with even more impatience.

"Well . . . something happened to him . . . that . . . I'm afraid . . . really affects *you*, Frankie. I think we got big problems. I mean *real* big problems!"

"What's happened? What's the 'big problem'?"

Greggy Richards finally blurted it all out quickly, like that would somehow make the news more palatable to Frank, or somehow help quench his wrath: "Tony Vero found Jimmy at Cherries last night and he shot at him a couple of times and he got Jimmy to tell him everything about you!"

Silence.

"Tony Vero knows you're Bernie Lokawski, and about you and Todd Falco! . . . Are you there? . . . Jimmy's real sorry, Frankie, but that Vero tried to kill him right in front of everyone in the whole bar! He said Jimmy had to tell him everything or he'd blow his head off . . ."

"Put Jimmy on the phone," came the low, satanic growl from Frankie.

"Uh . . . he can't hardly hear, Frankie, his ears are ringing so loudly . . . he can barely hear me! . . . uh . . . because of the gunshots Tony fired at him . . ."

"Put him on the line NOW!" he roared.

There was a long pause on the other end. Frank could hear Greggy ordering Jimmy to get on the line. Jimmy whimpered like a child, not wanting to take the phone. After about thirty seconds of that nonsense, Jimmy finally got on the line:

"Hey, Frankie . . ." embarrassment and shame quivered in his voice.

"What all did you tell Tony Vero about me?"

"What?" Jimmy shouted. "I can hardly hear you, Frankie! My ears are ringing so loudly . . ."

"WHAT DID YOU TELL HIM ABOUT ME?"

"Uh . . . I . . . can hardly hear you . . . you'll have to talk louder . . . you see, Tony Vero had a gun and shot it twice right in my face! And I haven't really been able to hear since then . . . and . . . Frankie? . . . are you there?"

An enraged Frank Kranac had grabbed an old metal stool in his kitchen and was bashing it on the floor one-handed, roaring with frustration . . .

"Frankie? . . . Frankie . . . ?"

Greggy grabbed the phone back. "Frankie? Frankie? It's Greggy . . . I can hardly hear you now! Are you there . . . ? We must have a bad connection . . . the line must be going dead . . . Hey! We have to get going to work, but we'll come talk to you later on today! How's that? Uh . . . the line seems to be going dea . . ."

Greggy quickly hung up.

Frank Kranac threw down his phone, tossed the tangled remains of the metal chair into the dining room, and punched a hole through one of his kitchen cupboards. His entire fortune was now in jeopardy . . .

Ray Kirkland felt terrible when he woke up that Monday morning. He went to get up to go to the study to read his Bible and pray. But instead of hopping to it like he usually did, he had to slowly slide his feet off the side of the bed and just sit there on the edge for a moment. His head hurt bad. And his chest and left shoulder felt real tight. He almost felt like he was coming down with the flu.

Shelly noticed, half asleep, that he was just sitting there. He never did that. He was a morning person who usually popped right up and got started the moment he awoke.

"What's up, Baby?" she asked in a groggy voice without rolling over to look at him.

"I don't know. I just don't feel good. Is there some sort of bug going around?"

"Noooo . . . but there's some sort of healing going around; it's called 'Jesus' healing.'"

"Well, go on and pray for me, Sweety. I need it. I ain't got time to mess with this."

Shelly reached a hand over and put it on his lower back. With a voice still slurred with sleepiness, she prayed, "Father . . . heal my Raymond. He needs it. Your Son provided it. Break the root of this curse and free him right now . . . in Jesus' name." She pulled her hand back and went back to sleep.

"Thanks, Sweety." He lifted his left arm in the air and rotated it, trying to work that tightness out of his shoulder. "Dumb old sick bug," he murmured. Ray Kirkland didn't realize that what was coming upon him was far more serious than any bug.

He thought about what a busy day he had ahead of him. He was going to get that search warrant to get into Tony Vero's safe deposit box at Reeves Bank. He knew the youngest Vero was hiding evidence there. He had to be.

He felt his forehead. It was warm and his temples were throbbing. His chest actually hurt.

"Man, Lord," he prayed aloud. "I can't mess with some dumb ol' sickness right now." He stood up, slowly. First he had to pray, meet with his Father for a while. Then he could work on busting open the Falco case and the Veros. He slowly sauntered out of the bedroom. He made his mind up as he painfully walked down the stairs: he was just going to go about his business, ignore how he felt, and accomplish all he had set in his heart to do.

But things didn't work out that way for Ray.

Tammi Bannerman was very nervous as she drove to the Holiday Inn to meet State Attorney General Michael Davis. Edgar Waters told the twenty-four year old undercover investigator to be there by 6:15. Davis wanted his "Carmichael Vero Task Force" to meet their inside link to VECO. And he had a specific assignment he needed her to fulfill. She had seen enough of the strange and mysterious going-ons at VECO to know something was up there. She realized she was the key to this investigation. If she fumbled the ball, the whole thing could blow up on all of them. Her heart beat wildly as she pulled into the Holiday Inn parking lot.

Edgar Waters met Tammi in the lobby. He couldn't contain his attraction to her when he saw her. She had on a dazzling business dress, ready for a day's work at VECO. He did try to bury his emotions and remain professional, though.

"You look great today, Tammi," he said without a smile as he led her down the hall.

She noted the spark of infatuation he was trying to bury beneath his stoicism, and was flattered. "Thank you, Eddie. Is the gang all here?"

"I don't know. I've not seen any of them yet this morning."

"I can't wait to meet 'Frick and Frack,' you were talking about on the phone last night. They sound like pistols."

"Captain Gandtz and Lt. Saucier? Doc Holiday and Wyatt Earp live again. Stay on your guard with them."

At 6:15 Edgar Waters brought Tammi Bannerman into the "war room" to meet State Attorney General Michael Davis. Davis had set up the room overnight. Pictures of Carmichael Vero and the Family members, all taken without their knowledge by Edgar, hung on a huge bulletin board. A table in the middle of the room had a laptop computer that contained the complete files of Carmichael that Davis and Waters had gathered over the years. The laptop was connected to a multimedia projector, which was aimed at a large white screen that hung from the wall. Beside it was another table with a small sound system to study the audio recordings Edgar had made over the years.

Michael Davis was already showered and dressed in a crisp business suit, busily writing notes at one of the tables. He was the consummate man of discipline.

"Did you sleep at all, Captain?" Edgar asked him as he and Tammi entered the room. Davis turned and smiled cordially at them both. "I got my customary five hours of sleep, Sergeant." He looked at the attractive, black investigator with Edgar. "This young lady must be our undercover agent at VECO." He stuck his hand out and introduced himself. Tammi shook his hand firmly. "I'm well aware of who you are, Sir. You got my vote." He chuckled. "I may not next time after what I'm about to put you through at VECO! I appreciate you joining us so early. It's imperative that I meet you before you go to work this week. We need to prep you about what we need you to do for us."

Edgar looked around. "Where's Gandtz and Saucier? Getting their beauty sleep?"

"You kiddin' me? They were down here at five reading all my files on Carmichael Vero. They also heard all of your recordings from this week. They're in the restaurant getting us all a bite to eat. You have that transmitter we need, Edgar?"

"Right here." Edgar pulled out a standard-looking VECO office pen from his pocket. He handed it to Davis, who held it up to Tammi.

"You recognize this?" Davis asked her.

"Of course. VECO has 'em on every desk and in every cubicle. Hundreds of them."

"Well, this one isn't like all the other hundreds. Edgar's wired this thing for sound. This is a transmitter with a microphone. We're going to need you to get it onto Carmichael's desk sometime today. That possible?"

She grabbed it and clicked it. Out came a working pen-point. She smiled proudly at Edgar. "I'm impressed, Eddie!" Then she turned to look at Michael Davis with a grim expression. "I'll make it possible. But do you have a wire order from a judge?"

Edgar looked embarrassed. "Tammi! He's the State Attorney General. He knows the law . . ."

"And I'm impressed that Ms. Bannerman does, too. She knows that anything we secretly record without a court order for the wire will likely be inadmissible evidence in a trial against Carmichael Vero. I'm working on that court order, Ms. Bannerman. As soon as I can get a judge's order we'll notify you." Now his expression turned grim. "You realize the risk you run by putting that pen in front of Carmichael? We believe Ed Larsky sweeps that office daily for bugs. If you get caught bugging it, I can't guarantee the posse here will be able to rush in fast enough to rescue you. We can't get too close to Carmichael Vero's office."

"Larsky's a professional killer, Sweetheart." Leo Gandtz startled the trio from behind. They turned and faced him as he and Saucier set several breakfast trays down on a table. "He's a dangerous man. He knows his business. I've seen enough of 'em to know the difference. You better heed the Attorney General's warning. Vero and Larsky play for keeps."

Tammi looked offended. "I'm well aware of Carmichael Vero and Ed Larsky," Tammi spoke up. "I've been watching them right under their noses for the past six months. And I'm not your 'Sweetheart.'"

"Uh-oh," Edgar mumbled to Michael Davis.

The Attorney General went to diffuse the tension. "Ms. Tammi Bannerman, this is Captain Leo Gandtz of the SBI, and his partner, Lt. Saucier."

Gandtz and Saucier merely nodded. Tammi nodded too, and said, "I've heard a bit about you two. Seems to all be true . . ."

"Tammi, it's okay," Edgar tried to stop her.

Michael Davis held up his hand sternly to them all and said, "That's enough." He looked disappointed at the four of them. "I've not even had the Carmichael Vero Task Force assembled for ninety seconds, and we're already divided." He looked at Gandtz and Saucier and pointed at the picture of Warren Zann on the wall. "You two are still shaken about being yanked from your investigation and sent down here to mine. You're taking it out on Sergeant Waters and Ms. Bannerman. Knock it off! They've been the ground breakers on this case ever since I found out no one in this State was interested in investigating Carmichael Vero. Leo, you may not favor private investigators, but you know me and *I'm* vouching for the credibility of Edgar Waters. The Marines decorated him for his work in Panama and Desert Storm. I hired him because I've seen his outstanding work. That good enough, Captain?"

Leo Gandtz's face was soured, but he nodded respectfully and answered "Yes, Sir."

Davis popped him on his shoulder. "Thank you, Leo! I knew I could count on you." He addressed them all, again, pointing to the seven pictures on the wall, including the deceased Pete Vero and his son Tony. "Don't you all want to put that conglomerate of criminals behind bars?"

The four of them nodded.

"Then we are unified! One last question: is there anyone here who objects to me praying for this task force before we get down to business?"

Gandtz looked speechless. Waters shrugged and Bannerman smiled a hopeful smile. Saucier looked a little green around the gills, though.

"Lieutenant Saucier?" Davis addressed him. "You got a problem with it?"

"Well sir," he said, "I don't really believe in God."

Davis laughed. "Well, He must believe in you, 'cause I prayed that He'd give me the best people for this job and I got you. Leo? You look dumbstruck. You got a problem with me praying?"

Leo shrugged indifferently. "You're my ex-oh. I'm game if this is what you want. Doesn't matter to me."

He looked around at them. "I want us to join hands, people. Lieutenant, you can step back. This is voluntary and I'm going to pray for you anyway whether you like it or not."

Saucier hesitated, then reached over and grabbed their hands. "Aw, I'll join in. I don't want us all to be jinxed."

"Yeah," Michael Davis laughed. "I don't want us to be jinxed, either."

He prayed an awesome prayer over the Carmichael Vero Task Force, qualifying them before God for the huge task at hand, asking Him for all His blessings, wisdom, and protection over them.

It was an effective prayer God was going to answer . . .

Larsky banged on Tommy Wheeler's back door for ten minutes. The hit man finally awoke and let him in. Wheeler's hair was going in twenty different directions. He wore only his boxers and tank top over his scrawny body. He led Larsky down into the basement. The place was musty, chilly and dimly lit. Bits and pieces of pistols, rifles, and machine guns lay atop workbenches strewn with electrical and timing devices. All that amid hundreds of tools.

Wheeler knocked off some filthy rags and shell casings from two dusty barstools to clear a place for him and Larsky. He rubbed the sleep from his eyes and bummed a cigarette from Larsky. "What gives, man? It ain't even seven o'clock yet."

"Listen up, Tommy! I ain't even had two hours sleep and I'm punchy. I'm here to tell you there's been a big change of plans regarding your contract to kill Tony Vero."

Wheeler looked even more confused as he sat up on an old stool. "What kind of change?"

"Carmichael Vero's taking over the contract."

Tommy Wheeler's mouth dropped open and the cigarette fell to his bare thigh and burned him. He slapped it off his leg with a jolt.

Larsky laughed at him. "Now that's the funniest thing I've seen all week!"

Wheeler spit on the burn and rubbed his leg. "You told Carmichael about your contract with me to kill Glory Boy? And he didn't kill *you*? I thought Tony Vero was the crown prince around all those snotty Veros. And now Carmichael's gonna pay me to carry out the hit? He must be smokin' dope . . ."

"It's his contract now. Meet me behind that construction site on Forrester Road off Route 51. I'll give your final orders there. But there's more to the contract, now."

Wheeler picked his cigarette up off the dusty cement floor. "I'm listening."

"Carmichael wants Tony to disappear. He wants no traces of his body ever found."

"Well, I was going to do the same for you . . ."

"You don't understand!" Larsky said, dragging off his smoke and staring a hole through Tommy Wheeler's head. "This is Carmichael Vero you're working for, now. If it was my contract and Tony's skeleton showed up a year later with a bullet hole or three through his skull, I wouldn't care. But if Carmichael Vero wants Tony to be killed and never seen again, you better make sure that's exactly what he gets for his money. There can't be any trace of blood or gunpowder or evidence at the murder site. And if his rotting corpse ever does show up somewhere, you can bet Carmichael will be paying *me* fifty thousand to put some holes in *you*! You dig, brother?"

Tommy got downright offended. "What are you lecturing me for? I've been a professional as long as you have . . ."

Larsky pointed his cigarette angrily at Wheeler: "'Cause you ain't ever worked directly for a man like Carmichael Vero! He ain't some second rate piker payin' you to smoke some lowlife in an alley. This is 'A' level you're playin' on, now. Everything has to be perfect. And since I work directly with Carmichael, my safety's on the line just as much as his. So that's why you're getting this pep talk from me whether you like it or not." He puffed his smoke one more time and stomped it out on the floor. "Now meet me at noon and be ready to get to work. If Tony has his act together, he should be finished with his work for us and then ready for you to come send him off to La-la Land once and for all." He held out his hand. "We on?"

Tommy nodded, still disgusted, and grabbed Larsky's hand. They went through the Plague's handshake, Larksy slapped him lightly on his forehead, and headed up the stairs and left. Tommy Wheeler stayed in his basement and updated his plans for killing Tony Vero and disposing of his body.

Frank Kranac burst through the back door of Greggy and Jimmy Richards' rural Wampum home; glass, wood splinters fell to the floor. Both Greggy and Jimmy had fallen fast asleep in their bedrooms after waiting all night to call Frank; they didn't notice the noise. Frank stormed through their kitchen and living room. This was his first "visit" to their home. The old place looked like some second-rate frat house. Neon beer signs flashed on the walls. There were posters and magazine pages of nude women and cars taped up everywhere. Pornographic magazines were stacked dozens high all over the place (ironically, the magazines were all purchased at the Beaver Falls outlet of Warren Zann's VECO-backed chain of pornography stores). Frank stomped down the hallway and straight into the first bedroom he found: there was Jimmy, passed out in his bed. The room was a mess and reeked of Jimmy's stale beer breath. Frank lumbered angrily over to his bed. He snatched the drunken twenty-six year old out from under the covers by his arms. Jimmy awoke . . .

"Ahhhhhh! Wha' is this? Help!"

. . . and struggled in his grip.

Greggy heard the commotion in the next room and snapped awake.

Frank dragged Jimmy violently out of his room and down the hall toward the other bedroom. Jimmy squealed like an animal caught in a predator's grasp.

Greggy grabbed his huge .44 Magnum from under his bed and pointed it at the doorway of his bedroom, waiting to see who had invaded their home.

When he got to Greggy's doorway, Frank hoisted Jimmy's flailing body out in front of him like he was a captured pig. Greggy realized he was sighting his gun right on Jimmy's chest as Frank carried him in. Greggy's eyes widened with terror when he saw it was Frank Kranac who'd invaded their home. Kranac saw the long .44 in Greggy's shaky hands and slammed Jimmy to the ground.

"Drop that gun before I rip your head off your shoulders!" Kranac roared at Greggy.

Greggy, scared out of his wits by the angry roar, threw the gun several feet across the room and cowered into the back corner of his wall on the edge of his bed.

Frank reached down, picked Jimmy up off the ground in one spectacular show of strength, and tossed him down onto Greggy's bed. The bed bounced up and down with the impact, bouncing both Jimmy and Greggy down on top of one another. They cowered together against the wall like two children being punished by an angry father. Frank leaned over them and pointed his thick, grimy finger in their faces:

"How could you two be so stupid?" he shouted. He grabbed Jimmy by the hair, pulled him over to him, and screamed in his ear as loud as he could, "CAN YOU HEAR ME NOW?" He pushed him back over toward Greggy. "Why did you tell Tony Vero everything about me?"

"He . . . he was going to kill me, Frankie! He was a madman, I tell you! He had a gun and fired at my head twice! I still can't hear, both my ears are still ringing so loudly . . ."

"Well, now that you ratted me out to him, who knows who he's ran to and told all about me! For sure he's gone to whoever was paying Todd Falco to buy my stash!"

"I'm sorry, Frankie!" Jimmy cried, tears of fear pouring from his eyes. "I'm so sorry! Don't kill me! Please!"

Then Kranac pointed at Greggy and yelled, "And I still hold you responsible for all this, big mouth!"

"What?" Greggy asked incredulously.

"Yeah!" Jimmy looked at his older brother. "This is *your* fault!"

"Shut up, weasel!" Frank swatted at Jimmy, then looked back at Greggy. "You are the big mouth who spilled the beans about me to Tony Vero the first time, when all you had to do was just blow him off! You are the one I hold personally responsible for this whole mess! If you hadn't 'a' told Tony Vero about me in the first place, he wouldn't 'a' been bangin' on my door all weekend and following me around! This is your fault!" He stepped back and kicked a chair across the room in frustration. "Both of you are mealy-mouthed weasels afraid of the likes of Tony Vero! Well, today you two are going to make amends for all this! Let me tell you what you two are going to do!"

They both looked up with ultimate interest. If Frank Kranac was about to give them a job, that meant he wasn't going to kill them. At least not right then in their own house.

"You two dummies are gonna go out and get Tony Vero alive for me! First, you're gonna go find him. Then, when no one's lookin', you're gonna snatch him up alive and keep him on ice for me until I can get ahold of him myself! I want him alive so I can find out who it is he's told about me! You two morons understand that?"

They both yessed with great reverence, sincerity, and gratitude, still trembling for their lives on the bed.

"And when you do get ahold of him you two nitwits better not let him outta your sight until *I* get there to take care of him. You got that?"

More yesses and groveling.

"'Cause if he somehow gets away from you," he grabbed Greggy by the throat and smacked his head up against the wall, "you, Greggy Richards, are gonna pay with your life! You got that?"

A bulging-eyed Greggy wheezed a tiny "yes."

"What happens to rats?"

Greggy tried to answer, but only a gasp came out.

"Answer me!" Frank yelled.

"Rats . . . get . . . stomped!" Greggy wheezed with the last of his breath.

Frank Kranac released his throat. Greggy bent over on the bed, sucking for air. Frank pointed at them one more time.

"You have until the sun goes down tonight to get Tony Vero on ice. If you don't and I have to go get him myself you can bet I'll be comin' right back here, now that I have an open door to come and go through when I want!" He turned and spotted Greggy's telephone on his bedroom desk. Frank snatched it up, yanked the wire out of the wall, and threw the whole apparatus at Greggy. It bounced off his leg with a ring-a-ling and slammed to the floor with a dull clang. "You're right, Greggy! You *do* have a bad connection!" He moved toward the door. "You call me when you have Vero! And you better not screw this up!"

With that, Frank Kranac left their room. Neither of them dared breathe or move, but listened until they heard him lumber out their kitchen, slam his car door shut, and start the engine. Then Greggy silently moved over to his window and looked out the blinds, hardly even breathing until he saw Frank's black Galaxie turn the corner of their house and speed off down the highway. Then they both fell back onto the bed, panting with relief.

Greggy massaged his chafed throat. He suddenly looked aggravated at Jimmy, then struck his brother over the top of his head.

"Ouch!" Jimmy yelled, reddening in the face.

"'Yeah, Greggy!'" his older brother imitated him in a mocking, whining voice. "'This is *your* fault!' You little moron! Why's he always blaming me for all this mess? Why doesn't he ever blame *you*?"

"Well, what about *you*, Dirty Harry?" Jimmy pointed at the .44 lying on the floor atop Greggy's dirty laundry. "Why didn't you shoot him when you had the chance? Then this nightmare would be all over!"

Greggy went over and picked his pistol up off the floor. He cocked the hammer back and pointed the gun angrily at Jimmy's head. Jimmy flinched with fright and covered his face. Greggy pulled the trigger. The hammer clicked lamely, all six chambers of the gun empty. Jimmy gasped and held his chest, white-faced, panting.

"You're wrong, Bro," Greggy said sadly, lowering the gun. "If we don't find Tony Vero and capture him alive today, our nightmare will just be beginning."

FORTY-FIVE

Sheriff DeBona was waiting by Ray Kirkland's desk when Ray got to the Sheriff's Department at 8:00 that morning. Ray arrived in great "discomfort" (he would never use the word "pain"). His chest was tightening even worse by the minute. His left arm was tingling, his heart felt like it was thumping up in his throat, and his forehead was beading with sweat. He had no idea what was going on or where these symptoms could be coming from. He took excellent care of himself. He was in perfect condition, in the top percentile of men his age.

Sheriff DeBona didn't look too good, himself. As Ray sauntered over to his desk he noticed the man's face was sheet white, and he had a queer, unconfident expression that was definitely out of character. They studied each other curiously as Ray plopped his briefcase on his desk. Then, eyeing each other intently, they both blurted out at the exact same time:

"What's wrong with *you*?"

Ray snickered as he walked around and unlocked his desk drawer. "We been working together too long."

"I guess so," DeBona acknowledged. "What is wrong with you?"

Ray shook his head. "I'm just not feeling too good this morning. You look like you've seen a ghost. What's going on?"

DeBona looked deadly serious at him. "You and I've been summoned to the Holiday Inn."

Ray did not look happy as he rummaged in his desk drawer. "Summoned? By who? You're the Sheriff, for goodness sakes. Who summons you?"

DeBona looked around to make sure no one could hear them. "The State Attorney General."

Ray looked up, shocked. "Michael Davis? What's he doing at the Holiday Inn? Holdin' a convention? I don't have time for this! I have a search warrant in the works that's gonna nail Tony Vero . . ."

"We're going to have to make the time. I spoke to Davis on the phone. He sent some private investigator out here to get us. He specifically asked for you and me."

Ray was really turning cranky by that point. "I am about to nail Carmichael Vero! This Todd Falco case and Tony Vero are leading me right to him! I . . ."

"That's exactly what Michael Davis wants to see you about."

Ray stood upright. "Huh?"

"He knows all about your investigation. More than I even know about it, in fact."

"How?"

"I don't know. But he was pretty specific about what you've been doing. He knows a great many details. You meet with Tony Vero out at Stop 'n' Sock yesterday?"

"Yeah!" Ray was surprised. "How's he know that?"

"I dunno. But he does." Sheriff DeBona suddenly got an embarrassed looked on his face. "That's not all."

"No? What else?"

The Sheriff looked nervously out the window at the overcast spring morning. "He . . . Michael Davis wants to know if you still have 'File 13' in your possession."

Ray could see the utter humiliation on the Sheriff's face. But Ray didn't gloat. He was too shocked by the fact that the State Attorney General knew about 'File 13' to gloat about it. He pointed to his bottom desk drawer. "I got the whole thing right down there."

"Well," DeBona said with a sigh of humiliation, "He wants you to bring it along, too."

Ray looked him in the eye. "What's going on here, Sheriff?"

He shrugged. "Something that's apparently a whole lot bigger than you and me."

Tony Vero was shaving in his bathroom, but he couldn't look at himself in the mirror. He felt too ashamed to look himself in the eyes. He was getting ready for his big ten o'clock meeting with Carmichael. He did indeed have the Todd Falco mystery wrapped up and was ready to plop it in Carmichael's lap. This was supposed to be his key to freedom, but instead it was triggering more confusion. Instead of making wonderful plans for his new life, he could only think of his Uncle Joseph's words from the night before:

"What do you think Carmichael and Larsky are going to do . . . when you turn over those people who whacked Todd Falco and stole our money? . . . You think they're going to give them some sort of holy absolution to pardon their sins against the Family?"

Tony's eyes watered as he tried to steady the razor on his neck. However, Joseph's prophetic, disturbing words were so vivid:

"No, you know what Carmichael's going to have Larsky do. Yet, even though you know what they're really going to do to these losers, I guarantee that you're still going to turn them over to Carmichael and Larsky in the morning."

A single tear rolled down Tony's cheek, absorbed by the shaving cream on his face.

"Because . . . you're more than willing to win your freedom by getting someone else's blood spilled! And then you'll have another Ft. Lauderdale type nightmare to deal with. Except this time, you won't be able to blame it on the Family and your own naivet•. This time, you'll be the one who shed the blood!"

Then Tony vividly saw himself firing that gun in Jimmy Richards' face the night before, willing to hurt someone else to get what *he* wanted.

"What kind of man are you?"

Now he did look himself in the eyes: "I'm a Vero!" he said out loud. And it hurt bad.

Edgar Waters met Sheriff DeBona and Detective Kirkland in the lobby of the Holiday Inn. He lead them back to the war room. Inside State Attorney General Michael Davis was looking at a computer file up on the projection screen with SBI Captain Leo Gandtz and Lt. Saucier. DeBona and Kirkland looked around at all the high tech equipment and the poster-sized pictures of Carmichael Vero and the other Family members. Their curiosity was greatly aroused.

Michael Davis went over to greet them. Gandtz and Saucier eyed them suspiciously.

"Gentlemen," the State Attorney General extended his hand to the Sheriff and Detective Kirkland. "I'm Michael Davis. I appreciate you two clearing your schedules to join us this morning."

They introduced themselves and shook his hand.

Davis stepped back and held his hands out cordially. "Welcome to the Carmichael Vero Task Force. This is our war room. Behind me are Captain Leo Gandtz and Lt. Saucier of the SBI. They are the best we have in the state." Nods and grunts of acknowledgment. Davis acknowledged their wide-eyed state. "You two look like Alice who just stepped into Wonderland. I know you have a ton of questions about what's going on. I will give you a full explanation. But the reason I summoned you both here is Detective Kirkland." He looked up at Ray, and realized the man looked ill. "You all right? We haven't scared you today, have we?"

Ray shook his head. "Oh, no, Sir. I'm just feeling uncharacteristically under the weather this morning, that's all," Ray underplayed the seriousness of his condition. His left hand was nearly numb by that point.

"Detective, we want to debrief you concerning the Todd Falco case."

"Okay," Ray said, his head woozy. "Then you'll tell me how you even know about it?"

"Yes. We will. What do you know about Mr. Falco?"

"He's a VECO employee. A marketing strategist for their subsidiaries. A womanizer who never spent a whole lot of time at home. His wife believes he's involved in drugs, but he apparently kept it well hidden from her. She doesn't know any details about his drug trade. She just greatly suspects he deals. There were only some minor traces of cocaine found in his home, so he wasn't running a drug lab out of his cellar or anything like that. Last Tuesday, Todd left home lightly packed and he and his car haven't been seen since then. He supposedly took a leave of absence from VECO last Monday, according to some paperwork I was shown, but that paperwork was dubious."

"Who was responsible for that paperwork?"

"The head secretary at VECO showed it to me, but it had been filled out and signed by Ed Larsky the office manager and Carmichael Vero himself with only a stamped signature from Mr. Falco."

Gandtz spoke up. "Where's Tony Vero fit into all this?"

"Tony is VECO's private investigator. They set up a private security and investigations business for him as a VECO subsidiary and retain him as their chief investigator. According to the hot air at VECO, Carmichael was suspicious of Todd Falco after he disappeared. Apparently Carmichael doesn't hire any troublemakers or people with records . . ."

"That's correct," Edgar Waters confirmed.

"So he wants Tony to find Falco and dig up all the dirt he can on him so Carmichael can expose him and fire him to prove he's the concerned citizen he's trying to appear to be."

"But you've seen deeper into Tony's investigation, haven't you Detective?"

"Yes, Sir. First of all, I believe Tony is hiding vital information taken directly from Todd Falco's home. I believe that information proves that Todd Falco's involved in narcotics. I also believe this information links him and his drug business directly to people at VECO."

Davis, Waters, and Gandtz all looked at each other and nodded at that bombshell.

"Like whom, Detective?" Davis asked.

"I believe Todd Falco deals drugs for Carmichael Vero himself, Sir."

More nods and glances of confirmation from the Task Force members. Edgar Waters pretended to pull the handle of a one armed bandit and sang out, "Cha-ching!"

Ray continued. "Those are my suspicions. Carmichael's had that pit bull Ed Larsky out grilling Todd Falco's wife and chasin' after Tony Vero. They don't seem to like how he's investigating things. I caught Tony and Larsky fighting at Kay Falco's Saturday night. I had to arrest Mr. Larsky. He's facing charges on threatening and assaulting an officer of the law."

Their eyes all lit up. Edgar Waters pointed at Ray. "You arrested Ed Larsky?"

"You didn't know that? I'm surprised. Yes I did. Carmichael paid his bail and he's out for now, of course. But there appears to be a lot of turmoil at VECO since Todd's disappearance. I don't think it's a coincidence. It really looks like they've hired Tony Vero to find out what happened to Mr. Falco so he can run interference between us and VECO, and keep us from finding out the truth. He certainly appears to be obstructing this investigation in a big way. Like that information from Mr. Falco's house. I believe Tony's hiding it in a safe deposit box at Reeves Bank. In fact I was putting in for the search warrant this morning so I could confiscate the box today."

"That all you know about Todd Falco?"

"No. Tony's also been to visit the number one G in the area about Todd Falco's disappearance. Tony went to see one Benny Miller, a major dealer who went down hard with his whole gang on Saturday night. He's been singing like a bird about Tony and Todd Falco. And he says Todd's been dealing him his weekly drug supplies for years, and he thinks that Todd is somehow working drugs for the Veros at VECO. He corroborates my story, believing Tony is trying to do the legwork for VECO to protect them from whatever's happened to Todd Falco."

Edgar Waters turned to Davis and Gandtz. "I read about that Benny Miller arrest. The police said in the paper that Miller and his gang were armed to the gills, and were preparing for a gang war because of those two other drug lords who were killed Friday night."

"I was informed of that," Davis said. "What were the names of those drug lords?"

"Jermichael DeVries and Stephen McClintlock," Gandtz spoke up. "I heard about 'em, too. DeVries was blown up by a car bomb, and McClintlock was gunned down on his property with several other people."

"All this the same week Falco disappears." Davis noted gravely.

Ray spoke up: "And Benny Miller told the Sheriff and me yesterday that Todd Falco supplied Jermichael DeVries and his drug gang, too."

"Whoa!" Davis said, stroking his chin. "This can't all be a coincidence."

"What do you think happened to Todd Falco, Detective?"

"Well, he could have cut Carmichael's throat and run off with his money."

"But you don't believe that, do you?"

"Well . . ." he looked over at Sheriff DeBona, who was pokerfaced. "No, Sir. I don't."

"You've been a proponent of something referred to as 'File 13,' Detective. Did you bring a copy of that file?"

Ray opened his briefcase and pulled out a thick manila envelope. He handed it to Davis. "I've never quite been fond of the title 'File 13', Sir. I like to think of it as 'The Black Widow File.'"

Davis opened the envelope and looked inside. "'Black Widow'?"

"Yes, Sir. Local gangland legend has it that someone's been luring our county drug dealers into buys then taking them out for their money and stash. Kind of like a black widow draws other black widows into their nests and uses them as prey. I have twelve unsolved cases there. All suspected drug dealers. All last spotted here in Beaver County. All disappeared without a trace. Eight of their cars with them."

Davis looked up at Detective Kirkland and Sheriff DeBona. "Well, how come this case file has never had a full investigation?"

Kirkland looked over at DeBona. The Sheriff looked embarrassed: "I've . . . uh . . . not felt that such an investigation would be prudent, Sir. Spending so much money and man hours trying to search out known criminals who've probably just fled the area to get away from suspicion or arrest. The taxpayers of Beaver County aren't interested in the welfare and well-being of known criminals."

Davis looked back at Kirkland who didn't hesitate to reply: "None of these twelve have ever turned up anywhere around the globe. I've done every sort of research I could on them. They are not showing up anywhere."

Davis looked over the file some more. "This all looks substantial to me, Sheriff."

DeBona shrugged, indicating that it didn't matter to him what anyone thought. "So what if it is? What does this matter to you, Sir?"

The Attorney General looked a bit irritated at the question. "It matters because of this: if there is such a character as this 'Black Widow' who's preying solely on drug dealers, and he's preyed upon Todd Falco, then we have more evidence against VECO and a possible witness who can testify that Todd was dealing for Carmichael Vero, or at least using his money. But," Davis sighed, "this is your jurisdiction over here. And your business. So, Detective, you're gut instinct is that Todd Falco took money from Carmichael Vero for some sort of drug deal and was taken in by this 'Black Widow' character like all these others?"

"Yes, Sir."

Davis handed Ray back the file. "You've been a tremendous help to us, Detective. You've filled in quite a lot of missing puzzle pieces for us, as I knew you would. I know you're anxious to find out what I'm doing here." Davis pointed to the photos on the wall. "What you see on the wall there is an organization called the Family. The Family has been operating a crime syndicate from within Beaver County for years, based in Carmichael Vero's VECO offices. The Family specializes in heavy narcotics trafficking and pornography. Their influences reach all the way east across the state and into portions of Ohio and West Virginia. They have eluded the law, suspicion, and investigation. Until now. Any questions?"

Sheriff DeBona slowly scratched the top of his head and looked up at Detective Kirkland. Ray shrugged at him and walked over to look at the photos on the wall. They were both completely overwhelmed.

"Pardon our speechlessness, Sir," DeBona smirked at Davis. "But you have our top businessmen of Beaver County up there on that wall."

"Not at all, Sheriff. I understand this is quite overwhelming. It has been for all of us."

"Carmichael Vero's made himself a living legend around these parts," DeBona said. "He's almost single-handedly been credited with turning Beaver County around because of the success of VECO."

Davis nodded in agreement. "VECO is a tremendous accomplishment, for a former Mafioso. But it's been built up to front Carmichael Vero's continued underworld activities. VECO is the great wall that camouflages the Family. Detective Kirkland has had insight enough to peer over that wall."

"Makes no sense, Sir," DeBona shook his head. "VECO's had to have made Vero a multimillionaire, several times over. He's had all the success a person could want. Why's he still need the drugs and vice?"

Davis nodded back to Captain Gandtz. "Tell him, Leo."

The bald-headed Gandtz crossed his arms. "It's the juice. These wiseguys can't live without the juice. Once they've tasted it, they're hooked for life. Carmichael Vero's got to have that power, that juice to keep him electrified. You can't get that legitimately. I've caught a hundred others like him. Once a wiseguy, always a wiseguy."

"How long's this been going on?" DeBona asked.

"I believe since VECO was founded, nineteen years ago," Davis said.

"Then why haven't you investigated it before now? Why haven't we ever gotten a whiff of the Family before? This is the first time I've ever heard of it."

"Star Trek!" Edgar Waters spoke up.

"What?" a confused DeBona asked.

"Star Trek. The Klingon cloaking device. The one that made them invisible. I've been secretly investigating Carmichael Vero and the Family for six years. And the one conclusion I've come to is this: they have some sort of weirdo protection, one that seems to make them invisible to everyone's eyes."

"Witchcraft," Ray Kirkland whispered, as he stared at Tony Vero's picture. It was all starting to make sense to him. Witchcraft manipulates and obscures the truth. That's why Holy Spirit spoke the word to him the Thursday before when he first entered VECO. Somehow there was witchcraft involved at VECO. He didn't bother to mention this to the others.

Davis continued. "Sgt. Waters is onto something, though I don't believe it's Captain Kirk and the Klingons. I've been unsuccessfully attempting to get a state-wide investigation of Vero and VECO under way for years. No one would cooperate. I've had every door slammed in my face. I've even checked to see if he was tied to high ranking law enforcement officials."

"Was he?" the Sheriff asked.

"Nope. No ties."

Ray Kirkland turned around and faced Michael Davis. "The Sheriff mentioned that you knew things about my current investigation. Things like my conversation with Tony Vero yesterday."

Davis nodded. "Yup."

"How, Sir?"

Davis pointed at Edgar Waters. Edgar was an ear to ear grin. "Sgt. Waters was the communications and surveillance expert in my battalion my last two years in the Marines." He pointed at the high-tech audio system on the table. "He can record a fly burping at five hundred yards."

"You've been recording me?" Ray asked.

"We've been monitoring VECO and the Family. As you've begun to investigate the disappearance of Todd Falco and uncovered things about the Family, we've caught some of it on tape, Detective. You've gone quite deep into the Family's business, without even realizing how close you are to it. I'm quite impressed with your work."

"I do have one question for you, Mr. Davis," Ray asked.

"Shoot."

"I remember Carmichael Vero's trial. You were the prosecutor in that trial. I remember the assassination of your witness, the trial being thrown out for lack of evidence. Now that you're State Attorney General, don't you think someone's going to bring up a conflict of interests in this investigation you're starting?"

"They might," Davis smiled slyly. "But there's nothing I can do about what people think. And I've got the governor's blessing. I'm not living in the past, Detective. Carmichael

Vero was in the Mafia back then. Now he's the godfather of his own organization. He's a lawbreaker, and it's my job to prosecute him. With your help, gentlemen."

"How else can we help you, Sir?" Sheriff DeBona asked.

"How do you think? I want you to join this task force. I want you two to help us bring down Carmichael Vero and the Family." He pointed at Ray Kirkland. "And I believe Detective Kirkland here has already begun making it happen."

Edgar Waters played all of his Family recordings for the two new members of the Carmichael Vero Task Force. They heard the late Pete Vero blabbing about the Family, proving its existence. The hair stood up on Ray's neck as Tony Vero gave his chilling monologue to Kay Falco regarding Ed Larsky's assassination of Michael Davis's key witness in the infamous Carmichael Vero trial. They heard the squabble at Tony's house on Saturday. Last they listened to Edgar's latest recording. The war room was filled with the sounds of Ray Kirkland and Tony Vero driving golf balls at Stop 'n' Sock. They heard Ray's extraordinary insight as he explained to Tony how he was being primed as the successor to Carmichael's crime organization. Then they listened as Ray began to witness about Jesus again. Sheriff DeBona continually shook his head with disdain during Kirkland's plea for Tony to be saved. Ray noted the Sheriff's angst. Nothing could be done about it, though. The recording ended as Ray left the driving range. Edgar Waters flicked off the audio machine. State Attorney General Michael Davis turned to Detective Kirkland.

"That, Detective, is why I want you on this Task Force. After only four days of investigating Todd Falco and VECO you can already see the truth behind the big lie. Where'd you get such a level of perception?"

Ray stammered for a moment, "Well . . . I . . . it's . . . it's the power of Holy Spirit is all I know. And I've been praying hard for Tony for the last few days, also. The Lord reveals things about people to the intercessor."

Davis nodded knowingly. DeBona looked ashamed of Ray, and Gandtz and Saucier looked at him like he was just plain nuts.

Sheriff DeBona broke in at that point. "Detective Kirkland is insightful, Sir." He eyed Ray angrily. "But I do not condone him proselytizing suspects on a case."

Davis nodded. "That does bring up a good point, Sheriff." The Attorney General coyly asked Detective Kirkland: "You don't think asking a prime suspect in a major investigation if he wants to be 'saved' is a conflict of interests to the duties you swore to carry out as a public servant?"

Ray didn't stammer or hesitate this time. With boldness he answered, "No sir, I don't. I'm not going to deny my God who saved me or be ashamed of the Salvation He's freely given to me and wants to give to all men. Even mixed up Mafia kids like Tony Vero need to be saved. If we can get 'em saved, God will change their hearts and we'll have that many less lawbreakers."

An embarrassed Sheriff DeBona shook his head and blurted out, "Sir, Detective Kirkland's done this before."

Davis looked at the Sheriff with surprise. "He has?"

"Yes, sir."

"Tony Vero isn't the first criminal Detective Kirkland's tried to evangelize?"

An ashamed Sheriff DeBona sadly shook his head. "No Sir, I'm afraid not. I've had to reprimand and discipline the good Detective for this type of behavior several times in his career."

"That so?"

"Yes, sir. I've even had the sad task of having to remove Detective Kirkland from the homicide division and put him in charge of our missing persons bureau because of his Christian behavior while on duty in a taxpayer funded job."

That was the first time Ray Kirkland ever heard the Sheriff admit this was so. It was quite a shock. And it hurt, too.

"Huh," Attorney General Davis pondered, slowly rubbing his hand over his chin. He looked back at Detective Kirkland. "And you continue to witness for Jesus while on the job, despite all this punishment your supervisor here has meted out to you because of it?"

Ray nodded with tremendous confidence. "Yes, Mr. Davis, I still do, and still will continue. I feel that my witnessing has never interfered with any of my investigations."

Sheriff DeBona slowly shook his head with shame and disgust for Ray. But he was grateful that one so high up in authority could witness first hand the sad disregard that Ray Kirkland had for the separation of church and state . . .

"Well, I'm impressed!" Michael Davis grinned enthusiastically. He reached out and pumped Ray's huge black hand hard. "The Kingdom of God and this backslidden nation need more men with backbone like you."

Ray was shocked. Then he noticed Sheriff DeBona's eyes bugging out of his head.

"You march on, soldier," Davis continued to pump his hand. "And if you get anymore reprimands for simple acts of sharing your faith while on duty, you contact me." He pulled a card from his wallet and handed it to Ray. "I know some of the best attorneys in the country who specialize in handling religious harassment cases against people in 'taxpayer funded jobs.'" He winked at Ray. "The Bible says that you're blessed for your persecution, Detective Kirkland. Stand tall and carry on the Gospel. And God bless you in it."

Ray nodded gratefully at the powerful man. "Thank you for the encouragement, sir. It means a lot to me."

DeBona was red-faced; flabbergasted. Not to mentioned embarrassed beyond belief.

Davis turned and breezed past the Sheriff. "Scrape your bottom jaw up off the floor and come over here with me, Sheriff," he said in his best Marine Captain's voice. "We've got a big case load ahead of us and no time to waste."

Captain Gandtz made his way over to where Kirkland was standing. "Detective Kirkland," he said.

Ray looked down into his eyes. "Yes, Captain?"

Gandtz smiled skeptically and shook his head. "I don't know how else to tell you this without sounding offensive: I think you're an absolute nut case. God talking to you, you trying to get some sleaze ball like Tony Vero to accept religion. I think you're wacko." Lt. Saucier snickered rudely behind him. "You think some sleaze ball like Tony Vero can accept religion and be rehabilitated?"

Ray looked down at him with a smile. "You've never seen any of the men you've had convicted go to jail, give their hearts to Jesus, and turn their lives around?"

"To be honest, Detective, after I get 'em in jail, I don't care what happens to them."

"I do. I ask the question, 'What if they die and go to hell?'"

Gandtz shrugged callously. "If they do, I can live with it."

Ray shrugged callously. "Well, if you think I'm a wacko, I can live with it. I'm not living to please you, Captain Gandtz. Excuse me." Ray turned and walked over to Davis, DeBona, and Waters.

Gandtz didn't look angry. He just pointed at Lt. Saucier and announced, "We're going to get a Coke." He sang very loudly as he and his laughing partner disappeared out the door: "Jesus loves me, this I know! For the Bible tells me sooooo . . ."

Ray told the others not to worry about it. Edgar Waters had witnessed the whole scene. He shook his head with disgust and looked up at Michael Davis.

"That Captain Gandtz is like having the neighborhood bully hanging around. Does he get along with anyone?"

"Never. But his colleagues at the SBI don't call him 'The Bull' for nothing. He's busted three of the most dangerous robbery rings in the history of this state. Leo's a tough, patient, and relentless investigator, one who's invaluable to me. Especially with this case. Leo's a tortured soul, though."

"What do you mean?" Ray asked.

"Leo and his wife only had one daughter. She was a rebellious thing. She got pregnant and had a baby girl when she was in high school. Courtney Lee was one of the most beautiful little baby girls you'll ever see. Leo fell in love with her from the start. She was the sunshine in his life. Well, his daughter never missed a beat of the party life, so he and Anna adopted Courtney Lee and raised her themselves in Philadelphia. Then, about ten years ago when she was four, she disappeared when she and Anna were at the mall one day. Two years later they found her remains nearby in the woods."

"Dear Lord," Ray shook his head. A tear formed in his eye as he envisioned Gandtz's pain. Edgar and the Sheriff looked equally as saddened by the tale.

"That's not the worst of it, believe it or not. A year after she was found, an SBI agent-friend of Leo's who worked vice spotted Courtney Lee in a child pornography film confiscated in a bust. They convicted the man who was responsible for Courtney Lee's kidnapping and abuse. Leo instantly transferred over to the vice division of the SBI, and has become the scourge of the child pornography industry in Pennsylvania ever since." "That's why you cut him so much slack," Edgar realized, out loud. "Yes, Sergeant." Davis pointed to Warren Zann's picture on the wall. "Leo's got a plant in Mr. Zann's pornography syndicate right now and he's about to nail him. That's why he's so antsy being here on the Task Force with all of you. But he's got demons plaguing him. He needs lots of prayer and care."

A long, sad pause followed. Michael Davis broke the silence.

"Speaking of plants . . ." He began to fill in Sheriff DeBona and Detective Kirkland on Tammi Bannerman, Edgar's undercover plant at VECO. As he was detailing how she got there and their plans for her to plant that pen in Carmichael's office, Ray suddenly got light headed. He didn't tell anyone, for he was trying to pay attention to the Attorney General. He casually pulled up a chair and sat down, trying not to attract attention. He was clammy all over. His forehead and neck broke out in a cold sweat. He couldn't feel his left thumb at all and his left shoulder hurt so bad he wished it would just fall off his body. He began to see spots before his eyes . . .

"Dear Jesus," he prayed silently, "What's happening?"

Michael Davis wanted to show them the court order for the transmitter pen Tammi Bannerman was going to use. He secured it through a local judge he had befriended when he was the Beaver County District Attorney. DeBona and Waters went to follow Davis across the war room. Ray mindlessly stood up to go with them. By that point, Cyrus Moreau's death curse on him was manifesting in its fullness. His life was literally being sucked out of him by demonic forces. Just as quickly as Ray stood up, his entire body gave way, unconsciousness overtook him, and he collapsed loudly to the floor in a cold, sweaty heap.

Davis, Waters, Gandtz and Saucier watched with deep concern as Sheriff DeBona sped out of the Holiday in parking lot with Ray in the car, sirens blaring and lights flashing. They had revived Ray rather quickly, but he vehemently refused their plea to call an ambulance. Instead he asked the Sheriff to get him to the hospital in the Sheriff's car. DeBona radioed for an escort from Rt. 18 to the Beaver County Medical Center and got one instantly. The four Carmichael Vero Task Force members stood and stared as two State Police cars met the Sheriff's vehicle just as he pulled onto Rt. 18 below them. All three cars sped out of view at over one hundred miles an hour.

The four stood speechless for a moment, stunned by the irony that their newest, most promising member was being sped off to the hospital after only less than one hour on the Carmichael Vero Task Force.

Edgar Waters looked around at them and finally broke their silence. "Well, I ain't afraid to say it: this absolutely gives me the creeps."

Davis shook his head in disbelief. "I don't know what to say, Edgar. This is so par for the course for our investigation. We shouldn't be surprised this is happening."

"Well, I know what to say: Carmichael Vero ain't human and the Family's not just the Mafia. They're like a pack of vampires or something, I'm telling you." He spat on the ground. "They got something ungodly protecting them."

FORTY-SIX

T ony Vero cruised up Rt. 51 toward VECO in his father's Mercedes. He tried to convince himself he was on the road to his destiny. Today he would be free from all that tormented him, he thought to himself. But it wasn't working. He wasn't convincing himself at all.

Despite the war that was going on inside him, he was going to tell Carmichael, Joseph, and Larsky all about Frank Kranac. Whatever they did to him, he was leaving town and would never have to see the results. Perhaps, if he made peace with God like Kay Falco had that weekend, he could get this right, too. But for the moment, he wanted freedom from the Family more than he wanted a clear conscience. So on he sped toward VECO. And five cars behind him were Greggy and Jimmy Richards in a rental car, following him, waiting for an opportunity to take him alive.

Cyrus Moreau was on a private jet bound for New York City at that moment. There he was meeting one of Wall Street's most respected analysts. They were to continue work they'd begun putting his occult businesses out on the public stock market. This IPO would be a huge hit, the analyst insisted. Oh, the money Cyrus would make then, and the lives he'd be able to control! The thousands of unsuspecting investors who'd be putting their lives under his spiritual authority! He'd have free reigns over countless masses, more people to be manipulated and controlled through his witchcraft. Aleister Estate would become the capital of an occult empire. Not even the notorious Aleister Crowley could make such a boast. He would become the greatest figure in the history of magic. After his immensely successful workshop weekend, where he made Carmichael Vero grovel at his feet and agree to perform the whole will of the Dark Lords, this indeed was going to be a perfect Monday for him. On top of all that he was wondering how that Detective Kirkland was feeling today! He would check that evening from New York City to see if the man was dead yet.

Cyrus smiled as he looked out his window all the way over New York state on his way to the Big Apple. He was on his way to ruling everything he saw on the ground below him. Or so he thought, in his arrogance . . .

Joseph Vero walked through VECO with great apprehension, an apprehension which was contrary to the cheery buzz in the office that day. Everyone was energetic, bustling with activity in preparation for Tuesday night's gala stockholders banquet. VECO employees were busy preparing final reports from the previous year's business records. Everyone was noisy. Everyone was cheerful. How amazing it was to him, then, that at a time when he should be so excited, that continued malaise of dread was overtaking him more and more each moment. Tony was on his way to hand over the goon who had so jeopardized the Family's future. They'd be able to deal with him swiftly, hopefully get their money back, and then regroup and re-plan the Family's narcotics structure. It all sounded good. But it just didn't feel good to Joseph. His discernment was amazingly accurate. He'd never been wrong before. And unfortunately for all the smiling faces around him, all whistling while they were working, he probably wasn't wrong this time. Before all these naive employees could realize it, the Family might be exposed, in which case VECO would collapse in a heartbeat. All these smiling faces could find themselves out of work in a matter of weeks, for the fire that could bring down the empire had already begun. Joseph knew it.

"Rome's burning," he whispered aloud as he made his way toward Carmichael's office.

Audra Dutton was in the fortieth hour of her fast. She had slept remarkably well all night, then woke up about seven o'clock that morning. She got up, prayed in her prayer language for a half hour or so to edify her spirit, and then she took another half hour to read her Bible. She went back and read all of the Gospel passages where Jesus taught on forgiveness, and then some of Paul and James' scriptural admonitions on prayer and warfare. At about 8:30, Audra continued her intercession over Benny Miller and the one to whom she referred as "that good lookin' white boy." She now knew these were the ones she'd been praying over since her son Orlando's death. And she could tell by the Spirit that something big was happening to them.

Joseph walked into Carmichael's office at ten minutes to ten. Carmichael was doing paperwork at his desk with head secretary Hilda Jessup. Larsky was getting the outside speaker system ready to blast away for their meeting with Tony. When Carmichael saw Joseph he looked at his watch and dismissed Hilda. When she was gone, Larsky switched on the outside music.

"The office swept and clean?" Joseph asked. Larsky nodded silently, chewing his gum.

Carmichael noticed Joseph's pensive state. "What's wrong, Nephew?"

Joseph was frank. "This whole scene that's about to happen with Tony is bothering me."

"How so?"

"We're about to send off my brother's son for the last time."

Larsky turned around, angry. "It's his choice, *Unca* Joseph! Your boy there made the choice to stab us in the back and leave us, just because we're not a bunch of goody-two-shoes. And your brother's the reason he is that way!"

Joseph chose to calmly ignore Larsky. He turned to Carmichael instead. "That doesn't make it any easier, Carmichael. Even though Tony's not right, he's our blood relative. Actually, besides you, he's all I got. And I'm about to watch him walk through that door for the last time. I'm sorry to be sentimental, but it bothers me."

"This is the business you've chosen, Joseph. You know how things are for people like us. Feelings of loyalty for the sake of emotions will be our downfall. Larsky's right. Tony's a big boy. He's made his bed and wisely chooses to lie in it. We're going to get our million dollars back now."

Joseph shook his head. "But what consolation is that? We won't have Tony anymore. He's our family. You and I can't keep a wife. We hang out with bimbos who don't really mean a thing. We have no one." He looked over at Larsky, then waved a hand at him with disgust: "Except Ed, there, who's about as warm and charming as a block of ice." Larsky snickered. "When's all this money supposed to bring us any happiness, Carmichael? I mean, if we're willing to sacrifice our loved ones for it?"

"'Love'?" Carmichael pondered the word. He smiled faintly. "I do believe you're going soft in your old age, Joseph. When has love ever been a priority to you? You are a stoic in the classic Greek sense of the word. Love has never been high on your list of importance."

Joseph just stood there looking out the window. He didn't want to be without Tony. Carmichael was trying to block out any feelings of love or loyalty toward Tony, knowing full well that he was about to have his great nephew murdered. He lied to Joseph to try and get him off the subject:

"And besides, Joseph: Tony will surely stay away from me, but I'm positive he'll contact you after he disappears. He's too lovey-dovey not to."

"Don't count on it, Uncle Carmichael," Tony startled them all from the doorway.

They all turned to look at him as he marched in and sat down near Carmichael's desk.

"When I leave today, it's for good, and when you told me never to show my face around here again, I took your order seriously."

Carmichael stared down at him. "As you should."

Tony looked at Joseph. "This will be good-bye, Uncle."

Joseph said nothing.

"Let's get down to business." Tony rolled up his sleeves as he looked over at Larsky. "You check this room for bugs? We safe?"

Larsky told him "Of course."

"Good," Tony nodded. "'Cause I have your man for you. The one who set up Todd Falco, killed him, and stole all your money."

Tammi Bannerman speed dialed the war room at Holiday Inn. Edgar Waters answered. "Mr. Rogers? This is Tammi Bannerman at VECO. I just wanted to inform you that there is a special meeting, fully catered, and that Mr. Thomas is joining the usuals." Edgar turned to Michael Davis. "The Family's meeting right now! They've got that loud speaker blasting outside, and Tony Vero's just joined them." He spoke back to Tammi. "You've not been able to plant that bug yet, have you?" Edgar said with great disappointment.

"Um, no sir. That has been an impossibility up until now. Hopefully, we'll be able to arrange such an appointment within the next two months."

"I know, Tammi. Let me know when the meeting breaks up."

"You're very welcome, Sir! And we'll do that for you. Good bye!" She disconnected.

"She doesn't have the bug in there yet, does she?" Davis was frustrated.

"No. You know she would have called to set it up. She hopes to have it planted within the next two hours, though."

"I sure hope she can." Davis sighed and scratched his head. "But why am I suddenly becoming so impatient now, after all these years of waiting?"

"Oh, I understand your impatience," Edgar says. "After all we've been through, and then especially after sending Detective Kirkland out of here with a heart attack on his first day on the job, it would be nice for something to go our way for once!"

"Hon," Ray Kirkland spoke into his cell phone to his wife from inside Sheriff DeBona's speeding, wailing police car, "I'm on my way to the emergency room . . ."

Ray calmly explained the situation to Shelly, who tried to remain composed. She praised the Lord when Ray told her it was some sort of health problems he was suffering, and not a gunshot wound as she first thought when he mentioned the emergency room. Through teary eyes she listened to his instructions. When Ray was finished telling her what he needed, she immediately began praying over her husband via the phone. Sheriff DeBona knew she was praying by the way Ray was openly "Amen!"ing and repeating "Yes, Lord! I agree with my wife!" She spoke the blood of Jesus over Ray and against any curse against his health. Shelly's instant prayers and pleas for Christ's all-powerful blood over Ray Kirkland bought him a few extra moments of life. Ray saw the emergency room doctors waiting at the entrance with a stretcher for him as the sheriff's cruiser and two state police cars roared into the hospital driveway. Ray told Shelly he loved her and would see her as soon as she got to the hospital.

Shelly hung up Ray's call and immediately called Covenant Church's office. She told the secretary and pastors what was happening. A prayer chain was instantly formed. Covenant Church cell group leaders were phoned. They phoned all their cell group members. Prayer warriors were notified within ten minutes of Ray's call to Shelly. The air over the Beaver Valley was soon filled with heavenly warfare on behalf of Ray Kirkland. It was effective warfare; the type of warfare that can not only turn the tide of a battle, but the entire war.

Even lifelong, hardened criminals like Carmichael, Joseph, and Larsky were shocked to hear Tony's lurid explanation of Todd Falco's disappearance. With wide eyes and gaping mouths they were glued to Tony as he told them all about Frank Kranac. Tony purposefully did not tell them about Greggy and Jimmy Richards, for they were the saddest two geeks he'd ever seen. He knew they didn't have the brains to set up a rip-off like Kranac pulled off with Todd Falco. Whatever the Family did to Kranac, well, that was one thing. But Tony didn't want the blood of those two idiot Richards brothers on his conscience. The Family would never have to know about them.

"Frank Kranac is who has your million and a quarter dollars, Uncle Carmichael."

After a moment of stunned silence, Carmichael ordered Larsky, "Get that creep's address." Tony recited Frank Kranac's 6th Avenue College Hill address.

"So you don't think this Frank Kranac psycho knows about the Family?" Carmichael asked.

Tony shook his head. "No way. This guy's a freak. He's completely out of any loop that might catch onto the Family. He lives in this dump and doesn't talk or associate with anyone. His neighbors even said so. He simply picked up on the fact that Todd Falco deals, zeroed in on Todd, lured him into his trap, and there went Todd and your money."

"You find out where this deal between Kranac and Todd went down?" Larsky asked.

"No."

"So you haven't seen the money," Joseph commented.

"Oh, he has it!" Tony perked up. "It may not be in his house, but he has it. Frank Kranac's too much of a loner to be working with somebody else. He wouldn't trust a million and so bucks to anyone. He has it. I just don't know where."

Carmichael turned to Larsky. "That's what you're going to find out, Ed! You're going to take care of him for us!"

Tony shook his head at Larsky. "You better watch yourself around this guy. He's huge! He reminds me of Frankenstein."

Larsky sneered at Tony. "He's gonna wish he was the living dead when I get through with him! Rippin' off the Family! He'll wish he was never born. I'll get him and our money."

Tony and Joseph traded glances. Tony wouldn't look at him long. He turned back to Carmichael.

"That's it. I've done my job, and I've completed it like I told you in just five days. If you get your money back and let Todd Falco remain wherever he is, you'll all be safe. Life for the Family can soon go back to normal and VECO will never miss a beat. If the local cops don't even know what this Kranac's been up to, they won't figure it out now. I told you I'd find your money and Falco and protect the secrecy of the Family . . ."

"What about that pest Kirkland from the Sheriff's Department?" Larsky asked. "What about the way you got him snoopin' all over us, raidin' VECO with that search warrant, gettin' me arrested? You call that keepin' things a secret?"

"That'll pass, too, Ed," Joseph piped up. "Carmichael built VECO to withstand an incident like that police search on Friday. We knew one would come, one day. They turned up nothing, I guarantee you. If we can withstand three IRS audits, we can withstand local police searches. And you got yourself arrested. Tony didn't make you hit that cop . . ."

Carmichael put his hand up to Larsky before he started arguing with Joseph. "I must agree with Joseph on this one, Ed. We're always careful and always ready for police interference at VECO. This too will all pass in time. The Family will just have to lay low for a while. It'll give us time to regroup. You worry about getting our money back and teaching that Frank Kranac what happens when people mess with the Family."

"What about me now, Uncle Carmichael?" Tony asked him. "Like I said, I kept my end of our business deal. I got you what you wanted. Now you need to keep your end."

They stared at each other for a moment, Tony adamant, Carmichael resentful.

Carmichael's eyes blazed red. "What you ask for, Tony, will be the end of life as you know it. You understand that."

"I *want* that!" Tony said without hesitation.

"You'll forever be a shame to your father's name . . ."

"I don't care about my father's name, or your name, or the Vero name! I want you to release me once and for all from the Family and any bonds we have!"

Carmichael leaned across his desk toward him. "I release you right now, Tony Vero!" he said through gritted teeth. "I release you from the best thing that's ever happened to you! I release you from the people who've supported you! I release you from your responsibilities to the Family! I release you from any loyalty to the Family! You aren't even worthy to be a Family member!"

"Renounce your Family oaths over me!"

"They are officially renounced!" Carmichael roared. "In fact, I even renounce you as a Vero! You are a disgrace to the Vero family name, a disgrace to your parents, a disgrace to us!" He stood up angrily and pointed his finger, "And from this day forward, in my sight, you are no longer a Vero! The first thing you are to do when you run away from Beaver Falls is change your last name!" He turned angrily to Joseph, continuing to point at Tony: "Joseph, this is no longer your nephew! He's to be a stranger to you if you ever encounter him again! For he's found himself to be too good for the likes of us! When he walks out of this office, I no longer want you to even think of him! He and his sister no longer exist!" He turned back to Tony. "There! It's done!"

Tony stood up suddenly, knocking his chair over behind him. "Good!"

"It's finished!" Carmichael shouted. "According to our deal, just like you wanted. You are officially a nothing around us. You no longer belong here."

Tony whipped out his wallet. He removed all of his Vero Securities and Investigations identification cards and licenses and threw them on Carmichael's desk. "Those are yours, now."

Carmichael pointed at them and yelled to Larsky: "Destroy them right now!"

Larsky took the pile of cards over to the shredder and ground them into twisted plastic and paper strips.

With that, Tony Vero was no longer under the sway and protection of the demonic entities that controlled and guarded the Family. Those evil ties that had bound him to these people he called his family were broken. Tony suddenly even felt different standing there in their midst. It was suddenly as though he was a stranger in a foreign land, like there was no place anywhere that he could call home or find people to welcome him.

Carmichael pointed to the double oak doors: "You no longer have any reason to be in my office, or on these premises, ever again. We don't know you. Go!"

He looked over at his Uncle Joseph. Joseph stood motionless, but his eyes were reddened and watery with uncharacteristic emotion. There was so much Tony wanted to say to him, but dared not. He simply turned, stepped over the chair he'd knocked over, and left, lightly closing the doors behind him.

Carmichael turned immediately to Joseph. The man looked bewildered. Tears rolled silently down his reddening cheeks. He understood the impact of what just happened from his days in La Cosa Nostra. What Carmichael just did truly did make Tony anathema to the remaining Family members. Even Joseph would be betraying them if he had any further contact with his nephew. Carmichael and Larsky were shocked at Joseph's open expression of emotion, as subdued as it was. It was the first time both Carmichael and Larsky could ever remember seeing him like this.

Joseph pointed to the doors where Tony had just left. He said, "He was the last thing that meant anything to me, Carmichael."

Carmichael held his hands up in a half shrug. He shook his head: "It was his choice. It was the only thing we could do, Joseph."

Joseph shook his head in disagreement. "If the hell of total isolation is our best choice, then we've truly run out of decent options, Carmichael."

Joseph left them.

Tony was dazed as he walked through the hustle and bustle of VECO. He looked around at everything for the last time. He was experiencing a queer contrast of emotions. He truly felt light, as though a burden had just been lifted from his shoulders. Yet inside he was empty, dry, and unfulfilled. There was a sense of both relief and grief, like a child who had just watched a horribly abusive parent die before their eyes. VECO reminded him of Pete. Memories of his father flooded his soul, and for the first time in a while he was sad about Pete being gone. If only he were still alive! Then maybe none of this would ever have had to happen. As Tony took VECO's flight of stairs down to the lobby to the parking lot for the last time, he realized that this whole place might someday have been his. Now, like his youthful dreams of the NFL, VECO was no longer his for the taking. And the Kid left the VECO building for the very last time.

As soon as Carmicheal and Larsky were alone in the office, Larsky grinned excitedly at him and said, "This couldn't be working out any better! The way you told Tony to disappear and drop his name and never to see Joseph again! Joseph would be the only one to eventually put two and two together and figure out that we've killed Tony. Now, he'll never even suspect Tony's dead!"

Carmichael did not share in Larsky's enthusiasm. He took no joy in any of the day's events.

"I'm going to go meet with Tommy Wheeler and get him moving right away," Larsky said, preparing his things to leave. "I'll have Tony killed by sundown. Then I'm gonna track down that Frank Kranac and get our money back . . ."

"No!" Carmichael suddenly became animated.

Larsky looked at him with concern. This was all going too perfectly. In the back of his mind Larsky was fearful Carmichael might get a sudden twinge of conscience and family love like Joseph had and call off Tony's murder.

Carmichael composed himself and explained. "We have too much work to do for this stockholders banquet tomorrow, Ed. You can't just leave for the day. I need you here."

"But what about Kranac? What about our money? We need to get to him as soon as possible . . ."

Carmichael instantly had the solution: "Here's what you do. When you meet with Wheeler you give him a grace period on taking out Tony. You put him on Kranac. Give him his address. Have him track the man down and follow him for us. Then you can call him later this afternoon when things die down here, go after Kranac yourself, and Wheeler can fulfill his contract then."

Larsky was openly disappointed at that plan. "But Carmichael! The longer we let Tony and Kranac go today the worse our chances become of whacking Tony and gettin' back our money! We've got to move *now!*"

"No!" Carmichael was vehement. "I know what I'm doing! You've got to be here today. We have VECO's banquet to worry about and you have too many responsibilities here. Kranac's been on the loose with our cash for the last seven days. Another six hours isn't going to change anything. You can be down his throat by supper time tonight. And Tony's got too much to do to make it out of town today. There's no way he'll be ready. Wheeler will have plenty of time to take care of him tonight. Put him on Kranac first. Tony can wait. You stay here and meet Wheeler at the appointed time . . ."

The oak doors swung open. Joseph Vero walked back in at that moment, and both Carmichael and Larsky were startled to see him. Joseph hadn't heard what they were talking about, but he immediately sensed that they were up to something. Their eyes betrayed them. The three stared at each other for a moment before Joseph broke the silence.

"I left my planner on your desk," Joseph said as he walked over to get it.

They all watched each other, Carmichael and Larsky with awkward expressions helplessly frozen on their faces. Joseph picked up his planner, looked them over again, and left.

When the oak doors closed, Larsky straightened up and angrily told Carmichael: "We need to do something about *him*! He's dangerous to us now!"

Carmichael became sarcastic. "You know, Ed, you're right! In fact, why don't you just take a machine gun and go kill everyone in this building for us right now! Then you and I can run VECO and the Family all by ourselves!"

"You said to me the other day that it was time to fix things so you and I could be at the top together! Didn't you mean that, or was that just some wick-wack to keep me happy for a while?"

Carmichael sighed and rubbed his eyes slowly, almost like he was defeated. "No. Ultimately you're right about Joseph. He is a perceptive man, but he's getting too perceptive for our purposes. But we're not going to deal with him yet. Not until we've finished dealing with Tony and Frank Kranac."

Joseph trudged down the foyer from Carmichael's office, stunned. His heart was heavy and he had a lump of apprehension in his throat. He feared for Tony. Suddenly he had to warn Tony about Carmichael and Larsky. He looked around. Had Tony been able to get out that quickly? Joseph pushed through the glass doors and started in a jog toward the stairwell. Halfway there he broke into a quicker trot, bouncing off several employees, not looking back to excuse himself or see if they were okay. He hit the steps running, bouncing down two steps at a time. He ran through the downstairs lobby and out into the VECO parking lot. He ran right into the pool of parked cars, looking all over for Tony's truck or Pete's Mercedes. Neither were to be seen. He ran toward the exit road that wound down to Rt. 51. No Tony. There were no signs of Tony anywhere. Huffing and puffing, the fifty-six year old man bent over and put his hands on his knees, trying to catch his breath.

Joseph had to warn Tony about Carmichael and Larsky. He had to. But first, he knew he had to take care of himself before the Family tried to take care of him.

FORTY-SEVEN

Tammi Bannerman had been watching head secretary Hilda Jessup all morning, waiting for Carmichael to call her into his office for anything. All she needed was one chance to plant that VECO pen on his desk. Her chance finally came right before lunch.

"Hilda," Carmichael's voice blared over the speaker at her desk, "I need that final Brighton Analytical report now. Is it ready?"

Tammi's heart beat wildly. This was going to be her chance. She was suddenly overcome with nervousness. *Don't fumble the ball!* she encouraged herself.

"I have it right here, Mr. Vero," Hilda replied. "I'll bring it right in."

As Hilda went to grab the file, Tammi Bannerman hit the speed dial button on her phone.

Michael Davis' phone rang in the "war room" of the Holiday Inn. He and Edgar Waters looked at the number on the call-screener connected to the phone.

"That's Tammi!" Davis said. "Go!"

Edgar Waters cleared out Tammi's call, picked up the phone, and hit his speed dial.

Hilda Jessup's phone rang at her desk just as she was getting up to take the reports into Carmichael. She checked her call-screener: it read "Holiday Inn" and its Beaver Falls number. She hesitated. "'Holiday Inn'? Who's calling me from there?"

Tammi was strategically walking behind her that moment with a huge stack of folders and clipboards, all bogus, with VECO pens clipped everywhere. She looked over Hilda's shoulder at the call-screener and said to her, "I bet its one of the stockholders in town for the banquet."

"Oh!" Hilda lit up. "I bet you're right!" Customers came first at VECO. She answered the phone.

Edgar Waters greeted her and began feeding her the biggest, fasted pile of malarkey he'd ever laid on anyone in his life. He pretended to be an officious, out of town stockholder who demanded to know volumes of inane information about tomorrow's banquet. Michael Davis stood beside him, praying that this would work.

Tammi watched Hilda. The head secretary was clearly torn: she wanted to help this stockholder with his questions, but Carmichael's request for that report was beckoning her. She said, "Ummmm . . ." and "Well, yes . . ." to Edgar on the phone while she nervously eyed the glass doors that lead down the corridor to Carmichael's office. Tammi grabbed the perfectly planned opportunity. Holding her giant stack of busy work, she nudged Hilda with her elbow to get her attention. Tammi nodded at the Brighton Analytical file in Hilda's hand and whispered helpfully so as not to distract Hilda from her "important" phone call: "I can run that into Carmichael."

Hilda "Uh-huh"-ed Edgar, looked at Tammi questionably, and looked down at her file. Carmichael didn't take well to any secretary or receptionist other than Hilda coming into his office without his request. Hilda was his second watchdog at VECO, next to Larsky. But Edgar was laying it on thick, beginning to fuss about his accommodations and questioning what in the world he was supposed to do in Beaver Falls to pass his time until tomorrow. He was talking so non-stop that Hilda couldn't find an opportunity to interrupt him. She looked nervously at the glass door to Carmichael's office again, back up at Tammi, and back down at the report in her hand. She was frantically trying to make a judgment call. Finally, she ruled in favor of Tammi's helpful suggestion. She handed the file to Tammi, nodded with a disdainful frown, mouthed "Okay," and waved Tammi off.

It worked! Tammi cheered inside. But as soon as she propped open the glass doors with her elbow, a near panic overtook her. Doubt, intimidation, and fear slammed her hard as she entered that last hallway to Carmichael's office. Halfway down the hall to those huge, dark, oak doors, Tammi Bannerman had to stop. Her heart felt like it was going to beat a hole through her chest and pop out onto that big stack of nothing she was carrying. A dangerous thought popped into her mind:

I can't do this!—the doubt that the devil brings to discourage every human being.

Aware that Hilda might be watching her, she bent over to adjust the pump on her right foot, as though it was causing her discomfort.

Pull it together, girl! she commanded herself. She had to overcome this. Carmichael and Larsky would see right through her if she didn't shape up. Suddenly, for some reason, she remembered Michael Davis's prayer over the Carmichael Vero Task Force early that morning. She remembered Davis' eloquent, encouraging invocation to God for wisdom, blessing, and protection over their venture. His prayer suddenly flooded her vexed soul:

God, if you're listening, honor that man's prayer now and help me not to screw this up for him!

Just as Tammi Bannerman had no way of knowing sinister spiritual forces were fighting against her, she also couldn't see Holy Spirit was now moving through Michael Davis's prayer and exhorting her. Suddenly, confusion became clarity, fear became determination, and the butterflies in her stomach became the energy Tammi used to march into that office and do what she had been planted there to do. On she went, stoic, determined, and tough.

She knocked lightly on the oak door and entered Carmichael's office. She instantly assessed the situation: Carmichael was on speakerphone to somebody, immersed in work, and Larsky was seated on the edge of his desk, aggressively looking over some papers, chomping gum. Neither noticed it was she who had entered the office and not Hilda Jessup. Pokerfaced, Tammi walked over to Carmichael's desk with that report resting on her huge stack of busy work. She was literally covered with VECO pens: there was one in her mouth, one in her ear, three lying atop her stack, and several more clipped onto all that work. She set her stack lightly on the edge of Carmichael's desk, grabbed the Brighton Analytical folder, and held it out to him. It was at that point that both he and Larsky looked up at her and noticed it wasn't Hilda Jessup standing in their midst. Carmichael didn't miss a beat of his conversation, but he eyed Larsky with an expression that clearly read, "What's *she* doing in here?" Larsky responded to his telepathic question:

"Where's Hilda?"

Tammi stood there holding out the folder, which Carmichael was purposefully not taking until she gave Larsky an explanation.

Help me, Lord! she quickly thought in her mind. She took the pen out of her mouth. "Hilda's on the phone with a stockholder who's chewing her ear off," she said to Larsky, nonchalantly. "She asked me to run this report into to Mr. Vero for her."

He stared a hole through her head for about ten seconds, trying to read her. He then nodded satisfactorily at Carmichael, who, without even looking up at her, reached up and grabbed the folder. The important man then waved Tammi off.

Tammy put up a silent "just a minute" finger to Carmichael. She cleared the three pens off the top of her stack and set them and the one she had in her mouth on Carmichael's desk, next to some other pens and pencils near his stack of work. She reached into her stack, pulled out an unimportant check requisition, and held it out to Larsky.

He looked up at her impatiently and stared at the requisition with a "Now what?" expression.

"This is from accounting," she said. "They misplaced the original and need Mr. Vero's signature to close out this account for tomorrow." Larsky glared at her and took the paper to examine it. She stared a hole back through Larsky's head with a bold "I'm just doing my job, grouchy-butt!" expression of her own. She pulled down the pen from her ear, clicked it open, and handed it to Larsky. "You can phone them and check on it if you wish."

What a lie to tell in this situation! she thought.

Without saying a word Larsky handed Carmichael the requisition and the pen. Carmichael looked it over quickly while he carried on his phone conversation, then signed it with the pen. Tammi quickly reached over the desk, grabbed the requisition with a whispered, "Thank you, Sir!" and laid it back on top of the stack. Carmichael tried to hand back the VECO pen, but she wasn't paying attention to him. He saw all the other pens she had, so he tossed it down on the side of his desk and continued his call. She picked up her stack quickly and turned and began to walk back to the doors, leaving the four other VECO pens laying on Carmichael's desk.

Yes! she thought as she was just about to open one of the oak doors . . .

"Hey, you!" Larsky barked at her. Her heart jumped up into her throat. She turned and faced him.

Larsky pointed to the edge of the desk. "Get these pens off of Carmichael's desk! This isn't your junk drawer, girl!"

She hesitated, then said, "Oh, sorry!" as she walked back over to his desk. Both Carmichael and Larsky stared her down. Carmichael looked irritated with her. She reached down and snatched up the four pens, placing them back on her stack.

Larsky shook his head at her and commented, "We got enough of those cheap, stupid pens everywhere." He went back to his reading and Carmichael to his conversation. Tammi turned and re-traced her steps back to the doors. She opened one of them and stepped out into the hall.

Triumph! She breathed a sigh of relief and nearly floated back down the corridor to the secretary's chambers, juiced up from her major accomplishment.

Back in Carmichael's office, sitting to the right of him within reach, was that VECO pen he'd used to sign that form. It was the transmitter pen. For the first time Edgar Waters had successfully planted a bug in VECO, right under Carmichael and Ed Larsky's nose.

Hilda Jessup was still on the phone with Edgar Waters, irritated to the bone. As Tammi smiled at her as she passed, Hilda held up her hand and made the international "blah-blah-blah" gesture. Tammi giggled and shook her head sympathetically. She went back to her station, laid down her stack, put on her headset, and dialed another number.

Michael Davis's cellular phone rang as he stood beside Edgar. He answered.

Tammi said to him, "This is Tammi Bannerman from VECO. Please inform Mr. Rogers that his message is in the mail and that he can put a cork in it, now." She hung up.

Michael Davis jumped and shook his fist, startling Edgar. "It's done!" he whispered at Edgar. "She did it!"

Edgar shook his fist triumphantly in the air. He turned his attention back to Hilda Jessup on the line. "Why, Ms. Jessup," he said, suddenly irritated. "Look what time it is! I can't let you hold me up any longer! I have to go now." Click.

Hilda cursed the man and slammed down her phone.

The transmitter in the pen on Carmichael's desk was tiny, of course. It only had a radio transmitting range of about one hundred yards, or so. Because of the big Tuesday banquet, Carmichael had Dalling Securities guarding VECO round the clock. Dalling patrolled the parking lot and checked all vehicles. None of the Carmichael Vero Task Force would be able to park a van in the VECO parking lot and listen to the transmission. So in the trunk of Tammi Bannerman's car was a big cardboard box, taped up and addressed to Grandma Bannerman in Kentucky. Inside the box was the digital receiver

ERIC FLORE

for the transmitter. The receiver was installed to a cellular phone hookup. Back in the war room at the Holiday Inn, Edgar Waters dialed the number to the cell phone hookup in Tammi's trunk from a telephone on the audio equipment table. That phone he dialed from was hooked up to the war room sound system. When the cellular connection was made, Edgar flicked a button on the audio equipment and proudly announced to Michael Davis, Captain Gandtz, and Lt. Saucier:

"Gentlemen, I give you the voice of Carmichael Vero!"

Suddenly, Carmichael Vero's voice filled the war room. Everyone whooped and hollered. Edgar played with some switches on a sound board, making Carmichael's voice smooth and clear. Digital recorders were rolling, and Carmichael Vero and VECO and the Family were wired for sound for the very first time.

The doctors at the Beaver County Medical Center pronounced Ray Kirkland was stable. They had him in bed hooked up to an IV machine and a heart monitor in a small room off the side of the emergency facilities. A team of cardiologists was scheduled to run tests on him after lunch. They were quite sure he'd suffered a major heart attack, which was the surprise of his life. He told them of his great fitness, yearly check-ups, low body fat and cholesterol levels, and the perfect bills of health his family physician had given him over the years. His medical records all verified this information. But the doctors didn't care. He'd just suffered a near fatal heart attack, according to their diagnoses.

Though stable, he still felt rotten. Shelly was by his side, and Sheriff DeBona was concerned enough about him to remain with them all morning, sitting in a chair off to the side. Ray was praying constantly in his prayer language, not understanding one bit what was going on. Shelly was continually laying hands on his head and his chest, declaring that her husband was the healed of the Lord, promised perfect health according to God's written word, and was healed by the stripes Jesus took on His back. Ray's forehead was shiny with olive oil from Shelly anointing him occasionally as she prayed the prayers of faith. Sheriff DeBona sat stoically, listening to the prayers. He didn't know what to think of it all, but he couldn't deny that these two were walking in peace at the moment, despite the horrible reports of the doctors.

It was at that point that Pastor David, Pastor Archie, and a budding young prophet named Darren from Covenant Church came into the room. They all hugged Shelly and slapped Ray's hand with firm handshakes. There was no fear in any of their faces, just love and concern. Sheriff DeBona found the whole scene very strange: a white pastor, a black associate pastor, and a young white man all coming to minister to the Kirklands. What kind of church was it that had that sort of racial mix? Ray introduced the Sheriff to everyone. Pastor Dave joked about how many times he'd voted for DeBona. The Sheriff watched for a while as they bantered and then got serious as Ray shared the doctors' reports. There was such a sense of true family among them, people who had little similarities. This concept was foreign to DeBona. He sat amazed and perplexed at this vision of the Body of Christ.

"We want to pray for you," Pastor David told Ray.

"I'm not stopping you!" the detective chuckled.

The three men and Shelly all gathered around Ray's bed and laid hands on his head, shoulder, and chest. They began by praying in their prayer languages for several minutes. For a while after that they praised the name of Jesus, and extolled God as the gracious and loving Father that He is. Then, after they had become still and quiet for a moment, Pastor David began:

"Holy Spirit, we thank You for Your presence here this morning; for the peace that You bring to us. Anoint our prayers, that they would be effective, powerful, able to reach down to the root of this sickness and uproot it before anything has a chance to set in on Brother Ray."

They prayed in their prayer languages some more. Then Holy Spirit began to speak to them individually, giving them wisdom and direction, pulling back the veil of the spirit realm so they could see what was really happening to Ray.

"This is an attack, a spiritual attack," Pastor David spoke the word of knowledge Holy Spirit gave him. "This is not a health problem, this is a spiritual assault."

They all responded with greater fervency, rebuking the attack, cursing the devil in Christ's name, taking authority over him, commanding him to give up the ground in Ray's life he had tried to take.

"This is a man of God!" Pastor Archie declared over Ray. "This is God's anointed. Touch not God's anointed, devil! You cannot have him! He is not yours! You must release this man and his health right now! I apply the precious blood of Jesus against you, enemy! The blood of the risen Savior, the Holy One who conquered you."

The prayers got much louder and more authoritative. It was clear that a war was going on and the tide was turning. Sheriff DeBona squirmed in his seat, uncomfortable with such an open display of faith in God, but fascinated by what they were all saying.

"My!" Shelly cried out at the revelation Holy Spirit gave her. Tears began to roll down her cheeks. "Death spirit! This was a death spirit sent out against my Raymond. A death curse! This was supposed to kill the man!"

They all began to rebuke the spirit of death. They declared the resurrection life of Jesus Christ over Ray and quoted many of His resurrection benefits promised in the scriptures.

"What's the root of this?" Pastor David asked the Lord out loud.

The buzz of their prayer languages filled the air, again. Then suddenly, after a moment, Darren the young prophet spoke one word: "Witchcraft!"

Everyone looked at him with surprise.

"Someone has sent this curse out to kill Ray. This is a witchcraft curse!"

They all stopped and looked at Ray. He nodded, confirming that word. He began to tell them of his Todd Falco investigation, how he'd run across Carmichael Vero, and how Holy Spirit had warned him of witchcraft when he first visited VECO the other day. Then, without naming names or going into detail, he told them all of Edgar Waters' testimony that morning about Carmichael Vero's 'invisible protection.' Sheriff DeBona even nodded in agreement, wanting to confirm Ray's testimony to them. He was clearly rooting for them, now.

"So these people that you've been investigating may have occult ties," Pastor David said.

Ray nodded. "I've not seen one shred of evidence in the natural to confirm it. I only know that's what Holy Spirit told me. But yes, I believe they somehow do hold ties to the occult."

A mighty wave of God's presence and power then swept over them. They were supernaturally endowed with Christ's authority in a way that was so tangible they could sense God's power in their midst. Every hair on Sheriff DeBona's body stood on end. He had never imagined there was a God as powerful as the one manifesting in that hospital room that moment.

Pastor David prayed: "We declare that the name 'witchcraft' is under the mighty name of Jesus, so witchcraft and its curses have to obey His supreme authority!"

"You must go, curse!" Pastor Archie commanded. "The curse cannot legally land upon us without a right to. Demon, you have no rights over what belongs to Jesus Christ! Go back out into the dry places of the spiritual world. You must go from Ray Kirkland and never return!"

"You have no authority!" they commanded. "Loose his health NOW!"

In the spirit realm there was a sudden mighty shaking. The glory of God moved against Cyrus Moreau's death spirit. Having no authority over Ray Kirkland, the demon lost some of its grip on him. In the natural realm, Ray's body suddenly jolted under the prayer warriors' hands. Sheriff DeBona nearly rocketed to the ceiling, it startled him so.

The tide was indeed turning in favor of the intercessors. They pressed in harder, commanding the spirit with tremendous authority.

"Leave him and go back to the dry places!" Pastor David said.

Darren spoke up: "We command you to go back to the source of this curse, demon! I command you back upon the sorcerer who sent you, curse!"

Ray looked up at Darren with shock. Pastor David looked at Ray with concern. But Pastor Archie and Shelly were amening Darren's command.

"Teach this sorcerer not to touch God's anointed!" Darren continued. "Let them be taught a lesson for this infraction against one of God's chosen children! Go back to that person who sent you, death curse . . ."

Ray Kirkland suddenly sat straight up on his bed, grabbed Darren by his arm and shouted: "No!" Darren's eyes lit up with unexpected shame at Ray's rebuke. "No!" Ray repeated. "We're not wrestling against flesh and blood, but against spirits of wickedness in high places! We *don't* curse that person back, Lord God! No, we speak mercy to them, Lord! We speak mercy to that sorcerer, whoever he or she may be. Mercy to their soul! Mercy to their life! We do not curse, but we bless this misguided soul who would try to use witchcraft to kill me! We declare God's infinite mercy in their life, Father!"

They all calmed down and looked at Ray. He nodded at Darren, who closed his eyes humbly and nodded back. Ray continued:

"We curse this spirit, this demonic curse sent to kill me. But we speak your grace and mercy to that person by whom this curse was sent, Lord. Protect that person, turn their heart to repentance, and bring them to salvation, if they can indeed be turned, Father. But Jesus, we speak Your mercy upon them right now. Mercy!"

They all began to pray in agreement with Ray, understanding his right heart before the Lord. Then Pastor David prayed once more:

"Now, Principality! You have been exposed by the living God! And just as the word says that Jesus stripped you of all your authority and humiliated you through His great resurrection, we now stand in the authority He's given us as His beloved children, and we now expose you for the lie that you are, and witchcraft curse-we break you RIGHT NOW by the anointing of Jesus that breaks every curse and yoke of bondage! We strip you of your power over Ray! We declare you humiliated and a failure in this situation! We declare your death assignment over Ray Kirkland is now and forever null and void! This death curse is BROKEN by the blood of Jesus! You are defeated, and YOU MUST GO NOW, by the name of Jesus Christ, the triumphant Savior of the world!"

Right then Cyrus Moreau's death curse was broken off Ray. The spirit loosed Ray's health completely and fled from the onslaught of God's glory and an innumerable army of His angelic hosts. Ray instantly felt something loosed off his body, like a smoky cloud in his midst was suddenly evaporated by a bright heat. His countenance changed.

They all began to clap and shout and praise Jesus joyously. They acknowledged the air of Christ's victory that was flooding that room. Even people out in the emergency room heard them, but no one dared rush in to find out what was going on.

Darren suddenly saw an overwhelming vision in his mind's eye. "The war is turned!" he shouted with glee. "The war itself is turned! I see the army of darkness fleeing before the hosts of heaven!" He began to laugh and cry at the same time. "Oh! I see the glory of God spreading everywhere! So many angels! So many angels! And I see the devil retreating in defeat! This war is turned! The tide is turned! Praise you Jesus!"

The others all sensed it too, and began jumping and cheering around Ray's bed. God's presence became so thick around them that Sheriff DeBona literally had to get up and leave the room. He knew something was happening, but did not understand what in the world (or heavens) it was.

Ray sat up as the power of Jesus flooded his body. He felt incredible! He was loosed! Aside from a slight headache and some lingering soreness in his shoulders and left arm, he felt a great relief. He lifted his hands and began praising the Lord . . .

Larsky finished his work in Carmichael's office and prepared to have it sent to another department. He stood up, folder in hand, and looked at Carmichael.

"I'm leavin' now. I've got to make my meeting."

Carmichael looked up at his henchman. "You make sure you come back. I need you here."

Larsky got irritated. "I know. I know."

"You remember what to tell him to do, right?"

"Yeah. Even though I don't think it's the right thing. We're gonna be wastin' too much time."

"So you told me. When you're in charge one day, you can do it however you want. Right now, I'm telling you how *I* want it done today. Tell him like I said, and then get back here."

The four men in the war room heard Ed Larsky sigh impatiently and leave Carmichael's office.

"Where's he going?" Captain Leo Gandtz asked with great frustration.

"Who's this person he's going to meet?" Edgar Waters asked the others.

State Attorney General Michael Davis stood up from his chair, a sudden knot forming in his stomach. "Man, we're missing something, here! They're up to something! And we've been stupid, gentlemen. Stupid!"

"How?" Gandtz asked.

"We've been so busy patting ourselves on the back all morning for getting that bug planted in Carmichael's office that we forgot to get you and Lt. Saucier out there to tail these people!" He sighed and shook his head. "Larsky's about to do something big. Something we need to know about."

It was a crisp spring evening in Bern, Switzerland. The European sky was crystalline, with millions of stars shimmering like precious jewels over that affluent Swiss city. An Alpine breeze made the three degrees Celsius temperatures feel more like an Arctic ten below. That didn't stop young Swiss banker Friedrich Roehler from trying to get his two dinner guests outside. Roehler, a successful banker in the private Swiss banking system, was entertaining the famous Benucci sisters from Italy. These thirtiesh beauties from Florence were descendants of the famed Medici family. They controlled an impressive portion of their family fortune. Friedrich Roehler's bank wanted their accounts. The bank president commanded him to do whatever it took to land the Benucci family account. So after a late day meeting he invited the sisters out for dinner and some drinks. To his surprise, the bratty sisters accepted his invitation. Like many Swiss residents, he spoke their native Italian, as well as his native German, and French. He conversed with them in their Italian dialect, which really impressed them. They had consumed a scandalous amount of expensive French wine with their light dinner, and were quite tipsy. He took them over to the famous Cacao cafe for mochas and pie. Both became very physically affectionate toward the charming banker, hugging him and kissing him lightly on his cheeks as the evening wore on. They were way underdressed for such an Alpine night as this, both foolishly wearing sleeveless sun dresses. He was hoping that by getting them out on the terrace, the cold air would make them beg him to take them someplace warmer. His condominium, perhaps? There all the paperwork from the bank had been faxed and was awaiting him. All he needed was the two signatures of these drunken Italian beauties. If Roehler landed this account, a handsome bonus awaited him.

To his surprise these gorgeous, drunken fools actually agreed to go with him out on the Cacao terrace. In a few short minutes he had them both cuddling him to stay warm, one beauty under each arm. He was just about to suggest that they return to his place for a night cap when his cell phone went off. It played Beethoven's third. Friedrich ignored it. He suggested the night cap back at his place before he returned them to their expensive hotel suit. They were hesitant, at first, to his surprise. But after some more smooth talking and cold Bern air they began to like the idea more and more. The phone went off again. The twins made him hush as it played. They commented on how much they liked Beethoven's third symphony. He bragged about his Beethoven collection and his high tech sound system back home. Not to mention, his wine collection. They were r...ly interested, now. A minute later it played again. He groaned, then excused himself. He went to the corner of the terrace and pulled out his phone. He dialed the answering service. There was a message for him, spoken in German:

"Rome's burning. Act immediately."

Friedrich's eyes bulged wide. "Josef!" he gasped with glee.

The Benucci account bonus was instantly insignificant. If he could pull off Joseph Vero's transfer command, Vero would pay Friedrich Roehler a fee quadruple what this Benucci bonus would be worth. He needed to get straight to his bank. All bankers there had global transactions capabilities available to them twenty-four hours a day. He could successfully fulfill "Josef's" international bank account transfer within a couple of hours. Oh, the bank president would surely be livid. The bank was about to lose Joseph Vero's vast account. Then the Benucci account would be delayed once more, perhaps for good. But who cared if the bank lost out? Friedrich was about to make a large sum of American dollars for a mere two hours work!

Friedrich didn't even make excuses to the Benuccis. He just dumped them flat. They protested angrily, being the prima donnas that they were, causing a major scene right there in the Cacao. But he couldn't have cared any less. He left them stranded there and headed straight for his bank as fast as his Porsche would get him there.

After all, Joseph Vero would make him far more money than these obnoxious Italians.

FORTY-EIGHT

G reggy and Jimmy Richards both sat in their rental car when Tony Vero finally appeared from around the corner.

"It's about time!" Greggy said. "What's he been doin' in there?"

"I'm hungry!" Jimmy whined.

Tony had spent the last forty-five minutes in Reeves Bank in downtown Beaver Falls. As he walked over to his car in the parking lot, he was carrying a cardboard liquor box packed full with something.

"What's he got in that box?" Greggy said. "I hope it's cash or something! We can get it from him before Frankie gets ahold of him."

"I hope he's going to eat somewhere! I'm starving!"

They watched Tony put the box in the Mercedes' trunk.

"Look at him," Greggy sneered. "He thinks he's all that."

"I can't believe that arrogant punk doesn't remember what he did to me in high school."

Greggy looked over at Jimmy. "What did he do to you?"

Jimmy shook his head, irritated. "It's a long story. There he goes!"

Greggy cranked the engine and they pulled out and followed Tony.

"Go get food! Go get food! Go get food!" Jimmy chanted hopefully.

But instead, Tony Vero went to a real estate office in Chippewa. Jimmy punched the rental car dashboard and cursed him as Greggy parked at the bank across the street.

"He's probably gonna be in there for hours!" Jimmy whined. "Let's go up to Al's and grab some pizza . . ."

Greggy interrupted him, pretending to be talking on the phone: "Well, you see, Frankie, we lost Tony because Jimmy had to go get something to eat. Do you want me to kill him for you now, or would you like to wait and do it yourself?"

"I'll get out and *walk* up there and be back in five minutes! Please, Greggy!"

Greggy firmly shook his head no. "No way. If he sees your fat butt walking up the road, we're sunk. You're just gonna have to tough this one out, little brother. You're life depends on it."

Larsky met Tommy Wheeler behind an old billboard near a construction sight off Rt. 51. They smoked a cigarette while Larsky gave him his new orders to follow Frank Kranac for the afternoon before he killed Tony Vero. Wheeler was not happy at all with Carmichael's new command.

"You gotta be kidding! I'm the number one shooter in these three states! And you want me to tail some freak!" He shook his head proudly and said, "Man, I ain't no flunky . . ."

Larsky, already angry with Carmichael, shoved his finger in Wheeler's face. "What did I tell you this morning about working for Carmichael, yin-yang?" Wheeler was startled by Larsky's ferocity. "When anyone works for Carmichael Vero, they automatically become his flunky. You follow that Kranac guy all day. I'll call you on that cell phone of yours. You tell me where you have him staked out. I'll come relieve you and take over from there. Then you'll go waste Tony Vero for us, once and for all! You got all that?"

"All right, Ed!" Wheeler snapped. "Why you have to get all huffy with me today?"

"Someone's gotta get people in line," Larsky sighed, blowing out cigarette smoke. "You and Carmichael both been givin' me too much attitude today, when this should be the happiest day of my life: the day Tony Vero dies!"

After an hour Tony stepped out of Chippewa Realty and got into his car. One of the realtors there was his arch-rival quarterback for Blackhawk when they were in high school. The two had become good friends when they were in college. Tony had the man draw up all the paperwork to sell Pete Vero's house and everything in it, then send the check for the proceeds to his sister Gina in Ohio. At least now she would be taken care of financially. This would be his last night in that house.

"There he goes!" Jimmy woke up his snoozing brother. Greggy cranked the engine and followed him again. "Please, eat, you idiot!" Jimmy said. But Tony lost them at the stoplight when they got tangled in traffic.

"He's getting away!" Jimmy yelled.

"He's probably going back to his house," Greggy said. By the time they passed McKinley Road on Rt. 51, Tony was no where to be seen up ahead. "He must have gone to his house. We'll grab a drive through burger up the road."

"Yeeeesssss!" Jimmy screamed triumphantly.

"But then we gotta go figure out a way to get him. Time's running out."

Tony parked in his garage. As he went to the back of the Mercedes, he heard his Family pager going off in his truck. He went over and snatched it out of the truck visor. It read that one of the Family members had paged him five times. Why would they be paging him? He was supposed to be like a dead man to the Family. Tony opened his garage door and marched down his driveway. There, he took the pager, dropped it to asphalt, and stomped it flat. He then picked up the broken remains and hurled the thing into the woods across the street as hard as he could.

Joseph slammed down the payphone. He knew Tony was too smart to answer his page.

Ray and Shelly Kirkland and Pastor Archie were in Ray's little room when the chief Beaver County Medical Center cardiologist entered. The doctor had a concerned look on his face that made Shelly nervous again. He silently pulled up a stool beside Ray's bed and folded his arms. He held the results of Ray's extensive cardiology tests that they ran earlier that afternoon. The young doctor looked Ray in the eyes and asked him to repeat, word for word, exactly what had happened to him that morning that got him into the hospital. Ray recounted the pains, fatigue, and dizziness he was experiencing when he woke up. He told how it only got worse, how a bad headache and chest pains increased as the morning wore on, and finally, how he passed out at the Holiday Inn. The doctor shook his head perplexed, opened the report folder, and held it up for Ray and Shelly to see. Pastor Archie looked over the doctor's shoulder.

"Well," the doctor said, unsure of what to tell them, "you may say that you experienced all that, and you certainly were exhibiting all indications of a major heart attack on your EKG's and blood pressure work when you first arrived here this morning," he pointed at the main page of the cardiology report. "But from all the tests we ran on you this afternoon, I have one thing to tell you:"

Shelly squeezed Ray's hand and silently prayed her trust to God . . .

". . . You have the healthiest looking heart I've ever seen in my entire career, Mr. Kirkland."

Ray sat up on the bed and glorified God with an ear to ear grin. Shelly screeched loudly, smiling and crying at the same time, and Pastor Archie fell to his knees, praising the name of Jesus and thanking Him. The doctor just shook his head and smiled lightly at their praise party.

"We can't find one thing wrong with you now, Mr. Kirkland," he continued. "The arteries in and around your heart are perfect. They're slicker than glass, with no signs of blockage anywhere. Your blood pressure's excellent, your EKG's are perfect, your blood sugar is normal, your cholesterol and triglycerides are probably the best I've seen in someone your age in years. All tests have come back negative this afternoon. We cannot find one thing wrong anywhere in your body."

Ray was tearing up, now. "It's the Lord, I tell you Doctor. He's my Healer."

The doctor then looked him sternly in the eye like he had something dire to say. Ray held back some of his euphoria and straightened up so he could receive whatever the doctor had to tell him.

"I just have one more question for you, Detective Kirkland," the cardiologist asked in all seriousness.

Ray and Shelly looked at him wide eyed.

"What are you still doing in this hospital?"

The Kirklands and Pastor Archie broke out in laughter.

"Go home and live a long life!" the doctor smiled gently at Ray.

At 2:15 Tommy Wheeler was stopped at a traffic light, three cars behind Frank Kranac's black Galaxie 500. The light changed. The Galaxie proceeded. Wheeler gunned his chopper and followed.

Frank Kranac peered into his rear view mirror when he heard the rumbling of that chopper from the traffic behind him. There went that scrawny punk again. This was the third time that day Kranac had seen him. Who was he? Kranac's mind worked it all over for a moment. Three times in one day. That biker was tailing him.

At 4:30 Carmichael and Larsky were completing work for the banquet. Carmichael suddenly looked at his watch and asked, "Have you seen Joseph around here this afternoon?"

"No. Why?"

"I haven't heard from him, and he hasn't return any of my calls." He looked up at Larsky. "Are you ready to go?"

Larsky sneered. "I been ready for eight hours now."

Carmichael looked at the paperwork before them. He sighed. "I can finish this mess. You get out of here. And Ed . . ."

Larsky looked at him with an impatient "Now, what?" expression.

"I need you back here at 6:30 tomorrow morning to sweep the office."

"I'll be here with a big smile on my face, by that point."

Larsky left VECO to go take care of Frank Kranac.

"What's he going to be smiling about?" Edgar Waters asked Michael Davis as they listened in on the conversation at Carmichael's office. They were alone in the war room. Captain Gandtz and Lt. Saucier had driven back to New Castle to work up their undercover agent for his meeting with Warren Zann on Tuesday.

"I don't know what he's up to today. But he and Carmichael are going to find that transmitter pen tomorrow morning at 6:30 when Larsky sweeps that office."

Edgar looked at the State Attorney General with alarm. "I hope you're not implying what I think you are."

Michael Davis nodded. "This is probably Tammi Bannerman's last day as a VECO employee. I'm not going to endanger her life when they find that pen tomorrow and figure out where it came from."

"But . . . !"

"No buts. She's outta there today."

"Well, she's my employee! You can't tell me what to do with her . . ." Edgar stopped.

Michael Davis smiled. "Don't get insubordinate on me now, after all these years, Sergeant. I'm the one who's footing your bill, remember? You're client is commanding you to get her out of there. Call her and go pick her up from work this afternoon, so her car will be there as long as we need to use that receiver in her trunk. We'll get here early tomorrow and monitor whether or not Larsky finds the pen. If he does, we'll have her call in sick for the day and she'll be safe with us forever more. If he doesn't find it, we'll send her to work and keep an eye on her while we continue monitoring Vero's office."

"If he has a halfway decent bug detector, he'll find it," Edgar said, frustrated.

"We'll worry about that when it happens. Right now, just make sure you pick up Tammi and get her out of there."

Edgar shook his head, deeply disappointed. "It took us all these years to get us up to this point. All those months getting Tammi ready and then getting her hired. Now that she fulfills her ultimate purpose for us . . . it looks like we've shot ourselves in the foot with this bug, Captain."

"Not yet, at least. We'll know tomorrow morning. If they do find it and Tammi's out of there for good, well, that's the surveillance business, for you."

Tommy Wheeler sat in a booth at the Edgewater Inn near the Beaver Falls city limits. He nursed a beer and read the paper, watching Frank Kranac, who'd been planted on a barstool for the last two and a half hours.

Wheeler's cellular phone rang. It was Larsky.

"Where is he?"

"He's here at the Edgewater Inn," Wheeler said, watching Kranac from the corner of his eye. "Been here a long time."

"Well, we're cuttin' you loose. Go get Tony. I'm gonna take care of Kranac, now."

"Finally! You just gonna leave this guy here?"

"I know where he lives. He's gonna have an uninvited house guest tonight! Now go get Tony. And make it count for *me*, would ya?"

Wheeler snickered. "I'll handle Glory Boy just like you would, Brother!"

Wheeler hung up, laid two dollars on the counter, and left to go kill Tony Vero.

As Tommy Wheeler gunned his chopper in the Edgewater Inn parking lot, Frank Kranac slowly rotated on his barstool and watched him through the window. Kranac took one last swallow of his beer and got up to leave, too.

Cyrus Moreau returned to his rented Hyatt Regency penthouse in New York City. His afternoon business meetings with that Wall Street guru were an exciting success. It looked like he would be announcing an IPO by the end of the year. His occult empire would go public, he'd earn millions more, and he'd make the spirit realm a tangible, marketable asset. Then he would cement his place in history as being even greater than the notorious Aleister Crowley himself.

Cyrus drank a mineral water and closed all the blinds in the penthouse. He wanted complete darkness so he could commune with the Dark Lords and find out how things went with Detective Ray Kirkland and the general goings-on of the Family in

Pennsylvania. When the late afternoon sun was darkened, Cyrus laid down his water and climbed aboard the huge king-sized bed. He began to relax, blank out his mind, and chant the ancient chants that always produced the Dark Lords. After a few minutes, nothing had happened. Cyrus opened his eyes, looked around the huge hotel room, and began to angrily curse the Dark Lords. *They had better learn to come immediately when summoned!* he thought. He began the process again. This time, there were different results. Cyrus sensed the icy presence of the summoned spirits nearing him. Usually the air of their presence gradually increased as they came forth to manifest themselves. Tonight, however, something was different. They were hovering somewhere close in the spirit realm. He sensed they were nearby, but they weren't fully disclosing themselves. He waited impatiently. They had never done this before. He didn't know what they were up to. Suddenly, an icy force jerked Cyrus's body, much like the tug of a fishing line when a fish first strikes the hook. A few seconds later it happened again. His head snapped lightly from the jerking. Cyrus sat up, wary now, not knowing what was going on. They were not trying to commune with him, that much was certain. Then the demonic forces pressed in violently on Cyrus Moreau, knocking him onto his back. He could not move. Fear began to flood his soul, for he was Cyrus Moreau, Master of the Spirit Realm. Why would his spiritual minions move against him so? But his minions quickly made clear who had been in charge all along.

"Warfare!" A spirit shrieked in Cyrus's soul. It was the death spirit he'd used so many times before; the same spirit he had dispatched to kill Pete Vero, the same one he'd sent after Ray Kirkland. But now, like a boomerang he'd thrown that had missed it's mark, this spirit had come straight back for Cyrus. The sorcerer's eyes widened with dread. The spirit spoke again:

"The Enemy has attacked us from all directions!" the spirit told him. "He's penetrated all of our strongholds! They are all crumbling around us! We are being defeated quickly! And this is YOUR fault! Now YOU will pay!"

Cyrus's windpipe was instantly throttled shut. It felt like a watermelon had just been bluntly lodged in his throat. He quickly began to asphyxiate. Writhing helplessly on his bed, getting weaker every second, clutching his neck, terror flooded Cyrus's spirit.

"How dare you so arrogantly disregard MY words of warning to you, Warlock!" the spirit screamed at him. "Now you shall pay the price for your impudence-ETERNAL DAMNATION! I AM NOT YOURS, FOOL! YOU ARE MINE FOREVER! FEEL THE FLAMES OF HELL LICKING AT YOU! YOU WILL BE LOST IN THEM FOREVER!"

Helplessness overtook Cyrus. He was no longer Cyrus Moreau at that point, but the weak human creation named Johnny Cirello. He experienced that horrible dread that an unredeemed human in the throes of death feels when the reality of eternal hell suddenly hits them. He suddenly remembered every word of salvation that Brother Maynard had ever spoken to him about the Risen Savior, trying to get him to let Him into his heart. Yet he rejected Brother Maynard's words, and now those words stood as a witness of eternal judgment against Johnny Cirello. He had surely heard every one of them and was eternally accountable for them. He realized now that it was God Himself who had put such a powerful witness as Brother Maynard before him, yet Johnny Cirello had willfully rejected him and Jesus. Now, in a deliberate parody of Faustus, the demons he'd always believed he'd controlled began to yank and tear at his soul as he choked to death. He felt his spirit being torn from his earthly body while hell yawned open, waiting for him like a predator its prey. And Cyrus, the dedicated servant of satan, knew he deserved the hell fires awaiting him as the Dark Lords dragged his spirit from his tormented body once and for all. He deserved hell, and could have no hope of redemption, now; it was too late to call upon the Christ he had so rejected. This horrible final moment was the one he always knew would occur but had deliberately blocked from his consciousness. Now he was actually living it out, and it was more terrifying than he could have ever imagined. As the final remnant of oxygen was used up by his brain, his spirit was loosed from his mortal body. Cyrus Moreau, the man born Johnny Cirello, could actually see the Dark Lords gleefully pulling him into the devastating blackness of eternal hell once and for all . . .

"MERCY!" came the call that pierced the horrifying scene of damnation. Both Cyrus and the Dark Lords who were dragging him to his eternal doom heard the cry in the spirit realm. They all froze.

"MERCY!" There it came again. The voice sounded dimly like the voice of Ray Kirkland, but beneath the prayer it sounded more like the voice of the Son of God Himself . . .

"THE MERCY OF GOD TO THE SORCERER!" The darkness of the hellish scene was suddenly split by a blinding Light. The words spoken by Ray Kirkland were empowered by the Spirit of the Living God Himself. Like a two edged sword they broke through the death curse that Cyrus Moreau had spoken against Ray Kirkland and was now receiving back upon himself.

"JESUS'S BLESSINGS OF FORGIVENESS AND MERCY AND LOVE TO THE SORCERER!"

Ray Kirkland's prayer over Cyrus Moreau in response to the curse against him fully manifested itself. The Dark Lords were suddenly scattered abroad over the mouth of hell, losing their grip on Cyrus. God's Light of Love illuminated that eternal darkness with a blistering heat of His Glory that caused the gaping gate of hell below to wither into oblivion at His Holy Presence. Cyrus Moreau found himself dangling literally between life and death. The Dark Lords were scattering in terror at the Glory of God around them. Cyrus could see them looking back at him, wanting to circle around and lunge for his spirit again, angrily aware that they were being robbed of what was legally theirs—a practicing sorcerer who deserved the eternal judgment of hellfire. But the God who was interceding on Cyrus's behalf wasn't as interested in judgment as He was in mercy. In fact, He had sent His only begotten Son to establish eternal mercy to those who would receive it.

"MERCY TRIUMPHS OVER JUDGMENT!" Ray Kirkland's prayer rocked the spirit world and sealed God's will in this situation. Because he had spoken that mercy over

Cyrus Moreau instead of condemning the man, Cyrus was freed from the Dark Lords' death grip. An innumerable army of holy angels swiftly entered the scene, filling all that realm now illuminated with God's glory. Before them Cyrus could see what he knew to be the remains of the Family's spiritual protection. Hordes of demons, the very ones Cyrus had loosed to protect Carmichael Vero and the Family, were fleeing defeated. They and the rest of the Dark Lords retreated forever from Cyrus Moreau, Carmichael Vero, and the Family as the countless bright angels laid chase. The Family was now completely unprotected and vulnerable.

Cyrus was quickly surrounded by God's angels. He sensed the holiness of these angelic beings. They were heading in his direction. He was so unclean! They couldn't possibly be coming to help him; that would require them to touch his unholy being. But touch him they did, to his surprise. Their touch was gentle and loving. Was this how God treated unholy people? These angels loosed by Ray Kirkland's prayer snatched up Cyrus Moreau's spirit and delivered him from this temporary limbo between life and death. They carried him back to the earthly realm. He could see the hotel penthouse quickly manifesting before them. He actually saw his long haired, blue skinned, tattooed corpse lying on that bed with a twisted expression of horror, horror now past for him. The angels deposited the real Cyrus Moreau, the spirit man, onto that bed, into his once dead corpse. Suddenly, spirit and body were reunited. Cyrus felt his body, soul, and spirit as one again. Life returned to his corpse. However, something was terribly different, this time. He didn't spring up on the bed and gasp for air, glad to be delivered from damnation and back among the living. No, he *couldn't* move his body. The demonic asphyxiation that caused the oxygen deprivation to his brain had permanently killed off whole sections of his brain and nervous system. He quickly realized his body was severely paralyzed. He couldn't move his face, arms, or legs. For all intents, his body was now a lifeless shell housing his spirit. He thought of people he had actually cursed into this condition before. Now he was in this state, and helpless to do anything about it. He knew he was no longer Master of the Spirit Realm; no Dark Lords would be coming to his rescue. He was not even master of even his own body, now. Fully aware and conscious in his spirit of everything around him, Cyrus Moreau was now trapped in a useless body. For life. With horror, though, he replayed the scene that he just lived through: he reminded himself that for some reason, when he was just about to go to hell, he was given mercy and delivered back alive in his body.

The one reason's name was Ray Kirkland.

FORTY-NINE

E ntering the third day of her fast, Audra Dutton was on her face before the Lord, tearfully interceding with incomprehensible groans for that young white man she'd seen in her Saturday afternoon vision. She felt such a burden for his well-being, like the devil was trying to snuff out his very life. With her flesh taken out of the way by her fasting, Audra was like a piece of conduit plugged directly into the Living God Himself. She was praying by the Spirit exactly what needed to be prayed concerning Tony Vero . . .

Unaware that two different factions were seeking his life, Tony Vero had gone straight back to drinking late that afternoon. By seven o'clock he was into his second six-pack and well drunk. He had his remaining five-hundred thousand dollars prepared to transfer and was ready to relocate forever. He decided to head to Myrtle Beach, South Carolina, to begin his new life as someone other than Tony Vero. He'd been to Myrtle Beach once when he was in college and loved it. There it would be nice and warm and he could spend a few weeks golfing and partying. If all went well there, he'd buy a place and stay. If things didn't pan out, he'd head elsewhere. Like much of his life since he abandoned his NFL dreams, he really had no vision about what he needed to do. Perhaps, and just perhaps, he thought he might give more consideration to this Jesus thing. If he could have the kind of joy and presence Ray Kirkland had, that would be quite an improvement. If God would even have him, after what he had just blatantly set into motion when he turned Frank Kranac over to the Family. Kranac was a dead duck, now. But too bad. He shouldn't have messed with Todd Falco. And Tony was leaving town fast, so he would never have to see the results, anyway.

He was packing what clothes he was going to take with him, what few personal belongings that meant anything to him. He walked past his demolished trophy case, at one point. He considered taking the picture of him and Pete and Joe Namath, but then thought otherwise when he remembered the things his father had done with the Family. He spat on the rubble pile, instead. Pretty much everything was going to be left behind when he disappeared in the morning. He wanted to call Gina, but realized she probably wouldn't be too thrilled to hear from him when he was so drunk. He'd get hold of her after he was settled down in his new life. Then there was Kay Falco. Suffice it to say, he knew he had a hopeless crush on the married woman. But she had found Jesus, and would probably be sick to her stomach to know that Tony knew exactly what happened to her husband Todd but wouldn't tell her. As much as he wanted to see her, he was drunk, and she was way better off without his company, anyway.

Everyone was.

His phone rang again for the fourteenth time since he'd been home that day. It would ring and ring and ring for minutes at a time. Tony figured it was his Uncle Joseph. But he wasn't in the mood for any teary good-byes. For some reason, though, he found himself drawn to the telephone. With no good reason he could think of, he answered.

"Finally!" Joseph Vero blurted out on the other end. "Where have you been?"

"Uncle Joseph?" Tony slurred drunkenly. "You must have dialed the wrong number! Don't you remember? I know longer exist to you . . ."

"Tony! You listen to me: get out of town right now."

"I'm going to! What's the matter? Am I not moving fast enough for the Family? Was I supposed to be out of town by sundown?"

"Tony, you do not understand me. Get out of town, now!"

"Why?"

Joseph paused. "I don't trust Carmichael and Larsky. You shouldn't either. Leave now."

"You think my life is in danger?"

"Yes," Joseph answered bluntly.

Tony laughed. "Wouldn't that just be the kicker, huh? The Family practically destroys everything I know, everything I am, and then they want to kill me, too. So what reason did they tell you they wanted to kill me?"

"They didn't tell me anything. Tony, Carmichael and Larsky are not right. They're in a corner right now, and anyone who they consider a threat is not safe. You are at the top of their list. Get out of town before it's too late. I can't do any more than that for you."

"What, should I be scared or something? 'Cause if that's what they want, I'm not!"

"No, Tony. I don't want you scared, I want you smart."

"Huh. Well thank you."

"And Tony?"

"What?"

"I'm gonna miss you."

With that, Joseph hung up and laid his cellular phone on the seat beside him. He had now done all he could do for his nephew Tony and niece Gina. He had been more loyal to his only loved ones than he had to the Family. To Joseph, that made him as noble and respectable as someone in his position could ever hope to be. He looked out the window of his Porsche as he gunned it across the Ohio Turnpike. His hair was shorn to half an inch and was bleached blond. He wore a fake blond colored gotee and golden rimmed non-prescription eyeglasses, as well. Dressed uncharacteristically in a leisure shirt, blue jeans, and expensive hiking boots, he had taken at least fifteen years off his looks. He was heading toward the Cleveland Airport for a 10:10 flight to Dallas. From Dallas, he would leave the United States for good. Friedrich Roehler in Switzerland had successfully transferred Joseph's multi-million dollar account to a location only the two of them knew. Joseph paid Friedrich well for his services and discretion.

Rome may have been burning to the ground back down the road in Beaver Falls, Pennsylvania, but all that was Carmichael Vero's problem from this point on.

Joseph Vero was now free.

Frank Kranac's house was the creepiest place Ed Larsky had ever seen.

It was so dark, dusty, and musty that Larsky half-expected a vampire to jump out at any time. He sensed such a cold evil about the place. He was used to the evil presence of the Dark Lords all around him. But all of his spiritual protection from Cyrus Moreau was long gone now, completely defeated and driven off by the prayers of faithful intercessors. He had no way of knowing they were gone, though, and he sensed the evil of Frank Kranac's house instead. Chills ran up and down his spine. What was this feeling he was experiencing? He couldn't put his finger on it.

Larsky had parked one of Tommy Wheeler's junk cars down a College Hill side street. He was dressed in black with his long blond locks of hair tucked tightly up under a rubber cap with a black ski hat over that. He'd walked down the alleys of College Hill to the back of Kranac's house. The man's back yard hedges were so high and unkempt no one noticed him back there. He easily broke in through the back kitchen door, knowing from Tony Vero's report that Kranac usually parked out front and used his front door. Inside, Larsky pulled out his 9 mm and explored the house, looking for the Family's million and a quarter dollars. He went upstairs and roamed the top floor. The only thing of interest to Larsky up there was a weight bench with three hundred and fifty rusty pounds on it. But there were no signs of money or any secret hiding places. He went back downstairs and looked some more. In a nook near the kitchen Larsky found the cellar door with the special key lock and deadbolt. Bingo! The money had to be down in that basement. It took him three hard kicks, but the powerful man finally splintered the shiny lock off the wooden door and busted the door open. There was no light switch anywhere to be found, so he descended the wooden staircase with his 9 mm in one hand, and a high-flaming lighter in the other to illuminate the way. This basement really gave him the creeps. He could see little before him. Maybe this was where Kranac hid that moron Falco and the bodies of all his other victims over the years! At the bottom of the stairs he shined his lighter all around. He found the string hanging from the overhead light and flicked it on. The dim basement was full of tools and other odds and ends. There were stacks of boxes on a red carpet. Larsky went over and kicked them all around. There was no money in any of them. He didn't think to look under the red carpet. He broke into several boxes and military trunks. He spilled their contents all over the filthy basement floor. At one point a set of military dog tags clinked to the floor. He picked up the chain and squinted to make out he name on it: "Bernie Lokawski." He remembered what Tony said about Kranac using this alias. Larsky shook his head with disgust. "What a freak!" he muttered. But after a few more minutes of searching, the money was still no where to be found. He went back upstairs to wait for Kranac.

He guarded the kitchen door just in case the man tried to come in from the back instead, but he kept his eye on the front door. He looked at his watch: 7:40. As the sun was setting on this busy Monday, Kranac's eerie place grew darker and darker. The man had no lights on anywhere. Larsky leaned against a wall, looked at his watch again, and began to chuckle. That spoiled brat baby Tony Vero was surely history by now, thanks to Tommy Wheeler. Just as he was about to bask in the thoughts of his wonderful life without Tony Vero around, Larsky heard the front door lock being undone. He scrambled for cover to the side of Kranac's kitchen and steadied his 9 mm at the front door.

Frank Kranac lumbered through the door with a heavy green military duffel bag slung over his shoulder. Ed Larsky's eyes widened when he saw the size of this creep. Tony Vero wasn't kidding when he described him. This guy could throw around that three hundred and fifty pound barbell upstairs with no problem. Kranac locked the front door behind him and took several steps into his living room toward the kitchen. Just when Larsky thought he would have to jump out and stick it to this freak, Kranac stopped in his tracks. He couldn't figure out what to do with that duffel bag. He looked toward the upstairs, then started back toward the steps by the front door. Then he stopped and took two steps back into the living room, trying to make a final decision. Should the bag go upstairs or down in the basement? He twisted his torso toward the kitchen once, and then back toward the steps again, the bulky bag bouncing off his back as he did so. Finally, he opted to go upstairs with it. He thumped up his staircase into the darkness. Larsky looked toward the upstairs, seeing that Kranac didn't even turn on any lights while he was up there. There were a few thumping noises, some shuffling, then things got quiet again. Kranac came back downstairs, minus the duffel bag. He stepped over to a dusty old table lamp in the living room and flicked on the single weak bulb. He doffed his coat, tossed it on the couch, and headed toward the kitchen. Before he got to the kitchen archway, Ed Larsky stepped out, pointed the 9 mm up at his face and growled, "Freeze!" Kranac stopped on a dime and stared down emotionlessly at Larsky. He looked neither scared nor intimidated, but concerned, like Larsky's presence meant a bigger problem than just having someone in the house pointing a gun at him. He was thinking only of the safety of his fortune in the basement, of course.

"Put your hands up high and get against the wall!" Larsky commanded. Kranac obeyed. He stepped to the wall. Larsky shoved him hard against it. "Put your hands up all the way and spread your legs!" Kranac didn't spread his legs wide enough for Larsky. "I said spread 'em!" Ed kicked both of the hulking man's feet further apart. He roughly patted down Kranac's body, looking for weapons. Right there in the back of Frank's pants was a silver 9 mm. Larsky snatched it out, emptied the ammo cartridge with one hand, and tossed the gun into the kitchen. Larsky then found a ten inch long double edged hunting knife strapped onto Kranac's right calf. He ripped it off and tossed it into the kitchen, too. He patted some more. Satisfied that was all Kranac was packing, Larsky stuck the gun up to the back of his head.

"Where's our money, freak?"

"What money?" Kranac bellowed with his deep voice.

"The money you stole from Todd Falco!"

Kranac angrily replied, "I don't know what you're talkin' about!"

Larsky took the butt of his gun and cracked Kranac hard over the back of his head. He cocked his 9 mm with a loud "SHNICKT" and jammed the barrel into the base of Frank Kranac's skull.

"I can get that money back with you alive or you dead. Either way, the choice is yours, freak!"

Kranac thought hard for a moment. Then Larsky saw his huge barrel chest heave slowly up and down with a sigh. Frank turned his head toward Larsky. "It's upstairs."

"Take me to it now!"

A drunken Tony Vero heard the noise for the third time. It sounded like it came from the garage. He went over, turned off his stereo, stopped packing, stood still. Ninety seconds later he heard it again. It was definitely in his garage. He staggered out of his room and down the stairs. He went through the kitchen and undid the garage door lock. His Uncle Joseph's warning rang in his mind, but he was so drunk and past the point of caring that he charged out into the garage anyway. He flicked on the lights. He looked around at his truck and Mercedes. There were no signs of anything wrong with them. Then he noticed the side door was half open. He always kept it locked. His heart began to pound with a mixture of both fear and anger. He reached up on the wall and grabbed a crow-bar. He walked quickly behind his cars over toward the door. Then Tony heard something behind him; it sounded like a boot scuffing on cement. He went to spin around to defend himself, but it was too late.

Tony Vero never knew what hit him.

Larsky walked Frank Kranac slowly up the stairs to his second floor. Kranac's arms were spread high in the air as Larsky pressed his gun firmly to the back of his head. Larsky controlled the big man's movements by jerking the back of his shirt collar with his free hand. Kranac wasn't really afraid for his life. He was too busy being furious at Tony Vero and those idiot Richard brothers. Surely this man with the gun at his head had been sent by whoever Todd Falco and Tony Vero worked for. If Tony had not been so nosy and Jimmy and Greggy Richards so inept, Frank's fourteen million dollar fortune wouldn't be in jeopardy at the moment. When they got to the top of the steps, Larsky flicked on a hall light and jerked him hard, asking, "Which way? Where's the money?"

Kranac nodded toward a closed door on their left. "Down there. In that closet."

Larsky walked him slowly toward the closet. "Get outta the way!" He pushed Kranac about two steps past the door and kept the gun aimed at his head. With his free hand Larsky opened the closet door. There on the floor was that green duffel bag Kranac had brought in. The bag was tied shut at the top. It stood three feet off the ground and was pretty bulky.

"Is that it in that bag?" Larsky asked.

"Yeah."

Larsky kicked the bag. "That doesn't feel like money!" For him to mess with pulling it out and looking into it would give Frank Kranac enough time to try and pull something on him. Larsky stepped away from the closet. Pointing the gun at Kranac he commanded, "You get over here and pull this bag out so I can see it and you."

"I can put my hands down now?"

"Yeah, moron! How else you gonna get it out?"

Kranac turned around and eyed Larsky for the first time. Their eyes locked in hatred. It was killer staring down at killer. Kranac slowly stepped over to the closet door and slid the heavy green bag into the hallway. He stood up and looked at Larsky, waiting for his next order.

"Slowly untie the top and open it up so I can see inside."

Kranac started yanking hard at the knot.

"Slowly, moron!" Larsky snapped, waving that 9 mm at him.

Kranac slowed down a bit, trying to undo the knot while watching Larsky from the corner of his eye. He needed to see exactly when he could make his move. He finished undoing the knot.

"Slowly open up that bag at the top now," Larsky ordered. He aimed the gun right at Kranac's face. "And you better hope that's our money I'm about to see in there, or I'm gonna empty this gun into your head!"

Kranac slowly pulled the rope open at the top of the duffel bag. It was still too dark to see down inside.

"Pull it down further so I can see the cash!"

Frank Kranac hoped he would say that. He yanked down the green canvas about a foot. There inside the bag was the lifeless corpse of Tommy Wheeler. His body was badly mangled. Kranac had ran over him and his motorcycle with his Galaxie 500. He'd caught up to him right after Wheeler left the Edgewater Inn that afternoon to go kill Tony Vero. Kranac rolled the remains of his motorcycle into a Big Beaver ravine below the roadside. He cleaned up the secluded crash sight, wrapped up Wheeler's body, and brought it home to dispose of later.

Larsky's eyes widened. He was uncharacteristically repulsed, and gasped. His shock was instant, lasting only for a second, but that was all the time that Frank Kranac needed. He swung up his left fist like lightning, connected perfectly under Ed Larsky's gun hand, followed through completely, and disarmed Larsky in the blink of an eye. The 9 mm sailed back down the hall, clackety-clacked down the wooden staircase, and bounced somewhere into the living room.

Being lightning quick himself, and refusing to be taken completely by surprise, Larsky instantly answered Kranac with a hard fast right to the jaw. Kranac's head snapped back like a punching bag. Larsky tried to follow up with a kick to Frank's gut, but Kranac stopped his foot cold with both hands, twisted Larsky off balance, and bounced him off the wall onto the ground. He charged to get on top of Larsky, wanting desperately to get him by the neck, but Larsky snapped up off the floor and head-butted Kranac up under his chin, knocking him backward about five feet. Both men straightened up, battle ready, and squared off. They each read the fight-to-the-death determination in their opponent's eyes, neither one yet showing any signs of fear. With that, they rushed upon each other like madmen. Kranac bowled over the smaller man easily, knocking Larsky backward several feet. The two rolled violently back down the hall to the top of the stairs. Larsky kicked Kranac off him with both feet. He got up to run down the steps to retrieve his gun, but Kranac quickly tackled him. They tumbled down the stairs one over the other like two out of control boulders. They landed in the living room, banging hard off the front door. Larsky got up and fought well to keep Kranac off of him, while Frank was looking for an opportunity to get him in a headlock. Had Kranac not been so busy trying to snap Larsky's neck, he quickly could have overpowered the man. If Larsky still had the Dark Lords with him, he would have angrily made short work of his bigger opponent. So the death struggle wore on longer than either normally would have let it, with Kranac trying for Larsky's neck, and Larsky bashing his face with powerful punches. Kranac lunged again for Larsky's upper body, but Ed stepped aside, leaving Frank's left side widely exposed. Ed quickly brought around his right fist as hard as he could into Kranac's rib cage. There was a loud snapping noise, and Kranac "OOF!"ed at the pain. The fracas spilled deeper into the living room, and there Larsky saw his gun near the couch. He sprang for it, but huge Frank Kranac tackled him from behind again. They both landed hard, Larsky on his stomach, with Kranac riding his back. Larsky lost all his wind on impact. He couldn't breathe, and had just given up the momentum of the fight. His right hand did land on the gun butt, though. So instead of trying to get Kranac off his back, he tried to pick up the gun. That was Ed Larsky's fatal mistake. Lying on Larsky's back, Frank Kranac worked one giant arm around his neck and swiftly reached up and grabbed Larsky's gun hand. They struggled over it, Larsky trying to get it in the air behind him so he could take a shot at Kranac. But Frank slammed Larsky's hand to the ground and the gun went off. The shot illuminated the living room. The bullet went under the couch flap and put a hole in the wall. Larsky, who still hadn't taken a breath since they hit the ground, was fading fast. He tried to bring the gun back up, but this time Kranac put all his strength into it and banged Larsky's hand on the ground once more. The gun fired again, but this time popped out of Larsky's hand and bounced a foot away. Still seeking the gun, Ed went to lunge for it once more, but it was too late. Kranac got his legs underneath them both and stood up with Larsky firmly in a headlock. That was all he needed. With the gun out of reach and stars forming in his eyesight from lack of oxygen, Ed Larsky felt the terrifying sting of hopeless defeat. His eyes bulged as he desperately tried to take a breath that wouldn't come. He reached his right hand out helplessly toward his gun on the ground. But it was futile. With one thick arm around Larsky's neck, Kranac finally worked his free hand up under Ed's jaw.

Utter terror was the last thing Ed Larsky experienced as Frank Kranac snapped his neck.

"Those were gunshots, I'm telling you!" Mary Craven whispered to her husband Mitch. She had them on the floor hiding behind two swivel chairs. Mitch was quite irritated with Mary. She had knocked him hard to the ground when she heard the muffled pops coming from Frank Kranac's house.

"How do you know those were gunshots?" Mitch asked. "That could have been anything!"

Mary was crawling over to the telephone. She was frantically hoping the kids were still asleep upstairs.

"I don't care what you say!" she whispered angrily to Mitch. "That man is evil, this is proof that I'm right, and I'm calling the police!"

Frank Kranac moaned like a grieving mother when he saw that Ed Larsky had broken into his basement. He touched the tattered wood on the door where Larsky had broken the locks off. He felt so violated.

"My money!" he whined.

All he knew was thrown into chaos at the sight. He jerked open the door and stormed down the stairs. His broken ribs throbbed with excruciating pain as he bounced down each step. He jerked on the light switch and moaned again when he saw all of the crates and boxes emptied out and strewn about the basement. The red carpet that covered his fortune was still laid out perfectly, but that made no difference in Kranac's warped mind. That dead man upstairs had probably ripped off the red carpet, found all the money, taken most of it out and put it in the trunk of his car somewhere, then replaced the carpeting neatly to fool Frank! He ripped the carpeting off, removed the boards, and stared down at his stacks of money. They were exactly as he left them earlier that day. But of course, that's not what registered in his paranoid mind. Somehow, it was all different. It was changed. It had to be. His house had been violated by an intruder.

Frank Kranac moaned sadly again.

The first of the two Beaver Falls police officers rang Frank Kranac's front doorbell for the third time. He and his partner had been at Frank Kranac's house for four minutes. There were no signs of life inside. The other officer came back around the front of the house shining his flashlight.

"His back door's been broken into, but it's been locked from the inside again. I don't see anything else wrong."

Just then Frank Kranac shocked them both when he opened his front door. Both police officers were taken aback by the size of the man. They tried to get a glimpse of his living room behind him, the second officer shining his flashlight all over inside. The living room was shabby, but there were no signs of anything being wrong.

Frank got irritated at the invasion of his privacy and stepped in front of the flashlight beam. "What're you doing?" he angrily asked the policeman.

"Sir, we've had reports of gunshots around here tonight. Someone reported that they came from your house."

Frank shook his head disgusted. "There were no gunshots. I forget my keys and I had to kick my back door open to get in here tonight! Two hard kicks."

The officer who'd checked the back of the house smiled with realization at his partner. He looked back into Frank's house. "Can we come in and look around, sir?"

"You got a warrant?"

"No, sir. We're just answering a call."

"Well, then, you're not coming into my house. I'm a law abiding citizen, a wartime veteran, and a hard working man who doesn't have time to be harassed by nosy neighbors!" Frank looked over toward the Craven's house, irritated. "That lady next door called this in, didn't she?"

Both officers smiled, now. "We can't tell you that, sir," one of them answered.

"Well, let me tell you about her: I'm forever seein' her looking over here, spyin' on my house. She treats me like I'm some sort of alien or something. She never says 'hello' or treats me nice at all. She's never liked me, and has it in for me, even though I've never done one thing to her. I'm a good quiet neighbor! There hasn't been any gunshots here tonight, I'm not some bad guy, and I don't appreciate being hassled!"

"We're not hassling you, Mr. Kranac. We're just answering a call about a disturbance."

"I was the disturbance! I gotta broken back door to prove it. Now if I had any other problems here I'd call you myself!"

The other officer shined his flashlight on Frank's face. It was swollen and bruised all over his jaws, cheeks, and forehead.

"What's happened to your face, Mr. Kranac?"

Frank put his hand over his jaw. "I got into a tussle with some loud mouth at work the other night. We worked it out. Why? It still looks that bad?"

"Yes!" the first officer said frankly. "Those wounds look fresh. And who in the world was bad enough to knock *you* around and bust up your face like that?"

"Huh," Frank smiled lightly. "You oughta see him!"

Both officers laughed and nodded. The second one turned off his flashlight.

Frank shrugged. "Is that all, then? 'Cause I'm workin' on a project in here and then I gotta go to work."

The first officer smiled. "That's all, Mr. Kranac. Thank you for your time."

Kranac shut the door.

The policemen went back to their cars, filled out a report, and reported back to the dispatcher that the disturbance turned out to be nothing but the homeowner himself. Both officers talked excitedly to the dispatcher about the size of Kranac.

Frank Kranac locked the front door securely. Those nosy cops hadn't seen anything, no thanks to that lousy Mary Craven next store! He knew the two bullet holes were well hidden. The one couldn't be seen behind the couch. The other on the floor he had covered with an old throw rug. He had quickly crammed Larsky's body in the closet upstairs with Wheeler's, and gathered up all the guns, ammo, and his knife that Larsky had strewn about. He had no idea who either one of those dead men were, just that they were both dangerous. Especially that intruder. He was a tough one. But now he was dead! They must be from some bad ol' drug ring, all right.

He staggered back toward the cellar door, holding his left side. Every breath he took was a new experience in pain from those ribs Larsky had broken. But Frank Kranac didn't have time to worry about his health. His fortune was in jeopardy. Whoever sent those two goons after him probably had more coming his way. He had to count all his money, secure his house again, and then get to the root of this intruder problem. That Tony Vero would surely know who Todd Falco worked for, and where these two goons came from. Kranac would torture every bit of information he needed out of Tony Vero once those Richards morons managed to snatch him up!

But first, there were more pressing matters. He descended his cellar steps again.

He stood over his money pit, shook his head, and moaned sadly. He looked down at all that cash and nearly wept with worry.

"My poor baby!" he said aloud to the lucre. "Daddy's gonna make sure everything's all right!"

FIFTY

Carmicheal Vero arrived at VECO 6:25 Tuesday morning. This was VECO's biggest day of the year: the stockholder's banquet. The investors who helped finance VECO's astronomical success would all descend upon the office building that day for an open house. Then, at seven o'clock that evening, the gala banquet would be held at the Wooden Angel restaurant in Beaver. There, the previous year's earnings would be reported and celebrated. Along with all that came a breakfast meeting, a luncheon, and an afternoon wine and cheese in the VECO offices entertainment room. Carmichael Vero's day was taken up by VECO. Unfortunately, his thoughts were occupied with a new Family crisis. He had not heard from Ed Larsky since he dismissed his right hand man 4:30 the previous afternoon. Apprehensive, he had tried to call Joseph several times to see if he'd heard from Ed. But Joseph could not be reached, either. He was also anxious to know if that Tommy Wheeler successfully finished his hit contract on Tony. So as Carmichael ascended the inner stairs to the main offices, he had three major unanswered questions plaguing him. Hopefully Larsky had just been busy with that Kranac oaf all night, getting back all the Family's money the man stole from Todd Falco and then disposing of Kranac's body. But if Larsky didn't show up at 6:30 like he'd ordered him to

The captain of the three Dalling Security guards was stationed upstairs at the secretaries' pool outside Carmichael's office.

"Have you heard from Mr. Larsky this morning?" Carmichael asked the guard captain. "No sir."

Carmichael went to unlock the glass doors to his office foyer. "Has anybody been by here since last night?"

"Not a soul, sir. Everything's been clear. No visitors."

"Well, send in Mr. Larsky as soon as he gets here."

Carmichael unlocked the glass doors and went to his office. The oak doors had been locked all night, too. He figured the room must still be safe from bugs. He went in and turned on all the lights. He waited at his desk for Larsky.

At 6:55, when Larsky still hadn't shown up, Carmichael got worried.

"This can't be happening," he mumbled.

"What can't be happening?" Edgar Waters asked Michael Davis, back in the Carmichael Vero Task Force War Room out at the Holiday Inn.

Michael Davis smiled. "Obviously Carmichael's worried about Larsky not showing up at 6:30 like he told him to yesterday."

"Where do you think he is?"

Davis smiled even bigger, now. "I don't care! All I know is Carmichael Vero's office is still wired for sound. He probably assumes since no one's been in his office since he left last night, everything's still all safe and secure. But he's living in a fool's paradise, right now. Call Tammi Bannerman and tell her to report to work same as usual today. If Larsky shows up sometime and does a sweep and finds that pen on Carmichael's desk, we'll get her out of there pronto."

"Carmichael's gonna trip up today," Edgar grinned. "You watch!"

Detective Ray Kirkland reported to work at 7:30 that morning. He was met with cheers and hugs from many of his concerned fellow workers. He recounted the story of his apparent heart attack for everyone and gave God all the glory for his healing, of course. He still had a headache and some soreness lingering in his left shoulder, but all the other symptoms were gone. Deputy Simmons was there to meet him, too. The deputy had a big smile on his face.

"Gotta present for you, Detective."

"What's that?"

Deputy Simmons produced an envelope from his pocket. "Search warrant, for Tony Vero's safe deposit box at Reeves Bank."

Ray reached over and put his hand on Deputy Simmons' shoulder. "I love you!"

"Don't kiss me, man!"

At 9:45 Carmichael Vero was beside himself. Larsky still hadn't shown up, and he wasn't answering his home or cell phone. Everyone at VECO was looking for the office manager. Carmichael didn't know what to tell them. He'd made it through the breakfast with the stockholders okay. But now that the employees all saw that Larsky hadn't shown up, a strange air of fear fell about VECO. And Carmichael was doing a bad job of masking his emotions. He wore this obvious look of concern, right in front of the visiting stockholders. As Carmichael tried to be chatty with the visitors, he would see the VECO employees whispering to one another. They were mingling with the stockholders, so the inevitable happened. One of the out of town female stockholders, an elderly woman who had chewed Carmichael's ear off at breakfast, drew him aside again.

"What's this I hear about one of our marketing executives disappearing last week?"

"Uh," Carmichael fumbled for words. "His name was . . . I mean is . . . Todd Falco. He didn't disappear. He's on a leave of absence."

"Yes, but one of your secretaries just told me that there's a major police investigation going on concerning his disappearance. She said that the Sheriff's Department searched VECO the other day and it's been all over the news."

"Um . . . I should have addressed all that at breakfast this morning. I guess I'll have to truly address it at our luncheon downstairs. It's quite complicated . . ." Carmichael's mind was fogging. Everything seemed to be closing in slowly around him. What was happening? What were these strange feelings of doom he was picking up on? Why was he picking up on them?

"How complicated, Mr. Vero?"

"Mr. Falco's character is in question, to be honest, Mrs. Dunthorpe," Carmichael explained. "His wife has some emotional problems, he's left town to sort some things out. She doesn't believe us when we tell her he's left town, and she's called in the police and made some bizarre accusations, I'm afraid."

Mrs. Dunthorpe looked concerned.

"But I'm absolutely confident we'll be vindicated and she'll be proved mentally incompetent."

Carmichael's throat began to tighten. He felt nauseous. He had to get out of this situation.

"Well I certainly hope so!" she said. "I wouldn't want any bad publicity destroying our profits next year! And now everyone here is wondering where Mr. Larsky is today. It seems he's now disappeared, too, and the workers here are all quite concerned . . ."

"The two incidents are completely unrelated!" he lied. "Please excuse me, Mrs. Dunthorpe. I have to take care of something right away . . ."

Carmichael left her in a huff, but didn't care. He couldn't take one more moment of this. He retreated swiftly to his office and locked the doors behind him. He went over to the stereo system and turned on the outside speakers.

"He's got his outside smoke screen blasting!" Edgar Waters called excitedly to Michael Davis. They rushed over to the war room sound system. They dialed Tammi Bannerman. Through one of their coded conversations, she let them know Carmichael was in there alone.

Carmichael dialed Cyrus Moreau's number. He was the only man who could help him, right now. A strange voice answered. It was one of Cyrus' two prodigies.

"Hello?" She sounded absolutely stoned.

Carmichael was shocked not to hear Cyrus. Who was this? "Uh . . . I'm looking for Cyrus."

"Who is this?"

Carmichael got impatient. "That's none of *your* business! Is this Cyrus Moreau's office?"

"Yeah, but Cyrus isn't here. It doesn't sound like he's going to be back. He was found in the New York City Hyatt a little while ago, half dead. He's in the emergency room right now. The prognosis does not look g . . ."

Carmichael slammed down the phone, his heart beating like a jackhammer. Cyrus gone! If *he* was gone, where was all of Carmichael's protection he'd been paying for? The walls were closing in tighter on him now. He couldn't believe all this was happening. His money, Larsky, Joseph, and now Cyrus, all gone. What in the world was happening?

"Who's 'Cyrus Moreau'?" Michael Davis asked Edgar.
Neither of them knew.

Detective Kirkland and Deputy Simmons left Reeves Bank in Beaver Falls highly disappointed. Their warrant was useless. Tony Vero came to the bank the afternoon before, closed out all his accounts, and emptied his safe deposit box.
Deputy Simmons was disgusted. "You gotta admit, boss. That Tony Vero's a pro. He's been a step ahead of us this whole time."
Ray shook his head. "I don't know that he's that good. It's the devil, I tell you. It's just like him to keep robbing me of what I need to break this case. He used that attack against my health yesterday to stay ahead of me."
They stopped out on 7th Avenue by their car. "Now what'll we do?" the Deputy asked.
"If Tony withdrew all his assets and closed out his safe deposit account, what's that sound like to you?"
"He's switching banks?"
"Or?"
"He goin' on a trip."
"A very long one, it looks like. Let's get out to his house."

Frank Kranac finished counting his money for the second time in two days. It was all there, all accounted for. Larsky's presence in his house left the big man feeling violated, defiled. This called for drastic measures. He called off work for the first time ever at Standard Steel. There was no way he was going to leave his cellar door broken open and his fortune unaccounted for and unsecured. And even now that he knew it was all there, he still felt funny about it, like his precious money was defiled, too. He replaced the boards and the red carpet perfectly, then he cleaned up all the crates and boxes and put them back into perfect order. He straightened up the rest of the cellar that the dead, nameless intruder upstairs had wrecked trying to find Todd Falco's money. Then Frank went out and spent literally the most amount of money he's spent in years. He went to the local hardware store, bought two huge, thick doors to replace his basement door and his backdoor. He also bought five of the most expensive, fail proof door locks the store manager showed him. He spent hundreds there, then zipped back home to install it all. He would not leave his house again until he was sure it and his fortune were secure against intruders.
Then he was going to go take care of Tony Vero.

Detective Kirkland and Deputy Simmons stood on Tony Vero's front porch. They'd knocked and rang the doorbell. No answer.

"You think he took off on us already?" Deputy Simmons asked.

Ray shrugged. "God only knows. He's got a whole day on us. Leg's go take a peak around the house, see if his car's still in the garage."

The main garage doors had no windows on them. They walked to the side door of the garage and found it half open. It had obviously been broken open.

"Bingo!" Ray said.

"Don't really need a warrant now, do we?"

"We have probable cause for investigating."

Inside the garage lights were on and the door into the kitchen was open, too. The garage was in impeccably good order.

"Both his Mercedes and his Ford're still in here," Ray commented as they entered.

They both went in opposite directions around the two vehicles. Simmons looked up under the pickup truck.

"What's that over there by you, Ray?"

Ray ducked down under the Mercedes and slid out the crowbar Tony had taken down to protect himself. "Why's this lying on the floor under here?" He laid it aside. "Let's go take a look inside."

They went into the kitchen.

"Mr. Vero?" Ray shouted. No answer. "Tony Vero?" No one.

All the lights that Tony had on the night before were still shining.

"Pretty well lit in here for this time of day," the Deputy commented.

"The man's definitely not worrying about his electric bill." Ray saw the trash can had about seven empty beer cans. "He's been hittin' the sauce pretty hard." There was one beer can sitting in a small puddle of condensation on the counter. Ray picked it up. "Still half full. Warm." There was lunch meat, deli cheese, a jar of mayonnaise, a jar of mustard, and some lettuce and tomatoes on the counter near the refrigerator. Deputy Simmons felt all them.

"Room temperature," he said.

"It's like he was here going about his business, then everything was suddenly interrupted."

They looked at each other warily. Both drew their guns.

"Call the station and let them know where we are and what's going on," Ray said. As Simmons explained their situation to the dispatcher and asked for backup, Ray peaked out of the kitchen and looked up and down the hallway. Simmons joined him from behind.

"You check the living room and the foyer," Ray commanded. "I'll check the hall and the rest of the floor."

As they began to search the downstairs, Ray's heart beat loudly. He wasn't really afraid someone dangerous was in the house. He was dreading finding Tony Vero dead.

There was nothing he found more unnerving than searching a home or apartment and turning up a corpse. That first sighting of a body lying dead somewhere was the worst. For some reason, Ray's discerner was tripping double-time. He knew something was wrong with Tony. The house just had that feel to it.

They met back at the foot of the stairs, both shaking their heads. Ray nodded upstairs and they ascended the steps. Lots more lights were on up there like it was the middle of the night. Deputy Simmons went into Tony's bedroom and called for Ray. They found half-packed luggage and two big moving boxes among more empty beer cans.

Ray put away his gun. "Wherever he is now, Tony was getting ready to leave. That much is obvious." He pointed at the luggage and the boxes. "My bet is that whatever he had in that safe deposit box is packed away somewhere in this mess."

They put the moving boxes up on the bed and began unpacking them.

Deputy Simmons whistled. "You were right, Boss. Look in this one."

Ray examined some of the documents and files Deputy Simmons was pulling out of the box. "These are confidential client files from his private investigation business." Ray threw them down and pulled the rest of the things out of the box. Down at the bottom, he found two thick manila folders. They were both full of stacks of photocopied papers. Ray opened them up and began reading through them. First his eyes lit up.

"What's up?" Simmons asked.

His mouth fell open in astonishment and he had to sit down on the side of the bed. "Lord Jesus! You are a good God! Thank you, Jesus!"

Deputy Simmons tried to read over his shoulder. "Well what in the world did you find that you're praising God for, the Lamb's Book of Life?"

"No, Deputy," Ray chuckled. "No! But I did find what we've been looking for all week. These are copies of the things Tony Vero found in Todd Falco's file cabinet from his house." He held up one of the folders in his left hand: "This is Todd Falco's personal journal that his wife burned up the other night." And in his right hand: "And this is a special file Todd Falco kept." He looked up at Deputy Simmons with a twinkle in his eye. "This is a detailed record of all his drug deals that he made for Carmichael Vero and an organization he runs called 'The Family.' Tony Vero photocopied every document and kept it for himself." He looked around the room. "We've found the missing treasure. Now, where in the world is Tony Vero?"

Tony Vero was in a coffin.

Somehow he knew exactly where he was when he woke up. Even though he could see nothing, for he was in complete darkness, he could feel the silky lining and soft bedding beneath him, and the tight quarters all around him. This container he was in had to be a coffin. And it didn't take a genius to figure out just who would put him in a coffin: Jimmy and Greggy Richards were in the burial business at Grand View Cemetery. His hands were handcuffed behind his back. They were numb from his body weight lying on top of them for however many hours he'd been unconscious there. The air was stale, too.

He wondered how much oxygen he had left. Had those morons actually buried him alive in a coffin? He tried to roll onto his side so he could get his hands back around to his front. But when he went to roll, an excruciating pain rocked his head. He had been slugged over the back of the head with a blunt object. Sharp pains cut from the back of his skull all the way through to his face when he tried to move his head. His guess was that Jimmy Richards was probably the one who clobbered him, getting his revenge for Tony shooting that gun off in his face the other night. The other night. What day was it, actually? How long had Tony been out? He had no concept of time, at the moment, he'd been rendered unconscious so long. He was also hung over and dehydrated from drinking, too. He had a bad case of cotton mouth, and everything tasted horrible.

After lying there several minutes, trying to gather his thoughts amid the cobwebs in his mind, he realized just how numb his hands really were there under his back. He literally could not feel them. As bad as his head hurt, he had to get his hands back around front of him and get the blood back to them. He tried to maneuver himself slowly at first, but that was only making the pain linger. So on a count of three he just forced himself to arch his back and slide his hands down past his butt until he could get his legs up under them. All of his weight was on the swollen back of his head and caused him tremendous agony, but in a few seconds he had worked his hands out from under his feet and got them back around to the front of his body. He lifted them to his face. His fingers were ice cold against his hot cheek. He wondered if they could actually be resuscitated. As painful as it was again, he forced himself to roll over onto his belly. He propped himself up onto his elbows so gravity would speed the blood circulation down to his hands. His head and shoulders pressed the silk-lined coffin lid above. As he lay there, so many thoughts raced through his head. Did anyone know he was missing? Since he told the Family he was leaving, they probably wouldn't even think of looking for him. And why did the Richards put him in that coffin alive? Why hadn't they just killed him? He couldn't think about all that right now. Shoot, the way the air in that coffin was so warm and stale, he might not survive to find out. After twenty or so painful minutes on his stomach, he had the blood circulating through his hands pretty well, again. They had warmed up, and though he could still only feel pins and needles in his fingers, he could at least *feel* again. He rolled onto his back once more. That felt a little better. For some reason, he wasn't terrified out of his wits by all this. Perhaps he'd been depressed so long now that actually facing death didn't seem so bad. He'd been experiencing a living death for two months. He did start thinking about one subject, though. One subject he'd been putting off and putting off. The subject that had lingered hard on his heart lately. For the next while he was awake in that coffin, he thought long and hard about one thing:

Jesus.

SBI Captain Leo Gandtz and Lt. Saucier pulled the Dodge van into Tony Vero's driveway. There were three Beaver County Sheriff's cars parked in the long drive already. State Attorney General Michael Davis had phoned the duo while they were on their way back from New Castle. He told them of Ray Kirkland's discovery and told them to get right over. He said Sheriff DeBona was giving the SBI full control over the investigation and would loan out any deputies Gandtz needed for the job.

"We have two other major developments, Leo."

"What are they?"

"Ed Larsky's turned up missing. He didn't show up for work this morning. We still have Carmichael live on the air from his office. He didn't think to check for bugs himself this morning. Tammi called and said everyone at VECO's having a baby today because first Todd Falco disappeared last week, and now Larsky can't be found."

"I bet Carmichael's the one having the baby."

"He's panic stricken right now. We can hear it in his voice. You should hear him on the phone with people."

"Kirkland got Tony Vero in cuffs right now?"

"No, Leo. That's the other development. Tony Vero's missing too."

Gandtz thought for a moment. "Well, by the sound of things, by the end of the day Carmichael Vero's going to be wishing he was the one who was missing."

He and Saucier were shocked to hear Detective Kirkland was out of the hospital, let alone moving since his apparent heart attack the day before.

"He got a perfect bill of health," Davis explained over the phone. "He says Jesus healed him."

Both Gandtz and Saucier were dumbfounded when Ray stepped out onto Tony Vero's front porch to greet them, looking fit and formidable. He smiled at them, not smugly, but with joy, knowing that God was able to use him to show off His amazing power to people like these two grizzled police veterans.

"You looked like a dead man when the Sheriff hauled you out of the Holiday Inn yesterday," Gandtz said in his usual blunt fashion.

Ray chuckled. "I felt like a deadman. But what you see before you is the evidence of the resurrection power of Jesus Christ. I had my church family come out and lay hands on me. God honored their prayers."

"Well," Gandtz looked him over, "you look good. Now what about Carmichael Vero's Family?"

Ray smiled and shook his head. "Oh, they've just received what could possibly be their death blow, today. Deputy Simmons and I turned up Todd Falco's private records. Seems Tony Vero intercepted them last week before I could get to them. He's pretty good."

"That's why Carmichael put him on the case."

"We have all of Falco's notes laid out on the dining room table for you to peruse. They're yours, now, SBI."

Gandtz and Saucier looked at each other and shook their heads astounded. "This is amazing. Sunday night when we got here this looked like a four year investigation in the making. At least four years. Now all of the sudden, the lid's blown off."

"Sounds like God, gentlemen. He brought you guys on board when the time was perfect."

Gandtz didn't know what to say. Deputy Simmons joined them all on the porch. He had the copy of Todd Falco's personal diary in his hands. Ray took it from him.

"We're going to make our leave, gentlemen. Todd Falco's other diary has given us some more leads regarding his disappearance."

"Where you off to?"

Ray looked at Deputy Simmons and winked. "A strip joint!"

Once again, he left Captain Gandtz and Lt. Saucier speechless.

Some of the retreating Dark Lords regrouped. The stronger ones, that is. The weaker demons were still wandering about in dry spiritual places until more powerful ones would be able to draw them into some spiritual gap at another time. If the Son Himself didn't return before then. All demons know that once He returns, their time is over. But until then . . .

The remaining Dark Lords could still hear the call of prince demons over the Western Pennsylvania region: Kill Tony Vero! The Spirit of the Living God was strong on him. God wanted to save him for His purposes. The demons saw that Tony had the God-created ability to lead masses of human beings. Chief demons and Cyrus Moreau knew as much. That's why Cyrus had commanded Carmichael Vero and the Family to raise Tony up to take over their demonic empire. Tony could have been powerfully warped to use his giftings to destroy even more human lives than Carmichael had. But now that God's prayer warriors had completely overthrown them and their purposes, it was clear that Tony was being marked for salvation by Christ. Once he was saved, God would mold him into the man He originally created him to be. Once He revealed Tony's true destiny, Tony would walk it out diligently, ultimately crushing the kingdoms of hell under Jesus's feet.

Hell couldn't stand that possibility.

The remaining dark lords gathered together, set their purposes to kill Tony Vero, and then searched for the one human vessel who could get the job done for them.

They found Frank Kranac repairing his home.

Audra Dutton was weeping loudly on her living room floor. Her curtains were drawn tightly, obscuring the afternoon sunshine. On this third day of her fast, she was weak in the flesh, but mighty by God in the Holy Spirit. Groaning the things of the Spirit which cannot be uttered, Audra was the vessel of intercession God was using to work all things together for the good of those who love Him and are called according to His purpose. She was laying hold of her vision of those two young men again. Benny Miller was still in jail, the judge having set a two million dollar bond that he and his lawyers were not going to try to meet. The other young man, the white one, she still didn't know. But she felt somehow that her prayers that afternoon were on behalf of that white boy. He had to be birthed into the kingdom of God. He had to! Her body would shudder. She'd feel what almost seemed like contractions in the deepest portion of her spirit. It was like she was the one personally birthing this white kid into the Kingdom. And for some reason he needed physical protection.

"Protection, Lord!" she'd blurt out every so often in the midst of her groaning intercession. "Protect him, Jesus!"

She was his intercessor that day, changing his life forever.

Detective Kirkland and Deputy Simmons descended the cement steps down into Cherries. The outer door was propped open. There was a carpenter's truck out front, and the sounds of an electronic hand saw buzzing inside.

"It's been quite a while since I been to a strip joint," Deputy Simmons chuckled as they walked into the foyer.

"Been my whole life since I been."

"You never been to one? Even when you were young?"

"You kiddin' me, Simmons? My mama would have tanned my butt a thousand shades darker than it is right now. Shoot. She'd still sting it, even today. That is, if there was anything left of it after Shelly got finished with me. Or Jesus first." He looked at his watch. "I don't think there'll be any nekked women in here at two in the afternoon."

The only person visible inside was the carpenter. He was busy at the far corner booth, replacing one of the wooden seats. Kirkland and Simmons looked around inside. Ray took spiritual inventory.

"Spirits of lust," he said aloud.

"How's that?" Simmons asked.

"Spirits of lust. That's what rules this place. Unweilded sexual lust. What God meant to be perfected in marriage is warped and undermined by places like this. Men gawking at women they aren't married to, committing sin in their hearts with these women. Everyone in here's defiled by it, and satan perverts God's perfect plans for the union of a man and woman and the reproduction of His greatest creation. That's what satan's good at. These folks in here are completely in bondage to it."

Deputy Simmons smiled at Kirkland and shook his head. "That's deep, man."

"That's truth." Kirkland walked over to where the carpenter was working. He looked at the booth seat he was installing, but then the seat he was replacing caught his eye. The man had removed it and leaned it up against the next booth.

"Looky here, Deputy!"

Ray bent over and examined the old seat. Deputy Simmons joined him. Ray pointed at two gaping holes blasted in the wooden bench. They were both outlined with black powder burns.

"Look at these," Ray said. "What do those holes appear to be to you, Deputy?"

"They don't *appear* to be anything. They *are* bullet holes."

The carpenter turned and was startled. "Whoa!" He yelled, his buzz saw slowing to a stop. "You two scared me!"

Ray pulled out his badge and identified himself. "What do you know about these bullet holes?"

The carpenter got red in the face. He nervously stammered: "Uh . . . I . . . really don't know a thing about 'em. This guy just called me yesterday and asked me to come out and replace this seat. That's all I know."

Ray reached over and touched the edge of one of the holes. He worked the black powder between his fingers, then brushed it off on his pant-leg. "Somebody's been a shootin' in here, Deputy. Call and find out if any shootings were reported here last weekend."

Simmons pulled out his cell phone and got to it. At that point Cherries owner, Danny O'Hurley, emerged from his office. He saw the Deputy talking on his cell phone and instantly got defensive.

"What's this?" he shouted. "You two got a warrant?"

Ray turned around and stared the short man down. "You Danny O'Hurley?"

"Yeah."

"Then I didn't need a warrant to enter here. I was just coming in to ask you some questions about this:" he held up a photocopied stack of papers.

"What's that?" Danny asked.

"It's a copy of Todd Falco's sex journal."

Danny's face got sheet white.

"Interesting stuff in here about this place," Ray said, not smiling. "Mr. Falco had a lot to say about the after hours activities around here. If I start diggin' around your other patrons and find out you truly are running a house of prostitution here, I'm gonna bust you, call the health department, and have this place shut down forever."

Danny looked scared. "You can't prove anything just because of somebody's phony diary. What do you want with me?"

"A whole lot of things. Let's start with Todd Falco. He's been missing a week. From his notebook I read he spent a whole lot of time here, instead of home with his family. I'm investigating his disappearance. Why haven't you contacted the police yet?"

"I didn't know he was missing!" Danny lied. "Who am I, his dad?"

Ray placed his arms akimbo. "Well, then. Since you're not going to cooperate there, how 'bout we talk about these bullet holes in this seat, here?"

"Those aren't bullet holes." Danny tried lying again. He hoped they wouldn't look up and see the huge hole Tony shot in the ceiling.

Deputy Simmons hung up his cell phone. "There was one shooting reported in Beaver Falls the last two days, Detective. And it wasn't here." They both stared down Danny.

"Lucy!" Ray said, "You got some 'splainin' to do!"

"No one's been shooting anything in here!"

"Discharge of firearms in a public building!" Ray said, pointing at the bullet riddled seat. "You are the owner of this joint. You're gonna face charges! Then I'm going to investigate these prostitution charges, and so help me, if I get one witness who'll testify against you . . ."

Danny, trembling, yelled, "I want a lawyer!"

Ray sneered at him. "We have to arrest you, first! We certainly have the charges with that seat right there! Read him his rights, Deputy!"

Simmons pulled out his handcuffs and approached Danny. But Danny backed away and put his hands up in the air.

"Wait a minute! Wait a minute!" he yelled.

"Wait for what?" Ray asked.

Danny pointed at the bullet holes: "This guy named Tony Vero did that!"

Ray and Simmons' eyes got wide.

"You know Tony Vero?" Ray asked.

"Yes! And I wish I didn't! He's been comin' in here for the last week harrassin' me!"

"Harassing you about what?

"Todd Falco! He thinks just 'cause Todd comes here a lot we must know why no one can find him all the sudden. Tony Vero's been a major pain around here," he pointed at the photocopied journal, "threatening me with that fake diary, harassin' all my patrons. Then, Sunday night, he comes in here like a wild man . . ."

"Tony Vero?"

"Yeah! Yellin' and screamin', he beat up my bouncer, nearly hospitalized him! Then I went and grabbed my gun outta my office to chase him out of here, and he beat me up and took it from me."

"And he shot your booth?"

"Yeah! He's been comin' in here looking for some guy named Bernie something. Polish name. He thinks this Bernie guy had something to do with Todd Falco's disappearance."

Ray remembered Benny Miller's testimony at the jailhouse on Sunday. "'Bernie Lokawski'?"

"Yeah!" Danny lit up. "That's the name. But I've never even heard of the guy. He's never been in here. Well, I got these two goofusses who come in here. They're brothers, name of Jimmy and Greggy Richards. They're the groundskeepers at Grandview Cemetery. Greggy's all right, I guess. Weird. But Jimmy's a little loser. No one can stand him. Well, Tony thinks they know this Bernie Lokawski. He's been harassing them about him all week. Then Sunday night, after he beats up me and my bouncer, he takes my .45 and grabs Jimmy and hauls him to that booth over there and starts shooting at him, threatening to kill him if Jimmy doesn't tell him about that Bernie Lokawski."

"Tony didn't shoot this Jimmy guy?"

"No. He just scared him senseless 'til he finally told Tony whatever he wanted to hear."

Ray got real interested in what Danny was saying. It sounded like Tony was right on this Todd Falco case. "What did he tell Tony?"

Danny looked over at the carpenter, who was sitting in the booth watching the three of them wide-eyed like they were there for his entertainment.

"Why don't you get back to work?" Danny barked at him. The carpenter hopped up and fumbled around with a caulk gun. When Danny was sure he wasn't listening any more, he told Ray:

"Those Richards brothers were bringing some other weirdo in here a few weeks back. A huge guy by the name of Frank Kranac . . ."

Deputy Simmons lit up when he heard that name. "Wait a minute," he stopped Danny. "Say that name again?"

"Frank Kranac," Danny repeated.

Simmons looked over at Ray. "That's the name the corporal just told me. There was a shooting reported at a Frank Kranac's house last night. Someone reported hearing gunshots there eight o'clock or so. The patrol officers checked it out but found nothing wrong."

Danny piped up, animated again: "Well, that's who Jimmy Richards told Tony Vero he was really looking for. He said that Frank Kranac was this Bernie Lokawski guy."

Ray let it all sink in. Realization hit him: if this was all true, Tony just may have stumbled upon the identity of the Black Widow killer of his File 13 cases. Could it be? After all these years of believing this cold-hearted killer did indeed exist, could Tony have uncovered his identity? His heart began pounding like it had yesterday, but this time he wasn't having a heart attack. He looked up at Deputy Simmons. "I'm going to get this Kranac's address and go visit him." He pointed at Danny. "Get this guy's gun Tony was using. Make sure it's licensed . . ."

"It is!" Danny shouted.

"Fine. Check it anyway, Deputy, then fine this man for unlawful discharge of firearms in a public building. Call in another deputy to pick up you and that shot-up bench there for evidence. I'll build the prostitution charges against him later."

Danny looked up at Ray like he'd just betrayed him. "But I helped you!"

Ray turned and looked at Danny O'Hurley. "You wanted a lawyer, I said we had to arrest you first, you sang like a birdie about what happened in here without me making you one promise. That was of your own free will. I offered you no deal whatsoever. I'm trying to find Todd Falco and whoever made him disappear. It sounds like Tony Vero already knows who did it."

"Tony Vero?" Danny shouted. "Tony Vero!" He shouted for God to send Tony to hell for all eternity.

Ray turned and looked Danny in the eyes as he was about to leave Cherries: "You're too late on that curse, Mister. I been praying Jesus will save Tony Vero."

Every once in a while Tony Vero would push on the coffin lid to see if he could get it to open even a crack. But it wouldn't budge. No surprise. He was pretty sure the Richards had him buried deep under ground. The air was alarmingly rank, now, smelling of his beer breath, hot, sticky. Time was running out for him. Fear overtook him. In a fit of panic he struggled violently against the lid, shoving it with all his upper body strength, then pounding on it furiously with his fists. After several moments of futile struggling and nearly injuring himself even more, Tony let his body go limp. He was using up whatever oxygen was left by raising his metabolism. He tried to calm down. After a moment's rest, Holy Spirit came over him, because of the people praying for him. Tony had no idea what was happening. He just began to meditate on all the conversations he'd had with Gina and Detective Kirkland regarding Jesus Christ and salvation. He suddenly felt impressed to pray, though he had no idea how to.

"God? I don't know if You listen to people like me, but I wanna talk to You. I'm just going on what Gina and Ray Kirkland told me about You. I'm not asking You to save me from these people who are killing me. I guess I deserve everything they're doing to me. I'm not saying, 'If You save my life and keep me from dying, I'll become a priest' or something. I just want You to forgive me. I want You to forgive me for ignoring You all my life. I want You to forgive me for . . . for . . . all my . . . sins? I've lived so bad. My family's been bad. Bad people. We hurt people . . ."

At that point his guilt over the death of Gus Savage rose to the surface of his consciousness. All that guilt and pain overtook him, along with hopelessness. How could he explain that one to God? That he searched out a man who was hiding from the Family, found him, and then was stupid enough to turn him over to them so they could kill him?

How could God forgive me for that?

He sighed and closed his eyes. Surely God couldn't for such a horrible thing. Tony didn't deserve forgiveness for Gus Savage's death. He was doomed forever. He deserved it.

But again, Holy Spirit came over Tony Vero. He began to stir up the seed of the Word that had already been implanted in Tony's heart. And suddenly Tony remembered the words that Ray Kirkland and Gina Vero both told him:

God will forgive all sins!

With those words stirred in his soul, Tony was suddenly not willing to relegate his spirit to hell for eternity. "Forgive me, God!" he cried out. "Forgive me, Lord, for . . . Gus Savage. For his death. It's my fault, Lord. I caused Gus to die. I could have prevented that. I didn't. Gus's blood has been on my head. And Gina and Ray have told me that You can even forgive sins like that. Murder. I'm a murderer. I work for murderers. We've killed people, destroyed people. Forgive me for Gus's death. They told me Jesus would 'wash our sins away.' Wash mine, God. I'm coming to You, Jesus, no fooling, no death bed confession here. I want to know Who You are. I want to be with You, God. I want to know Jesus. Jesus, save me! Save me! If You save me, Lord, and I get outta here alive somehow, I promise you I'll get everything right! Gus Savage, the Family, my crimes, every bit of it, as long as You're with me through it all. I'll let the truth be known and pay the price. But I want You to make me just like Ray Kirkland. That would be the biggest honor I could ever have, Lord, is if You'll make me like Ray Kirkland. He's so cool with You. He's at peace with You. He loves You. He has a presence. He and Gina both do. It's Your presence they have. Save me, Jesus! I need You! Save me! Come into my heart! Make me a new person. Save me!" Suddenly Tony felt something as though it were rushing through his innards. It was a feeling . . . a feeling of . . . joy? . . . cleansing? It was Love, joy, and the cleansing of his sins, and at that desperate moment in his life, Tony Vero asked Jesus to come into his heart and save him, and He gladly obliged him.

The Messiah saved another lost soul.

After the VECO luncheon, Carmichael Vero hastily called the remaining Family members into his office. Though Anthony and Warren Zann and Marv Lenstein were the guts that made the Family work, Carmichael never confided in them. He'd always had Joseph and Larsky for that. Now that they were gone, he had no one but Lenstein and the Zanns.

"You don't look good, Boss," Anthony told him. All three of them stared strangely at Carmichael. He was pale and worn; his eyes glazed with an anxious preoccupation.

"Any of you seen or heard from Joseph?"

They all shook their heads.

"Where's Larsky?" Marv Lenstein asked.

Carmichael stared off to the side and shook his head slowly, with disbelief.

"We . . . we could have some real troubles on our hands right now."

They all stared blankly at him.

"Tell us all about it, Mr. Vero!" Edgar Waters grinned as he and Michael Davis listened.

Carmichael told the other Family members about Tony Vero's investigation and what he had turned up regarding Todd Falco's disappearance.

"This guy Tony found out about, it appears he's done this kind of thing before. Tony says he lures dealers into a buy then kills them for their money."

"What a scam," Anthony Zann said.

"That cocaine sample Todd Falco showed us several weeks ago," Carmichael began.

Michael Davis looked at Edgar Waters with disbelief, knowing he was about to live out the moment he'd been awaiting for years: "This is it!"

. . . "this Frank guy from College Hill used it like bait with Todd; lured him into his trap. Took all of our money."

"Frank who?" Edgar Waters asked aloud.

"And Tony found all this out for sure?" Warren Zann asked.

"Every bit of it." Carmichael went silent for a moment. His eyes were sunken and bloodshot. "So I ordered Larsky to go take out this guy last night and get our money back." Carmichael looked back up at them. They could see the dreadful realization on his face. He could not speak.

"But you think it turned out the other way, instead," Anthony Zann said gravely.

Carmichael eyed Anthony, but couldn't speak. He began to tear up; he turned his chair toward the window so they couldn't see his face. They were shocked at him. They had never seen him devastated before, and it made them all nervous. Their seemingly unflappable leader was falling apart before their eyes.

"I think Joseph realized how bad everything was. He's got like . . . ESP or something."

"You think Joseph took off on us?" Marv Lenstein asked with shocked offense.

Carmichael didn't answer him. He was contemplating their future. It didn't look good at all. Finally, staring out the window, with cheery voices chirping away out in the VECO offices, Carmichael gave the order he thought he'd never have to give:

"Gentlemen . . . the Family's in danger. Self-destruct immediately. Shut down everything. Destroy all evidence of the Family."

They all stared at the back of his head, their mouths gaping in shock.

He didn't look back at them. "You heard me. Do it now. Time is of the essence."

Michael Davis stood up. "There we have it. An admission from Carmichael Vero himself to drug trafficking, conspiracy to commit murder, and that the Family does exist." He turned to Leo Gandtz and Lt. Saucier. "I want warrants drawn up for Carmichael Vero, Joseph Vero, Tony Vero, Anthony and Warren Zann, Marv Lenstein, Todd Falco and Ed Larsky. Get search warrants for their homes, businesses, properties, everything. Put together the best local State Police unit you can assemble and start raiding and arresting them."

Edgar Waters looked up at Michael Davis. "But Todd Falco and Ed Larsky—it appears that Frank guy they were talking about has killed both of them."

Davis firmed his jaw and shook his head tersely. "Until I have their corpses, I want warrants for them. Especially Larsky. If he's still around lurking in the background somewhere, one of us could wind up dead. I'm finished with Larsky's menacing ways. Put out an APB on him. Find him and bust him or give me his corpse, but until then, consider him armed and dangerous." He turned back to Leo Gandtz. "Captain, once you acquire those warrants, go after everyone but Carmichael. I'm going to oversee his arrest myself. You understand me?"

Gandtz nodded and smiled slyly. A man not afraid to take down a dangerous sort like Carmichael Vero. This was why he was such a great fan of Michael Davis.

As Ray Kirkland cruised up to College Hill, he listened to his cell phone as a Beaver Falls police dispatcher read the entire report from the two officers who investigated the shots heard at Frank Kranac's house the night before. Kranac had pretty much played it off as him breaking into his back door because he'd locked himself out. His next door neighbor, one Mary Craven, had called in the report. Ray parked his car in front of the Kranac and Craven homes on College Hill. The Craven's home looked like the Beaver

Cleaver residence. Kranac's house looked like the Munster's. The stark contrast was uncanny. A huge row of high hedges separated their properties. Ray walked up to Frank's front door. There was no car out front. Ray knocked and rang for a while, then started to make his way to the back when Mary Craven suddenly showed up from around the hedges. She stopped Ray as he was halfway around Frank's house.

"I'm sorry to act so nosy," she said after they each introduced themselves. "But when I saw another police car here I just had to know what Mr. Scary was up to again. I have two children I fear for."

"Why do you call him 'Mr. Scary'?"

Mary Craven explained her litany of reasons why she feared Frank Kranac so much while Ray investigated the back of the man's house. Ray noticed that the cellar window wells had iron bars over them and the glass below was tarred black. On the back stoop he inspected the new back door Frank had installed only an hour before.

"Back door here is brand new." He tried to peak into the darkened house through the door windows. He could see nothing. The door was locked, of course.

Mary Craven crossed her arms. "I don't care if that door is new and I don't care what he told those police officers last night. I heard two gunshots in that house. I know what a gun sounds like."

Ray wanted to go into Frank Kranac's house in the worst way. But he had no warrant and no probable cause, especially after two police officers claimed everything checked out the night before. He looked at Kranac's dilapidated two car garage. He went to it and tried to look in through the back door. To his surprise the back door pushed open, though it was locked. Ironically, though his house was locked like Ft. Knox, Kranac's garage was not. Ray went into the garage and clicked on a light. The place looked like it hadn't been cleaned since it was built. An inch of dust blanketed everything. An old car rusted on cinder blocks. Piles of rotting lumber, newspapers, and paint and oil cans lined the walls.

Mary Craven followed him in. "Any rotting corpses in here?" she asked sarcastically.

"You certainly don't hold Mr. Kranac in any high esteem, Mrs. Craven."

"As much as I'd hold Frankenstein's monster in . . ."

Ray's cell phone rang in his coat pocket. At the same time he spotted two doors against the back wall. They were not dusty at all. He pulled out the phone and answered it as he walked over to the doors.

"Kirkland," he said, not really paying attention to the call.

"Ray, this is Michael Davis."

Ray was surprised to hear the State Attorney General's voice. He became more alert as he bent down to examine the doors. "Hello, Sir! What can I do for you?" Ray saw that one had been the back door that was just replaced. It's glass was broken in the lower left hand corner. Someone had indeed broken into it.

"I have some very important developments to report to you that I believe directly affect your Todd Falco investigation. Listen carefully. Carmichael Vero spilled his guts to his remaining Family members this afternoon."

"Remaining, Sir?" Ray pulled the back door off the other door behind it. The one underneath was an old thick wooden interior door.

"Yes. Both Ed Larsky and Joseph Vero are missing today. No one can locate them."

That did shock Ray. "No kidding? Tony Vero's gone somewhere, too. What do you think happened to those two?" He saw the inside door was broken into several pieces. It appeared to have had a powerful deadbolt lock that had been shattered out of the wood by some violent force. He couldn't figure out what the deal was with those doors. Why had they both been broken into, and why did Kranac admit to one of them? The doors were puzzling, to say the least.

"Well, as far as Joseph Vero's disappearance, we don't know. But the bit we learned about Larsky appears to connect Todd Falco to that File 13 case you've had on ice. That's why I'm calling you."

"Well, let's hear it!"

"Carmichael Vero said that his nephew Tony had found out who set up and robbed Todd Falco of his cocaine money the Family had given him to make a buy."

Ray stood straight up and forgot about the doors. "Carmichael actually said all that about my Todd Falco?"

Davis laughed. "All that and more. He didn't just shoot himself in the foot today; he shot both his feet completely off. And we got it all on tape. But that's not all. Carmichael said that he sent Larsky after this guy Tony said set up Falco, the man I believe is your Black Widow killer in File 13."

Michael Davis's words suddenly jarred Ray's memory regarding what Danny O'Hurley had just told him back at Cherries.

Ray looked over at Mary Craven and sobered. "Tell me who it was."

"Carmichael said it was some guy named Frank who lived over on College Hill. That's in Beaver Falls, isn't it?"

Mary Craven watched Ray Kirkland's eyes bug out of his head and his jaw go agape as he looked through the garage door back at Frank Kranac's house.

Tony was slipping in and out of consciousness as he used up the last of his oxygen. When he was awake he was praising God, just telling Him how great He is and how grateful he was to Him for saving his soul. Sometimes he'd ask Him if He would arrange for someone to open that lid and get him some fresh air. He had passed out again when the casket holding him began rumbling violently. So violently, in fact, that it shook him conscious. Light headed and dizzy, he spread his legs against the silk-lined walls to steady himself as the casket vibrated with a loud crunching sound. Jimmy and Greggy Richards were sliding off a two hundred pound cement slab that held the coffin lid shut. Tony heard the sounds of someone unsnapping the lid locks. Some one was about to open the casket! *That was a fast answer to prayer, God! Thank you!* He had the final presence of mind to close his eyes and feign sleep. The lid suddenly opened. Light and glorious cool, fresh air fell over his face. He heard the whiny voice of Jimmy Richards:

". . . remember Suzanne St. Claire?" he was saying to Greggy. "She was the homecoming queen and prom queen my senior year?"

Greggy grunted inattentively as they leaned over the coffin to check in on their captive. Tony held his eyes shut and lay perfectly still.

"He still alive, Jimmy? He don't look too good."

Jimmy reached in and smacked Tony hard across the face. Tony didn't even flinch. "Who cares! I'm trying to tell you why I hate this guy so much! What he did to me! This punk is the cause of all my misery in life! I can't wait to watch Frankie work him over!"

"Look at his hands! They're in front of him! Remember? We cuffed them *behind* him!"

"Who cares! He's out cold and he's still alive. Now I'm trying to tell you what this punk did to me to ruin my life! Are you gonna listen, now?"

Greggy sighed, bored already with his little brother's ancient sob story. He put his hand on Tony's neck to make sure he still had a pulse. He did. "Okay. Tell me your story."

"Well do you remember Suzanne St. Claire or not?"

"You talkin' high school?" Greggy said, disgusted.

"Yeah!"

"You're twenty-six years old, Jimmy! This was eight years ago you're talkin' about." He pointed down at Tony Vero. "You tellin' me you hate this creep so bad because of some chick he stole from you in your senior class almost a decade ago?"

"Would you listen!"

"Get over it!"

"Listen! Suzanne was a major babe. She was the homecoming queen during football season! And she was in four of my seven senior classes with me. I sat near her and talked to her all the time! We were *seniors* together!" He waved a hand at Tony like he was a piece of trash: "And this punk here was only a sophomore! A *sophomore*! Well, I asked Suzanne to the senior prom in January. She told me she already had a date. She didn't! She lied to me! And then she turned around and asked this sophomore to the prom. She turned me, a lifelong fellow senior, down first, and then the girl gives me the ultimate insult by asking this two-bit underclassman here to go to the prom with her! A sophomore! The girl asked the guy! Two years younger! After she lied to me to turn me down! A senior!"

"He was a football star in tenth grade! You were some dumpy kid with a crew-cut and zits!"

"He didn't even have a drivers license! His rich Papa rented them a huge limousine with a chauffeur! And I heard he had sex with her in the back of that limo!"

In his mind, Tony immediately began repenting to Jesus for that sin: *Sorry Lord! Sorry! I shouldn't have done that! It was a sin! Forgive me, God! Forgive me!*

"I was the senior! She should have been with *me*! But this moron, here, Mr. Hotshot, Superstar football player, had to get in the way! What should have been my perfect evening turned into a nightmare! I had to watch at the prom while Suzanne was crowned prom queen . . ."

"You took that ugly McNair girl, didn't you?" Greggy laughed. "Boy, what a dog!"

". . . and Mr. Wonderful here got to escort her all around the gymnasium, crowned the most beautiful girl, while they played my favorite song, Whitney Houston's version of 'I Will Always Love You,' and this SOPHOMORE was the one waving at everyone with her on his arm, not me!" He smacked Tony again. "You deserve everything you're going to get!"

Greggy stared at his younger brother. "You're pathetic, Jimmy. Grow up." He went around to the head of the open casket. "Grab his legs, Ding-Dong. We gotta get him in that pit. Frankie'll be here any minute."

Greggy grabbed Tony by his shoulders, and Jimmy grabbed him by his feet. On a count of three they hoisted him out of the casket.

"Man, he's solid!" Greggy moaned.

"He's a woos!" Jimmy sneered.

Tony relaxed his entire body, hanging limp like he was unconscious. He cracked his eyes for just a split second. He saw cinder block walls, a cracked, cob-web covered window, and rusty digging tools hanging from hooks. They had been holding him in a casket in Grandview Cemetery's maintenance garage.

They carried him out the front door. There Greggy's car was waiting, engine running, trunk open.

"Watch him if he wakes up," Greggy warned Jimmy.

Jimmy unexpectedly but purposefully dropped his end of Tony. Greggy, surprised, lost hold of his end. Tony slammed to the ground with a thud. His already cracked skull sent agonizing pain signals all over his body. It was unbearable, but Tony forced himself to lie still and show no signs of consciousness. Jimmy pulled out their Dirty Harry sized Magnum and pointed it directly at Tony's crotch.

"What are you doing?" Greggy yelled at his younger brother.

"I'm showing you and him what's gonna happen if he wakes up! He'll wish he was dead!"

"You are a psycho! Put that thing away, pick him up, and let's get him in this trunk before someone shows up!"

Detective Ray Kirkland shot out Frank Kranac's back door handle with his 9 mm. He tried to kick open the front door, but it must have been reinforced with kryptonite. The new back door proved to be even worse. He used a rusty crow bar from Kranac's garage to try and get it open. It didn't work. He was able to pry out one of the locks, but one or two others wouldn't budge. He needed to get into that house pronto. He'd had enough.

"Mrs. Craven?" he yelled to the snoopy woman who was hiding behind the hedges.

"Yes?" she answered, embarrassed that she was found out.

"Please go back into your house. I have to shoot this door open."

Mary Craven happily obeyed, validated by the violent force being used regarding Frank Kranac. Wait until her husband Mitch got home! she thought.

Ray fired the gun from five feet away. Four shots, splintered wood and shredded metal flying everywhere did the trick. Sheriff's detectives and Beaver Falls police backups were on the way, but he didn't have time to wait. He pulled open what was left of that new back door and entered the house, gun drawn.

Jimmy and Greggy dumped Tony Vero into the trunk of Greggy's car (more excruciating pain for Tony) and slammed the lid. Tony was not happy to find himself in a tight enclosed space again. They got in the car, and Greggy drove them over to an open grave they had dug for a recently deceased plot-owner. The plot was right beside Grandview's main drive. Greggy backed the car up to the huge grave. Jimmy and Greggy had purposefully dug the hole three feet deeper than needed. After Frank Kranac tortured Tony for the information he wanted about who the young man was working for, he would kill Tony, they would lime his corpse, bury him in that extra three feet of hole, and then the plot owner's casket would be buried over him after a funeral ceremony the next day. Tony's body would be never be found.

Greggy opened his trunk. Tony was elated once more to feel sunlight and fresh air on his face. They each grabbed an end of Tony again, and hoisted him out. They laid him on the grass beside the hole. Jimmy stared down into the nine feet deep grave.

"Let's make sure he gets hurt when we drop him down there!" he said.

Tony hadn't looked to see the deep, gaping grave yet, but he didn't like the sound of what they were about to do. He readied himself for them. His hands were cuffed, but he would have to make do.

Greggy leaned down and placed his hands on Tony's shoulders.

"Help me push," he said to Jimmy.

Before Jimmy touched him, Tony sprang to life. With one quick, fluid motion, he reached up, grabbed Greggy by the shirt, and flipped the man over top of him directly into the grave. Greggy didn't even realize what was happening until he was airborne, plummeting nine feet to the bottom of the pit. Greggy hit the bottom with all of his weight landing on his left heel. He felt something snap deep in his knee and screamed with agony. His leg was locked tightly as he fell over into the earthy pit. Jimmy stepped back, wide-eyed and startled, trying to withdraw his .44 Magnum to put some daylight through Tony. However, the metal sight on the end of the long barrel snagged on the inside of his pants and he stood there yanking and fumbling while Tony sprang forward on him. Tony went to tackle Jimmy, who was helplessly groping at the gun lodged down his pants. Tony's handcuffs prevented him from wrapping around Jimmy's waist, so he wound up knocking the stocky man down on his butt. At that point the .44 came loose and Jimmy tried to point it up at Tony. But Tony had already made it to his feet and saw the gun barrel being aimed at him. With a hard right kick to Jimmy's gun hand the .44 fell to the ground. They both went for it, Tony reaching it first. He tossed it hard behind him. The gun disappeared behind a distant tombstone. Jimmy lost sight of it. Tony went to hop into Greggy's running car. Jimmy ran after him, leaping on top of him from behind when Tony was halfway inside the driver's door. Jimmy grabbed him by his hair with one hand and punched him several times with his other. Despite the excruciating pain of the blows to his head, Tony got his cuffed hands over the steering wheel, grabbed the gear shift on the steering column, and yanked the car into gear. He pulled his other leg out from under Jimmy's weight and stepped on the gas pedal. The back wheels violently sent dirt and grass up into the air, where it rained down on Greggy deep in that grave.

Greggy screamed for help as he heard his car speed off, his voice muffled in the soft dirt walls:

"Don't leave me down here! I can't get out!"

He saw the shadow of the car disappear and the sound fade off somewhere in the graveyard. He cursed loudly, fearful and in deep pain.

Ray Kirkland nervously prayed in the Holy Spirit the whole time he went through Frank Kranac's creepy house. He had a bad, bad case of the willies. He remembered a frightening journey he took as a boy through one of those local charity Halloween haunted houses. This was worse. Everything was dark inside. He yanked open curtains and blinds in the kitchen, dining area, and living room. He could spot nothing but thick clouds of dust floating throughout the air. He found the other new replacement door in a nook by the kitchen. It had three more locks on it than the one it replaced out in the garage. Kranac had something major to hide in that basement. He would wait for his backups, though, and have them batter the door open for him. He didn't want to shoot up any potential evidence inside the house. Much to his chagrin, Ray knew he'd better investigate the upstairs. Gun in front of him, he made his way back over to the staircase near the front door. The entire upstairs was pitch dark, despite the afternoon sunlight outside.

"Jesus, you've not given me the spirit of fear, but of power, love, and a sound mind," Ray earnestly prayed as he slowly began his ascent. "But you gotta help me! I haven't seen anything like this place since I saw *Psycho*!"

Tony was dragging Jimmy from the side of Greggy's open car door as he sped up Grandview's Gravel road. Tony's left leg was still trapped halfway out of the car under Jimmy. He stretched his right foot at an awkward angle inside, pumping the gas pedal, trying to steer the car with manacled wrists. Jimmy was wrapped tightly around his torso, holding on for dear life while Tony was dragging his legs out on the dirt road. Tony saw that he had slammed the car all the way down to first gear, so it would only go so fast. He wasn't steering very well, either, for he was slamming into grave stones and an occasional tree off the side of Grandview's main drive. He steered the car up the dirt road toward the highest point of Grandview, about seventy yards from that open grave where they'd left Greggy. He realized he was going the wrong way. The only exit road was down past that grave in the opposite direction. Escape was now an option! He hadn't thought it was back there in that casket. But to escape he had to get Jimmy Richards off his back and speed out of there as fast as he could. So he slammed brakes hard. His head banged off the steering wheel (*Could I possibly put myself in any more pain?* he thought upon impact). Jimmy Richards lost his grip on Tony's torso and flew forward, bouncing hard off the open door and then falling to the ground. Tony shook himself to. He climbed all the way into the seat, now free of Jimmy Richards, and pulled the door shut. He reached over the steering wheel again, put the car in reverse, and stomped the gas pedal. He spun the car around backwards, knocking over another tombstone, pumped the wheel hard in the opposite direction with both cuffed hands, and reached back up to slam it into overdrive so he could get out of Dodge

In a flash Jimmy was at him again through the open window. He cold cocked Tony hard in the left side of his face. Tony nearly lost consciousness, stars floating to and fro across his line of vision. Jimmy went to swing on Tony once more, but this time Tony swung his arms around instinctively, and blocked the blow.

"That's it!" Tony growled as he snatched onto Jimmy's wrists. "I've had enough of you!" He pushed Jimmy down outside the car and crawled out as fast as he could. Jimmy saw the rage in Tony's eyes and quickly lost heart. He fearfully tried to slide away in the gravel, but Tony was all over him. The two tussled for a few moments, trading punches, but then Tony got the better of him, so desperately wanting to escape that he was going to put Jimmy out of commission. He would have, too, if it weren't for the handcuffs. Jimmy snatched hold of the chain between Tony's wrist with both hands to stop the blows. It was the only thing that prevented Vero from pummeling him. They spun each other around in a macabre waltz near the car, a wild-eyed Tony frantically trying to lay hold of a very frightened Jimmy Richards. Tony was putting all he had into the fight, ignoring his injuries as an athlete would. Jimmy held onto the chain, moaning "No! No! No!" as his grip loosened more each time they spun around one another. Just as Tony was about to free himself from Jimmy's grip and do great harm to the younger Richards brother, a bright flash down the road caught their attention. They both froze and looked in the direction of the light. And there, turning the bend near the top of the hill at Grandview's entrance was a sight that made both their hearts sink. Cruising slowly like a viper on the hunt was a black Ford Galaxie 500, the bright sun shining off its windshield. It pulled to a stop beside the open grave where they'd left Greggy.

Frank Kranac had come to call.

Two Beaver Falls police officers battered open Frank Kranac's cellar door for Detective Kirkland. Ray, two other Sheriff's detectives, and the two patrol officers looked down into the blackened basement. They could see nothing.

"Well, just head on down there, Ray," one of the detectives joked.

Ray was looking all over the place for a light switch. "I would, if I could see."

One of the patrol officers produced a flashlight. Ray took it and they all six filed down the staircase. At the bottom Ray and the other patrol officer shined their lights about for a minute before they finally spotted that single light string hanging from that old fixture. He pulled it and dimly illuminated the basement. They looked around for another moment, but were all drawn to those crates Frank Kranac had stacked on top of that red carpet.

"Let's bust open those crates," Ray ordered.

Tony Vero and Jimmy Richard watched in horror as the enormous Frank Kranac stepped out of his car, the whole vehicle bouncing up off its shocks as his immense weight was released from its frame. He left his door wide open and walked around to the back of the car. He popped open the trunk and began to pull something out of it. Tony and Jimmy couldn't make out what it was. Frank was hidden by the open trunk. Suddenly, muffled shouts could be heard coming from the grave. Frank's head popped up from behind the trunk lid. He stopped messing with the load in the trunk and sauntered over to the open grave. Greggy was shouting his head off for help.

"Shut up, Greggy!" Jimmy whispered in fear for his brother.

Frank looked down into the hole for a moment. He said something angrily to Greggy. They could hear Greggy nervously explaining something back to him, but couldn't make out any words. Frank looked up the road, spotted Tony and Jimmy, and then looked back down at Greggy in the grave. He walked slowly around to the front of his Galaxie. He stood there calmly, glaring up the road to the hill were Tony and Jimmy were standing perfectly still in each other's clutches beside Greggy's car. Even from seventy yards away his murderous stare sent chills down their spines. Frank looked back over at the grave, back up at Tony and Jimmy. Then he pulled out a shiny, silver 9 mm. The gun gleamed in the late afternoon sunlight. He marched over to the open grave, pulling the top of his pistol back to cock it.

"No," Tony whispered, realizing what Frank Kranac was about to do. He and Jimmy let go of one another.

Frank barked something down into the hole. Greggy suddenly shrieked with terror below.

Jimmy couldn't make out what Frank Kranac said next, but Tony did:

"What did I tell you I was gonna do to you if this happened?"

Greggy shrieked some more, pleading for mercy.

Frank barked something else down at Greggy, aiming his 9 mm toward him.

"Greggy?" Jimmy whined with a hopeless finality.

"No!" Tony said aloud, helpless to do anything.

Tony and Jimmy heard Frank say one more thing, nodding his head in anger as he spoke, and then the man pulled the trigger six times in a row, blasting bullets down into the deep grave. Tony and Jimmy both flinched at the loud pops, muffling as "THUMP"s into the grave, yet their reports reverberated loudly off the maintenance building nearby. From their distant vantage the shots didn't coincide with the white flashes rapidly exploding from the gun barrel. The gun would flash, the sound would follow.

Greggy's voice was instantly and eternally silenced.

Tony screamed a long, drawn out shout of protest, tears in his eyes, his heart sinking in his chest as he had to personally witness yet another senseless murder.

Frank Kranac heard the shout. He turned from the grave and looked back up at Tony and Jimmy with an expression that read, even from seventy yards away: "YOU TWO ARE NEXT!"

But Tony Vero had enough.

He'd had enough of killings over money. He'd had enough of gangsters and psychos ruining people's lives. He'd had enough of Frank Kranac. He had enough! Now he was going to do something about it. So what if he died trying? Supposedly, he'd just given his heart to Jesus. *Let's see if this Salvation thing really works!* was his instinct. He was going after Frank Kranac.

His first impulse was to save Jimmy, who was still frozen in shock at witnessing the death of his brother. Tony snatched Jimmy by his shirt, shook him violently to snap him back to alertness, and then shouted in his face:

"Run for your life!" Tony pushed him over toward the woods on the hillside. Jimmy stumbled, stopped, looked at Tony, bewildered for a split second, then heeded his order. The surviving Richards brother disappeared into the trees.

Tony then marched angrily over to Greggy's car, which was still running and facing down the hill. He hopped into the driver's seat, pulled the door shut with both hands, pulled the gear down into overdrive and snatched the wheel: the car was aimed right at Frank Kranac. Tony stomped the gas pedal and roared with all his might as the car fish-tailed then caught control of itself. He gunned it over that hillside road. He saw Kranac's eyes widen with shock when he realized Tony was driving right in his direction. He was fifty yards from Kranac. Kranac kept his eyes on Tony. He quickly pulled out a fresh clip, jammed it up into the butt of the 9 mm, and slammed it home. Tony was twenty yards from him now, and closing in faster each second. Kranac stood directly in the road, spread his legs, and got into a perfect Marine firing stance. He aimed the gun sights right at Tony Vero's face through the windshield, and steadying the weapon with his free hand, opened fire with Tony only ten yards away. Tony held the steering wheel tightly in place and ducked below the dashboard when he saw the first flash from the gun barrel. Five bullets ripped instantly through the windshield, spraying Tony and the rest of the car with glass. When Kranac realized Tony wasn't veering the car but was staying his course, he fired three shots into the front grill (there was a loud "HISSSSS" as two bullets plowed straight through the radiator) just before Tony could run him over. He jumped for his life as Tony nearly pummeled him. Greggy's car whizzed past Kranac, but slammed directly into the side of the Galaxie 500. The impact sheered off the open door of the car, knocking the vehicle sideways and severely bashed in the back half of the car. Kranac landed and rolled hard several times, and fell into the deep grave with a thud. Tony sat up, realizing he was past Kranac, now, and slammed on the brakes. His windshield was almost completely gone. The car did a 180 and skidded violently to a stop, radiator steam beginning to puff out from under the hood. Tony sat still for a moment, surveying the graveside for any signs of Kranac. He was glad to see what a mess he'd made of Frank's car. He punched the gas again and started to turn the car down the exit road. He was fifteen feet from the Galaxie and the grave. He slowed when he couldn't see Kranac anywhere. But suddenly, Kranac's huge hands appeared on the rim of the grave. Then his head popped up, mired with dirt. He pumped his feet hard into the earthen walls within the deep pit, half burying Greggy's body. When he was halfway out, Frank Kranac spotted Tony sitting in Greggy's car, not three yards away, sneering at him. They stared, then Tony yelled: "You missed!"

He gunned the gas to get out of Grandview. However, there was a disappointing amount of power when he did so. Instead, the car chugged, sputtered weakly, then reluctantly picked up speed, steam now pouring from the front. Tony steered the car hard down the winding hill, exhilarated at the prospect of his escape. But the car was continually surging then sputtering, picking up speed, then not responding at all. He punched the gas hard once more as he neared the sharpest bend of the road. This time, the car reacted perfectly. He had given it so much gas to compensate for the sputtering engine that as the engine caught as it was supposed to, he went too fast, couldn't navigate the sharp turn, and sent the car sideways off the road into the trees on the hillside. The car slammed to a halt at a forty-five degree angle.

"Oh, help me God!" he mumbled. He looked back up the hill toward the cemetery. No signs of Kranac. He put the car in reverse, backed up about five feet deeper into the hillside brush, and then put it into second gear and stomped the pedal. The car roared, then sputtered, then roared again, the steam from the damaged engine so great that it poured in through the broken windshield so Tony couldn't see in front of him. Finally the car made it up the hillside and back onto the winding cemetery road. He spun gravel, did a fishtail, jammed it back into overdrive, and headed down the last stretch toward the Grandview entrance onto Old Route 18. All he had to do was turn right, head straight into Beaver Falls a few blocks, and there he could call the police, turn himself in for protection, and he'd be safe from that murderous lunatic Frank Kranac.

Detective Kirkland and the other five policemen in Frank Kranac's basement found nothing interesting in Frank Kranac's crates. They were either empty or full of worthless junk. But all six policemen stopped cold when they heard the Beaver Falls police dispatcher talk loudly over several of their walky-talkies:

Gunshots reported at Grandview Cemetery by a neighbor up over the hill.

Ray Kirkland stood up as though hit by a brick. He quickly remembered Danny O'Hurley's words at Cherries earlier that afternoon: Jimmy and Greggy Richards worked at Grandview. They were somehow in cahoots with Frank Kranac. Tony Vero had apparently caught onto them all.

Jimmy and Greggy Richards worked at Grandview.

Ray Kirkland suddenly realized he was in the wrong place.

Tony was nearly home free. He sped Greggy Richard's car down to the Grandview Cemetery entrance and pumped the steering wheel to the right onto Old Route 18. But the engine was hissing so loudly and the steam was so thick that Tony could neither see nor hear Kranac's battered Galaxie 500 as it zoomed down the hill behind him at forty miles an hour. Kranac, with his missing front door, rammed the back right fender of Greggy's car as Tony started for Beaver Falls. The high impact of the crash shook Tony to his core, racking his already aching head. Kranac steered into the impact of the hit, spinning Greggy's car around 180 degrees. The Galaxie fishtailed and Kranac spun it back around behind the Neon. Tony Vero suddenly found himself facing the wrong direction, with Frank Kranac blocking his path behind him. He looked northward up Old Route 18, now, knowing that the next mile or so was nothing but brush and trees until he could get to the Homewood suburbs where there would be houses and a place to call the police. For a split second he thought about trying to get the car turned back around and making another break toward town. But there was a loud "CRACK" behind him and something whizzed past his right ear so hard that it made his hair flutter. Frank Kranac was shooting at him again. He quickly ducked down across the front seat and jerked the gearshift into reverse as two more shots came through the rear, blasting out what little was left of the back window and windshield. Tony stomped down the gas pedal. Gratefully, the car reacted perfectly this time. The Neon slammed backward into the Galaxie. Kranac's head bounced off his steering wheel and he dropped his gun out the open doorway. Tony sat up, turned the steering wheel hard to the right, and rammed Kranac's car completely off the road into the ditch, throwing Frank across the seat. Tony put the car back into overdrive, punched the gas again, and squealed off north up Old Route 18. The steam from his engine was still so bad he couldn't see, but the bullets had stopped. He looked in his rear view mirror. The Galaxie 500 was still in the ditch. Kranac had jumped out and was picking his gun up off the road. Soon both he and the black Ford faded into the distance behind Tony.

Frank Kranac's College Hill house was actually only four miles from Grandview Cemetery. Ray Kirkland ran from Kranac's basement and was quickly in his police car with sirens wailing and lights flashing, weaving through traffic on Route 18. He was frantically praying in his prayer language the whole way, while he pieced the puzzle pieces all together in his mind. They were fitting perfectly, and they linked Frank Kranac, Jimmy and Greggy Richards, and the now missing Tony Vero.

Homewood, Pennsylvania was a township divided by the Pennsylvania Turnpike. The Turnpike was blasted through the mountainside upon which Homewood was founded. So the Beaver Falls suburb, a mile and a half up Old Route 18 from Grandview Cemetery, was connected at the middle by a seventy-feet tall bridge spanning across the Turnpike. The bridge connected Old Route 18 from Beaver Falls out to its northernmost suburb, Koppel.

However, the bridge had been out for fourteen years, the victim of erosion, a state legislature fight that tied up repair moneys, and the fact that it was little used. Reconstruction had begun, and part of the bridge was deconstructed to be reinforced before the money ran out. Therefore, the middle of the Homewood bridge, well visible from the PA Turnpike, was completely gone; the steel girders at the sides of the bridge were still intact, but there was a nine-feet gap with crumbled cement and rebar at each tattered edge, and a clear seventy foot drop to the Turnpike below. Both entrances were blocked off with orange work barrels and huge "Bridge Out" signs. To the right of the Homewood bridge on the Beaver Falls side were a large group of houses built on the hillside. They overlooked Route 18, the Turnpike, and the Beaver River valley. To the left, down a dirt road leading under the bridge near the Turnpike, there was a park and two little league fields.

As Tony Vero arrived at the Homewood bridge on its Beaver Falls side, Greggy's steaming, smoking car breathed its last. It just wouldn't go any more. He didn't even shut it off. He just jumped out and abandoned it. He ran toward the two-story house to the right of the bridge. On the road behind him he could hear Frank Kranac's bashed-up Galaxie making its way up Old Route 18. Tony had to get help. His head hurt so badly and he felt so weak he didn't know if he had the strength to tangle with Kranac anymore. He rushed for the driveway to that house and ran up to the back door, the Galaxie getting closer. He was just about to bang on the screen door when he saw a family of four inside. They were eating supper, filled with fright at the sight of this filthy, handcuffed stranger suddenly staring in at them through their back screen door. He was going to rush in and lock the door behind himself, but he quickly imagined Kranac kicking the door in and shooting all five of them, including the two little children.

"There's a crazy man chasing me with a gun!" He yelled at them. The mother squealed with fear. "Lock your doors and call the police!" But nobody moved.

"NOW!" he yelled, again, and started to run for the bridge. The father did get up and lock the door, as Tony commanded.

The battered black Galaxie suddenly appeared around the bend, as Tony ran across the entrance to the bridge, past the orange work barrels that barricaded it. He got to the pathway on the other side that led down the hill to the park below. Just as he was about to run down there, he saw two different tee ball teams practicing, little children with ball gloves running and jumping and playing on both fields. He had visions of Kranac mindlessly opening fire on them, too. He couldn't put them in such great danger by going down there. The bridge was the only route of escape Tony could take that would not endanger other people. The Galaxie was fifty yards away and closing fast.

Frank Kranac sighted Tony Vero at the bridge entrance. Demonic rage flooded his soul at the sight of him. The evil spirits who wanted Tony Vero dead all manipulated Frank Kranac's warped soul like master puppeteers. There, according to Kranac's twisted mind, was the cause of all his problems. If it wasn't for that meddling Tony Vero, Frank and his money would all be safe and secure. He had to kill Tony Vero to protect all that he knew and make things right again. Tony Vero had to die. He gunned the car for him.

Tony burst between two of the barrels, hands cuffed in front of him. Ignoring the pain of his injuries, he sprinted across the bridge. As he did, that nine feet gap loomed clearly before him. He ran right to its edge and stared down below, seventy feet to the hard deck of the Pennsylvania Turnpike. Cars and semi trucks zoomed by like Match Box toys. It was almost ten feet from where he stood to the other side of the gap. Frank Kranac plowed through the barrels at the mouth of the bridge behind him. Tony turned and looked as the orange barrels bounced up and down and off one another, flying through the air as the Galaxie sped for him like some hellish apparition. He had no time to try and shimmy across the steel girders that were still intact on the sides of the broken bridge. Kranac would get out and shoot him like a sitting duck. He instantly knew there was only one way to escape. Tony ran backward about ten steps. Kranac had him in his sights and gunned the Galaxie even harder as he sped toward that gap with a vengeance. Tony turned, and just before Kranac would have run him over, he charged the gap. His eyes targeted the other side of the bridge as he sprinted. His foot reached that last piece of bridge on his side and with all he had Tony stretched his arms, threw his right leg out in front of him and leapt:

open air all around him . . . pavement seven stories below him . . . he never looked down . . . always targeting that other side . . .

Frank Kranac slammed on brakes. The Galaxie screeched, leaving four thick strips of rubber on the road. The two front tires went over the edge, the car bottomed out, crunched into the cement and came to a halt, dangling halfway over the edge of the seventy foot precipice.

Gravity's pull brought Tony lower than he should have been on the approach. He landed on the other edge of the crumbling bridge, not having made the whole distance. His stomach smashed into the broken cement, painfully winding him; the jagged rebar scraped his belly. His hands latched onto the road above and stopped his fall to the turnpike below. His feet pumped like pistons, desperately trying to find him some footing with which to support himself, breaking up all that exposed rusted rebar wire.

Kranac jumped out of his car and pulled out his 9 mm, watching Tony hang onto the other edge for dear life, trying to work his feet into the cement and rebar, kicking up dust and debris. Finally, he did find some decent footing under his left shoe and he flung his right leg up over the edge, his hands pawing the road for support. With the last of his strength, he painfully pulled himself up and rolled over safely onto the bridge. By that time Kranac was back in his Marine stance, steadying his 9 mm to fire at Tony. Tony jumped up from the ground, legs trembling like wet noodles. He stepped back away from the edge and looked up at Frank Kranac ten feet across the chasm. Frank had his pistol sights on Tony's chest, his eyes full of hatred and murder. Tony's eyes widened, but then Holy Spirit quickly gave the newborn in Christ the gift of faith:

"Jesus!" he yelled and raised his hands high up in the air to God, "I'm Yours!" That's all Tony knew as Frank Kranac went to kill him. If God wanted him alive, He'd save him. If not, God would take him to heaven, according to the promises Gina and Ray Kirkland had told him about this loving God. Tony closed his eyes.

Frank Kranac pulled the trigger with rage. The gun hammer snapped to. But the muzzle sparked instead of exploding a white flash; only a muffled "piff" could be heard. The gun didn't recoil in Frank's hand like it was supposed to; it merely trembled a split second.

Tony heard the gun misfire and opened his eyes, shocked that a slug hadn't knocked him ten feet backward. He looked down at his chest, half expecting a bullet hole: nothing. Nothing! He looked across at Kranac who was now pulling the trigger violently. By now the pistol hammer wasn't even snapping. Kranac held the gun up to his face and looked down the lightly-smoking barrel. He tried to cock back the hammer manually, but couldn't. The gun was permanently jammed.

No bullet could come out. Years of precious saints interceding and speaking the word of God over Tony's life had just manifested in the natural realm in a mighty way: God stopped a bullet with Tony's name on it.

Tony couldn't believe it. He wasn't shot! The gun didn't work! He looked across the gulf at Kranac.

"Today ain't your lucky day!"

Frank Kranac stopped toying with the gun and growled at Tony. The spirits of hatred and murder rose up with fury at this baby Christian who was mocking their failure. Frank tossed the impotent weapon into the front seat of his car. He looked back at Tony with determination in his eyes. He bent down, pulled up his right pant leg, and pulled out that huge, shiny knife from its holster. He pointed it at Tony.

Tony's countenance fell once more. But there was still that seventy foot drop to the highway between them.

Frank Kranac stepped backward about fifteen feet and eyed the side of the bridge where Tony stood.

Tony shook his head discouragingly at him. "What're you gonna do, old man? You'll never make that jump over to here!"

More determined than ever, Frank Kranac took one last deep breath, focused his gaze on Tony's side of the bridge, and took off running for the edge. Tony got scared all over again as he watched this hell-bent man making a lumbering dash for it, silver knife gleaming in his pumping hand in the late afternoon sun. Tony stumbled backward a few steps, wondering if he had the stamina needed to outrun this murderous goon should he successfully make the leap from his side of the bridge to Tony's. Frank Kranac ran his last step off the dilapidated edge and took the leap with a loud grunt.

Tony watched the absurd vision of this gigantic man flying through the air at him from across the gap, knife out in front of him, his face glowering, focused on Tony. Frank would have easily made the leap, he was so demonically charged with energy.

"Save me, Jesus!" Tony prayed aloud as he stepped backward several more feet, preparing to run for his life once more.

But just as Frank would have reached Tony's edge, it was as though he suddenly hit an invisible brick wall. When his momentum should have brought his upper down toward that crumbling edge, he was suddenly flung backward like he was hit by some unseen force. Tony saw his natural momentum through the air quickly change in an impossible manner. His feet, which would have easily cleared the gap and landed flat atop the bridge, caught low on the deconstructed side. His stomach slammed hard into the top edge, at the same spot where Tony landed in a similar manner. Frank "Oooof!"ed as his already broken ribs sent even more anguish through his body. His hands smacked down on the top of the bridge. He struggled to get a hold on the cement. He still had a firm grasp on the knife, though, refusing to let it go. His feet caught hold of the rusted rebar wiring sticking out from the side, but Tony had worked it so loose it was snapping and crumbling under Frank's immense weight. Persistent as always, though he was struggling, Frank's eyes were locked on Tony the whole time. Tony was the cause of all his problems. If Frank could only kill him and bury him in that grave-hole at Grandview, he and his money would be safe forever.

Detective Kirkland's wailing siren could be heard coming up Old Route 18 in the distance behind them.

Tony watched from about twenty feet back as Frank struggled to hold on as he hung halfway off the edge of the bridge. Then a large chunk of rebar and cement crumbled out from under his feet and he lost all footing. He began to fall. His hands scraped the cement road to hold on as his upper body slid out of Tony's view over the side. Frank stopped his fall at the last second, laying hold of the cement at the edge of the precipice with his left hand, and digging the pommel of his knife down into the cement with his right.

"No!" Tony shouted. Frank had fallen so far back only his hands and that knife could be seen. But Tony was relieved when he saw that Frank has successfully stopped his fall and still had a grip. His heart couldn't take seeing another human die, even if it was this maniac bent on killing him. Against his better judgment, Tony ran forward toward the tattered edge of the bridge. Frank had one hand gripping the cement, his other hand gripping that knife. Tony looked over. Frank was dangling straight down off the edge, his feet swaying back and forth over that seventy foot drop, traffic racing below him. There was no fear in his eyes, though. As single-minded as always, he still looked ready to kill Tony. The police siren was closing in on Homewood.

"The cops are coming now," Tony said to Kranac. "Let me save you. You can turn yourself into the police and live. Let me help you."

Frank was silent. Stretched as far as his body would go, his great weight pulling him hard, his hateful gaze never left Tony.

"You're not going to be able to hang there forever. Drop that knife and let me pull you up here."

Despite Kranac's continued glare of hatred, Tony got down on one knee and went to grab Frank's left wrist.

"C'mon!"

When Tony touched his wrist the demons in Frank's heart erupted with rage. They wanted him to kill Tony NOW. Frank was the demonic realm's last chance at wiping out this human. Offended that Tony would even get that close and dare to touch him when he was trying so hard to kill him, Frank Kranac took one last shot at him. He loosed the knife's pommel in his right hand that was supporting most of his dangling weight, and swung the knife up at Tony. Tony saw it coming, with great disbelief, and jumped backward onto his butt as the knife whizzed past his throat, missing only by an inch. Frank Kranac's futile effort cost him his life. Gravity won out over his two-hundred and seventy pound body. The final momentum of his swipe at Tony shifted all of his weight to the left side of his body, quickly causing him to lose what little grip he had with his left hand. Frank Kranac suddenly found himself slipping away from the jagged cement edge of the Homewood bridge and free falling to the hard deck of turnpike below. His only thought as he plunged seventy-feet to his death:

All my money . . . !

Tears filled Tony's eyes when saw Frank's fingers slip out of sight. He didn't watch Frank Kranac plummet to his death. He remained sitting five feet back from the edge where he landed when Frank stabbed at him. He was deeply saddened. Not that Frank Kranac was gone; he was quite relieved that the madman's relentless efforts to kill him were over. But as he heard the sound of horns blowing and tires screeching on the turnpike below, Tony completely broke down. He fell over to his side and wept bitterly over all of the death and the loss of lives he'd encountered over the last few months, all over nothing more than filthy money.

In his wailing police car, Detective Ray Kirkland passed Greggy Richard's gunshot, smoking car on the side of the road in Homewood. He looked and saw all the work barrels scattered at the mouth of the bridge and turned in there to get a better look. He saw the battered black Ford Galaxie 500 hanging halfway off the edge. He accelerated and pulled up behind it. He couldn't see anyone, for the Galaxie was blocking his view of Tony across the other side of the chasm.

"Dear Jesus . . . am I too late?" he said as his parked the police car. He killed the siren and got out. He ran over to the Galaxie, and there he spotted Tony Vero on the opposite side of the bridge, laying on his side, weeping.

"Tony Vero!" Ray cried out with great relief. "Man, am I glad to see you alive! Thank you Jesus!" Tony didn't respond. Ray looked over at him, then at the ten foot gulf between them, and then at the Galaxie. He was confused for a moment. Then he stepped over to the edge of the bridge and looked below to the Pennsylvania Turnpike. Three cars and a semi-truck were stopped in the middle of the westbound lane. Three people were behind the cars, waving white rags and a red flag to caution speeding motorists behind them to slow down. There in the middle of all that chaos was a huge body on the road with four other people standing around it. They weren't touching it. Some of them were looking up in the air at Ray and the Galaxie, both visible out over the precipice. Ray looked over at Tony.

"Who is that down there? That Frank Kranac?"

Tony finally looked up at Ray with red, tear-stained eyes. He sat up and nodded slowly.

"That's Frank Kranac . . . AKA Bernie Lokawski; AKA the Black Widow killer from your File 13 cases."

Ray could only stare over at Tony, sadly dumbfounded.

State Police cars and an ambulance arrived below on the Turnpike and attended to Frank Kranac's corpse. Against Ray Kirkland's orders Tony went to climb back over to the Homewood side of the bridge. He looked very injured and Ray was afraid he might slip and fall himself.

"Wait for a back-up car to pick you up on the other side!" Ray ordered.

Tony silently ignored him and walked along the steel girder of the right ledge, holding onto the pointless guard rail above. When he was safely on the other side, Ray made him immediately sit down and examined him. He looked into Tony's eyes. Both his pupils were fixed and dilated.

"You have a concussion for starters," Ray reported. "You look pretty beat up."

"The last couple of days haven't been too kind to me."

Ray smiled. "It shows." He pulled out his cell phone and called for another ambulance for Tony. "Don't move. Sit right there," he warned Tony. Ray walked over to the driver's side of Frank's car. Tony ignored his instructions once again. He got up and followed him.

He asked Tony what had happened. Tony briefly told him of being kidnapped from his home and the rest of the horrifying incident with Kranac and the Richards brothers. Over Ray's police radio they heard Beaver Falls police officers arriving at Grandview Cemetery.

"Tell them they'll find the body of Greggy Richards in the open tomb across from the maintenance garage," Tony said. "And Jimmy Richards is hiding in the woods up there somewhere." Ray looked at him sadly. He told the deputies about the body and informed them to look out for a kidnapping suspect on the grounds.

Ray looked at Kranac's Galaxie. He stepped around to the open driver's side. He put some pressure on the roof of Kranac's car, carefully making sure it was well settled on the side of the bridge. The vehicle wouldn't budge. He leaned in across the steering wheel and pulled Frank Kranac's keys out of the ignition. He was amazed at the huge jangling collection.

"He has the keys to the whole world on this ring," Ray commented as he walked to the back of the car to the trunk. After four tries, he successfully found the trunk key and opened it. Inside were two tightly stuffed military duffel bags.

"What's this?" he asked aloud. Ray reached in and strained to pull the biggest one over to him. "They're very heavy, whatever they are."

"I don't feel good about this," Tony said gravely.

"Me either. This feels like a body up in here."

Ray Kirkland got the duffel bag up to the edge of the trunk. It was tied off tightly at the opening. He pulled out a pocket knife, cut the draw string, and pulled the top wide open. Long blond hair spilled out. He pulled it open further. They could see the top of this person's head, also blond, but neatly crew-cut. All the long hair flowed from the back. Ray and Tony leaned over top to see who this corpse was, but they both had already knew:

"Ed Larsky," Tony said.

"Cold dead."

Ray investigated the body in the other bag. He couldn't identify that person. Tony could.

"That's Tommy Wheeler. He's one of Larksy's biker buddies from the Plague. They pull off hit jobs together sometimes."

Ray's eyes widened and he slowly pulled his head out of the trunk, staring at Tony incredulously. "Do you have any idea what you just implied, young man? You're not right in the head, now. I need to inform you that you're under arrest. I better read you you're rights before you say anything else . . ."

Tony stared down emotionlessly at the two bodies in Kranac's car trunk. "Larsky is a hitter for my Uncle Carmichael and his crime organization called the Family."

"Tony . . . !"

"The Family runs drugs and owns a pornography chain through VECO. I think the pornography stores front some illegal materials, too. They hide their ties to VECO from the public . . ."

"Stop! You don't realize what you're doing!"

"And Todd Falco worked for them all."

"Tony!"

"He sold drugs for them! And Frank Kranac killed him for all his money, like he did all those other missing men in your File 13 report. And I told Carmichael and he must have sent these two dopes to kill the creep themselves."

Ray put his hand on Tony's shoulder and shook him lightly to get his attention. "You have rights to protect you! You're implicating yourself by telling me all this! You can be legally charged for everything you're admitting you know . . ."

Tony pushed Ray's hand off his shoulder and looked up at the huge detective. "I gave my heart to Jesus when I was in that coffin, Detective Kirkland."

Ray was truly floored by that one. He didn't even know what to say.

"I did. Just like you and Gina have been telling me I needed to. I asked Him to come into my heart and He did. I made Him Lord of my life. And it was real! Just like you two said it would be. I really felt His love and forgiveness when he took away my sins! And He did take away *all* of my sins. I really feel His Presence in me even right now! I told Him I'd get everything right. All the lies and deceptions and crimes I been a part of. I promised Him my heart and told Him I'd get it all right if only He'd be with me through whatever it is I'm facing. And now I'm going to do just that. I don't care about any charges I'm facing. And I sure don't care about jail;" he pointed at Kranac's Galaxie. "These people were going to kill me! And now," Tony pointed at Kranac's car trunk, "especially since Larsky's dead, I don't care for my safety." He put his hands up on Detective Ray Kirkland's wide shoulders. "You, Detective, promised me that Jesus would save me and that the 'truth would set me free'." Tony smiled a little smile of inner joy. "Well, I've trusted you about Jesus, and you were right. Now I'm trusting you about the truth. I'm gonna tell everything that's gone on with the Family, anyway. So you can go on and use anything I've just said against me. I just want to be free. You've been right about everything so far. I thank you for telling me."

And Tony Vero surprised Ray Kirkland even more: he leaned in and hugged the big man. Ray could hear the back up squad cars screaming down the road toward him. What would they think about all this? *Ultimately,* he smiled to himself, *who cares!*

Ray hugged Tony back, a big brother in the Lord loving on his new baby brother. "Praise Jesus," he smiled.

For the first time in months, Tony felt safe.

"Gun, Partner!"

The two deputies at Grandview Cemetery both pulled their pieces and aimed them at Jimmy Richards. He sat dazed on the edge of the grave where his brother Greggy lay dead at the bottom. Jimmy's legs dangled over the edge, the .44 Magnum sitting in his lap. He'd retrieved the gun Tony'd disarmed and was going to hide behind a tombstone and blow Frankie away when he returned. Instead, the police arrived. The deputies held their sights tightly on the younger Richards brother, and made their way around each side of the grave to where he sat.

"Throw the gun and put your hands in the air," one of them calmly commanded Jimmy. He looked unstable to them.

Without looking up at them, Jimmy asked, "Did Frankie kill Tony Vero? Is Tony Vero dead?"

The deputies eyed one another. One of them shrugged and answered: "Tony Vero's still alive. He's in custody as we speak. You're about to be dead, though, if you don't throw that gun behind you and put your hands up in the air as high as you can!" They were both within point blank range of him now.

Jimmy shook his head with disgust and droned, "He's still alive. I can't believe it." He cursed Tony Vero and slapped the gun off his lap into the grave.

The .44 landed beside Greggy's corpse with a thud.

As the ambulance workers examined Tony on the Homewood bridge, Ray Kirkland dialed up State Attorney General Michael Davis back at the Holiday Inn. He told Davis all about Frank Kranac and finding Ed Larsky and Tommy Wheeler in his trunk.

"But you helped me to break my case earlier this afternoon. Now I'm calling to help break yours. I want you to know you have the great favor of a good God, Mr. Davis."

"How so, Detective?"

"Tony Vero just confessed everything about the Family to me. He said he didn't care if I used his words against him. He promised he was going to cooperate fully with any investigation against Carmichael Vero and the Family. He's going to be your number one witness against Carmichael Vero."

Davis could say nothing at first, he was so floored by it all.

"God's bringing this whole thing to you, Mr. Davis," Ray smiled.

"After all these years, He's placing this whole case in my lap in a matter of days."

Ray laughed. "Sounds just like Him!"

FIFTY-ONE

*Y*ou're done now.
   That's what Audra Dutton heard Holy Spirit tell her. It was that blunt and that quick.

"Just like that, Lord?" she asked out loud from her living room couch. Could He cut off her fast and intercession that quickly? After three days? She got up from the couch, mouth pasty from three days of no food, and stood on wobbly legs.

"I'm done now?" she had to ask again. She didn't know why she was asking. She knew in her spirit it was the voice of her Father releasing her from her fast. She felt His release and knew it was Him. She shrugged and said, "All right!"

Within five minutes she had a nice little rib-eye steak broiling in her oven. She would break her fast with that and a light fruit salad. She giggled to herself when she thought of how quickly God just ended it. It was just like Him. And though He currently wasn't conversing with Audra like He had been during her fast, she could without doubt sense that He was very pleased with His faithful daughter.

Captain Leo Gandtz called in many favors among the SBI that day. He quickly organized three teams, warrants and all, to raid the Zann brothers' offices, Joseph Vero and Marv Lenstein's law offices, and the New Castle headquarters for the pornographic book chain. The Carmichael Vero Task Force was going to shut down the Family for good that evening. The Family was finished.

SBI and State Police teams raided the three offices in Beaver Falls and New Castle. The president of Warren Zann's pornography chain was there when SBI agents stormed the building. He was destroying illegal web-sites on the company computer that linked child-pornography sites. Van loads of child porn had been shipped out of different warehouses to be redistributed to new hiding places. Gandtz's undercover agent knew about the different hiding places for the materials. He slammed his gun up to the head of the president and demanded the names of all the van drivers and their destinations. The president refused at first, but when the agent told all the other officers to leave the room and he cocked his pistol, the president reconsidered.

The vans and all their horrible wares were all recovered by the next morning. The Family's chain of porno stores was systematically shut down, store by store, across Western Pennsylvania.

The elegant Wooden Angel restaurant in Beaver, Pennsylvania, played host to the galaxy of wealthy VECO stockholders. Great lengths were taken to prepare the classic restaurant for the gala stockholder's banquet. Interior decorators, florists, sound technicians were hired to redo the restaurant for the event. Special menus were prepared. Some of the best wine from the Wooden Angel's wine cellar was bought by VECO to be served at the celebration. Carmichael had ordered that this evening be made a night to remember for everyone.

Limousines and the most expensive cars known to man began to arrive around six o'clock that evening. Dalling Security officers were there to valet park the cars and guard them during the celebration. Reporters and camera crews were allowed to film the arrival of the guests.

By seven the Wooden Angel was packed. Inside the celebration had begun, despite some of the low notes at VECO that day. People were willing to temporarily put aside the controversial disappearance of Todd Falco, and the no-shows of Ed Larsky and Joseph Vero.

Carmichael Vero, donning an expensive tux, looked dour at best. The weight of the day's shocking events had taken its toll. He welcomed his coveted guests at the door, trying to make small talk and appear joyful. But inside the kingpin knew everything was crumbling.

The ceremony started. Carmichael had to take the stage and introduce the master of ceremonies. VECO had hired a Pittsburgh comic who'd recently made it big out in Hollywood. This rising star was well known and quite popular. After a weak introduction by Carmichael the comic grabbed the microphone and began to roast the elder Vero, joking about his former Mafia ties and his inexplicable grim mood that night.

"You'll have to excuse Carmichael tonight, ladies and gentlemen," the celebrity quipped. "The police just found Luca Brazi's body floating with the fishes in the Beaver River. Carmichael Vero's their number one suspect."

The crowd roared. Carmichael smiled weakly. Then he grabbed one of his top Dalling Security officers and slipped back out of sight.

The Beaver Falls Police Department took over Frank Kranac's home. Detectives and forensics experts were going over every inch of the house. An exonerated Mary Craven stood on the sidewalk outside, chiding her husband Mitch for all the years he wouldn't listen to her. After a long browbeating, he wisely repented to her about his doubt.

Police cars lined 6th Avenue on Kranac's block. Detective Ray Kirkland parked a block down the street, due to the lack of parking spaces. Ray flashed his badge outside Kranac's home and was instantly escorted inside by another detective.

"You're not going to believe what this creep's hiding in his basement, Ray."

"Thirteen rotten corpses?"

The fellow detective laughed. "No. Something much sweeter."

The Beaver Falls Police Captain shook Ray's hand. "You need to see all this. This confirms your theory, Detective."

Ray stopped in Kranac's front doorway. "What theory?"

"Sheriff DeBona gave me the skinny on that 'File 13' you put together. Our discovery downstairs confirms it."

Ray couldn't believe the Sheriff's turn of heart. The man had so rejected his report. He could have easily kept mum on it now to save his face, which would have been typical for DeBona. But instead, the man was being atypical. Ray grinned and prayed aloud: "That's gotta be You, Lord."

On the way through the living room the Beaver Falls Police Captain pointed out two bullet holes near the couch. One was in the wall behind where it had been sitting, the other on the floor in front of it.

"Two shots," he said to Ray. "Just like the lady reported hearing the other night."

Must've been a scuffle with Larsky and that other guy we found in the trunk, Ray thought. *Carmichael Vero sent him to kill Kranac. Kranac got the better of him.*

They descended the basement stairs. Kranac's cellar was brilliantly illuminated with police lights so they could investigate the dank place. Twelve investigators were down there. Ray saw that they had uncovered a pit beneath the crates where he and the other men had wasted time looking into all those empty boxes.

"The crates were nothing but camouflage to distract us," Ray told the captain.

They approached the pit. "Hold your breath, Detective Kirkland." Ray walked between some of the policemen and stepped over to the pit. There, in all its filthy glory, was Frank Kranac's money.

"Jesus help us," Ray whispered.

"Can you believe that?" the captain asked. "We've estimated just by looking at it that there's over ten million dollars down there. Easily. No wonder this guy went on such a rampage. He was protecting this fortune."

Ray shook his head sadly. "This is nothing but paper and green ink, Captain. Where Mr. Kranac is right now, he's not gonna be able to spend one dollar of this pile of cash he's been killing people over."

Forensics experts had begun to remove some of the cash on the other side of the pit.

"May I suggest something, gentlemen?" Ray said.

They were all ears.

"Treat this like a dinosaur dig."

They looked at Ray like he was nuts.

"When they remove fossils and bones at a dig, they have to try and remove the parts that go together, to help the scientists correctly piece the creature together. I believe Mr. Kranac's been building his cash collection over the years as he's been luring drug dealer's to fake buys and killing them for this cash. Check the dates on all the bills in there. This guy's been at this for almost fifteen years. I believe the currency will be stacked together according to the time period Mr. Kranac offed the victims. There are going to be certain parts of this pile that go together according to the dates on the bills. Be sure to remove those similarly dated piles of money together."

The Beaver Falls Police Captain nodded in agreement. "If he killed a guy in 1985, there should be a pile of cash in there with treasury dates from 1985 and before. If he killed someone in 1991, the dates should coincide with that time period. Makes sense. Do it his way."

After ten hours of undoing the piles and counting the money, they found out that Ray Kirkland was indeed correct.

Tony Vero lay in bed in a private room at the Beaver County Medical Center. He had tubes hooked up to the veins in his left arm. A Beaver County Deputy sat in a chair by the door guarding him. Ray Kirkland had officially arrested him on obstruction of justice charges because of all Todd Falco's materials they'd found at Tony's house. They also charged him as an accessory to drug trafficking because of his knowledge of the Family, and conspiracy to commit murder for his part in the Frank Kranac affair with Larsky. Wanting to get his life right he also gave a deposition against the Family. Ray took him from the Homewood Bridge to the Holiday Inn to see State Attorney General Michael Davis. To Davis's surprise, Tony refused a lawyer and told all he knew about the Family.

"You're not afraid for your life doing this?" Davis asked Tony.

"Is that Ed Larsky's corpse in the back of Kranac's car?" Tony asked back.

"Yes."

"Then I have nothing to be afraid of regarding my life. Carmichael doesn't have another enforcer."

When he finished the deposition, he told Davis: "I'm expecting a greatly reduced sentence in return for my testimony against Carmichael."

Davis nodded. "I give you my word. You're gonna do time, though."

"I want my time reduced even more." He paused somberly. "I can give you the answers to an unsolved murder in Florida."

Their eyes all lit up.

"What are you talking about, Tony?" Ray Kirkland asked.

With that, Tony Vero told them the entire Gus Savage story, with great sobs and many tears. Michael Davis and Ray Kirkland were mesmerized by the tale.

A very somber Michael Davis remarked, "We didn't even have any idea such an event was going on. That's how well protected the Family's privacy was."

After Michael Davis left them alone, Ray put an affirming hand on Tony's shoulder. "That must have been a horrifying event for you."

A broken Tony could only say, "I've never felt so guilty in all my life."

"Tony," he said. "You told me that you gave your heart to Jesus in that casket today."
Tony nodded enthusiastically. "I did! And it was real."

"Then He's washed away your guilt about this Gus Savage man, whoever he is. I want to pray for you, boy."

Tony agreed. He couldn't believe it when the Detective charging him laid hands on him and began praying deliverance to Tony's soul. He called forth Holy Spirit to break the spirits of guilt, torment, and condemnation from Tony's life. He asked the Father to cleanse him of all his guilt. Ray prayed that God would destroy Tony's ties to the Family. Then he got a word of knowledge, and asked that Christ Jesus would "put an end to the nightmares" Tony was having and allow him "peace that passes understanding" while he slept. Tony looked up at Ray, shocked. He'd not mentioned one word of the tormenting dreams to anyone.

Tony thanked Ray profusely when he finished. He made Ray promise him he'd take care of him "spiritually" while he was in jail. Ray agreed. "You're gonna need someone to disciple you in the Lord. I'd be honored to do it."

With that, Tony Vero was arrested and charged, but had to be taken to the emergency room as the victim of a kidnapping. The doctors found that he had a severe concussion and was dangerously dehydrated. He needed surveillance for the skull fracture and an IV to replenish his body fluids. The Sheriff's Department had to furnish a deputy to guard Tony so he wouldn't try to escape. But Tony wasn't going anywhere. He suddenly had a new outlook on life. He was so excited about asking Jesus into his heart, and having Ray Kirkland agree to teach him about God and the Bible. He tried to call his sister Gina to share the good news with her. She'd be elated, but she wasn't home. So he lay in his bed just beaming. Beaming about knowing he was in good standing with God, thanks to Jesus. He was also beaming because for the first time since his horrible experience in Ft. Lauderdale, he felt forgiveness and cleansing for the death of Gus Savage. He may have sent Gus to his grave, but Jesus had surely forgiven him for that sin. Gus's murder was no longer an issue to him. He was free from that horrible ball and chain of blood guiltiness over someone's death. Tony would struggle with other sins as time wore on. He'd spend years reading the Word of God, getting it down into his soul, and renewing his mind. Many struggles and battles awaited this newborn Christian. But one war over Tony Vero had been instantaneously obliterated by the Messiah, Christ Jesus: there was no more condemnation.

Guilt free and loving it, Tony giggled on his hospital bed while the IV dripped fluid into his veins. The deputy guarding him heard him laugh and looked over at him curiously.

"What's so funny over there, hotshot?"

Tony just blew him a kiss (which really irritated him), rolled over, and went to sleep. There were no more nightmares of Gus Savage. Just peace.

Edgar Waters and Tammi Bannerman were cruising across the Pennsylvania Turnpike in Edgar's convertible Mustang. Wind whipping at their hair, they were all laughs and grins. State Attorney General Michael Davis gave Edgar his orders:

"You've successfully given us our suspect confessing to major felonies on tape. You've given us our insider at VECO and she planted a wire on Carmichael. You've blown this case wide open for us, Sergeant Waters. It's in our hands from here on in. Now, take Tammi and get her out of town. Tammi will be a key witness for us in our case against him. Hide her away safely. Carmichael Vero should still be considered highly dangerous. Get her out of town, contact me when you're safe somewhere, and protect that special woman with your very life."

Edgar's brother was also a Marine, stationed at Camp Lejuene, North Carolina. He and his wife lived in a beach house at Topsail Island. It was a perfect place to hide Tammi. His brother and his wife were all for it. The twelve hour trip with Tammi at his side after their incredible victory over Carmichael Vero was very romantic. Their hearts beat hard the whole trip. First over their success, second, over their secret feelings for one another. The more they talked during their drive the more they meshed. Dreams, goals, secrets came out. Finally, at one point on I-95 in Virginia, Edgar looked straight over at Tammi. This time, she looked straight back. Thunder and lightning struck in their souls. Edgar melted as he stared into her eyes. He couldn't hold back his secret any longer.

"I've . . . I've gotta tell you something, Tammi . . ." the big confession about his true feelings began. He poured out his love for her in surprisingly poetic language.

Tammi's heart melted. She smiled ear to ear, tears forming in her eyes.

"I . . ." he tried to finish explaining, "I just didn't know if you'd be interest in some white guy almost twice your age."

She snickered, grabbing for a tissue in her purse. "I didn't think you'd be interested in a black woman half your age . . . and a much better investigator than you!"

He laughed, and reached over and held her hand tenderly.

"I feel the same way for you, Eddie . . ." she smiled.

They held hands the rest of the way to North Carolina.

They found Topsail Island to be a very romantic place to get to know one another. His brother and his wife, devout Baptists, requested that Edgar and Tammi keep their hands off each other and build their relationship. They honored the request, and were later so glad they did.

Six weeks later they were married at a private ceremony at Camp Lejeune. Tammi was a gorgeous bride: a chaste soul in a white gown, her cocoa skin glowing.

God blessed their marriage greatly.

Leo Gandtz, Lt. Saucier, and fifteen SBI agents in three cars and three vans pulled into the Wooden Angel parking lot. The Dalling security officers guarding the property saw the SBI vehicles speeding up to the gate. One of them radioed their chief officer inside. A pair of Dalling guards stopped the first vehicle at the entrance. Gandtz, Saucier, and two hulking agents stormed out of the van and ran right up to the guards, who were demanding identification. Gandtz flashed his badge and identified that they were SBI and were going into the restaurant. The guards, under heavy orders to defend the event, foolishly refused to stand down. The SBI agents both pulled guns, got the guards' hands up in the air, and quickly tossed them face down onto the cement. With the way cleared, the SBI vehicles pulled into the lot and parked at the Wooden Angel's front doors. The second in command Dalling guard stormed out of the restaurant just as the SBI agents began pouring out of the vehicles. He had three other security officers with him. The rest of the Dalling agents patrolling the parking lot all converged at the front door of the restaurant, looking like they were ready for trouble. But Captain Leo Gandtz pulled out his badge, the warrants, and his 9 mm.

"Rent a cops," he shouted at them, "You are finished for the evening. Go home. The State of Pennsylvania is taking over these premises, and we're making arrests. You will be arrested the second you get in our way."

The second in command Dalling officer was undaunted. He got up into Leo's face, ignored the 9 mm, and snatched some of the warrants from his hand. As he read the names on the warrants, his face began to lose all its color. There were warrants for Anthony and Warren Zann, Marv Lenstein, Joseph Vero, and last but not least, a warrant for the arrest of none other than Carmichael Vero himself.

"You're insane," the man told Leo Gandtz. "Do you know what's going on in there? You're going to have to wait for this to end before we can let you in there."

Gandtz stood firm, stared down the guard. "You're the one who's insane. I've just identified us as SBI with warrants on a raid. You'll be our first arrest this evening."

With that, two agents sprung up on the Dalling leader and slammed him up against one of their vans. They cuffed him and arrested him with obstruction of justice charges. Three other SBI agents pulled out pistols and Leo Gandtz looked around at the rest of the Dalling Security guards.

"I've ordered you all to get out of our way and go home. You don't have any idea of what's going down here, tonight. For you to get in our way would be the greatest and final mistake of your rent a cop careers." The SBI agents shoved the Dalling leader into one of the other vans, handcuffed, while they loudly read him his rights. The other Dalling guards watched, jaws agape, hearts sinking in their chest. Now that Gandtz had their undivided attention, he continued: "Now: stand down, get in your vehicles, and get out of here this minute!" They hesitated at first, but then, one by one, the Dalling Security guards all slowly walked away from the restaurant entrance, and left the SBI agents alone.

Satisfied, Gandtz ordered: "Put your guns away."

They went inside.

The VECO stockholders were having a great time inside the Wooden Angel. The food and entertainment was so spectacular and VECO's previous year's financial reports were so superb that every one there had forgotten about Todd Falco and the week's bad press. The crowd was laughing hysterically at the comedian host. He introduced the singer for the second time that evening. The lights went dim. She took the stage and began singing one of her popular R&B ballads in her powerful soprano voice. Gandtz and his team did not make their presence known at first. They stood quietly in the shadows where the Dalling Security guards would have been, scanning the restaurant for the men named on their warrants. No one took notice. Gandtz had drilled his team before they left the State Police barracks, showing them photos of the Family members. As the pop diva crooned, Gandtz began picking the Family members out of the crowd one by one and pointing them out to his SBI agents: Warren Zann first; then his older brother Anthony. Then Marv Lenstein. Joseph Vero was still AWOL. Ed Larsky was cooling off at the morgue. But where was Carmichael? Leo scanned the entire restaurant from his vantage point. No sign of Carmichael. He left his dark corner and began walking about the dinner guests, scanning about for the Family head. He was no where to be seen in the restaurant. Gandtz went back over to the rest rooms. He went into the men's room. No one was in there. On his way back out into the dining room, he snatched a program off one of the tables. Inside it he read that Carmichael Vero's big speech was next on the agenda after this singer. Maybe he was in the kitchen warming up. Gandtz went back over to his SBI agents assembled near the darkened foyer. He assigned certain men to take the Zanns and Marv Lenstein.

"Bring 'em quietly out here, away from the crowd. Show them the warrants, and arrest them." He looked back to the stage near the kitchen entrance where the diva was belting out the last of her hit song. "Carmichael's mine."

The diva finished her song to a wild standing ovation. She stood on stage for almost a minute, bowing and blowing kisses to the stockholders enthusiastically cheering her. Two of the VECO employees graciously handed her a huge bouquet. She accepted it, they gave her two pecks on her cheek, and she exited the stage, where her manager briskly escorted her back into the kitchen away from the cheering crowd.

The comedian took the stage once more while the crowd was still cheering and began to hold his hands up like they had been cheering him. They all laughed, quieted down, and took their seats again.

"Now that we have all the exciting music and entertainment out of the way," the comedian deadpanned, "it's time for a boring speech from our host."

Everybody laughed, especially the VECO employees.

"In all seriousness, though, Carmichael Vero doesn't really need an introduction. This amazing man has overcome horrible odds against him to create this incredible company. VECO has not only been the saving grace of many of your wallets . . ."

The crowd howled with laughter.

". . . but it's also been credited with the turnaround of Beaver County's economy." Everyone stood to their feet again and applauded enthusiastically. The comedian nodded in agreement to the crowd. They sat again.

"Yes. VECO is a remarkable company. With a remarkable creator. Carmichael Vero is just what the Business Quarterly Journal dubbed him back in 1993: a financial genius." Everyone nodded in agreement.

"And this remarkable man, who has graciously footed the bill for this shindig tonight . . ."

Light applause from the crowd.

". . . has also graciously shared his financial genius with all of you. We're all winners by Carmichael Vero, by his inventiveness, his risks, his very life. He's had you here tonight to honor you. But in my estimation, Carmichael Vero is our man of honor."

He waved a hand at the kitchen door where Carmichael Vero was to make his appearance. The crowd stood and began to applaud him before he even made his entrance.

"Honored ladies and gentlemen, let's now honor the man who made all this possible. I now welcome to this stage none other than Mr. Carmichael Vero."

He stepped aside and began applauding, looking for the grand entrance from the kitchen as the crowd was cheering wildly.

Captain Leo Gandtz watched carefully. *I'll let him make his speech, clear out the crowd, and then we'll quietly call the Family aside to bust them.* He eyed the kitchen door, as did everyone else.

No one appeared.

People were still wildly applauding and whooping, the comedian was leaning off the stage, looking for Carmichael, but no Carmichael Vero appeared.

After a moment, Leo Gandtz knew something was up. Thunderous applause, still no Vero. *He's pre-empted us*, Gandtz knew.

The applause began to metamorphosis into light murmuring, then loud buzzing as it became evident after ninety seconds that Carmichael wasn't coming out. The comedian grabbed the mic.

"Excuse me," he said as he began to exit the stage toward the kitchen door. "Carmichael must be tied up with a few waitresses. I'll go divert his attention back to us."

As the comedian stepped off stage, Leo Gandtz and Lt. Saucier bolted across the dining room toward the kitchen door, too. Gandtz pulled out a walky-talky on the way.

"We have all entrances sealed and the restaurant surrounded, right?" he asked his officer out in the parking lot.

"Yessir. We do now."

"What do you mean, 'now'?" Leo shouted as he hit the kitchen door.

"They didn't secure this place in time," Lt. Saucier said angrily.

In the kitchen the comedian was talking to the surprised restaurant manager and several cooks and waitresses. There was no sign of Carmichael Vero anywhere. Gandtz pulled out his SBI badge and identified himself, shocking them even more.

"Where's Vero?" he asked the man who appeared to be in charge.

The owner pointed toward a back hallway at the far end of the kitchen. "He and one of those Dalling Security guards went back there about ten minutes ago. Mr. Vero said he had to make a cell phone call and didn't want to be disturbed."

Gandtz and Saucier made a dash for the hallway, knocking the comedian out of the way.

"Tell me there's not an exit door back there, please!" Gandtz shouted as he ran to the hall.

"There is," the owner replied. "But it has an alarm lock on it. It would have gone off if someone opened it to get out."

Of course, Gandtz and Saucier found the hallway empty and the emergency door hanging open. The Klaxon alarm above the open door was mute. The two wires from the exit door bar to the Klaxon were severed.

"Dismantled!" Lt. Saucier reported.

Gandtz burst out the door to the darkened rear exterior of the restaurant. He couldn't see a thing, except a huge row of pines that separated the restaurant property from the bar up the hill beside it.

"I need lights out back here!" Gandtz shouted into his walky-talky. "Carmichael Vero's escaped." He paused and looked around. "Apparently, he was one step ahead of us."

In the rental van, State Attorney General Michael Davis was listening to a police scanner. He merely laughed at Captain Gandtz. "Welcome to the club."

Back inside the Wooden Angel SBI agents began making their way into the confusion of the moment. Guests murmured loudly, shocked expressions lighting their faces. Lt. Saucier first pointed out Anthony and Warren Zann to the agents, and then Marv Lenstein.

"You see those three? They look like the sky's falling on them? Here are their warrants. Serve 'em, bust 'em."

Concern was rising among the dinner guests. It was obvious that Carmichael had disappeared. The comedian and the VECO representatives in charge of the banquet were huddled near the stage. They didn't know what to do. VECO employees were buzzing about, remarking about the apparent vanishing epidemic that was striking their executive officers that week.

"First Todd Falco . . ."

". . . today Ed Larsky and Joseph Vero . . ."

". . . Now Carmichael!"

"What's going on?"

"On what charges?" Anthony Zann yelled at Lt. Saucier and the two SBI agents with him. Saucier slapped the arrest warrant hard into Zann's chest. Anthony stumbled backward. His thick black glasses slid off his nose.

"It's all on the paper, Poindexter. Racketeering. Accessory to buying and selling narcotics. Money laundering. You can read it yourself. The Family's been busted."

Anthony Zann was shocked to hear this law enforcement officer utter the Family name. Obviously they were on to them. Probably thanks to Todd Falco and Tony Vero.

Lt. Saucier pulled out a pair of handcuffs. "You have the right to remain silent . . ."

Captain Leo Gandtz and three other SBI agents with flashlights ran up the hill past the pine trees toward the old bar above the Wooden Angel in search of Carmichael Vero.

"This is the only place he could've gone. He made it up here before you bozos sealed off the rear of the restaurant."

The bar parking lot was half full. There were a handful of people standing around talking near the bar entrance. Gandtz went over to them with his badge and identified himself.

"Any of you seen a man about this tall, salt and pepper hair, dressed to the nines?" Gandtz asked them.

They had. Along with some big security looking guy. They said the two jumped into the back of a waiting limo. It took off about ten minutes earlier.

Gandtz cursed and threw his wallet down onto the ground in frustration.

Carmichael Vero's limousine sped up Rt. 51 past Brady's Run Park. In the back seat Carmichael Vero sat frightened, impatient. The driver was taking him to the Beaver County Airport. There, Carmichael's Lear jet was awaiting him, fueled, cranked, and packed with his personal belongings by another Dalling agent. He looked nervously at his watch: in less than ten minutes he would jump from this limo into his jet and fly off, safe and sound. They would fly him to Europe in secrecy. There he'd withdraw his huge accounts from Swiss banks, and then he'd relocate for good. Plastic surgery and a complete make-over would render him unidentifiable as Carmichael Vero. He would retire, begin life over again, and enjoy the massive fruits of his years of labor as a criminal.

In a few minutes he would be home free . . .

The limo's phone rang. The driver answered. A moment later, the tinted window that separated the driver's seat from the passenger's area retracted.

"Mr. Vero?" the driver said timidly, holding the phone away from his head.

"What?" Carmichael answered, irritated.

"I . . . I think you better take this call back there."

"Wha . . . ?" Carmichael looked at the car phone beside him. "No! Hang up on whoever it is!"

The driver shook his head: "You . . . you don't understand, sir. You better talk to this guy. He says he's right behind us in that club wagon."

Carmichael turned around and looked out the back window. There was indeed a club wagon van right on the limo's tail. The driver, only a silhouette through the darkness and headlight beams shining in on the limo's rear, waved friendly-like at Carmichael. Hesitantly, the elder Vero picked up the phone.

"Who is this?" he blared angrily as he looked back at the mystery driver.

"Hello, Carmichael Vero. It's been a long time. This is Pennsylvania State Attorney General Michael Davis. Remember me?"

Carmichael was speechless. His bottom jaw dropped.

"I'll take that silence as a 'yes'," Michael Davis chuckled. "Going somewhere, are we? There's a whole restaurant full of guests waiting for you to give your speech."

Carmichael was desperate at that point. He commanded the Dalling agent: "Draw your firearm, lean out that window, and shoot that pest in that van behind us!"

The Dalling agent was mortified by the command. But just as Carmichael was about to bark it out to him once more, the agent's cell phone started ringing. Grateful for the distraction, the agent quickly answered the call. He listened for a moment, cursed, and held his phone away from his head in shock.

"Mr. Vero!" he said with great alarm. "This is our man at the Beaver County Airport! He says that a whole squadron of State Police cars have just stormed the airport. They have warrants. They've confiscated your Lear jet, sir! They've forced the pilot to shut down the engines and clear out! They're searching it . . ."

Dumbfounded, Carmichael simply put his hand up for the Dalling agent to shut up.

"Mr. Vero," Michael Davis spoke through the limo phone, "We've just arrested all the remaining Family members back at the Wooden Angel. The Zanns, Lenstein, they're all in our custody. Tony Vero's in our custody, too."

Carmichael couldn't believe it. Tony was alive! So now Larsky and Joseph were gone, Cyrus Moreau was as good as dead, and Tony Vero had escaped death . . .

"We've got the warrant for your arrest, too, Carmichael."

As the two vehicles approached the intersection of Rt. 51 and Rt. 60 to Pittsburgh, a slew of flashing lights lined both sides of the road. Carmichael couldn't even count all the police cars up ahead.

"Meet me at VECO." Michael Davis spoke with gravity: "It's over, Carmichael."

Captain Leo Gandtz was still busy yelling at the SBI agents for not securing the Wooden Angel and the adjacent properties in time to apprehend Carmichael Vero. He'd given precise orders to them at the station on how to proceed. Someone had dropped the ball. He got back on the walky-talky and cursed out another set of agents on the other side of the property from him.

"Captain Gandtz," came Michael Davis's reassuring voice.

Gandtz picked up his radio. "Yes, Sir?"

Davis was friendly, calm: "Stop cursing everybody, Leo. Get up to VECO with that arrest warrant, pronto. Carmichael and I will be waiting there for you."

Gandtz was flabbergasted. "You got him?"

"Yes, Leo. You didn't think I was going to let him get away again after twenty years, did you? Get up to VECO, now."

Ten Pennsylvania State Police cars, lights flashing, escorted Carmichael Vero's limousine and Michael Davis's van up the blacktop road to VECO. The limo stopped right in front of the VECO office doors. Michael Davis parked his van behind the limo and got out. He walked over to the limo and waited by its back door. State Police officers came and joined him at his side. Davis asked them to step back. They chased off the Dalling Security agent who was watching the property. No one emerged from the limousine. Michael Davis couldn't see any movement inside through tinted windows. Two minutes passed.

An officer stepped up to Michael Davis: "You want me to get in there and yank him out, Sir?"

Davis pursed his lips and nodded calmly. "No. He'll come out."

"Is he armed, Sir?"

"I'm sure someone in there is. But I don't think we're in any danger."

"What if he's . . . you know . . ."

Davis shook his head confidently, again. "I highly doubt Carmichael Vero is suicidal. Distraught, maybe. But he values his hide too much to off himself."

Carmichael slowly emerged from the limo. His skin was white. His eyes wide, bloodshot, filled with confusion and . . . Michael Davis could read it: defeat. Vero, shorter than Davis by almost a head, looked up at the Attorney General. Their eyes met: Davis was the patient, enduring victor. Carmichael Vero was the unbelieving prey; shocked to see such an old nemesis standing over him victorious.

Michael Davis broke their silence. "I don't gloat, Mr. Vero. I'm not going to make this a circus. Let's you and I go wait in your office. The SBI captain in charge will be here in a moment to serve you your papers and take you into custody."

He made Carmichael unlock the VECO front doors. Carmichael's hands trembled. Davis made the State Police officers attend to the limousine.

"Captain Gandtz will have a search warrant for this vehicle," Davis announced. Carmichael opened the front door. Davis held it open for him. They disappeared together, inside.

Captain Leo Gandtz and Lt. Saucier entered Carmichael's office through the oak doors. They silently glared at Carmichael Vero, sitting defeated behind his desk in a daze. Michael Davis stood silently off the side of his desk. He didn't greet his lead detectives. Gandtz walked up to Carmichael and pulled the arrest warrant out of his pocket. Carmichael looked up at him with contempt in his eyes. He broke the silence:

"Do you know who I am?"

Gandtz shrugged. "I don't really care who you think you are. I hope you're not waiting for that Larsky guy to come to your rescue. He ain't coming around anywhere anymore."

Carmichael looked up at Gandtz with shock.

Gandtz nodded his head. "Yeah, that freak you sent him to kill snapped his neck like a twig. He's cold and blue down at the morgue."

Carmichael turned grief-stricken. "Ed Larksy's dead?"

"Dead as dead can be. He won't be coming around here to assassinate any witnesses for you, this time. You're under arrest."

"Mr. Vero, stand up, please," Michael Davis ordered him.

Carmichael looked around the room in a stupor. Davis, Gandtz, and Saucier all watched the color fade fast from his face as he stood up out of his chair, trembling. He looked at Michael Davis, scared, angry and humiliated as Captain Gandtz stepped around his desk toward him.

"Put up your hands, Mr. Vero."

Carmichael slowly complied. Gandtz frisked him roughly, thoroughly.

Lt. Saucier pulled out a note card and began to read it: "You have the right to remain silent . . ."

As Saucier finished reading the Miranda Warning, Leo Gandtz pushed Carmichael face forward toward his desk and pulled both his arms behind his back. He pulled out a pair of handcuffs and manacled Carmichael's hands behind him. Carmichael was in a deep fog.

". . . I said do you understand your rights, Mr. Vero?" Saucier yelled that time. Carmichael snapped up and glared at him.

"Yeah," he wheezed lightly. It was all his constricted throat could manage.

Gandtz snatched Carmichael up by the handcuffs and the back of his tuxedo jacket and forced him back around from his desk. Michael Davis stopped him.

"Bring him here, Leo."

Gandtz marched Carmichael right up into Michael Davis's face. Davis looked down at Vero with deep conviction.

"You listen to me, Carmichael Vero: you can hire an army of assassins to come after all of us this time. But you're going to get a counter strike like you've never seen before. Isn't that right, Leo?"

Gandtz thrust Carmichael up onto his toes. "Bring 'em on, little man!" he whispered into Carmichael's ear. "You'll be going to a lot of funerals if you do!" He let him back down.

Davis spoke the last words he'd ever personally speak to Carmichael Vero: "You and your empire are finished. And to God be the glory!"

By that time all of the local news media had heard about the SBI breaking up the VECO banquet and arresting all the top VECO executives. So when State Attorney General Michael Davis, Lt. Saucier, and Captain Leo Gandtz emerged from the VECO office building with Carmichael Vero in cuffs under arrest, an explosion of camera and video lights lit them up with a blinding white flash. Reporters screamed inquiries to Carmichael and Davis, police officers everywhere demanded calm, and a media circus that would go on for months was birthed. But there was a State Police car sitting not ten feet from the VECO office doors, and according to Michael Davis's orders, Carmichael was immediately and safely placed inside the back of the awaiting vehicle. The tinted glassed door was closed and Carmichael was protected from the rabid swarm of journalists.

Just as Michael Davis had promised.

EPILOGUE

The Beaver County judiciary system had never seen so many court cases fill its dockets in such a short amount of time. Carmichael Vero's fall and the Family's collapse literally produced hundreds of charges against dozens of people. The remaining Family members were all charged and had to be tried. The Family pornography chain, including the child pornography arm of that business, faced countless charges. Jermichael DeVries, Stephen McClintlock, and Benny Miller's drug gangs were all busted, rounded up, and charged with every kind of narcotics charges ever brought into a courtroom. And then there was Jimmy Richards left to face the aftermath of his and Greggy's involvement with the demented Frank Kranac.

Christians had been interceding for peace over Beaver Valley for years. God was bound by His word to honor those prayers, as sweet as perfume to Him. Therefore, His anointing suddenly rested on judges, prosecutors, juries, and courtrooms to establish peace and punish lawlessness on the earth.

Jimmy Richards cooperated little. He did tell authorities that he and Greggy met Frank Kranac through their father. He'd worked in the mill with Kranac. Later, when he got a job as groundskeeper at Grandview Cemetery, Kranac showed up again and paid their father to be a part of his murderous schemes. After their father's death, they took over his place in Kranac's tangled web.

Other than that, Jimmy Richards, embittered soul that he was, would only give false testimony implicating Tony Vero for Todd Falco's death. Therefore, Jimmy rotted in prison.

Detective Kirkland and a forensics crew searched Jimmy and Greggy Richards' home. He found a plot map of Grandview Cemetery in Greggy Richards' bedroom. On the map, Greggy had placed little red dots on thirteen of the graves. Ray remembered what Tony Vero said the Richards brothers were trying to do to him when he escaped them. He took the map to Grandview himself, along with File 13. He located all thirteen graves that were marked on Greggy's map and wrote down the death dates engraved on their tombstones. Without failure, all of the deceased in those graves died within at least ten days of when the missing drug dealers in File 13 disappeared. Holy Spirit confirmed Ray's suspicions.

Police cars were scattered about Grandview Cemetery. Three Bobcats with hoes were rumbling away as they dug up earth over designated graves. Detective Kirkland had obtained the necessary court orders and permission from the families of the deceased to exhume the thirteen caskets marked on Greggy Richards' map of the graveyard. The late June sky was overcast and dank with the threat of rain. The air was chilly. Kay Falco stood holding Dylon near Mary Gray's plot. Looking grim, wearing one of Todd's gray overcoats, she had told Shelly and Ray Kirkland that she wanted to watch the exhumation of Mary Gray's casket alone. They prayed with her, then they returned to Ray's car to honor her wishes.

"She's had such a rough time of it these last two months," Shelly said as they watched her from the car.

"I'm proud of her, though," Ray said, "with the way she's dug in her heels and made such a deep commitment to know the Lord and get joined to our church. She could have chucked her conversion as some do, and brooded alone. But she's refused to let her flesh get the best of her in these difficult times. She's one tough cookie."

Kay stood still as the hired hands jumped into the hole and connected chains to the cement casket. The wind blew her sandy hair away from her face, revealing dry eyes. She didn't know if she had any more tears for her wayward husband. All she wanted now was closure.

"They've got the casket on the winch," Ray said. "I've gotta go." He kissed Shelly and got out to go over to the grave. He radioed one of the three medical examiners who were present. He made sure he steered clear of Kay on his way to the deep hole. The examiner joined him. Ray put on heavy work gloves. He spoke to the workers:

"Let's be careful not to break the seal on that casket. I've promised all these families the bodies of their loved ones would not be disturbed in any way unless we absolutely had to."

When Mary Gray's huge cement vault was safely on the ground, Detective Kirkland and one of the workers jumped down into the hole with shovels.

"Be careful. There should be a duffel bag right below the surface here." They began to dig gingerly around the bottom of the pit.

"The earth's white with lime," the medical examiner remarked to Ray as he dug around.

Suddenly, Ray stopped his digging and began prodding the ground.

"There's something right here."

They dug lightly around the discovery. Suddenly, an earthy green canvas material appeared below them. A faint but ugly stench arose. Ray stopped the worker.

"You need to go on out of here. This ain't gonna be pretty."

The worker and the medical examiner traded places. Ray called the police photographer over to the open grave. The photographer joined them and began flashing pictures. Ray and the examiner crouched down and began to move earth away from the duffel bag. When they had it cleared, they undid the ropes that tied it closed at the end. The stench grew worse. They carefully opened the end of the duffel bag and examined what was in it.

"It's a corpse!" Detective Kirkland yelled from within the pit.

Kay Falco walked a few feet closer to the grave. She had given the description of the clothing Todd wore that Tuesday he disappeared. Detective Kirkland had obtained Todd's dental records, too. So verifying whether or not the body was Todd's would be relatively simple. The body was badly decomposed, but it was fully clothed.

"The clothing matches perfectly," Ray noted.

The examiner pried open the bottom jaw of the corpse to examine the fillings in its teeth.

Moments later Detective Kirkland crawled up out of the open pit. He pulled off his work gloves and brushed the dirt off of his body. He started walking over toward Kay. She held Dylon up high at her side and noted Ray's expression.

"It's Todd," she said without expression before Ray was even ten feet close to her.

Ray nodded. "I'm afraid so, Mrs. Falco. The clothing and the teeth and fillings all match perfectly. I'm so sorry . . ."

Kay turned quickly on her heel and walked straight to her car. Ray stopped in his tracks, surprised at her flight, but honoring her privacy. He didn't try to chase her down. Shelly began to get out of their vehicle to run over to Kay, but Ray waved her off. Kay swiftly fastened Dylon into his carseat and slammed his door shut. She got into the driver's seat and cranked the engine.

"But Raymond!" Shelly protested as her husband neared. "She needs someone now!"

Ray shook his head sternly. "No, she doesn't. She's had ministry. She knows what she needs right now. Leave her be. If she wanted us, she'd tell us. She's gonna go handle this her way. She's a widow, now."

Kay Falco sped out of Grandview Cemetery as fast as she could. She could see her eyes tearing up in the rearview mirror. Oh! How she didn't want to cry another tear for this wretched man she'd married. But memories of better times and early romances in their relationship filled her head. Todd's strong demeanor and confident air filled her senses once more. She could see his gorgeous face, his masculine hands. And the original man who had deteriorated into her worst nightmare flooded her mind's eye: Todd Falco, the only man she'd ever really loved, the man who took such good care of her so early on.

The tears came, one last time. These would be tears of closure.

Kay Falco would weep over Todd no more.

Deputy Simmons oversaw the search of the chemical dump at the Koppel strip mines. Coal was raked from the land there during the thirties and forties. The mines overran a deep cavern under those Koppel hills. At one point in time a well of water nearby was ruptured by the mining and the cavern was flooded. Divers were called in once to do a depth chart of the water. They descended ninety feet, still saw no sign of bottom, and quit their search. Local steel companies dumped barrels of toxic chemicals into the seemingly bottomless expanse during the fifties and sixties, hence the nickname "chemical dump." The deep water pool was discovered by local teenagers in the seventies and eighties and used as a summertime swimming hole. It was Greggy Richards who introduced Frank Kranac to the chemical dump. Greggy knew it well: it was a boyhood diving accident there that shattered his hip and left him with his lifelong limp. Greggy knew the bottomless pool would serve Frankie well as a place to dispense of his victims' cars. Frank Kranac and the Richards sank eight cars into those depths.

Deputy Simmons hired a local diving team to search the underwater dump. The search didn't take long. At forty feet they found the wreckage of three cars. At sixty feet they found four more. Beyond that there was a rocky gap in the cavern leading to an even deeper abyss. They and Deputy Simmons concluded that one of the eight cars must have made it past that point and floated deep into oblivion. Having discovered seven cars in there was satisfactory. They were not going to risk sending divers deeper into unexplored waters to locate the eighth wreck.

"Is the one we want reachable?" Simmons asked the diving crew.

"It's one of the deeper ones, but we definitely have a clear shot at it."

Minutes later, a tow truck reeled in a huge towing cable sunk deep within the pool. Then, from out of the gurgling water, the cable pulled Todd Falco's white Camaro slowly to the surface.

The building formerly known as "Cherries" was boarded shut. The health department closed the place down after many people disclosed Danny O'Hurley's after hours activities. Danny was convicted of running a prostitution ring and jailed for a short sentence. The ironic thing was that one of his lead "dancers" soon got saved at Covenant Church. She turned out to be quite a testimony to Jesus, and within a couple of years even got two more of her fellow dancers saved.

The deputy lead the handcuffed Benny Miller into the visitation room of the jail. A very nervous Audra Dutton smiled with great love from the other side of the glass partition when she laid eyes on him. Benny didn't recognize her, and looked confused as he sat down across the glass from her.

"What you want with me, Granny? I don't know you."

Audra Dutton smiled bigger at him and leaned forward. "But I know *you*, Benny Miller. And I've been prayin' for you for years!"

They talked for a long time.

Everybody turned on Carmichael Vero. Everybody. All the people who had operated under the cover of his empire fell, and like dominoes they all fell in his direction, bent on toppling him. Everybody arrested in the Family and the three drug rings and the pornography business they fronted were more than willing to finger Carmichael to save their hides.

The remaining Family members, Anthony and Warren Zann and Marv Lenstein, all wanted to cut deals with state prosecutors. They would testify against Carmichael if guaranteed lighter sentences in minimum security prisons. Attorney General Michael Davis agreed to Anthony Zann and Marv Lensteins's pleas. He cut deals with those two. But he nailed Warren Zann to the wall. No child pornographer's testimony was worth letting him escape full justice. He received several twenty-five year sentences and was sent off to hard time at West Penn Penitentiary.

It took the State of Pennsylvania almost a year to develop its case against Carmichael Vero. Months of depositions and records were mounted against the elder Vero. Their masses filled rows of file cabinets, promising weeks of air-tight prosecution against him. Michael Davis stood in awe of how smoothly everything went. After years of battering invisible brick walls protecting Vero, it was amazing to see so many people suddenly so willing to testify against this once dangerous man. That's what happens when satanic strongholds are brought down through prayer, though. Michael Davis was left scratching his head and praising God daily for the rapid progress and sudden turn around of his investigation.

Surrounded by a squad of deputies, the silver bullet witness wore body armor and a bullet proof helmet as he was rushed from the police van into a back entrance of the courthouse. Hallways were cleared before the rushing mass of deputies protecting him. Armed officers stood blocking every doorway to the halls from the back entrance of the building all the way to the courtroom. The witness and his protectors had a straight shot through the building. They ushered him safely into the judge's chambers next to the courtroom. There the helmet and armor was removed, revealing a handsome, tailor-suited Tony Vero. He looked up at the deputies, all dressed like SWAT team members, and grinned: "That was fun! But don't you know that Ed Larsky's dead?"

A likewise dapper Michael Davis walked over to Tony and straightened out his tie for him.

"Larsky may be dead," he told Tony, "But Carmichael Vero's still got money somewhere to hire another Ed Larsky. I made my big mistake twenty years ago, and this whole region's suffered for it under the grip of the Family. I won't have Carmichael putting any holes in your head during this trial."

Tony playfully pretended to fix the State Attorney General's tie: "I sure hope not! I already have a big enough hole in my head!"

Thus went the first arrival of Tony Vero for Carmichael Vero's trial. This scene was repeated for the next eight days as the state's key witness was delivered to the courthouse to give his testimony.

The fun was taken out of Tony Vero's sails when he caught his first glimpse of his Great Uncle Carmichael sitting at the defense table with his high powered attorneys. Tony had not seen the man in almost a year and a half, since that Monday morning that he left Carmichael's VECO office for the last time. Carmichael looked like he'd aged almost twenty years since then. His once stylish, salt and peppered hair was now all white and cropped short. His face, once youthful and smooth for a man in his sixties, was pallid, dry, and wrinkled. His green eyes that were always bright and clear despite the sinful life he lead, were now dull and bloodshot. And Carmichael was deathly gaunt. He had no meat left on his bones. Tony realized the fourteen months spent in jail had been quite rough on the man. Tony remembered Uncle Joseph telling him how the two eldest Veros thrived on "the juice" of their criminal lifestyle. Joseph said they'd die if they couldn't have it. Death was certainly working over Carmichael Vero. Tony thought of how great he felt, despite his fourteen months in jail. But Jesus had been working on him, not death. He was free from guilt, free from himself, free from sin and death. The contrast between him and his great uncle sobered him. It was at that instance that Tony took up the burden to pray daily for Carmichael Vero's salvation. Gina later told him how long she'd been praying for Carmichael, and she and Tony joined forces to touch in agreement for Jesus to save him.

"The State of Pennsylvania calls Michael Anthony Vero to the witness stand."

Tony took the stand calmly. Carmichael looked him straight in the eyes. Tony looked him back. Neither wavered. Carmichael stared with disappointment and betrayal. Tony wasn't intimidated in the least. Carmichael was the founder of this whole nightmare. Though Tony loved the man as his great uncle, Tony, Pete, Dot, Joseph, and Gina had all suffered because of his illicit schemes. He had single-handedly destroyed the Vero family. It was time for the truth about Carmichael Vero to come completely to the surface.

Tony gave nine full days of testimony.

Carmichael's expensive defense team tried to paint Tony as a disgruntled traitor, one who wanted VECO handed over to him but who wasn't willing to work for it. His alcoholism and agoraphobia were revealed, and how he blew a major college scholarship and a possible NFL career. They ended the trial by declaring Michael Davis a vengeful politician who was bent on using his high powers to corrupt people into railroading the "innocent businessman" Carmichael Vero. They noted how all of the Family members who testified were all so willing to pin so many of the Family crimes on a deadman who couldn't defend himself: Ed Larsky. A dead scapegoat, they contended, did not prove Carmichael Vero to be a criminal.

Carmichael Vero never took the stand. He never uttered a word in his own defense. Tony and Gina often discussed how the man didn't even look the same anymore. His confidence was gone. He just sat at that defense table, a gaunt, defeated man with no fight left in him.

"We the jury find the defendant, Mr. Carmichael Vero, guilty as charged on all counts." That was the final word on the trial. All appeals were shot down. Three consecutive life sentences were handed down to the man who for twenty years ruled the Western Pennsylvania criminal world. Tony and Gina Vero watched their weakened, frail, defeated great uncle handcuffed and hauled out of the courtroom for the last time. He didn't look at them or anyone.

They never saw Carmichael Vero again.

Audra Dutton saw Tony Vero on the TV and almost fainted. She instantly recognized him as the other young man in that vision Holy Spirit gave her during that time of intense warfare. At Tony's right side was Detective Ray Kirkland, a Godly man Audra knew when he used to attend her church. On his right was his sister Gina Vero, a pretty brunette. Audra looked closely at the screen as the trio was escorted out of the courtroom by deputies: on Gina's sweater was a huge, glittery "Jesus Is Lord" pin. Audra laughed ironically at first, then broke down into tears. Tony and Gina Vero were both children of some of the people responsible for her son Orlando's death. Gina apparently knew the Lord, and if Tony didn't yet, he was surrounded by two people who surely did. Audra knew God had given her a role in their salvation.

The Beaver Valley greatly improved through the demise of the family. But this is not a fairy-tale, "they lived happily ever after" world in which we live. There was a huge gap in the drug trade in Beaver County and Pittsburgh since the collapse of Jermichael DeVries, Stephen McClintlock, and Benny Miller's gangs. But satan is tenacious, and he doesn't allow voids in the spirit realm to stay empty long. Other criminals were willing to quickly rise up in place of those thugs. But none of them had the demonic firepower to protect them like the Family's empires did. But no Benny Millers ever lasted in Beaver

Falls again, since God moved to topple all demonic activity in those spiritual heights once and for all.

Pastor Dave and Covenant Church saw a marked increase in the number of salvations and visitors coming in for services. Drug addicts, homeless, and ex-gang bangers appeared more frequently for ministry. Some requested counseling and prayer, requests for which Pastor Dave and his talented, anointed staff were ready. Much seed was planted during this time. The Kingdom of God increased.

Sister Katherine Elaine joyfully sang praises to Jesus as she made her way through Mercy House. Mercy House was an old school turned "rest home" in a wooded up-state New York township. The thirty-six year old nun strolled past dozens of invalid Mercy House patients. Many of them were young children born with horrible birth defects that left them catatonic or paralyzed. Many others were elderly victims of severe strokes or debilitating diseases. None of them could function even slightly by themselves. They were all bedridden and needy of the most diligent care. There was little if no hope for their recovery. Many had been abandoned by families who could no longer bear to look after them, or just plain refused to. At Mercy House, Catholic nuns, nurses, and volunteers cared for these helpless souls. Mercy House provided human dignity and love for these people nearly destroyed by the curse of sin and death.

Sister Katherine Elaine made her way through the long dormitory. She praised God with a grateful heart as she passed many bedridden patients. She headed toward her favorite patient. She pulled up beside his bed at the end of the row and smiled down at the inanimate man. Gaunt, in his forties, he was propped up, shirtless in the bed. The long, black hair this patient had when he arrived at Mercy House had been shorn to a crew cut. Caring for long hair was too much of a burden there. Now his spiked, un-dyed hair revealed more gray hairs than black. Sister Katherine Elaine examined the many black, blue, and red occult tattoos on the man's body as she sat down to minister to him.

"Hello, Johnny Cirello!" she greeted the severely paralyzed Cyrus Moreau. "Isn't it a glorious day? Praise God for it, huh?" He, of course, could not move or communicate with anyone in any manner. His body was lifeless and he was mute. She didn't know why she was so drawn to him. Perhaps it was because he appeared to have lived a lifestyle so parallel to the one from which Jesus delivered her. Sister Katherine Elaine had run away from home at age fifteen and became a groupie, bouncing from one famous rock and roll star's entourage to another. Her life was a hell of drugs and abusive sex. But at age twenty-six, she found Jesus! Or was it the other way around? He gloriously saved her and delivered her from a heroin addiction. She gave her broken life back to Him. She longed to serve Him and Him only. He revealed His destiny for her. Carrying several incurable sexually transmitted diseases, and having had her fill of men for so many years, she didn't want a husband. Soon Holy Spirit lead her back to her Catholic roots. He wanted her to be a shining light in the Catholic church. She decided to become a nun. There she could serve Him, live high expectations of purity, and devote her life to helping others. It was perfect!

Cyrus reminded her of the many rock stars she'd known, with his gaunt, tattooed body. Perhaps that was why she was so interested in him. She wanted to see him delivered from whatever hell had gotten him into this place. No one knew anything about this Johnny Cirello's past, including his alias, Cyrus Moreau. The sorcerers from his old coven made sure any records of Cyrus Moreau were erased. The young witch and warlock he was raising up had taken over Aleister Estate and his businesses. Using the witchcraft Cyrus had taught them, they stole Cyrus's entire life from him. They created a false will with a perfect likeness of Cyrus's signature. In it they gave themselves everything he had and was. And there was nothing he could do about it. It all backfired on them, though. Vicious in-fighting among the coven members over control of Cyrus's estate broke out. Ultimately, all plans for the New World Alchemists IPO collapsed and the company was never put on the stock market. None of their schemes worked, and the occult empire that Cyrus spent his life building collapsed.

Sister Katherine Elaine tried to minister to this Johnny at least once a day. Some days she would sit for a half an hour or so and just read the Bible out loud, declaring God's word over him. Today, she pulled out some anointing oil and began to pray over Cyrus. She anointed his head with oil and prayed Christ's salvation and healing over him. She often anointed his occult tattoos and rebuked the curses behind them. Many days she interceded for his safety. She didn't know what was up, but some days she could sense demonic forces trying to get to him. She sensed they were not only trying to torment him, but they wanted to kill him. She battled on his behalf, praying holy angels around him and blessing him with God's protection.

She stared down into his catatonic face; his eyes lifeless, his mouth agape in paralysis.

"Johnny," she smiled at him, "Do you know what? For some reason you just seem to have God's favor about you! Someone special must have been praying for you during your life."

All Cyrus Moreau could do was think about Brother Maynard . . .

Detective Ray Kirkland was blown out of the water by the praises he received regarding his Todd Falco case and File 13. Ironically, File 13 wound up having thirteen victims. Greggy Richards map was quite accurate. All of Frank Kranac's drug dealing victims were found buried underneath caskets in Grandview Cemetery. Ray was able to stamp all thirteen missing persons cases "solved." The story even made the national media. Tabloid magazines and television news shows were especially interested in the story and Ray. He carefully avoided any spotlight attention, and always gave Jesus all the praise and glory. That usually discouraged journalists.

Just when his glory in the news media peaked, an eleven year old girl from New Brighton disappeared. Her concerned parents were all over the news. Ray was instantly brought back down to earth. File 13 was no longer of importance. Finding this missing girl became his focus. Keeping himself humbled before his Father remained his obsession. For Ray Kirkland knows better than anybody, the Kingdom of God does not stop for anyone.

The mountain village of Gabon, Columbia is a hidden paradise. The temperature remains about 70 degrees year round. The town is well secured. Many wealthy citizens and property owners make sure of that. Gabon's security forces are made up of ex-government intelligence employees from South, Central, and North American countries. Many of these security officers maintain their links to Colombian military forces. This enables them certain liberties, like banning all paparazzi from the pleasant village. Reporters and photographers are never welcomed. Rights of the press are purposefully oppressed. Therefore, rich and famous people world-wide are drawn to Gabon to either retreat from the high price of fame or retire there anonymously. Gabon is also a neutral zone. Leaders of rival cocaine cartels will summit there, their children playing together during their stays. Safety and privacy come first in Gabon. But the price is high. One has to commit several million to one of the local banks to be welcomed. "Association" fees are astronomical, too. But those prices are minor compared to the freedom and peace of mind they buy.

Joseph Vero paid for his morning coffee at the local Gabon cafe in the village square and returned to his small but luxurious condo. Joseph Vero didn't look like Joseph Vero any more. His nose was smaller and his lips were fuller. He'd had a major face lift and liposuction, too. He was fifteen pounds lighter and his hair was much darker. He was no longer known as Joseph. The villagers knew him by an alias he'd created. He was also known as a philosopher, an avid chess player, and an expert on international laws. He was well-liked by the villagers, and he had struck up acquaintances with several internationally known business tycoons who frequented Gabon, Columbia. He enjoyed many mornings with coffee and a chess match, and many evenings with a glass of wine and good company at one of the local outdoor restaurants.

On this particular morning, however, Joseph was particularly anxious to return to his condo. He declined chess invites from his usual opponents, and a breakfast offer from an amorous senorita he often courted. No, this morning, he wanted to take his coffee straight home.

He turned on his computer and logged onto the internet. He went straight to his bookmark, tagged *The Beaver County Times*, and down-loaded the newspaper's electronic publication. He had been waiting for them to post their latest edition on the web. The newspaper appeared, and it was indeed the latest update. Joseph anxiously scrolled down the headlines, until he found the one he'd been waiting so long to read:

"Local Sports Hero Sentenced."

He clicked on the headline. Up came the story. He was only able to read the first line:

"Former Beaver Falls High School football star Tony Vero was sentenced to seven years in prison on Wednesday for his guilty plea to second degree murder charges in the death of Gus Savage in Ft. Lauderdale, Florida . . ."

And then something unexpected happened to Joseph Vero: he broke. It started as a sudden knot in his stomach when he read that first line. That knot quickly rose up to his chest and into his throat. Out it came as a sob. It so shocked the stoic that he slapped his hand to his mouth to mute it. But his face reddened, tears welled in his eyes, and his emotions erupted like a flash flood through a weak levy. To his embarrassment, Joseph Vero wept violently. All of his identity changes, his facades, and the barriers of deceit that he erected to protect himself could not withstand one profound fact:

Joseph Vero was still a human, and he was overwhelmed by his true love for his nephew Tony.

EPILOGUE 2

September, 2002

The center snapped the football up into Tony Vero's waiting hands. Linemen exploded across the line of scrimmage with violent thuds, grunts, and stomping feet. Benny Miller, who was split wide right, darted along the sidelines, quickly outpacing the safety who was trying to pick him up. Tony Vero's eyes locked on target. Benny Miller was sprinting precisely according to his pattern. Tony's brain flashed impulses to his body. His linemen fought to hold off defensive tackles and a blitzing linebacker. Tony eyed his mark forty yards down field. The linebacker broke away from Tony's left guard and was charging with a roar. With perfection Tony hurled the football into the air. It spiraled with dazzling majesty. Although Tony was rid of the ball, the linebacker hit Tony full force and drove him into the ground. But it was futile. Benny Miller hit the mark precisely, the football arrived in his dexterous hands simultaneously, and he was five yards ahead of the safety. He laughed and danced the remaining fifteen yards into the end zone, breaking the tie and winning the game. There he knelt, prayerfully thanked Jesus Christ his Savior for this opportunity to excel, and then got up and danced about the end zone triumphantly with his fellow wide receiver.

Both Tony and the linebacker looked up from the ground as Benny made the touchdown. The linebacker cursed and jumped up. He bent over and extended a hand to Tony:

"Nice throw, Quarterback."

Tony took his hand and read his regulation t-shirt. "Nice illegal hit, inmate number '07541'."

The linebacker helped Tony off the ground. "Too bad these correctional institutions don't provide us referees to protect you quarterbacks." He popped Tony over the head to congratulate him.

Tony ran down the field, grinning at Benny Miller. Benny laughed and ran out of the end zone to meet him.

"Wasn't I great, Tony Tiger?" he mugged as they bumped chests and hugged.

"Yeah," Tony said with sarcasm, "I really didn't have a whole lot to do with that touchdown."

They walked together off the Beaver County Correctional Facility recreation field.

"You think West Virginia can take us back?" Benny asked.

"*Us?*" Tony laughed. "Don't remember you on my WVU roster, Pal."

Benny cackled loudly. They gave each other some dap.

The camp loud speaker crackled: "TONY VERO TO THE VISITATION CENTER. TONY VERO TO THE VISITATION CENTER."

Benny's eyes lit up: "Your woman's here!"

"She's not my woman! She's just a friend." Tony's face turned red.

"Right. Run on and see your 'friend,' Tony Tiger!" Benny smiled.

"Catch you at Bible study."

Tony was filthy. His sweat-soaked clothes were covered in grass and dirt. He didn't want her to see him like that. He ran across the yard to a building that had a spigot. He stuck his head under it and turned on the water. He soaked his head and hair clean. He ripped off his shirt, ran back to his dorm room, donned a clean prison uniform, and bolted over to the visitation center. He definitely didn't look and smell his best. Good thing there would be an inch of Plexiglas between them.

He'd seen her at Covenant Church about seven weeks earlier when he was released to speak there one evening under Ray Kirkland's care. He and she talked. She agreed to exchange letters. They wrote each other aggressively ever since, and had even made several phone calls. This was her first visit to the correctional facility. He couldn't believe she was actually coming.

Tony was so nervous.

Kay Falco stood smiling at Tony from the other side of the partition. Tony's mouth fell agape when he saw her. Even through an inch of prison Plexiglas, she looked like a dream. Her hair was long, with dark streaks that highlighted her sandy and light features. Her brown eyes shimmered, her smile dazzled. She was dressed in stylish, dark fall wear with black boots. Her beauty took his breath away, and once again, Kay noted it. She smiled so pretty at him. He was so handsome and rugged. He was lean and rock muscular from daily weight training. She couldn't help but stare. His eyes gleamed with joy, a joy Kay never thought she'd ever see in them. He just stood there dumbfounded at the sight of her.

"How about a 'hello'?" Kay laughed.

"Hello! I'm so glad you came! I didn't know if you'd feel comfortable coming here to see me."

"I can handle coming to see a jail-bird."

Tony paused, looking her over. "You look wonderful."

She blushed lightly. "Thank you. You look pretty good yourself. For a jail-bird."
He turned with a flourish, mock-modeling his outfit. "The finest in prison wear!"
She giggled. They took a seat on either side of the Plexiglas.

"How's Dylon's pre-school going?" he asked softly.

"Oh, he's loving it! Most mornings I don't even have to coax him to get up and get dressed, he's so jazzed about going to school."

"I couldn't believe that was him at church that night! He's so big."

"Four years old!"

Tony was blushed, silent for a moment. Then: "You getting along okay?"

"Great. I do a lot of volunteering while Dylon's at school and take care of him at night. My parents make it up from Florida quite often."

"You . . . you doing okay financially? I don't mean to pry, but I've noticed you're not working."

She laughed a light giggle. "Tony, Todd left me a fortune in insurance and savings accounts. Dylon and I will never want for anything. I'll never have to work again."

Tony smiled with embarrassment for prying.

"It's okay, Tony," she reassured him. "I don't mind you asking things like that. I know you're nosy, you private detective!"

They both smiled.

"How about you, Tony? Are you doing all right in here?"

He nodded confidently. "Yes. I really am. This place sure stinks at times. I mean, it's prison! It's not supposed to be easy! But I'm blessed despite all that. I've met so many brothers in the Lord here who've helped me grow in my faith. God's really doing a work in me . . ." He stopped, moved with emotion, embarrassed.

"It's okay" she grinned at his humility. "Oh! I was watching one of those 'most wanted' shows the other night. They had another feature about your Uncle Joseph. There's still quite a reward for anyone with information on him."

"I pray for him a lot. Gina and I both do. I doubt anyone's ever gonna catch Uncle Joseph. He's too smart for that. He's one of the coolest there ever was."

There was silence as he could only stare at her. He suddenly felt the urge to tell her how he felt. How could he bring it up? Again, she rescued the conversation.

She got a confused look on her face. "You said on my answering machine the other night that Benny Miller might have an opportunity to play for the Pittsburgh Steelers?"

Tony chuckled. "Yeah. But not the Steelers you're thinking about. After his next sentencing date, he might get sent to West Penn Penitentiary. They have an intrastate squad called the 'Stealers' . . ."

Kay smiled: "I see. That's S-T-E-A-L-E-R-S."

"Exactly. Pads and all. It's a pretty big operation. They don't just let any inmate play. But Benny's playing like he's at his prime right now, since the Lord's delivered him from smoking weed."

"But isn't West Penn pretty rough? Isn't he scared?"

"Benny's got a real evangelical anointing. He loves to share the Gospel. God will clear the way for him and get him through the rough stuff. Plus, Benny's pretty tough himself. And shrewd! He didn't get to the top of the drug world around here by accident. And he's got such a powerful testimony to share."

"So do you! You were wonderful at Covenant Church last month! That whole service was!"

Tony blushed once more. "I . . . I . . . uh, can't take much credit for that. That was God's doing."

"How many kids got saved that night?" she asked.

A tear formed in his eye. He shook his head, humbled even more. "I don't really know. I didn't do that, I'm tellin' you. That was Jesus working through the situation . . ."

"Ray Kirkland said like fifteen or more of those kids from Tiger Pause came up to give their hearts to the Lord after you gave your testimony."

He shook his head, not seeming to believe it. "All I did was share what had happened to me . . ."

"But *what* a story you have, Tony! Your football career, your family, the Mafia, that maniac who tried to kill you, everything! Everyone was mezmerized, Tony. You have quite a story to tell about how you met Jesus. Can't you see that?"

"I . . . just don't deserve that sort of reaction, not after the life I've lead . . ."

She hushed him. "No one deserves the grace God gives us, Tony. But he's chosen you to use in His work. That was obvious to everyone at Covenant Church that night. Now accept it!"

He shrunk back and grinned. "Yes, Sir!"

She waved him off with her elegant hand. "Well, if you'd just listen to me you'd be a whole lot better off! You're too stuborn! You don't know what's good for you."

He trembled with stifled laughter and shook his head. She knew what he was thinking and spoke it out loud, nodding her head: "But I do!"

They laughed, then smiled and locked eyes in silence for a long moment. There was more between them than friendship. He so wanted to reach through the Plexiglas and hold her hand. He had to speak.

"You know . . ." he tried to begin. But Kay was a tough one. It was intimidating to open up to her.

She leaned forward and gave him an enticing look that melted his heart even more. "Yes, Tony?"

He took a deep breath: "I . . . I just wanted to tell you . . . I . . . I think about you all the time. I mean *all* the time."

Kay's eyes lit up with pleasant surprise, but she didn't respond. Tony waited, but Kay remained silent, wishing to yank his chain as hard as she could. Tony got uncomfortable. He'd just put his heart in the open, and Kay wasn't responding. He wished she'd throw him a life line.

"Well," he said shyly, "do . . . do you think about me?"

Kay tilted her head and frowned as if she were flogging her memory. Finally, she just shook her head, smiled politely, and answered nonchalantly: "No."

Tony's face turned bright red. She didn't know he could blush like that. He looked both disappointed and humiliated all at the same time. She had got him good.

But then Kay Falco smiled her sexy smile and said, "But I really like that you think about me!"

BVG